The Book of Mrs Noah

Michèle Roberts was born in 1949 and lives and works in London. Her previous novels are *A Piece of the Night* (Women's Press, 1978), *The Visitation* (Women's Press, 1983) and *The Wild Girl* (Methuen, 1984). Her volume of poetry, *The mirror of the mother* (Methuen), was published in 1986, and together with Judith Kazantzis and Michelene Wandor, she is the author of the poetry collection *Touch Papers* (Allison and Busby, 1982). She is also co-author of the short story anthologies *Tales I Tell My Mother* (Journeyman Press, 1978) and *More Tales I Tell My Mother* (Journeyman Press, 1987). She has contributed essays to *Walking On The Water* (Virago, 1984), *Gender and Writing* (Pandora, 1984) and *Fathers: Reflections By Daughters* (Virago, 1984).

The Book of Mrs Noah

Michèle Roberts

A Methuen Paperback

For Joanna Defriez and Helen Walton

Thanks to Howard Burns, Sarah Lefanu and Anne Morgan for reading and criticizing early drafts. Thanks to all the friends who sustained me with encouragement and hot dinners, and to those who helped me find rooms to write in. Thanks to Salvatore Camporeale and Melissa Bullard for sharing with me their interpretation of the Annunciation. Thanks to all at Methuen and in particular my editor Elspeth Lindner.

A Methuen Paperback

THE BOOK OF MRS NOAH

British Library Cataloguing in Publication Data

Roberts, Michele
 The book of Mrs Noah.
 I. Title
 823'.914[F]   PR6068.0155
 ISBN 0–413–58190–X

First published in Great Britain 1987
by Methuen London Ltd
This edition published 1988
by Methuen London Ltd
11 New Fetter Lane, London EC4P 4EE
Copyright © Michèle Roberts 1987

Printed and bound in Great Britain
by Cox & Wyman Ltd, Reading

'That floating Colledge, that swimming Hospitall–'
John Donne, *Elegies*

1   Noah died last night. Surely I should have prevented it, but did not.

We stand on the riverbank, quarrelling. Our bare feet share the same patch of silky mud that squirts between our toes as we shift back and forth, towards each other and away again, and his brown fingers hold mine until I pull them away from him, and the rain beats on our shoulders and on our hair. The green rags of the palm trees bend under the water that pours from heaven as though the sky is a split skin, and the bright grey clouds are reflected in the gleaming puddles on the ground.

I argue that it is time to board the Ark, to make the voyage. Noah promised to accompany me. Now he says he has changed his mind. It is too soon. He is not ready. He's not sure he'll ever want to come with me.

In the end I leave him behind. I teeter across the slippery gangplank into my wooden shelter, hastily closing the door after me as thunder and lightning begin to surround me with flashing blue zigzags of light, long low growls like sheets of corrugated iron being shaken up and down. From one of the hatches I peer out, seeking Noah's figure on the shore.

A silver pin sizzles down from the heavens, fallen from the quiver some god of destruction rattles at us so viciously. It strikes Noah between the shoulder blades with a fizz of blue light, and cracks him in two. Flames burst up from what was his spine and is now a long split, gaping emptiness. Flames form him: flesh and bones and hair are drawn in leaping fire. For a moment he wavers, and is still upright, and has shape; and then he crumples, sinks to the ground, a small heap of black ashes that the wind lifts and scatters on the river.

Noah has been wiped out. There is no dead body to prove he

has ever been alive. I am alive, and he is not. I put my hand to my side, which is seared and raw, as though my skin has been torn off, as though Noah has been unpeeled from me by the fire. I am burning too. Loss is more than absence: it is the fire.

I open my mouth to begin screaming, and wake up.

Noah lies asleep beside me, his round face peaceful, his black hair sticking up in spikes, his mouth open. I touch his cheek with my finger. I should ask for forgiveness. But I can't. Not yet.

2   My story begins in Venice.

Noah and I travel there on the little local train from Verona. We jolt along, stopping at villages that seem to consist only of a church, a scatter of pink concrete villas. It's a steamy, sticky day: the mountains on the horizon are misty blue shapes against a golden sky. The ditch running alongside the railway brims with purple mallow, pink campion, lavender thistles. Light blooms in the grass. Green light, that pours onto the glassy twists of the olive trees, onto the tobacco-coloured hilts of the swords of maize stuck in rows, onto the vines spreadeagled and sagging on their wires. The tall maize, ear-high, rustles all about us, stretching away across the vast plain, an ocean of green and bronze.

Our compartment, empty apart from us, is fitted out in silvery aluminium. Our seats are of maroon leatherette, the elbow-rests fat as aubergines, a strip of white linen antimacassar running behind our heads.

Noah is sitting opposite me, his attention on the newspaper in his lap. His hair is standing on end as usual. His blue eyes are screwed up against the sun. His hands caressing the smudged newsprint are brown flags defying me to approach him too closely, to say what's on my mind. He sighs, sags, looks tired. I wear him out with my demands. The air between us bristles with outrage.

Don't start again, his silence pleads: I know what you want to say. We've been through it all before. Every month for the last two years.

Walking on the water. I stand on the deck of the *vaporetto*, packed in amongst Venetians serenely going about their

9

business with briefcases and shopping bags as though immune to this miracle, and I laugh and laugh, staring unbelieving at the façades of palaces gliding by like theatre sets on the greeny-blue waters of the Grand Canal.

Our room is in a *pensione* behind the Accademia, on the wide Zattere waterfront facing the Giudecca. The walls are washed salmon pink, and a pink glass chandelier frilled and floppy as a giant squid hangs over the huge bed with its brocade-covered headboard in blue and pink and turquoise. The bedside lamps are cut from amber perspex and wear black and gold masks, and the radiator has cream accordion pleats. Below the window a narrow canal slaps at the weedy stone wall, and, opposite, a walled garden is full of flowering trees and stone statues. The air is as milky blue as the water in our bath. We sit at opposite ends of it, washing each other's feet, tickling each other with soap. A truce.

The city smells of cats' piss, yeast, rotting rubbish, coffee, fried fish, blossom. Noah leads me out into it, taking my hand and drawing me along. He's been here many times. He knows every path through this labyrinth of water, and so I allow myself to become passive for once, swept along behind him. We measure the city that floats, the city of carved pink islands and oily green canals. We travel through burning streets of yellow and rose façades, glittering churches, small blackened palaces. We plunge down crowded passages that twist and turn and double back. I lose all sense of direction. Venice loses me. Hanging on to Noah's hand.

Noah leads me, certainly and repeatedly, back towards our bed. Through courts and alleys striped by black shadow and sharp sun, up and down narrow stairways, over tiny humped bridges, along water corridors. Our bed is a four-poster sailing along the canals through the afternoon, and we on it are lulled by the rocking of the water, the swinging and clanging of the church bells, sweaty and hot and languid, our bodies taking and taking their holiday. But I can't abandon myself completely. Noah has betrayed me, and now I'm on guard.

We go down to supper in the dining room below. Noah's conference doesn't start until tomorrow morning, so we've got this evening to ourselves. Green light from the canal just beyond the ornate arched windows ripples in green waves

10

across the white walls and floor. The waiter is detached and severe, a priest saying Mass. He bends over silver trays, he flourishes silver cups, he flaps linen napkins, scrapes and bows and sweeps through the watery green room.

We eat chicken. I remember how I took Noah's flesh between my teeth, biting him gently, licking him, teasing him with lips and tongue, sucking up his juice. Spirals of black hair pattern his chest, arms, legs. I groom him, comb him with my fingers, pretending to search for fleas, pulling each curly black hair until he yelps and grabs me. His fingers sidle into me, a longboat riding my canal. He tells me I can have whatever I want, that he will give me whatever I ask for. (Except . . .) I don't know what to say. I drink wine in the *pensione* dining room, swirling the yellow liquid in the shining cut glass.

We walk out again, into the sparkling dark city. The night pulls us, unresisting, down tunnels of lights and laughter, past open-air restaurants where red mullet crackles on grills over beds of charcoal. We find a café in a small *campo* lit by flaring torches, and sit down outside and order coffee. The air laps at us, as warm as the sea, a black deep through which glide strings of lights, strolling people, gondolas, on which the churches sway up and down, docked for the night. I stretch out my legs in front of me and look around at the golden and black plane trees, the stone benches under them, the well in the centre of the little *campo*.

Then I see her. My grandmother, walking rapidly past us, her head down. There's no mistaking her face, her shape. Even as I turn my head and stare after her, she's gone, gliding down a narrow passageway.

– That's Nana, I exclaim, getting up and knocking my chair over in my hurry: what on earth is she doing here?

– How can it be your grandmother? protests Noah: you know she's dead.

He glances at his watch.

– Time for me to get back to the hotel. I want to put in a bit more work before going to bed.

– It *is* her, I insist: I *must* speak to her.

Ignoring his protests, I run across the *campo* into the shadows under the plane trees. There are seven exits; I counted them when we sat down. The *campo* is a kaleidoscope, shifting,

11

turning, offering seven times seven ways of experiencing it, seven ways in and seven ways out, a crystal constantly changing, linked to all the other crystals that make up Venice. How can I be sure which way my grandmother has gone? I stare down the black mouth of a *calle*. Was it this one?

Behind me Noah is calling me to wait. I run.

I fly, full tilt, after the sturdy figure always just in front of me, whipping round corners just ahead, her face resolutely set forwards though I cry out her name and, behind me, hear Noah call out mine. I increase my speed until his voice dies in the distance. I knock into strolling people and send them stumbling. My heart beats in my throat.

She leads me towards the Grand Canal. I skitter through an archway, down a greasy stone ramp, and onto the bobbing raft at the end of it.

It's very quiet here, the palaces behind me closed and shuttered, noises and lights far away across the dark water. There is no one about. I can hear the creak of ropes, as the invisible gondolas moored by the stakes stuck into the mud tug at their fastenings and the ropes grow taut and then slack. I can hear the slap-slap of water on stone, my own harsh breathing.

My grandmother is not here.

I peer at her absence, the pitch-black night at the end of the raft. The Ark is moored there, way out somewhere in the lagoon. I know it.

I strip hurriedly, tearing at buttons and fastenings. Cotton frock, underwear, espadrilles drop, a crumpled heap of darkness.

A cry. My name called.

Noah stands, panting and dishevelled, at the top of the ramp.

– Don't do it, he shouts: don't be stupid. Come back. It's dangerous to swim in the canal. You could be killed.

He is starting down the ramp.

– Keep back, I yell: or I *will* jump in.

He halts.

– I know you're upset, he shouts: we can talk about it. Let's go back to the hotel. You need to rest.

Under my bare feet is the cracked splintery wood of the raft, dry and warm. The night air, fragrant with the smell of ripe

12

fruit, caresses my skin. I shiver.

I stumble forwards to what I judge must be the edge of the raft, one foot pressing into the night in front of the other. When my left foot comes down on nothing I teeter, almost fall in. I stop, balance myself, raise my arms above my head. No moon, no stars. Just this cloudy blackness.

I launch myself forwards and down. Noah's cry behind me is cut off as I enter the water. It smacks my ears but can't hold me back.

3   If I have my grandmother's blessing I can leave for
the Ark without too much fear. I need my ancestor at
my back.

This is the way I imagine it.

I take the lift down inside myself, pressing the button marked
Help. I drop past floor after floor of memory, down past death,
down to the bottom floor of the unconscious. I step out into a
large square room. The sign over the door reads *Ladies*.

I have arrived in a veritable college of grandmothers. Seated
in rows on old-fashioned commodes are scores of stern old
women with bright eyes and white hair. I start laughing. These
are real thrones all right.

Here's my own grandmother, sitting in the middle of the
room, filling in her football coupon.

She frowns at me, holding my hands.

– Get on with you, you storyteller. Become a journey-
woman. Build your Ark. Sail off in it. Get going.

Then she smiles.

– When I'm on my own, she says: I make whatever I like.

She shakes her biro as I kiss her soft cheek.

– Hop it. Be off with you. You've got to invent your own life.
It's up to you.

It could also happen like this.

The lift carries me very high, up through layers of white
cloud. I step out onto a terrace walled in glass. Up here it's
night, the darkness pressing cool and moist on my skin.

My other grandmother is perched on a stool, eyes clamped to
the telescope she has trained upon the distant stars. She swings
around to face me, and sighs irritably.

14

– Well? What do you want?

She's as remote and indifferent as snow piled on a Himalayan peak that no one has ever climbed: that's the cold place she's won for herself in her old age. She's left us messy and emotional young ones in order to dwell in a fastness of prayer and ice; it's an effort for her to readjust her eyes and focus on me rather than on wheeling empty air, on stars. Her face is austere: all neediness has long since been scoured away from it by the winds she lives amongst and loves.

– I've no time for children and grandchildren any more, she remarks, frowning: young people today are graceless, ungrateful and spoiled rotten. I've spent my life in the pursuit of wisdom, but none of you cares for that, or listens to me. Too difficult for you, isn't it? You're still children, all of you, playing your silly games of sex and politics. Why can't you grow up? Why can't you leave me alone? Why must you still come running to me and expect me to do it all for you?

I open my mouth to speak, but she shrugs me into silence and goes on.

– I know what you're going to say. I've heard it all before. I can read your thoughts. They don't interest me. I'm weary of the world you still choose to live in. I have nothing to say to you except this: you are naïve and stupid and ignorant; you have never listened to me or taken my advice; and so now I wash my hands of you.

Now she glares at me.

– I don't *like* you very much. So get *out*! Get *out* of my house!

4   I swim out along the Grand Canal, towards the Lagoon.

How shall I recognize the Ark when I reach it? It's certainly no good relying on Arkitects to design it for me ready-made. They all disagree on every aspect of it and spend their time squabbling over how to interpret the specifications laid down by the great Client in the Sky.

For example, the great Origen imagines the Ark as a sort of truncated pyramid, a classification system in three dimensions of the hierarchies in the natural world. On the top deck there is a cabin for Man, and beside that, space for Woman and their three sons and their wives. Below this comes the deck where the clean beasts are kept, and below this again a deck for the carnivores and reptiles. Origen draws a horizontal line through the middle of the Ark at this point, to demonstrate the need for a strict division between Above and Below. Under the dividing line is a storage deck, where food is kept, and under this, the place of offal.

St Augustine is convinced that the Ark should be built according to the proportions of the human body, and St Ambrose agrees with him, at great length. St Augustine points out that there is no need to have a deck full of fish tanks on the Ark, since the fish can swim alongside through the waters of the Flood, and that it's unlikely God means Man to take the insects on board since they breed on putrefaction and will be catered for by all the corpses floating about. St Augustine also thinks that Man can feed the carnivores from his stores of fruit and chestnuts rather than tackling the problem of preserving fresh meat on a long voyage.

Hugh of St Victor designs an Ark with stalls on the outside

for frogs, seals and sirens.

The poets Prudentius and Avitus both imagine the exploits of the raven to be sent forth from the Ark to see whether there is dry land in existence. Prudentius and Avitus reckon that the raven can perch on floating carcases and gorge himself for the duration of the Flood. They do not, however, tell us much about his hutch or cage. I think this must be the same raven who turns up on the battlefields of the Anglo-Saxon heroic poems, picking out the eyes of the dead.

Tertullian is terse, but he reminds us that the Ark will be built before the founding of cities and is therefore unlikely to look like one.

Buteo remarks that no special arrangement is needed for the reptiles, actually, because they can easily just twine themselves around the beams and the rafters (presumably on the third deck).

Tostado describes a higgledy-piggledy of animal arrangements, with Man walking between the asps, dragons, unicorns and elephants at feeding time; thanks to God they will not harm him.

There is no consensus on whether the centaurs, sirens, satyrs and fauns will actually be on the Ark with special living quarters provided for them.

On the other hand, everyone agrees that the Babylonian Sibyl will certainly be on board, for she has been commissioned to write a long poem about it all afterwards.

When we come to visual representations there is even more confusion.

The Ark is an enormous chest, banded with iron.

The Ark is pretty much like an ocean liner.

The Ark is a longboat with a prow carved like a dragon's head.

The Ark is a floating castle, a small city of wood and stone with towers and turrets and gates.

The Ark is a detached suburban house.

These are the main types I have been able to detect.

I'll add a few of my own.

The Ark is a huge seed, tossed along by the waters, carrying its cargo of new life.

The Ark is a bestiary, of beasts domestic and fabulous. Here are, preserved for ever more, not just the Unicorn, the

Dragon and the Bonnacon, but also the Phoenix, the Loch Ness Monster, the Bearded Lady, the Siamese Twins, and many more. The Ark is a series of allegories, a Sunday newspaper, a zoo.

The Ark is a coffin bearing dead bodies out to sea.

The Ark is the coracle in which the hermit saint sets out for paradise, rowing away from this earth, which is the condition of exile from the city of God, towards freedom and the enchanted isles with their mountains of glass, their talking birds.

The Ark is a sieve.

The Ark is the cradle of Moses, the basket caught in the bulrushes, and it's the manger in which Jesus sleeps. On second thoughts: I didn't make this one up. St Augustine probably did.

The Ark is the nuclear shelter of the survivalists, defended by machine guns.

The Ark is an inner-city neighbourhood fighting back against poverty, unemployment, racism, police raids.

What kind of Ark do *I* want?

I depend on books to help me out when I'm stuck. I dive between the covers of a novel, my foldaway house that travels in my pocket, my cool tent that I can put up wherever and whenever I choose. I trained as a librarian thinking it would give me time to read, but I spend most of my days, in the public library where I work, checking that books have been correctly re-shelved, showing readers how to use the catalogue on microfiche, chasing enquiries and loans.

I've taken two months off work to travel around Italy with Noah while he researches his book on the Italian health service and attends various conferences. My bibliographical skills have come in useful; I help him organize his card index, classify his hills of files and notes.

But in the evenings, when Noah pores over statistics in our hotel room, time hangs heavy, tugs my empty hands. I've already finished reading all the novels I brought with me.

I need work to do. I need books. I'll invent a library.

5   The cabin smells of dust, leather, furniture polish. I pick my way across it in the dark, fumble at the catch of a porthole, swing it open.

Sudden white light, hurting my eyes. I blink, refocus on walls lined with wooden shelves behind glass doors, packed with maroon boxes labelled in white. *Mazzo* LIII. *Mazzo* LIV.

In the centre of the archive a baize-topped table on wrought-iron legs bears two large open volumes of manuscript, two brass lamps with parchment shades, a paper press, various lumps of rosy marble. A leather sofa with a ripped yellowing seat and a carved back is set against one wall, flanked by two shabby velvet-covered armchairs. A spotted china globe dangles from the ceiling, which is painted with four female figures, faded and flaking, representing the seasons. The wooden deck is scattered with worn rugs.

I seat myself at the mahogany desk I have placed underneath an enormous oil painting of Judith slaying Holofernes, donated by Artemisia Gentileschi. Deep soft armchair upholstered in cracked battered leather. In front of me is a pile of cataloguing slips in blue cartridge paper, a green blotter bound in half-calf, a flowered china inkpot with a quill pen balanced on top of it, and a plastic tray heaped with nibs, rubbers, a bottle of glue, a pair of scissors, and a stapler.

I try out my signature on a piece of blotting paper. Mrs Noah, Arkivist of the Ark.

I draft notes for the brochure outlining the Ark's function and services.

The Ark of Women is the Other One. The *Salon des Refusées*.

Des Refusantes. Cruise ship for the females who are only fitted in as monsters: the gorgons, the basilisks, the sirens, the harpies, the furies, the viragos, the amazons, the medusas, the sphinxes.

Where shall we go, the women who don't fit in? Those of us who are not citizens but exiles? Those of us who are not named as belonging, but as outcasts, as barbarians?

Into this Ark of Women.

The Ark of Women has been founded by an international committee of sibyls in order to guard and encourage women's creativity. Every women who has ever lived has deposited here her book: her story or novel or collection of poems or autobiography. On the Ark time doesn't work normally and nor do clocks: all the stories, from past present and future, are here, rubbing shoulders in the dark. Some composed at home, some dictated to friends, some written during the writer's stay on the Ark. The Ark is not only an archive: it is a rest-home that swims, a workshop that floats, a bubble of temporary retreat for women who need time to write away from their families and domestic cares.

The Ark's bookstack, extending over many decks, contains all the varied clashing aspects of women's imaginations expressed in books. These can be called up by a classification system of great subtlety, based on the crystalline thought processes of the unconscious, designed by a committee of poets. Men's books are of course available, on inter-library loan. Please see the catalogue.

Aids to study on the Ark include comfortable cabins, beds in the reading room for those wishing to rest or dream, food and drink always available (supper, however, prepared on a volunteer rota basis), and a crèche for those needing to bring their children.

Writing materials on offer include knotted strings, circular seals, blackboards and chalk, wampum belts, message tallies, tablets of clay and ivory and wood, oracle bones, slabs of gold and silver and wax, shards of pottery, strips of cloth and papyrus and paper, sticks of bamboo, palm leaves, bits of birch bark, leather scrolls, rolls of parchment, copper plates, pen and ink, palettes and paintbrushes, sticks and dust-trays, printing presses, typewriters, tape recorders, word processors, etc.

Women come on board the Ark for a bit of peace and quiet in

which to think about their lives and question them.

Women come here to develop their craft, to discuss work in progress, to give and take criticism and advice on redrafting, to share fears, failures, ideas.

Women who hate the very idea of writers workshops come here to get away from other women, to live in cells of silence and isolation, to be as selfish and unsisterly as they like.

Women come here to find out what it means to be a woman writer, whether in fact that matters, whether we aren't all just writers.

Women come here to free their imaginations, to learn to play again, to destroy.

Some rush home again. Some leap over the side in rage and despair. Others enjoy themselves. You can read all about the Ark in our records. Please ask at the main desk for further information.

I get up, and prowl along the bookshelves until I find the leatherbound brass-cornered volume that is the index to the sibyls and their works. Soft thick pages: rag paper, lovely to touch. The entries are written in my clear neat hand, wide margins left around them, each name underlined by flourishes in faded brown ink. I'm impressed by my handiwork: no blots or crossings-out. I run my index finger down the columns, pausing over particular names. The Nubian Sibyl, the Persian Sibyl, the Bombay Sibyl, the Guatemalan Sibyl, the Brixton Sibyl. I know them quite well, have read their works in a tumult of sorrow, laughter, rage. They've come, in the past, to give talks at the public library where I used to work. But I see that opposite their names I have scribbled *Gone out of town*. So. What about some of these others? The Babble-On Sibyl, the Correct Sibyl, the Deftly Sibyl, the Forsaken Sibyl, the Re-Vision Sibyl. I'll try them. I scribble down the shelf-marks of their works, then hunt along the shelves again until I find the corresponding numbered boxes which I lift out and put on my desk.

Inside the boxes, under each cardboard lid, are masses of tightly rolled parchments, some no bigger than cigars, each one tied up with string and labelled in black ink. I select at random, undo the strings and unroll the parchments, flattening them with my fingers and weighting the ends with the lumps of

21

marble I fetch from the centre table. I browse. Some odd titles here. Unmemorable. It's a biggish book, people say, coming up to the desk in the public library: with a red cover, you know? But these sibyls will do. They are the companions I want.

6   This morning the Deftly Sibyl has woken up hating her husband. Lying rigid, a foot away from him, she feels her heart pump with anxiety. His back is turned to her, only his shiny bald patch visible. She shudders. She'd better get out. Run away.

She has an escape fund. A secret building society account, added to monthly. Rarely touched, in fact, except to buy clothes for the children, Christmas presents, birthday gifts for family and friends. But it *is* her money, produced by scrimping and saving on the housekeeping, working odd nights as a barmaid when her sister will baby-sit, writing reviews and articles for magazines she despises. It's there for her if she ever needs to run away. Enough for a ticket to Newcastle, where her best friend Emily lives. Single.

This morning she decides to run away into the field backing onto their (George's) little house at the end of the village street. She effaces herself in sweatshirt and jeans, ties her hair back. Slips out of the back door, down the path, over the stile.

Early morning is cloudy, the grass smelling fresh and moist. She would like to walk barefoot in it, to lie down in it, to rub her face on the earth, to stuff it into her mouth. She starts to run round the edge of the field, the hedgerow a blur of olive green, the cold air stinging her cheeks. She wants to be a good person, loving and unselfish. But at the moment she is possessed by hate. If she runs fast and long enough, perhaps she can sweat out the hate, trample it underfoot and leave it behind, return to the house a kind mother and wife with a sense of humour.

She wants to leave her husband and children. She wants to live in a house that is *hers*. That she pays for with her own money. A place in which only she lives, where no one else enters unless invited to do so. George has the power in this house: he earns twice as much as she does. Living with George, in George's space, at George's rhythm, it is impossible to concentrate properly on her writing. He's so proud of the elegant avantgarde novels she writes, but nonetheless his needs have to come first. Since he works freelance, his hours are unpredictable. She can't start working until he's left the house, left her in peace. She has to stop as soon as he comes home and re-possesses the kitchen where she writes. She can never plan her own work, can never be sure of a long stretch of hours ahead into which she can slowly sink, submerge herself, reach that level, far down, where she makes contact with what wants to get written today. She hovers on the brink, head raised, unable to let go, waiting for the crash of his step on the path. Then the children. Off at school all day now, giving her clear limits of time, but still needing to be fed cleaned up after cared for listened to played with accommmodated. Oh yes she loves the children and George but that's not the point.

She slows down as she passes the gate and sees the bullocks in the corner. Old friends. They lumber towards her, eager and curious, bawling, some of them with coats of black satin, others auburn and ruffled like doormats on stocky legs. They push their snub heads at her caressing hands, lick her with rough tongues. Tired of the game, she smacks their backs, waves her arms at them, and they lumber off. She pads on again.

If she lived alone, meals would not be such a fuss. She'd eat if and when she was hungry, a bowl of pasta and a salad, her elbows on the table, no need to talk to anybody, a book open beside her. None of this searching the supermarket for economical cuts of meat, searching the recipe books for a hundred exciting things to do with mince. Once she heard a man complain that women on their own don't dine, don't know how to. We don't always want to dine, you poor fool, she screams into the wind: it makes a change, not bloody dining. *Dearie*, she addresses a thistle as she gallops over it.

George's face at dinner last night. Sulky, cold. Yes, she admits it: she had too much to drink, lost control, poured herself out like spilled wine onto the white linen tablecloth. Which she'll wash, dry and iron. It will take longer to launder things with George. His disgust at her as she sat pounding the

table with her fist, blethering on about her need for uninterrupted work, for silence and solitude, not letting him talk back,
interrupting him, speaking to the soup tureen not to him. She
slid into bed as a criminal. Unreasonable, rude, unkind,
surprising herself as much as him with her carping, her
complaints. Bad bad bad. She knows it, even before he tells her.

Which is why she is out here this morning, racing the devil
around the muddy track circling the field, her lungs burning,
her throat raw and dry, her legs aching and shuddering as she
urges herself on.

She's begun to need to complain. Better to do it out here,
where no one can hear her, where she can't hurt those she
loves, won't let them down.

Around and around she runs.

Running away. Around and around.

The Re-Vision Sibyl needs to be careful. Don't quarrel with
Jim when he forgets to send three maintenance cheques in a
row then points out how hard up he is with a second family to
support. Don't let on how interested she has recently become in
feminism, how her current lover, to her own surprise, is a
woman, lest Kitty be taken away from her, in her best interests
of course. Work hard, yes, get on with her writing, yes, but
never forget to put Kitty first, prove to the school and the social
workers that single mothers can cope. Just. Provide the child
with adult male company, uncle figures, to ensure she won't
turn out queer; on the other hand, don't let them stay the night
lest snooping neighbours report you and you're seen to be
doing it for money. One day someone will find out that she
augments her meagre maintenance and social security payments
with writing stories for women's magazines under a false name,
and then she'll be for it.

Today it's her birthday. Her mother, bless her, has sent her a
cheque for twenty pounds and she's blown the lot on food.
Rarely able to get out at night, she misses her men and women
friends; but tonight she's having ten of them round for supper,
and for the rest of the week she and Kitty will survive very well
on the leftovers.

She's stuck in the middle of a story. Doesn't know how to end
it. What a relief to put her pen down and take up a knife instead.

25

She's going to make a real French meal, posh food, the sort she cooked when she was married and bought all the newest cookery books.

She starts with the apple tart.

The table top is white formica, cool to touch. On her right, the basket of apples. In front of her, the wooden chopping board; in her hand, the savage black knife. To her left, the blue-rimmed china dish.

She pares the apples, one by one. The sturdy russet coats, rough-textured and scarred, all colours between yellow and red, fall off as the ragged edge of the worn blade reaches under them. The peel slides over her fingers, sticky with juice. She eats a sliver, licks and wipes her hands. Then she chops the round white bodies of the naked apples into quarters, and halves these, and then scoops out the core, the black shiny pips. Now the apples lie in the china dish, rows of crescent moons.

She melts butter to a pale gold foam in the big frying pan, lays the slices of apple in it, sprinkles sugar over them, pokes them gently with a wooden spoon. They start to take on a deeper colour, a rich yellow. Scent of butter and apples and caramel.

Another slab of butter into the white china mixing bowl, quickly cut into small pieces with the tip of her knife. Swift snow of flour, a little sugar, gritty, glistening, rubbed together to make sand. Egg and water mixed in with a fork, the crumbly mess rapidly gathered into a plump buttery ball she tosses from hand to hand before rolling it out into a thick circle she picks up and flaps like a pancake, tosses into the aluminium tin which she shoves into the oven.

She switches on the radio while she makes the *crème patissière*. Evensong from St John's College, Cambridge. The voice of a male priest invokes God the Father and God the Son. The male choir, so hushed, so reverent, murders successive antiphons with a prissy breathing in and out of notes, a cricket team masquerading as coy nymphs. Hefty boys in frilly white drag, she imagines them, massed solidly in the safety of their oak pews and choir stalls, high-faluting, up up up and away their voices intone, deliciously shivering at how precious and right their prayers are. No women here.

She breaks egg yolks into a bowl, whips them with sugar and flour, boils them with milk. Beats and beats with her wooden spoon to remove lumps. Lumpy female bodies. Lumpy bellies and breasts. Eggs breaking and splattering, warm mess of sweetness on the sheets, warm flow of sweat and blood. We can't have *that* in our nice Anglican chapel. Only male chefs please.

She composes the tart. Layer of crisp pastry. Layer of cognac-scented egg cream. The apples on top, arranged in overlapping circles brushed with apricot glaze. It is ready. Her devotions are over. She takes off her floury apron.

Tonight they will eat it. The labour of several hours will vanish in ten minutes. Rather like her stories, she supposes, read in the hairdresser's under the dryer and then discarded. What would it be like to produce great novels? Real art? She shrugs and laughs. She's a good cook, anyway. Perfect results every time. She wishes she could say the same for her stories.

Soon they will all be home from church, stampede of parents-in-law, nephews and nieces, Neil and his brothers. The Babble-On Sibyl smiles to herself, the cats stirring around her feet as she stands at the sink washing parsley in the tin colander. In the meantime, she has the whole house to herself, the stillness of the empty room scoured by light, the white curtain lifting at the window.

The glass doors of the dresser swing open at her touch. She pulls out a red and blue paisley cloth, spreads it on the round table, places a vase of bright leaves and ivies in the middle. She loves coming to stay with Neil's family. Image of unbroken happiness she hasn't quite found in her own life so far, that she worships in this kitchen shrine. Now she has it for her own. Now she has Neil.

Departing up the path to the car in a flurry of silk headscarves, leather handbags, walking sticks, white socks, they exclaim how good she is to stay home and make the lunch, releasing them to the pub on the green, after sermon and hymns, for gin and tonic, cheese squares arranged on saucers, air thick with plummy voices and cigarette smoke, the children bribed with crisps to run and squabble in the garden outside.

What she had meant was, she would stay behind and *write*. But it is inconceivable to Neil's mother that a real woman could ever do such a thing on a Sunday morning. Real women either go to church, or get the dinner on. Preferably both. And the Babble-On Sibyl very much wants to be loved by her mother-in-law, very much wants to be a real woman. So she will cook the lunch. Her new family regard her hobby with affection, amusement. She's an authoress, you know, they say at drinks parties, pushing her forwards: quite a civilizing influence on our Neil here, eh? Neil's eyes signal: don't be upset; I love you. So she smiles. Yes, two collections of stories, slim ones, published, despite her youth. No, it doesn't bring in much money, writing. Good thing Neil's got a steady job, yes.

She's glad, anyway, to have got out of going to church. Only Neil knows how churches frighten her, that cold space between nave and chancel which holds nothing for her now, since Fanny's death, but a tiny wooden box set between tapers and stiff white gladioli. She fought Neil's parents for that, insisted it mattered that there was a funeral, that the dead baby had a name. The cold, coffin-shaped space is inside her still, a year later. Womb frozen, so that no sick baby can grow. Cervix clenched, so that no baby can slip out before time. She hasn't told Neil he's loving a wife with ice inside. She still can't talk about it. He's very patient. He makes love to her often. She knows he wants her to know how loved, how safe, she is.

How often she dreams of death, getting it muddled up with life: Fanny bursting up through the flowerbed with a hideous grimace and wizened limbs. She whisks an egg yolk with a drop of wine vinegar, adds oil drop by drop, beats at the thickening mixture, the cold glassy pleats of mayonnaise, greenish, smelling of olive. The dead salmon lies on its silver bier, parsley at head and tail. She has laid him out between the flowers and the candles. Now she anoints him with her home-made chrism.

Car tyres skidding and crunching on the gravel outside. The dogs (who terrify her) barking. Rattle at the latch as the door opens. Neil's footstep in the passage outside, his cheerful voice upraised.

– Where's the worker, then? Where is she? Curled up in a corner, I bet, with her head in a book. Where are you, Ba?

Her mother-in-law's voice, brisk, complacent.

– She won't have much time for *that* when the next baby arrives.

28

She snatches up the cut-glass decanter of sherry, swings it wildly above her head as though to throw it. Puts it down, shaking, just in time, as the kitchen door bursts open and they all crowd in about her.

On her way to the conference, the Forsaken Sibyl cycles past the park. Its colours draw her in. Irresistible. She dismounts, wheels her bike through the gate onto the asphalt path. Why worry if she is late? Being here is suddenly more important. She needs to calm down, anyway. Too churned up by last night's telephone conversation with Julia to concentrate on political theory.

She's strolling along a wide avenue edged with ornamental maples turned into translucent clouds of yellow sharp as lemons, fine as glass. The trees glitter like metal in the intense light of the sun, yet their colour is also soft, the yellow of chemicals, shiny as butter. The oval leaves of a cherry dangle, single flames, strange hot pink fruits. The trunks are a clear black, wet licks of paint. Luminous yellow. Splashes of rose, sour lime.

I'm afraid of loving you too much, Julia says, and laughs. Her olive eyelids cast down, her beckoning glance. Then her hands outstretched, forbidding contact; rapid talk of male lovers. Then the midnight phone call, newly seductive. I can't stay away from you, you know?

It's Saturday morning, nine o'clock. Few people about yet. She patters along in the troughs of dry leaves at the side of the path, lifting her cold face to the glare of the sun. Gold handcuffs. Gold chain around her neck. Runny gold light, leaking from her eyes. Leaves whirl about her, one by one surfing down from the blue sky, crackling under her boots, under her bicycle tyres.

She halts, to draw in the sweet smoke of a bonfire. November is bitter medicine in her mouth: the taste of chrysanthemums' cold russet hearts, the spicy burning smoke. A squirrel flows across the olive grass, waves of movement passing from body into long fur tail, rippling it. The brown of beeches separates into glowing scarlet, bright apple-skin, then blurs back into bronze.

I won't press you. I won't make demands. I'll keep my

distance, the one you indicate. I'll tie my hands behind my back, gag my open mouth. I just want to be with you sometimes.

This must be the last day of autumn, this radiant spending of colour, this transfiguration by light, this nail of sun banging the cold treacle of the air and smashing it to splinters. Tomorrow there will be rain, and sodden leaves squelching, dark mush underfoot, cold torrents of wind sweeping the last leaves from the trees. But this morning she treads, forgetting Julia at last, along a gold tunnel, no different in herself now from the sealskin tree trunks, the fresh earth of the flower buds, as the yellow park fringes her, then enters her, and she takes it inside. No more difference between outside and inside, no separating skin; just this flow of goodness, sweetness, self and words gone.

You can't control these moments; they lift off swiftly as they come; however much you long for their return. She sits in the conference hall, filling the thick notepad on her knee with abstract and technical words. Loss. Loss.

Walking back to her shabby flat after delivering the two children to school, the Correct Sibyl decides to stay outside. She, the old pro, famed among her friends for her capacity to stick at it rigorously, to write her thousand words a morning come what may, to produce a meaty piece of social-realist fiction every two years, is admitting defeat. The empty white space of the paper rolled into the typewriter terrifies her. She has nothing to say. She has dried up.

But she cannot afford this self-indulgence. Packets of words circulate in the bookshops like packets of Cornflakes in the supermarkets. She must stay on the production line, produce this season's new variety, special offer. Or she will be discarded, obsolete. No new Correct this year? Well, switch to Weetabix. Spot the difference. Correct drops to the trash can. No recycling in the Grub Street economy.

Clicking along the busy little road between the Victorian tenements gradually being prettied up for the influx of gentrifying home-owners pushing out poor tenants like herself, she wards off panic by reciting the litany of shops. On the far corner is the off-licence run by Mr O'Ryan who drinks in the Three Compasses next door and who is to be seen on Sundays buying a bunch of tulips from the flower stall to take to his mother. Next comes the Spanish deli, spice cave from which Mr and Mrs Garcia and their teenage daughter dispense chorizos, olives, honey-cakes, glutinous sweets. The West Indian restaurant opposite doubles as mini-cab hire office and as breakfast parlour: families hire beaten-up limousines here for weddings and funerals in their local church, the sumptuously panelled Tabernacle painted with apocalyptic texts. Next door is the Turkish fish and chip shop selling Jamaica patties and Chinese spring rolls; the Scottish grocer stocking everything from plimsolls to lemons to brillo pads; the chair-mender who works amidst enormous gilt-framed looking-glasses and broken chaise-longues; and the tailor whose window is adorned with a portrait, wreathed in plastic roses, of his mother, Kathleen O'Donoghue Tailoress, propped by old dress patterns from the forties. And lastly, just underneath the flats where she lives, the West Indian video hire shop, outside whose windows the local children gather for free film shows, and where the police come screaming up to investigate Black men in parked cars, to accuse them of theft, to turn the boots inside out, to search their pockets.

Unemployed youths and children skiving off school have turned the paved space in front of the Anglican church into a piazza for running races, for playing hopscotch and riding bicycles and skateboards. A lone roller-skater executes a figure of eight backwards with swooping grace, ears plugged by music muffs. The Correct Sibyl lingers to watch. Perhaps that is the way to do it; turn it the other way round.

I belong here, she reminds herself: this is my home. Out of this emptiness, somehow a story will come.

7   Outside the porthole, gulls loll on currents of air.
      I scribble, on a blue cataloguing slip, the message
      I want to send.

Dear Sibyl: this is an invitation to join me, Mrs Noah, on
board the Ark. The purpose of my voyage, though not
necessarily of yours, is to solve a problem: to discover how
other women survive; to sail towards, and explore, the Western
Isles, in order to arrive at a solution. I need companions. I'll
leave you free all day to get on with your writing; I simply
suggest that in the evenings we could get together and tell each
other stories. I need to hear your stories. Will you come with me?

Now I need to send out my invitations.
I open the deep drawer in which I keep my collection of
ephemera: bits of printed matter I am convinced will soon
become obsolete. I preserve them as museum relics, memory of
the time before paper is replaced by plastic in all its forms.
Bus tickets, *vaporetto* tickets, entry tickets to churches, the
zoo, art galleries.
Squares of tissue paper, picked up in markets, used for
wrapping oranges and lemons, printed with exquisite fifties
and sixties designs, stamped with gold. Similarly, labels off tins
of tomatoes and bottles of olive oil, and butter papers printed in
old-fashioned typefaces with blue designs of cows.
Holy pictures picked up in churches: pale pastel representations, wreathed in flowers, of swooning saints, with prayers
printed on the back, details of indulgences, tiny inset relics.
None of these will do.
Here's a stack of old airmail envelopes, fragile blue paper
boats striped in red and green, stuck with large glorious stamps

franked with wavy black lines and circles, adorned with prints of red pointing fingers, eagles, aeroplanes, wings. Artifacts giving pleasure to the ears hearing the rustle of the flap, the tongue licking the sour-sweet gum, the eyes feasting on the words *Espresso* and *Via Aerea* in bold scarlet, the nose scenting the fresh ink, the fingers smoothing the grain of the delicate, almost see-through paper. Soon these will be replaced, I'm convinced, by spools of tape; we'll marvel at the absurdity of sending words as physical objects in packets from hand to hand. So I hang on to them. Sentimental? Reactionary? I suppose so. I console myself in advance for the time when the surreal poetry of addresses, written in words, will be replaced by rows of dreary numbers. Postcodes are bad enough, but things will get even worse.

Here is my collection of antique London telephone directories with their beautiful plain pastel covers: dusty pink, banana, olive, sky blue. The details of exchanges are given in words: PRImrose, BLUebell, SPEedwell. Of no use any more to anyone but me. I shall flip through them in the evenings as a change from reading the dictionary.

They won't do either. To send out my invitations I'll rely on an old technique that's coming back into fashion, newly granted scientific respectability.

I shut my eyes, and concentrate.

8   The Re-Vision Sibyl is swimming through sleep, rolling over and ducking, gliding along on her back, easy, feet flicking up and down in the water. A knobbly sack is lying across her legs, a burden weighing her down, bringing her head up from dreams.

– Mum. It's me. Let me in.

Feet treading her ribs. Kitty wriggles under sheet and blankets and down by her side. Small warm body pressed against hers. Head laid on shoulder, silky hair lapping face and neck. Kitty's hand pats her cheek, dances along her collarbone, flicks her ear lobe.

– Mum. Wake up. Cuddle me.

She shifts, slides an arm out under Kitty's body, pulls her closer. Kitty buries her face against her mother's skin.

– You smell nice.

– So do you.

Sleepy satisfaction. Powerful perfume of their naked skin released by the night, soap gone, sweat in the creases, pores breathing warmth. She draws it in, sour-sweet, milky.

– Mum.

– Mmmm.

Now Kitty's on the move again, propping herself on one arm under the heave of blankets. Fiddling with her hair, stroking and lifting it with her fingers, separating the strands. She starts to twirl it, plait it. Slow shivers along the back of the neck and down the spine, her bones pouring away, trickles of pleasure starting up all over as her daughter's hand caresses her head.

– There. You're done now.

Hot breath blowing in her ear. Sensation of sweetness dissolving in her throat, dissolving her.

34

That reminds her. For once, she has not been dreaming about her overdraft. Sleep-fuddled, heavy, she considers, clambering after the memory up a swaying rope stair.

– I had this dream last night, she tells her daughter: I was on board Noah's Ark with a bunch of friends.

Kitty's sucking her thumb and the edge of the sheet, both at once. Not interested. She lays her head back on her mother's breast, pulls her arms around her. They fall asleep again.

Morning. The Correct Sibyl walks around her room with no clothes on, enjoying the brush of the rugs on her bare soles, letting her stomach relax and flop out, plump and wrinkled. She's got a dirty face and she swings her arms to the music in her head and feels the sun on her skin and hair.

She lies on the unmade bed and looks at the green and gold tangle of the maple tree outside the window, the sharp jigsaw of its leaves, points jagging the blue sky. The light slides, sliced into oblongs, through the bits of stained glass Tom has propped on the windowsill: plum, orange, strawberry, apricot. Light lies like water on the fat blue arm of the chair, on the bits of carpet on the white painted floor.

She picks at her toenails and scratches her head. The sheets are full of the crumbs left from her long, lazy, uninterrupted breakfast. The tray of dirty dishes is still by the bed. Greasy thumbprints on the newspaper.

Twelve noon, and she's still lounging about. Delicious. With Tom and Jessie away at their father's for the weekend, she's having a morning off work goodness cleanliness godliness. Just as well, since she's got writer's block. Daydreaming. Doing nothing of any value whatsoever except pleasing herself. To hell with the muse.

She decides to take a bath. The window in the bathroom that she shares with the tenants downstairs is cut low, just beside the bath, so that she can turn her head and look out at the thrashing green branches of the maple tree through the open casement. Baby in a glass womb. She floats in the water she has scented with prodigal handfuls of bath salts, dissolving mauve grit. Cool air blows in from the window around her neck and shoulders. Lapped in wetness and warmth, fragrant steam, she joins two worlds: the air and the clouds and the racing green leaves, and the deep enclosure of white enamel. She swims in and between both. She lies in her bath imagining she is the Ark plunging through rain and oceans, and the wind sweeps over her and through the house.

The Deftly Sibyl adjusts the straps of her pale blue nylon swimsuit, pads across the dimpled rubber tiles of the changing room and out into the great domed hall echoing with the shouts and splashing of the schoolchildren having a lesson at one end, lowers herself down the little aluminium ladder.

Now she's in her element of sloppy turquoise, legs and arms propelling her through liquid glass, chlorine smarting at the back of her throat as she dips her chin and the water slaps in. Above her, a wooden sky, and below, navy lines that wobble and loop. She keeps to her traffic lane, doing a neat breaststroke up and down, timing her lengths by the clock above the diving board. Important to keep fit. To keep things in perspective. George is working at home today, so she's taking time off. For herself. She will *not* worry about money.

Besides the youngsters at the shallow end, the pool is full of other fish. Girls streamlined and silver-bellied as mackerel stroke past, white arms lifting in a shower of drops. An older woman in a pink turban. A youth doing butterfly, head and shoulders darting absurdly up and down, eyes goggling on rubber stalks. A narrow-waisted man with a pointed black beard flexing his muscles before dropping his goggles into the deep end and diving to retrieve them, waving them above his head, looking around to see who watched. Now they're nicely wetted, he dons them, does a showy crawl to the far end, dispersing the little ones with the spray he raises. He does like to make a splash, this one.

She forges through the blue water that is both translucent and opaque, marvelling at the lightness and ease lent her body, the closest she can come to flying, her thighs and arms flexing with a power that pleases her, stomach sucked in by her movements, wet hair in a heavy dollop on her neck. Then she relaxes, rolls onto her back, glides idly, just twitching her toes and fingers, letting the other swimmers' currents carry her through the choppy pool and so to the ladder again and out back up.

36

Standing naked under the hot hiss of the shower, she bends this way and that, the steamy jet of the water hitting her like darts. At first, shy, she keeps her eyes on the cream tiles of the wall. Then, bolder, she glances at the other women in line beside her, each twisting and turning, skin gleaming under a lather of soap. Smooth outlines, each one different, some curved and rippling, some lean, some fat. Each one naked and uncaring. She peeps at the triangles of hair, black and brown and golden, the slump and slack of bellies, the swing of breasts. Watches a face upturned, eyes closed, for the stream to rush over, hands smoothing back shiny black tails of hair, wringing the last drops out, reaching for the thick towel. They're nymphs, she thinks: or mermaids, swimming around the Ark. She surprises herself, feels gently amorous. Shocked, cross, she stomps into a formica-walled cubicle and bangs the door.

Once she closes the shabby front door of her squat and steps outside the white stucco block, the Forsaken Sibyl is walking in morning air blue and shiny as porcelain. Her determined steps crack it. Then relief takes her over: she's shut the eviction notice away behind her. She's out. The world touches her: cold air tangy on her lips, the sun hot on the back of her neck, relaxing her body. She skims along the pavement, caught up in a wave of green light as pure and clear as glass, as water, veined with yellow. Antique-shop windows display oil paintir.gs in gold frames, Chinese jars in red and blue, ebony cabinets inlaid with mother-of-pearl.

She will *not* torment herself with longings for Julia. She will exorcize them. She needs a treat. She buys tulips from the man on the corner by the cinema. He sits among orange plastic buckets packed with flowers whose colours glisten fresher than wet paint. A water-sprinkled rainbow hedge. A wall of perfume: she is eating white narcissi petals. One bunch of tulips is tawny and striped, an armful of red and yellow tigers splitting open pale green sheaths, and the other is a collection of pearly pink eggs. She buys fat rosy hyacinths too, juicy trumpets toppling above fleshy stalks, and a scarlet geranium shooting away from its frilled fan leaves, and a cyclamen violently pink as a flight of flamingos over a pond.

That's this week's gas and electricity money almost gone. To hell with it. To hell with Julia. Today she's going to be a lily of the field.

Today she wants chaos: every possible combination of colour and form whirling together. She stopped painting at puberty, when she grew frightened of colours. That red Flood swept her towards the knowledge of death. All the colours got mixed up, no boundaries between them, blurred into each other and lost their names, a dark smear on the palette. She wanted to enter the dance of colours, to go beyond the severe line traced by others' words around that white space, her female body, to explode it. That way lay madness. So she drew back, stopped painting, used words instead, unravelled the wild complex whole into limping lines of words that belonged in time and space and could only say one thing at a time.

She fills her room with the flowers she has bought until it looks like a funeral parlour only waiting for the corpse laid out in the middle. Hers?

Now she is able to let herself remember her dream of the night before.

She meets her own ghost.

Asleep. The room grows first chill, then icy. Body jerks with fright. A cold hand on her naked back, waves of ice, a glacier forcing itself through an unwilling valley. Words spoken.

– Remember the dead woman artist.

She has lined up a row of jugs containing tulips, hyacinths, geraniums and cyclamen. She will learn to live in the rainbow. To find the end. She wants rain. An Ark.

The mountain falls, sheer, down to the sea. Picking their way down it, hopping from slab to slab of white rock carved into the semblance of steps, they keep well into the lichened wall. The heat beats up at them in waves. The Babble-On Sibyl licks her cracked lips, imagining salt on them, shifts her smart scarlet holdall from one brown hand to the other. The dry flowers of the seaside, gorse and pinks, fringe the way plunging ahead, and umbrella pines lean over them, scant shade.

There's no beach at the bathing place. The rocks have been levelled out under a platform of concrete, just enough space for the café thatched with grasses and bamboo, a strip of blue wooden beach huts with yellow shutters fronted by an emerald-painted verandah with a lime canvas roof, two rows of mats and deck chairs in scarlet and indigo, sun and shadows striping the wooden staircase leading to the tiny jetty.

Fifty yards out from the shore, looking back, the water is navy, dancing with figures of eight and circles in bright blue as it catches the sun. Then, when she swims nearer the landing place again, and dog-paddles along the steep rocks she climbed down earlier, the water is transparent green, the seabed lit up as though there are lights hidden in the coral. At first the heavy flippers she has borrowed from Neil cumber her, the goggles clasped too tightly to her wet head, the eyepiece misted by sea water. Then she gets the hang of it, beats her rubber fins up and down, takes a deep breath, and submerges herself.

The underwater world is illuminated, magnified. The mountain sheers down, knobbled and weedy, in a sharp slope she bumps against. She hangs in blue space, can see her legs dangle, rounded and pale brown. Far below her, a bright carpet: a play of broken crystals, gold bits, fragments of sapphire, emerald, jade, turquoise, all flashing and changing as the water gently moves over them. Neil swimming in front of her looks as though he is flying in a vast blue sky high above this jewelled earth, his skinny white legs kicking lazily above a flowerbed of white coral.

Back on her red cotton mattress, skin basted with cocoa butter and coconut milk, she roasts, the sun licking the water off her with a scorching tongue, drying her harshly. She lifts an eyelid, contemplates her scarlet satin bikini with pleasure, her deepening tan. They have saved for this holiday for three years. Oh, to stay here always. To live on an Ark, to dive off it daily into this sparkling sea, to drop down through it to that iridescent bed. She reaches for Neil's hand.

9   I design a chapel for the Ark.

It's a non-denominational one, available to anyone or any group wanting a quiet place in which to pray or think or write. Not everyone uses it. The Buddhists, the Hindus and the Daoists have built their own temples at the other end of the Ark. From time to time processions wend their way along the deck, as the devotees of different faiths visit each other and attend each other's ceremonies. The Muslims have likewise erected their own place of worship. The Sufis don't need temples or churches and prefer to dance and sway aloft in the rigging. The Theosophists use the saloon. The Quakers meet all over the place, building soft walls of silence and attention around themselves.

It's mostly the Protestants and the Roman Catholics who use the chapel. Like a theatre, it adapts itself to the requirements of the different rituals enacted in it. It can be stripped bare for the Methodists, filled with flower arrangements and Mothers Union banners and Pre-Raphaelite stained glass for the Anglicans, packed with plaster Sacred Hearts and lacy altar cloths for the Papists. Sometimes it shudders with the exaltation produced by Black Gospel choirs; sometimes a spiral of plainchant coils up through a smoke of incense; sometimes brass band and organ together blare out their praise; sometimes jazz, skiffle and rock music pound and thump in the aisles.

Today, the chapel has been reconsecrated for use by the Roman Catholics. Although I no longer practise the religion of my childhood, I still find Catholic churches holy places in the way that Protestant ones are not. There is an absence in a Protestant church, an emptiness. It is not marked with the presence of God as I was taught to understand it: the winking red light in front of the tabernacle of the Blessed Sacrament. Nor does a modern Protestant church testify to the action of God in creation through the presence of works of art. It is the statues, the altar-pieces, the sculptured tombs, the decorated walls, doorways and roofs, created by the struggle of human minds and hands to express the relationship of human beings to food, sexuality and death, that brings God into a church. The Catholic churches I have seen in Italy, however tacky and over the top in their decoration, hush me, make me reverent, fill me with pleasure. In fact, the tackier the better.

I am not disappointed. Today the chapel's gloom is dispelled by bursts of light from the black iron racks of candles before the shrines flanked by tall columns clothed in red brocade leggings bound with fringed gold cords. I recite the litany of ornament; I catalogue church furniture. Here are baroque lanterns on poles, monstrances wreathed in tarnished golden leaves, dusty red velvet cushions edged with gold braid arranged on elaborately carved prie-dieux. Here are magnificent black oak confessionals with bolted doors and windows, domed tops, iron grilles, and purple silk curtains. Here are walls hung with silver ex-votos: hearts and legs and stomachs and arms. Here are floors chequered in rosy marble and planted with memorial tablets, ceilings offering a glimpse of heaven swagged with flowers, ornate doorways alive with saints perched on the spandrels swinging their long legs as though out on a picnic. Here are altars dressed in lace and satin skirts, set out with candles and books and gilt cookery utensils.

Here is Our Lady with a freshly painted wax face and silk robes embroidered with gold thread, a ruff of tin lace at her neck, jewelled rings on her fingers, her thin blonde locks streaming from under her white muslin veil and spiky crown, and all of humanity sheltering under her upraised arms. Here is Our Lady again and again: with her china face contorted by grief and her long hands lifted lamenting over the dead son in her lap; with a black skin and coiffure and glittering gold eyes outlined with black kohl; with a pasty-faced porcelain baby in her arms. Here are dead bishops incorrupt in glass cases, dead virgins scattered with crepe roses, dead nuns cruelly crowned with thorns. Here is the cold scent of dust and myrrh, and the slow heavy speech of the organ, and a flaming heart transfixed by an arrow of gold.

I sit down in one of the pews. The Roman Catholics are singing the Litany of the Blessed Virgin Mary. They are praying that our voyage may be fruitful and safe.

Holy Mother of God
Holy Virgin of Virgins
Mother of Christ
Mother of divine grace
Mother most pure
Mother most chaste
Mother inviolate
Mother unblemished
Mother worthy of all love
Mother most wonderful
Mother of good counsel
Mother of the Creator
Mother of the Saviour
Virgin most wise
Virgin worthy of all reverence
Virgin of renown
Virgin of power
Virgin of mercy
Virgin of faith
Mirror of justice
Seat of wisdom
Cause of our joy
Shrine of the spirit
Shrine of honour
Betokened shrine of devotion
Mystical rose
Tower of David
Tower of ivory
House of gold
Ark of the covenant
Gate of heaven
Morning star
Health of the sick
Refuge of sinners

Comforter of the afflicted
Help of Christians
Queen of angels
Queen of patriarchs
Queen of prophets
Queen of apostles
Queen of martyrs
Queen of confessors
Queen of all virgins
Queen of all saints
Queen conceived without original sin
Queen assumed into heaven
Queen of the most holy rosary
Queen of peace
pray for us

I want to join in. I want to worship, to praise. My own mother. All mothers.

I want everything: I want to be virgin, amazon, lesbian, mother, lover of men, artist, friend.

Here are the feminist Roman Catholics opening their mouths wide to praise the Great Mother.

bright goddess
black goddess
companion of sibyls
lover of difficult daughters
truth-teller
ark of all life
hunter of meanings
sister of sisters
moon-swallower
blessed black triangle
blessed black O
precious vessel of blood
hill of sweetness
dark cave of becoming
maker of God
secret pearl
virgin of silence

whore of wisdom
mother of many words
juggler of atoms
land of milk and honey
house of warm flesh
gate of paradise
be with us

I am holding a lit candle between my hands, as are all the women around me. Pearls of transparent wax fall down it, harden, grow cloudy, thicken. One by one we are blowing the candles out. Moment by moment the darkness encroaches. All of us go on together now, our voices thin and hoarse.

preferrer of sons
despiser of women
breast of marble
lover of patriarchs
blocked ears
blocked mouth
blocked shout
jailer of daughters
bag of emptiness
transfusion of bitterness
tongue of ice
spine of rigidity
fearer of chaos
fearer of darkness
hood of loss
foot binder
soul binder
let me not become that

10   I say hello to the five sibyls as, one by one, they enter the chapel. We introduce ourselves to each other. Then we push back the front pews and arrange a circle of chairs. Perhaps some of the sibyls might consider a chapel a strange place in which to hold a writers meeting? It will do for our first session, I decide. We can switch venues for the next one. Just to make my position clear I pop my typewriter cover over the tabernacle on the altar.

We seat ourselves, and I survey my new companions.

The Babble-On Sibyl chooses a basket chair packed with fat silk cushions. She wears a faded blue dress of Indian cotton in a swirling paisley design, flowing and loose in the sleeves and skirt and gathered in at the waist by a tasselled gold cord hung with tiny gold bells. Her straight brown hair drops over her eyes and down her back. Ornate gold earrings, which don't suit her at all, dangle from her ears, and her arms are laden with heavy gold bracelets. She plays nervously with these, twisting them round and round and pushing them up and down her slender arms. Her round face is young and unlined, and her bare feet are shod in Indian sandals of plaited brown leather. She twists her feet around each other, ankles and calves into a tight knot.

The Deftly Sibyl sits upright on a canvas director's chair with her name stencilled on the back. Her knees are pressed together, in exact alignment with each other, and her hands are clasped over them. Her hair, dragged back and fastened in an untidy coil at the nape of her neck, reveals the alert expression of her face, the crease above her brows, the lines drooping from nose to mouth. Her eyelids are painted pale blue, and her lips pale pink, like her fingernails, and her nose is dusted with

45

translucent powder. She wears a trouser suit of flowered green and purple corduroy, green slingbacks, and a wedding ring.

The Forsaken Sibyl ranges to and fro, picking at her fingernails. She has cut her hair short, in two different lengths; one side of her head bristles in a crew cut and the other sprouts with curly red tufts weighted with amber and turquoise beads. Her green eyes glare out from her pale bony face, and her wide mouth opens over strong teeth. Her ear lobes are hung with loops of silver wire from which dangle black feathers, and her long fingers are braced with fluorescent plastic rings. Tall and thin, she wears a floppy black jumper, skinny black slacks, and big black crepe-soled shoes, and she pads up and down, up and down, watching.

The Correct Sibyl hides her eyes and most of her face behind a large pair of red-rimmed sunglasses. Short curly fair hair, a delicate mouth with tightly compressed lips, high cheekbones with hollows under them; not much else can be seen. Her small hands fiddle with the notebook in her lap. She wears a grey wool jumper, a well-cut grey flannel skirt, a shawl striped in brilliant red and orange, and knee-high leather boots in shining chestnut. From the embroidered shoulder bag slung over the back of her plain wooden chair there peeps a grey manila folder and a large desk diary.

She glances at her grey metal watch.

– Shouldn't we get going? If we're all here, which I assume we are? Let's make a start.

She looks pointedly at the Re-Vision Sibyl who is scrabbling around on her knees on the floor, picking up the clutch of gaily coloured felt-tips she has allowed to spill out of her white plastic carrier bag.

The Re-Vision Sibyl looks up.

– Sorry.

She seats herself hurriedly in the only remaining chair, a rocker made of pink steel tubes. She is wearing a brown linen fifties jacket tightly nipped in at the waist and decorated with cream lapels and cream pocket flaps, a long tight skirt slit at the back for easy movement, cream cotton lace stockings, brown schoolgirl's lace-ups. She settles herself, pulling at her padded shoulders, twitching at her stocking seams. Then she looks around.

46

– Right. I'm ready.

I utter my carefully rehearsed speech of welcome, repeating my desire for the voyage, its proposed function, and my need for the sibyls' help. Everyone nods, apart from the Forsaken Sibyl.

– Aren't *you* going to tell any stories? she asks me: how can we function as a real group if you hold yourself apart and just listen to what *we* say? I think it would be better if you joined in.

– You're assuming, points out the Babble-On Sibyl: that we're going to function as a collective, in the traditional feminist way. I'm not sure that I want to. I met plenty of feminists at college, I was quite interested at first in going to their meetings, but I ended up feeling completely rejected by them. Feminists don't like women like me. That group at college were a really hostile bunch, I can tell you. They didn't approve of my need to wear pretty clothes and make-up and do my hair nicely. They didn't give me their support at all, when I needed it so badly! It's so unfair. The trouble with the women's movement is that they don't like heterosexual women. Women like me, who really like men, who really like being women, we're made to feel we don't belong. Why *should* I be a lesbian? I just don't feel that way about women. I'm heterosexual through and through. My husband's not sexist, yet when I took him to a feminist bookshop to choose me a birthday present, he wasn't even allowed into the café! I *did* decide I would like to be in this group, because as far as I know you're all professionals and I wouldn't want to be in with a load of beginners, and I could do with more support for my writing. I'm feeling completely stuck at the moment. But I wouldn't mind at all if there were some men involved too.

– Quite right, says the Deftly Sibyl: I must say I'm rather irritated by the fact that there aren't any men here. I call that sexist, excluding men. I felt that attending a writers group might help me, since I'm also blocked right now, but why do we have to be all *women*? What matters is simply being a *writer* and striving for excellence. We're just creating a ghetto if we don't join in with men. If women want to be taken seriously as writers it's the quality of their writing that decides it, not their sex, and certainly not membership of a movement or group.

She looks severely at the Forsaken Sibyl before going on.

– I have to admit I'm rather disappointed by the quality of the work produced by the so-called feminist writers. It's hard not to feel that, first, they are more concerned with a political message than with the fact that they are working with language, and second, that they are limiting themselves unnecessarily by concentrating on questions of gender. I'd be the first to admit that women haven't always had equal opportunity and so on, but once they become writers they can be as good as any man. The imagination is a liberating force, don't you see? The writer, as Virginia Woolf said, is androgynous. Quite honestly some of these feminist writers would be better called hysterics, the way they fulminate on in the most angry and unpoetic way about their own bodies all the time. We simply can't have a horde of strident whining frustrated neurotics pushing into Parnassus and claiming that they are writers. Quite frankly, not everyone can make it. There's not enough room at the top. One's got to preserve standards after all.

She pauses to draw a breath. True to ourselves as would-be sisters, we wait for her to finish.

– Some of my best friends are men. Writers. They don't call themselves *male* writers. Why should they? And they treat me just like one of themselves! Not as a *woman*. That would be patronizing, if they judged me by anything but their most exacting standards. It's a mistake, I'm afraid, to demand special treatment for women. A weakness. And d'you see, in any case, it really is so boring, what so many women write about. Themselves. The small world of the home. Whereas in fact, one's just as capable as a man, if one has a good home help or an au pair, of thinking and travelling about and going to pubs just like men do. And, if I may say so, writing about *real* oppression, if one wants to write committed works, rather than going on about being a woman. That's rather self-indulgent, in this day and age, what with war, and poverty, and the Bomb, and totalitarianism, and so on. Those are the *real* issues. It's nothing to do with being a woman if you see your children dying of hunger, or if you have mice put up your vagina in prison, or if you're a Black maid raped by the son of your white employer. One's simply a human being. Not a *woman*.

48

Out of the corner of my eye I notice a red-faced middle-aged man peering around a column, a sheaf of papers under one arm. No one else seems to have seen him. They're all too intent on the discussion.

The Forsaken Sibyl hisses and spits.

– Neither of you should even be in this group. You're traitors to your own sex. I may be the baby in the group, seeing as I haven't had anything published yet, but I'm absolutely clear about what we should be doing. Men have dominated literature with their fantasies and lies about us, they've invented their phallic language to silence us and put us down, they've constructed a ridiculous grammar based on male subject and female object, denying the body and repressing the female point of view, and all you can do is say how wonderful men are! Men with their cold rational minds and their dreams of genocide and their pornography, they are dangerous I tell you. What we've got to do is forget their literature and write our own. And that means inventing a whole new female language. Incoherence and irrationality and syntactical violence and multiple word-orgasms, that's what we need.

– Excuse me, says the Re-Vision Sibyl: sorry to butt in and all that, but I really haven't any idea what any of you are talking about. Do you think you could try and use ordinary language? It leaves me cold, the way you go on.

She looks at us.

– What's the problem? We're all lucky enough to have been able to take some time off and get down to some writing, and here you are wasting your time scoring points off each other. I came here to work, not to talk about it. All right, I admit, perhaps I don't take my writing as seriously as you do, because I don't suppose you'd think of what I write as proper writing, anyway. Not like yours. I can see you've all got fancy ideas about being real writers. I just write stories. I do it for the money as much as anything. I just get on with it. Well, I used to. Recently I haven't been able to write a word. I *would* like to try something longer, a novel maybe, which is why I'm here. I could use the free time. And I'm quite happy it's a women's group. It's women who read what I write, after all. But I can't see the point of this sort of discussion before we've actually done any writing. Let's get down to it! Let's get *going*.

– Don't you think, the Correct Sibyl replies: that it's rather simplistic to talk as though common sense were all we needed? Will that really help us bridge our differences? How, for example, do you propose we should set about judging each other's work? What are our criteria? In what terms should we discuss our problems with writing? I may be unhappy at being told that some of us have this mysterious quality called talent whereas others haven't. I'm equally dismayed to hear that the biological fact of being a woman automatically produces good art. My own writing is going really badly at the moment, as it happens. I could do with hearing some properly rigorous arguments on what constitutes creativity. Somehow, I'm sure, gender and the imagination are linked, but I don't think any of you have theorized it correctly as yet.

– Who cares about theory? yells the Forsaken Sibyl: I'm not a bloody academic. I'm a writer. If you're going to wait to write until you've formulated a theory on how to do it, you'll never get anywhere.

The middle-aged man, who can clearly bear it no longer, rushes out from behind his column. He halts in the middle of the space between our chairs and holds up his hands in protest.

– Ladies! Ladies! Let's not get too excited. Let me give you *my* point of view. You shouldn't have started without me.

– I never invited you, I exclaim: who on earth are you?

– What are *you* doing here? chokes the Forsaken Sibyl: this is a *women's* group. Get out!

– Aha, murmurs the Babble-On Sibyl: a man. Things are looking up.

The Correct Sibyl stirs, and opens her notebook.

– What is *your* position on this question? she asks: I'd be interested to hear you define it.

– Do come in, says the Deftly Sibyl: we've only just started the meeting. Your point of view is crucial. Do take a seat.

The Re-Vision Sibyl begins to rock her tubular chair back and forth. The creak of the rockers is a calming sound. We all watch her, as she considers what to say.

– I was dead scared of coming here, she informs us: I was sure you'd all disapprove of what I write and think it's a sell-out of your politics. Well, now it seems to me that we've all got quite different views on what the group should be like, whether it

50

should even exist, and that's a relief. So why not let a man in, as an experiment? It might be interesting, to match our writing against his, and to see to what extent they're different. As long as he promises to behave properly and has some work he's seriously interested in doing.

She looks at him sternly.

– Please, begs the middle-aged man: let me stay. I need this group, I'm sure of it.

– Tell us all who you are first, I burst out, furious at his interruption of *my* project: go on, introduce yourself.

He draws himself up.

– I am the speaker of the Word of God.

– All men think that, scoffs the Forsaken Sibyl: pull the other one.

The Deftly Sibyl leans forward in her chair, studying our visitor closely.

– I don't see, she declares: why you shouldn't be allowed to explain yourself and your narrative theory. As a modernist, of course, I've never believed in omniscient narrators, but I hope I'm tolerant.

– I think we should take a vote, growls the Correct Sibyl.

– No, I insist: let's ask for inspiration.

I point at the brazier which I set up earlier in front of the altar on a tripod. At its foot is a wreath of laurel. I pull a spray of leaves out of the wreath and cast them onto the glowing coals, causing smoke, a sweet stench, to eddy forth.

– I don't accept inspiration coming from anyone but God the Father, grumbles the middle-aged man: sheer idolatry.

– Be quiet, I snap: if you want to take part in our group then you must have the courtesy to abide by our rituals.

I turn to the others.

– Who wants to be priestess? Who will consult the sacred fire?

The Forsaken Sibyl's voice is unexpectedly confident.

– You, Mrs Noah. You must become a sibyl too, like the rest of us, as I told you before. After that we'll all take turns.

The others all agree, silencing my protests. So I approach the tripod.

They are all quiet and still now, watching me. I tremble, not knowing what god I shall summon up.

I lean over the tripod, and breathe the fumes in deeply. My body starts to shake, to jerk, and then a thick cloud of smoke pours from the bitter burning leaves and hides the sibyls from my view. My feet dissolve, or the floor does, and I'm falling, down into the pit that's opened up beneath me. Someone is holding my hands lightly and whispering to me: let go, let go. And then I'm off, cutting downwards through the whistling air. My voice leaves me. I hear it talking to the others, hoarse and gasping.

– Hear me. This is the story of the burning laurel leaves. This is the story you may have read in the library, in the books written by men.

The god Apollo, who was poet and musician, loved the beautiful nymph Daphne. She did not return his ardour. Fleeing from his embraces, she prayed for help to Mother Earth, who transformed her into a laurel tree. Disconsolate, Apollo made himself wreaths from its branches, and so the laurel became the emblem of poetry.

Hear me. This story has an earlier version. Rewritten, it has been almost erased. Its forgotten words, trampled in the dust of the male scholars' sentences, yelp in their elegant pauses, poke through the gaps between their graceful lines.

Grasp the laurel branch, you women, the laurel named as Apollo's sign (the male poets are crowned with laurel wreaths). Sit under the laurel tree. Put your ear to the trunk and press it to the bark, which is Daphne's book, Daphne's body, and hear her speak. The girl stilled in the tree. The virgin with a heart of wood.

I want to get out, she cries: I want to get out. My mouth is full of green sap, of green words.

Pick up your pens, and transcribe the creak of the branches, the rustle of the leaves. Hear me.

Daphne, fierce priestess of the women's mysteries. Daphne, with a knife in her hand and her face daubed with blood. Daphne, who leads her troop of maenads up to the hills outside the city, in the grey smoke of dawn.

They cut young shoots from the laurel tree, and chew the fresh leaves. The sour juice tips down their throats and sharpens their senses and their minds; the sap of the laurel darkens their eyes and quickens their tongues.

They are poets now, hunting their meanings across the high wooded slopes, on the stony mountain-tops, along the dry beds of streams, through flowering meadows and fields full of wheat. While the drug of the laurel works in them they are frenzied, eager, fast.

At evening they carry back down to the city the poems and stories they have captured, and sing them to the waiting people. They go home with bloodstained mouths, and their husbands and lovers walk warily around them.

Every month they repeat the rite, chewing on the tough laurel to release the fierce spirit, to find their power, express it; hunting for images and tales, dipping their fingers in blood and painting their mouths, then singing. Who does not fear them, envy them?

Apollo has stolen Daphne's laurel branch to make his own crown, has locked up her version of the story inside his, has pretended she is captive and silent inside the tree, has claimed that women do not make poets and storytellers, that poets and storytellers make women.

Hear me, you women. Hear the laurel tree speak. Let me seize you too, and infuse you with my power. Pity the male god, who searches for the woman he has lost, for her harsh magic, for her healing words. Pity him. Do not be bound by him.

– Me? shouts the middle-aged man: searching for a lost female? What nonsense! I can get a woman any time I like. Women adore being fucked by writers, especially women with aspirations to write themselves. You trying to accuse me of impotence or something?

His crimson cheeks puff out with rage.

I feel sick. Laurel-leaf sickness. Seasickness. This is our first real squall. I wouldn't mind morning sickness. If it were a baby heaving up and down in me, doing a sort of dance, I wouldn't mind. But not this pulse and swell of anger.

– You and your interruptions, I shout back at my uninvited guest: you'll spoil everything.

He subsides, looks at me pathetically. I know his type. All he wants is that I should match him in passion, join him in his arguing which is his way of showing he's interested in what I've said, be as ferocious as he. He's not a bully. He just likes a good fight. So do I, but marriage with Noah has shown me the

53

dangers. Once I get angry and start shouting I say things that wound deeply, send him white-faced from the room. Then silence for two days. So it's better to keep a rein on my temper.

– You behave yourself, I warn our visitor: and then we can talk. For a start, I'm not addressing you by this ridiculous title you've assumed. Voice of *God*. Who d'you think you are? As far as I and this group are concerned, you'll be known as Gaffer from now on. Meaning one who makes gaffes.

– People keep telling me I'm dead, he complains: twice over, once as God and once as Author. But I'm damned if I'll lie down and hand over my creative function to any pipsqueak thinking that her garrulous confessions or streams of consciousness constitute a proper act of creation. They don't! You need talent and craft and enormous patience to be an artist. As I should know, none better. Didn't I end up creating a near-perfect account of an entire world? It's true that I had to destroy what I wrote, more than once, and try again. I admit that. There's nothing wrong with redrafting. It's necessary. First I invented a world and some action, then I wrote it all down. I did have some secretarial help, a few scribes who took dictation. But *I* am the Creator! I take responsibility for the whole thing. I've never pretended to be less than dedicated. You can't combine creation with a whole lot of other hobbies. All these silly people going to creative writing classes. They don't understand that you've got to give up everything else if you want to be a serious artist. It's all a question of imagination, you know. And mine's the best.

– So what's brought you here, then? I sneer: why bother trying to join our writers group?

He looks sheepish.

– Actually, he admits: I'm having a few problems with my writing right now. I did all right when the Bible first came out: I collected a lot of royalties and retired to a tax-free haven. Heaven. I was read by everyone in the old days. I was on the curriculum at universities, critics squabbled over my message and my prose style, other writers copied me, I was rewritten countless times by people inspired by my story, people even named their children after my characters. All very flattering, even if I disagreed with a lot of the reviews and thought that half my fans hadn't got the point. But now, having published

54

one big blockbuster going from the beginning of the universe right through to the end, I'm not sure how to go about writing a sequel, whether I've left myself anything to write about. To put it frankly, I'm stuck. Writer's block. People always say the second novel is harder than the first, don't they? So I thought I'd attend a writers workshop, see if I could pick up a few tips. I was just passing and I saw the notice saying *Writers group this way*. So I nipped on down. I do think you could have waited for me, though, before you got going.

– You weren't supposed to come, I mutter: I never thought of asking *you*. Now you're here, I suppose you should stay.

– Good, he beams: now, tell me, which of you is the tutor?

– There isn't a tutor, I yell at him: this is a *group*.

– Don't be too hard on him, the Babble-On Sibyl rebukes me: he's not used to our ways yet.

She smiles at him.

– Come on. Tell us what you think about this whole question of women's writing.

The Gaffer coughs, and looks around.

– Well, he begins: I'll have to tell you the truth. I am truth incarnate. I'm incapable of lying.

– You can tell us *your* truth, sneers the Forsaken Sibyl: but I'm afraid you'll find it's partial.

The Gaffer looks pained.

– Listen, he says: some of you aren't going to like this, but I'll have to say it. That's how you operate, right, saying what you think? Well, my problem is that I don't know any women writers, for a start. Where I live there aren't any. So of course it's never crossed my mind that women, and certainly not *mothers*, could create whole new worlds. I *do* sometimes think of my imagination, the Holy Ghost as I like to call it, as having a female aspect, in a purely allegorical sense of course. To that extent I think of the writer, ie me, as androgynous. But I've never needed to imagine women creating because I can do it all by myself. Women are *receptive*, yes. They're great at listening for my Word and taking it in. Take Mary, for example, this girl I knew years ago. She was this terrific incubator of my ideas. She gave them a nice warm place in which to grow. But she was empty to start with. I mean she couldn't have done anything

55

without me. I had to sow the seed. It's the *male* who represents humanity, creativity, spiritual quest, after all. How could a *woman* possibly do that? How could a *mother* know anything about human growth? Any fool can give birth. Writing a book is *labour*.

He lowers his voice.

– I have to admit that the thought of what goes on inside women turns me right off. Women writers, well, they're like leaky wombs, aren't they, letting out the odd stream of verbiage, the odd undisciplined shriek. They don't *create*. They just spill things out of that great empty space inside. It's babies they hold, not books. It's only frustrated neurotic women who write, women who can't have children, or who are scared of their normal feminine fulfilment. I'm sorry, ladies, I'm sorry. I'm sure most of you are planning to do sterling work. But I'm convinced you can write properly only when you rise above your bodies and forget them, when you get to the proper height from which you can survey the whole human race and speak for it, when you become, yes, androgynous. More like me. To put it bluntly, when you are *virile*. Of course I like to think of myself as having a womb. But it's *imaginary*. A real one can only get in the way.

I howl with laughter. I can't stop. I can feel my face turning red, tears coursing down my cheeks as I rock from side to side and then fall on the floor and pummel it.

– You see the danger? the Gaffer sighs: this unfortunate tendency to overstate? to overreact? to exaggerate?

– Please, the Deftly Sibyl says to me: control yourself. You'll give us all a bad name.

She turns to the Gaffer.

– Mrs Noah is not a writer. She's a librarian.

– You shouldn't judge *us*, adds the Babble-On Sibyl: by *her*.

I'm surprised. It's the Correct Sibyl who comes to my rescue, helping me off the floor and onto my chair again.

– I'm sorry, I mumble: I'm feeling a bit sick.

– Don't be sorry, snaps the Forsaken Sibyl: you should be *angry*.

– Let's call a halt for the moment, I suggest, wiping my eyes: I think we've got as far as we can for today. Let's go and have supper. I need an early night. I'll be all right in the morning.

But I can't sleep. I'm too confused.

Here I am, returning to a nice warm womb full of the nourishment and sweetness of women, a fine safe place in which to grow and change, and what do I find? Not only disagreement and conflict (women's groups? give me a coffee morning any day) but also untruths. To speak is to lie. To over-simplify. I don't believe in that conversation we've just had. The taking up of positions as in a war, no ambiguity allowed. Ambush of the images streaming up along the narrow pass, polemical boulders dropped on them, crushing them. I spoke more truth when possessed by the inspirational leaves. Who are the sibyls and the Gaffer? I don't know yet. I'll have to find another way of getting to know them.

I prowl the dark passages and companionways of the Ark, nightmare tangles of decks and steps, identical layers. No numbers. No signs. I can't tell which deck I'm on. From time to time, through a closed door, I hear snores and mutters, my sister dreamers mapping their sleeping worlds. From far below me, many decks down, in the depths of the bookstacks, the bowels of the Ark, come muffled roars, screeches, bellowing. The utterances of hysterics. Their crazy complaints, pre-verbal. I refuse them. I escape up a ladder, towards a higher deck. The hold is safely locked, and it can stay that way.

Here's my cabin at last. Falling onto my bunk I bury my head in my pillow, press my fingers into my ears, will myself towards oblivion.

11 The first thing the Deftly Sibyl does, once the Ark has left the Venetian lagoon and is heading out to the open sea, is to fall ill. To fall, down onto the deck of her cabin. Bending to find her slippers under the bunk, then straightening up again, she is gripped by violent pains in the lower back, and falls.

She staggers up. Someone is sawing her in half; she's the lady in the circus trick only it's real. She lacks backbone; a section is missing. When she tries to walk a step, her bones melt in heat, pain at the point of collapse, the base of the spine. She is a ruined column, toppling. She lurches towards a chair, sobbing, unable to stop the tears washing out of her eyes and down her face. Crying does not stop the pain nor ease it, just accompanies it. Her hips grind. Her bones wrench apart.

She shouts for help. The other sibyls come out of their cabins along the companionway and carry her into the sickroom.

She invents it, according to what she wants: a quiet place. The white walls are bare. Thin white curtains drift against the open portholes, letting a breeze stir about her aching neck. The wooden deck is painted pale pink. A bamboo screen hides the door, shapes the sickroom into a hollow of privacy and rest. No clutter of ornaments, pictures, books. Just this enclosure of bare wood.

The Deftly Sibyl lies flat on her back, staring at the ceiling, and remembers the sickbay at convent school. Mysterious place that she entered only once, after fainting at early Mass. Tiled red floor, folded white counterpane at the foot of the high hospital bed, tall window blocked by red serge, smell of disinfectant. Coolness and peace; a picture of the Virgin on one wall. The kindness of tiny wizened Sister Joan, the infirmarian, after the sternness of the other nuns in the classroom.

Is the Ark a floating convent then, full of sisters? Is she on retreat amongst them? Sisters are the last thing she's ever wanted. Not her style, those gossipy female friendships, hint of Lesbos with the grumbling about men, the threats to a safe, well-ordered marriage. Yet the other sibyls behave as though she's invited them to be her nurses: lift her up and down, carry her to the lavatory, wait outside the door while she grips the cold enamel edge of the washbasin and tries to lower herself onto the pan without screaming. Agony. She sweats. Then the women's hands raise her again, cart her along the companionway back to the sickroom. She refuses a bedpan, that humiliation. One of the sibyls has remade her bed. Even though it hurts so much to sit down, lift her legs in, lie back, shove herself lower down the bed, the clean sheets feel wonderful: cool scratch of ironed cotton and the light floating weight of the quilt like a cloud settled on her stomach.

The sibyls leave her alone, as she asks them to.

Am I being ill, she wonders to the yellow afternoon: simply in order to be taken care of?

It is extraordinary to lie in bed, not in too much pain as long as she does not move, and wait for dinner, lunch, breakfast to arrive. She marvels. Meals she has not cooked herself. For the first time in twenty years.

She has not been ill in bed since she had chronic tonsillitis as a child. Once she stays off school for two whole weeks, and her mother takes unpaid leave from work to look after her. Her mother is pinned to her bedside for half an hour at a time, reading to her, telling her stories. The late dark afternoons of that winter illness are the worst, when her mother's downstairs catching up on housework, and the grisly radio play she dare not switch off tells of murder, and her bed and body are too heated, flush of fever swilling the room, her fear lying panting in the corner, and not enough lights on, and her brothers and sisters have all gone away and left her alone. Fourteen days like that she passes, throat aflame, head bowed by concrete weights, eyes rolling over the ceiling like escaped marbles, arms sometimes long enough to scrabble on top of the wardrobe, and once her self floating high above the bed and looking down at the body tossing on it.

One time her mother's ill with a bad back. Not for long; she has too much to do, is scared of losing her job, can't leave the running of the household to her husband for too long. The children surge into their mother's room, never wondering for a moment whether she wants peace and solitude. They've got her, pinned down again; she's still theirs, there for them to love and cuddle, no escape.

The Deftly Sibyl stares at the walls, grateful for their lack of demand. At home it is impossible to be ill. The children wouldn't understand, would fret. George wouldn't be able to cope. She wouldn't be able to cope with him not coping. Bad mother. Bad wife.

She likes it here in bed. She doesn't have to hold everything together. She doesn't have to hold anything. One by one the burdens topple to the floor: shopping, cleaning, cooking. All the responsibilities. She has nothing else to do but lie here and watch how the light filters between the white curtains into this empty space which she does not fill or disturb. When something is empty then you can see its shape.

Into the emptiness swims the meaning of her illness. She invents it. It may or may not be true; impossible to know. What matters is that she's found it, believes it.

She's finally got herself a room of her own, which no one enters without her permission, which belongs to her alone.

The home of her childhood is all bustle and movement. She shares a bedroom with her two sisters. Inside her rounded bedside cabinet lives her doll, the curved cupboard her room where she sits peacefully alone. From time to time she opens the white door and peeps in at her, then closes the door again quickly, not wanting to disturb her solitude for too long. What does the doll do behind the closed door when she can't see her?

It is necessary to have a secret, and a secret place. The houses in the suburb where she lives are not designed to accommodate mystery, the unconscious. Downstairs is open-plan, every corner visible, large plate-glass windows on two sides hiding nothing of the garden's bland flowerbeds, cropped lawn, concrete patio. Upstairs, the bedroom is filled with her elder sisters experimenting with make-up, new hairdos. This house, this suburb, make her ache to be unseen, to be able to invent a movement incorporating both display and retreat, both silence

60

and speech: *choice*. The suburb is too public, too falsely communal, too bright white clean glaring hygienic.

Diligently the child invents her escape. She clears out the coal hole, furnishing it with wooden boxes, chipped mugs rejected from the kitchen, a strip of old carpet. She makes dolls' rooms in cardboard boxes, a chair a chestnut on pin legs, postage stamps for pictures, chest of drawers of a stack of matchboxes. She squats in the cupboard under the stairs between the massive hoover and the old sunburst bakelite radio. She buries treasures under the trees in the park. None of these retreats lasts. She's unable to stake a lasting claim.

When she gets married and acquires, through her husband, a home of her own, she doesn't realize at first that that doesn't give her a private room, and that she hasn't, as young wives are supposed to do, grown out of needing one.

But now, at last, she can sleep by herself in this single bed, for as long as she wants, without feeling guilty, without betraying her marriage. Hours to spend as she likes, daydreaming, dozing, being a child again. Illness has given her the power she was unable to claim when well: the power to refuse others' demands sometimes, to go away by herself, to be free to do what she wants, which is to be still, and dream.

The pain has been useful. It's made her slow down, stop, be silent. It's let her withdraw from her family into this retreat. It's absolved her from guilt about not working hard enough finishing her next book, not earning enough money. It's forced her to admit, grudgingly, her gratitude to the others for looking after her when she needed it.

She starts to get well, and to want to write. Images begin to emerge, diving up from the deep to break the surface of her mind, turning over and lolloping in the green waves, showing the flick of a fin, of a tail. She's fishing for them, casting her line, waiting patiently for a bite, a tug, a kick, reeling in, rod bent taut, uncertain what she's hooked: an old boot, a lump of seaweed, a mermaid.

Quilt pulled up over the head, a soft cave. Bed is a good place for writing: why did she never realize that before? Hesitant scratch of pen on paper, the loose sheets scattered across her stomach as she tries out two words at a time, rejects them, starts again, a fresh sheet each time so she can see properly what the words look like. Haul them in gently, coaxing, a net of words sprawling. The deepest pleasure there is, this certainty that the words are there, hidden underwater, and will come when she calls, when she stops still and listens for them. Four hours of alert concentration, the music in her head sounding stronger and clearer as she goes on, led by its rhythm to shape one phrase, one sentence at a time. A paragraph gathers form and speed, leaps forward shedding silver adjectives, sinewy, bony.

She stacks the pile of scribbled-over sheets together, her sieve of words: two words on the top one, a hundred on the bottom one. Later she'll re-read and sort and discard her gleaming catch. She's tired now, needs to sleep, to dream her way into the next shoal of images. It doesn't do to hurry, or you lose it, that new meaning that gleams, phosphorescent, in the ocean lapping her body, her bed. She floats between her scrawled drafts, sinks down to the seabed of words, lets sleep quench her and turn her loose.

12 When I'm seven, I'm given an Advent calendar for the first time. The four weeks before Christmas are represented by numbers printed on the doors and windows of the façade of a paper house, one opening for each day, the whole design framed in glittering silver holly leaves. The calendar hangs in the sitting room above the side table where we shall build the crib later on.

Each day I pull open a new door or window, carefully moving around the house according to the dates on the paper casements. Inside each one I find an image printed: a lamb, a star, a shepherd's crook, a bunch of grapes, an angel. And so on through the month. When at last I open the door marked 25 December I find the Child inside.

I am a house with many windows and many doors. Each day I must pull one open and peer inside. This is my time of Advent, of preparation. I have work to do. If only I knew what that work is.

I'll start with today's door. I'll reach for it.

It bursts open.

Memories of my last conversation with Noah, on the train going to Venice, leap out.

– In any case, he asks: what makes you think you'd be able to be a good mother? Are you really sure you want a baby? It's not just a passing whim?

In the archive I discover an ancient volume of riddles dedicated to the Sphinx. She may be on board with us but I haven't seen her yet.

When is *a confinement*, I read: *not a confinement*?

13 At sunset I climb to the very top of the Ark, open the trap door there and peer out, watching the sun fall heavily into the sea and disappear. At dawn I watched it struggle up again out of the deep. What happens to the sun when I can't see it, sunk in darkness, traversing the land of the dead, the underworld? I want to find out. Tonight I want to reverse time, and follow the sun.

I climb out onto the roof of the Ark, the guidebook which I have found in the archive clutched in one hand. It doesn't tell me much. A scanty volume. I dive into books and fish greedily for treasures. At primary school, having read all the books in the school and hungry for more, I was put to reading the Bible. To slow me down a bit. Very well then. A plunge back into Genesis; into sub-plots and sub-texts.

I dive into cold blackness. I part the steep hills of water on either side of me. Down and down I fall, to the deep seabed.

My bare feet touch gravel. The sun rolls along far ahead of me, a wheel glowing in the darkness. In its muffled light I see bright fish dart upwards in wriggling shoals. I walk in slow motion, my hair floating up in the water like weeds, my arms stretched out for balance, my legs pulled along by currents of curiosity.

I halt. In the distance, shining through the green screen of the sea, is a palace as vast as a city, hidden behind gleaming battlements, scales of mother-of-pearl.

The way in is by water.

To Atlantis: also called the house of memory and of forgetting; the fossil of the old world.

I come closer. The thick walls are pierced by a colonnade

64

faced with marble. A high doorway claps its wooden tongue behind twin red columns.

Once through the main entrance I cross a courtyard, weedy and barnacled, now an aquarium for slow-moving fish, and come into a great hall set with obstacles of white coral, twisted white branches bursting up through the marble pavement, delicate forests of knobbled whiteness dancing underneath my feet in the clear water. And now the palace discovers itself to me, a labyrinth of revelations turning over and sliding like the inside of a Chinese puzzle box carved in ivory, as one saloon opens out of, and into, another.

I find interior gardens slung one above the other, a waterfall of courtyards planted with roses and lilies still impossibly blooming and set with pools once stocked with carp. Now the bright carp are everywhere about me, exclamation marks in gold and red. Orange trees launch up from earthenware pots; vines twist along gilded lattices; red persimmon fruits dangle from black branches. Each of these gardens is a secret and a surprise: I come upon them unexpectedly, as they open up at the end of a gallery or a corridor. As I climb higher and higher in the palace, so the gardens tumble past me, a rain of scents, of butterflies and ferns and bees.

I float through a loggia of creamy stone into a tiny court, the fountain at its centre half buried by a drift of sand, broken shells, polished white bones. These must be the gardeners, I decide, looking at the clean dislocated skeletons: this is their tomb.

I swim through a low dank tunnel, its walls painted with *trompe l'oeil* landscapes of the outside world, and emerge into a grotto. Water slides over the white pebbles underfoot, over silver gravel, over the creamy cockleshells decorating the walls in patterns of arabesques and fans. From niches of mossy stone satyrs peer at me, their long mouths curled up and grinning. Lady satyrs too, with muscular legs, little breasts peeping out of their thick fur, and big pointed ears. One of them looks rather like me.

In the beginning, I remember: as in the end, the waters covered everything, and all kinds of creatures flourished in them.

I bounce slowly through a passage hung with mirrors and

painted with all kinds of fish and waterfowl leaping in lakes and streams, stags and boar and deer chasing each other across the ceiling and around the door at the far end.

Now I come to the room of metamorphoses.

Here all the rules are broken, joyfully. Here chaos reigns for the sheer pleasure of it. Here are men turning themselves into gods and gods into men. Here are creatures that are half-beast and half-man, with pink naked feet and thick swishing tails.

Here are male gods, disguised as bulls, dragons, showers of gold, attempting to seduce women. A fleshy hand grips a delicate white chin, forcing it up. A great phallus waggles. Shrieks and laughter. Games of kiss and chase. Gestures that beckon and repulse.

Here are nymphs, hiding behind rocks, in the depths of streams and pools, combing and plaiting each other's hair, riding on the backs of dolphins, blowing sea-music out of conch shells, playing with each other in a tangle of breasts and necks and knees. Here are goddesses bathing in the company of their maidens, tipping water from silver basins over their heads, or striding the hills wearing gilded helmets and kilts, a froth of hounds at their ankles, long-haired women running behind them with outstretched arms, darting over the dewy grass.

Here are heroes and heroines, legs entwined, falling back, gasping and sweaty, onto gold couches. Hands part plump thighs; tongues plunge into dripping wet openings; clever fingers make the juice run, the heat mount, the flush spread. Beside them, lovely athletic boys wrestle, oil each other, lick and fondle each other, give each other voluptuous slow massages. Reclining on silk mattresses, ringleted girls spread their legs wide, admiring each other's cushiony lips and springing triangles of hair, enjoy each other's display. One woman puts her mouth to another's, touches her all over.

You may look, you may touch, you may tease, you may bite. You may experiment with being held down and tied up with strings of coral beads, with being blindfolded, with being fondled by strangers. You may invent any game you like, for three or four or more to play.

God the Father didn't approve of this state of affairs, so he sent the Flood. It's all there, in chapter six of the Gaffer's novel. God the Father wanted order. So he invented heterosexuality, monogamy, and the family.

Into the hall of the giants now, a vast, dark, windowless place whose walls are painted with images of enormous grotesque figures cowering, terrified, under boulders and broken columns and thunderbolts being hurled by the king of heaven. I escape up a staircase so narrow it seems to have been made for dwarfs. I bend my head; my knees brush my chin. I catch glimpses, as I squeeze past low openings slit in the stone, of thumb-sized chambers and chapels, of throat-like corridors branching off. The miniature palace within the palace. A new crystal growing, a new cluster of cells. A pregnancy flowering in the stone.

I push open the golden door at the top and enter the hall of the expectant mother. This is a long gallery with tall arched windows on one side reaching from ceiling to floor, tall mirrors between the windows throwing back the images of the frescoes painted opposite, other mirrors tilted to reflect the swags of fruit carved on the bosses of the high ceiling.

A naked goddess is painted in the centre of the long wall, her arms outstretched towards me as I enter. As I walk down the gallery, and past her, never taking my eyes off her, her arms swivel and stretch after me, as do her eyes. How's it done? I can't believe it. Laughing, I swim back through the cool green waves, and watch the painted beauty turn and languish after me. It is not possible to be other than desired by her, sought by her, reached for by her: she turns, and turns, and turns, keeping me always in the circle of her arms and eyes.

Further, and higher, into the twelve-sided zodiac room, to scrutinize the baffling chart of the stars, of the child I want to bear. The domed ceiling peels back in a welter of vines and flowering boughs to reveal the night sky, curved expanse of deep inky blue, sea trawled by nets of golden constellations, each knot a star. Gods and goddesses in faint gold outline move across the blackness, starry profiles. The depth and reach, the unfathomable time and space of the universe, is caged in gold wire, unimaginable distances flattened out into two dimensions, the human body patterned onto the night and patterned by it.

A narrative is simply a grid placed over chaos so that it can be read in descending lines from left to right, if that's what you want to do. Some writers prefer the chaos, prefer simply to record, rather than to interpret, the interlocking rooms and staircases and galleries of this palace, this web of dream images that shift and turn like the radiant bits of glass in a kaleidoscope. Others, like the Gaffer, make a clear design, slot incident onto a discernible thread.

I understand the Gaffer's point of view, because now I want to retrace my steps and find the way out. But which way did I come? There is no sign saying Exit, no red arrow pointing.

I choose a door and plunge through it. This isn't right. I'm in a vast saloon, draped in crimson silk hangings, that I haven't been in before. I go back, but I can't find the zodiac room, or the long-mirrored hall. Passage after room after staircase beckons me, mocking, only to present me with a dead end, or an unfamiliar suite of lavishly decorated chambers whose doors give on to yet more splendid corridors and galleries.

The palace broods over and around me, tightening its grip, chuckling: I've got you now, and I'll never let you go. Panic whistles up in my throat, and I let go of my last vestige of a sense of direction. I'm running, but I can't escape the palace: it's swallowed me up, and I rattle in its dark belly. I'm alone. I could die here, and never be found, my body withering to a pile of scattered bones like those of the gardeners in the courts far below.

Is this the mother, then, this horror? This hold? This great gloomy imprisoning embrace that hangs on, that won't let the child step out free? That sits, and waits, implacable as death?

How could I ever become a mother, let myself become that embodiment of possessive power, fortress jangling with locked gates, sealed windows? Never. I'm the child running away from home, from the enormous voracious controlling mother, drumming my fists on the bolted door: *let me out*.

Mothers are not free. A woman entering pregnancy is entering time, and history, process whirling her inexorably towards the moment of giving birth, that long road of mothering, her life altered irrevocably and utterly, no going back, no returning the baby to the shop, sorry, I've changed my mind. Women who do are monsters.

To become a mother is to become unfree; tied down; committed, as to prison. A confinement. Leaving the crossroads, the myriad beckoning possibilities; choosing just one not hovering over many.

68

To become a mother is to own up to having a female body and the social consequences of that: invisibility. Mothers exist only on mother's-day cards, on telly ads for margarine. Mothers don't have jobs, do they? Mothers have no money.

Therefore mothers are boring and unsmart and have tiny minds. Mothers are cabbages buried in the mud of suburbs.

Therefore motherhood is a woman's mystical destiny, her fulfilment that puts her in touch with the rhythms of the cosmos, a glory men can't aspire to. Therefore any woman not choosing motherhood is not a real woman. Therefore any woman not choosing to have children is taking the easy way out. Therefore mothers don't need to be paid and should not complain. Therefore mothers distrust women who are not mothers. Therefore women are scared of mothers. Therefore it's the mother's fault. Therefore mothering comes naturally.

Therefore a mother's life is already over. Therefore mothers can't invent their own stories. Therefore mothers can't live their own lives. Therefore mothers should not want paid jobs.

Therefore it is better not to be a mother but to remain a child and remain free. Therefore it is better to imitate men. Therefore it is better to dream of a thousand possibilities, to fantasize omnipotence, to deny death.

Therefore to become a mother is to accept death. Therefore it is better not. Therefore men preach the resurrection and eternal life. Therefore women are not men. Therefore women are not.

Therefore I will not become a mother. Therefore I want to become a mother. Therefore I cannot find the way out.

– You left a lot out of Genesis, didn't you? the Forsaken Sibyl remarks to the Gaffer once I'm back on board the Ark and telling the others, over breakfast, what I've seen during the night: there's almost no description there, if I remember correctly, of Atlantis, of what the world was like before the Flood.

He looks pleased.

– So you *have* read my book. I wouldn't have thought it would have appealed to you, somehow.

– It was a set text throughout my childhood, the Forsaken Sibyl growls: I couldn't avoid it. It was there, like Mount Everest, so I climbed it.

The Gaffer reflects.

– You could say I discarded a chapter. I don't approve of pornography, you know. My book was written for a family market, after all. I didn't want to encourage youngsters to try out perversions, all the wrong things. I wanted to show the purity and beauty of married life. I saw the Flood as a sort of correction fluid, blanking out all the bad bits, the parts of creation that had gone wrong. In later chapters of my novel, of course, I stressed how perverts always come to a sticky end. Torn apart by dogs, stoned to death, killed off by plagues, and so on.

– Censorship! exclaims the Correct Sibyl: I can't possibly accept that. It may well be useful sometimes to divide writers into progressives and reactionaries, but things should *not* be taken further than that.

– Censorship can be enforced, the Gaffer says, coughing: rules and regulations, you know. Acts of Parliament. Zealous police and customs officers.

– You'd censor male writers, wouldn't you? the Babble-On Sibyl taunts the Forsaken Sibyl: if you had the power? I bet you'd be the first to demand that male pornographers should be punished and their books and magazines burned.

– You'd like to censor other women writers sometimes, wouldn't you? the Deftly Sibyl insists to the Correct Sibyl: you pretend to be a liberal, because it looks good, but you'd write damning reviews of bad girls who wrote things you didn't like. If they experimented with pornography, for example, or criticized feminists as puritanical and sentimental. Oh yes, you would.

– But why should you want to read what I left out? asks the Gaffer: why try to rewrite my story?

– Perhaps this is the moment, I say: for someone to *tell* a story?

– Someone tell a story, the Forsaken Sibyl suggests: about one of the characters the Gaffer completely forgot to put in? Fill in one of his gaps?

14 I am a wanderer. The soles of my feet are yellow with callouses, my body is lean and muscled, my brown face is polished by the sun and wind. It is the changing seasons that are my constancy. I and my people are always on the move. We drive our sheep and goats along in front of us, as we trek from one watering hole to the next. We butcher them for our food, make cheese from their milk, and our tents and bed-coverings from their hides.

We travel through the wilderness, seeking water. A parched riverbed spells death, an oasis life. Always in my mind I carry the image of the shimmer of light on a deep pool, green grass at its edge. Fresh water trickling over my dry tongue, loosening it to prayers and songs. My life is a long thirst.

Linked together by our need for water, my people are also linked by blood, the ties of kinship which separate us from the other nomads wandering this harsh world. Blood is spilled when we defend our claim to pitch camp at a particular watering hole, a particular spring. We slaughter our animals with clubs and knives. We kill our enemies. We offer blood sacrifices of lambs and kids. Our people are stern with wrongdoers. Robbers and murderers, who add to the weight of suffering we carry, have their hands cut off, are stoned to death.

Blood also separates women from men. When my monthly bleeding begins, my mother gives me a bundle of rags and tells me to sew them to make my bandages. I sit and do it so proudly, outside, where anyone can see me, my father, my brothers, my uncles. My mother hits me and hits me.

I am afraid of growing older, of the years of hardship stretching ahead, of a painful death that will perhaps come early. I tell no one this. There is no point.

I accept leaving my people and being given to Jack as his wife. He watches me from behind a tree one day, when I sit in the shade of a rock and wash fleeces. I pretend not to notice his eyes running over me, measuring my strength, my youth, as I swirl the heavy wool in the green water at my knees. I know him: his route has often crossed ours.

He is kind to me. He does not beat me. He is anxious that I stay with him, for his children have been killed by thieves, and his wife has run away into the desert, crazed by grief. He wants more sons. When I bear him three in five years, he treats me with respect. In bed at night he becomes more gentle, less desperate, and I start to like being with him there. He says it is our duty, that his God wishes it, and I certainly don't mind.

Raising our children, preparing and cooking our food, making blankets and clothes, caring for our livestock, all this carries me through my life. I cradle my sons, one by one, in my arms, then have to let go of them, slap them into shape, watch them grow. Not exactly pleasure but a sort of satisfaction arrives for me out of my work. I am creating the survival not just of myself but also of my children. So far I am winning against the cruel nature stalking us with the threat of death. And so I gain the courage to go more deeply into my life, and start to feel less afraid, more capable, more powerful. I start to reflect on the world around me through concentrating intently on whatever it is that I am doing. I flow out of myself and become pot, hide, fish, earth, leaf. I worship the creation of the world day by day by letting myself become part of it, by working. God is in my hands as they scrub, wring, knead, scour, caress, sew, carve. I act, I create, and God pours through me. At these times I am not-myself, I go into a strange country. Sometimes I come to with a shock, to find myself kneeling, my forehead bowed to the ground.

When Jack catches me at my wild prayers one day he is worried I have fallen ill. I reassure him, but after that he watches me secretly, not wanting a second wife to lose her wits.

For Jack God is different. He is a mighty father in the sky, who punishes us when we do wrong, and sends us diseases and plagues and famines to show us his power. I can't understand

72

why that's necessary when the terrible beauty of God shimmers as close to us as the raindrop on the end of a twig, burns in the grass. You only have to sit still and *see*.

Jack walks and talks with his God. Sometimes, in the evening, at sunset, he goes off out of sight and stays away for a whole night. In the morning he comes back and announces that we have to offer a sacrifice or else we're in trouble. It's confusing for the boys, I think, Jack telling them one thing and me another. As they grow older, though, they decide to follow their father's example.

– What does your God look like? I ask Jack.

– I don't *see* him, he replies: he's too magnificent for that. I hear his voice sometimes, like the ringing of cymbals and harps and trumpets. Or he comes veiled in a golden mist, like the smoke of a heavenly fire. He wraps himself in the clouds and holds the sun in front of his face. His eyes are stars. And yet he is greater than all of these. His splendour is so great that if I looked at him I would surely die.

Jack's God is up, and mine is down. That seems to be one of the differences between the two. I wonder whether there are in fact two Gods, and whether they know each other. I wonder whether without knowing it Jack and I worship the same God. I don't think of God as a person but I might be wrong. My God is all over the place. I keep tripping over God at the oddest times, and not always in secret holy places or when I am by myself. Sometimes God is in bed with us.

– There is only one God, Jack repeats to me: and he lives beyond the sun and the moon and the heavens and sees everything we do and wants us to obey him and love him and behave properly.

– Well then, I reply: he'd be pleased, I'm sure, if you gave me a hand with the milking.

I have a picture in my mind of Jack's God as out to get us. Ready with his thunderbolts. He frightens me. Whereas when I meet my God in the middle of doing something ordinary I am flooded with happiness like sweet fresh milk. Jack says mine is a childish vision. I am not sure.

Time passes. My sons reach manhood, and take wives. I slow down a little, stop counting the silver strands in my black hair, feel restless. When my monthly bleeding lessens and then finally stops, I feel like a girl again, skinny and nimble. I am not sad. I rule over three fine sons and their wives. Jack and I still make merry at night. But I catch myself thinking: so what now?

One night I have a dream. The earth appears to me as a woman groaning and arching in labour. She twists her hands in the tops of trees, which are her hair, and bites hard on the mountains, which are her arms, while her belly shakes, threatening earthquakes. Her waters breaking are a great flood. For nine months she has carried the seed of new life safely inside her, letting it float on her waters. Now it rushes out on a flood-tide of water and blood, while she heaves and shouts. And then the waters subside, and the waves are stilled, and the new child lies on her breast.

In the morning I tell Jack my dream. He is troubled by it, and goes off at evening to commune with his God. On his return he is white-faced and shaking.

– A great disaster is on the way, he tells me: God has warned me that he is about to destroy the world. People are so wicked that he is sorry he ever created us. There will be a great flood, and the whole race of mankind will be wiped out.

That night I have a second dream. This time the earth again appears to me as a pregnant woman, but this time at the beginning of her pregnancy. Inside her womb she holds the whole of creation, all forms of life dancing and growing within her. Jack and I and our children are there too, swimming on the waters inside her belly until we are ready to be born.

In the morning I again tell Jack my dream. Again, he is troubled by it.

– If your God is serious, I say: and he really intends to destroy us all with a great flood, we could escape if we built a boat with a roof. A house that could float. These tents would be no use in a really bad storm, they're far too flimsy. But a covered wooden shelter that could go with the storm and ride it, that might save us.

– I'll go and ask God what he thinks, Jack says.

He comes back next morning.

– God is willing for us to be saved, he announces: since we are less wicked than the rest of mankind. What we have to do is

74

to build a big wooden Boat with a roof and go into it with our sons and their wives and all our animals and livestock. That way we can see it through.

That was *my* idea, not your God's, I think. But I hold my tongue. This isn't the time for a quarrel.

Building the Boat is a real problem. Jack is handy at building sheds and cages for the animals, of course, and fences around our tents, since whenever we settle anywhere we always make ourselves secure against winds and robbers and storms. Our buildings, such as they are, are light, being woven of saplings and plastered with mud. Similarly, our rafts, whenever we settle for a time near a river or a lake and want to catch fish, are simple light craft, woven from lashed saplings like floating carpets.

We scratch pictures, in the dust, arguing. In the end we copy the shape of the closed earthenware pot we use for baking fish in the fire.

The people camped nearby help us. We pay them in sacks of wool. They laugh at us as they work. They declare that they would rather die than be shut up in a wooden box. They are used to the touch of wind and sun on their faces, and they are frightened of the dark. In the end I hold my peace, just thinking: they'll be glad enough to be saved when the time comes.

First of all we build the skeleton of the Boat, a spine with ribs arching above and below, and then we fit curved planks over it, making a large door in one side and rows of windows high up under the eaves of the roof. We paint over the entire vessel with a special waxy paint we make from tree resins mixed with egg white.

Inside we construct three tiers, the lowest one of stables and cattle sheds, the middle one of poultry houses and bird-cages, and the top one of living quarters for us. I paint the walls of our rooms with pictures of the world we are about to leave. I dip my brush in the pigments I have mixed from berry juices and earth and I paint tents and water pots, the sun rising over the purple mountains, the flowers waving in the grass. I think that perhaps the Boat will be our burial place, our coffin, and so I also paint pictures of people dying, falling sick, drowning. To give myself courage. I lay our best rugs on the deck, and hang

75

others on the walls, and I bring in our mattresses and pillows and cushions. I stack cooking utensils in a corner, and I help my three daughters-in-law carry in sacks of dried fruits, grains and flour, casks of oil, barrels of water.

When all is done, we gather on the riverbank and pray. Jack kills a lamb and offers a sacrifice, calling on God to be our good shepherd and take care of us, his faithful flock. The smell of the blood turns my stomach, and so I look away towards the green weeds under the fast-flowing river, the sand and rocks at its edge, the bushes and grasses dry and dazzling in the sunshine. I pray too, keeping my eyes averted from the bowl of blood at Jack's feet and putting my fingers in my ears so that I can't hear the sizzling of the burning lamb. Then I crouch down on the dust of the earth and commit us to her care, begging her not to be barren but to deliver us, to bring us through.

Then I pack my own private goods: my best linen robe, my blue eyelid paint, a bracelet of shells, a game of spillikins, a basket of embroidery threads. At the last minute I stuff a basket full of herbs, flowers and vegetables, I am not quite sure why, and then I am ready.

The weather changes. Violent storms by night, sticky heat by day. The earth is shaken by tremors stronger than we have ever experienced before, and the big mountains to the west begin to smoke a little. It is a sign. We know it, even before God tells Jack it is time to board the Boat. God is scolding and impatient, urging Jack to get a move on before it is too late.

Then the rain begins to fall, and does not stop.

We visit all our neighbours in turn, begging them to join with us. They sit tight in their tents and refuse to budge. They have never seen weather like this, they admit, but they see no reason to believe it won't clear. They can't hear God speaking the way Jack does, so they have no inkling of what is going to happen and don't believe Jack when he tells them. In the end we leave them. I am sick at heart, but I can't see what else we can do.

In the afternoon of that day an arch of colours appears in the sky, a bridge between heaven and earth. It twinkles in the rain, with the sun behind it, like strings of polished stones. One end of it touches the roof of the Boat and the other is hidden in the grey clouds.

– It is a rope, I declare, gazing at it: with God holding the other end. We shall be safe.

Jack goes off to ask God what it is all about.

– It's a sign, he says on his return: that God won't let go of us. He is our father, and he has put the arch of colours in the sky to show us that he will save us. It's a sort of heavenly rope.

– That's just what I said, I retort: your God is just copying me.

Jack goes as pale as sour milk.

– Don't blaspheme, he cries: or you'll be cursed and thrown off the Boat.

He looks so fierce that I decide to keep my opinions to myself. Two of my daughters-in-law are whimpering and blubbering with fear, and I relieve my feelings by turning on them and telling them to be quiet. Sara, my third daughter-in-law, tosses her head at me, and I slap her, I am that upset.

In one way I'm not at all sorry to have to go on board the Boat. I am fed up with hardship, with cleaning and cooking and scraping a living, with the constant battle against flies and dirt and illness. Don't ever let someone try and convince you that living close to nature in tents in the open is some sort of picnic. It's not. Either we are wading through seas of mud when it rains, or we are being bitten to death by insects when it's hot. The milk is always going off, and the tents leak, and I am forever washing and tidying and mending, forever making do, always trying to keep my self-respect by keeping a nice home. What for? I think to myself sometimes: why bother?

Sometimes I dream of running away, just going off and leaving them all to it. On my own I could live as I like, eating when I want to, skipping meals if I feel like it, sleeping and getting up when I want. Sex? What you don't have you don't miss. I know how to give myself pleasure, anyway. Sometimes that's all that's necessary, the quick solitary hand up the skirt and as many shudders of ecstasy as you feel like.

What I really want is a Boat of my own. I want to sail off all by myself, to abandon myself to the seas and the winds and go exploring, with no worry about where I will end up. But Jack thinks it's our duty to save the world; we have to try and entice all our neighbours on board, let alone our family and all the animals. He won't hear of our building two Boats, and I can't build my own without his help. So I have to drop my plan and go along with his.

We fight about which animals to take.

– The fewer the better, I say: who'll clean out their pens and cages? Me, of course. So let's leave most of them behind.

Jack is horrified. He's a kind man, and he can't bear to think of our cattle drowning.

– No, he insists: we must take two of each sort, so that we can mate them afterwards and be sure of a renewed stock.

– Just like us, one man and one woman? I say: we've done our mating. By your logic we're too old to be saved. We should just put the youngsters on board. And let's not forget to take as many nasty creepy-crawlies as possible, two cockroaches and two mosquitoes and two spiders and two fleas.

What a strange way to live, I suddenly think to myself: couples couples couples. I want to live on my own.

I shut up about all this because Jack is getting upset. But when the heavy rains come, and turn into the Flood, I feel relieved. More than that: I am excited and pleased. The world is getting washed and scoured and rinsed for the very last time, and then God pours it all away with the dirty water, as sick of it all as I am. The world is a stack of pots I shall never have to scrub again. I enjoy the prospect of destruction. I don't get on to the Boat feeling like one of God's elect, some sort of holy being. I am escaping from a life that wearies me.

The noise, once we are on board and have shut the big wooden door, is terrific. The animals down below are bellowing in misery, not used to being cooped up in such a small space, and the birds are squawking as though they are being torn to pieces. They quieten down a bit after we feed them, but it makes me realize how difficult the voyage is going to be. I don't want to think of it.

None of us sleeps that night. Jack pretends he does, to set the rest of us an example, but I can tell he is awake because he isn't snoring. I lie listening to the rain drumming on the roof, and think about the neighbours we have left outside. Just before dawn the swollen river bursts its banks and takes us and sets us free with a great lurch and a bump. Trapped in the dark, we all shriek and hold on to each other, while the animals below set up their noise again.

When morning comes, Jack and I decide to climb out on to

78

the flat space we have left, as a sort of observing post, on the roof of the Boat, to see what can be seen. The moment we open the trap door we are drenched. We give up the idea of climbing out any further and just stick our heads out into the gale.

There is nothing there. The world has vanished. All around us, as far as I can see, straining my eyes in every direction, are the waters of the Flood. I can't see where sky ends and water begins. The horizon, if there is one, is grey mist. The Boat is a child's toy made of straw, bobbing helplessly up and down on the waves. I peer downwards, thinking of my neighbours with the water first creeping into their mouths and then filling them up. They are below us now, sinking down onto a cold bed. We have not heard their cries in the night.

For the rest of that day, and the next one, we slump in despair, only rousing ourselves to feed the poor beasts below and to swallow a bite ourselves. We fall sick with guilt and remorse. The will to survive leaves us, just as we have deserted our neighbours. The tides of the Flood enter my soul and drown me too. Welcome, death, I say to myself: I am no better than the slayers of animals I used to despise.

My daughter-in-law Sara saves us. I do not like her much, have never done. She has a sharp way of looking and speaking which bothers me, especially when I think it is aimed at me. She is a restless girl, bitter and dissatisfied, and she never bothers to hide how she feels. I am angry with her when I remember my own struggles, as a young woman, to become a good wife and mother, to put up with Jack's ways, to learn to suffer in silence. Sara makes me remember these things which I would rather forget. When I explain to her the best method of making yoghurt, or bread, she looks at me with a sort of veiled insolence, her hands demurely clasped but mockery darting from her eyes. I dread that look of hers, so I speak sharply to her always, just to keep her in her place. My other two daughters-in-law cause me no such trouble, but they are no company either, with their meek and mild ways. Sara, for all her sauciness, at least has a mind of her own.

On the third day she saves us.

– Mother, she says to me, giving me that awful sly look of hers: you didn't shut the trap door properly when you came back down from the roof, and it's leaking. Just look at the mess on the floor.

I jump up scolding. Seizing a rag, I begin to swab the puddle I am sitting in, and then Jack groans and get up too, and re-closes the trap door and makes it properly fast. Then I realize that I am both hungry and thirsty.

– Come on, Sara says: I'll make you something to eat. A real meal. And you can tell me whether I'm doing it the right way.

She feeds us. She kicks us out of our gloom, and goads us back into living. Every time she sees us ready to drop back into weakness, she mocks us back onto our feet. We dislike her for it, but it works. She organizes us. She makes us all take turns, Jack and my three sons included, in preparing our food and feeding the animals, in clearing up afterwards, in washing our dishes and clothes.

– This is women's work, not men's, Jack and my sons protest: this is the end of civilization as we know it.

– That's right, Sara says: if you want to survive, do it.

Sara becomes our leader. She is mother and father to all of us. A strict parent, always ready with the whip of her tongue. We know that without her we would die.

Time passes, passes. Days, weeks, months.

Sara looks less restless and dissatisfied. Nowadays she walks about with lighter steps, humming, and sometimes she sits with me in the afternoons when all the others are asleep, and we talk. We mellow a little towards each other, recognizing our need for one another. I notice how she is beginning to stand in a new way, with her belly thrust a little forwards and her hands resting on it. She has a new smile, very different from her old one. Still secretive, but pleased.

– You'll have to take things a bit easier, I remark to her one morning while we are forking filthy straw out of the sheep pen: with the baby coming. Save some strength for him.

She turns scarlet.

– I didn't think it showed yet.

Then she looks at me in her old way.

– How do you know it won't be a daughter? That's what I want. A daughter. If it's a boy I'll throw it over the side.

I am shocked. She looks down, and I am shocked again to see that she is crying. I can't bear this. I have never been able to endure the sound of my children crying. Something tiny and

80

monstrous and dark within me wakes up and joins in, and then I have to slap it back down, slap the children to stop them crying. I hold my hands together in my lap, itching to slap Sara as she goes on weeping, her face ugly and red, and that terrible sound coming from her.

– You didn't welcome a daughter, did you? she says: you were happy with your three fine sons, and you've never thought much of the worth of daughters-in-law.

We spread the clean straw on the floor of the pen in silence. Then, exhausted, I sit down in it to rest. I want to tell Sara to go away, but I'm unable to do so. She sits down beside me. I fear her now. She is my accuser, my judge.

– When I came to live with you all, she says: I was so lonely. I missed my people so much I could hardly bear it. I wanted my husband to love me and to be loved by him, but he took little notice of me. Except at night when he would climb on top of me for a few minutes and then fall asleep. All day long it was nothing but work work work. I wanted kindness from you but you kept scolding me. Everything I did was wrong. I felt stupid and useless. So I gave up trying.

I am struck by how young she is. Younger than I when I married Jack. Cautiously I grope my way back to that time and try to remember what it was like. I expected so little. That was what saved me from too much sorrow.

– What about God? I ask her: isn't God a comfort?

– I don't believe in him, she says: I want my mother.

She starts crying again. I want to shake her. I stop myself, and take her hand. I expect her to withdraw it, but she doesn't.

– We had a song, my sisters and I, she sobs: handed down from one of our ancestors who was stolen away into captivity and made to marry her captor. She sang how she was as lonely as a water lily whose stem is gnawed by a beetle. That was how I felt. Living with your son, before the Flood came, I used to sing it to myself every day, for comfort.

She blows her nose on her sleeve and looks at me defiantly.

– I want a daughter, she says: I'll love her properly. The way no one loves me. And then I'll let her go. I'll let her leave me. I know it's got to happen.

She's on the verge of tears again. I can't bear it. I search hurriedly for something to say that will stop her.

– You're my daughter now, Sara, I say: please stay with me.

We haven't any choice, anyway, I think. We just have to make the best of it. But I promise her in my heart: you have looked after me, and now I will try to look after you.

We begin to rely on each other in a new way. Sara is someone I can really talk to. Jack is depressed, and isn't much good to me. He doesn't tell me his thoughts in the old way, and he stops coming to me at night. I miss him.

– What's your God thinking about things? I ask him one day.

His face grows even more miserable.

– I can't hear what God's saying any more, he confesses: there's too much water in the way.

I find this odd. To my way of seeing we are surrounded by Jack's God. I believe in his power and anger as never before. Whereas my God seems to be sleeping or dreaming. I have to take it on trust that the earth will deliver us again out of her womb. There is no sign I can see that this will be so.

We have to wait. We have to be patient. It isn't easy to stay cooped up in a small space with the fear of death tapping at your shoulder night and day, after a lifetime of running about outside and going pretty well where you want.

We remain in the Boat for nine months in all; for the length of a pregnancy. When we are not working we sit and gossip, or we play at spillikins, or we try to pray. I embroider linen for the new baby, or I just sit in silence. That feels good.

I need nothing now but this water surrounding us.

I develop eyes of piercing vision, capable of seeing down through the wooden hull of the Boat, through the fathoms of ocean underneath us, right down to the stones and gravel and sand that once formed the earth, the dry land. I build a new world there, one of my own choosing. A childish vision, idealistic, impossible. I know that. I fill it with people who are as fluid as water, flowing past each other in peace and letting each other alone.

My world allows people to choose how they will live: by themselves, or in groups, or with one other person. People are allowed to be flexible, to change, to change how they live. There are no rules about having to get married and have

82

children, having to leave your mother if you don't want to, having to live with a man if you don't want to. In this deep-sea place Sara and I can keep house together, and no one minds. I give us fins on our backs and tails, like fish, and I build us a cool cave decorated with coral and shells, with a floor of silver sand, and green weeds waving around the entrance. The water slides all over my body as I lie in it and am carried along by it. Water is my mother, my lover, my bed. My element, which gives me the freedom to swim off wherever I want to go. Water is my food and drink. Water is my god.

I've had enough of being a woman, with being confined in a clumsy body, with being defined by men. Yearning and suffering and dying on the harsh earth. Just as when I am a child I yearn to escape upwards and join the birds in their airy element, when I pretend I can fly, so now, as an adult woman, I am reborne from the Boat into water. I become fish. Untroubled by the Flood, which, after all, is merely my home. I go with it.

We carve a tally of the days we spend afloat, using Jack's knife to notch slashes in the doorpost. Every morning one of us marks the wood in this way, while someone else peers out through the trap door to see what the weather is like. We invent a lot of new words for different sorts of rain.

After nine months have passed it stops raining. We look at one another. Without saying a word, Jack goes down to the middle deck and fetches out a raven and a dove. Opening one of the casements he lets them go. That evening, only the dove returns. It bears a sprig of olive in its beak.

Next morning, when we wake up, we find that we have been put ashore in the night. Perhaps Jack's God has pulled us from above and mine has pushed us from below. I don't know. But here we are, wedged between two enormous rocks. At first, looking out of the trap door, we assume we have landed on an island. Then, when we emerge, we discover that we are balanced on the tip of a mountain. Fancy that, I think: a Boat on a mountain-top. How ridiculous. I start laughing so hard I can't stop. Not until Sara shakes me. Then I begin to weep.

We clamber out of the Boat onto dry land. There, shining above us in the grey sky, is the arch of colours. A thin sun glimmers behind the clouds, and the air on our faces is fresh and damp. Way down below us we can see the tops of trees.

The waters, ebbing and receding from the mountain, have left a trail of litter. The rocky ground is sticky with slimy green debris, rotten vegetation. Bones, clotted with lumps of hair and gristle, poke up out of it. Here and there are the corpses of men and animals, bloated and stinking, whose rotting flesh has turned all manner of bright colours, as though it reflected the arch of light above.

How does a baby feel when it is born, propelled from the safety of the enclosing waters into the enormous dry world? Beside me Sara is being sick all over her feet.

I want to go back on the Boat. I don't want to see the ruin of the world, these scraps of clothing caught on the rocks, this broken baby's rattle a body's length away. Jack has his face turned away from mine. I know he is trying not to weep.

– Wife, he says, gripping my hand: we should offer a sacrifice. Go and fetch a lamb from the Boat.

– No, I say.

I point at the band of colours hanging over our heads. One end hides in the clouds, and the other touches the roof of the Boat, just as before.

– The earth is a hard mother, I say: but she has delivered us, just as I dreamed she would, and we've been born onto this mountain for good or ill. She will cut that shining cord in her own good time. When she does, it's up to us to get on with living. There is no need to kill an animal. I want no more death.

Jack stares at me, his face wretched and uncomprehending. Then his shoulders sag.

– I can't bear this. I'm going off to find a clean place in which I can pray.

He blunders off, crying.

The rest of us bury the dead. We dig one large shallow grave as best we can, and roll the bodies into it, then cover them with earth and stones. A little way down the mountain we find a big puddle of water. In silence, we strip off our filthy clothes and wash ourselves, all of us going in together. It doesn't seem to matter, that we show our exhausted naked bodies to one another. It is a kind of prayer for the dead, and for ourselves, to

84

pour scoops of water over each other's heads. It confirms us as a family, as survivors. Then we go back on the Boat to feed and water the animals, and to prepare a meal. It smells too bad outside to stay there for long.

Jack comes back after dark. My sons and daughters are eating supper, but I can't touch a thing. The meat stew nauseates me. As though it were boiled up from dead babies.

Jack stands in our midst and raises his hands, palms upwards.

– God has spoken to me, he announces: he is very terrible, but he is also merciful. He is our shepherd, and he has brought us here, through the waters of the Flood, so that we may know his might and tremble before him. He has put the arch of colours in the sky as the sign of his pledge to us, of his new alliance with us. He wishes us to offer him burnt meat as a sacrifice, so that he may enjoy its pleasant odour. And he commands us to go forth and be fruitful and multiply. We shall become the masters of the earth, and hold sway over it. We have dominion over all the animals and birds, over all the fruits of nature, over the fish that swim in the seas. Everything that lives will serve us for food, and will tremble before us and be filled with fear at our approach.

– This way of talking is a disaster, I retort: what good can come of our setting ourselves up like lords? The animals have suffered just as much as we have, and have been reborn just as we have. It's wrong to make them our servants again. We need to treat them differently now. They are our companions, not our slaves.

– God has decreed it, is all Jack will say: as the rule of our new life.

I heave myself to my feet and raise my arms just as my husband has done.

– Then I too, I declare: have a rule for my new life. I swear that I shall never kill an animal again, shall never shed blood again, shall never eat meat again. I am sick of killing, and so would your God be if he had any sense.

This argument confirms the division between Jack and me. I still love and respect him. How can I not? We have come through so much together. But our opinions are leading us along different ways.

85

After supper, the others fall asleep. I stay up, unable to sleep for worrying about what will happen to us next. The wooden ceiling above my head shuts me into a space of sour breath and sweat, of torment. I open the trap door and clamber out onto the roof.

The cool evening wind has swept away the foul stench of the day, and the darkness has blotted out the ugly view. I sit cross-legged, the breeze fanning my face. I listen to the silence of the night and throw myself into its untouchable blue distances. I look up at the stars, my eyes walking amongst them, hopping from one to the other as though they are stepping stones. Perhaps we are not alone, after all. Perhaps there are other living creatures on those stars. Perhaps all this business of living and dying goes on all the time among the stars. The earth is only one place among so many.

Night has cut the bright cord, and set me upright. Now I need a name. I need names.

I decide to give the earth and all her creatures new names, as you do with a baby when it is born. I jump up, and begin to pace up and down on the roof. I think first of the arch of colours we have seen twice, once before the Flood and now after it. It links our new life to our old one, ties heaven to earth, knots us to God.

– God's bow in the rain, I call out: God's rainbow.

For the rest of the night I wrestle with words, trying to find new ones. The names are a string with which I tie together my understanding of the God I know in this new creation, my way of connecting us all with each other and with God, humans and animals and birds and plants, none of us superior to the others however different we may look. Naming the names is a form of worship. I grow drunk on it.

– God's rainbow, I chant to myself: God's knot, God's promise, God's-not-forgetting, God-not-forgotten.

Also I mourn. This work of renaming includes contemplating all that I have lost: the old world with all its beauties and sorrows. The people we knew and travelled and laughed with. The drowned beasts. Also my hopes for a new and better world which would not include killing, the ruthless mastery of nature. Jack said to me before he slept: it is necessary to dominate nature in order to live from it; how, otherwise, shall we start

86

our new life and survive? I had no answer for him. I dream of a harmony between all created things, a state of peaceful growth, of unity and kindness and no killing. I know I shall not see it.

In the morning I take Sara aside and tell her I've renamed the world while she was asleep. She looks astonished at first, then worried.

– No, no, I'm not ill, I say: just listen, will you?

In the end, perhaps just to humour her crazy mother-in-law, she agrees to teach the new names to her baby once it is born. She is doubtful about how many she will be able to remember, when she's no longer looking at the things I've named, or should illness or death prevent my being there to remind her, and so I start thinking of a way to help her do it.

I go back in my mind to the time when we started building the Boat, how we drew pictures in the dust on the ground of what we thought we wanted.

I take dollops of wet mud in the palm of my hand, and shape them into little slabs. I sharpen the end of a stick into a point. Then, with the stick, I draw pictures on the mud slabs, one by one, of all the new words I've made up. I keep the pictures as simple as possible: a few strokes and curves. Some of them are just straightforward drawings of things, or part of a thing, as I see them in my mind's eye, like *bee*, or *leaf*. *God* is a circle. Then I work out I can use sound as well as sight. So *belief-in-God* comes out as a circle holding a bee and a leaf. I enjoy myself doing this, playing games again. An aged child I am, squatting on my haunches getting my hands all clotted with mud. When I've finished, I lay the slabs on the roof of the Boat to dry in the sun and grow hard. Then I collect them up in my apron and give them to Sara. And I give a name to what I've done: I call it *writing*.

– See, I show her: this mud brick is a *word*, and it means *my-love-for-you*. And it will replace me when I'm no longer with you. It will survive our separation. It will survive my death. This is my gift to you, daughter, and to your children and to their children.

I laugh at myself. I wanted to save and change the world, yet all I've been able to do is make up a new kind of toy.

That's more or less the end of my story. I decide to stay on the mountain-top and end my days there. It is no longer unpleasant to me, now that the filth on the ground has been dried by the sun and wind and the bodies have been shovelled into the earth where they belong. I am filled with weariness. Perhaps I just lack the courage to struggle on. The weather is turning colder, and the others want to get down the mountain with the livestock and find shelter, found a settlement. No more wandering: we are all agreed on that. Sara wants a wooden house, like the Boat she's grown used to, not a flimsy tent, to shelter her baby in. She wants to stay in one place, to become a farmer, to plant the seeds we have brought with us, to see them grow. She wants crops, and a harvest, and a barn full of wheat, and an end to wandering.

So they leave me, as I ask. They build me a little hut near the Boat with a few provisions stored in it, and they tether a couple of goats nearby to keep me in milk and cheese. Then they take the rest of our goods and animals and move off down the mountain to find the place where they will build a home.

My parting with Sara is as sad as that with Jack. Both of us weep.

– I shall return and visit you very soon, Sara promises me as she embraces me: after the baby is born. I'll bring her with me.

I don't want to lose my newly found daughter so soon. I begin to love her, then have to tear her from me. She talks of staying with me, but I pack her off. I drive her away, using some of my old harshness, complaining that all I want now is to be left alone. I know it is right that she goes with her husband and family. Hers is the last human face that I see. She waves goodbye, then drops out of sight behind an outcrop of rock. What hope would she have, staying with me? That is what I say to myself when I find myself missing her.

A strange time begins for me. For the first time in my life I am free to do what I like all day long. My increasing weakness means that I can't get about very much, so I stick to my little patch of mountainside near the Boat. I like being surrounded by nothing but wind and sky. I sit for hours watching the changes in the clouds, the shifting of the light, the play of sunsets and dawns. Daily I witness the creation of the world. When I pray, it is not with words. When I talk, it is to praise God, by which I mean the action of creation. I don't try to draw a picture of this. Sara will need to break the circle I drew in two, and find a new word. But I don't need words any more. I'm alone, and I've given my words to Sara, to do as she likes with.

I don't last long in my solitary retreat. Cold white pieces of sky fall down day by day, smoothing out my world, blotting out my thoughts. God's silence wraps me up, hushing me, putting an icy finger to my lips. I open my mouth and the whiteness of the sky falls onto my tongue, dissolving, pouring down my throat like sweet milk. Welcome, death. In you I drown. Until I'm reincarnated, born again into the next story. I'm the ghost in the library, cackling, unseen, from between the pages of the sacred texts, waiting my chance to haunt a new generation of readers. I'm what's missing. I'm the wanderer.

15   The Babble-On Sibyl sits tugging a comb through her hair in the communal bathroom that she has dreamed up on the Ark: cavern of red brocade encircled by pink-tinted mirrors and red and gold shaded lamps that is set with Art Deco vanity tables and red plush pouffes and sofas, and crowned with a jingly crystal chandelier swinging from the gold-encrusted ceiling. Her source of inspiration is the Ladies Boudoir in the Lyceum Theatre on the Strand, but she has added a couple of touches of her own: enamel baths behind red brocade screens; free-standing wooden towel-horses bearing piles of fluffy white cotton and linen.

She has always loved other people's bathrooms, loves seeing what they keep there. Visiting new acquaintances for the first time, she makes for the bathroom as soon as possible, opens the cabinets to discover secrets: the packets of hair dye, the ladies' razors, the laxatives, the discreet bags in flowered cotton containing rubber domes and tubes of foul-smelling cream. Her voyeurism is a mark of love, an effort towards intimacy she cannot always make in a sitting room. Using her hostess's hairbrush, patting on her moisturizer, sniffing at her cologne, inspecting her range of eye-shadow colours, she gets close to this woman she does not yet know. Back in her armchair, sipping a cup of tea, she is cool, watchful. A woman may be a rival for Neil's attention; she cannot afford to relax her guard.

One Italian couple she knows have a bathroom each, all black tiles and gleaming chrome, and special men's and ladies' toothpaste. She and Neil, moving hastily in their need to find a home together, are stuck with pale orange vinyl bath and bidet, always a little greasy to the touch, chocolate and orange-flowered plastic shower curtains, camel tiles around the

90

washbasin, and wallpaper jazzy with enormous cream and orange lozenges. She doesn't mind: having to use a bathroom of someone else's choice means she's not responsible, doesn't have to reveal her own taste, commit herself. No one can snoop in her bathroom and secretly claim to know her. She hasn't plunged for baskets of ferns, china dishes of pretty pastel soaps, hanging bamboo shelves, like some of her friends. She hasn't gone all bohemian, with the radiators painted gold and hung with old bead necklaces and grotesque raffia masks dangling from the high lavatory cistern, like Neil's ex-girlfriend. Nor has she not bothered at all: stained cork mat, yellowing bath with brown streaks under the taps, piles of old copies of *Private Eye* in a corner, plastic beakers crusted with toothpaste, wastebin overflowing with bits of used cotton wool and empty cardboard lavatory rolls. She has seen beautiful bathrooms, too: one walled in plain shining mahogany, a man's room this, with his silver-backed brushes of pure bristle lined up next to his silver-topped bottles of eau de Cologne and aftershave under the thick square mirror secured with silver studs. She could never afford anything like that; useless to dream of it. And that bathroom she saw once in a house in the country: enormous, carpeted, with armchairs and pictures, bath proud and nude in a corner on curled feet, long windows open onto a view of lawn and flowerbeds. Better to stick to her tangerine vinyl suite; like her clothes and hairstyle, she suddenly thinks, safely sweet, tasteless and out of date.

She crumples a fistful of pale frilled cotton. Her curiosity begins not in bathrooms at all, but in her mother's bedroom, clean shrine in the afternoon, the bed looking as though it's never slept in, net curtains hazy at the window, clear space full of light, of absence. She tiptoes across the furry carpet to the little antique chest of drawers, pulls out, one by one, the shallow tiers. Handkerchiefs, ironed and folded monogrammed squares, kept in an embroidered linen sachet, a sprig of lavender laid on top. Petticoats in pastel nylon with pencil straps. A drift of silky nightdresses, pink and blue and lemon. One black one with red bows. Row of sturdy cotton bras, cups reinforced with circular stitching. A pink corselette with hooks and eyes gripping the elastic, wrinkled suspenders dangling. A fragrant pile, interleaved with ribboned bags of lavender, of knickers, enormous they seem to her, like shorts, the legs edged with lace, little pleated nylon skirts with cotton gussets. There is such order here, such spotlessness, such care taken with this store of underwear whose quiet arrangement no one will ever see. The daughter sighs, running her fingers through orlon and silk, lifting each pile out, then replacing it.

When she is older, she confines herself to other women's bathrooms. Hard to explain if you're discovered going through a wardrobe.

How is it that other women have the confidence to make such clear-cut choices about their clothes, their possessions? She knows, from her delicate rummaging here, that the Forsaken Sibyl has a secret stash of powder and lipsticks, that the Deftly Sibyl sometimes takes sleeping pills, that the Correct Sibyl uses washing grains to remove blackheads, and that the Re-Vision Sibyl travels with a child's slimy flannel bearing the picture of a panda. She herself carries a neat zipped plastic case, free from Elizabeth Arden once sufficient purchases have been made, stocked with lotions, creams and make-up bought from a chainstore combining quality with low cost. Anyone might have such a blandly pretty outfit of conventional equipment; it gives nothing away.

She is so eager to please; not to shock. The two collections of stories she has published were written before she met Neil and fell in love. She has written hardly anything since. Why?

She grimaces at herself in the mirror. Suddenly she hates her face, smooth screen which she has defied time and experience to mark, whose bones she has not allowed to emerge, whose lines and crows-feet she has worked tirelessly to erase. What's behind her face? What cries, what laughter wait there to be expressed, to carve a personality onto and out of her round pink mask, to give her her own distinctive individual beauty?

Her mother uses Nivea Creme, cupping the shallow blue tin in one hand, prising off the round lid with its elegant fifties logo in swirling white lettering, peeling back the thin disc of silver paper with a fingernail, digging her fingertips into the glistening surface of the cold cream, roughing it up, scooping up a fingertipful which she dabs onto her face, around her eyes. Her mother's eyes are brown, deep-set, sunk into shallows of bone, surrounded by webbed lines. Eyes that look unflinchingly at her husband's minor cruelties, at her own yearnings and silences, at her children's squabbling. Tired eyes sometimes, beautiful eyes, eyes holding an infinity of knowledge.

The Babble-On Sibyl is frightened of writing honestly about her own sexuality; about what she has learned about men after loving, and therefore studying, quite a few of them; about what can happen, spoken and unspoken, between a man and a woman. Things a woman can be ashamed of, in herself and her man; things she is confused or embarrassed by. Things which, if she admitted their burning existence inside her, might force changes in her life. Things she has discussed with no one. Things which could hurt her lovers, her family, her friends.

So why talk about them? Better to write about sex in conventional feminine terms, discreet and romantic, giving nothing away, nodding towards received wisdom and common sense. Or to write about sex in the rip-roaring way some women writers use, objectifying herself, seeing herself through men's eyes, in their terms and language, thrusting nipples, wet cunt, taut breasts, a lover no more than a cock driving like a piston, a woman's response the echo of his. No doubts, no fears. None of those moments in between, which carry perhaps the truth of the experience but which are so hard to catch, to put into words, flickering just out of sight, glimpsed from the corner of the eye, off-canvas.

Most male writers do not seem to have this problem. They expose their nearest and dearest in the frankest way without worrying whom they hurt, true to the dictates of their art which transcend those of ordinary bourgeois morality. Is that really true? What do *they* leave out? Plenty, she's certain. Or else, *pretending* to be frank, they reproduce the conventions which enmesh her: man as intelligent ironist, woman as sticky fly-trap; husband as adulterer, all those campus novels, young students his prey and so flattered to be so. Boring silent frumpy wife. Nothing changes. Pursuit, gratification, boredom, pursuit. Female characters complying. Of course. Let's not be sentimental.

Why write about sex at all? Every novel with its obligatory sex scene, hero's fucking odyssey in between his thoughts on life money death god irony. Sex as decoration in the twentieth-century novel. Sex put in as spicy ingredient because it sells.

Fantasy sex for consolation of male readers, character armour of machismo left intact, the women characters either a projection of a feared and repressed part of the author or dream figures plucked from the childhood level of the unconcious. Where are the modern male writers who write honestly about their own sexuality? She can't think of one. Stendhal, Balzac, Sterne, all did better.

Isn't it rather neurotic to write about sex, to isolate it artificially from the rest of life? Shouldn't sex be just one aspect of a well-ordered well-balanced life, and so, in context, not really that remarkable? Why all the fuss?

Sex seems to be the dominant contemporary emblem of the psyche. To explore sexuality seems to open the way to exploring what makes people tick. If the psyche is part of the universe, there need be no shame in exploring the 'inside' as opposed to the 'outside' of the great realist writers? But 'outside' remains more respectable. If you want to write about 'inside', better project it, put a man on the moon, on the Russian frontier, on the seabed?

Why is it that she wants to talk about what is called perverted sex, sinful sex, immature sex? Is the writer's finger that of the masseuse, the doctor, unerringly finding the wound in the psyche, the bruise, and so, in the examination, bringing healing, restoring wholeness? No; that begs the question; too romantic. Who defines health anyway? Why is one form of love sick and another not?

The feminist group at her college believed that women wrote about sex in self-defence. Tired of men's ignorant fantasies, they wrote 'the truth'. What words are capable of doing that? Start by exploring, perhaps. Take that word *woman*, and squeeze every last drop of meaning out of it? That will take her a lifetime.

She throws away her comb and stands up. Sheds her clothes, the crinkled dead leaves of several seasons back. Dons a bathrobe she selects from the rack by the door, voluminous garment in heavy checked wool, comfortable, warm. Then she picks up a pair of scissors, blades like two legs dancing. Flexes them. Begins to cut her hair off. It's too long, almost down to her waist; a child's hair, not a woman's.

She shears her fringe. Startled face springs out at her in

the mirror. Clips the tendrils curling on her neck, delicious shivers of pleasure as the cold steel grazes her skin. She leaves one long lock, plaited, to remind her of what's gone. Her make-up looks wrong now, too pink and blue. She soaks a sponge in soapy water, clears it off. Not nakedness, not true self, not essential core: just a new image. To start with. She picks up her pen and writes.

Her pen is a dagger. Her father lies dead at her feet in a splatter of blood. She is a murderess.

Hand shaking. Dip your pen in your father's blood and write another line. Watch your husband's face tighten with bemused pain as your nib jabs at his soft secrets, the most vulnerable parts of himself; the places he let you see because he trusted you. You have betrayed him. You have destroyed his trust in you. Is this really what you want: to ruin your marriage? to expose how nasty you yourself are?

She needs to find another way. Truth is not obvious or straightforward. Sneak up on it, sideways, from behind? Tell the truth but tell it slant? Confessional writing, the belief in truth found through simple straightforward outpouring of feeling, won't do, if it reproduces the sinner in the confessional, the accused in the dock, the madwoman in hospital. Speak not to your enemies, your judges, the snoopers and voyeurs with power to arrest, punish, define, drug and prevent you, but to your allies, your friends. Discover a language that *they*, listening intently (you hope) for your words, will understand, take in, recreate, give back to you. So that true conversation can begin. Sabotage the enemy's language, disguise yourself in it if you must, play spy at the enemy's dinner table. Observe him. Make up your own code under the enemy's nose, pass your secrets in the images he is conditioned to find banal and absurd and therefore undetectable, uncrackable. Send up metaphor flares which he will think are just decoration not urgent complex signals of desire, intent. Smuggle your weapons under aprons of gossip, your diplomatic bag. *Begin*.

Her words make such a clatter. Who goes there, friend or foe? Password!

She sweats. What shall she say?

Start with a few lies?

To invent simply means *to find*. What's inside.

16 When I was twenty I started my librarianship training, in the Department of Printed Books in the British Library.

My bunch of keys enables me to unlock the hidden doors in the walls of the public galleries, to swing back a section of bookcase and vanish behind it, to disappear into books, parting their pages and walking into them. I am Alice. My bed has paper sheets.

The unconscious of the library is held in the bookstacks. Iron ladders thread through it; I peer down through the open grille-work rungs at the floors falling away under me, six layers, a transparency of books. I clamber about Western culture's brain. I find the locked room of uncatalogued, inaccessible and forbidden erotica, and I read these books too, poring, in musty dimness, over excited guilty tales of whipping and slit-silk knickers and maids giving their all on back staircases for a few pence stuffed up their cunts.

The conscious mind of the library is contained in the Reading Room, vast circular space under a lofty glass dome. Rows of desks and armchairs radiate out from the centre like threads in a web, and the superintendent, black hairy spider, crouches in the middle in a glass cage. Around him curve the stands of catalogue volumes, labyrinth that the alphabetical order of author entries unravels. James Brown, Murderer, precedes James Brown, Pederast, and James Brown, Poet.

No classification system. Just a subject index: more alphabet.

Here on the Ark, in my Arkive, I can search through B until I come to Baby.

*

– But the world's such a terrible place, Noah complains: why bring a child into it? That's irresponsible.

I consult the book of riddles.

Does *want* also mean *want*?

17   On our seventh day out in the calm blue sea, we spy land. An island, sprawling in a froth of breakers. We see its palaces from far off, glittering and crystalline against the clear sky, the sun bouncing off their marble domes and porticos and flashing us a message: come closer. I fetch the guidebook from the archive and study its maps closely. I don't think this is the land I'm searching for. Nonetheless, no harm in having a look.

We moor in the tiny harbour. Leaving the sibyls scribbling in their various hiding places and the Gaffer sunbathing on the roof of the Ark, I go ashore and walk into the city down streets lined with buildings of a severe beauty, a restrained grace, their classical portals and windows flanked by elegant columns flowering with leafy capitals. Some of these palaces are in a good state of repair; many others are crumbling, mutilated by weather and corroding time, their stone decoration blurred and broken, cracks in their façades, roofs gaping open. A programme of restoration has clearly been started, and then abandoned.

I reach the main piazza, an enormous rectangular room. On one side is a basilica, a Renaissance stone veil thrown around a medieval building and pierced by a double tier of *loggie*, a pattern of white arches and columns in clumps like the stalks of giant flowers. On the other side, forming a large squared-off corner, is the wide terrace of a café. Away down the other end, past the elaborately decorated façades of churches and palaces, is a tall clock tower, and two statues, one of a lion and one of a dragon, set on top of two lofty slender columns. Under my feet is a carpet of white stone, and above, the ceiling of blue sky.

It's utterly quiet. No dogs barking to break the hush. Nothing stirring in the sharply cut shadows. The basilica floats across the piazza as serenely as our Ark has sailed across the sea, but there is no sign of life behind her high windows. Not the flicker of a handkerchief. Not the sound of a single footfall coming down the long external staircase under its arched canopy. The siesta hour.

I move out of the white dazzle of the sun into the cool darkness of a colonnade, and sit down on the stone pavement, resting my back against a column. I unfurl the Italian newspaper that someone has left lying there, and laboriously push my brain through its closely printed columns. Leaping over words and phrases I don't understand, leaving gaps in my reasoning, I make my own translation.

I am a citizen of this proud city; and my ears are clotted with wax. Better that way. Then I can't hear what the wind is saying. The sirocco blows in on its way around all the continents in the world, and covers the cars with a fine layer of red dust brought all the way from Africa. A strong, harsh wind, whirling in from the sea, bringing whisperings and mutterings from lands I have never seen, insistent warnings hinting at the imminent outbreak of yet another war rooted in the spiralling greed of the great empires for money, profits and power. More lands and villages bombed and burnt, more women raped by soldiers, more people starving and thirsting in refugee camps, more corpses riddled with bullets, fried by napalm, poisoned by gas. Sooner or later will come the war to end all wars. One last great ejaculation of fire, the world crumpled and burnt out, our rulers emerging from their shelters to sift our ashes. If one green leaf pokes up through the cinders and grows into a tree, I shan't be there to see it and nor will you.

The wind scratches the heart, strikes the breastbone, whimpers down chimneys and coils around the cots where children sleep. Sometimes it chuckles. Sometimes it sobs. I mourn too, reading the newspaper's list of the dead, the dying, the about-to-die. I'm a hypocrite. I'm a citizen of the First World. I'm responsible. What have I ever tried to do to prevent the rulers of my country from waging war and death?

I want to go on living my nice comfortable life. If I read the newspapers every morning, the complacency of that life is destroyed. I can't bear it. I clap my hands over my ears, rush indoors, seal my ears with wax, great gobs of brown glue sticky as burnt sugar. I am beginning to forget how to speak, because, with my gummed-up ears, I can no longer listen. I am beginning to die, because I am no longer listened to. I can't write: the only word I can spell is *death*.

Folding up the newspaper, I shiver. The afternoon sun paints the inside of arches a dark gold. It is conceivable that the world will suddenly end, that the Bomb will fall. It is conceivable that all these peaceful streets of palaces will burn to ash.

How could anyone let herself have a baby once she knows it's likely that the world will be blown up in that child's lifetime? The shadow of the Bomb falls across my ovaries. I shan't conceive. Death, the guerrilla, has got me, scuttles through my dark interior, booby-trapping my desires for a child, setting mines to kill the life that stirs in me every month. He's winning. He's captured my territory, and my hands are lifted in surrender.

I never wanted to come here. I'm in the wrong place. I turn to flee. Then I remember. Before I go, there is one more monument I must visit here.

I go out of the piazza and down a deserted and colonnaded street, into the great church at its end.

It's cool and peaceful inside, out of the blaze of the street. Smell of damp, old stone, incense. The rosy floor is slippery. The door in the side aisle has been propped open, letting in brilliant light. Just outside is a fountain, a single jet of water tinkling into a basin of white marble set on green grass.

I sit down, in one of the front pews.

There she is, the Queen of Heaven. Seated, cradling her divine child, on a low stool which her draperies flow over and almost conceal. Her pale oval face is grave and sweet, and her head is bent a little to one side, reflectively, her eyes glancing towards the spectator. The veil covering her hair and shoulders and sweeping down around her feet is of a blue so dark it is almost black, edged with gold and lined with olive green. Her dress is crimson, stencilled with a pattern in gold. She is very grand. Around her head shines a gold halo, flat as a plate, and she is seated against a splendour of dark gold streaked with orange. Within this fly two burly cherubs with

100

blue wings, dressed in green frocks, holding a triple crown above her head.

A flying carpet carries her up, and separates her from a tranquil landscape painted in soft blues and greens that shows this city with the harbour in front and the dumpy blue mountains behind. The clouds extend upwards and surround her, so that she flies up inside a mandala of whiteness framing her gold radiance. And on the clouds, and in them, almost part of them, are angels and cherubs, looped together in a tangled necklace of legs and wings. A school of them, lively as dolphins, playing flutes, harps, cymbals and dulcimers, and their mouths opened wide and singing. These cheerful babies are all colours: red or blue or green faces and wings, tunics of pink, plum, lime, violet, lemon. So round and soft are the contours of their faces and limbs that they are like plump fruits hanging in a woven garland, ornamental swags, bearing bright peaches and nectarines, flung about the Queen of Harvests.

Then I suddenly see it. The rope of cherubs is the rainbow, arching, in all the rainbow's colours, entwined with the white clouds, around the Madonna and her Child, enclosing them.

So the rainbow signifies the rebirth of humanity. Not just once, as the Old Testament has it; or twice, as the New Testament commentators argue; but over and over again.

The Madonna in this church feeds her baby from a tiny white breast pointed like a pear. The sixteenth-century artist is in no doubt that the new birth which will save the world is that of Christ.

But perhaps renewal has to be achieved repeatedly, by each of us, by each community. The divine child has to be born, with labour and struggle, in each of us: the discovery of how to create a world of freedom and justice, how to live fully, how to stop hating and killing, how to prevent the planet from being blown up.

I sit and look at the Madonna and her bambino and feel doubt rise in me, as green and bitter as bile.

18   Back on board the Ark I cook supper for us all. The Ark
as crammed larder. At least one sensual treat a day aids
the creative process. So I serve the others with *bigoli*, a
local speciality I have brought back from the market on shore:
thick yellow spaghetti made with egg, with a hole down the
middle. Next, *baccalà* with *polenta*, cod soaked in olive oil, and
maize pudding. I shan't learn the word for meat: the sight,
smell and taste of it have begun to disgust me. Though reading
meat recipes used to be my form of pornography. I still kill
mosquitoes every night, smashing them, with a wetted
handkerchief, against the cabin wall, in a splatter of blood (my
blood). But I don't want to eat meat any more.

 – The imperialism of cookery books, I say to the others: with
the words of exotic recipes we invade the Third World yet
again. Rich whites knowing the names of Javanese dishes pluck
money from wallets, food from shops, while the Javanese
peasants starve and do not discuss anorexia or vegetarianism.

Clatter of scraped clean plates.

 – Eat up your meat, the nuns used to tell us, says the Correct
Sibyl: think of the starving millions who'd be glad of your
leftover scraps of gristle and fat. Mortify your body. Spoon up
the food that revolts you: the slime of tapioca lumps at the
bottom of the soup bowl; the tinned sweetcorn, tasting of
polish, that you choke on; the glutinous jam congealed like
blood on dry pastry. Get a holy soul out of purgatory with every
flaking butter bean you swallow, every gob of vomit you hold
back. Eat this spoonful for me, darling. This is my body and my
blood. Do this in memory of me. The blood and body of the
mother nourish the child inside. That is the true holy
communion. We're sailing past butter mountains over an

ocean of milk, while babies die safely out of sight.

– The meat market, says the Forsaken Sibyl: is marriage. Virgin cattle branded in red. My mother failed the test. My adoptive parents *chose* me. Picked me out. Plenty of white babies available in those days before the abortion law was loosened. My mother was damaged goods. Bruised like a fruit in the gutter tasted once then thrown away.

– My mother started married life in lodgings in Fog Street, Manchester, says the Re-Vision Sibyl: she wasn't used to such cold. All through that first winter, she told me, when it rained every day and got dark at three o'clock, she sat in the kitchen wrapped in her overcoat and cried. For her mother, for the apple orchards of her native Normandy. Love lugged her across the water and made her strong. Her first child, a boy, died at three days old. She was alone, among strangers, my father away having to travel on business. She endured her grief and pain all by herself, taking them into her, stoically. They became her framework, a second skeleton. She survived, to have more children, to find a job, to make a home. As I hoped to do. As I wanted to do.

– A woman I know, says the Deftly Sibyl: went through the marriage ceremony while having a miscarriage, standing upright in her white brocade tent while the blood coursed through layers of sanitary towels and seeped into her satin shoes. She stumbled to the hospital, not to the reception. A man I know left the registry office with his finger swelling up around the platinum wedding ring. Later he was discovered in the bathroom with a woman friend and a tube of KY Jelly. In the end he went to a jeweller's and had the ring sawn off. Then at last he went to the reception.

– A woman I know, says the Babble-On Sibyl: had an affair with her butcher. At noon he pulled the iron shutters down, then fucked her on the tiled floor among the heaps of sawdust, in the cool gloom, the taut red carcases swaying above. Her husband found a brown paper bag in her knicker drawer, containing her photo and that of the butcher placed face to face, two kissing squares of celluloid. So he beat her up. When I got married I wanted a wild pagan ritual with me in a low-cut silk frock and my friends dancing and singing. I checked out Kensington registry office. No one could call that a holy place, with its red flock wallpaper and bouquets of artificial tulips and officials in bulging satin ties. In the end I got married in a little Anglican church in the country, wearing a wreath of lilies, a veil, the lot. I mourn for the ceremony I did not let myself have. I mourn for the fact I can't marry all my women friends. No public ceremonies to celebrate the passionate love between friends. Our real wedding was in bed. We held each other's ears and whispered into them the words we made up. Neil's idea. I love him for that.

— What is a husband? asks the Gaffer: the one with too much power. I don't understand why you women want to get married. What's in it for you? Status? Money? Security? You itch, you get married. You do your mating dance, produce your children. What then? Those years stretching ahead. Dryness, no passion. I know this. I've pressed my face against the bedroom windows. Better not to marry, and not to burn. Better to be safe. Better not to have that power. Better not to hurt the women. Better not to let your needs out. Better to be like me.

I serve green salad, pears, more wine.

— Time for a story, the Deftly Sibyl suggests: about a woman who's *not* married?

19 Death. Think on it, as I have been instructed to do. Hovering above the bed, I shall take leave of my body, the spittle-flecked lips, the thin cropped hair sodden with sweat, the wasted scarred limbs, the rolled eyes. Then up, into the night, and up, further up, past the chapel tower, above the realm of moths and bats, up the staircase of the stars, to the place where there is no night and no crying out and no hunger for kisses.

If I am sent to hell. I have seen pictures of it. I remember the one painted on the right-hand wall of the apse in our old parish church. The doors of hell are open, and I peep inside. I meet two naked women, both of them graceful and fair, with gleaming silky flesh and unbound golden curls. They wear ropes of pearls about their necks, rings on their fingers, jewels in their ears. One of these ladies is held down by two scarlet devils, while a third tears off her breasts with red-hot pincers. The other lady, tied to a gridiron, is having her eyes put out, and a glowing poker thrust between her legs. Swirls of smoke obscure the other tortured souls; it is these two naked ladies only who represent the torments of the damned. As a child I do not understand why this should be so. Our parish priest, a holy man who does not keep a housekeeper-whore as so many clerics do, explains to me that women's beauty evokes men's lust, and drags them down to vileness, away from their search for God. I watch these ladies in their agony. Every Sunday for sixteen years. My father has told me how pretty I am.

I shut my eyes in order to meditate and to prepare for sleep by thinking of the Four Last Things: death, judgement, hell, and heaven. I open them again, unable to bear the horror. I am an exile from heaven, beating on its closed doors. Will they

105

remain closed to me when I die?

God is not here with me. I see only furniture. This bed, my prie-dieu. I don't like the crucifix; it dominates my cell, but I won't look at it. I won't be responsible any longer for his pain, my poor torn brother. Nor can I console him. I have abdicated my position at the foot of the cross. For me, now, Jesus is only one more wretch condemned to death by a cruel Father-God in the name of a corrupt religion that crushes the spirit rather than freeing it. Crushes the body. Maims and rips it in the name of love. I can't love a God who requires such suffering, who wills his son to be tortured to a slow death. I can't purchase salvation that way. I have given up that God. My visions over my years in this abbey have taught me different truths, and I trust them more. But the God of the priests does not let go so easily. I shall be punished, I know that. Tomorrow morning, when I kneel in the chapter-house in front of our Abbess and all the Ladies of our community here I shall learn what my punishment is to be. I am a heretic who refuses to recant. I do not expect mercy from him whom I have abandoned.

On my sixteenth birthday, I walk to St Paul's to attend Mass, with my sister Joanna and our aunt Dame Alice. It is a spring morning. May. Our Lady's month, and mine. The city rises about me, roofs and tiles and thatch washed by the cold light, the stone of the great church scrubbed by the sun to the colour of milk on oatmeal. After Mass, I kneel in front of the Virgin Mother and light a candle and pray. A lay brother pushes a twig broom across the wide flags, and the dust dances up in golden grains. The choir, practising for vespers, uncorks a sweet and piercing music that explodes in a froth of spine-tingling sound over my head where I kneel at the Lady altar and see the light splash in, red and green and blue smudges on the clean stone floor. The columns arch above my head, whippy and thin as young willows in the fields. God swings about in the sculptured air like a child on holiday.

The cloud of gold dust hangs between me and the Virgin's kind face like the pillar of fire the Israelites saw as they tracked across Egypt searching for the promised land. I close my eyes, and see a pillar of gold smoke against my eyelids.

We stand outside the west door, enjoying the sunshine. The

yard smells of fresh-cut grass, manure, baking bread. Seagulls and pigeons hop and peck, seeking crumbs in the cracks between cobbles. Joanna dusts her palms together, beats her hands on her heavy skirt and laughs as the birds scatter upwards. They make a flashing pattern of white embroidery, glossy linen threads looping and darting and then settling on the grass again, stitches in an orderly row.

Then the three men come into the courtyard, beating drums and crying out in a strange tongue I cannot understand, and we, with the rest of the strolling crowd, turn to watch them.

They are friars, I think at first, for they wear rough habits of brown wool, and deep hoods drawn forwards over their faces. On the back of his robe each man bears a red woollen cross, and in his hand each one carries a scourge. The sun flashes on the hooked metal barbs embedded in the leather thongs that swirl up and down in the air as the men march forwards, shaking them. At first I think only how pretty they look, like bright ornaments, like the thorns of rose bushes when raindrops hang on them and they glitter.

The three men circle the courtyard, their sung prayers issuing in hoarse cracked voices from thin lips. They limp, and their bare feet are dusty and scarred.

Then they halt, quite near us. Without speaking, they throw back their hoods in a single gesture, and wriggle out of the top part of their habits, so that they stand naked from the waist upwards, their brown robes hanging down over their girdles. For a moment they stay thus, in silence, and they kneel down and raise their flails.

They have their backs to us. We are too close not to see. I hear Dame Alice and Joanna gasp in the same breath as I, and we clutch each other's hands simultaneously. Each of those poor penitents has a back covered in unhealed wounds, the flesh torn and red in layers of pus and suppuration. Patches of dried blood crust around places that are open and raw and still bleeding. As we gape and watch, they begin to whip themselves. Steadily, methodically, the black snakes of the scourges whistling over their shoulders, first to the right and then to the left, as they take up their chant again. Each metal hook bites and grips the edges of wounds, and tears them a little wider, raking across fresh undamaged skin at the same time and ploughing it into channels of blood.

– Come away, my aunt chokes, tugging on our hands: come away, children.

I cannot. I am taken by the harsh music of the flagellants, the song of their whips in the air, the hiss of leather, the rattle of the metal tips clashing together and then descending onto red meat. I believe I can hear the harmony of the black barbs as they drag across bleeding wounds that are open like ecstatic mouths. And the men keep up their singing, their high complaint, whose rhythm orders and measures the pace and fury of their strokes.

I wrest my hands out of the hold of my sister and aunt, and move sideways. I need to see the men's faces. I want to know how much they hurt.

I know death already, of course, and corpses. I hear my mother's shrieks as they try to pull the stuck baby out of her, and I see the sopping red mess she lies in as I am hurried in to say goodbye to her. Her bed is like a butcher's shop, and the dead baby lies on a cushion like a joint of meat waiting to be carried home. Also I have seen animals slaughtered, and beggars rotting in the street, their flesh stinking, and my aunt's husband before he died, with the bone sticking out of his gangrenous leg. I know suffering.

I know suffering as a blow to be resisted, by cursing, by yells. At the most, endured. The chicken pinioned on the chopping block by my aunt's hand, the fish still wriggling in anguish in the basket, my mother arching her back and thrashing on the bed. I understand that for all of them a moment comes when struggle ceases and the spirit seeks only to be released. But this voluptuous abandon to torture is new. These three men bend forwards into their pain, inviting it, supplying it. And so in turn I bend towards them, wanting to understand.

Two of them have their eyes closed, sweat and blood running in white and red rivulets down the grime of their faces. They are sealed off; their ecstasy is private. But the third has his frenzied eyes wide open, and stares at me, and salutes me with them as one who is kin to him. He summons me, his little sister of the precious wounds. Though my sister and aunt snatch me away and bear me home with them, angry and scolding, his message stays with me, inscribed on my flesh in letters of red.

*

My father has been teaching me to read, and in the evening he sends for me as usual. I am his favourite child, being the elder and more closely resembling my dead mother than my sister does. He is a man who greatly loves learning, and at night, when he has shut up the shop at the front of the house, he retires to his private room at the back and is transformed from apothecary into wizard. He calls me his little scholar. Already I know Latin, and some French. Along with new words he feeds me sweetmeats made by my aunt, little balls of paste flavoured with almond and rose-water. Learning is no hardship, for it means time alone with my father, his finger guiding me along the brown loops and curls of the page, his palm offering me my reward. Language tastes of frangipane and peppermint and sugar, and I roll it over my tongue, the words dissolving into me. My aunt mutters that I am lazy and spoilt, and my father laughs and pulls my hair.

At the moment we are reading an encyclopedia listing the properties of precious stones, plants and planets, a work that knots the universe together into harmonious music. Naming is power: the hidden world yields up its secrets when you link the right names in nature together, when you trace the correspondence, taut as a fishing line, between star, herb, season, humour and beast. I see God as a doctor and philosopher, as a teacher like my father. I trust my father, that he will sew up the jagged edges of the morning, wipe away the blood with a dry maxim, cover the torn flesh with the cloak of scholastic truth.

There is a new lesson this evening, with no sweetmeats to follow. Instead I taste bitterness. I swivel around on my stool and stare at the great bed in the corner, and imagine two heads laid on its pillows. I look at the wooden clothes press, and see it full of the new wife's things. I see her fur slippers tumbled on the floor, her cup of spiced wine set next to my father's, her fat arse resting on my stool, in my place, next to him. I see myself outside the door in the dark, pressing my ear to it, hearing their laughter, the disgusting noise of their kisses, the creaking of the bed. Perhaps there will be a new baby, a new bloody mess on the sheets, more screaming. Another death.

My father's hasty words tear strips off my heart, but I keep my back as straight as the flagellants'. Like them, I kneel down.

Like them, I apply lashes of hate to myself.

– I shall never marry, I blurt out: I wish to dedicate my life entirely to God.

My father raises me from my knees and sends me to bed.

– We will speak of this in the morning, he says: after I have talked to your aunt.

Joanna and I discuss the news in whispers, mindful of Dame Alice snoring in the other bed. My sister is not disturbed by our father's intention to remarry. She expects an indulgent stepmother who will give her new clothes and caresses, who will allow her to have a pet dog of her own, who will be different in every possible way from our strict aunt. I despise Joanna for these simple wants, but I keep silence, thinking: she is only twelve years old, after all. My sister wriggles her plump body closer to mine and blows her hot breath into my ear, telling me of the other things she also wants, giggling. A doting husband, a house of her own to order as she pleases, servants to skip to her whims, mornings of lying abed dandling her little dog. The secret delights of the night.

I have seen our dogs engage in their hasty, indifferent coupling. I have seen the pictures of devils on the walls of our church, with female faces painted over their private parts. I have heard our priest describe, many times, the shameful itch, the hot allure of women for men. I am familiar with the half-naked idiot youth who sits at the end of our street and begs from all who pass. Once or twice I see his wrinkled purplish member, ugly and comic, dangling from the rags around his waist. I want to touch it, in case it is as soft as a rotting rose. Once, while I look at it, it rears and swells into an enormous rod, and Mad Jack puts his hands on his hips and smiles at me.

My father. Joseph's flowering rod. In the bloodied bed, with the new wife. I do not know what a woman is supposed to do when a man smiles that particular invitation. Mad Jack stretches out his arms to welcome me, and my father feeds me sweetmeats, and my insides dissolve to wet sugar.

I try to pray. Joanna is fast asleep, her head on my shoulder, and Dame Alice breathes heavily next to us, her mouth open. I cross myself and call on God.

He comes in the shape of the three flagellants. They stand in

110

a row at the end of the bed, their scourges neatly rolled up and tucked under their arms, and they nod a greeting to me.

– Little sister of the precious blood, they whisper: we will teach you the true ecstasy of the flesh, the dance of numbing and forgetfulness, the high song of pain. We will show you the strait and narrow way to perfection, the bliss to which only the pure of heart arrive.

They shake out their scourges in a single beautiful coordinated gesture.

I have already been taught to meditate on the passion, wounds and sacred blood of our Saviour Lord Jesus Christ. I have spent hours in church kneeling under the enormous crucifix, gazing at the thick nails driven through his hands and feet, the gashes torn in the soft flesh. I have learned to enter his suffering, to share it. So it does not seem strange to me that my new brothers show me the way further in.

At first their whips only tickle me. Then they drive me up a red spiral of agony. Only the chosen, they whisper to me: can follow this path, can trust that God is surely at the other end. The lashes sting my flesh and make my feet nimble. But I faint before I reach the top. I wake to find Joanna shaking me and Dame Alice standing by our bed holding a lit taper. Someone is screaming, and I do not at first recognize my own voice.

Two months later my father accompanies me to the Cistercian abbey at Bidewell in Kent. My eyes dry, I strip off my velvet mantle, the gold ring and chain he has given me, my embroidered coif and girdle, my silk purse with silver drawstrings. I pile all these items into my father's arms, asking him to sell them and give the money to the poor. My sister does not need more finery, I assure myself. Better to cover Mad Jack's nakedness. Then I go through the door into the enclosure. I have forgotten to ask for my father's blessing, but I do not look back.

I follow the Mistress of Novices along the cloister as eagerly as my sister will go, when her time comes, to meet her husband. Behind me is colour and glitter, the changeability of weather and affections, the surge of pleasure and pain. Henceforth the Office and the Liturgy will provide me with seasons, will mark off day from night, each hour ordered by the Rule, each minute taken care of by Mother Church, my time divided by her into

111

passages of work and prayer, study and contemplation. I throw myself into my future as though into a bottomless sea. Safety as the waters close over my head and I die to the world, to time, to the flesh.

God plucks me from drowning and baptizes me with the sea of my sorrow. God sets me in this abbey, which is an Ark of Ladies sailing towards salvation.

In the centre of this Ark is our cloister, the place where I most often meet God. He wears a red robe and is borne up by four pairs of fiery red wings. He hovers above the grass of the cloister garth, and I look at him out of the corner of my eye, for I do not dare approach him face to face. He is warmth, and great sweetness inside me, and steady light, and he breathes on all the plants growing in the garden so that they flourish and bloom. Even in wintertime the air of the cloister is fragrant with the scent of balsam and roses, lilies and cedar, jasmine and frankincense.

But when the bell in the chapel tower rings, summoning me back down into time and duty, the gates of paradise close against me and I drop, disconsolate, into God's absence. Hurrying along the cloister, to the chapel or the refectory or the chapter-house, I hear snickering laughter behind me, the flick and click of metal on the tiled floor, and I smell foul air, as though the devil has farted. Then I choke and freeze, while icy invisible hands grip mine or pull at my habit. Sometimes they lay themselves around my ankles so that I am obliged to stand stock-still and rigid, listening to the voices that hiss in my ear and whisper to me to lash myself until the blood comes.

The other Ladies, seeing me suddenly stop rigid and then jerk my body from side to side, think that I flaunt myself as some sort of visionary, that I am rotten with spiritual pride. I am often late for the office in chapel, or for meals, and so I have to perform constant penitences. I dare not confess my trouble lest I am charged with possession by demons, and though I know this to be true, I fear that exorcism will not help me. I am already lost.

All of the Ladies practise mortification of the body. We keep Lent twice a year, and in addition we fast every Friday. We sprinkle vinegar and bitter herbs on our food. In the fresco painted on the wall in the refectory, Our Lord eats supper with his friends, smiling, passing baskets of cherries, flagons of amber wine, dishes of nuts and fine white bread. Our supper is spread below: thin gruel or porridge, hard salty cheese. We wear spiked chains twisted about our arms, and hairshirts, and we scourge ourselves once a week in the privacy of our cells.

I have three male helpers in mine. One brother deftly strips me of my habit and folds it neatly on my bed, then caresses my naked limbs with his cold hand. I like his touch; I shudder with pleasure, waiting for what will come after. The second brother takes me in his arms and hugs me to his breast, holding me so tenderly, making sure I cannot break free. I do not want to. I tremble in his embrace, my head on his shoulder, my face smelling the dirty wool of his habit. Then the third brother lays on the whip.

The pain is my consolation for the time I cannot spend with God. I can tell no one this. But my three brothers know it. They know how to touch me delicately as though with tongues, until all my flesh tingles and cries out for more, more, harder, harder. They know how to turn me round and pinion my arms afresh and tickle my breasts with their thongs, how to send the lash whispering around my private parts and between my legs. I grow to need them holding me down, holding me back, and I plead with them in ashamed and disgusting language that they will go on and hurt me more. Then they do. They hurt me and hurt me, and I sing and sob along with the pain until the tide of pleasure rises in my running blood, in the urine I cannot stop myself from passing, and overwhelms me, and I drop to the cold floor, panting and crying out. Then the three brothers mock me, calling me their vile animal, their little sister of filth and excrement, and I roll and grovel at their feet.

This goes on for five years. God slips away from me. I can no longer rise above my throbbing and tormented body into that high pure place where God flies gaily in the green sweet-smelling garden. I live only in my dreadful body. I punish it, through redoubled fasting and mortification. I become very thin. My monthly bleeding stops. I set exquisite stitches, in gold and silver threads, in a white silk stole our Bishop will wear. Is not this sacrilege? I live in hell, no longer daring to appeal to Our Lady and the saints for help, for have I not betrayed them, and my vows? I cannot expect them to visit me in my house of foul delight. Trying to expiate my longing for my brothers' company, and for that of my fourth brother and lover the whip, I grow sick. And by now I know my brothers' names. Our Lady Abbess has warned us against the blandishments of the heretics spreading their contagion through our country as they arrive from the Low Countries and distribute their message through their disciples and their books. There can be no mercy for a nun convicted of following the Fellowship of the Atonement.

One December, in the season of Advent, my sister Joanna comes to visit me. The trees are leafless and black, the earth rigid with frost, the days short and dreary. It is the long night of the year. Snow falls, and melts to dirty slush, and falls again.

On that particular afternoon I am walking, as usual, in the dark cloister, making my cold legs move me around and around. A cloister is a kind of prayer in stone. I cannot pray; I let the force of the cloister pray me. I stumble along under the vaulted painted roof, looking through the repeating slender columns at the little garden and at the well set in the centre of the grass.

I am awaiting the birth of the Christ Child. I believe he will lighten my darkness, and loosen the grip of winter, and plant me with new green shoots of hope. I hope I believe this. I need him to be born. I need to hold him, the new fire, to the ice in my soul. I need him to melt me, to free me.

The iron handle of the well is very black against the white square of snow that blots out and redefines the little courtyard. Whiteness replaces black. White lines spell out the curves of the opposite side of the cloister, and white wedges and triangles and squares are its jutting roof and the cell windows above it. I need blackness, the darkness in which things germinate and grow. The world is spoken through white, and I need it to be balanced against black, set against black, the one giving a shape to the other. I watch a sparrow hop through the snow to the well, leaving a trail of tiny precise black prints. I am clothed all in white. I want to be both the snow outlining the dark shapes of stone, and the stone that the snow clings to. I want to be both the cloister encircling the garden, and the space thrusting out

114

against the pierced stone walls.

One of the lay sisters, muffled up in a thick mantle and felt boots, stumps towards me, her frosty breath hanging before her in the air. She pulls at my sleeve, and then gestures with both hands, signing to me that I have permission from the Abbess to break enclosure for an hour in order to speak to my sister and her husband, who have travelled out from London to visit me.

Joanna sits by the parlour fire, wrapped in furs. Her cheeks are pink, and her eyes sharp and brown. Her husband, the merchant, who stands behind her chair, looks to be a kindly and prosperous man, but after our brief salutation I have no eyes for him. We Ladies are not supposed to touch people, but I kiss my sister's cold face, and hold her hands in mine, and then drop to my knees in front of her. The warmth of her presence thaws me. I burst into tears. I feel her recoil from my noisy grief, and from my sick, emaciated body, but I cannot stop. I burrow into her lap. Unlike me, she smells so good, of fresh sweat and cold fur and wood-smoke. I snort at her like a pig rooting for truffles, I eat her and drink her in, and I go on sobbing until she pushes me away.

– All this snot and tears will ruin my clothes, she reproves me: I have enough of that already.

I look up, gulping, as the nurse comes out of the shadowy corner and puts a plump white bundle into Joanna's arms, turning back a corner of the silken wrappings so that I can see the tiny face.

I am astonished by my meeting with this child. He is already himself: delicately formed, all his features clearly marked. His dark blue eyes stare gravely at me from under the black tufts of his hair, and his brow wrinkles as he considers me. I do not know what to say to him. I am silent in front of his questioning eyes.

– Go on, Joanna urges me: hold him.

I wrap my sleeves around him, for greater protection from the whistling draughts, and sit back on my heels, looking from my sister to the child and back again. The child's eyes seem to me full of wisdom, and experience. Yet his tiny rosy mouth, opening and closing as he sucks the air, and his little fist darting out from his bindings and waving, make him nothing but small

115

new animal.

– It's a miracle, I breathe.

Joanna bursts out laughing.

– I remember how unpleasant you once considered it, she mocks me: all the business of making babies. You never said a word to me about it. But I knew from the look on your face how you felt.

Her husband looks a little sorry for me, and bends forward to touch Joanna on the arm in reproof.

– Of course we thank Almighty God, he declares: for his goodness in giving us this child.

My sister tosses her head at him. I see how she pleases him, how she has mastered him. I imagine their deep soft bed, its curtains drawn against the cold winter night, and their two bodies riding and tumbling over each other. I understand, suddenly, their kindness to each other, their courtesy, their pleasure. Then the baby vomits a thin stream of milk into my lap, and his nurse snatches him away.

Joanna helps me wipe myself. This establishes some friendship between us, some calm. I settle myself on a stool, and wave her husband into a chair on the other side of the fire. I sit between them, warming myself in their company, and we talk. Master John tells me something of his life as a merchant, his travels to the Low Countries, and what he has seen there. He tells me of the communities of holy women called Beguines whom he has visited in Flanders and Brabant. He interests me particularly by his description of their goodness, their prudence and economy, for I have heard of them only as loose women, as heretics, and he insists instead that they are lovers of God and sisters to each other, bound by no vows, submitting to no rule except that of friendship, and collectively earning a living.

– I wish I could be a Beguine, I blurt out: my life here constrains me too much. It is full of too much pain and hardship.

Joanna and Master John exchange looks.

– Be careful, Master John cautions me: what you say aloud concerning these matters. Many of the Beguines, though not deserving it, are arraigned for heresy, especially when they travel to beg for their alms. They are suspected by many, and

116

suffer for it. You too will come under suspicion if you speak freely of your admiration.

– I will pray for them, I say, sighing: I wish them very well, poor ladies.

– You should pray for yourself a little more, my sister retorts: you look so thin, so ill. What has happened to you? I never thought to find you so pitiably haggard, so wretched. I suppose you have been mortifying yourself with penances. What good does that do? Surely it is far more worthwhile to praise God through a healthy life, with a healthy body. A soul who truly loves God has no need to fear the body's desires. Why have you been tormenting yourself?

Master John's upraised hand checks her. I am so surprised by her blunt words concerning my physical welfare that I do not take in the rest of what she says. Not until I am alone again in my cell when I have time for slow reflection. But now the Office bell is ringing, and I am rising to my feet and hurrying towards the door.

They leave the following morning. While Master John supervises the loading of their horses, Joanna leaves her son in the care of his nurse and insists on coming with me to see the guesthouse garden.

– There is something I must say to you, she says: where no one can hear me. It is better to go outside.

The lay sisters have shovelled the snow off the path the day before. Now it sparkles with a sheen of frost in the pale sunlight, its yellow sand overlaid with silver bits of ice which crunch under our wooden soles. The pleached apple trees trained along it are gnarled plaits of pale green and grey, and I stroke the cold roughness of their trunks as we pass between them. I drink in the clean chilly air, holding it in my mouth like a swallow of the Moselle wine my father used to let me taste from his cup. The brick wall separating us from the Ladies' garden glows red, the moss and lichen in its cracks as bright as turquoise and jade. One of the lay sisters is burning rubbish, the smoke of her fire as thick and sweet as incense in my nostrils. She smiles and nods to us as we pass, and I am filled with shame. I am lacking in charity. So long involved with my private misery, I have not made friends here, have not loved the women I live among. Yet this nun still smiles at me.

117

I have not loved my own sister properly, either. I know it. I understand the reasons for her reserve with me over the past five years, I think, the lack of letters or visits. Her coming to see me now, her soliciting this final interview, means that at long last she has forgiven me. Happily I seat myself next to her on a stone bench set at the end of the path in the shelter of the garden wall.

– Before our father died last year, God rest his soul, Joanna says, crossing herself: he asked me to come and visit you. He had had no news of you for a long time, and he was anxious. I sent you the news of his death by a servant rather than coming myself because I had only recently begun to carry the child and was very sick. I told myself that I preferred to wait until my baby was born and that I would come to see you then so that I could show him to you. But there was another reason that made me delay my visit. I have only come at all because Master John said it was my duty to do so.

I can hardly bear to listen, but I force myself. I am afraid that my sister's words will summon up my three brothers to punish me again as I deserve. It is better to stay quiet, for I can think of nothing to say.

My silence drives Joanna to further anger.

– Of course you were always the one our father favoured. I suppose you thought I neither noticed nor cared. I wanted to learn to read too, but there was no chance of that. You stood always in my light so that I was merely your shadow.

She sits with averted face. I make myself speak.

– Forgive me sister, I say: for all the times I wronged you in the past.

Now her voice is quick and harsh, like a cartwheel jolting over loose stones.

– You think it's so easy to be forgiven, don't you? You think you just have to ask and it comes to you. You holy Lady wrapped in proud purity! When I sent messages telling you of Dame Alice's death and then of our father's, you sent none back. Did you imagine my husband too could not read? Could you not imagine we needed word from you?

She kicks at the gravel at our feet with her fur boot. Furiously, so that the small stones skip in all directions.

– You did not love me, she accuses me: you scorned me. And

118

now you expect me to forgive you. Tell me why I should forgive you after all the times you have neglected me. Even after our mother's death, when I cried myself to sleep every night, you never once tried to comfort me. You sat with our father in his room instead. Why did you never think I might be grieving for our mother as much as you and he? You thought I was too little and too stupid to feel anything. Only you were allowed to have feelings. You left me alone, when I needed you.

Her face still turned away from me, she draws her feet back close together and thrusts her hands more deeply into her fur sleeves. We both sit very still, but the air between us crackles.

Black earth and green grass are closely fastened under transparent ice. A blackbird strikes its beak against the silence of snow, the garden a forge for his silver notes. My sister's words touch my skin, enter me. My mouth is sore with the need to speak true words, not to lie, to acknowledge my sister in the angry place I have driven her to and from which she reproaches me so bitterly. I am trying to make reparation, and I do not know how to do it. I have been stuck in the mud of despair for so long. Joanna's passionate cry tugs me out of it, breaks me open.

– All those years I hurt you and failed you, I say: I am very sorry for. I can hardly tell you how sorry.

– What's done, Joanna mutters: is done.

– Will you forgive me? I ask her: I have punished myself arrogantly and uselessly for my sin rather than try to mend things with you.

I can see the struggle in her face now, as she turns to me and I see that small crying child missing her mother, uncomforted. I have learned the pleasure there can be in not forgiving, in not allowing oneself to be forgiven. In refusing that grace. Have I not inflicted that on myself for the past five years?

– I suppose I do forgive you, my sister murmurs at last.

Her kiss is formal, dry brush of lips. She touches my hand. Pauses, then puts her face close to mine.

– With Master John, she whispers: I have begun a new life. No, not just the married one. A spiritual one, a rebirth. He has converted me to the true faith. I am happier than I have ever been.

I stare at her in shock and unwilling comprehension. She

hurries on, telling me what I have already begun to suspect, that she and her husband have secretly become adherents of the Brethren of the Free Spirit, in so far as, being a married couple, they can.

My own sister a heretic. Therefore in danger of death. But she shrugs off my anxious questions. Back straight, eyes gleaming: she is the beautiful one now, the strong sister, the clever one.

– Do not betray us, she says: and do not fear for us.

She gabbles to me of incomprehensible doctrines. How humans can attain a sinless state, in which sensuality is so guided by the soul that the body can be allowed any gratification it likes. How these liberated souls are not subject to ecclesiastical authority, being blessed in and by themselves. How free souls can enjoy heaven on earth. How the carnal act is not a sin, but, on the contrary, a route to God. How the perfect have no need of the Eucharist and the Mass, nor of the Passion of Christ.

– Why are you telling me these things? I ask, full of terror: how can you speak thus in this place dedicated to holiness?

My sister's grip on my wrist tightens. Her eyes flash scorn.

– I am offering you freedom and consolation, she breathes: the happier life you spoke of yesterday. Can't you see?

Her husband calls from the other end of the garden, startling us both. Such a confidence in his voice that he will be listened to. Such assurance that she is here, waiting for him. I am envious.

– Listen to me, Joanna hisses: will you? Before I go I have a present for you.

She fumbles inside her furs and extracts a velvet bag laced with leather which she lays on my lap.

– Don't let anyone see it. It comes from our father's library. Our new mother has sold most of his books. Master John helped her. He kept this one, thinking it safer. I am not able to read it, and so now I want you to have it.

She gets up. I clutch the little bag.

– Our father made his own translation into English of the *Miroir des Simples Ames* of Marguerite de Porête, Joanna says in a voice sharp with excitement: in secret, for his own use, and now for ours. He must have meant to tell us before he died. It is

120

not too late now. He was one of *us*. *He too.*

– But who is Marguerite? I ask: how do you know her?

– Marguerite was burned alive in Paris thirty years ago, my sister says: in 1310, as a heretic who would not recant. Also she was a Beguine.

Then she is gone, tapping down the path in her wooden-soled boots, to rejoin her husband and her child.

The three flagellant brothers do not visit me again.

I stop using my scourge, and hide it under my bed, along with my hairshirt and my spiked chain. I stop sprinkling bitter herbs on my food, and eat with relish, savouring the taste of bread, of milk, of the pure water from our well. I grow breasts again, and I begin to bleed again every month. I no longer meditate in front of the crucifix. That bloody flesh hanging from the nails disgusts me. I do not need it for my salvation. My own blood is fresh and sweet.

Spring comes. The orchard is thick with pear blossom, the bare trees suddenly flowering, rods dipped in white stars. I ask permission, for the sake of my health, to work outside, with the lay sisters, in the fields and the kitchen garden. I kneel on the earth, smelling it, crumbling it between my fingers, breaking open the moist clods and digging my nails into them. At first my back and legs ache, but this is pleasure not pain. And now, rather than pleading with God to listen to me, I begin to listen to God. So my visions arrive.

In the first vision I find myself in a basilica shaped like one of the beehives in our garden and made of rosy bricks fitted closely together, bricks baked onto a thick rope which coils around and around. Bricks coiling to make a basilica, a beehive.

Columns, sturdy as the bodies of women standing in a circle with joined upraised hands, support the upper gallery. Between them are arches as tender and fine as the place at the back of a knee, the dip in the shoulder, the turn of the neck.

The small church closes around me like a second skin, closes not around empty space but around fullness.

A staircase hidden in the thick outer wall takes me up to the circular gallery. I pace it, around and around. I find God here,

God quickening in this kiln of dark pink bricks. Just above my head is the vaulted roof, whose curves repeat, loop, arch away and back again, divide each other, join each other, intersect. Fans of sinew and muscle, balancing of bones, warmth of flesh. Clear limits and edges of stone, but not sharp.

On my right the leaping columns open onto the deep interior space of the church. I can float out into it, fly in it, turn over in it. On my left is another circle of columns bracing the outer wall. In their recesses are empty niches shaped like egg halves, shaped as though a huge thumb has gently pressed itself into the inner rim of a clay pot, decorating it around and around. Pinpricks of light in the centre of each recess let fall lozenges of gold onto the tracery of cracks in the pavement. Darkness except for these tiny diamonds that are the windows.

The little basilica is blown like a bubble in stone, rounded and airy, swelling upwards, suspended, caught. It holds me. I can play in it, roll around in it, pray in it, dance in it, sleep. God is born here. This place enables God to be born: crouches, squats, pushes God out, embraces God. These bricks are woven together to make God's basket, God's Ark.

This church is the woman's body, where God begins.

In the second vision I stand enclosed by a box made of dark blue glass, opaque and shining, a slippery and precarious container, with nothing for my outstretched hands to hold on to. The glass box, and I inside it, hang suspended in a deep shaft, down which we suddenly start to fall at great speed.

The blue glass walls surrounding me become transparent, so that I can see the pictures, incomprehensible and bright, painted on the wall of the shaft. As I drop past them, these pictures run together and blur, forming the image, in white brilliance, of a tall shape. An angel? A human being? The image detaches itself, passes through my blue glass wall, and enters me, mixing its substance with mine. It is my soul.

My soul: a necessary word. My soul: meaning the memory of myself in my beginning. How I became. How two struck and fused, how a seed of life sprouted.

Our great Doctors teach that the woman's body is merely the bed of earth which receives and grows the seed of the man, merely the container for his power. He gives her a baby, they say. But they are wrong. The seeds of new matter spark in the woman's body as well as in the man's. They mix their seeds together. Thus I too began.

My soul is my remembering how at that time what I call I was not I, how I was kin in my being to earth, rocks, sea, trees. How I leaped and grew from being that towards being female, passing through thousands of years of change, living two times. How I might have become a mackerel or a dandelion or a man.

My soul simply holds my memory together, is the knot tying me into the dancing web of creation. Through my body I am part of the universe in its constant becoming and changing and dying and transformation, and my soul is the word that tells me that.

Creation happening. Now. Creation happening over and over again, unceasingly. Seven days and seven nights! I could laugh out loud. A thousand thousand years, and nine months, and a single second, and I am in all of these and I dance.

The soul is born as the body is, down the birth canal. The channel joining heaven and earth. The slippery bridge. The rainbow. The sign of birth, when the waters break and the sun shines in all its radiance, the fire in the sky, the joining of the elements anew as the child is born.

It is the woman who reminds the child of the soul, by giving birth to the child. That struggle of creation. That labour. The new body delivered in its wet shining memory of connection to everything else that has been and will be and is. The dancing.

In the third vision I see Lot's wife looking back. Looking back at what lies behind her, at what she has lost: that great fair city of infancy, the strong mother-city holding the child and keeping her safe.

Lot's wife turns her face away from the present, towards the past. Her feet are stuck. She is too frightened to move. Frightened of change, of newness, of suffering.

Her mother is gone. She weeps, and she beats herself because the mother she would like to beat instead is not there. And her tears, flowing copiously, harden and set, until she has turned into a pillar of salt.

She is alone now. A rock in the desert. Her husband and

family, losing patience with her crying, have gone on without her. Dogs sniff and lick at her, and raise their hind legs and piss against her. She leans into the wind, which carves her a face, a body, the semblance of a woman.

Now she can't cry any more. She is dried up and hard. She can't feel.

Yet salt can melt. If the Flood comes again. If water surrounds her and overwhelms her and lets her dissolve in it. Sea water. Salt tears. Swimming strongly on them to a new life.

I am Lot's wife. Learning to mourn.

In the fourth vision a woman whose nightgown is soaked in blood clutches me by the hand, and won't let me go. I struggle to be free of her red embrace which stains my white robes. I turn my face away from her and the stink of the blood streaming down her legs and puddling at her feet.

– Daughter, she reproaches me: don't you know me?

Holding her at arm's length, I look at her.

– Mother, I cry out: let me go. I never wanted to be like you!

She drops my hand and pulls her tangled hair forward to hide her eyes. I suppose she is crying, but I'm already moving away from her. I must not look back.

Her voice follows me.

– I am Lady Wisdom. Who else should I be? You have spent your whole life searching for me, and yet I was close by you all the time.

Aghast, I turn round, ready to run back towards her and to kneel at her feet. Too late. She has disappeared.

I have no more visions. I should have burned Marguerite's book, instead of keeping it in my cell where it could be found, and produced in evidence against me. I did not trust Marguerite's words enough, that they would stay in my heart if I let the parchment they were written on go from me into the fire. I could not bring myself to burn her book. Any book.

Marguerite has gone through the fire before me. I have this one night left to me before I find out whether I am to follow her there. I want to use this night for prayer, but I cannot. I have no time. It has been more important to me to write this account of my history. I have bribed the nephew of one of the lay sisters

124

with the promise of a rich reward from Master John if he can get this writing safely out of the convent and into my sister's hands. I want her and her husband to know my thoughts. I want their child to know. I want my life, with all its errors, to have been of some use. Perhaps its use is simply that now I have earned death, and am ready to die. I pray that my words will reach the ones I love even if I have to die. I pray that my life has not been one long mistake.

I wish I had been able to leave here, to spend time with my sister talking; to find those other sisters, the Beguines. It is too late now.

I am a stranger in this world. I am an exile from heaven, beating on its closed doors.

20 The Re-Vision Sibyl sprawls in the Ark's kitchen, finishing a late solitary breakfast. A sit-down affair, leisurely, no Kitty to get ready and rush to school.

The kitchen is the sort that the heroine in one of her stories might choose. A slightly romanticized version of her grandmother's kitchen in France. The table, spread with a yellow oilcloth stencilled with wreaths of red and pink and white flowers framed in dark blue, bears a double-decker tin coffee pot marbled in pale green, a chipped white coffee bowl banded in navy and decorated with stylized clumps of blackcurrants, a basket of glossy croissants, a gold-flecked china dish full of apricot jam, and a red and white checked napkin. No plate. Crumbs on the cloth, a cat sidling at her ankles, a tin pitcher of milk.

Above her, the smoke-blackened ceiling, and high shelves bearing iron cooking pots, this year's supply of jams, the brass pans of the heavy kitchen scales, their golden weights marching alongside. Lower down, the row of china canisters, white glaze stamped with blue squares, bearing flour, spices, tea, coffee; and the racks of metal ladles and whisks. A tiny basket, shaped like a holy water stoup, holding boxes of matches, hangs above the gas stove. Frilled muslin curtains at the windows, floor tiled in stiff arabesques of yellow and blue. Clutch of brooms in a corner, tower of aluminium buckets, boxes of string, old jam jars and carpentry tools cluttering the little tin table near the furnace and the ancient washing machine.

The Re-Vision Sibyl dawdles her spoon in her bowl. Swirls of milk scum, coffee dregs. She could happily stay here all morning rather than getting down to some writing, feasting her eyes on the carelessly exquisite still life on the dresser of those

126

onions tumbled into a wide shallow basket, brilliant brown skins nestled against tissue paper of a thrilling indigo, the creases glistening and darkly blue, and, catching the light from the window, transparent and rich as stained glass.

Language is as changeable and delicious as food, coming from outside her to inside. Many times as a child she puzzles over this, trying to discover why certain sounds, certain words, fascinate her, and why she wants to make them part of herself. *Carpet*, for instance. How, why, does the sound manage to convey the meaning? No other sound, she is convinced, could get its essence across so well. Then, in French lessons at school, she learns the word *tapis*, which carries an equally mysterious weight of truth (the close-cropped pile that, brushed the wrong way, sets her teeth on edge, the oblong shape, the geometric pattern of faded scarlet and blue), and becomes confused. She discovers the opposite: that words dissolve into absurdity if she repeats their sound over and over again, their shape and colour detached from their context of meaning. *Biscuit*. She chants it, sings it, looks at it, and the precise meaning crumbles, a blur of yellow, into incoherence, and she's bitten, eaten the word; and her body, her self, is as fluid as carpet, biscuit, meaning as little, as much.

Playfulness vanishes during years of English lessons in primary school. Write a poem, the pupils are urged: about spring, about autumn, about Christmas. Sharp, eager to please, she discovers that the poem is a gift to the teacher, a gift to the mother. Like the sampler produced in sewing classes, the bean sprouted in biology lessons. It's meant to be pretty, to confirm her as the good loving daughter, and she's encouraged to decorate the borders of her words with little pictures of ladies or holly leaves or snowmen. She conjugates the verbs of her pleasing: crazes for collecting miniature teddy bears, ornamental soaps, glass jewels in matchboxes; desklid decorated with pictures of pink ballerinas, kittens, puppies; poems about roses, that rhyme, in regular rhythm. It all comes so easily. The knowledge she had before about words slips away under an avalanche of pink niceness. She is grateful, veiling herself, during the march up to puberty, with signs of a pleasing femininity (pleasing others); veiling her fears, the boy in herself, with images of cute curly-maned ponies.

127

Blank years until she is fifteen, when a heaven-sent English mistress (a dyke – she knows that even when she has no words except *spinster, eccentric, desirable, fiery, demanding*) rescues her with poetry. Poetry snatches her out of the banalities and deprivation of her everyday speech based on self-repression and polite dishonesty. The poetry of Donne and Hopkins (no women – she's never heard of a woman poet) sings to her, wakes her up, makes her grasp that she could *live* if she could ever invent a language to speak her like this. She could spend the rest of her life searching for words.

She starts to write stories and poems, in secret, trying to recapture the lost world of her childhood in France. Is it just the sound of the French language, or particular words spoken in it, she's never sure, that catches at her heart, that transports her to a place that is simultaneously a state of mind? A street in Toulouse, early morning, cobbles under the plane trees swept clean by rain overnight, now speckled with sun chasing shadows, the green leaves blowing, the rosy church washed by light, cool wind on her neck and warmth on her face . . . No, that's wrong, those words aren't quite it . . .

Is it that the French language summons up a particular relationship between, say, *sun* and *stone*? Is it that the words spoken in the French language reassemble that particular beloved landscape of place, of the heart (*France* meaning *mother*) and fill her with consoling joy for its loss? Certain words give her back the mountains, cold bony austere, give her back herself measured by the wind against their slope, their shape. No, that won't do either . . .

Simply by chanting certain words to herself, or by coming across others unexpectedly in a book, she can re-evoke the sensation of *being-in-France, belonging-with-mother*, and that conjunction of language/place ravishes her with pleasure yet as though she's dying, a shivering all over and then orgasm felt in the throat, fountain of sweetness overflowing.

Leaving her mother in order to love her husband (no of course it's not that simple) she abandons that language, that usage, picks a way out: stay inarticulate about desires and feelings that don't fit the romance of marriage she's dreamed, that she talks her way into; sweep gritty rebellion into a diary dustpan; write stories of a galloping naturalism that are clear-

128

cut about *he* and *she*, *he-and-she*, yet hide the longed-for body of the mother under Regency buckskin breeches and caped greatcoat; endure her husband's gentle jeers at what she writes; pick up a romance to read and see *him* become the baby, furious at her lack of attention; forget how to speak French.

She goes on making her childish gifts of pretty words, which upset nobody and which cloak her conflicts just as they did when she was a little girl, which are despised just as the collecting crazes and reading habits of little girls are despised even as they are encouraged as suitable. And she makes her gifts of food, which are necessary; soluble art.

If she is a good wife and mother then she is like her own beloved mother; feminine, a real woman; and will be loved by her.

She cherishes the tools of her trade, picked up at junk stalls in the market, keeping them clean, polished, sharp: the wood and bristle basting brush; the tiny nutmeg grater; her 1930s apple corer and potato peeler with their fine red wood handles; her collection of bizarre egg whisks all spirals and loops; the metal lemon squeezer; the plywood flour sifter with its fine mesh. It is her trousseau. Her mother adds to it, giving her treasures from the old home in France; blue and white lace-edged napkins she hemmed herself; heavy teacloths with a thick red stripe down the middle; a damask tablecloth. Her mother loves to give to others, to fulfil their needs; her mother practises the generous, unselfish arts, cooking and sewing for others. Oh the pleasure of this receiving; of this being given to; of being loved by her. Do nothing to break the beautiful cords of this love, this definition of yourself; for without it you are outcast, dying, monster, bad daughter. Done for.

When she is first married, she scorns machines in the kitchen, convenience foods: no, she will do it all herself, like her grandmother and mother did, and enjoy.

Then she discovers she can't cook well for people she doesn't know as friends, doesn't join in inviting. Jim's business associates, at first feasted on home-made puff pastry and pâtés and pasta, are now fed grim gourmet meals concocted from packets and tins. And when Kitty arrives, she buys a liquidizer for those endless purées of spinach and carrots. She buys chocolate biscuits as bribes, fish fingers, crisps, instant caramel whips, takeaway hamburgers and chips. The food Kitty likes.

She starts to revise her opinions as she starts to revise her writing. Her precious kitchen tools lie in the drawer, blunted and dulled. The kitchen table is littered with papers and typewriter ribbons. She worries about white sugar, adjectives, carcinogenic additives, tenses, cholesterol, paragraphing. But Kitty seems to be thriving on the new diet, even if Jim starts to grumble.

She starts to avoid butchers' shops, those white-tiled laboratories of death: stink of blood, sodden sawdust clotted with bits of skin and gristle, racks of cruel hooks from which dangle headless rabbits and skinny pink and yellow chickens strung up by the feet, whack of knives onto bone, onto raw flesh, sloppy piles of purple liver, dripping red hands fumbling for change in the till, dishes of tripe like white knitting, stained aprons, trays of pink trotters, glistening kidneys, tiny trussed quail, chunks of dead lamb marbled with thick fat. And oh those terrible women peering suspiciously at the corpses, picking them over, inspecting the tender morsels they will carry home and cook and eat, swallowing death: she rejects them too.

Now she spends her time in stationers' shops, gorging her eyes on sheets of marbled and hand-blocked paper, notebooks bound in satin and silvery plastic, silky purple carbons, fresh rubbers, thick-snouted felt-tips, black-eyed pencils. The white pages open under her gaze, inviting: write on us. She comes home with armfuls of A4 pads, pocket-sized notebooks, gold-beaked fountain pens. She deprives her daughter of sweets and gives her cards of coloured stencils instead. She cuts down on Jim's beer and buys him rainbow stacks of blotting paper.

Her neglected marriage starts to break down. Jim wants to lie with a woman between ironed cotton sheets not ruled paper ones. He wants a woman with powder not ink on her nose. He wants a woman who looks at him more often than she looks at a book. Who can blame him? She almost breaks down too, discovering her old desires now flourishing openly in the notes she scribbles in the bath, on the bus. Terror, and guilty joy. Will her mother still love her once she reads what she writes?

Poetry breaks back into her life, poetry written by women this time, poetry, written over the centuries, that acknowledges

130

her submerged experience, keeps her awake at night, sends a fizz down her spine.

She has taken a woman lover and cannot write romances any more, cannot write a lesbian romance either much as she would like to. That struggle and soar and rock of body against body, mind against mind, demands less smoothness, dangles loose ends of words all over the place. She does not know how or what to do.

She stares at the onion-enfolding radiant dark blue tissue paper, and searches for words, new words, to twist the paper into the wick of a rocket and shoot her, firework scared of exploding, into the night skies high above that street in Toulouse.

21   During my librarianship training I became aware of the Woman Problem.

Leafing through the volumes of the subject index in the Reading Room, I discover, as Virginia Woolf did long before me, the hundreds of entries referring to books on Woman, most of them written by men. There are no entries for Man, which puzzles me until I think about it.

The following year, at library school, I study classification theory. The Dewey system, used in all the public libraries in Britain, places Woman in a sub-section of Sociology along with Lunatics and Gypsies. (Wanderers.) Our lecturers encourage us to criticize the rigidly hierarchical pyramidal model of knowledge favoured by Dewey (he would have approved of Origen as an Arkitect, I'm sure), to prefer the modern flexible systems based on computer programme theory which allow you to link one aspect of a subject with any other in crystalline fashion.

For my special project I design a classification system that puts Woman at its centre and allows her to relate to anything under the sun.

Here on the Ark, in my Arkive, I can connect I *want* with innumerable other words.

– But if you have a child, Noah warns me: you'll see it suffering, and be powerless to prevent it. How will you bear that? Why bring a child into a world of suffering and pain?

I search the riddle book.

Life. Sentence. Life-sentence?

132

22   We sail on, towards the next island. I'm not much of a navigator: I steer by intuition; desire my compass North, true North; and dreams my maps.

The harbour opens neatly around us, swallows us in with a single gulp, closes behind us in a belch of waves. I leave the Ark moored there, the Gaffer and the sibyls its sleepy guardians preferring shut-eye to this night excursion, and walk inland, towards the great capital.

Darkness surrounds me, a glimmer of lit boulevards ahead. This city at night is the colour of dried blood. Smell of charcoal, and pines. Whisper of my rubber soles over paved roads. The air is smoky and damp as I go down tunnels of blackness, dark green weeds of trees woven over my head. The suburbs are dull yellow and black, neon lights reflected on pavements of amber satin. I slide in just before dawn, huddle on a stone bench in the centre of the hushed city, wait for the light to irradiate the streets, for their massed buildings to take shape around me. I pick up the tattered pamphlet lying just beside me on the pink granite of my seat, and open it. This is how I practise Italian: conjugating all the verbs meaning: to produce pain.

A scream is abroad in our streets. Our city is haunted by a continuous ravaging scream, dragged out of the mouth by a sharp thin quickly coiling corkscrew of pain.

Torture: the refined systematic politically approved application of pain to the body of a man or a woman or a child. Increased reliance by the State on the extraction of a statement or a confession of guilt from the accused means increased reliance on torture in the prisons of East and West. Everybody's doing it doing it doing it the expert stamp grind hop of the

133

foxtrot of pain, yes even the smug democracies. Read all about it. Listen to the scream. Bear witness. The flesh bears witness. The cracked open mouth screams *no* while the State brands its lies on the tender body and calls this truth, calls this confession. The truth of the body uttered by poets in their struggled-for words counts for nothing here in the strip-lit hygienic cell where the police doctor stands by to monitor the pain inflicted on the body being oh so delicately torn and twisted into a rhetoric of lies. I have not had to bear this pain myself. I hear the screams of my sisters and brothers who do. They will cry so, when the torturer takes them in his arms, when the second torturer comes with his quick instruments, and Death strolls past, a glossy catalogue of sadism in his hands and a carnation in his buttonhole.

I could be one of his victims, or one of his pupils. I could be a torturer too. A woman's place is in the home. I could saw off my daughter's clitoris with a razor, my friends holding her down while she screams. To cleanse her, to rid her of that horrid little flap of excess flesh, to make her pure, to make her grateful enough to do it herself in her turn to her own daughter when the time comes. I could punish her just with words: tell her she's *nothing*, with *nothing* down there. I could, very carefully, burn her legs with glowing cigarettes, to teach her not to cry all night, not to soil herself, to be obedient when I tell her to stop crying wanting wanting wanting. I could shut her away in a drawer for the night, her mouth clogged with cotton wool so that I can't hear her choking screams. I could tie her to the bed, naughty chicken, to poke and scratch amongst her excrement. I could bind her dead body in clean white bandages, small stinking mummy, and prop her in the armchair opposite mine, perfectly behaved doll watching telly with me and no longer disrupting my nights with her crying, her intolerable wanting I can't satisfy. For who will satisfy *my* crying, *my* yearning, *my* wanting? Better to cut it out, carve it out, burn it out, batter it out. I am human; and so I can do all of these things.

I can't control the scream. I can't stop it. It withers the vines on the hillsides outside the city, so that the grape harvest is destroyed. It shrivels and blackens the olive trees in the orchards as though with frost, so that the fruit can't mature. Pregnant women miscarry, hearing the scream, while others

134

become infertile. All the young men have lost heart, and have run away into the mountains to hide.

We don't scream back at the scream. Possessed by its echo, we have fallen silent. We can't love: we are dumb. We hide ourselves inside our homes, tidying ourselves away from the knowledge of torture and pain, and yet we cannot, however hard we try, avoid the scream.

I spend the rest of the day exploring the city. Weeds choke the public gardens. Grass grows thickly in the cracks between paving stones. The fountains are dry. A dead horse, covered in black flies, sprawls outside the State Museum.

In the late afternoon I come to a large piazza surrounded by dying palm trees. The crumbling rose and orange stucco fronts of its buildings are washed in light. I climb the rippling stone waterfall of a magnificent decaying staircase, and stand in front of the State Palace. The huge doors are open. I pass through the marble hall, honey-coloured and dim, braced by springing columns, and go through another pair of double doors and so out onto the wide terrace, set with two crouching stone lions. The stone wings of the palace open out on either side of me, long and graceful; there in front of me, stretching away like corresponding wings, are the gardens.

The neglect here is not so obvious, as though the State rulers were the last to succumb to apathy and fear. Their army of gardeners can have laid down their rakes and spades only recently: the weeds are just a pale fuzz, like a newborn baby's hair.

Directly ahead of me, beyond a gravel walk, is a huge patterned oblong of grass and earth cut by narrow paths into privet-walled boxes, the low clipped hedges twisted and curled into complicated bows and knots of dark green ribbon. To my left is a long row of tall cypresses, their inky plumes nodding and swaying against the brilliant blue of the sky. A high privet hedge runs behind them, a series of archways cut in its green thickness giving glimpses of long green corridors, the middle one lined with orange trees, a tiny white stone nymph dancing at the far end. To my right, a forest of greenery is separated by another walk of orange trees. Through this planned wilderness broad green paths pull the eye onwards towards statues set at

135

the junction of green alleys, towards a small temple crowning a moss-covered flight of steps launching steeply upwards between green walls that rustle and hold green shadows and green light.

There is no one about. The gardens are completely deserted. I walk forwards, into them.

The air is golden now, going from warm towards chill, and it smells of oranges and flowers and smoke. I go down the broad shallow steps from the terrace, and plunge through a green doorway on my left.

The walls of the privet avenue rear high above my head, so thick that I can't see through them. Marble benches are placed along it at intervals, their curved feet deep in glossy acanthus leaves. I turn, and walk, and turn corners, and walk, and am soon lost in this labyrinth of green privet rooms opening off the branching green corridors. Each garden room is a green square space, overgrown with tangling plants. Some are waist-high in brambles, some contain flowering thickets draped over trellises, some are studded with lumps of broken columns, all are carpeted with lush green grass.

The light is a deep gold now, the sun sinking lower and its radiance flooding the sky, dissolving its blue. The privet walls throw long sharp shadows, and the green darkness between them is cold and deep. A wind swishes the tops of the cypresses. I begin to shiver. I need to find the way out. I halt, uncertain which way to go, then plunge through the nearest opening.

A shock. The dead are alive, and dancing.

Facing me, at the far end of the enclosure, are white bodies glimmering against the dark green fence at their backs. Ghosts, summoned up by twilight. Half-naked ghosts, draped in fluttering white robes.

There are no birds singing. The scream I hear comes from my own mouth. The long grass smells sweet, like fresh peas, and is chilly on my ankles. I walk slowly forwards.

The group of marble statues is solid and white. Here is a nymph, her dress half torn off, her arms jerking helplessly, her mouth open in a soundless yell, being carried off by a burly male god. Here are her mother and friends mourning and gesticulating, running alongside amidst a welter of stags and dogs.

136

A sound behind me turns the back of my neck to ice. I spin round. Dark silhouette, faceless, in the privet doorway, the last gold streaks of the sun outlining his head and shoulders. My guts soften with fear.

Then his hand goes up in a greeting. I see Death there, leaning against the green wall, watching me.

23 Back on board the Ark, I tell the others what I've seen. We eat supper. I'm as hungry as usual. The food doesn't choke me, though perhaps it should. The Babble-On Sibyl has cooked *carciofi alla Giudea*, artichokes deep-fried in olive oil, crisp and golden as sunflowers.

– The sadist as gourmet? I say: take one brown or pink or black body, grill well over charcoal until the flesh blackens and peels off easily in long strips. Rub salt well in the wounds. Beat out flat with a wooden steak-hammer and lard with live electrodes. Truss well, then plunge head-down into boiling urine or oil. Garnish with gouged-out eyes and severed genitalia. Torn-off breasts may be served on a separate plate. Or cure in the sun. Tie to a stake. Smear with honey, then sprinkle with hungry live ants. Don't carrots feel pain when you pull them up? Where are you going to stop? my aunt used to say to me: the trouble with you is, you read too many books. I am Mrs Noah, and I want to be an Ark for souls. But as yet I don't dare.

– I am afraid of pain, says the Forsaken Sibyl: I am afraid of not bearing it, and afraid also of bearing it. First of all books made me cry. I cried not for my own life but for that of others. I read books in order to discover the world. I cried at what I found there. I cried when I finished a book, because it was sad, and because I had finished it, because it would never represent the unknown again. I cried when I had read all the books in my house, all the books in my school, all the books in the children's library. I joined the adult library. I wore my first pair of high-heeled shoes, winkle-pickers. I used my parents' tickets as well as my own, and carried home a basket of twenty new books. My new shoes rubbed my heels raw, pinched my toes. I refused to take them off and walk home barefoot. Blisters formed and burst and bled, and the shoes rubbed up and down on the bleeding flesh. I reached home and did not cry. I discovered how much pain I could bear. I read non-stop all weekend lying on the sofa, my feet bound up with Elastoplast. Whenever my mother found me crying over a book she snatched it away. Run out into the sunshine and play with your friends.

– Most of my friends are mothers now, says the Babble-On Sibyl: with two or three young children. At college we sat up half the night talking about the books we read. Now my friends are walled in by children, tiny hands plucking at skirts. So we talk to the children or about the children. Our conversation is broken. My mother once told me: what women talk about is so boring, I prefer the conversation of men. See a mother at a party, her eyes anxiously on her children: will they break something or make a mess or be sick? Who'd choose to talk to *her*? Mothers are not available. Who mothers the mothers? If I go and baby-sit to give my friend some free time for herself, then I don't see her. How can mothers make time for women who are not? How does the friendship survive?

– The voice of the angry daughter, says the Correct Sibyl: is the only one heard in our land. What of the mother? The woman who sees her childless women friends draw back in distaste from her hands that know piss, shit, vomit, milk, blood? The woman whose women friends give her rendezvous in wine bars three miles away when she has no baby-sitter and no transport? The exhaustion. The not being understood. The rage. My mother made friends with other mothers. My mother dumped me in a carrycot and took me to Africa. My mother strapped me on the back of her bike and wheeled up the hill to Gran's. My mother plonked me in a box behind the counter while she served customers, and I played sailors. My mother brought my baby brother to Brownies: he sat on the toadstool in the middle of the fairy ring while my mother organized us hefty little girls to dance around him with our pennants; kelpies, gnomes, pixies, sprites. My mother was a great inventor. My mother doesn't believe in feeling sorry for herself.

– I don't like my children much at the moment, says the Deftly Sibyl: this makes me uncomfortable. Also I do not like

139

deodorants, sweet white wine, milk in coffee, word processors, biros, women who smile too much, hot weather, crimplene, church services, men who talk too much, chocolate cake, Wagner's music, fleas, gladioli, sleeping less than eight hours, Walter Scott's novels, single beds, nylon sheets, soap operas, reviewers, other people's dirty kitchens, people who send me unsolicited manuscripts for comment, string vests, cocktail parties, telephones, stripped pine, plastic cups, piped music in public, shopping malls, central heating, politicians, smokers carriages, cocoa, poodles, blue eye shadow.

— I used to hang onto words like hooks, says the Re-Vision Sibyl: other people's words. I was cloth cap, torn mackintosh. I was classified: a nag, shrill, strident, hysterical. I still hang myself onto hooks: I must control myself, not get drunk, not spill out my needs and desires as mess on the floor, not laugh too loud, not cry out too high, not make too many demands or be impatient. If I begin again. To choose words. In the mini-cab, sharing a lift home, after the party, with Maria. Towards our separate flats a mile apart. The radio sings, it's 3 am, net lace curtains at the back window frame a jointed model of an Alsatian dog in plush, head nodding. Scent of air freshener. Shadows and light from the streetlamps flickering over us. This is the moment, but we don't know it, you never know it, ever, at the time, only afterwards when you select it, when you're lying with your face buried in her breasts, when you think oh yes, that was it, when I suddenly realized how things were between us, how they might be, and the moment's gone, the one which changes present into future, you're not there any more, you're looking back seeing the cab speed away up the dark street, looking at her face and words stuttering out, you've already entered what will be.

— I'll never understand it, sighs the Gaffer: women loving other women. How can you love someone who is the same as yourself? Sexual *difference* is what excites *me*. Beauty: everything that I'm not. Nor do I fancy a cock up my arse, no thanks very much. I like women, you know; I always have done. I've never considered them inferior. If anything, women are *superior*. Their powers of endurance! Just look at the women characters in my novel. What puzzles me is your attitude. If, as a reader or a critic, I deny sexual difference in writers, then you

140

complain I'm treating women as pseudo-men and using a false concept of neutrality to disguise my contempt for women's work. But if I notice sexual difference and applaud women writers for their feminine style, then you assert I'm being patronizing and pushing you into a ghetto. I can't win! You're a contradictory lot, you know. You should try to be more reasonable.

– For you, *feminine* doesn't just mean different, the Forsaken Sibyl informs him: it means worse. That's why it can be a double-edged compliment. I should like to re-invent *feminine* so that it simply meant: pertaining to a woman. Then it could mean whatever the life of a particular woman made it mean. And we could keep it as a word we could use without feeling so ambivalent.

– Impossible, declares the Correct Sibyl: given the structure of language and of the unconscious. Far better to drop it.

– The *history* of women's lives, the Re-Vision Sibyl says to the Gaffer: the lives that they actually lead – that history tends to be different from men's. That's what *feminine* means to me.

– So what would a mother's history be? I ask the others: can one of you tell us a story about a mother?

24   Sending God's blessing and mine to you, my most cherished daughter whom I shall never see again, unless by God's grace the Queen's heart be softened, which is a cause I think hopeless, I write you this letter, which I have asked shall be delivered to you once you are of an age not solely to read but also to comprehend it, should you survive, by God's grace, the years of your childhood, as I pray, tonight, you may survive this present time of trouble and terror. I have charged those who will have care of you that you be taught your letters. I have sent money for that. I have said goodbye to you already, my beloved first-born, though I doubt you will remember it. Now I grant myself the indulgence of addressing you one last time.

I need to write to you more for my own sake, perhaps, than for yours. Yet I would not have you ignorant of your mother, of what made her, as she swore she would never do, send you far from her. Others will tell you, perhaps, false stories of your beginnings, of me. I pray you to forgive me if I set down my truth of it for you to read. You are my judge. When you know the story of my life, and of the first years of yours, which I shall try to record as honestly as I can, I pray you will not condemn me, but will find it in your heart to forgive your mother's weakness, and to pity her present wretchedness.

I am sending the miniature portrait in the basket I have packed for your journey to France. Do you still have it? Take it out. Look at it. I remember it well enough. Myself as I was then. The age you are now.

Two young women, dressed exactly alike. Black farthingales faced with dark pink velvet, black-sleeved gowns laced on with

142

gold cords and slashed to reveal the white lawn undersleeves, black caps, white lace collars and cuffs. Hair parted in the middle and pulled back. Long almond-shaped eyes, long noses. The eyelids lowered, half-smiles playing over the lips. Their hands tightly clasped in each other's, white skin of the long fingers set against the billowing black skirts.

The painter has lied, of course, in order to follow his patrons' whim, to flatter my parents. In fact we are not identical. Only one of us is beautiful. I'm the ugly one.

Twin sisters. Margaret and myself.

I am sitting in a garden, on the grass, with a privet hedge behind me and a long flowerbed beside me filled with lupins, hollyhocks, sweet williams, gillyflowers and roses, all mixed up in a pleasing profusion of bloom. I watch the bees dive in and out of the bright petals; their scent makes me a little sick. The orchard screens us from my father's house, and the oak trees, behind the hedge, marking the beginning of the farmlands, are a further shelter. Hard green acorns rattle occasionally into my lap, and I raise my hand to sweep them away from Margaret's face.

She lies there with me, her head on my blue stuff knees and her feet tucked up under her skirts. She wears blue too, with a black bodice just like mine, and her cap is tumbled on the grass beside her. Her hair is loose: it flows over my hands as I dip them in it, and has acorns and leaves caught in it, and smells of sun and of the rosemary wash she rinses it with. Her eyes are closed, the lashes a pale fur, and her cheek is warm to my touch.

Around us the bees swerve and drone, parting the flowers and gulping their nectar. Flies from the cows grazing in the neighbouring field circle our heads, buzzing noisily, and I flap them away. Ants creep over our ankles, nipping our stockings. Summer is ending: the edges of the oak leaves are rusty brown, and some are already fallen on the grass like tiny wrinkled books. I peer at them; then I see poems, made of stems and pebbles and dry petals. When Margaret wakes up, I will repeat them to her in the private language we share for telling each other stories and whispering secrets at table or in bed.

Margaret moves her head in my lap, opens her eyes, smiles

143

at me.

— Sister, she says: I'll make a daisy chain for you to wear at your wedding, and you make me one to wear at mine.

— Never, I cry out: never.

When we are little, I talk before she does, and have to translate her grunts and cries to our nurse. She walks before I do: when I rise, plump and wobbling, to a standing position, she pushes me over and laughs.

We sleep in the same bed, in the little room we share with our nurse behind the parlour. A dark, comfortable place like a shelf in a cupboard, with a sliding wooden door. Behind this, we curl in each other's arms on our feather bed, the tattered damask coverlet pulled up to our chins. In the morning I smell her sour breath on my face as she must smell mine. She clings to her bolster when it is time to get up, fingering the treasures she has hidden underneath it after yesterday's play outside, pretending to be asleep, her eyes tightly closed. It is our game, to see how long she can resist my rousing her with tickles and caresses. Sometimes I lose my temper, the game having turned into a task, and pinch her soft flesh through her nightgown. Then she kicks me, or cries. To punish me, she refuses to speak to me for an entire day, while I trail behind her like a whipped dog, blubbing.

As she knows how to make me suffer, so she also knows how to give me delight. Sometimes, at night, her thin fingers trace my collarbone and spine, caress my back with long slow strokes that soothe me into a grave pleasure. There are the two of us in the same bed, a fact simple as breathing, as necessary. I try to fit myself into the dent made by Margaret's body, curve myself into her part of the feather mattress, imagine I am she. Then she rolls back and repossesses the dip she has made, and I sniff at her, lick her, trace with my tongue the outline of her nose, her ear. Sometimes I want to eat her. Sometimes I dandle her like a baby. Always she is there for me.

Sometimes I wonder: how do my parents know which of us is which? Suppose that soon after birth we were turned about, in those first days before we received names? Suppose that I really am Margaret and she me? Suppose our parents were confused, right at the beginning?

144

Our father once told us: when you were born we were all so grieved that your mother had missed her mark, we prayed that at her next shot she might hit it.

I do not mind that I am not the male child they wanted, for I have Margaret. I do not mind my parents' indifference and coldness to us when we were small. I understand that too much affection cannot be wasted on children who may not thrive: it would hurt too much. Three of my mother's children have died in infancy. Can I blame her that she holds us at arm's length, watches our growth with a harsh, suspicious eye? I do not look to her for love. I am far luckier than most, for I have Margaret. We have not been sent away to school, like so many. We have not been separated. My two younger brothers, aged eight and seven, will soon leave home to begin their education, fostered out in my uncle's house in London. My mother has chosen to keep Margaret and me with her, to train us at home. We are fortunate. We have each other.

Light flashes on the blades of our knives. Nurse stands at one end of the table, scraping at the loaf of sugar. Margaret and I lean opposite, our sleeves pinned back, chopping up damsons, quinces, plums. We lick the juice of the fruit, sticky and red, off our fingers, then ladle the sweet pulp into the black iron pot hung over the fire. Belch and seethe. I poke at it with a long wooden spoon, skim off the fresh pink scum which smells of cloves and ginger. The mixture boils and boils. Our faces red and wet in its steam. Then we test it, dropping a little into a basin of water to see whether it will set. Golden strands of the sun imprisoned in a pewter dish. I cleaned that dish yesterday, scouring it well with sand. Our lady mother ordered it, a punishment to teach me humility. There is little in me this morning. I would rather be outside, lying in the long grass in the orchard, watching the wild dash of the April clouds across the sun, the shaking of the white blossom on the pear trees as the wind throws itself on the garden and the light breaks through the canopy of branches. My mother is famous for her marmalade. I am famous for my laziness.

After dinner, we bend to our sewing in the small back parlour. Little light finds its way into this low-ceilinged recess. We drag our stools over to the window, which we have set open

145

for a glimpse of blue. Cold air rinses our necks. These dark walls hung with threadbare tapestry repel me. I'd rather be surrounded by the trunks of trees. I've dusted the oak chest and brushed the stiff Turkey carpet that drapes it. I've washed the precious bowl of Venetian glass in the cupboard. Now my needle pricks in and out of linen, grubby from its daily mauling in my fingers. Margaret, opposite me, sighs in a private dream. I launch myself through the window, fly out to go riding with my brothers. My fingers canter over glazed linen fields. A glossy hedge, the raised border, to leap. The silver stab. The red line pulling through. Each stitch is a beagle with a bloody mouth. Baying. I kill the bedsheet I am supposed to be hemming. Over and over again I pierce it. Blood springs up, a row of dead birds, a string of scarlet beads. So pretty.

The birch whistles over my shoulders, not gently.

– God help me, my mother laments: how will you ever find a good husband when you resist all my efforts to teach you seemly ways? I'll beat God-fearing manners into you yet, you foolish gentlewoman.

One last whack on my shuddering neck, then she throws the birch from her, as though disgusted with it. Which I do not think she can be since she applies it so often to me.

I perform my part, as she performs hers. I understand that it is necessary. She has taught me that much. I stay kneeling on the cold flags which bruise my knees, and join my hands, keep my back straight. The needle and the birch, between them, lead me to decorum. Those harsh sisters.

– Dear madam, I growl between clenched teeth: most humbly I beg you to forgive me.

Then she's gone, her skirts rustling towards the door, a chill draught wheedling in as she opens it and passes through it. Bitterness sticks in my throat like a sour nut.

Margaret is the older of us two by half an hour. Now she is mother for me, kissing me, caressing me.

– So much trouble you make for yourself, she chides me in a whisper: can't you see how worried our mother is?

I know that my father is in the thick of arranging a marriage for the elder of our younger brothers, the heir. Young he may be, but he must be married. *We* are already fifteen. But

146

daughters matter less. Letters fly back and forth between my father and his brothers, the gods who control the estate, who secure the best interests of the family, who protect our land. I suppose they will get me a good settlement when my turn comes. I don't want to think of it.

I dream of the betrothal long before it takes place.

Time collides with us, sends the oak leaves spinning from the trees in spirals of bronze, rots the rose petals fallen on the black earth, hauls the apples from their branches, scythes the stiff corn in the yellow fields. Time is my mother in a golden gown with a wreath of oats and barley on her head, nodding and blessing me, and my new husband picking me up in his arms and carrying me away.

It surprises me, his strength, the power in his indolent limbs. He goes striding over the ploughed fields, over the long silky curls of clay under the bare oaks and elms, carrying me lightly as a bag of plums he has stolen from my father's orchard.

– I'll be your twin, he whispers: let me be your twin.

I spit into his face, so that his grip loosens. I bite his cheek, so that he stumbles. I spring from his arms and run as fast as I can back the way we have come, tripping over clods of earth and roots, holding up my skirts with both hands and jumping from furrow to furrow of the ploughed ground.

I escape him. I find Margaret high up on the hillside behind our house, beside the waterfall. She is dressed in cloth-of-silver, her hair hidden under a winged silver cap, a frosty veil streaming down her back, a silver breastplate fastened on over her glittering misty gown, and silver shoes tied around her ankles with silver wire. We stand in silence beside the waterfall, watching its thin line of water and spray plummet past us and down the hill. If I had a sword with which to defend myself I could stay here, speechless for ever, locked into this companionship of silence, of silver.

– It's no good, Margaret says, sounding troubled: it is time.

– You don't love me any more, I accuse her: you're sending me away.

I start singing then, a song of loud defiance. So of course my husband hears and finds me.

My new home is a large house. Too large, with many

windows and doors and innumerable suites of rooms in which I fear I shall soon get lost.

My husband takes something out of a bag and hands it to me.

– Here. Put this on.

It is a false head, like something out of a puppet show, moulded from leather, wadded with gauze inside, and painted with a sweet smiling expression. I am afraid that if I fit it over my nose and mouth I shall suffocate and die.

– No, I say, and push my husband's hand away.

He disappears then, and I am surrounded by strangers. Servants I suppose them to be, as they hurry past me, pushing and shoving me where I stand clumsily in their way. I have been set down in the middle of a play, or a masque, like those performed on summer evenings outside our old house, in which the painted and costumed performers move elegantly through dances and mime. I do not know my part; I have no idea what my character is supposed to be. I have no friend to turn to for help: my companions bustle past me, carrying steaming pots of soup, bowls of custards and fruit, platters of meat and vegetables. None of them take any notice of me; they are all too busy.

This is my life now, I tell myself: so I had better learn what do to.

I begin to copy the actions and movements of my fellow servants. Very soon I am in a line, helping to pass dishes. A fist in the small of my back makes me lurch forwards. Two hands dump a basket of plaited loaves into my grasp. I find myself going through a curtained doorway, treading carefully on the swirling patterns of the pink marble floor so as not to slip. I enter the dining room, a huge rectangular space with many doors and high windows, gold-framed paintings hung around the tops of the walls, and below them, carved wooden sideboards displaying gold plates and majolica ware. Down the centre of the room runs a long table, its damask cloth hardly visible under its array of dishes of gold. There are lamps burning, and their light dazzles back from the golden forks and spoons and plates.

There are only two people eating. The great hall is empty of other guests. I trudge to the head of the table with my offering of bread. When I am nearer, and dare raise my eyes

148

to peep at the two seated in their carved wooden chairs, I understand from the splendour of their clothes that this is a wedding feast.

My husband is the bridegroom, dressed in a rich purple suit. He dabs at his mouth with a lace handkerchief, wiping away the grease from his lips. Beside him sits a beautiful woman, whose expression is smiling and sweet. Unchangingly so. She does not eat; she sits still, as though replete or a little bored.

I come nearer, and see that the doll-like bride wears the leather and gauze head I have refused. I throw down my basket, and tear off the head from the simpering woman who has usurped my place. My sister Margaret sits there, staring back at me.

Then I am back in the garden of our old house. The oak trees are completely bare now, curled yellowing leaves stuck to their gleaming trunks in the fine rain, mashed to a swamp at their roots. The flowerbed is empty, all its green cleared away. The rose bushes rear wizened black stumps, each thorn a shiny triangle hooking the cold air. No birds sing, and no cattle bellow in the field beyond the hedge, and the rain runs into my mouth and down my neck. But the flies are still here, a dark busy cloud of them hovering above the wet grass.

Margaret is still there too. She lies on the ground on her side, her feet tucked up under her red skirts, her long hair fallen across her face. I bend down to touch her shoulder and wake her, and she topples over onto her back. Her sockets are sightless, eyeless. Ants swarm there, and in the cavities which were formerly her nose, her mouth. Ants pick at her cheeks, unpick her bones. She is immobile, but also crazy with insect life. Her face has almost gone, her toes and fingers are vanishing fast. Her body is black with ants, as though she has grown new hair everywhere. You cannot say which is garden and which is grave: her rotting body joins them.

– There is only one marriage bed, Margaret, I say: and we cannot share it.

Daughters are a difficulty, a drain on family resources. Dowries to be found and argued over, jointures to be agreed. Luckily there are only two of us to be settled. Harder on my

149

second younger brother, I think to myself, who has to make his own way in the world, no estate at his back. Everything goes to the heir.

– You're healthy, Nurse tells Margaret: with beauty enough. You've learned all you need to know. You'll do.

Margaret preens herself, laughing. At Nurse, and at me. Alarm is a weed sprouting in me when Nurse clacks her silly tongue in my direction.

– But what shall we do with you, chick? Still so careless of your manners. So often untidy and rude. And no one could call you anything but plain. Strange how most of the goodness has gone into your sister and so little to you.

There's only so much goodness. I shouldn't have been born. My poor mother, landed with such a mistake.

– Hold your tongue, you gossiping old busybody, I shoot at her: I am a grown woman now, and shan't heed you.

– Fifty years ago, she grumbles: you could have made a fine life for yourself in a convent. Nowadays what's to be done with a girl who lacks beauty and a fat dowry, with not even a sweet temper to recommend her?

I could make do with little: a couple of rooms to call my own, enough pasture to graze a cow on. Why should Nurse imagine I want more? I disdain marriage, that race towards the marketplace, young daughters sold off like cattle into endless childbearing, sickness, early death. I start up, to box Nurse's ears for her impudence, but Margaret, suddenly my defender, restrains me. She's the only one who's allowed to tease or taunt me. Now her authority, borrowed from our mother, rat-tats in her cold voice, subduing the old woman better than any blow.

– My sister is sure to be found a good husband. In any case, that is my father's business, not yours.

Margaret is never envious, never spiteful. Why should she be? She's beautiful, she's virtuous, and therefore blessed. Sudden hatred of her is another bushy weed I find flourishing inside myself, whose head I must lop off, whose roots I must grub up. I wonder how long it has been rampant, unsuspected, in my heart. Certainly it's not a sin I'll bring to my father's attention when he reads prayers to the household tonight and asks us to lay our consciences bare before him. My little garden may be barren and bleak, but it's mine. I protect it from the

150

winds of loving paternal chastisement with high walls of sullenness and silence. If only weeds grow in it, at least I alone shall be its gardener.

Relief and rejoicing in our family. Congratulations from all our relatives. My father has secured a substantial addition to his estate; the new bride will bring a large dowry in farmland for our younger brother, the heir. My father is no great landowner. But now he has shaped a solid sufficiency for our brother to inherit. The patrimony, augmented, will survive. My father pulls off a second triumph. Margaret is married, in the spring of the year we turn eighteen, to James Grenby, whose father owns land in the north adjoining a farm brought by my mother as her dowry twenty-three years before.

I send away my nurse and the maidservants, insisting that I alone must perform this last office for my sister: to help her put on her wedding clothes.

The silver chains, the ropes of pearls, don't weigh her down. She stands tall and straight, the cloth-of-silver falling down her like moonlight.

– Sit down, I order her: and I'll do your hair.

I peer over her shoulder into the little mirror she holds up in front of herself. My reflection scowls behind hers. For so long we have been mirrors for each other: identical, if not perhaps in looks, then certainly in wishes, in friendship. Now I am not-her. The shadow; the failed copy. My eyes narrowed and hostile, my mouth turned down, a pimple bulging at the side of my nose. Beside me, in front of me, this shining stranger all expectation and triumphant looks, pearls in her ears and at her throat, a collar of starched gauze rising behind her head like a peacock's tail. She is smiling at me. She knows how I feel. That's the worst thing: her pity. That passive goodness of hers, which lets her accept her destiny, which will let her be happy.

– Be careful! she cries: be more gentle. You hurt me.

My mouth is full of pearl-headed pins. I mumble back at her, laying down the comb and starting to anchor her silver cap to her hair. Stab. Stab. Stab.

– Be quick, she counsels me: or we'll be late to the church.

I pluck the mirror from her hands and stamp on it. Bright slivers of glass crunch under my heel. The noise pleases me. I want more of it. I grind my foot on the silver shards fallen all about us. Blood blooms up through the toe of one velvet shoe. The broken glass severs my will to punish. I crouch on the floor, sobbing. Blood leaks along the hem of my new dress. Margaret gets up, pushes away her wooden stool, stands over me, rustling and silver. Cuffs me on the ear. Then she drops down beside me and is crying too, holding onto me with a grip that hurts.

I'm told I never cried for my three dead brothers. Nor, apparently, when, aged two, I was brought home from my kind wet-nurse. I didn't cry for the deaths of my aunts and grandparents. Grief only hardened me, chilled me. I'm not used to grief that's hot and runny, that tears open my body and plucks my soul out. I'm not used to crying.

My mother's two sisters and their women fetch Margaret away. All the light in the room goes out, leaving me dreary, in the dark.

One of my feet is bound with bandages; the other is free. Only one of my feet is wounded. I can walk, with a limp. I stroke the little wooden statue of the Virgin Margaret has given me, kissing me goodbye, bidding me keep it safe, in remembrance of her.

But when I put my hand out in the night, she is not there. My fist closes on emptiness. When I turn to look for her quick smile, there is only the hanging shifting in the draught from the open door. Margaret never walks through the doorway, though I sit on my stool watching it for hours each day, waiting for her. She must come back, and I must be here to attend to her. Her glance will kindle my life again, set my legs moving, give back my hunger and thirst.

Now I sew all day long. My mother, my nurse, even my father and brothers, all try to tempt me out. Fools.

– Come for a walk in the garden, my mother invites me: to see my new plan for the flowerbed.

My needle is a lance I hold in front of me. Never a tongue so sharp.

– Come for a ride, my father offers: we'll take the dogs, and

152

my new falcon.

I am much too busy. I have these yards of linen to hem. I won't stir before I'm finished.

– Play cards with us, my brothers suggest: lay a wager with us, as you used to do.

The white material flows over my lap, and I stitch myself to it, very neatly.

– Eat, commands my nurse: you must eat. I've brought you a dish of fat quails, your favourite.

How can I eat? I don't want to get grease marks on my work. I knot and bite off the silk thread, and choose another length, licking the tip smooth so that it will pass through the eye of the needle. I, in my purity, will pass through the eye of the needle, and into the kingdom.

I need silence and stillness for this journey. And great courage. I am voyaging through a darkness beyond which lies death. I carry the knowledge of it in my eyes: I fall into their deep black pits when I look into my mirror, which I do not dare do too often. My new beauty frightens me: my flesh shrinking on my bones to bring me slenderness, my unruly hair so much neater now it is falling out and there is less of it, my wasted hands so elegant and pale. My silence is exquisite, a finely wrought music only I can hear. There are different sorts of silence, which I listen for, head cocked to one side. A silver spoon knocks on white ivory. Mist hums and vibrates just behind my head. A pebble whistles to itself before it hits the water at the bottom of the well. I offer myself to this silence. I must make myself empty in order to receive it. I must fast.

My silence, so proudly chosen, is powerful. It lets no one near me.

Sometimes, fists knuckling my lap under the heavy drift of the damask curtain I am embroidering, I allow myself clarity. I know what I am doing. Methodically, month by month, I am shoring up my defences. For I am besieged by my family, my walls attacked by their insistence that I tell them what is wrong. I stick it out. I want to die quietly, with the minimum of fuss. For aren't I the murderer? There isn't space enough for two daughters. For twins. Isn't my greedy body trying to swell up, to get fatter and fatter, despite all my care and restraint? I am the monster, the cuckoo in the nest, sucking up all the milk and

153

goodness Margaret needs. Before I remember, and spit it out. I must protect her from me. I must control my anger. Keep it inside. Where it wastes me. As I deserve.

Who can heal such a sickness of the soul? I know its name but my friends and family do not.

I am the good daughter, because no one knows I am angry. Except for Margaret. She has stolen my soul away. She knows.

In my dream I see Eve pregnant. The mother of us all wishes for sons so that she may find favour in her husband's eyes and in those of God. She picks up a fistful of yellow sand, watches the grains trickle through her fingers. Contented, her hands folded over her work, she weaves flesh, blood, bones. Absent-minded, thoughts filled with her son's future, she drops the shuttle, picks it up again, weaves her pattern twice over by mistake. Eve sits in the desert and weeps. Adam comforts her. Two sons are even better than one. They will call their sons Abel and Cain.

Margaret, born first, is Abel. I come second, and am Cain.

The mother of us all has vanished. It is my job to dig for her, to find her. I'm alone in a square room that is slowly silting up, in one corner, with sand. The angry desert has swallowed Eve, and is hungry for more deaths. My hands are spades, torn and bleeding, as I tunnel through the onslaught of grit.

It is my body that is in the way. Very well, then. A sacrifice, to appease the ravening desert-god, to stop his mouth. He doesn't want life.

The mountain of sand swells, slowly filling the room. I try to crawl up it, to stay on top of it, but it's too loose, too shifting and slippery. My hands scrabble at it. My feet find no hold. I slide down to the bottom of the travelling hill, which gathers itself up and stoops over me, prepares to dive into my mouth.

Now Margaret is crouching beside me. Her skirts are soaked in blood. The sharp skewer is in my pocket. If I stab her and throw her body down before me on the sand then the desert will pause for a second to snatch her up, and I can escape, and find my mother.

The sand has our legs fast. Is creeping higher, clutching our waists.

Margaret kisses me on the mouth, pushes her spit between

my lips, breathes into me. The mountain of sand engulfs us, flows over our heads. Inside the flood, we are safe, mouths glued together, the air of life passing to and fro between us. And then we breathe out, hard, a tempest that blows the sand away until it smashes the walls of our room. Our feet hobble over the golden ground. The desert lies all around us, tamed for the moment, rippled into dunes. We're still in the wilderness. But we're both alive. I know this is only a dream.

– Do you want to die? my mother shouts at me, shaking my shoulders: you will die very soon, unless you begin to eat.

So I consent, wearily, to live. I pick my way back along that hard path. I'm weak. My arms are like sticks.

My first Ark is our mother's body, the womb I shared with Margaret. Now I've jumped ship. I'm in the water, thrashing and flailing, afraid of drowning. On my own.

But it seems I shall have a companion after all. My second Ark is marriage. We enter in couples. My parents have found me a husband. The double-headed hybrid, the twins, has been cut in two. I am a woman. Not half of one. Woman: a strange name. I stretch out my hand to touch that of a stranger. I dream that my dowry is sand, ticking through an hourglass, safely contained.

I press my nose to the cold windowpane, seeing nothing but the mist of my breath. Frost has scratched the glass with a pattern of delicate fern, curly fronds. I hold a penny to the flame in the hearth to heat it, press it against the pane. I melt myself a peephole, set one eye to it, peering out. Blackened tree trunks. A few yellow leaves pasted to the withered grass. I can hear horses trotting on the road behind the garden wall. My fingers, swollen with chilblains, play with the silver chain dangling from my waist that carries my household keys. Will gave me the chain when our parents betrothed us.

Will sits behind me in the far corner of the room, playing the virginals. I settle myself on the window seat to listen, my head against the heavy blue curtain that I embroidered, in the long years of my girlhood, with animals and flowers. This is my favourite place, half in and half out. I am the room, and the garden. I am the window, and I am she who looks in and she

155

who looks out.

The music uncoils itself from Will's fingertips. His rapid hands unpick the locks of silver boxes: the notes spill out, unroll, fall into the air, liquid balls of mercury, ice petals. He at his instrument is open-mouthed: a stream of cities, pepper-pots, larks, pours from him. He is playing a dance written at the court of Spain. His fingers are slithering over a guitar, knocking on tambourines and castanets. Music that buzzes and grunts, jangles its bracelets, stamps its feet, clicks its heels together. Listening to him play, I become free: a bottle unstoppered, pouring out inarticulate sounds. I rise, and dance for him, inventing the steps I don't know, laughing.

His hair is blond and bleached as the wooden panelling of the wall. His blue eyes are intent. His hands move faster over the ivory keys. I've been for too long the silence in this room, sticky with sorrow. Now I'm the dance, a gold comb to part the air, a plait of gold wires singing. I pull the music, a gold cloud, around me, then beat it into shape with the hammer of my feet.

When the music stops, its echo rolls like a wheel into the corner. My arms chase it. I stand behind Will and bend over him, wrapping my arms around him, pressing my cheek to his. He catches my hands in his, and puts them against his breast. He's a boy only, I think suddenly. He needs comfort as much as I. Tonight, when dutifully he comes to my bed, I won't only pretend to accept his nervous skinny body. I'll dance for him again.

Will reads me the letter at dinner. I could read it myself, for he has taught me how to, but he likes to read to me. Margaret is expecting her second child. Will looks at me, loving and miserable. Three years of marriage, of managing his tiny estate, have thinned and sharpened him. God knows, I am often bad company for him. Disappointment sours my love, turns me away from his friendly hand. He never reproaches me openly, but I am convinced that in his heart he must. He needs heirs. Margaret's child is to be born in five months' time. She did not want to let us know before, the secretary writes to her dictation, in case she was mistaken.

I push back my chair, pleased at the angry scrape of wood on wood.

– I must be off to the kitchen, I tell Will: to see to things.

Things. I do not know what they are as I stand in the empty hall. I fill it with self-reproach. Childless. Childless. The pain is a cord twisted about my throat, choking me, a red-tipped skewer in my ribs, shrivelling my heart, a knife plunged into my belly. Ashes on my tongue. A barren woman finds no favour in the eyes of others. I have tried prayer, wringing supplication from myself like water from a cloth. I have swallowed all possible remedies and medicines, their potency sworn for by the friends who supply them, to no avail. Be patient, I tell myself: accept God's will. But I don't. I question it. Why should my sister have children, and not I?

I have grown so ashamed of myself that I do not like to meet other women's eyes, in case I see their pity, their scorn. Even facing my own serving-women has become a test of courage. I am as stern with them as I know how to be, in case they don't obey me as they should, in case they mock me. I take a deep breath before opening the kitchen door.

Smell of boiled mutton, old beer. Smoke haze. Familiar, consoling. The two maidservants are busy unwrapping several great parcels, tied up in sacking, that have been dumped on the kitchen table. Three stout barrels stand nearby, and a pile of calico bundles. Will's steward, John Whittle, is there, with a paper in one hand, a pen in the other. I suddenly remember, then. The goods I ordered to see us through the approaching Christmas season. The dried fruits. The pickled herrings. The lengths of velvet and silk. The caps and purses, the bonnets and stockings, embroidered by the nuns in Brussels with their inimitable skill, which I shall send to all the members of my family as gifts. I must stop feeling so sorry for myself. I have work to do.

John Whittle puts down his writing materials and comes to greet me. I smile at him. I like this man. He is of middle age, with bushy black hair and eyebrows, much physical vigour, simple and honest manners. I trust him. He has our interests at heart. Will pays him well, and is rewarded by his faithful service.

I stand and watch him go carefully through his inventory, checking every item against the merchandise strewn around us. I grow cheerful, feel less empty. My larders, at least, will be well stocked. My storerooms will bulge with plenty. I and my

157

household, with our lusty appetites, will not starve this winter, though many poor wretches will. I give them all the alms I can spare, then shut them out of my heart. They enter my dreams instead, an army of misery dressed in vile rags, who loot my barns and then set fire to them.

– There is one thing more, madam, John Whittle says: which my master ordered me to get for you.

He lays the knots of ribbon on my cupped hands, a soft, glittering pile. Black velvet, threaded through with gold, each one fastened at the centre with a tiny black and gold-headed pin.

– My master, John Whittle continues: told me to procure you some pretty ornament, some extra thing for the Christmas holiday. I hope they please you.

I lift my head and look at him.

– How did you guess? These are just what I need to fasten up the sleeves of my new gown.

– Madam, he replies: I commend myself to you, most earnestly. It is my joy to serve you.

Winter plods on into what should be spring. Snow drains from the sky like the watery whey from a cheese held in a cloth. Icy winds batter our doors and windows. Glass daggers hang in the porch. Will's horse slips in the snow, throwing him. John Whittle carries him home, binds up his broken ankle. He does not need much nursing. Mostly, he dozes, waking only to call fretfully, like a child, for sips of wine and water. In the intervals I can spare from my household work, I sit by his bedside, in the shadow of its drawn-back curtain, sewing or just sitting still, thinking, moving only to throw more wood on the fire. The room is dim, and warm. It is peaceful in here, sitting staring at the flames, time measured only by the scarlet heap of embers sinking slowly down, to collapse with a soft crash, or by the weak voice calling from the bed. Will is very tired. He is recovering more slowly than he should. Self-reproach flares up in me like sparks spurting in a fireplace. With all my moping and pining, I have not been a good wife to him these three years. Sometimes I take his hand in mine, very gently, and hold it, resting on the bedclothes. Sometimes he is shivering and chilled, and I heap the heavy covers about him to guard him from the draughts he insists he feels. He is very young. But suppose he were to die?

One night, having sent my maidservant to bed and taken her place at Will's bedside, I wake suddenly from a heavy sleep, hurtling out of a dreamless darkness into this room ringed round with red circles of pain. I discover that the pain is inside me. I am the room, and the fire is burning me. It jabs my back, my belly. I am most uncomfortable. I want to cry, and to laugh. I can't sit still. I twist in my chair, not knowing whether I want to get up or to lie on the floor. Something is knocking inside me, seeking a way out.

I breathe deeply, trying to keep calm, to consider what to do. Will is asleep. I mustn't disturb him. But the pain disturbs me, insistent, grinding me, a grain caught between millstones.

I hobble to the door, a hand on my waist, feeling my stomach hard and swollen. My monthly time is not usually as bad as this. A glass of wine. Hot wine, with spices in it. Perhaps that will dull these pincers gripping my insides. I get myself down the stairs, step by heaving step, stumble towards the kitchen. No strength to shout for a servant to aid me. If I can reach the kitchen I will be all right. I will lie down on the cold floor and drum my heels until someone hears me.

I launch myself at the door in one last effort, knocking it open and falling inside. My glance, swinging wildly around the room as I burst into it, trips over tapers burning on the table, a litter of papers and account books, John Whittle, wrapped in his furred gown, jerking up, open-mouthed. He catches me as I reel towards him.

He won't let me lie down. He won't let me die, as I implore him to let me do. He grips my arms, marches me up and down the kitchen, from the door to the window and back again, our black shadows staggering in front of us, monstrous shapes dancing on floor and wall. The sour tallow smell of the tapers sickens me, but I need their flame, need to know that not all the fire is inside me. Sweat pours down my face, over my wrestling hands, as the pains bang my spine. All my bones yawn, regularly, a kind of music, surprising me.

– Keep walking, madam, my steward urges me: you'll be all right. Just keep on walking.

My feet slide like a broken doll's along the floor. Knees

159

buckling. An iron arm holds me up. He has driven pins through my joints so that I can't fall down. Lurching along like this with the pain, I am forced to learn its rhythm, start to lean into it, to let it pour through me and over me. Like Will's Spanish dance. The tinkle of virginals timing my breath, my hoarse gasps.

A great cramp seizes my belly, an eagle's beak picking me up and holding me over the abyss. My body is going to fall out of itself. I am opening, opening.

A high voice calling out. Mine.

– Take me to the jakes. Then leave me.

We totter together across the room. The chimney breast glistens with my sweat; I have leaned right across the kitchen and laid my wet forehead against it. I am very tall, because I am being stretched. A gold scroll unfurls in my throat. My toes are chopped-off pieces of white marble. I am paper, fire stinging my edges. Then silver scissors clip me, cut me up.

No fire in the jakes. Burned out. Cool blackness. Squatting in the blessed dark, arms outstretched, hands flat against the wall to brace me, I feel the great lump of shit leave me. I stand up then, lean on the cold wall, a sweat of lightness and relief bathing me, my dissolved bones reforming. My flesh shaped back to itself.

John Whittle hovers by the kitchen door. I sink down on the oak settle by the dead ashes of the fire and put my head in my hands until the faintness passes. My steward's voice, anxiously questioning me, plucks me back. I look up, wave my hand at him.

– I'm all right, I say between laughter and crying: this night, I know it, my sister Margaret has been delivered of her child. That's all that has been the matter with me. God be praised! My sister is well, and so am I now.

– Madam, he insists: let me leave you now. Let me fetch your woman. She should be with you.

My hands fly up, gesturing *no*.

He waits.

My mouth opens and shuts. My hips shiver. I let my eyes speak for me, compel him closer. My fingertips whirr in the air between us, searching for his.

– Madam, he whispers: command me. Only tell me what you wish me to do.

*

160

Three days later, the messenger on his panting horse kicks through the snow to the house. I myself see the poor brute stabled and fed, then take the letter from the messenger and despatch him to find food and warmth in the kitchen. Slowly I climb the stairs, turning over in my mind the news from London I extracted from him in the stable yard, well out of hearing of my servants, who are all Protestants. Now, to remain a Catholic is to become a traitor. The Queen has decreed it so. Therefore death. And before it who knows what agony under questioning? My knees shake. Would I be brave enough? I do not think so.

Will reads me the letter. Three days previously my sister has been brought to bed of a fine boy. Will is surprised by my calm, turns his pale face to peer at me. It annoys me to see him still so weak, to watch his thin fingers collapse on the bedclothes, his head flop back among his pillows. I need a protector for my household, not this sick child.

– God help me, I burst out: I don't wait for letters from my sister to discover how she is. I knew about this birth. I laboured through the night with her. I shared her pain. I understand her triumph.

– Hush! Will says, lowering his eyes: that's talk of witchcraft.

In nine months' time my own child will be born. I am as certain of this as I am of the sun rising tomorrow. These hands of mine can beat, brew, stitch, whip, cook, caress, embroider. This body of mine is a maker.

I stand over my husband.

– Today you must get up. Try to walk about a little. Then you can rest in your chair, by the fire. It's time you were stirring again.

Will's world has shrunk to his curtained bed. His little warm sphere where he lies lapped in warmth, cosseted, consoled for my irritable fits, taken care of. I'm impatient with him. I've other responsibilities to think of now. My child must have a future. No breath of scandal must sidle in between her and the arrangements I shall make to ensure her position and security in this world of such rapid and terrifying change.

I slip my arms around Will and lug him upright, ignoring his curses.

– Come on. Where's your gown? And your slippers?

I kiss him on the mouth.

– Sweet husband. You must get well for my sake. I need you in my bed again.

My bed is spread with the finest cloths in the house. New damask covers for the bolsters at my back, fresh hangings above me. I am attended by two midwives, also by three of my women neighbours and by my mother-in-law. In the intervals between pains, I play cards with them. I lose a pair of gloves, a fan, my enamelled belt. The others laugh at me, teasing me for my inattention. I don't care. It passes the time. I'd rather keep the conversation off other subjects. When they fall to fits of praying, as from time to time they do, I see them watching me slyly. Will's mother is most anxious. She and her husband have converted. Yes, I tell her, to shut her up: of course we're no longer Catholics. I ask the women to recite me some psalms.

I have hidden my little wooden Virgin deep down under my pillows. I have shut her into the dark, whispering to her that it's not safe for her to be seen. Asking her to forgive me my treachery, my lies.

In any case, Margaret is with me, her boy in her arms. She doesn't speak. Her dark eyes fasten themselves on mine, encouraging me to hold on, to endure. She has arrived in a hurry: her feet are bare, and her hair, unbound, flows down her back. Her nightgown, bordered with lynx fur, shows her white nightdress underneath, embroidered with silk thread. She floats in the darkened far corner of the room, her head brushing the ceiling. I lift my arms to her, welcoming her, as a fresh wave of pain tugs me open like a stiff gate. The child's cry in the dawn echoes mine: the sharp wail of the newborn whom I have learned, through a day and a night, how to bring out.

I bid the nurse set the cradle near the fire. My daughter is asleep, lashes like smudges of dirt on her blotched red cheeks, one tiny ear showing under her white cap slipped sideways, tiny limbs wrapped rigid and still. I have prised her from my breast, as I must, have delivered her into the arms of this sturdy woman whom I supply with plentiful meat, fish, eggs, to ensure

162

that her milk flows freely to nourish my child as well as her own. My mother-in-law has shown me how to bind my breasts tightly so that my milk stops. I have watched the babies guzzle at the nurse's fat breasts. I utter a confused prayer, silent, for Elizabeth. That she will prosper. That she won't suffer too much. That I won't need to beat her. That she will survive the calamities crowding in upon our troubled land.

– Little black thing, croons the nurse, rocking the cradle with her foot: where did you come from, you little changeling, with your father so handsome and fair?

She looks at me sideways.

My legs are wobbly. This is my first day out of bed and downstairs, and I am unused to going upright. I clutch at the back of the nurse's chair to steady myself.

– None of your old wives' tales in this house, good woman, or I'll have you dismissed. There'll be no talk of witchcraft here.

Hoity-toity, her back says to me, but she huffs into silence. That's the way to treat idle gossip. Stamp on it.

Will is the other one I have to deal with. After dinner he hands me a present. A small black bottle sealed with wax. I suppose, at first, that it is perfume. Symbol of my being churched tomorrow, of his return to my bed, of my becoming his wife again. I break the seal, raise the dark lip of the bottle to my nose. Strange odour, medicinal, of bitter herbs.

– It's for women just out of childbed, Will explains: it tightens them up again, inside.

He blushes as I stare at him.

– Who got you this? I exclaim: not your steward, surely?

He stares back at me, pale brows lifted.

– My father had it sent from France. He says that it also helps lift the breasts again. Not that you need that.

He lunges forward, pats my stiff bodice. My sharp breath constricts my bound breast even further. I walk to the fireplace and tip the contents of the bottle onto the flames. They hiss, flare up blue and smoky.

– I'll bear you fine sons yet, I declare: you wait and see what I can do. I'll prove to you what a man you are.

The flush on his cheeks spreads to the rest of his face. My cruelty doesn't even scratch him. He's too puffed up with pride

163

at the birth of his first child. Too innocent. I am not innocent. I have decided, since my husband cannot get children on me, to get them elsewhere. It's my duty to bear children. Very well then. I'm doing it.

Lying alone in my bed that night, my arms clutching at nothing, I know myself for a liar as well as an adulteress. My sin brought me a pleasure I want to taste again. I had it years ago, with Margaret, when she swept her hands along my back. Now I have it with John Whittle.

The darkness presses down on me. I give it eyes, a mouth, a name.

At midnight, laughing, I send all my household to bed, protesting that Hallowe'en is well over for this year. A pagan feast. But I couldn't resist the chance of celebration. Heated and thirsty after our long evening of dancing and singing in the hot kitchen, the servants happily take the last cup of punch I serve them. Strong ale, that brings heavy sleep, that I brewed myself against such an occasion as this. They pass the red poker from hand to hand, plunge it, hissing, into the spiced brown swirl in their pewter tankards.

I stand in the hall, yawning, bidding them each good night, Will red-eyed and unsteady at my side. I extinguish their watching eyes like the candles I snuff between wetted fingers. I pack them away into their beds like leftover cakes into the cupboard.

Now the house rattles with their snores. May their stories of hobgoblins and fairies, told in stertorous whispers around the fire in the dark, curdle their dreams. May my drug hold them fast in their beds. The neighbours have departed into the frosty night, shouting and stumbling. Pray God they don't inform against us. My husband and child are asleep. My steward has gone around the house, fastening up windows and doors.

My velvet-soled shoes hush the creak of the stairs. My gown slides after me. My straining ears catch the rub of fur on wood. I close my fingers over my little Virgin whom I carry in my pocket. Sweet Lady. Help me. Pour your grace onto me, a sinner. You're a woman like me. You understand. Don't let them catch me.

The mastiffs sprawled on a heap of sacks in the hall mutter at me, cock an ear, subside again. Why should they stir? They know me. I glide past them to the heavy door.

Too risky, we agreed, to leave it unbolted, lest someone see. I grease the great iron bar with dripping hastily scooped from the dish in the larder. I turn the bolt with both my hands, draw it back.

As the door swings open, the hinges creak. I have forgotten to smear them with the pork fat. The cold air smacks my face. I halt. No sounds from upstairs or from the servants' sleeping-place beyond the kitchen. I creep forwards, drawing my gown closely around me, shivering, pull the door to after me.

The farm dogs catch my scent, my footsteps, and set up a questioning growl. My low call quiets them. The new moon is up, thin as a silver ring. And now the night, rustling, unfolds itself around me, draws me into it. My eyes pierce holes in the blackness, see the creases of the sky thick with stars, the roofs of the outbuildings angled and sharp, the trees beyond the garden wall flattened into black paper cutouts. I pick my way across the dark puddle of the yard, drowning between cobbles. Splinter of gold light at the barn door.

I've torn the thin soles of my shoes. John holds my feet in his hands, warming them. My teeth stop chattering. I lift my legs over his and wriggle closer to him. Astride his lap, face to face, I knot my arms behind his back and hold him to me, kissing him, lolling in his mouth that tastes of sweet warm ale. Then he pushes me backwards, pillows me on straw. This is a game I like: taking turns to play master. Except that which of us is master I can't always tell. Am I master when I signal to him to undress me and he obeys me, pulling at ties and laces, opening my bodice and sliding his hand inside, setting his hands to my hips and rustling my gown slowly, so slowly, upwards? Am I master when I lie there on my back and stare at him, all my power in my eyes, pulling his hands towards me? It is a sweet power, that one, to make a man desire you just by looking at him. We call each other *master*, and we laugh.

His hands are warm and firm on my back, his caresses long and slow, moving over my spine, my shoulder blades, the curve of my waist. Straw pokes my skin through the blanket. I race with currents of water, of light. This is kindness: John soothing

165

and waking me together, speaking to me through his capable hands. It's hard not to be quick, after we have waited for so long, but we manage it. We let the pleasure between us mount up, up, up. We follow no special path: we hang and rock in the moment. This second of touch is what matters, and this one. We're going in no particular direction. Until wanting takes me over, and I take him into me, guiding him with my mouth and hands, then riding with him on our bed of straw. The force of my wanting makes me gentle, makes me big. I swell up, happy and fat, around him, letting the sweetness inside build up, my harvest, the good grain piling up in my barns, no more starving, no need to hurry, the darkness I'm in turning blue as fire starts in my toes and ankles and swarms up inside me and I spill into him and he into me.

The gestures, the poses, the play, I learned with Margaret. Will seemed to have no such knowledge when he came to me, and I did not know how to share mine, for fear of shaming him, for fear of what he might suspect. It feels so good to be playing again. To be a woman who dances and plays and laughs. Not to be always the mother, so strong, so responsible, cradling the husband-child. To get back a bit of wildness.

We lie still, letting ourselves turn fond and silly for the few minutes more we can risk staying together. I want to lie here with him all night, contented and wet, unceasing these endearments of the farmyard, the nursery, to hear his stories and to tell him mine, to talk more of our child. But there's not time. I hoist myself onto one elbow, and sit up, and start to pick bits of straw from my sleeves.

– What's this? he asks, plucking at my knobbly pocket.

The little Virgin lies on his palm.

– My little heretic! he says, laughing: my little Catholic!

I try to hush him, but he puts his hand over my mouth instead.

– You must give her to me, he insists: as a memento of you. As a consolation during your too frequent absences from me.

I've given him the most precious thing I have. Fool. I've given him too much.

Our farewell is brief, a touching of hands and lips. I drag myself to the door.

166   *

I snatch at chances like these as they dart past me, dangerous, enticing. Also I watch over our farm and our affairs, I make marmalade the way my mother taught me, I replenish my stock of linens and hangings, I fight with our neighbours over the fishing rights to the river that flows past the boundaries of our land, I ride out with Will, I send presents of birds and game to our friends in London, I watch out for spies amongst our neighbours' servants who might betray our allegiance to the forbidden faith. I manage things. I try to keep us safe. Also I present my husband with two more bawling black-haired children. The sons he needs. I weave careful dreams around their small heads, planning their welfare.

I manage my husband too. Will is gentle, a dreamer. He is my fourth child. In this way, standing between him and the world, I come to love him. His health is frail, and, seeing my capability, my industry, he lets the reins slip from his delicate hands into mine. Increasingly he takes refuge in his collection of maps and books, his music. He writes dances and songs, and sends them, with respectful and loving dedications, to the one or two friends left to us at court. Our daughter, a fat pretty bundle tied up in stays and ribbons, perches on a stool next to him, listening as he plays. She wriggles from the arms of her nurse and bounds onto his lap, her favourite place. He loves her tenderly. I watch them tease and play with each other. I don't spend as much time as I'd like with her. I have too much to do.

My third ear keeps on listening out for Margaret, for the words unspoken in the letters passing between us.

One morning I find her in bed with me, cuddled up against me for warmth. But we're no longer girls together, playing our bittersweet games again: my sister frowns at me, in a way she never used to do.

– Why are you putting your family at risk? she whispers: why are you being such a fool?

– I never wanted anyone but you, I blurt out: I never needed marriage after our nurse explained to me that I couldn't marry you. I lost you when you were married. All my life I have been wanting you back again.

– Don't be more stupid than you can help, she retorts: and

167

don't blaspheme. Listen. You've got a kind husband, a good house, three servants, and your children. Why can't you be content with that? You're willing to lie, cheat and steal in order to have more. Think of the danger! Think of the consequences for all of you. Suppose Will puts you away, like the Queen's father did his wife? How would you live then?

I avoid her eyes. She digs her fingernail into my arm.

– Be careful, she pleads: be careful.

Then she takes my chin in her hand and forces my face round. Hissing at me now, with hot breath.

– Where is the Virgin I gave you? Where is she?

– I don't know, I mumble: I've lost her.

– And so you've lost me, says my sister: you've turned me loose.

She vanishes, and I rub my eyes, waking to a bleary grey dawn. A red crescent-shaped weal on my forearm, two dents in the pillow.

When our younger son is ten months old, Will rouses himself to make a journey to London, to visit his father, and to sue, with the help of his kind offices, for an audience with one of the powerful gentlemen in close attendance on the Queen. We have plotted this together. The masque, with songs and dances, that Will has written on the theme of Virginity Triumphant, and dedicated to Her Majesty. An additional gift of a pair of black satin gloves, marvellously embroidered with gold. We're not quite sure what we're asking for. Without giving ourselves away, we're begging not to be suspected of treachery; for a little extra time.

Not once has Will suggested that we convert in order to save ourselves. I love him for this. His courage props up mine.

For we're in great danger now. Somehow, and we don't know how it's happened, we're openly known in the neighbourhood to be Catholics. Despite all our precautions and secrecy, someone amongst the people here we thought were friends has betrayed us. News travels fast enough to court. We need to move faster. We make preparations to send the children into France, to Will's cousin at Argenteuil. Should it become necessary. Though we try to believe it will not.

– I'll take my manservant with me, Will instructs me: but I'll leave John Whittle with you. I'd rather you had him here, to keep a watch over you all.

He doesn't look up as he speaks. He is seated at his table, sorting the sheets of his music, rolling them up carefully inside a square of silk which he ties with a ribbon. I examine his profile. He can suspect nothing. I have been too discreet. With him, I am always compliant, gracious, the pattern of an obedient wife. Surely he is not laying me a trap. I make sure that my voice is unconcerned and gay.

– We could manage very well without him. Don't deprive yourself of his services, I beg you, for our sakes.

He whirls round, smashes his fist on the table. The inkwell jumps. A sheaf of parchment slithers to the floor. I dart to pick the spilled papers up. Kneeling at his feet, my skirts billowing and crackling around me, looking down so that I don't have to meet his eyes. He knows. Somehow, he knows. But as yet he has no proof. Surely he has no proof.

His hand closes on my ear, pinching it hard until I yelp with the pain. His fingers shift, jerk my earring. I don't dare to move lest the gold wire tears itself out, rips through my flesh. I crouch before him, fear rising like vomit in my throat, waiting for his blow.

– Dear wife, his voice scrapes at me: don't argue with me.

He lets go my earring. Still not daring to look at him, I feel his movement, the air pushed aside as his arm swings back and up. I dodge just in time. His knuckles catch my cheekbone as I swerve from him and fall sideways on the carpet. Tears drop down my face, of rage and surprise. My bruised cheek smarts, the flesh instantly puffing up and half closing my eye.

Now he's huddled in his chair, crying.

– You made me do it, he weeps: whereas you should mind me. Do you think I want to hit you? You should obey me.

I crawl to the door, where I'm out of his reach and he out of mine. For I'm minded to cuff him as I never do my children. I pull myself to my feet, and look back at him. My contempt dwindles him. Puny child sitting in father's chair pretending to be master. My fault, is it, for not loving him properly, not letting him grow up into a man? For certainly I've managed him. I've kept him young, protected him, I've dandled him in deceit, and coddled him with lies. I tell myself I had no choice. I

169

did what he wanted, didn't I? He let me do it, didn't he? He wanted to be weak.

Grief overcomes me for what might have been between us and never had a chance to grow, because of our fear. I'm crying like my daughter does, in great noisy gulping sobs. I can't bear it. I stumble back towards him. Wanting to babble that it's not too late. That we can start again. To begin to know each other truly this time. To find a better way of loving.

He holds his hands out to stop me.

– Who do you think has betrayed us? he shouts: if not your lover? Who else had a chance to know all your secrets, you bawd?

He wipes his snot and tears on his sleeve. I'm freezing, numb.

– It's a lie, I stutter: you know it's a lie.

– Don't think, he whimpers: that I don't know what you've been up to, you witch. You laid spells on me, to make me powerless in bed with you, to hold me fast, asleep, while you slid off to meet your lover. Of course I knew. My shame was too great. I told nobody.

He lays his head on his arms and blubs.

– You've destroyed us all.

Will is arrested while he is in London, and put into the Tower. I could not keep him at home with me. He would ride off. I disgusted him too much. John Whittle has disappeared. I know I must hurry. Soon the men will come for me too. The day after I get the news of Will's arrest, I complete my arrangements to despatch the children, in the company of the two servants left to me, to France. I make the servants swear the most terrible of oaths that they will fulfil their duty to me. I give them all the money I have, and promise them more from Will's cousin when they shall reach France. I don't send for help from my family. It's too late for that, and I fear involving them. I pack a basket with my few pieces of silver plate and jewellery, hiding them well under layers of the children's small-clothes. Then I put the children to bed one last time, and come into my room to write this letter.

Elizabeth, my first-born. It's cruel of me to make you bear all this. I should let you forget me, or invent me, in peace. For you I am a blank: absent. Dead. I want to fill in that space of your

170

ignorance, to write my name there and offer you my history, which is yours too. I want you to inherit me. A daughter needs a mother. A daughter should know who her mother is. In order to accept her, or to reject her.

Let this letter be a bridge between your future and my past. Let this letter join the small child that you were, when I sent you away, to the young woman you have become and whom I shall never know. You're sleeping, so small and plump, as I write this. I imagine you tall and well formed and beautiful as you sit and read it. My darling, we haven't met. Writing this letter, I pretend that we have; that we might; launching it like a paper boat to carry you into your new life with a cargo of knowledge, enough strength to claim what is yours.

Conceived in such a passion of wanting, in such a joy of giving and receiving, how could you not be laid, now and for ever, at the centre of my heart?

I pray that, one day, you'll meet Margaret.

She's with me, in Will's book-lined room, as I sit writing this. Will's books and papers are strewn everywhere about us. Margaret is wearing a billowing scarlet gown, and a flat scarlet cap with black markings on it. She's my mistress. She's my perverse Mistress of Letters.

– Change all the names in your letter, she instructs me: it's safer that way. By your voice alone they'll know you.

I've thrown all her letters to me onto the fire. I don't need them any more. It's time to go with her, through the fire, up the dark tunnel behind it, and out into the sweet air of the night.

Elizabeth. I'll leave this letter behind.

25 The Correct Sibyl is looking through the racks of clothes in the great wardrobe of the Ark that runs the entire length of one of the decks. Instead of bookcases, here are long rows, narrow corridors between them, of dresses, coats, suits, arranged in no order at all but according to some glorious carnival rule of sexual and social confusion. Dress-suits press up to ski outfits. Policemen's uniforms are mixed up with those of chambermaids and nurses. A judge's splendid robes hang next to a maternity smock, a university chancellor's scarlet gown next to a nun's habit, a businessman's sober striped trousers and dark jacket next to a baggy harlequin costume. Drag abounds, if that's what she wants to call it: sequinned and beaded and feathered evening frocks, butterfly-collared shirts with pleated starched fronts, purple cassocks, jodhpurs, velvet smoking jackets, Boy Scout shorts, taffeta crinolines. Racks of shoes underneath match, or mis-match: country brogues, high boots, silver sandals, carpet slippers, running shoes, loafing shoes, walking shoes, shoes that raise the heel five inches or squeeze the toes into a triangular point, shoes decorated with gold buckles, shoes that look like Chevrolets, satin espadrilles, shoes of plaited straw, shoes of rubber and plastic and brocade.

The Correct Sibyl has so few clothes at home that she does not bother with a wardrobe. An old hat-stand bears her jeans, one well-cut pair of grey flannel trousers, her one smart suit, her few shirts, her two skirts. At a loss for words, she has invented this wardrobe in order to enrich her vocabulary. She is searching for inspiration. For a new voice. Her old one has died away and left her hoarse, monosyllabic. She moves along the closely packed rows, passing her hands over the swaying hangers, parting and separating them, throwing her catch over one arm and then moving on again.

Arms overflowing, she flings the clothes she has chosen onto a big armchair, noisy heap of squabbling colours, crazy grammar of silk, linen, felt. Then she strips naked, and pauses, wondering what to try on first.

As a young girl she adores clothes. She starves in order to buy them, lies in bed in the morning for half an hour putting an outfit together, witty, stylish, irreverent, in her mind; never appears in public without making some sort of provocative and punning statement. She understands the risks a woman takes if she dresses up sexy and wild and then goes out into the street; she accepts the consequences, the wolf-whistles, loud comments, lip-smackings. Fair enough, surely. She dresses to express her own moods; she's glad when her audience responds. If she wakes up feeling happy, sensual, confident, then she dresses in revealing shapes and fabrics, in colours that suggest her gaiety, her involvement with what is around her. In this frame of mind, she's touched and pleased when men notice her as she goes by, acclaim her with rough male kindness, say hello, affirm her as person, as sexual being.

It's an exchange, she works out. Men whistle at women because they are desperate to be noticed by them. Men are babies with fragile egos, needing mother to smile and coo. Preferably a pretty and well-dressed mother. Well, she doesn't mind. She sways past the workmen and their eyes and mouths swap jokes and liking with hers.

But the babies can turn nasty if mother doesn't behave as she ought. When she is in a thoughtful, introspective mood and dresses accordingly, in something oldish and shapeless, jeans and a raincoat perhaps, the men are enraged that she is hiding herself, not noticing them, not caring that they exist. Cheer up darling! they snarl, as she drifts past in a private dream: it might never happen. And then she wakes up, shocked and irritated, and hurries past with bent head while they pursue her with irrelevant advice, new labels: she's the bad mother, the one who goes away from baby; the whore.

It's not that men can't read women's signals; it's not that they're illiterate. They prefer their own meanings, that's all, and, since the street, they have decided, belongs to them, feel

173

free to impose them. They write her in on their pavement page.

Once she's become a professional writer, more of her energy goes into composing arrangements of words than into creating flamboyant selections of clothes. Hurrying back from the supermarket she's already, in her imagination, at her desk. She doesn't care what she looks like at these times. It's irrelevant. Shiny nose and unkempt hair, laddered stockings, droopy skirt: why bother? As far as she's concerned she's invisible. Grub, not butterfly. But the men in the street don't understand. And punish her with their name-calling.

One of her pleasures is to roam the streets of her neighbourhood at night, alone with the race of clouds and moon. She's not a fool: body blanked out by her greatcoat, she's anonymous, no man's prey, scudding along dark and silent as a cat. This is freedom: to walk for hours in the city through the darkness, at peace and excited, feet flying rapid in their soft-soled shoes, unseen, her mind streaming with images, her body dissolved into shadows. This is the freedom that men enjoy without ever having to think about it, unless they're wearing drag, unless they've dressed to express their gayness. One night she walks a woman friend to the bus stop, arm in arm, and they're abused by a gang of drunken youths spilling out of the pub. She reads in the papers of a judge's comments on a rape victim being dressed up and asking for it. Stay home. Mind your baby-man.

She doesn't want to have to disguise herself, to deny her occasional, rhythmically dictated need to wear pretty clothes. She sits at her desk studying the local newspaper's report of the man who is methodically raping his way along the street in which she lives: breaking and entering by day, waiting for each woman to come home from work, then, armed with a knife, raping her. She's always thought herself inviolable, because sensible. But a rapist rapes little girls of five, old ladies of eighty, as well as women of forty. Why should she imagine she'll be spared? New locks on her windows and doors. But not always a friend to see her home. That moment between turning in at the gate and fumbling for her keys in the porch. The Ripper, according to certain male journalists, was forced to become a murderer because of his too-loving mother and dominating wife.

174

Rape, by definition, means that a woman hasn't asked for it. Except, of course, that so many men don't understand what the word means because they refuse to read a woman's signs, refuse to recognize the sign *no*. Women can't create signs, can they? Women are silenced by male speech, aren't they?

She takes to wearing dark glasses. She stops being able to write the novels she once turned out with such professional regularity. Words don't flow. She wants to spit and curse, to mourn, to write gruesome revenge stories filled with hatred and sadistic sex. Well, that won't do, doesn't fit her civilized tolerant self-image. So she shuts up. Then learns to speak a new language: dry; unfeeling; technical terms rigorously arranged; over-controlled. She reads the critics: today's high priests. They know it all.

She stands in the wardrobe of the Ark, and wrestles her way into a pair of shabby corduroys, an Aran sweater, a large pair of suede lace-ups. She picks up a pipe and waves at her reflection in the long mirror opposite her. First Deadly Sin: laziness.

– It's simply a question of self-discipline, of setting yourself a regular schedule, she declares: nothing to it. Nine o'clock every morning I'm at my desk, rain or shine, and come lunch time there's my thousand words ready for my wife to type out after she's done the washing-up. None of this fluffing about thinking up excuses to waste time, pretending you're too depressed, feeling guilty about neglecting the housework or your family. You've just got to get down to it. You've got to get used to making your work an absolute priority. You simply need to train people not to interrupt you. Let your wife answer the telephone! Your job is to be in your study, steadily writing. It's as straightforward as that. Nothing to it. If you can't handle marriage and motherhood as well as being a writer, then you shouldn't get married and have children. At least you women have that choice. Male writers don't: they have to write *and* support a family. So get on with it, why don't you?

(The First Deadly Sin has suddenly fallen in love with another man, and does not know what to do about it.)

She adds a spotted bow tie, a green velvet waistcoat, a gold fob-watch. Second Deadly Sin: intensity.

– My dear, the person in the mirror addresses her: do try to be a *little* less serious all the time. It's so fearfully boring

175

listening to you droning on and on about your deepest feelings. You seem to believe that what you say has the status of some sort of *truth*. Whereas of course we more sophisticated types know that fiction is merely a tissue of *lies*, a *game*, and that's why it works. You don't know how to *play*. You're so grim. Do strive for just a *little* more humour, just a *touch* of irony. Your writing is so *frightfully* narrow and banal without it. We've heard *quite* enough, thank you, about the agonies of the housewife frustrated in her creativity. *Try* to be a little more original, can't you? What's wrong with writing a *comic* novel, for instance? A few *jokes*?

(The Second Deadly Sin is undergoing rigorous psycho-analysis and is somewhat dismayed by the ferocity of his atavistic desires for Mum.)

She conceals these first two layers of clothes under a huge donkey-jacket, sticks on a droopy false moustache. Third Deadly Sin: lack of political bite.

– You know the trouble with your writing? she admonishes herself: it's becoming out of touch. Not what we want. Not what we like. What have your self-indulgent narcissistic musings about your interior life to do with social reality? Not much. Completely irrelevant to most working people's experience and sufferings. And this mystical religious strain that's creeping in: *ugh*. Very nasty. Reactionary. You want to be careful, girl. We're beginning to find you trite and *boring*. We like our progressive writers to be accessible, too, not relying on bourgeois forms and images meaningless to most of the population. Who weren't paid to sit around for three years at Oxford reading medieval poetry, remember? If you must write poetry, let it be ranting and rhyming. If you must write novels, for goodness sake try to remember your audience wants a *plot*. You're not angry enough, either, any more. And you've started to write about bourgeois pleasures. Tsk. Tsk. Who the hell cares what you think about breakfasts, or the colour blue?

(Last night the Third Deadly Sin had a vision of the Angel Gabriel.)

Next she throws on a tweed suit, feathered hat, sensible brogues, brown stockings, clutches a crocodile handbag in one stiffly gloved hand. Fourth Deadly Sin: arrogance.

– Who d'you think *you* are? she asks, peering scornfully at herself: to think you've got the right to write? Who asked you to? What makes you think anyone wants to listen to what *you've* got to say? Giving yourself such airs. Cocky, I call it. Waste of your education, hanging around in pubs pretending to be a writer and not earning a decent living, letting the State support you while you do it. What have you got to offer that's of any value to ordinary hardworking people? Why not take up voluntary work if you want to do something useful? What's wrong with looking after your family, like decent women do? All those women who never had your chances. And you sit whining about your problems! Who *cares* about your meaningless self-inflicted problems? Mad, you are. Bad. Thank heavens no daughter of *mine* would ever *dream* of going in for such nonsense.

(The Fourth Deadly Sin knows that her husband no longer loves her.)

Now she dons a roomy suit of well-cut coffee-coloured overalls, a glittering silver belt, a pair of pink sneakers. Fifth Deadly Sin: unsisterly behaviour.

– Call yourself a feminist? Hmmm. You're not *my* idea of a feminist, I can tell you. For a start, you're much too fond of the sound of your own voice. You're too ambitious. You don't work collectively any more. You want to be a star. You've stopped caring about your struggling sisters. Women all over the world are trying to fight their oppression and you sit at home cosily writing novels. You'd never have become a writer if it wasn't for the women's movement, yet where's your gratitude? Look at you, trying to grab the limelight, wanting to pose as some sort of *leader*. Bourgeois individualism, that's called, dearie. And secondly, if you insist on writing, you might at least try to betray feminism less. All this romantic garbage you churn out about heterosexuality, real men and real women and the orgasm as every woman's fulfilment. Yuk. Nor can you even find new forms! When you're not spewing out your messy confessions you're falling back on patriarchal myths that are obsolete. Who gives a damn about the bloody Greeks or the Bible? We want *new* images, ones that suit *women*, not the men you're so anxious to impress. Take your nasty traditional feminine stories away. *And* your phallocratic psychologizing and your rubbishy religious images. You're old hat, dearie.

177

You've been left behind. We have a younger generation of writers who are *much* more interesting. And I can't say I've noticed you giving them much of a helping hand. Too busy looking out for number one, aren't you?

(The Fifth Deadly Sin works nights as a striptease artist, and is very good at it.)

She swathes herself in a black cloak, ties on a black headband, straps heavy chains around her waist and ankles. Sixth Deadly Sin: lack of avant-garde originality.

– You're not very *wild*, are you? she asks: not really weird and violent and post-modernist. You never got even as far as modernism, did you, poor thing? You're pretty middle of the road. I mean, you're still using quotation marks and narrative and conventional sentence structures and conventional ideas of character. Haven't you heard of Gertrude Stein and William Burroughs and de Sade and Bataille? Aren't you embarrassed, deep down, by the sweet safe sticky sentimental stuff you write? You should be. You've never experienced real life, of course. You've never lived in the depths. What do you know about the truth of urban survival, you babbler about nature and love? How can you expect to write a work of true passionate bitterness until you've been a hooker and gone in for S-M and been a junkie and sold your blood and refused a clear gender identity? I bet you still think of yourself as a woman, don't you? I bet you love your family. I bet you've never been to prison. You don't really *know* about much, do you?

(The Sixth Deadly Sin is a virgin. Weekends, she visits her beloved elderly aunt, and they sit and read the Bible together.)

She adds a white beard, a black gown and mortarboard, an eyeglass. Seventh Deadly Sin: lack of true artistry.

– Foolish left-wing perverted rubbish masquerading as art. Thank God there's some sanity left in this world and that books like yours don't sell, don't get reviewed, don't win prizes, and don't get taken seriously as literature. Polemical tracts, they are, not *novels*. Who wants to read banal snivelling rhetoric about ugly man-hating lesbians with herpes and dandruff raising their foul illegitimate brats on social security? You have a modicum of talent, I agree. With time, with effort, you might, if you dropped all this stridency and whining, write a second-

178

or third-rate book. But you prefer to grumble, don't you? It's easier than the struggle the true artist has to *transcend* his self, his personal egotism, and create an enduring work of the fullest humanity that will be recognized as *great*, as *authentic*. You just aren't in that class, dear. You never will be. Why fool yourself?

(The Seventh Deadly Sin would love to be able to write.)

She bends forward and gazes at the mirror.

– You've had it, dear, can't you see? all the Seven Deadly Sins murmur at her: you're not up to it. You lack the stamina necessary for sustained creative work. You lack imagination, confidence, originality, wit. You're too genteel. You're too hysterical. Why not give up now, gracefully, before you make a complete ass of yourself?

She is stuck to the mirror, to its definitions. She flails her arms but the layers of clothes she has assumed, one by one, swaddle her, wad her, helpless and fat as a bound baby, do not let her move away.

– I want to please everybody, she screams: I want to say the right thing and be approved of and loved by everyone and it's IMPOSSIBLE. That ideal mother, ideal listener, *doesn't exist*.

Her scream shatters the mirror. Now she can pick up a shard, cut off her clothes, piece by piece, and let them fall under her feet. Now she can be lonely, and begin to hunt for her own words.

She starts again, strolling through the racks of clothes to find something she might want to wear.

She reaches her hand into the past. The caress of memory. Her favourite clothes. Why is it that nothing she possesses now gives her an equivalent pleasure?

Here's the long white linen nightdress, tiny pleats falling heavily from the low wide neck, that she bought from the antique stall in Carnac market that summer she went on holiday with Jenny, and which she wore as a dress in the evenings, sitting in the café under the pines drinking Kirs and feeling the rough linen fall over her bare calves. As she washed it, so it frayed, went into holes, wore out. At last she had to cut it up for dusters.

Here's that cotton skirt in dull brick red, just above ankle-length, very tight and small at the waist, very full and gathered, with big pockets, that she wore for years until she spilled oil on it, making mayonnaise for Paula's wedding party, and the huge dull stain would not wash out.

Here's that cotton dress cut like a French schoolchild's overall with square shoulders and a square yoke and little buttons, in the rich blue of French workmen's jackets. She left it behind in a bed-and-breakfast in Cornwall and never got around to writing to ask for it to be sent on.

Here's that tubular dress in cream linen with a cutwork yoke, wide shoulders, wide scooped neck, sleeveless, mid-calf length, that she bought for her grandmother, who wore it a couple of summers then gave it back. How she loved that dress. The dry-cleaners ruined it, marking it with pale purple dye.

Here's the black 1940s suit she bought for three pounds in Camden market in imitation of her mother, who married in wartime in sumptuous sexy black. Buttons of black jet, curved pockets and shoulder yoke outlined in overlapping rows of black silk ribbon, narrow skirt with a single kick pleat. She lent it to Laura to wear to an interview. Then Laura went to Australia and took the suit with her.

Here's that 1920s sleeveless waistcoat made entirely of sequins of mother-of-pearl, soft, gleaming, pink merging to silver. It was the most precious thing she had, so she gave it to her lover Marie. When they split up she didn't dare ask for it back. She regretted its loss more than that of Marie, she sometimes thought.

Here are the summer sandals of pale olive-green leather, with a closed toe and closed heel, woven in plaited straps, that she spent a week's earnings on one summer. They were stolen in Paris when Greta's car was broken into overnight and the cases they hadn't bothered to take into the hotel were snatched. The case was full of books mostly. It was the shoes she grieved for.

Here are those other shoes, enormous absurd platforms in bright apple-green, which she used to wear while making love with Mick. Nothing else: just the shoes. When they went out of fashion she turned them into flowerpots and grew geraniums in them until they rotted.

Here's her huge man's tweed overcoat, bought in a War-on-Want shop one autumn in Leeds for one pound. She wore it to the Guy Fawkes party at Chapeltown: the slip and hiss of
180

fireworks, the song of bonfires, the strangers bumping against her in the dark. The sleeves became marked with wax dropped by candles at midnight Mass and at Greenham Common demonstrations; the buttons dropped off. In the end the moths got it.

Here's that pair of olive-green ex-army shorts, picked up in another market, in Aix-en-Provence. With Jenny again. Long, almost down to her knees, pleats belted tightly into her waist. Sometimes she wore them with a red forties blouse, red fishnet tights and shoes. Mostly she wore them in summer, so that she could have the deep pleasure of feeling the warm air caress her bare knees, calves, ankles, as she ran along the street or bicycled home at night through the black sweet-smelling park, and knew herself a boy again, or a boy-girl, the free rapid long-legged creature she had been before periods came with lagging steps and fear. Aged thirty-five, scampering up a hillside in Provence, she finds that boy again. She stops wearing the shorts when her daughter complains she is too old, they make her look ridiculous.

Words can be given away, lost, put out with the rubbish. Words can rot and need replacing. Loved words, favourite words. One of the pleasures of being a writer is that you can take power, please yourself and nobody else, choose your own words. So, come on, girl, get on with it: start enjoying.

26   A lot of sex used to go on in the Reading Room.
The joy of reading and researching has to be translated into action. Like new wine in old bottles: I understand that people may explode with excitement. Male scholars prowl the gangways between the desks, ostensibly tracking down obscure volumes of bibliography or lost books delivered to the wrong seat. It is easy to allow my eye to be caught, to find companions for lunch or coffee. Most of them have shoulders speckled with dandruff or bad breath or blackened teeth. That doesn't matter: they hint at sexual matters with shining eyes.

I choose one of these scholars, a clean funny one, as my first lover. I peel off the elastic panty girdle which is as awkward as my virginity in a dusty cubbyhole in the bookstacks unlocked with my bunch of keys. I lean against the scorching radiator on which we boil up illegal kettles of tea, and lift my antique crepe de Chine dress around my waist.

Foreplay goes on in the Reading Room, intense discussions about Bibliography which is Ken's subject too. After half an hour's whispering about silken headbands, rubbed and spotted and foxed pages, laid paper, we are at such a pitch that when we get to the cubbyhole and the radiator we are speechless, frenzied, our pleasure increased by the need for secrecy and speed. Downstairs again, flushed and languid, I leaf through the letters of bibliographical enquiry from foreign scholars that I am supposed to answer.

I don't come with Ken. It doesn't bother me. I'm a beginner, with a lot to learn. I've got to Advanced Bibliography, and will eventually get to Coming. But it worries Ken. Is that better? he asks hopefully. In the end, to silence him, I begin to fake orgasms. I deduce from novels in the erotica section how to act. Some people are experts at faking texts. I become an expert in faking orgasms. But I lose interest in my acquired gestures, and after a while we give it up.

Here in my Arkive on the Ark, books on sex are allowed to stand next to books on procreation.

– But the world's a poisoned place, Noah reproaches me: full of illness and death. How can you be so irresponsible as to bring a child into it?

I skim through the riddle book.

Does *to bear* mean also *to bear*?

27   The next island lifts itself, beaky and bony, from the blue seas surrounding it, two huge caverns in its white cliff. The port is on one side of the great bay, and the city straggles up the steep hills behind it.

The city is an enormous tropical fruit: a durian, yellow and rotting. The smell envelops me as soon as I step onto the quayside, and for a moment I want to turn tail back to the Ark where the others are hard at work, no time for this tourism. The smell pushes up my nostrils: moist decaying vegetable matter; urine; over-ripe fruit; dying flowers, slimy-sweet; incense; sickness; and, laid over the top, a thin vapour, the smell of chlorine and disinfectant.

It's raining. Under my feet, a brown squelch of mud, sludge of cardboard laid over potholes, dark mash of trampled litter, wet cigarette stubs, wet sand and grit. The narrow streets are tumultuous, thronged with hurrying people elbowing their way past each other, shouting and gesticulating across the heave and blare of traffic at acquaintances on the other pavement. They don't seem to mind the smell; they're armed with pomanders studded with cloves, and wear nose-masks of black cloth tied on with golden ribbons, of black silk decorated with gold lace and sequins.

Fighting my way forwards in the pushing, clamouring queue, I board a clanging tram. As it whines and sways up the steep hill I rub clear the steamed-up window next to me and gaze out at the tall shabby tenements. Traces of rich colour remain: burnt yellow, orange, dark red, grey. Palm trees, branches a bunch of untidy rags. Sodden lines of washing sagging between apartment blocks. The paint peels off windowsills in long curls. Cars hoot shrilly in the hot wet traffic

184

jam, swerve to the wrong side of the road to overtake, zip through red lights. Bruised cars; dents beaten out, panels patched up. A dump of old tyres with a handwritten notice above saying RIP *le gomme*. Stalls selling plastic baskets and sandals and necklaces. We rattle up, up, up. Craning my neck I see the bay far below, small silver crescent.

I struggle out of the crowded sweaty tram and down the folding steps. The tram swings off along its shining rail. I'm standing in a little curving piazza just below the brow of the hill. Dusk: the hour of deep transparent blue. Sharp outlines of roofs and parapets. Youths on motorbikes roar up and down, their exhaust fumes bitter in my unprotected nose. I walk away, over to the centre of the piazza where a baroque monument to some long-dead general is encircled by benches and where I can sit down, the rain slowed to a drizzle dampening my shoulders. Up here, so far above the seething fishy smells of the port, the air is a little clearer. It's possible to breathe without immediately wanting to retch.

Perhaps, once upon a time, this city smelled of chestnuts and wood-smoke, of vanilla and almonds, in those far-off days before the chemical factories made the air stink. Perhaps people used to bathe in the sea, in the time before it was used as a dump for sewage and industrial effluents and nuclear waste. You can buy expensive designer perfumes in the shops, to wipe out the disgusting natural smell of female bodies; the perfumes are processed in that factory over there, look. It's a good thing; it's meant a fall in the local unemployment figures. You can sit in a beach-side café, wearing your mask and sipping synthetic orange juice full of carcinogenic additives, and watch the sapphire-blue waves lapping on the shore littered with turds and clots of oily mud washed in from the tankers sailing by.

I read the poster stuck on the monument behind me.

Oh dear. There's been an accident at the local nuclear power station. Don't panic. Nothing to worry about. The radioactive cloud hanging over the island won't stay for long: the wind will soon blow it somewhere else.

I have the smell of death in my nostrils. Invisible death, falling gently with the rain onto the parched earth, blown with the sea breezes into the city. Death carried in the cows' milk, in

185

the new crop of spinach and lettuce, in the air I have to breathe when I go out shopping. I swallow death. I inhale it. I'm helpless in the face of it. It presses into me: a rape. Death working in my cells, against my will, to make me infertile perhaps, or to give me, or the child I want to bear, some form of cancer. I have to live with death. I can't escape it: how can you evacuate an entire nation? There are no nuclear shelters here.

The government does not wish to alarm us: no figures are released; no studies published. Jocular ministers appear on the television news programmes, telling us to take a few sensible precautions, the crisis will be over soon, as the wind shifts and bears the cloud away towards the north again, as the radioactive matter in the atmosphere and on the ground gradually decays.

One of the worst things is not knowing exactly what is happening. I can't help suspecting that in some areas the level of radioactivity is so high that the government is deliberately keeping silent, deliberately keeping us in ignorance. My fantasies grow unchecked. I can't sleep at night. The invisible dust settles on my eyes, my lips. I don't want to speak of my terrors to others and make them feel worse than they already do. We can't console each other. We are blank-faced, silent.

Oblivion is the way out for some, through sleep, drink, drugs. Some go mad, and have to be shut away. Others, with desperate gallantry, dress in their best and go out into the town to stroll up and down and chat to friends, to pretend that all is as usual. Business as usual. The shops stay open. Policemen with guns and sheafs of official papers inspect the greengrocers, to ensure that no fresh leafy vegetables are on sale, then issue the day's certificate of healthy trading. In a couple of weeks, they promise airily, we can eat raw green food again. The lettuce sown just before the cloud came, and heavy with its cargo? I am heavy with sorrow, and heavy with rage. I cry in private.

Demonstrations occur daily in front of the Ministry of Health, in front of the foreign embassies of those countries who have installed nuclear power stations. *Danger*, we cry out. *Danger*, we signal, as we don grim carnival masks and skeleton costumes and dance our dance of death. How would *you* like to dress for death? In white silk? In black tails? Here's a death cocktail, and a death dice, and a death cue.

186

It's too late, say the world's governments: we're already committed. They don't care, can't admit their grave mistake, refuse to reverse policy. This is just an isolated disaster. Of course further precautions will be taken to ensure such accidents never recur. Nuclear power remains clean, effective, cheap, efficient, safe. Your diseased child will be born too late to be counted as a victim. Statistics, after all, can be destroyed or lied about.

I go into the great gloomy church set back on one side of the piazza. Temporary shelter from the soft radioactive rain.

Cavern of darkness, lit with bunched sticks of glitter, trembling silver flames. I slide across the stone floor towards the high altar garrulous with coloured marbles, bronze angels, falls of lace. The chancel walls are lined with row upon row of framed cavities, like boxes in a theatre. In each one a skull set on a starched ruff, padded velvet shoulders. Sightless eye sockets gaping at the drama of death daily enacted there in front of them, on the brightly burning altar-stage, to the sound of cries and trumpets. The crucifix swings down out of the blackness. We must all die some time, the man on the cross reminds me: why make such a fuss about it?

Relics in boxes of crystal and gilt leer at me, like deformed babies, pathological specimens, swimming in stoppered glass jars.

28 We're going to have fish for supper. Caught by the Gaffer, who has spent most of the day sitting out on deck with rod and line.

I inspect the sparkling haul in his basket. Tails still flapping, until I pick up the fish and knock them out one by one, while the Gaffer flinches and looks away. Then he turns his head back towards me with a smile.

– I see you believe in mercy-killing, at least. And what about the cruel barb, dragging the throat? If you're going to continue to eat fish you should catch them yourself.

– I'm not prepared to, I say: shut up, can't you? All right, I'm a hypocrite.

Scales rippling in blue-black silver, in mother-of-pearl, in opal, shading, in gleams of light, to rose pink. The eyes stare at me, reproachful and dead.

– You'll have to de-gut them, the Gaffer says: I don't know how.

All the others watch me as I lay out the fish on a board on the kitchen table, and pick up my knife. Turn the fish belly upward. Grip the slimy corpse in one hand, slit it open with the other. The knife isn't sharp enough: I have to jab, then raggedly saw, unpicking a silver seam. Spurt of greenish goo. I reach my fingers into the red innards, curl them around the slippery entrails, squashy and yielding. Two swift tugs, my hand filled with a knot of wet sacs of jelly and white filaments, dripping blood and a dark green liquid. I scrape the innards with the knife, then rinse the empty fish under the tap. I repeat the procedure twelve times, until there's a large pile at my side of sloppy shiny guts, smelling high and raw, and two neat rows of floured fish ready for frying.

I hold up my reeking hands and arms, gloved in red blood up to the elbow, towards the Gaffer, and laugh.

– Easy, once you make up your mind to do it.

He shudders.

– You women! It's like some hideous pagan menstrual rite.

– A good job for a sadist who's out of work, though, I say, wiping my fishy fingers: or for a sadist who's trying to kick the habit. Keep your hand in. Displacement activity.

– I'd rather not have to read about menstruation, says the Deftly Sibyl: I quite see that it was a revolutionary topic when first introduced into women's writing, but now it's become *de rigueur* I'm bored with it. I'm also bored by throbbing wombs, moons, grandmothers, lesbians, the lost mother, nuns, witches, food, and orgasms. They're all feminist clichés. All right, no subject is inherently boring; it depends on what you do with it. But still. I'm bored with the subject of women. I'm also bored by war, tarts with a heart of gold, fathers and sons, visiting academics, bullfights, erect penises, spies, and bank accounts. But I don't suppose that will stop male writers from writing about them.

– Don't bully me, shouts the Gaffer: I'm not ready, not yet, to write as a man on taboo subjects. I need to be sure there's a market, first, for that sort of writing. I suppose sooner or later one of the women's presses is going to start a men's list. We've got spinster classics by dead spinsters, spinster modern classics by living spinsters, the spinster youth list, the spinster teenage list, the spinster children's collection. What about spinster bachelors? Spinster bachelor babies, spinster bachelor boys, spinster bachelor mature writers, spinster ageing bachelors? Somebody, sooner or later, is going to make a fortune promoting books in these categories. And then the whole bloody mess can start all over again.

– Womb envy? says the Re-Vision Sibyl: it's not a male prerogative. I've got it. A catching disease. My hands are claws curved ready to strike. Curdle of sour grapes in the stomach. Green is the colour of life, also of envy. Thwarted life, desire gone mildewy or covered in greenfly. I must hold fast to the fragile trust we build between us here on the Ark, for the winds of my envy want to blow our house down. Publishers scramble for our books, now briefly fashionable, make us compete for contracts. Reviewers compare us to each other and to straw hysterics who can be knocked down, we're grateful not to be like *them*. One of you has your new novel selected for the best-twenty-books-by-women promotion: I want to lash out and hit, preferably you. One of you already has a cult following, based on only two books of stories: I want to see you fail. One of you is chosen as flavour of the month and hyped everywhere: I say I despise publicity. My envy destroys my growing love for you, shuts me up. I might kill you if the beast jumped out with her claws and teeth. I might stamp my foot on your neck. My breath is fire, and blasts you. I don't admit this; haven't men always said women are bitchy, envious and competitive? I punish myself instead. I stay away from you. The boulder of rage is stuck in my mouth, choking and silencing me. A faceted stone that fits. Gobstopper lodged in the windpipe. Breast-jet of bad milk forced at my face. Why does she hold herself so aloof, you wonder: why is she so awkward, so guilty, so distant? What shall I do. Suck on the stone, and let it dissolve, green sherbet firing my tongue. Write it all down and let you read it. Then walls of glass break, and I can touch you, and new words can come. I roll my envy lightly around my tongue, just one more taste for the palate to savour. Not bad food. Not poison. Just a part of myself. I can kiss you and not sting.

– Penis envy? says the Forsaken Sibyl: yes, that too. I envy their bodies, long and lean, patched with fur. The absence of fullness and curves, hips and breasts. Often I envy their control. My body explodes, over and over again. I open, I stream forth, urgent rhythms of blood, sweat, spittle, piss, shit, milk. I dissolve into air, then recreate myself. Stop up the exits and entrances, block the pores. Man is a signpost, one white finger pointing. Clean and lean. Less flesh to him. Less mess. Less of himself to lose. What shall I do. Go on a diet, discipline my body through weightlifting, have a sex change, wrap myself in chains so that I can't spill out. Arranging words on paper helps me to feel safe.

– I believe in God, the Father Almighty, creator of heaven and earth, says the Correct Sibyl: do I? *He* is just a word. The Word that structures difference, that structures language for everyone. *He* defines all that is not-him. What can I possibly write that does not take its shape, its bent, from accepting or rejecting *him*? Can I really write *I* and mean something else? I invent *him*, I write him in. So I can also forget him, erase him, cross him out. He's just a word. Is *she* enough by herself? The goddess worshippers say *She* made the world. Is that any better than saying *He* did? The myth starts when *he* meets *she*? Centuries of trouble, rival versions of the truth. How can I invent *she* without exploring what she touches or yearns to touch, the *not-she*, the *mother* who goes away and touches *father*? *Man* and *woman* so distant from each other in the dictionary, such a lumber of meanings in between.

– I don't like printed books, says the Babble-On Sibyl: I like a text like a letter or like a diary. Receiving the letter, snooping in the diary, I am close to the hand of the body that made it. Just one set of marks on paper, no need for duplicates. No buying and selling, the book as a commodity that circulates. Instead, the body impressed onto paper. I study the author's fingerprints. Directed towards me. I should learn to love word processors. Do I fetishize the hand that writes? Can I learn to love the brain, and print-out? Multiple copies at the flick of a switch. Just one baby? Or sextuplets? Are they all different? Do books also have souls? Now there are no more originals. Just flickering green screens.

– What about women who can't read or write? the Gaffer asks: how do they tell stories? A story, please.

29   Meg Hansey decides, after only a year in his service, to kill her master. But it's not for *his* murder that she's taken up in the end.

I visit her in Bridewell. I have a lot of sympathy for these poor women, pushed to take desperate measures in order to survive, and then cruelly punished for it. And, after all, I know Meg well, having visited her master so often at his house. Certain French books I used to bring to show him, smiling to myself to see him grow so red, so hot and so excited, and afterwards so ashamed, when his wife tripped in to lisp her compliments and to see what we were up to, and he blushed and hid the book under the tablecloth. Or when Meg came in, with a tray of wine and sweets. I take Meg wine now, when I can afford it, or beer. It comforts her. I take her bundles of bread and sausage, and I play cards with her to take her mind off her troubles. Of course she's grateful. Though at first suspicious of my motives, as she has every right to be, poor wretch. After a couple of weeks she relaxes. Then it takes only a bit of coaxing to get her to tell her story. It's a short one, an ordinary one, like her life. But I think I can do something with it.

I don't take notes. I don't want to play the journalist too obviously. I've got a good memory. I write it all down on this grubby manuscript at night, here at home in my rooms, where I'm undisturbed. My debts don't let me out too often to my old haunts, and I want to keep away from the Allens for a bit. So I shall spend my evenings writing about Meg. These rough notes, which I shall reassemble into a story. My idea is to combine the sensational details of popular novels and broadsheets with the sober nature of religious confessional tracts. I want to tell a woman's story. I want to create a

192

woman's voice. Of course I have to invent Meg's style. In real life she's not got much of a way with words, bless her. I polish up what she tells me; I give it a shape; I make her up. You have to.

Meg's a country girl, from Kent. Not a dullard. Clever enough to snatch at the chance of a decent living, a spot of excitement, when she comes up to London to visit her aunt and sees that Mrs Penn, herself an abigail, can put her in the way of earning more than she'd ever do at home. Meg's parents are dead of the pox, and her crew of sisters and brothers hanging on by fingers and toes under the unwilling care of their grandfather. Meg abandons them, seizes her own chance. They'll end up, most likely, in the poorhouse. She tells them: I'll save money. I'll send for you. Then she flits. From far away, looking back, the house is small enough to hold in the palm of her hand. Then she drops it.

She learns fast: how to curtsey and keep her mouth shut; how to wash muslins and starch lace; how to freshen up old satin gowns rotten with sweat under the armpits; how to arrange a head, more or less; how to stir up messes fit to be carried into the chamber of one seeking to be treated as a lady. How to lie, how to look sharp, how to duck and swerve.

Mrs Penn recommends her as waiting-woman to her own mistress's cousin, concocting a neat story of Meg's former employment under a rich merchant in Bristol, now alas suddenly drowned in the West Indies with a cargo of Black slaves and his widow too distraught to furnish a testimonial. Meg's clean and sober, not pretty. She's a thin little woman. Her complexion is dark, her mouth is twisted awry. She doesn't yelp at the prospect of low wages. Her future mistress stares at her and decides she'll do.

– You'll have to sit with me at night, Mrs Allen warns her, sighing: my health is that delicate that often I can't sleep. Especially when Mr Allen is out late, or from home.

Meg likes the house, set back behind a tall brick wall from the bustle of Well Lane in the shadow of St Paul's. A small square house, solidly built of rosy red brick, with white wood casements and a fine brass knocker on the door that Meg polishes every morning. In front of the house, behind the wall, there's a garden with three lime trees and a fine flowerbed and a stone bench. Meg pegs out the washing, once the washer-woman's been on a Monday, on a line she stretches between two of the trees, and draws in deep draughts of the scent of their flowers.

She makes herself indispensable to her new mistress. Mrs Allen is rising thirty-five, a faded beauty grown fretful. Yellow curls fall on a white neck. Hard eyes flicker away from too much contact. Rarely stirring out, and eating too many sweets, she's growing fatter. Her skin is still soft, but shows every mark: so many bruises. One of Meg's tasks, she discovers, is to assure her employer she's still beautiful, and this is true in the evening once the candles are lit. Then she's a pink and white girl, all dimples when she laughs at the antics of her puppy.

Mr Allen has several faces. In the morning he slouches at table in his old gown, unshaven, dipping his soft roll into his cup of chocolate and swallowing noisily, then belching. Meg, who's quickly taken on her mistress's fine manners, turns her eyes away from the slop of half-chewed bread in his open mouth, his lips slapping loosely, blocks her ears to the sounds of his chewing, to the gurgles of his stomach. He's afflicted often with indigestion, and fussy about what he eats, though not about how he appears in front of his womenfolk. In the mornings he takes it easy, with stooped shoulders and a slack belly.

Then he dresses to go out, and is transformed. He's a goldsmith, doing good business. He dresses well, to impress his clients. In his best velvet suit and his curled wig he looks a real gentleman. Not very tall, perhaps, but a fine figure of a man once he squares his shoulders and twirls his cane, his rounded stomach hidden under his purple waistcoat and his handsome calves displayed to their advantage in white stockings. He's a vain little man, pointing his toe to show off the red heels of his new shoes, pirouetting at the door for his wife's delectation. He likes her to be happy when he goes off: he chucks her under the chin and kisses her cheek before he minces down the street in a trail of lace handkerchiefs and the scent of Eau de Venus.

Mrs Allen loves him well, and sure, he's devoted to her. That first day, Meg sees what a good mood he's in when he comes home for dinner, rubbing his hands and chuckling, tweaking her ear as she stands back to let him pass her in the hall. Meg

194

shakes out the cloth and lays the table while Mr Allen pulls his wife on to his knee: oh my pretty bird, my little popinjay; paddling his hand in her bodice, putting his mouth to her neck. She twines her arms around him and they cuddle as artlessly as a pair of children. They don't care that Meg's watching. Perhaps, she thinks: they like an audience.

– So you do love me? Mrs Allen asks, patting her tumbled hair: just a little bit?

And for answer he pecks her, and tickles her, and nips her, until she's squealing with contentment. Not entirely satisfied, though.

– Tell me you love me, she coos, caressing him with her fingertips as daintily as a sweet she'll pop into her mouth: tell me.

– My darling poppet, he says, kissing her nose: my little honey, of course I love you.

Then he leans back against the fat cushions of his chair and tells her the story of his morning, glancing away from her needy eyes, chafing at the soft bonds of her arms, holding her at arm's length while she wriggles happily on top of him. He tells her of the splendid and enticing allure of the lady he saw driving down the street in her carriage, leaning forward to look out of the window so that he saw her white uncovered bosom, her opulent mouth. He mentions his dream of the night before, too erotic to be fully revealed to his virtuous listener. He peeps at his wife sideways, to see how she's taking it. Flick, flick. Just a little stroke of the lash. Mrs Allen's eyes fill with tears. She struggles to get off his knees, while his arms, suddenly embracing her tightly, restrain her. She tries for pride, saying nothing, but her tears betray her. That satisfies him. He redoubles his pats, his kisses, soothing her back into complaisance: little chickabiddy, little silly, sweet goosie.

Then they're both ready for dinner.

Meg slams down the plates. Mrs Allen fiddles with her food and watches her maid, watches where her husband's eyes go.

– Meg, she frets: you've spilled wine on my sleeve. It's too bad. Why must you be so clumsy, you great gawk?

Her face, pouting with ill humour, is all lines. She catches sight of herself in the mirror hung over the sideboard, and crumples her napkin between her hands.

– It's my favourite gown, she weeps: and the stain won't wash out. You slattern. You wretch. You did it on purpose to annoy me.

Mr Allen covers her hand with his.

– Now then, now then. Don't cry, ducky. I'll buy you another.

Mrs Allen's sobs melt into smiles. Mr Allen's eyes meet Meg's, and she looks away quickly.

Mrs Allen does indeed have delicate health. Once a month she is confined to her bed with severe pains. Meg wraps heated bricks in sacking, then in linen towels, and places them at her mistress's feet, at her back, at her belly. She piles the covers over her, beats up the pillows, brings her hot broth and oranges and gossip.

– Don't go away, Meg, Mrs Allen pleads: I like having you here with me. You do me good.

Her washy blue eyes: frightened; watchful.

– There, my dear madam, Meg exclaims: I'll sit with you willingly.

She fetches the basket of mending and settles herself next to the big bed in a low chair.

– I miss my family, you know? Mrs Allen confides: they all live so far away, except for my cousin. And she's so often unkind to me.

She bursts into tears.

– Now then, madam, now then, Meg reproaches her: crying won't do you any good.

She speaks absent-mindedly; her mind's on her darning.

– I need a friend, Meg, Mrs Allen says: I need someone I can talk to.

Meg shifts in her chair.

– Well then, madam, I'm sure you can rely on me. I'm at your service.

Mrs Allen tells Meg of her courtship by her husband.

First there is the gravity of the flute music, and my mother's bare shoulders above the silver lace of her busk and loose gown, her white skin, seriously powdered, matt not shining in the candlelight. A summer night beyond the tall window, the long curtains flung back, the moon slides behind a flurry of cloud; a

196

dark mirror; blue-black ripples.

He sweating. Well I could see it. Hand fidgeting with the sharp-edged ruffle tickling the opposite wrist. Pleated linen, starched. Settling the plum velvet sleeve over it.

My mother's eyes are dark slits shiny as apple pips. Her skirts rise over the bolster tied around her hips and fall in thick folds of embroidered blue satin around her tiny feet in gold high-heeled shoes.

She rises, and collects the others with a gesture of fan and quick fingers. Supper laid out on tables in the room behind the folding doors. Mr Allen waits, to hand me from my chair, I suppose.

What have I to offer? A willingness to trust.

I say to him oh I've dropped my handkerchief oh what a weak ploy his eyes say oh say I thank you my eyes respond now we can talk.

There is a mole at the side of his nose that sprouts with two stiff black hairs. I don't mind, I have one too, on my inner thigh. What else do I know of him? He's as pretty and as tricksy as his clothes. Changes from sober broadcloth to bright silk in the twinkling of a mood.

Chairs in their sullen brocaded positions opposite the marble fireplace. By day this room is high-ceilinged, cold, bright, large. Tonight, the streaming fires of the branching candlesticks touch the edges of the sofa back I grip in both hands, mark out a space just big enough for we two to manoeuvre in.

Laughter from the next room, where my father turns the tap of the silver urn of wine. I'm alone here. None of those people matters to me. I curtsey to Mr Allen, have my hand kissed. The hangings shift at the window, and the moon shines in, a gold square on the carpet, and I am impatient.

Can you understand this? To stake your life on the gleam of moonlight on a man's shoulder as he holds aside a fringed curtain and waits for you to pass?

I have to make some room for my own imaginings. I need to invent him. I need to believe that I meet him naked and free as one of those nymphs in the tapestry hung on the opposite wall; and that I make my own decision. So I choose him for the way the moonlight falls on his braided coat (there are shadows thick

197

in the corner, and they scare me), for the way he looks around seeming so free. So I too could feel free.

I rise from my curtsey, and approach him, while he looks at me.

That room. Heavy with crimson on the walls, and carved doorways, and carpets. My heels clack across the parquet then the carpet muffles them. I reach him. I look at him. I hold him eye to eye. I'm drowning. If he does not respond what shall I do?

He drops the curtain and pulls it across the doorway, so that we're securely enclosed. He puts his white hand out, and takes mine, and this time he does not let go. He kisses my neck, my forehead, my lips.

Really this happens in public. All the rest of our party, ten or more persons, stand just beyond the door, talking and laughing, the clash of spoons and glasses.

I invent my own story. I need to love him. How else can I give myself away, into his keeping? I see us in the mirror, with our hands joined in an emblem of marriage, and I feel at first sick and faint, and then: that this must be so. Then we go into supper.

Afterwards he stays behind while the others crowd into the hall to say their goodbyes to my mother and father. The room is almost dark. He captures my hands again in his and whispers so low I can't hear him, then presses his mouth on mine again. This time he puts his tongue in my mouth. It is fat, like grapes. We're alone. This is how it will be. His eyes scatter me into corners. What else is there for me, besides him? I have to go forwards. What else can I do. I do not say one word. I consent to a destiny, knowing no other.

Matters run swiftly on. My body is as smooth and new for him as the sheets and towels I bring with me. I am his bed, and he slides into me. I spread myself for him. I want the treasure I have guessed at from poetry, the jokes of servants: the sweetness and the fire. Well. I learn how odd, how awkward, the way there is. Madam. He parts my thighs. Your obedient servant. He jabs a finger in, to open me up. I want to go with him, because this is what I believe I was born for, my life's summit. We're dancing a strange step. I don't know how to move, and he hasn't noticed. He is plucking at me, and I'm a
198

cold instrument, unresponding; ignorant because too innocent. Oh I'll learn won't I? Give me a few months and I'll learn this language, this music; how to answer; and joke; to bring him delight. Oh I must. I'm embarrassed. His naked body, hairy, on mine. Panting and gasping. I'm still. What has this to do with me.

This happens at night. The days are my own, when he's out on business. The days bring me duties, my power in the house to order and chastise servants, to choose dinners, to sort through my wardrobe and then select colours and stuffs for new gowns and dresses. I'm happy. Then at last the days join up with the nights, and I'm happy at night too.

After the first stillbirth I sit in the bow window in the little room upstairs, watching the birds in the garden. I wish I were a ship with three great white sails turning her prow towards unknown lands to garner a harvest of spices. I wish I could sail away and never come back.

There are no more surprises in wait. One day I will eat baked fish or stewed mutton for dinner. Another I will wear the new green satin waistcoat my husband has had made for me. Another I will touch the bricks of the passageway outside the house and wonder who touched them before me.

I don't mind this as much as I once thought I should. If only I could conceive another child, and carry it through to full term. I try not to think about it too much.

I don't like the moonlight streaming in from far across the river to fall on my bed. I close the curtains tight. The moon plays a high thin eerie music, a silver music, like a flute, and my heels lift despite themselves, my feet arch and begin to dance. I hold on to the pillow lest I'm swept across the floor by the music. I jab an elbow in my husband's ribs to wake him up, and then I dance with him. Both of us are blind in the darkness, our breaths twisting together, struggle of knees on the soft mattress. Like two rats in a cellar after our squabbles of the morning. He never takes so much pleasure in me as after I've fought with him, disobeyed him. He subdues me here in my bed, in the sweetest way. Sometimes I hate him, because he has learned how to speak to me in moon-music, in flute-language, and I can't hide from him anywhere. We understand each other too well.

*

Meg summons a polite voice.

– Poor madam. Well, we've all got our way to make in this hard world.

– Meg, Mrs Allen complains: you don't understand what I suffer.

Meg picks up the scissors to cut a fresh length of darning thread.

– No madam, she agrees: for I am not wed, and not likely to be, either. What man would take me?

She sends her wages home to the country. Bread for her brothers and sisters. This month she has kept some back, persuading herself the children will not go hungry. Scarlet ribbons to brighten her drab Sundays, to let her pretend she has a fresh petticoat. New woollen stockings. She looks with disgust at the fine silk one she is darning for her mistress. At night she hears the children crying, wails that scavenge in her heart like rats. Or she dreams of their wizened bodies strung up in the butcher's by red cords. Perhaps she will ask for a holiday. To go and see them. Her hands slacken in her lap as she considers what to do. Try Mr Allen first?

– So you see, Meg, Mrs Allen drones on: you should not speak that way of the most holy estate to which women are called. My father read to us, every night, Dr Benson's *Homily on Matrimony*. Thus I learned a wife's duties. Submission. Cheerful patience.

Her hands are fat and white as they grope for another sweet. Meg's hands fumble for the scissors. She holds up a stocking almost severed at the ankle. Oh.

She carries the bowl of slops down the back stairs, so busy fuming she doesn't see the bulky shadow looming ahead.

Her foot's on the bottom stair. The shadow comes away from the wall and embraces her, tongue pushed into her mouth, one arm about her waist, a shadow that giggles, and whispers what a fine girl she is. Not unpleasant. No one's ever praised her. And he smells warm and good. Then his hand bundles up her skirts and she panics.

She acts before she thinks. Raising the slop bowl held in her free hand. He's cursing and slipping in the wet mess in the dark while she's round the corner and safe, into the kitchen.

– You're better staying up there with the mistress, at this

time of the month, Alice comments: where you can keep out of his way.

She's stooping to blow up the kitchen fire with the bellows. Her face is shiny and red, and her hair dank with sweat. She smells of it, too. Old sweat. A month of unwashing.

– Hand up your petticoats as soon as look at you. Of course the mistress knows. She sent Jenny packing, didn't she? He laughs at her. Tells her she's imagining it. So you be careful. If they turn you off you won't find another place.

– Mr *Allen*, Meg marvels: but he's so old. Who'd fancy him?

In the dark, I might. Where he cannot see me either.

– Not too old to do as he likes in his own house, comes the surly reply: so don't say I didn't warn you.

Meg considers Alice's straining back and arms, and goes forward.

– Here. Let me do that.

Alice looks up, pleased.

– Thanks.

She watches Meg pump energetically, and the red flame start up amongst the wood and coals. Then she seizes a floor cloth and goes out to clear up the mess in the hall.

Meg is well scolded by Mrs Allen for her carelessness. Then the matter's dropped. Mr Allen burns a suit of old clothes in the back yard.

Six months pass. Meg deals with her mistress's moods and whims, coaxes her out on short walks to go shopping. She learns the beauty of the city, slowly revealed to her: the river slipping past in silver flashes at the bottom of a narrow street between tall buildings, the clean stone of the spires of new churches tugging upwards like kites, the tide of bodies flowing through alleys and courts, declaring their shape. She likes being a stranger, carried forward in ignorance of all the people pressing up against her and passing her. She likes the quick ring of money tilted onto counters, and the heaviness of the purse she carries for her mistress. Money stacked up to make chimneys, spread out to shingle a roof, whirling down as rain to pock the mud under her feet.

The ruts freeze to ice. Winds jerk at the kitchen window. Meg and Alice toast bread and nuts at the fire, skirts kilted up to let the heat mottle their thighs. They gossip, and tell fortunes. Mr Allen's friends sit with him, snug in the parlour upstairs, playing cards over their mulled wine, laughing. Mrs Allen sulks prettily in her room. Some nights Mr Allen sits alone, writing his diary, and shouts for Meg to bring fresh coals. Then he'll give her a kiss, a pinch or two.

When Meg catches a bad chill and falls sick, Alice accompanies their mistress to church that Sunday, wearing a big clean collar, carrying Mrs Allen's fan and gloves. Meg tosses on her little truckle-bed in the cupboard-room opening off the kitchen she shares with Alice, and hears Mr Allen's heels tapping down the stairs.

– I'm your friend, Meg. Let me be your friend. Be a good girl.

One hand over her mouth so that she can scarcely breathe, the other ripping back the blankets, hoisting her shift up over her shivering knees. Legs trembling with fever. Head boiling. Arms too weak to push him off. So she submits. He's her master, isn't he? She does not struggle. She stares at him. Yes. I need a friend. When he's finished his business and is climbing off her, she spits in his face. You should not have looked at me. I am too ugly. He slaps her lightly and goes away.

Meg's big belly is the worst insult she can offer her mistress. She understands that. Mrs Allen's outcry, followed by hysteria and fainting, doesn't surprise her.

No point in trying to defend herself. She has seduced her master, and must quit his house. The night before she is due to leave, she crouches in the dark passageway outside the privy, listening to Mr Allen grunt and strain inside. When he comes out, she springs at his throat. She flies at him with the bread knife. Their dance is silent, intimate, arms round each other, tangle of hands and feet. Then Mr Allen finds his voice. Hoarse screams. Lights along the passageway and down the stairs. Alice tearing them apart, her hands gleaming with dark red blood. Meg falls to the ground, her strength spent, and her master staggers away from her to the arms of his frantic wife, his bald head shiny with sweat, blood all over his shoulder. Alice hauls Meg to her feet, scrambles her into the kitchen. They stare for a moment. No word. No kiss. Alice shoves her out of the back door. Then Meg hears her raise her voice too in the general clamour. Murder goodbye help mercy goodbye.

It's raining. Meg lumbers along back ways in the darkness, rough breaths coming and going, enough sense left to her to know that she must keep in the shadows, and keep going. She makes for Mrs Penn's. Refuge, from which, surely, she'll not be turned away.

Standing, panting and swaying, in front of the house where her aunt works, seeing the closed shutters with no chink of light showing, she loses the courage to rouse up a house full of strangers. There's blood all down her bodice, and on her hands. She crawls into the tiny alley that opens, a black cavity, beside the house, sinks down on a heap of stinking rubbish. She must rest. In the morning she'll discover what to do.

She gives birth there, under the grey sheet of the dawn sky. The baby comes out easily, her exhausted body relaxed into the pains, no fight left in her. She dandles the baby, puny body smeared with her shit, her blood. She looks at the mewing face, and reaches out her hands. She strangles it; swiftly; cleanly. So that she won't be able to feel any more. She wrings her daughter's neck, just like a chicken's, and the head flops back on its broken stalk. Now she has cut herself off from all help. She buries the body in the rubbish, hauls herself to her feet, gasping. She dare not try Mrs Penn. She drags herself further on down the alley, deeper into the waking city where she has no home, to find a hiding place.

Mr Allen writes his account of this in the diary he will never let me read despite all my persuasions. He likes to talk of it; to tantalize me. He has some leisure for writing whereas I must make a living by my pen. I wonder what he has written of Meg. Not the truth, I daresay. I kissed her too, whenever I got the chance. I knew she liked me. Perhaps she would have let me have her. Probably glad to, poor wretch. But Allen got there first. I took care not to let him know that I made as free with his servant as he. And my story of Meg will see the light of day. Not his. I'll watch his face as he reads. And that of his dear wife. I'll change the names, but they will know. Nor will they dare admit it.

Mr Allen and I, together, compose the advertisement stating

his loss. I carry it myself to the *Postman* office, and thence to the printer's.

Gone away. And her mouth a little awry.

A servant girl turns her in. Found fainting behind a bale of silk in a warehouse off Cheapside.

She was hanged yesterday at Tyburn for infanticide, and is already immortalized in broadsheet ballads hawked about for a penny each. One of the oldest and commonest stories told along these streets. I'll write her life. In my hands her poor body will live again.

30   The Forsaken Sibyl's favourite place is the little flat roof, or deck, at the very top of the Ark. Here she has conjured a garden into existence: both enclosure and wilderness.

A garden compensates for loss of the countryside, not just here on the Ark, but in her life. When she is a child, her adoptive parents' back garden suffices. The inch-high doll enters the crack in the low mossy wall surrounding the lawn, moves through the towering grass, spreads her tiny fingers over the apple tree's bark, stares at the veined green hairy moons of gooseberries. Her eyes level with the earth, she peers up at the underneath of blackcurrant leaves, the strings of the net spread to keep the birds off. There are no fences around her mind; the garden is big enough to roam in for a whole afternoon without exhausting its routes. Yellow flare of peppery nasturtiums, close-packed orange dazzle of marigolds, dry crumbs of soil big as boulders springing with blue forget-me-nots.

When she's older, she likes to walk by herself out into the countryside. Ten minutes by bicycle from the university town, and she's out in a landscape of gentle hills set with woods and farms, the river winding below. Leaving the bike in a ditch, she climbs the lane white in sunshine, springs over a stile, and falls into an enormous meadow, stretching away to the horizon and tipping over it, thick with buttercups. Glossy flowers high to her knees, knocking gold pollen against her as she wades through them, the sun hot on her face, warm breeze flowing over her. She lies down in the very middle of the meadow, a grassy hump at her back, rasp of crickets, hum of bees. Her book is on her lap, but she doesn't want to study. She drowns in yellow, listens intently to the sounds of the afternoon, dissolves into it. That is joy: to be completely alone under the sky, to let go of everything, not to think, not to dream, just to be there. A part of it. Essential for this is the fact that no one is watching her.

So much chatter of birds and insects that she doesn't hear him approach. She feels him standing over her, and looks up. Middle-aged man in a grey raincoat, flies open, penis dangling.

– Please go away, she tells him.

But he's in the mood for chat, for company. So it's she who leaves, angry but also scared, all her mother's warnings ringing in her head.

Since the countryside seems to be peopled with lonely men needing girls to talk to every time she goes out for a walk by herself, she gives up her solitary adventures. She's really in prison now. The warders peer at her from behind hedges and trees. She goes walking with friends, but it's not the same, because they always want to talk. Of course she likes talking to her friends, but. Lucky Emily with the wild moors just outside her house, free to walk them alone, to lie face-down on a rock and dream for hours without fear of interruption or assault. Lucky Simone, tramping the hills of Provence, all by herself, free to think her own thoughts and boldly impervious to danger. She is a coward, lacks their courage. She reads too many newspaper reports about what happens to girls walking home by themselves.

Her circular garden on the Ark has no entrance, so that no voyeur can enter it. She sits on the close-cropped turf that she has sown with thyme and camomile and presses her bare soles against the springy stems to release the strong scent. A privet hedge surrounds her, set with arched pergolas thick with climbing roses, and in front of it the flowerbeds, a forest of delphiniums, cornflowers, irises, lupins.

Her London squat, from which she is soon to be evicted, has a garden. She's kept it wild and tangled, the way she likes it, clearing back the tall grass and weeds just enough to make a cave to sit in on long summer evenings, blue dusk above her, the pink brick wall at one side, reggae and pop drifting across the neighbours' open windows. She will obey the council's summons and move out. The house is due to be renovated and turned into flats, and she understands only too well the rage and anxiety of local families waiting to be rehoused. She won't take what is theirs. She herself is not on the council waiting list, because the council does not house single people. She can't afford private rents. The housing associations have closed their lists, as have the housing coops. She'll join the drifting desperate mass of the homeless. Stupid and foolish to want to live on her own. In the past she has stayed with friends, in spare rooms, on sofas; or she has lived with others in shared houses and flats. She has no choice. That's what she'll have to go back to, just as she'll have to go back to a proper job. But she can't stop wanting her own kitchen, her own room, her own bathroom, spaces in which she can't be disturbed, in which she can practise her own secret rites.

She supposes she is mad. That's what her friends would certainly call her, if they knew what she sometimes does when she's alone. If she begins to publish what she writes, then the whole world will know she is mad too.

Very often, when she's by herself and safely invisible, she gets the urge to fall on her knees and pray. To something both inside her and outside her. The summons comes abruptly, and she lets herself obey, falling down, joining her hands together, feeling flooded with sweetness and pleasure, wanting to cry out in praise of whatever it is that suddenly opens her, inside her, and calls. In the middle of the city, the street and traffic noises bruising the window, the race of work and shopping and money-making going on just outside, she surrenders, is surrounded, opens her mouth wide and gulps in, and then a landscape of open hills, sun and cloud moving over them, enters her, and brings her joy.

Of course she tells no one. Her friends would edge away, if she admitted to having religious experiences and desires. With her friends she discusses sex, death, relationships, money, the unconscious, art, politics, books. The only taboo subject is spirituality. To be interested in this is to be priggish, neurotic, repressed and reactionary. She's done her fair share of sneering at Christians, who eat their God's flesh and drink his blood, who tend to be so depressingly unsensual and dowdy even when they try hard to be trendy with guitars in church and updated prayers and images. For her atheistical ex-Protestant friends religion means Christianity and backwardness. Other religions, foreign exotic ones, are on the other hand sympathetically respected, as being part of Third World cultures oppressed by imperialism. What hypocrites, what snobs we are, she thinks: to patronize in others what we deny in ourselves. Yet she doesn't want to be a British pagan and worship some sentimental icon of a lost Mother Goddess, she doesn't want to wear robes and sandals and be a Druid or moon about in the Celtic twilight or search for Pan, she doesn't want to be a fanatical embarrassing bore. So she keeps quiet. She wears the savage satirical costume of her peer group and generation, she goes dancing as often as she can afford it, she has her love affairs, she hopes she looks normal. The experiences keep happening, and she lets them. Deep down, she trusts them, because they bring her joy, because they allow her to let go of herself and to get lost.

Homeless, she fears being nowhere, having nowhere to go. Homeless, she starts to understand the true condition of physical existence: we are all part of one another and part of the universe. How banal that looks, written down. She ought to invent a specialist language, like the mystics did, the ones she studied at university, trying to set down their truth as precisely and scientifically as possible; rigorous systems of understanding; no despising of logical language. Concepts. Heat, sweetness, and light. To be understood by the *rational* mind.

The self can become lost, can be safely homeless. Writing is like meditation: you focus, concentrate on the breath going in and out of the body, accept the stream of images passing through. You record them, then play and pare. Not only must you let yourself be a conduit for that flow of images moving from outside to inside and then out again, crystalline and dancing; you must translate it, anchor it in your own bodily existence in society and history, bring all of yourself to bear on it as you search for metaphors.

She laughs, and tears at her hair. This is all very well, but hadn't she better get down to some writing? Enclosed in the perfect O of her garden, no exit or entrance, she is a stone, a blade of grass, a flower, a tree. It is also true that she is human, and can speak, can tell her difference from stone, grass, flower, tree. On one level she is them, knows their inaudible speech; on another, she must struggle to create her own, name herself as

208

human, find out what the hell that means. Find the way out. Find speech.

She opens her mouth.

This is the truth of it. Want.

She wants to flow out and touch that world outside herself, that m/other; surround it, merge with it. She wants to take it all into her mouth open to the air sucking biting chewing swallowing. Because she is starving. All mouth. Nothing but this wide open mouth. She is greedy, too: she'll never have enough, wants to eat the whole world, everything in sight.

The pleasure of it, on her tongue, as she eats: mother meadow mountain. That's the good moment, those few seconds of delicious taste, the juices running; before she swallows, loves the world to death, and it disappears inside her, gobbled up, inside her the corpses of beloved dead mothers bloody and chewed. Then she's all alone again, still wanting, still wanting to eat. Her mouth closes on air, on nothing. Still hungry. Unsatisfied. Desperate. Too powerful. Too destructive. If the thing she loves would only *stay*, and not vanish. If the moment of tasting it would not slip away.

She wants to disappear. She wants to let go of this greedy mouth, to flow out of her body and become part of the other, the meadow, the mountain. Will she ever come back if she lets that happen? How will she find her way back again, into the body/self that is necessary most of the time for living in this world?

She needs an umbilical cord, joining the anchored body of flesh to that other imaginary one that flows out and becomes part of what she loves. Don't cut it. Or she'll never be able to come back.

Out of this chaos inside, make a pattern. Out of the timeless perfect whole of the internal world, pluck two or three symbols at a time. Let yourself make a mess, make mistakes, fail. Laugh at yourself. Fall from paradise, from the enclosed garden, and write words. She scrabbles with her hands at the green hedge. Making a gap.

31 When I was at university I was happiest in libraries. I sit in the Bodleian, the pages of books raining through me. Books are food: I open my mouth and am filled and snort like a baby. Reading is joy felt in the body. I feast at a banquet, can feed uninterruptedly, pleasure flowing through me in wave after wave as I'm caught up out of myself into the company of poets, philosophers, mystics. I walk with them, and am one of them, and learn from them.

I remember a male student shouting at me in the courtyard: you cold virgin sitting cooped up in the library reading medieval love songs, how can you understand them when you know nothing of sex?

I join the Society of Bibliophiles. The other members are all men, booksellers and dons. Much older than I. On Sundays we take small local trains into the heart of the Cotswolds and visit shabby old homes housing famous private collections. The teas are always good: thin sandwiches filled with savoury relishes, scones and cream, walnut cake. My companions wear black overcoats rusty and greening with age, treat me with cautious courtesy, suspicious attention, unbend when they realize my passion for typefaces and paper, every aspect of printing. I learn to speak the language of my love: sheer poetry of new words precisely articulated with one another. I speak to these men, shyly, the dialect and code of books, and they let me in. It does not matter that I wear a pink mini-dress and parrot-coloured high heels: my devotion is my habit, like that of a nun in the world wearing a tiny cross on her lapel.

Here in my Arkive on the Ark, mind and body are not split.

*

—I don't *want* a child, Noah says: and there's an end to it. D'you hear me? *I don't want a child.*

I consult the riddle book.

So why does *to conceive* also mean *to conceive*?

32 I go ashore by myself. The island is all lit up, golden sparks in winter darkness. The narrow streets of dirty grey and yellow *palazzi* are choked with exhaust fumes and dogshit, webbed with gold strings, huge single crystals strung above my head on gold laces. As I look down the street, the delicate gold snowflakes stack themselves into a forest of frost; marks of the way through. The air is hoarse, dark as chocolate, smelling of petrol and cinnamon, slivers of silver shaved off it by the rasp, rasp of a plane in a carpentry workshop, door propped open. Corset shops. Wheelchair shops. Gold windows jiggle in the river. A scull, passing under the arch of the bridge, pulls a peacock tail of coloured lights.

In the early morning, the air is still clean. The winter sun falls on conical piles of yellow apples in the market, on heaps of walnuts, brazil nuts, almonds, chestnuts, dried dates and figs. Smart women in fur coats carry bouquets of artichokes and broccoli, poke at russet pears and scraped yellow potatoes, run their fingers through green peppercorns and black ones, weigh pods of carob, sausages on a string, bunches of violet onions. A warehouse, its metal front rolled up, is dense with the fires of red chillis hung from the rafters.

Smoke from the glowing embers heaped in dustbins, burning to keep the stall-holders warm. It's Christmas Eve. I want to buy a spruce tree, and shining glass balls to decorate it with, I want to buy wreaths of mistletoe and holly, and pots of scarlet flowers, and candles, and silver tinsel. I want my own children around me.

Absence of stars. Absence of joy at this midwinter festival. A dark place inside me: empty; cold ashes in the grate.

212

Plastic carrier bag heavy with grapes and oranges in one hand, I wander into a church in a side street in order to inspect its *presepio* and sit down for a rest. Crib-crawling is one of my favourite occupations at this season: every church has one, tries to out-rival its neighbours. Toys for adults, not just children, to enjoy.

The crib here dominates the whole of a side chapel. Framed by lofty serge curtains of deep blue, it presents a country landscape. Far above it and behind it the night sky, mistily blue, is pierced by stars that twinkle on and off. Regularly, every few seconds, a luminous angel with outspread wings moves across it in a steady arc, gently pulling a banner of light like the tail of a meteor. It disappears, reappears, disappears again, always on the same track. An invisible choir croons that it's dreaming of a white Christmas. On the rocky ground of crumpled brown paper in the foreground, underneath that vast blue dome of sky, innumerable peasants go about their business: small wooden models of men, women and children fish in streams of real water, boil pots over fires emitting real smoke and flames, hew wood, cart it home on their backs. Sheep, donkeys and cows are graded in neat rows according to size. Tucked away, very much on the sidelines of all these important activities, Mary and Joseph admire their new baby. He's a big boy, with fat knees, curly black hair, and a real silk nappy. I put a two hundred-lire piece in the slot below the crib. And then the sleeping baby opens his waxen eyelids, bats his long curly eyelashes at me, and jerkily lifts his wax arm up and down to bless me. Until the money runs out.

Noah's present to me is disappointment; bitter and deep, curdling my love for him, souring it to resentment, anger. I want him to want a baby too, and he doesn't: too much responsibility, too much curtailment of his freedom to roam the world. He doesn't want to be tied down by a child's needs for regular school attendance, a stable home life in one place, friends and family around. He wants to remain the child, not to become its father.

I could steal a baby from him: make love without contraception and without telling him, and so get pregnant. He never knows when I'm ovulating or when my period's due. So far I haven't done it, feeling it's wrong, that I must wait,

213

persuade him. Getting pregnant that way would be disastrous, as he has warned me: he'd be outraged, would cease to trust me, would give me scant support during the pregnancy and the birth, wouldn't help me bring up the child.

When he comes inside me, I think he is impregnating me with sterilizing fluid, or with an abortifacient. No longer that good sweet milk of his that once filled me with delight, but death. That's the way I see it now.

How long does he think I'll wait? Time's running out for me if not for him.

I could get pregnant by him and then leave him. Or leave him and get pregnant by another man. Or have A.I.D. Bring up the child by myself. Oh you selfish irresponsible girl cry all the agony aunties: deliberately to become a single mother and not give your child a father and the chance of a normal life.

Far worse: my fantasy about stealing another woman's baby. A dear friend dies, and so I adopt her baby. I kill my friend, and steal her baby. This fantasy recurs, though I try to kill it.

I'll be a single mother if I have to. Lots of women are. By necessity, when their men abandon them. Or by choice.

The Virgin Mary was a single mother. Here she is in this church, in the big oil painting hanging on the wall of the side chapel opposite the crib.

I watch the women on the canvas: the one with wings, and the one who sits under a dark green tent, eyes lowered, reading her book. The fold of a knee, the flow of a thigh; the angel insisting, making her point with a raised hand, adamant gesture of long index finger; she's thin as a boy, with a curled wig and a tasselled cloak.

The girl opposite her grips her book, and imagines. She is reading the story of the Boat. Meditating on words, her half-shut eyes cast down, seeing nothing but the black marks on the white page, she conceives other words; new words. She creates the Word inside herself, by herself, using her *own* power.

The angel with rainbow wings represents her inspiration: the words of the other/the book, that she hears in conversation/ in reading; and takes inside. Then the alchemy: new words made out of old; new words she will offer others in her turn.

Who is she, this virgin? She who broods under her green

214

tabernacle, her dark imagination?

She is the proud hunter-goddess who walks the mountains with her companions. She has many lovers but belongs to no man. She scorns marriage, preferring freedom. She is the one who turns away her face. She is the virgin; which means the whore. She is the Ark, the maker of the Word. *She is the author.* Meditating on the Old Testament, then discarding it, she will write a new text, with herself as the subject that speaks.

This is the meaning that pushes me out of the church.

33 For supper the Deftly Sibyl has made a dish of green ribbon noodles with *pesto* sauce. Afterwards comes a tomato salad served with a big piece of Pecorino cheese, and then the fruit I brought back on board with me.

– My days of discreet starvation, I tell the others: are over. For two years, when I was living on social security while I finished my librarianship thesis, I survived on brown bread, carrots, apples, and cheap coffee. I paid my rent and bills; just. When friends came, I fed them well, then starved for the rest of the week. I was lucky: my friends could afford to lend me my rent money when things were tight, to cook me supper sometimes, to take me out to a restaurant occasionally. My friends helped me survive. Other people, commenting on how thin I was, assumed I was dieting. I knew that this period would end; my middle-class education would help me find a job when I needed one again. Single mothers I knew were permanently hungry; they fed the children first. When my giro arrived every fortnight, I transformed it instantly into my favourite food, feasted for three days, then went back to brown bread and carrots. Feckless, unable to budget, people like me were called in magazine articles. A rich person can't know that pleasure: the plate heaped high on Monday after the scanty weekend, the delight in forgotten tastes, greediness permitted to jump out and enjoy. Full larders amazed me. When I went out to supper I ate more than I wanted, storing fat against a lean tomorrow. Now I've got a job and an income, I no longer need to gobble: the food will be there again next day. I still gobble books. Hunger that never goes away. My body is sturdy, well rounded. My desire is keen and lean, a paperknife cutting through pages, slicing up the text, the book falling apart like a cut loaf. Holy

216

communion once a day was never enough. My husband feeds me well. He likes to see me eat. He courted me by cooking me supper every night for six months. *Yes*, I cried: *yes*, I'll have you. He licks me and whispers: I could eat you all up. I laugh: go ahead.

– I want to be ordinary, the Deftly Sibyl says: I want to be normal. Like other women. I believed that marriage brought me the possibility of coping with a reality shared by countless other women across the world, of sticking to a commitment, of engaging in the struggle to invent a morality I could honestly live by. Happiness: the capacity to accept reality. I did not want to be mad. I left her behind when I married, the mad girl of my early twenties. Yet she's been lying in wait in the cupboard all this time. When I'm alone, she jumps out, and gibbers. I should stay in the library, and read my book; I should control my body with contraceptive devices, not smoke, not drink too much, eat properly, get on with my writing. I don't like the story forcing itself out of my pen. I want to write a story in which the heroine does not have to leave the man she has married. She can find independence, autonomy, some freedom; by *staying*. So many women write of the necessity to *leave* men. I want to be different. For what is this freedom and self-actualization some women write about? The freedom to be selfish? To leave my children? How can it be combined with loving others and allowing their claims on me? When my friend phones to say she's sick and can I pick up her children from school, should I say: no, my time is for me? What would a man do? Would he be there to be telephoned? Are men more free? What for? To make money? Not to spend time with their children? To chase that ideal lover?

– I want to be the author of my own story, says the Forsaken Sibyl: and of my own life. I can't bear the thought of a life which finishes well before death, such as I perceive the life story of so many women to be. To be perhaps forty, or fifty, and to know: this is all. I want the power to make things go on happening. Becoming a writer protects me from happy ever after, from death before death is due, from the stopping of adventures. It's better for me not to be married, not to be tied to a lover, male or female it doesn't matter which. Yet if I become a narrator and tell a story, I'm talking about something that's over, something

217

that ends. I can't bear endings. I'll stick to the present tense. I want to be the author of my future: closed book I'll open and read, text I shall write myself.

– The dream of adultery, says the Babble-On Sibyl: the repeated desire to get away. Baby in Mum's lap, whimpering if Mum goes off, quickly finding a substitute. Is that it? I'm not sure. Certainly if you're the one playing Mum then you need to move sometimes. Often. Well, I am not pure. I have helped to make my own situation, to place myself as Mum, always available to Neil's needs. What will I have to break in order to change my situation? Will I break too?

– I'll tell you about the woman who goes away, the whore, says the Re-Vision Sibyl: it's simple as ABC. Like the ABC of Women I read about once, composed in the fifteenth century by St Antoninus as a meditation aid for his lady parishioners. Penitents. A is for Animal, B is for Beast, C is for Cupidity; and so on. Amazon, Bitch, Cunt, Devil, Fiend, Gossip, Harlot, Idiot, Jilt, Lesbian, Mollycoddler, Nymphomaniac, Nag, Pervert, Queer, Slag, Tart, Vixen, Witch. Feel free to fill in the blanks.

– You see men so crudely, cries the Gaffer: enemies to be kept at a distance, studs to be used for breeding purposes, children to be patronized. What about the men who love women yet are rejected by them? You don't care. That's *your* problem, you say scornfully. I could spend days on your picket line, helping in your crèche, servicing and protecting your peace camp, and you wouldn't bother to thank me. Haven't you lot got any men friends? Most women, normal women, would never agree with you. They like men. They don't have your problems.

– Guilty men are silent, says the Correct Sibyl: scared to say the wrong thing, scared of Big Feminist Momma beating them around the head with her stick of ideological purity. They're the worst. Holier than thou. I'd rather have you any day, Gaffer. At least you say what you think. I don't want to be any man's mother. Never again. I want men not to be scared of my power, to enjoy me, to leap at me, to play with me, talk to me, listen to me, read me, desire me ardently, notice when I'm in the mood for their company, leave me alone when I'm not. I would like men to enjoy being men: it would make life easier.

218

I like some men. Quite a lot of the time. I also like solitude, country walks, travelling, eating, drinking, reading novels at breakfast, digging the garden, all the usual things. But I have no desire to punish anybody. No, that's not always true. Let's say: no desire to act on that desire.

— I would like a story about food, the Re-Vision Sibyl says: and about punishment.

34   Already they are lost, and quarrelling.

– You're the driver, Francis accuses her: it was up to you to remember to bring the map.

– You're the navigator, Barbara snaps back: you should have thought of it.

She hunts in her bag for a cigarette, lights one, refusing to notice Francis's frown. He winds down the window, and the icy afternoon air strikes in. Barbara shivers. They are still below the snowline, but she is not adequately dressed for this weather. The cold enters her thin leather boots, her black lace stockings, her fine wool tunic, her leather jacket. She shivers again, and draws her paisley shawl around her neck. Even her hands are goose-pimpled. How disgusting.

She has pulled up on one side of the road which zigzags vertically up from the valley floor. The top of the mountain, which she can see when she cranes her neck, is a row of great jagged teeth. Thin waterfalls foam down it. The road below is a crumpled grey band, and red-roofed houses hang above them as though dangling from the sky.

– We must be on the right road, she says: that turning there can't be the right one.

The unsignposted track goes down to the left from the heart of the V of the next turn, just ahead. Crestino can't be down there. Where or how could it perch on those fluent masses of rock?

Francis runs a hand through his hair.

– You're probably right. Let's go on until we come to the next village and we can get directions.

– If we can understand them. So few people up here seem to speak English. They're so backward.

220

Barbara sighs, and stubs out her cigarette.

– Some New Year's Eve it's going to be if we can't even find our hotel. Wind up that window, can't you? I'm freezing.

She eases the car up into the next bend. They travel on in silence, climbing steeply up an interminable series of loops and bends. Twilight advances on them, the pale sun swallowed by blue mists, the edges of overhanging rock blurred by shadow. It is much colder now, and the road is glazed by ice. Snow films the crags ahead, marking their hollows, and crisps of white drift past the windscreen.

– The chains for the wheels, Francis exclaims: we didn't hire any when we got the car.

– I didn't think we'd need them, Barbara defends herself: they should have told us.

Sweat starts up in her armpits, dampening her silk camisole, probably ruining it. On the next bend, the car slithers a little. It is not dangerous yet, Barbara tells herself. She holds her breath. Concentrates.

– Careful, Francis warns her: go slower.

– Shut up! Barbara yells at him.

They emerge from their twisting ascent onto a narrow plateau, where the road, though glimmering with black ice, is mercifully flat. On their left, the mountain sheers on up, clothed in dark pinewoods, and on their right is a wide meadow edged by small pines and scrub. Tufts of grass poke up through patches of frozen snow. The meadow ends abruptly, tipping over the invisible abyss of the valley they have just climbed out of. Far beyond it, on the other side of the drop, blue mountains rear their sharp profiles like the heads of old women flung back, ready to bite, chins and noses in clear outline against the grey sky. What was that book she read recently, about a plane crash in the Alps? The survivors, lost in the vast snowslopes, huddled together under the grim needle tips of uncaring rocks, began eating their dead comrades in order to stay alive. Corpses laid out in the snow, slivers of flesh shaved off them and dried in the sun. Then the meal.

– Look, Francis exclaims: a house.

The end of the plateau widens out. On their left, between the mountain and the road, a small hill, round as a pudding, lifts itself, snow sifted onto it like sugar. A paved track, edged by low stone walls, curls around it and away between tiny sloping meadows scattered with snow. The bare black branches of little thorny trees are clear as liquorice against the white and brown earth, the blue air. The house squats at the base of the hill, square and two-storeyed, a row of round windows under its sloping roof. Two stone columns, topped with leafy capitals, frame the door, and wooden shutters, painted dull yellow, are folded back. The small garden is adjoined by a pocket-handkerchief orchard, wizened apple and pear trees splayed and bent by years of wind. On the other side, a vegetable plot, sheeted by ice as clear as glass, encloses whorled turquoise cabbages, fat plaits of leeks toppling across each other, the spikes of onions.

– It's like the gingerbread house in the fairy tale, Barbara says, laughing: it's so pretty.

Looking, she can taste the earth, the cold air, the vegetables under their lid of ice. She wants to eat the little house, its cream-coloured stone, its raspberry wooden window frames, its plum-raftered roof. Her fingers itch for her notebook and camera. Later, she tells herself: first things first.

– Let's knock, she decides: and ask our way.

Even before they are out of the car, lights spring out in the house, each window an oblong of warm gold. The front door of the house opens wide, displaying the sturdy black silhouette of a woman who stands still, one hand on the latch, steadily watching them.

– There's the witch, Francis says.

– Of course you must stay here tonight, Angelina insists: we can ring your hotel. I have plenty of room. And you are too tired and cold to go any further.

– That would be wonderful, Barbara says: this is such a lovely house.

Her eyes travel round the room again, checking. The walls and ceiling are panelled in silvery pine, worn smooth by the passing of three centuries. A green-tiled stove bulges in one corner. The gleaming dark planks of the floor are scattered with woven rugs in faded primary colours, and the walls are hung with eighteenth- and nineteenth-century examples of folk art: heavily varnished and cracked holy pictures of saints

222

done on wood, scenes of country life in naïve oils, all surrounded by ornate frames of gilt and shells and tin lace.

– This house belonged to my grandparents, Angelina explains: nothing has changed since their day.

She gestures at the muslin and lace curtains hung at the two tiny square windows, the wooden benches, the porcelain jugs and bowls arranged on the shelf above the stove.

She sighs.

– Often I think of selling this house. It's too big for me now. Too much work, after my husband died so long ago.

– I'm sorry, Barbara says.

It's awkward having to converse in broken French, their only common language. Things come out clumsily, over-simply, the wrong way round. Barbara tries to work out the sentence in her head before she speaks.

– My fiancé is an antique dealer. Please. If you want to sell anything, perhaps he can help you?

Francis kicks her ankle. But Angelina does not seem upset. She sits back in her wooden chair, her palms on her thighs, smiling.

– This house has such integrity, Barbara hurries on: it's so unified, so complete.

– I am glad to have visitors who appreciate my home, Angelina answers: I shall open some wine, and we shall drink a toast to our new friendship, and then I shall cook dinner.

Barbara follows her into the kitchen. Its smoke-blackened walls are hung with copper moulds, racks of antique cooking implements, iron pots and pans. The stone fireplace is set with meat-jacks and fire dogs, a wicker basket of logs. A shallow stone sink in one corner is piled with pottery dishes. Pine shelves are stacked with earthenware jars and china. The table is spread with a red and white checked cloth.

– It's perfect! Barbara exclaims: marvellous!

Angelina smiles politely, picking up an unlabelled green bottle from the table and wiping it with a corner of her striped apron.

– I write about cookery, Barbara explains: for a magazine in London. A monthly supplement about life styles, with lots of colour pictures. I've come to Italy to do a series on Italian regional cooking. Italian food has become very important to us.

This kitchen is so right, so authentic. I wonder, would you mind, could I take some photographs?

– Please! Angelina says: I would be so happy.

She puts thin-stemmed wine glasses on a tray together with the bottle of wine, half a salami, a brick of pale butter, some white rolls, and picks it up with her strong hands.

– If you are interested in cooking, she says, nodding to Barbara to open the door: you must learn some of my recipes.

The salami is fresh and delicious, containing no artificial flavouring or preservative. Hard to import into England, Barbara thinks regretfully, as the *exquisite tastes of pork and pepper and garlic* burst inside her mouth. But at least she will be able to describe it in an article, give her readers a hint of the flavour of the real thing, make them salivate with longing for her recipes.

– Leave your cases downstairs, yes? Angelica suggests: let us have dinner first, and then I will show you your room. There is a little place to wash next to the kitchen. Barbara, perhaps you will like to help me? Francis, we leave you here with the wine, to do as the men do.

Dinner is served in white china dishes hand-painted with flowers and gold flecks. Francis has insisted on laying the table, despite Angelina's protests that it is not a male job. He strokes the scorched-linen tablecloth, the black-handled knives, the wrought-iron candlesticks, the silver spoons thin and sharp with age.

They eat *home-made pastry cushions stuffed with cream and spinach and nutmeg and then fried in olive oil until they puff and swell and are removed from the frying-pan to a cloth-covered basket*. Barbara has watched this operation and taken careful notes. The heel of Angelina's strong hand smiting the ball of dough, stretching it away from her across the scrubbed table top. Angelina's big fingers handling the rolled-out dough lightly, so lightly, cutting it into paper-thin diamonds with her long knife.

After this a *bollito of beef, chicken and tongue. Another simple and delicious dish, and one not sufficiently appreciated by visitors to Italy. Perhaps not even by Italians themselves. The*

224

rich stock is ideal as the basis of a risotto the following day, and can be kept for several days in the fridge.

– How did you happen to have all this food in the house? Barbara asks: it's as though you expected us.

– Aha, Angelina smiles: I like to eat well, that is all. A woman on my own, I like to take care of myself and cook myself nice things.

– I worry about putting on weight, Barbara says: I have to, in my job. I have to look good. But tonight I'm going to forget all about my diet!

After the bollito, a salad of fresh green leaves tossed with olive oil and flavoured with *rugeta, a bittersweet herb unfortunately unobtainable in England. Its strange taste of walnut and egg adds the final authentic touch. No mustard in the dressing. A drop of lemon juice may be added if wished.*

Finally, *a chocolate cake, cold, with rum in it (recipe on next page). No cream. The plainness of the bitter dark chocolate, the smoky rum, is quite enough. Inelegant to overdo it.*

All through the meal flow the wines Angelina insists they must taste: red wine *earthy and strong and heavy with tannin; white wine delicate and golden, with a dry sparkle, a hint of petillance.*

Black coffee, served in thimbles of white porcelain. No saucers. That is the traditional way.

– Why don't you stay with me tomorrow night too? Angelina suggests: and celebrate New Year's Eve here? I can phone your hotel for you again. There will be no trouble, I am sure.

Francis and Barbara exchange glances.

– Thank you, Barbara says: we'd love to.

– It's unbelievable, Francis declares: we've struck gold.

He and Barbara are sitting up in the high wooden bed in the guest room upstairs, propped by square white pillows whose cases are edged with drawn-thread work and bands of delicate lace. The linen sheets are similarly decorated. The coverlet of the bed, which they have folded carefully back, is made of rubbed purple velvet threaded with stiff gold, and the quilt beneath is of padded pink cotton stitched with a pattern of scrolls. The panelled headboard of the bed, stretching up almost to the ceiling, is made of the silvery pine they have seen downstairs. One of the panels opens, to reveal a rosary of amethyst beads and a prayer book with gilt clasps. Francis, who has been examining the rosary as he speaks, twists round and replaces it in its tiny hiding place.

Barbara stretches and yawns.

– She can certainly cook. Her recipes will keep me going for three issues at least.

She pinches her waist.

– I'm getting so *fat*.

– Look at the pictures up here, Francis says: you can't find stuff like that any more. It'd go for a fortune.

The pictures up here are masterpieces of the intricate crafts worked by women in their homes in the eighteenth and nineteenth centuries. Framed in velvet and mother-of-pearl and beaten silvered tin, they are done in cut paper, in marquetry, in embroidered stump-work, in appliqué. Over and over again the Good Shepherd summons his flock, the Virgin holds out a stubby baby, the Son dangles from his cross.

– You'd better go carefully, Barbara warns him: don't rush it. If we want to walk away with some of Angelina's goodies we'll have to plan carefully. She's a grasping old bitch, I can tell. These peasants always are.

– I'm depending on you, Francis says, snuggling up to her: you're the interpreter.

– She's so *gross*, Barbara shudders: did you look at her neck? She's built like an ox.

She spreads her limbs out in the bed, one arm around Francis, her mind busy manipulating and discarding phrases and words. *Peasant aristocrats, sacrament of eating, ancient life of the forest, fossil shapes reflected in the forms of pasta.* She'll do better tomorrow, after talking to Angelina a little more.

– Time for a little fun and games before sleeping? says Francis, pressing closer: what d'you say?

– It's too late, surely, protests Barbara: aren't you too tired?

– I'm never too tired, he says, getting out of bed and going over to her suitcase: and besides, I want to make it up to you for being so horrid and unhelpful on the journey up here. Hmmm?

He turns round, brandishing the whip.

226   *

For breakfast they have big cups of ferocious black coffee tempered with frothy milk, fresh rolls with butter and home-made cherry jam. Barbara tries to punish her appetite, draws deeply on a cigarette. Fresh nicotine. How she loves that smell. How she loves its effect: swift laxative, voiding her of all that dangerous food. She looks around at the panelled walls of the little parlour. The polished wooden surfaces gleam back at her.

– It's like the Ark in here, she remarks in her bad French: you've rescued us and taken us on board, and the snow outside, it's like the sea.

Angelina, sitting opposite, inhales on her own cigarette, which she has rolled from coarse black tobacco taken from a tin. She holds the cigarette between thumb and forefinger. Her hands are revolting, Barbara decides: too broad, too red and coarse.

– You're a real earth-mother, she goes on: you remind me of my grandmother, you know?

She translates her comments for Francis's benefit.

– The animals went in two by two, Francis says in her ear: you've forgotten there's no Noah here.

Angelina smiles at them, visibly searches for French words.

– I just finish this cigarette, then we go for a walk. You will like to be in the snow.

Muffled in borrowed overcoats, their boots packed with layers of socks, they plod after their hostess. Up and up. The world has gone into negative: pale monochrome of peaks, the valley far below them scooped out of white blocks, speckled with the brown grains of houses. Pines bristle on the mountain's flank, each black branch lined exactly with white plush. They walk for an hour, in silence, their breath coming and going in hoarse gasps. They push up into steep woods, toecaps cutting steps in the blank ramp ahead. No path is visible. Only the walls of snow plot the curve of the vanished track. What were meadows are now full wedges of white.

The temptation is irresistible. Barbara runs heavily, floundering in whiteness, to the middle of a snowfield, lies down in it, waves her arms and legs carefully, in and out, in and out. When she gets up again, she has left behind the imprint of a creature

227

with a long triangular skirt and pointed wings.

— It's called a fallen angel, she tells her hostess, giggling: it's what we used to do as children, every time it snowed. It's a fallen angel, Angelina. It's like your name.

Angelina smacks her gloved hands against each other.

— It's very cold, isn't it? Perhaps it's time to go home.

The others wheel and follow her. Barbara is secretly relieved. She doesn't like walking much, and certainly not in this weather. It's much too cold. She bumps against Francis and takes his hand. Wet wool against wet wool.

They have seen no other walkers all morning. Now, the figures of three men, bulky in sweaters and padded jackets, red woollen caps on their heads, are climbing up towards them along the corridor of snow between the pine trees.

Francis drops Barbara's hand.

— Hang on a minute. I've got a lump of snow down my boot. Wait for me while I get it out.

He brushes the snow from a rock and sits down, begins to unlace his boot.

— We must hurry, Angelina announces: it will snow again very soon. Look at the sky.

She starts off again down the track, pauses, looks back.

— Barbara! Come with me, please. I need your arm. I am tired out with all this walking. I am too old.

Barbara grimaces at Francis and shrugs.

— She wants me to go on ahead with her. We'll go slowly. You catch us up. You're not going to be more than a minute.

Coming abreast with Angelina, she takes her arm. The older woman is breathing heavily, clearly in distress. She leans heavily on Barbara, who staggers a little under her weight. They set off together, Angelina maintaining a steady pace.

— I'm sorry, she pants: I just need to get home. To rest a little.

The three men meet them and pass them. Angelina turns her head away. No greeting is exchanged. Barbara, looking after them, is surprised to see them staring at her. I suppose it's because I'm a stranger, she thinks: they must know everybody around here. But the expression on the men's faces alarms her a little. Why this look of gloating contempt?

Angelina stumbles. Barbara rights her, then glances back

228

again. The three men, who have halted to watch Francis struggling with his boot, are marching away again, their backs broad and dark against the snow.

—I have a weak ankle, Angelina explains over a hearty lunch of *eggs fried with peppers and onions*: and it gets worse in the cold. I shouldn't walk on it too much. It is silly of me.

She will not let them help her wash up, shoos Francis out.

— No, she says to Barbara: let me do it. This is your holiday.

Clearly, she does not want to talk about whatever it was that upset her on the morning walk. Just as clearly, bustling about her domestic tasks is her way of soothing herself. Barbara settles herself more comfortably in her chair, watching Angelina pick up the greasy pan and begin to scour it under the tap.

— So then. Tell me what we're going to eat tonight.

Angelina ticks off the courses on her fingers. *Raw red beef carved into paper-thin slices, these delicious morsels then being salted and scattered with shavings of parmesan cheese*; next *a rich venison stew flavoured with red wine, cloves and celery*; then *a salad of curly red radicchio*; then *a dish of red lentils to symbolize good fortune in the coming year*; finally *pears cooked in red wine and served cold, with cream.*

— It's a very *red* meal, Barbara remarks.

— Quite so, says Angelina: that's how we do it here, for New Year's Eve. It's our tradition.

— What else do you do? Barbara asks: this is all so helpful for my article. I'll send you a copy, of course. I'd like you to see it, at least, even though you can't read English.

Angelina considers.

— On the stroke of midnight we open a bottle of Prosecco, that's our champagne, and sing a special song. Sometimes we yodel also. Then we all kiss one another and shake hands, and drink the wine. Always a white sparkling one, a dry one.

— Not a red one? Barbara teases her.

— No, Angelina replies: it's eating the red food that matters. The red wine we take outside and pour on the ground. Afterwards. Then we talk and dance a little.

229

She shrugs.

– For as long as we want. Then we go to bed.

She sighs.

– You can't believe how splendid it was in the old days, when my husband was still alive, before the children left home. All our neighbours and friends came for the evening, to celebrate with us. We would be twenty, thirty, for supper.

She brightens.

– But you will be here. This year it will be like it was before. When the children were here.

She peers at Barbara.

– You have children? You like children?

– No, shudders Barbara: too much mess.

Angelina smiles.

– Now I must begin my preparations. There is so much to do.

– Shall I help you? Barbara asks, fingering the notebook in her pocket: I'd love to see how you do it.

– No, no, Angelina chides her with a warm smile: go and enjoy yourself. This is your holiday.

Shouts, childish laughter, outside the window, draw Barbara's attention. She brushes past Angelina, lifts the little checked curtain, peers out. At just past three o'clock, it is already getting dark, a silvery gloom swallowing the garden, the mist beyond making it impossible to see.

– What's that noise? asks Barbara: what are those children up to?

Angelina does not cease her busy to and fro between table and stove. Her voice, when she speaks, is indifferent.

– Oh, it's just a children's game. Another tradition. On the eve of the New Year, one of the children dresses up as an old woman, to represent the Old Year. Then the other children chase him, and pretend to kill him. That way, the New Year can be born.

– How quaint, Barbara exclaims: how delightful.

– It's just a custom, Angelina says: something for your notebook, yes?

Barbara looks at the older woman's back. She shivers suddenly.

– I think, she remarks: I'll go and see what Francis is

up to.

Francis is sprawled on the bed, flicking through one of the magazines he brought with him. Barbara fiddles with the iron latch, making sure that the door is closed properly, then kicks off her shoes and curls up beside Francis on the bed.

– I'm beginning to think, she remarks: that there's more to our hostess than meets the eye. It's going to be more difficult than we thought, you know, to persuade her to sell us some of her stuff. She's pretty smart. She must know what it's worth.

Francis looks up.

– Funny you should say that. Those three men we met today, out on our walk, were talking about her. I didn't have a chance to tell you before.

– How do you know what they said? Barbara says: you don't speak Italian.

She feels quite breathless and cross.

– I understand a tiny bit, she insists: whereas you can't speak a word.

Francis rolls over onto his back, his eyes glinting.

– You'll have to take my word for it, won't you? What I *think* they said was that she used to be a film director before her husband went off, and that she's pretty rich. Hence all the bibelots. We've been idiots, you know. No simple peasant nonna could possibly possess all this stuff.

He pauses.

– They also said that she's mad. Her husband leaving her turned her brain.

He is watching her, wanting to see her get upset. She controls herself, smiles at him.

– How can you possibly know what they said?

He shrugs.

– Gestures. The expression on their faces.

– I don't believe you.

– Sweetie, you don't need to. It doesn't matter. We're off tomorrow morning. Put it down to experience.

He slides a finger along her chin.

– I know what you need. Something to take your mind off all this.

*

No more vanilla sex. Red-hot chilli. Ginger me up. Barbara finds more phrases for the recipe. *Ropes, hot wax dripped onto nipples, pincers, tongs, contract, consent, freedom, submission, cry, blood, enough, orgasm.*

Here is her own willing victim. A white backside offered like *an iced cake to be decorated.* Friend invitation tryst. Trust? Trussed. Triste? She will discover. *Athletes musclemen heroes childbirth anorexia stigmata sword-swallowers crucifixion corsets.*

– Shut up! she shouts to the cookery writer inside her brain.

She picks up the whip, and stands behind Francis. It is only a game between friends. To find out about power. Why get so het up?

She is always nervous, at first, of hurting him too much. Giggles. Feels clumsy, unschooled. Undisciplined.

– It tickles, Francis says, his voice muffled by the silk cushions of the chair.

His glossy porno mag lies open on the floor beside him. There's mummy, stuck to the page. Stapled in place. Eternally available. No whore she, going away and leaving her baby yelling and unsatisfied. Good mummy, who stays with baby. Breasts eternally on offer, legs spread wide to welcome her little man, cosy womb all ready for him, always a hot dinner on the table and a hot kiss.

Barbara sees that the twin fat cushions are Angelina's breasts. She whom the growing boy does not want to leave. Mummy mummy mummy don't make me part from you don't make me be a man.

Bad boy, Francis. Be a man, Francis. Take it like a man. Barbara takes responsibility. He is her child.

She lifts her arm again, more determined this time. She has been cheated. Her warm peasant granny is just another neurotic successful woman. Like herself. She smacks Francis harder for asking her to beat him. Your fault your fault your fault. That this is the only game we play.

Barbara is such an efficient lover. So responsive to her men's needs. She leaps springs bounces sucks. Beats when asked. Stays in control. Looks after them, holds them, brings them to orgasm, fakes her own, praises their sexual performance. Stays in control.

She does not know how to ask for what she wants. She does not know how to stop playing this game. Give to your baby. Give him what he wants. Beat him for wanting to stay with you. Beat him for wanting to get away.

Delicious smells, of *onions and garlic* frying, drift up from the kitchen below.

We are brother and sister, she thinks: both of us wanting the same thing. Both of us lost in the woods, and starving. Beware of the witch's house.

She puts down the whip. Francis is still moaning with pleasure.

– I would like, she begins to say: I want –

The scream beats at the window, asking for admittance. The children's voices whoop, triumphant.

Barbara runs downstairs, past the open kitchen door from which streams radio music and gusts of steam, and outside, into the blue darkness. Snow is falling. The moon is up, a slender crescent high in the sky with a single bright star at its heel. The icy air strikes her cheeks and neck. She blunders towards the garden gate, her slippered feet skidding on the glassy path, snowflakes whirling against her open mouth and melting, crisps of water, on her tongue.

She plunges across the deserted road and down the bank into the meadow. The row of pines at its far end hides the drop of the valley, and the great jagged mountains rear dimly behind, monochrome of paling blue. The meadow, deep in snow, gleams in the moonlight, the falling snow already blotting out the dents made by the children's boots. The children have vanished.

The old woman lies spreadeagled on her back, arms and legs flung wide, undignified. She is all in black, and her grey wig is askew, revealing her short grizzled hair.

Barbara kneels by the body and puts out a hand to touch it. It is Angelina's face she is looking into, and it is Angelina's hand, big and red, she is holding in her own.

Angelina's clothes are tumbled and disordered. She has torn her skirt in falling, or perhaps one of the children has slashed at it with a knife; it is spread out on either side of her like a pair of ragged black wings. Her white petticoat is similarly ripped, and her baggy bloomers. The penis pokes out sideways, limp and wrinkled.

233

Barbara goes on kneeling there, holding the hand of this person she does not know, while the snow falls on both of them.

This week we visit a district, famed for its peasant cuisine, in the mountainous north of Italy. Barbara Cheriton reports on fragrant ways with food and wine in the province of Adelmo, and describes rituals and festivals, unchanged for hundreds of years, in which food plays a crucial part.

35   The Gaffer sits in the Ark's Reading Room, shoulders hunched. He has decided that the best place to make a start is amongst all these writers who have come after him, find out what they have been up to. Convinced that his own book is the last word on the subject, he's puzzled that others have felt able to go on stating the obvious over and over again.

But he's depressed. There are too many books here. Too many books by women. He's tired out already, can't stretch open wide enough to take it all in. He can see the point of focusing on a few new women writers: like adding salt or sugar to porridge. A little more *crème de la crème*. Spice up the familiar tradition. All right, he's prepared to taste books by six, seven, even eight women writers he's never heard of, but any more is too much. He'll be overwhelmed. They can't *all* be good. So why should he have to read them all to find out? He might be wasting his time. He might get bored. It's force-feeding, that's what it is.

Surely, it stands to reason, the feminist publishers, and the mainstream houses with women's lists, are publishing women writers simply because they are women. An insult to any decent writers among them. All these publishers claiming to discover five or six brilliant new novels by women four times a year. Surely there can't really be that many new women writers? There isn't room for all those books in the shops. How can all those writers become equally famous and admired? It damages the entire concept of literary quality.

These days, he broods, male writers don't stand a chance. You're only published if you're a woman, or Black, or gay. Nobody's interested in white men's writing. There white men

235

have been, slogging away over the centuries to investigate meaning and enrich the pantheon, keeping the flame alight, and no one's interested any more. What's a man to do?

He strokes his chin. First of all, some research. How to define men's writing? What do men write about? What is this thing the sibyls keep banging on about called masculinity? He could start here, in the Reading Room. A man is: not-a-woman. Scan all these female texts, discover what they leave out, then plunge into that blank space and explore.

First of all he needs to transcribe these texts, make notes. He plugs in his word processor and computer. Once he's got all the women's words in his computer memory, he'll be able to search, compare, scan, index, collate. Books are such an untidy way of storing information. Better to have it all in one place, on his floppy disks. Then he'll know everything.

He plucks a book at random from the shelf beside him. An anthology of Egyptian tomb inscriptions concerning women. He laughs. Why not dogs, or camels? He'll find out eventually. He spreads his hands over the keyboard and starts to copy out the book, word by word.

By lunch time he's tapped out half a chapter. He runs his fingers through his hair. At this rate it will take him several thousand years to get every book in the archive into his memory. Better find another method of research.

He wanders over to the male author catalogue. Rows of grey metal cabinets with deep drawers. The *obvious* thing to do is to start with the great classic authors, those agreed to constitute the pantheon. Most of whom just happen to be male.

He pulls open the drawer marked SH.

Death stares up at him. Waxen embalmed face, white hands folded over velvet stomach under the cellophane wrapping, locks of grey hair, severed by decay, fallen onto the yellowed ruff propping the shrivelling head.

He slams the drawer shut. Pulls open another marked WO. Bald skull, yellow tooth sockets, one cracked tooth stump still in place, but no lips. A maggot waggles in the nose cavity. Rotten cambric of the shirt parted and rent, arch of ribs showing amidst shreds of flesh.

The metal rattles back from his fingers. He tries a third. GR. Blood dried around the nostrils, in thick clots at the side of the mouth, plastered like a poultice across the chest. The wounds all smiling at him, little red lips. Fast, delicate work: knives and razors.

What about his book, then? The foundation and source for subsequent literature in the West? His name must be on a card in this catalogue. He hunts back along the drawers to GA. Pulls it open.

Oblong grey metal crib in which a dead baby is laid. Satin bonnet edged with pleats of stiff whiteish lace frames a celluloid mask, cheeks tinted bright pink. Around the head a halo of twinkling gold stars, around the neck a necklace of gilt and pearls. The tiny body is wrapped in white satin, a sausage parcel, tightly bound with ribbons of gold thread tied in a large bow on the stomach. Pearls and gold beads decorate the silk mattress on which the little corpse lies, and the sides of the casket-drawer are lined with quilted pale blue brocade.

The Gaffer shoves the catalogue drawer closed, stumbles to the nearest wastepaper bin, vomits. He's trembling and faint, in need of fresh air. His hands stink of formalin and incense when he raises them to wipe his face, and his stomach still heaves.

He leans over the rail on the roof of the Ark, strains his eyes towards the shoreline just visible in the distance. Yet another island.

Those bloody sibyls. After all his efforts at making friends. To play such a trick on him.

What *can* he write? He's no nearer an answer.

Staring at the sea tumbling past the anchored and stationary Ark, he slowly becomes aware that it is alive with mermaids, a shoal of them swimming lazily to and fro and waiting for him to notice them. Raised arms splash silver drops of water, graceful necks twist and arch from side to side, amused eyes beckon him closer. He grips the rail, and peers over it. Real women, they look like; like the topless bathing beauties on the beaches he and his companions have sailed past and which he has longed to visit. Of *course* Mrs Noah only docks the Ark at islands conspicuously lacking pretty women disporting themselves at the sea's edge. How charming, then, that these girls have let their curiosity propel them so far out from shore. Their brown skins, veiled and then revealed by the green waves curling and

237

breaking above their heads, are gleaming, their little breasts so pert, the nipples lifted, dark brown, haloed by rose. No tails visible below their skirts of green water. Not monsters, these ladies. No cold cunts, tight, rejecting. They lift their chins at him, and laugh.

The Ark is moored near a large rock. The mermaids swim up to it, loll at its foot, half out of the water and half in, on cushions of seaweed, the white spray pearling their shoulders. Each one produces a circular mirror, into which she looks while starting to comb her long salty hair. They sing now. Sweet voices tossed away on the wind, melodies of longing, of promise. Each one is lonely, and wanting a companion. Come to me, dear man, come. He smiles, tickled by their openness. It's a difficult world for women alone, he has learned that much on this voyage.

He has been broken into little pieces by lack of nourishing love. He doesn't know who he is any more, if women don't need him. Those harsh earnest sibyls. He leans over the rail, and harkens to the mermaids.

The mermaids stretch out their arms and hold up their mirrors and sing. Help me, please help me. Help me to find a kindly editor for my work. Help me to get my poems published. Please give me an introduction to a publisher. Listen to my tales of woe. Believe me, I'm not like other women. I am so much more sensitive, so much more intelligent, so much more appreciative of you.

He can be loved by all of them at once. Standing on the deck of the Ark, dazzled by their smiles and by the light flashing off their mirrors, turning round and round in an ecstasy of being looked at, held, cosseted in their regard, he can see himself reflected in all their looking-glasses at once. He is whole again. He is holy as a host.

All this nonsense, the mermaids sing: about gender and sexual difference and the oedipal moment. Don't believe it. A trap constructed by women envious of your genius. Designed to pull you down into what's falsely called reality, to drown you in cold waters of common sense. It's not necessary to enter the human world. Remain a god, laughing and playing above it. Refuse to be named in their terms, to be reduced, part not whole, man not cosmic voice. Don't let them suck you in. *Choose*: to stay outside the ugly diminished house of human

238

language, to remain androgynous; which means *omnipotent*; *free*.

The mermaids twirl their mirrors in the sunshine.

If you want stories, they call softly: listen to ours. If you want songs, we'll carol you a lullaby. We'll carry you down to an underwater bed where you can dream and never wake up. We'll take you back to Atlantis, your forgotten home, the land that existed before time began, true paradise, perfect womb where childhood never ends. Come to us, dear man, come.

The Gaffer has never been able to remember his past. Only the words he has written on paper. He started with the beginning of the world, and he was always there. Now, as the women's voices call to him, terror pokes him in the back of his knees. Where *did* I come from? How *did* I begin?

The voice of a mother. Come to me, my darling, come.

He remembers the story he told in his novel.

Then he starts to imagine a draft of a new, unauthorized version.

In the beginning there is Mother. Omnipotent, maker of everything. Her right eye is life and her left eye death. She is both beloved and terrible. Her son hangs from her breast and she loves him. She is the whole world to him and he to her. Promised land. Milk and honey. Garden of Eden. Paradise.

His childhood is filled with petticoats and soft arms, table top in the kitchen he peers over to discover his aunts shelling peas. Their arched feet in peep-toed high heels, swirls of pleated and polka-dotted skirts. They lift him up; pass him from lap to lap while they talk. Mother's hands are dusty with flour, the strong fingers kneading. Look, baby, here's how to make a pastry doll. In stalks a column of wood, very tall and smelling of coal-tar soap, hedge of hair bristling above mouth, surely he scratches mother when he bends to kiss her.

In the cool of the evening Mother abandons her son and walks in the garden with this stranger. What can he offer that Gaffer lacks? He *must* know. He eats the apple, peers round the bedroom door.

The intruder has three legs. And he has a fiery sword which he flourishes in Gaffer's face. Watch out. I could cut your head

239

off with this. Gaffer is expelled from paradise: Mother unties her apron strings and he tumbles out, no longer her treasure. He's a big boy now. Banned the lap, banned the hiding place under the kitchen table, banned the gossiping circle of aunts and best friends, banned the double bed on weekend mornings. Shut out from mother's country, of which this person called Father is king, to which only Father can command entry; country that smells of sweat masked with lily-of-the-valley talcum powder, where nylon stockings and bits of cotton wool and cut-glass bottles grow.

In the beginning there is Father. Omnipotent, maker of everything. Terrible, and wise. Far away, untouchable. Except when he chastises the son he loves and Gaffer is held in his arms across his knees. The rod that leads the chosen one across the desert, away from mother.

Gaffer resists. He likes girls, hangs around them. They do sensible things like talking to each other, reading, inventing games he enjoys. One girl shows him how to draw cartoons and do magic tricks. Her friends giggle, hostile, and she withdraws.

Mother brings home a new baby. Over and over Gaffer asks: where did it come from? How did you know to expect it? An angel told me in my sleep, mother says, smiling over his head: and babies come from God. Father is God. Father makes babies. God plants the baby in mother.

Mother? Or Father? He can't see the connection. Can't remember it: the vision through the half-open door of the wild coupling of that monster with two backs Adam-and-Eve.

His mother takes him and his two friends out into the country for a picnic tea, with her neighbour from next door. The two women loll on the tartan rug, play with the baby. Cool shade under the scrubby oak trees, yellow gorse at their backs. Tea from the thermos sipped from plastic cups, white sandwiches bulgy with marmite and fish paste and sandwich spread. The little boys tangle with the woods, bury a split ball in the roots of a hollow tree, get lost, find the way out through thickets of purple rhododendron. He buries his face in his mother's lap, and she rocks him idly while she suckles the baby and chats to her friend. Then she pushes him away: go on with you, you're much too old for that nonsense.

The postman rings early in the morning. As Gaffer runs to

open the front door his mother flies out of the kitchen and up the stairs, wrap falling open to reveal black bra and camiknickers, long white legs.

Father goes away on business. Gaffer buys a Charlie Chaplin mask in the local toyshop, a plastic pipe, practises a strutting walk, pipe waved in one hand. This week I am Father, he tells his mother: this week, let me sleep in your bed with you. The baby is asleep: non-existent. His mother snores lightly, face greasy with cold cream. Tenderly he pulls the pink satin quilt up over her. That old witch from next door comes for lunch, and he hears them laughing in the kitchen. Then the mask and pipe disappear, put out with the rubbish. They do not speak of it.

Rescued. Father. You can be like me. My power is greater than that of the female. I will show you the way out of Egypt and into the real world. I will give you a second chance. Have I not formed you in my image? I will cleanse you of the stain of the woman. I will make of you a hero; sending you forth into battle so that your blood will baptize you, redeem you, mark you as mine. Forget your knowledge of the woman, for sex means corruption and decay. I will give you eternal life; am I not the Father who makes all things? The woman's blood is the sign of death: your wounds and your blood are sacred, the signs of life.

Jam-rags and tits. Bitches in heat, stupid with giggles as he goes by. Their terrible power to reject him if he admits to needing them. The ones who do it are slags and the ones who don't are frigid. Eve is bad, and Mary is good. The terrible devouring mother glowers in the background.

He could marry one, get his mother back. Weigh her down with babies so that she can't leave him, can't leave the house. Find cosseting again. Be in control of the woman; keep her in her place. Always ready for him, permanently available. Crucify the image of the Father and get his mother back. On his terms this time. Become the Father himself. Into the Kingdom. Heterosexual male. Saved.

He could father a son on his wife. When the child asks: who made me? where did I come from? what is sex? what is death? the new Father can hand on the Christian story.

*

The Gaffer stares over the rail at the cold perfection of the mermaids, and remembers.

When she holds him in her arms. When he lies back and is still. When he does not have to prove his strength. When he does not have to do anything.

She's the one he's lost. He bears the mark of her absence. The space of loss inside him has her shape. His bawling mouth and weight of tears. His sour mouth and pricking skin. His emptiness. There is just this gap, and this crying. Parting from her is necessary. It is over. It is over.

He cries, gulping into his brown silk handkerchief. Tears break the spell. The mermaids dissolve into foam.

He stomps down the companionway. Real sob-stuff, eh? All right, sob-sisters, listen to *this*.

36 At library school I learned more about sex.

Not only am I working on the Woman Problem in classification theory, I am making a lot of women friends. I tell one of them I fear I am frigid, and she gives me Masters and Johnson to read. My imagination fills with flashing neon pictures of women strapped to machines measuring their every response to stimulation. I wonder whether machines are more effective than men. I am certainly aroused by the idea of jerking, naked, on a table, with a lot of serious white-coated male doctors watching, and envying, my multiple orgasms which apparently men don't have. I don't have them either but I like the idea. I don't tell my friend this in case she disapproves.

She lends me another book: *The Myth of the Vaginal Orgasm*. Apparently I have been doing it the wrong way. More technical information. Women are like cars, with starter buttons. All a man has to do is press the right button for long enough. I discover how to come by myself. This encourages me.

I try to put these theories into practice with my next lover, a Marxist who lends me *Das Kapital*. It's a wonderful book, full of jokes. I notice that Marxism does not attend to the Woman Problem, and have many fiery arguments with Bill about this. Extended foreplay of ritual exchanges of teasing words is followed, one afternoon, by bed. By this time I am so panting with desire that I simply lie back and open my legs and he dives into me, in and out, in and out, while we stare at each other and drown, looking. I forget all the instructions about patient stimulation of the clitoris. I just open up and suck him into me, in and out. When orgasm sweeps through me I yell with surprise, sit up and say: that was not technically possible, the

243

vaginal orgasm doesn't exist!

I decide that the pleasures of sex are like those of reading: you hunger, you yearn, you open up, you swallow, you take it in. The body, the book.

Bill leaves me the following week because I want him too often and too much. Men are not as reliable as books. I convert my suffering into something tolerable by beginning to write about classification systems. I am at the centre, and I am allowed to relate to everything under the sun. Writing is more difficult than reading, but brings the same sensation of blissful release. Oh wise nuns at my convent school who warned against lolling on sofas before lunch with novels: I understand the dangers now. Too much pleasure makes you want more.

The Ark's Arkive hums with desire. Desire off the leash and given its head, making all the books jiggle up and down on the shelves and jump out of order.

– I'm not convinced by your arguments, Noah says: it's all too pat, too simplistic.

– Part of me agrees with you, I force myself to admit: I'm beginning to think, as a result of all you've said, that perhaps I shouldn't have a baby. That perhaps I don't really want one. I'm destroying my desire. That's what you want, isn't it?

I search the riddle book.

Can he *come to terms* with my *coming to term*?

37   We creep across the bay. When the mist surrounding us dissolves, we see the island rear up, a single mountain with a dented peak rising sheer from the encompassing sea.

Leaving the others on board the Ark docked in the tiny harbour thick with tourists enjoying the crowded cafés and shops, I take the funicular railway up to the village that constitutes the capital. Craning my neck, I see a bus launch itself onto the road ahead and dive upwards, hang over the precipice of the cliff at my side, zigzag further up and out of sight.

I wander through a honeycomb of tiny *piazze* connected by paved lanes, archways, tunnels. Over the top of the high walls on either side of me spill bright flowering creepers: blue *campanelli*, clusters of pink oleanders with stiff dark green leaves. The houses are plastered in rainbow colours. Balconies, terraces and exterior staircases are set with tubs of geraniums and begonias. Trellised vines crawl across loggia ceilings; palms and cacti grow on the flat roofs. Painted tiles are stuck above doorways. Baskets of lemons stand on doorsteps.

The street turns, winding around a corner, into a colonnade, the deep blue of the sea suddenly visible through a pierced screen of white marble columns twisted about with purple flowers. The branches of umbrella pines sweep sharply up. Scent of basil.

I climb the steep hill. At first there are still houses on either side, and tiny orchards planted with apricot trees, little triangular vineyards heavy with fat blue grapes, dusky bloom under their pointed green leaves, rows of silver and turquoise cabbages, aubergines, asparagus. The stone passage loops around the walled garden of an old villa, solid L-shape with

245

ultramarine shutters and white plaster dirtied to a pleasing grey, tall nodding cypresses on two sides of the courtyard framing a well surrounded by squat palms, rust-coloured urns overflowing with aspidistras and a few pink geraniums. Peering through the wrought-iron gate, I see blue-grey shadows dance along the wall as the wind rustles the leaves of a wild plantation of tall pines and holm oaks and blows through the long grass invading the paving stones.

Now the hillside opens out: steeper, stonier, less fertile. Fig and olive trees cling to the parched earth scattered with cacti and low thorny bushes. The path turns into a staircase with broad shallow steps flinging itself up and up. Cocks crow. A man whistles somewhere out of sight. The sun is pallid gold in the moist blue air, a dusted blue, a blue mist. Dry rasp of crickets, chirp and buzz of grasshoppers. The stone steps are silted with dark red pine needles. White patches of boulders stick up through the brown grass.

I reach the plateau just below the very top of the mountain: the dented space I saw from the harbour. On one side, the ruins of a once-vast villa now reduced to curving corridors of broken columns. On the other, a rustic balustrade of lashed saplings invites me to leap into the sea down a sheer drop of several thousand feet. Leaning over the flimsy paling, holding onto a palm tree for safety, I can just see a white lace of breakers around a rock a little way out from the very bottom of the cliff. Everything else is sheer blue: sea and sky are the real world up here, earth just a foothold in blue space.

I want to go further up. The way is by chair lift. I stand on the little oval platform, ducking as the iron chairs whirl up, round, and off again, never stopping. I launch myself at a chair and scramble into it as it swings past scooping me up as cargo. Two wooden slats under me, one at my back, a strut locked over my lap to keep me from slipping out.

I'm away. I'm in a flying armchair, a little spacecraft open to the sun and wind. I'm flying. I'm flying alone. Just above the tree tops, skimming up a deep green cleft in the mountain, reclaimed from desert and planted with trees. I dangle my feet over the swaying tops of chestnuts, I hover through the sunlight and the dry air, the heat branding my bare shoulders and knees, my legs hanging in the void, my arms stretched out wanting to touch the mountain walls but unable to; flying gravely and slowly and silently along.

It's the only way; to step out into the empty air and trust that I will not plummet down. My wings are quill pens, and bear me up. I tiptoe on nothingness.

Then earth rushes at me and knocks me to my knees. I stumble up, and find myself on the very highest point of the mountain.

This is a lonely place. Patches of bare rock, of scrub. The wind plucks at dry grass, at the leafless branches of a black thorn tree. Up here there are no books, newspapers, pamphlets or posters to give me a clue, no rope of words to lassoo the unknown and make it tolerable.

Up here there's nothing. No one. Except myself.

That 4 am feeling, when you wake suddenly with a parched mouth and thumping heart. Troubling dream you can't remember projects itself into scrape and scrabble of mice overhead in the roof, a stranger's fingers delicately testing your front-door lock. Take it all back inside you and what have you got. Your lack of certainty about what you want and what to do. Your lack of hope. Your lack of strength, energy, commitment. Your lack of a sense of humour about yourself. Your priggishness. Your lack of kindness, generosity, warmth towards others. Your blind seeking egotism. Your lack of love. Your lack.

So that's that.

38   The Gaffer cooks supper, using some of the food I have brought back with me from the island. Fat pizza, the dough crisp and biscuity, laden with seafood. Slices of tomatoes and dripping fresh *mozzarella* decorated with basil leaves. Aubergine marinated in vinegar and chilli, and stuffed yellow peppers, rolled in breadcrumbs and fried. Two sorts of figs: purple ones that are darkly rosy inside, and green ones splitting open to reveal white flesh shaded with pink. Cold wine.

My plate clean, I lie back in my chair. Try to tell the others what I found out.

The Gaffer puts down his toothpick and grimaces at me.

– That's rather like what happened to me today. I got no writing done whatsoever. I felt really depressed.

The tears gush out of me, running warm over my face. I can't stop them. It's like slitting a sack of water. Someone's hauling me to my feet. The Gaffer puts his arms round me and I sob into his shirt that's clean and ironed and smells of fresh air. He's so big that I don't have to worry that he's not strong enough to hold me while I blub. It's comforting to lean against his plump body and feel him sturdy as a wall propping me up and letting me rain tears down him.

Then I'm back in my chair, sagging, all the tightness gone, no need to pretend.

– I had an abortion ten years ago, I tell the others: an illegal one. My period was only ten days late, but I *felt* pregnant. I was convinced. I remembered the night I got drunk and probably put my cap in wrong. I wasn't ready to become a mother: I had little money, only temporary accommodation, I was struggling to write my thesis and qualify as a librarian. Tim always

248

refused to use sheaths. He agreed I should have the abortion. He was sleeping with two other women besides me. I rang up a woman I knew who had trained in the States as a paramedic and performed safe early abortions for women who couldn't get them on the NHS. My male GP was against abortion. The woman came to my house where I was living and tickled my womb with straws until the blood came, answering the expert jiggle of her fingers. She showed me a clot of blood no bigger than a seed pearl and said: that might have been a foetus. I told no one. I hardened myself, and felt only the relief. The guilt has lain deep in me, like a bone, and the sorrow. Now, at last, I can speak of it and take responsibility for what I've done. I am not a victim. I *chose*. Inside me is a harsh female god who straddles life and destruction and tells women to *choose* what we do.

– I've had an abortion too, says the Correct Sibyl.

– And I, says the Re-Vision Sibyl.

– And I.

– And I.

– And I.

We look at one another.

– That Boat I invented in the Old Testament, says the Gaffer: floated on dark waters. Underneath its hull were all the lost cities of the world. Now I wonder: how were they found, and tested, the elect? Did God grieve for the ones he killed? I didn't think about that. I didn't make him weep.

– I want someone to tell a story, the Correct Sibyl says: about a man and a woman making friends.

39   He finds the baby only because it starts crying so hard. Otherwise it would be impossible to know it is there.

The rubbish heap leans in the darkness, a hill of darkness itself, against the corrugated-iron fence erected by the building company in a vain attempt to protect the builders' supplies against the gangs of boys who scavenge at night. It's an unofficial rubbish heap, unsanctioned by the council, patronized by the people living around the crossroads on one side of which it sits broodily, an urban compost of old prams, cider bottles, broken ironing boards, gashed sinks, black plastic sacks of discarded clothes, rotting cardboard boxes heaped with used sanitary towels, worn-out stilettos, empty make-up containers. At dusk, the women creep from the flats to chuck the rubbish out. The council vans with their grinding maws, their high whine, don't visit these streets often enough, and the dustbins get stolen. The rubbish heap functions as swap-shop, free jumble sale. Most of the local homes are furnished from it. The pickings are left to the homeless to sift through, a pecking order everybody obeys.

The boys don't bother, usually, with the spilling smelly dump. They prefer the challenge of proper stealing, leave the art of rubbish sorting to women, older vagrants, kids. They prefer to swarm over the fence at the tip's back and prowl through the deserted building site, mindful of the Alsatian dogs on guard, loose and hungry, to look for materials light enough to be carried back over the fence for re-sale. Every couple of months one of them gets savaged by a dog. Every so often the council sends its men to clear away the foetid, decaying mountain of domestic refuse, post notices warning of fines, of imprisonment.

Nobody knows what the new building will be. Mounds of earth, stacks of cement blocks, give little away. Some say it's the new district brothel. Others insist it's the council's nuclear shelter. They don't care much. They have plenty of other things to worry about.

The moon ripples silver along the corrugated-iron wall that sings and rattles in the wind. Bored with a night of no booty, Turtle stops his mooching progress to contemplate the graffiti scrawled along its undulating length. There's a new one since last night. *The daughters of Isis will eat your heart out.* The red loops of the script wobble, and the message ends in a cascade of blood red drops.

Turtle traces its syntax with difficulty, only just having learned to read. It might come in useful, Dog pointed out: for keeping one step ahead of the other gangs. Survival depends on speed and accuracy; being able to read the police posters warning of imminent clean-up campaigns will show them when to vanish, decamp to another neighbourhood a few streets away, lie low until they judge it safe to return. The Little Sisters of Liberation run a library in the nissen hut at the corner a block away. They hold evening literacy classes, after the dole-out of soup and bread, and so Dog and Turtle start to slink in at the back, hands and faces hastily washed to achieve some semblance of normality. The Little Sisters ask no questions, embarrass no one, offer their vision to any who will listen. I struggle, they spell out: I fear, I desire, I cooperate, I love. When the police raid the centre, burning the books of poetry and the novels, removing the files before tinning up the entrance and ushering the three Sisters on duty that night into an unmarked black van, Dog and Turtle, still small enough to scramble through lavatory windows, escape with pockets stuffed with bread and pamphlets. And a sketchy knowledge of how to read. The bread vanishes immediately. The tracts linger: fire-lighters, lavatory paper, shoe-wadding.

Turtle scowls, unable to comprehend the threat that bleeds across the silver barrier in front of him, worried at the idea of a new gang arrived in the neighbourhood. Possibly older and bigger. Possibly better armed. He lashes out, kicks at an abandoned box at his feet. Its fabric yields, as soft as plastic, and immediately a wail goes up from its depths. He peers down,

251

investigating. It's a suitcase, an open suitcase, squashed between a pile of empty catering tins and a torn lampshade sticking black ribs into the night. The wail deepens, steadies into an intolerable cry. Cautiously, Turtle advances his hand, touches a blanket tucked around a small breathing shape.

Shit. A baby.

He'll have to shut it up fast, before some nosey-parker warden arrives on the scene sniffing trouble, has him arrested for being out after curfew. He hesitates, then puts his hand over the baby's mouth and nose. He misses his aim in the dark, grabs its hand instead. Tiny fingers curl around his, and the anguished crying dies.

Relieved, he lets go and steps back, eyes darting along the deserted street to clear his escape. The baby begins screaming again. Enraged, he picks it up, crooning hatred into its damp woolly hat. Again, it stops crying. Gurgles. Turtle is astonished at the power he discovers in himself, and with the astonishment comes a feeling he has no name for, a clutching of the guts, his bowels softening. This frightens him, and he looks around, uncertain what to do.

There are lights flashing at the far end of the main street, the livid pink of a police beacon turning, a high scream of sirens going up. The curfew patrol. Somehow, as he gathers himself to run, Turtle forgets to drop the baby. Shoving it under one arm, he ducks around the rubbish heap and scampers into the mouth of the alley lined on one side by the building-site fence, runs head-down into safety, away from the cars, into the dark.

Dog hovers on the other side of the packing case they have laid the baby on, holding a lit candle. Its flame jumps in his uneasy hand, causing shadows to swirl and dance on the bare brick walls of the basement, hot wax to run and stick on his fingers. When he curses, Turtle, gingerly unwrapping layers of sodden yellow nappy, assumes it's with pain.

– Shit, Dog says: it's a girl.

Beneath them, the baby kicks and crows, delighted to be rid of her stinking bandages. The two boys look at one another. Turtle is short and skinny, with white freckled skin and marmalade hair. Dog has seen this expression on his face before: the snub nose wrinkled in puzzlement, the pale blue

252

eyes slitted under thick white lids, the bony jaw tense with concentration. Turtle survives street life only by a miracle, so prone is he to stop short in the middle of a thieving expedition and be thrown off course by a dahlia in the gutter, by a change in the air, by a sudden idea. Sometimes, Dog has to admit, his friend's hunches, new trains of thought, are productive, lead to an improvement in their life style, extra pickings from a fresh source hitherto unconsidered; but mostly they don't, they just root Turtle to the spot, wondering and entranced, prime victim material just begging to be picked up. Dog fears for him, tries to teach him, by dint of insult and sarcasm, the likely consequences of his carelessness, succeeds only occasionally. He ends up playing mother to the younger boy.

Mother. He glances round, as though he has spoken the taboo word aloud, as though there are great ears pinned to the sheets of brown paper they have stretched across the doors and windows to resist the draughts whistling in.

– Get rid of her, he commands: quick.

Women of Class D are subdivided into *breeders*, *feeders* and *tarts*. If they are *bleeders*. *Non-bleeders*, depending on age, are classified as *holes* (pre-pubescent) or *sacks* (post-menopausal). Women of the superior classes are called by names Dog does not know. He has never met any. They live in a different section of town. The Prime Ministress has, as one of her titles, *Big Mummy*. But these are sacred words, reserved for her alone, and rarely spoken.

Turtle's expression does not change. He goes on looking at his friend in silence. Dog, at eleven, is a year older than he is, they have worked out, but he looks older. The structure of his face is purpose congealed like rock into apparently immovable direction. His brown eyes are usually blank, carefully concentrated into a stare, and his mouth is firmly closed over his teeth. The tic at the corner of one eyelid betrays him, and the hand, which constantly goes up to push aside the flopping strands of black hair, the stubby hand with its sore cuticles, its chewed nails.

– No, Turtle decides: she's mine. I found her. I'm going to keep her.

Dog drops the candle, whose flame sputters out as it hits the wet nappy on the floor. The wick sizzles as blackness drops on-to them, their little bit of bright home reduced and snuffed out, the basement once more a cavern of cold and menace. The baby screams.

— I'll manage, Turtle asserts, groping for the matches: I'll look after her.

That forbidden word roars louder than the child.

What does Turtle remember? Not much. The New Era, its dawning carefully set out in the definitions of the New Era State Dictionary, has pulled a curtain across all their pasts. Grey shapes move behind his eyes. Five children crammed into one double bed. The social worker arriving to take him into the Youth Treatment Centre. A woman bunched in desolation over a sputtering gas fire. His escape from the social worker as they emerged from the lift at the bottom of the flats and she turned aside to show her pass to the policeman on duty there.

He re-lights the candle and sets it on a saucer. What to use for nappies? He looks around. There's nothing. They sleep in a huddle of ragged blankets stolen from the Salvation Army, possess no linen. He shrugs. The baby's arse will have to go naked and unwrapped for the time being. Meanwhile, he swaddles her in his one spare jumper. In the morning he'll return to the tip and see if the suitcase is still there. Till then, his arms, the nest of blankets, will serve as a crib. He settles himself and the whimpering baby, hungry for milk they'll have to steal tomorrow, on the ground, next to the worried Dog.

— What will you call her? Dog asks: you'd better give her a name.

Turtle considers. His sisters, he suspects, once had names, now converted into numbers on state orphanage registers and therefore erased from his memory. The Little Sisters of Liberation whispered about heroines, nervous fingers covering their lips: Rosa, Eleanor, Winnie, Sylvia, Sojourner Truth. From somewhere else swim up Grace, Florence, Teresa, Joan. Impossible now. Conspicuous. Forbidden.

— She needs a name like ours, he pronounces: we'll call her Mouse.

Such is the beginning of Mouse. When she is old enough to talk, Dog and Turtle tell her where she comes from, teach her to utter their three names. By the time she is five, she knows many things: how to boil water in a can over a fire, how to scavenge for fuel and rubbish, how to linger around food queues, pounce at just the right moment, escape with an egg or two, a loaf, a can of beans. She keeps her curly hair short, like Dog and Turtle do, and wears, like them, trousers kept up with string, jumpers salvaged from the dump, plimsolls lined with old newspaper taken from their steadily diminishing store. Newspapers are not printed any more. Council announcements are made through loud-hailers or pasted up on walls.

The three young vagrants keep themselves as clean as they can, in order to pass for normal, meaning Class D poor, on the street, to avoid the vigilance of social workers, community wardens, police. To the casual eye they are like any other kids on the street: Youth Treatment Centre detainees out on an afternoon's parole for Community Training. So far they have not been caught and found out. So far, like the members of the other lucky gangs, they have avoided arrest, the discovery of their lack of ID cards, classification numbers, street passes.

Mouse learns to run. Fleet and silent on her black rubber soles, she speeds behind the boys on their nightly excursions for scrap. She loves the night, being lost in it, bodiless, yet rapid as the clouds scudding overhead. She knows every brick, every windowsill, of the neighbourhood, tracks the movements of others, notes their changes of health, their acquisition of pots or weapons or bicycle tyres, can often tell by a footfall who is likely to turn a corner. Brat the dwarf en route for his evening performance at the freak show in the community hall; woolly-hatted Mr Simpkins in his three-wheeled invalid cart, being taken out for an airing by one of the social workers from the geriatric ward; Big Lucy, popping out from the brothel between shifts for a packet of fags.

Big Lucy is the only woman in the neighbourhood who dares to walk around alone at night. Any child under twelve, any old person, found wandering the streets after curfew is asking for trouble. But a woman, in addition to a heavy fine extorted by the Night Police, will be *given bliss* by any passing male. *Tarts* perform a useful social function, in channelling and containing male aggression, and are therefore reasonably well paid. They are supposed to stay inside the brothel, where the men come with their cards that are stamped weekly with red stars by the authorities to indicate that *servicing* has been achieved. Since sex is organized, and legal, inside the brothel, *tarts* cannot be raped. Therefore *rape* is a concept not included in the New Era State Dictionary. *Servicing*, and *giving bliss*, are of course heavily contracepted activities. Most of the *tarts* are given sterilization. Fertility and reproduction are the tasks of a different section of the female population, controlled by a different state department. If a tart goes on the street, it's her own lookout if she gets *blissed-out* and not paid.

Big Lucy enjoys her forbidden strolls. No one dares bother her: she's too quick with her knife. So far, she's safe, and not sorry. She displays her red star, worn on the right shoulder, her long dyed yellow hair, her fat white shoulders and calves and pumpkin-bosom, with insouciance, a cold blue stare. Even the policemen leave her alone. Not their type. Too big. Too powerful. Too ugly, they tell each other.

Dog and Turtle have explained the complex street rules to Mouse. She understands. She's frightened when Lucy tries to make friends with her, coaxing her like a puppy.

– Here, babe, she croons, extending a plump palm on which lolls a square of chocolate: come to Lucy.

Mouse, who's never tasted chocolate and doesn't know what it is, backs away scowling. Big Lucy laughs, and swings on by.

It's Lucy who saves Mouse when the boys vanish.

Mouse is eleven years old. Small for her age, thin. She stays home one night with a stomach-ache after eating hard green windfalls filched from the community allotments. Crouched, wrapped in blankets, she watches Turtle don jacket and sweater, slip his knife inside his breast pocket, tie a scarf around his neck against the chill of the rainy August night.

– I wish I could come with you, she complains.

Turtle's face softens, as it always does when she addresses him, but he goes on collecting up his equipment: a plastic carrier bag, a bunch of skeleton keys, a length of chain.

– You wouldn't be able to help tonight, he says: it's a big raid. We're joining forces with the Sewer Rats. You're too young.

She watches them leave, absorbed in the coming adventure, and bolts the basement door behind them before returning to her bed in the corner. From here she can survey doors and windows, her back to the wall, eyes sweeping in arcs like headlights, body tensed against possible intruders. On several occasions in the past, passing tramps have attempted to force an entry, tempted by the prospect of what looks, from the outside, like a reasonably dry shelter. So far, Dog and Turtle have always been there, armed with knives and heavy sticks, to drive the intruders off.

She cries a little, clutching her painful stomach, snuffling into the bundle of her clothes that serves as pillow. Oh, she knows. Dog and Turtle confer together in corners, whispered conspiracies that shut her out from their plans for the future. She is too young, they keep telling her, for this or that exploit, and she understands how she has outgrown her baby charm, her function as mascot, as pet. Nowadays she's a drain on their resources, a too-hungry mouth, a dragging responsibility.

When she was smaller, as recently as a year or so ago, Turtle would still sometimes take her on his lap and tell her stories. Episodes from comics and newspaper strips used in the literacy classes, flashes of video programmes winking on screens behind the plate glass of corner shops before such places were closed down. The children lined up in front of the window, impassively watching crazy axe-men, dressed in the calico smocks worn by doctors, lingeringly dismember blondes trussed like fragile quail. The New Era changed all that.

She shudders, hearing floorboards creak above, the rain driving in long gusts at the loose panes of the basement door. Her candle is burning low, and she has no other. One of the reasons for the boys' sortie tonight is to replenish their stock of candles and matches, but they didn't tell her what time they would be back.

She sucks her thumb, closes her eyes, tries to sleep. In her dreams at night she becomes many Mouses. Mice. Her dreams are filled with nothing but Mice, a clock tower with her own face telling the time, a bright palace whose wide portal is her own mouth, a galloping horse coursing on four of her legs, a river which is her own body flowing along. Tonight, Mouse has gone, replaced by jagged dark shapes running in endless pursuit of something unseen and whimpering, patterns of blood running down the basement walls, enormous mouths cackling and grinning, flecked with spittle in which she will drown.

Now the stories rise up and leer at her. Dog and Turtle have

257

told her all about the expected, the commonplace, the *asked-for-it syndrome*: the women brutally attacked on the streets at night, left to die slowly in puddles of their own blood, their bellies and vaginas gashed, gushing. A warning. A warning. Don't go out. Don't go out. Now the violent sexual murders of men have begun to happen too. The authorities pretend to know nothing about it. The neighbourhood discusses the news in whispers, inspects the corpses before the refuse cart clears them away. Ritual tortures, ritual deaths. The genitals hacked off, laid on the dead face. The killers' signature daubed in blood on the forehead. D.I. Daughters of Isis. Nobody knows who they are. They are not in the Dictionary.

As Mouse opens her eyes, her heart thumping, she hears the feet stumbling down the basement steps. A trip and a curse. Then the hand trying the bolt. Her candle has guttered out, a warm pool of wax in the saucer when she searches for it blindly. She shrinks into her corner as far as she can, pulling the thin blanket up to her chin, ready to vomit as the hard green apples of the morning rise sourly up her throat and she tries to swallow them back down again. She clenches all her muscles, but the warm piss streaks down her legs anyway.

The feet retreat from the door. Now the hands are at the window. She imagines the monster as patient, huge, able to tiptoe down the iron area steps and at the same time magically lift off the ceiling of the basement, rummage for her with a glistening scaly paw.

Hissing whispers. A giggle. The catch on the window is easily wrenched and snapped. The window is pushed up, and it, they, are in.

A match flaring spatters her briefly with light before she dives under the blanket, eyes tightly closed. Her scrabbling, her gasps, alert her guests to her presence, and they stand still by the window as the match flickers and its quick radiance dies. She can hear the pumping of her heart, the rain beating down on the steps outside, someone else's jerky breathing. The night air rushes in through the open window and coils itself, a cold tube, up her nose, down into her stomach.

– What's that? A rat?

A man's voice, hoarse, sounding as afraid as she is.

The scrape of another match, this time applied to what must

be a candle-end pulled from a pocket. The light lifts her eyelids.

– We'll soon see, never mind.

She knows this voice. Lucy's. She hisses and spits, fist flailing, as the blanket is torn away from her face.

– Why, it's the little boy. So this is where you live, dearie. Clever little mouse, to find such a snug hidey-hole.

She kicks and struggles, but it's useless. Lucy knows her name. Lucy's bulk overwhelms her, and Lucy's hands lift her effortlessly up.

– Isn't he sweet? Look at his curls. And his big eyes.

Lucy's deep fringe is brassy in the candlelight, which warms her pasty skin thickly coated in powder. Her lipsticked mouth dribbles tender words while her eyes watch, measure, consider.

– I haven't got all night, her companion complains: how long are you going to be messing with that bloody kid?

Lucy turns the glare of her smile onto him as well.

– Now dear, who are we to get upset? Here we've found this nice dry basement away in from the rain. And a bed, here, look. Don't go spoiling things.

Nevertheless, Mouse, watching her, can see she is annoyed, perplexed. This isn't what she hoped for, that's obvious. Her smile keeps slipping.

– All right, Lucy decides: since we're here, we may as well get on with it.

Mouse, strapped to the table leg by the man's raincoat belt, watches them. If she keeps her eye on them, perhaps they won't kill her. Who knows what they might do if she shuts them off? Despite her terror, leaking down her legs and out of the corner of her mouth, she is curious. A new lesson to learn.

It takes about five minutes. Lucy rolls her coat and dress above her waist, grunting, lowers her knickers around her ankles, kicks them away. The man unzips his fly, clambers on top of her where she lies on the bed. She heaves her plump arms around him, issues instructions.

– That's right, dear. Oh, aren't you big, aren't you a fine fellow. Oh, what a whopper. There we are. In you come. I've got you. Come along then. Come on. Hurry up. That's it. Nicely now.

The man's white arse bobs up and down several times. Lucy gazes idly at the ceiling. The man climbs off her and stands up,

259

stuffing his shirt back into his trousers.

Mouse is puzzled. A man turned into a baby. Weak and wobbly. Needing. Dog and Turtle are not like that. The male body has always been her haven. Not the other way round. Hands which pick her up and stroke her cheek. Arms that hug her. A lap that holds her. Until a year ago, when the sad Turtle told her she must grow up, stop being a baby. Does Turtle, she wonders, do this? Does Dog? Is that why they go out at night? But it's forbidden, to do this. It's dangerous.

– And now, Lucy addresses her: what shall we do with you?

Mouse drops her eyes. It's then that she sees the blood seeping through her trousers, the dark stain on her thighs.

– You little *bleeder*, Lucy curses softly: you little *bleeder*.

– Cunt! the voices cry out in chorus: cunt!

Cunt is one of the most powerful words in the language, explains the Dictionary. Whereas in former epochs in the West, backward and illiterate ones, it was used mainly by men as an insult to one another, it has now been rescued and restored to its true meaning. It denotes Woman. Whole Woman. Real Woman. What every woman should aspire to: that essential and complete female Beingness. But since the females of our civilization are still, unfortunately, in a state of only gradual evolution towards full consciousness, the title *cunt* is reserved for the Prime Ministress alone, she who, embodying female perfection, acts as an example to the weaker members of her sex. Nobody has ever seen Big Mummy. Nobody else deserves her Name. Her palace is heavily guarded. She is worshipped at a distance. A statue of her, or a portrait, stands in every home, every institution, in the country. Some of the tarts in the brothel have whispered to Mouse that Big Mummy is dead. But nobody really knows. And it doesn't matter: dead or alive, she is an allegory of virtue. Omnipotent. Eternal.

– Cunt! Cunt!

The daily reading from the Dictionary is over. The final hymn has been sung. Morning prayers are finally ending. Mouse, still on her knees, glances at the plaster figure on the bracket high above their heads. The blue eyes are both kindly and piercing, the chin thrust forwards, the hands raised in loving admonition. The sky-blue robe, falling from chin to

260

ankle, moulds the slender girlish body, its barely perceptible breasts and hips. Over one shoulder drops a sash of white silk, inscribed with the motto of the State: Consciousness; Cleanliness; Correctness; Caring. One bare foot, slightly thrust forwards, rests on white roses. The neat blonde hairdo is crowned with a circle of stars and lilies clasped at the front by a silver crescent moon. The smile is unfalteringly sweet, with a hint of toughness. Every day, morning and evening, Mouse and the other tarts kneel in front of this image, repeating the brothel prayers, asking for forgiveness, begging that they may become more like Her.

The tarts haul themselves to their feet. Lucy slams down the lid of the piano. The first shift begins in ten minutes' time.

Lucy catches Mouse up in the corridor.

– You managing all right? Happy?

Mouse keeps on walking in the decorous line, eyes fixed on the grey overall, red star just visible on the shoulder, of the girl ahead. She tries to consider Lucy's words, what they might mean, tries to undo them, take them in one by one. She shakes her head in bewilderment. Lucy squeezes her arm.

– Cheer up, chicken. You'll get used to it soon enough. It's not a bad life, you know. No one will hurt you.

She jerks a shoulder in the direction of the uniformed male guards, guns at their hips, who are stationed at intervals along the white bare corridor. A tart has only to blow her whistle, should a client prove violent, and he is quickly dragged away and dealt with. On the other hand, any tart blowing her whistle too frequently is liable to be suspected of *non-compliance*, and had up for questioning, and possible punishment, by the superintendent.

Mouse has reached her cell door. She pushes between its minimal swinging halves and looks at Lucy over the top of them.

– Let's talk sometime soon, Lucy suggests: I could be useful to you, and you to me.

– I've got to work now, Mouse mutters: thank you for your concern.

She waits for the other woman to depart before stripping off her overall and donning her work clothes. Silver leather bra, silver leather G-string, fake tiger-fur gloves, high-heeled shoes, tiger half-mask. She checks her appearance in the mirror hung at the end of the bed. Good. Slender thighs, concave belly. Most of the tarts, Mouse included, are on permanent slimming diets, to make sure they don't become too plump. A few, like Lucy, are allowed to remain large. They cater for the special interests of certain members of the officer class. Only last week, one of these was found murdered on the wasteland just behind the brothel, beside the rubbish tip. It was hushed up, of course. But everyone knows.

Mouse yawns, applies fresh lipstick, then arranges herself carefully on the bed to await her first client of the day.

– Come to mother, she whispers to herself, very low in case she's overheard by one of the guards patrolling outside: come to mother.

Turtle stands in the queue, shivering. Jacket sleeves too short, no gloves, scarf stolen last week from the factory canteen when he went back to the serving-hatch for a clean fork and turned his back on his chair for two short minutes. He folds his arms across his thin chest, sticks his hands in his armpits. Head down, whistling to keep his courage up.

– Number. Card. Health certificates.

The queue of young men shuffles forwards, one by one sucked out of the biting wind scouring the concrete walkway into the strip-lit relative warmth of the reception area. At first Turtle can't hear what the white-uniformed woman in her plate-glass booth is saying to him. She turns up her microphone and points. He enters the steel-walled lift and is carried upwards. The automatic doors close behind him and he's in a white corridor lined with mirrors. He can't escape himself: short, skinny, hunched, carroty hair cropped short, blue eyes watering. He walks forwards, in accordance with the instructions boomed over the tannoy just beside his head, halting obediently outside a door marked Temple of Joy.

Clothes stripped off, revolve under an icy swoosh of chlorinated water in the tiny shower, don white towelling bathrobe reaching barely to his thighs. Wait, shivering uncontrollably now, in the cold cubicle walled with plastic. Lino clammy under his bare soles. Exit as his number is called.

The bearded doctor is genial, letting Turtle take his time to doff his skimpy robe, fingers trembling, climb up onto the high couch and arrange himself, lying down, on its scratchy paper sheet. Knees bent, open and apart.

The doctor waves a cheerful hand at the crowd of white-coated students pressing intently forwards at the foot of the couch.

– You don't mind them, do you? They've got to learn.

The examination would be a short one, were it not prolonged by the need of every student in turn to approach, don the thin rubber glove, probe for himself Turtle's most vulnerable places. Their fingers measure, pinch, tap, squeeze, rootle. Turtle is rolled onto his front, onto his back, onto his front again. A nurse, in the white nylon jacket and trousers of his elite profession, leans against a side wall, sardonically watching.

– They told you this examination's necessary, didn't they? soothes the doctor: just a matter of hygiene. Don't let it worry you.

He massages Turtle's penis, which has wrinkled back on itself like a snail trying to escape inside its shell.

– I tend to find that some clients even learn to enjoy this experience. A certain pleasure can be gained, a certain erotic response set up. Better to let these things out. All the more for our girls to deal with afterwards. We wouldn't like to leave any perverse fantasies lurking in the unconscious. Better to rout them out as early as possible.

From behind the students' masked male faces come their clinical questions.

– A virgin, are you then?
– Masturbate, do you?
– Masochistic fantasies, have you?
– Know what good sex should be, do you?
– Been to a tart before, have you?

Their breath smells sour. Turtle answers yes, no, no, no, no, never. They laugh at him, camaraderie. The doctor slaps his right nipple.

– You'll do. Get your blood tests and jabs from the nurse, and then have a good time.

Clothed again, arse sore, mouth dry, Turtle walks down

263

another white corridor, this one patrolled by uniformed armed guards and set with swinging half-doors with numbers painted on them in gold. He checks the card in his hand. Number seventeen. Nearly there.

Don't panic, Dog had counselled him before he was sent off to winter camp for retraining: there's nothing to it. The tart does it all. Once you've got her underneath you just lie there and close your eyes. Then afterwards you get your certificate and your new card, and your new set of clothes and your video recorder and your alcohol allowance, and you've done it. Done what? Turtle asked. Passed your puberty rite, Dog said, grinning: become a man, like me. You'll get used to it. We all do.

Turtle stands in front of number seventeen. The guard stationed some way down the corridor notices his hesitation, turns, begins to stroll towards him. What else had Dog told him? *Give them bliss* if they're too passive, if they don't pretend well enough. Perform. Don't let them know you're scared, the bitches.

The guard is coming closer. Turtle plunges through the swinging doors.

Huge red mouth, open, tongue playing over glistening lipstick. Eyes glittering coldly through black and yellow stripes. Thick fur, silver strappings at breast and ankle and crotch. Small furry hands playing with a heavy silver chain, links clinking against each other. Body of a half-tamed beast lying on the fur-strewn bed, ready to pounce, tear, devour. Get in there first, Dog warned him: before she springs, or bites.

Turtle approaches the bed without fear. He knows her.

– Mouse, he whispers: it's me.

Mouse adjusts the lighting with practised fingers. The strip light dims. Now the cell has shadows.

– We'll have to do it, she mutters, her breath tickling his ear: because of the camera. They give you a video of it afterwards as a souvenir. Then when we've done it they turn the camera off and we'll have a few minutes to talk before the guard comes and fetches you away.

She jerks her head towards the electronic eye above the door. Click. It tilts and swerves; they blink and brace themselves.

Turtle follows Mouse's silent instructions: the twitch of a wrist, flicker of an eyelid, grip of a knee. He remembers her. He

264

knows her, a little. Under her savage costume she is as nervous as he: he watches the pulse beat at the base of her throat, shifts his glance towards her eyes, which are very bright. He lets go into her with a cry of grief, and her hands tighten for a second in his hair. She hasn't bothered putting on an act with him, and he's grateful.

– On the wasteland, she's whispering to him: behind the car dump. I've got a hiding place there. I'll show you. I'll meet you tomorrow night, around eleven, after lights out here. At the car dump. I'll see you.

The cab of the broken-down lorry holds them snug, a frail tent pitched against a stormy night. Outside prowl the Night Police with guns and batons, starving dogs, sleepless derelicts. Inside, they are warm, domestic. Mouse has pulled the cab's curtains, frilly cretonne stitched by some long-ago wife or girlfriend, and has lit a stub of candle. They curl on the little bunk high up behind the driving seat, faces close, under the coats they have laid on themselves as blankets. Tonight Turtle has his own smell back, undisguised by carbolic and cold water, and Mouse, sniffing him, is torn open. She has meant to be cautious, but now her hands fly free, suddenly frantic, and explore his shoulders in the half-dark, his neck, his ears. Her mouth, daring, rubs against his. This time unskilful, lingering, inventing each step of the way. His fingers slither around buttons and enter her overall. Her skin shouts out with a hundred voices: touch me. Kissing him, she is astonished by the flock of birds that rises inside her and migrates. Hasty, and confident now, they wriggle arms and legs free of clothes, pull the loose coats back over their bare shoulders.

They lie on their sides, facing each other, legs laced, and Turtle dips his fingers inside her and she holds him there, wanting more, more. Pleasure is easy, born of memory, of this comfortable liking, this hunger not held back. Turtle is light, moving beside her and on her, his hand caressing the place she has shown him, the little bud blossoming plump and wet, and they move over and against each other, intense heat at the core, that hand her anchor of sweet sensation as they ride and ride, she enclosing him, he leaping gently into her. Coming is just a continuation of this slow dance, first a tingle from the seabed,

265

then a warm current lazily pushing up and through her, finally a pouring deep inside. Mouse feels enormous, full, the long valley pulsing while she lies there and laughs, while her knees are liquid and the explosion melts calves and thighs, electric.

– Let's rewrite the bloody State Dictionary, she says, giggling: let's rewrite every single damned word in it. Let's make our own meanings.

She can talk now. So much to say, to tell. Turtle is bringing her all of himself, approaching her with heaped hands, offering his gifts, his plenty, his kindness. She has not known this. She lies wrapped up with him, while they play with words. Loud laughter as the poems spill out of them, the images they bounce back and forwards, the jokes that make them wobble, almost tearful with delight, with disobedience, with loving rudeness. They name each other, and each other's bodies, slapping each other with new names. They turn policemen into milk bottles, butter up tarts, make men soluble in tears, stick red stars onto the matt black sky.

– Mother, calls out Mouse over and over: mother.

– I've written it all down, Turtle tells her: every word. But we need a safe place to hide it in. It's treasonous to write poetry.

Mouse opens her mouth to reply. I know that, stupid. Give it to me. I'll bury it somewhere. But the cab door speaks instead, a screech of rusty hinges. Then the flashlight, blinding them for a second, zigzagging across their faces.

Lucy's face, startled and white. Lucy's other hand coming up to her mouth. A red hand. Blood, glistening and fresh, like a rubber glove. And behind her, not very far away, a play of yellow searchlights, the hunting cry of the sirens of the Night Police.

40 No island visible this morning. We're lost, becalmed in glassy green sea.

I don't know what to do once I've finished my chores. Not in the mood for reading or cooking. Too cloudy to sunbathe. I decide I need company, and go off in search of the others.

Here they all are, descending the companionway leading down from the cabin deck.

– Where are you going? I ask: can I come too?

– Sure, says the Deftly Sibyl: we're going down to the hold. Of course you can come.

Down to the hold. Down to that dark windowless place ribbed like an upturned church, where those who have upturned reason and sanity disport themselves. I've heard them. The hysterics, uttering their cries and groans, stamping their feet in bitter rhythms, beating at the walls of their wooden cage. They've kept me awake many a night, kept me tossing on my hot bunk and worrying about how securely the hatches are battened down and whether the whole mob of them won't burst out in mutiny and commandeer my ship.

I shudder.

– We can't go down there. It's dangerous. And it's filthy.

– We've been going down there regularly, the Forsaken Sibyl soothes me: we know what it's like. Don't worry. Come and see for yourself.

The hold is the one place I didn't want to design. All the Arkitects were brisk: let us take care of it; sanitation and sewage disposal, not a job for a woman. In the end I did do it myself. A large cellar-like place, to take all the rubbish. Then I locked the door and forgot about it.

– Down into the bowels of the Ark? I cry: whatever for?

I don't know how the hysterics got in there and I don't care.

– Come and see, says the Gaffer, holding out his hand: you might find it quite interesting once you get used to it.

– Why didn't you tell me? I demand: where you've been going all this time? You've never said a single word about it.

– You never asked, says the Correct Sibyl: did you?

– You'd come back on board in the evenings, says the Re-Vision Sibyl: bursting to tell us all about your adventures, and somehow we never got to telling you about ours. We assumed you weren't interested. Or that you'd disapprove. So we kept quiet.

– It's quite difficult to explain the writing process to other people, adds the Babble-On Sibyl: I always assume they'll get bored. So I tend to shut up about it.

– Come *on*, shouts the Gaffer: get a move on, girls.

I'm dumb. But I don't want to be left out this time. So I follow the others down the companionway. The iron rungs are slippery. I lose count of the steps. Down one steep ladder-like decline, then down the next, gripping the cold rails with both hands. Smell of wet tarpaulins and wet ropes. The deck slimy under my bare feet. Greasy puddles slicked with oil and smeary rainbows.

We halt outside a massive iron door. I know how the bolts work: I tested them long ago, concerned for security. I slide them back, then touch the great ring handle.

– You're the only one of us, Mrs Noah, the Deftly Sibyl tells me: who hasn't told a story yet. Yours is the one that's missing.

– But I'm not a writer, not really, I hiss at her, almost weeping: I'm a librarian. I like things to be orderly, especially on my own Ark. I'm not sure I want to go in here.

– Time you got started, the Babble-On Sibyl says.

All my companions lay their hands next to mine on the iron handle. I nod my head. Then we all pull together, and the door swings open.

I close my eyes.

What a mess I'm going to find. My mess, that I brought with me onto the Ark without knowing it. This is the room I have never entered; the last place I ever wanted to be; the junkroom of old newspapers, heaps of torn lino, old vests and underpants stained yellow; the cave alive with spiders and cockroaches; the

268

coal cellar where the bogeyman lurks.

I like to have everything neat and tidy about me. I've dusted the chapel, done out the kitchen and the sickbay and the bathroom, cleaned the big step-in wardrobe, weeded the little roof garden. So it's time to go in here.

I open my eyes, and blink.

The hold is as bright and alive as a railway station, as crowded. There seems to be some sort of party going on. The dance floor is thick with performers costumed in garish silks stepping hard under spangled spotlights, under a central twirling lantern of stained glass that scatters the dazed faces with veils of colour. To one side, a man in a periwig and a blue satin coat plays raucous organ, accompanied by a woman on tenor sax. Smell of sweat, French cigarettes, Eau Sauvage, lilacs.

No one has noticed my entrance. A breathing space. I start to make my way around the walls. A quick snoop, discreet. Then I'll make my escape. The sibyls have already vanished. I can see the Gaffer on the dance floor, shirt unbuttoned to the waist, arms flung up above his head as he tosses and stamps.

Here are my two grandmothers wedged into armchairs, hands clawing cups of tea, heads nodding over the blue flame of an oil stove.

– You should have seen this place when I moved in, Nana is exclaiming: piles of tack everywhere. Balls of fluff under the beds, no hot water, the cold tap leaking through rag bandages, layers of filth on the floor. I gave it a good going-over. Rotten as a compost heap it was. Heigh-ho, look sharp, I told them, give us a hand. Then with my spit-and-polish memory I set all straight.

– The youth of today, scoffs my other grandmother: I wonder you bothered asking them to help. Self self self, that's all they think about.

She catches sight of me and scowls.

– I want, I want, I want, she mocks: that's all you can say, isn't it? I'll tell you this much. You won't get it.

– I swept up the abuse, Nana chatters on: and I burned it. Every scrap. But there was too much work left over for one person to do. So I got sat down here to rest my old bones and left it to the young ones to finish. Ten o'clock struck at the castle gate. What, girl, you dare to thwart me thus?

She laughs at me, waving a dismissal, and I wander on.

269

Here's the child I aborted: a tiny girl whimpering in a corner, snot congealed round her nostrils, over-large jumper crusted with food and sick. Waaa. Waaa. The plaint winds my forehead in barbed wire. When I put out a hand to her she tries to bite it. I pick her up, calming the flying fists, patting the furious red face hot with tears. After a while she stops crying. I set her down again, and she waddles off, nappy bulging at her knees, to watch the circus acts succeeding each other in a nearby alcove. A four-legged body splits apart then re-joins itself: identical twin jugglers in glittering leotards toss batons and balls at each other in a swift strobe, mirror-reflections for each other. Which is which? I can't tell. Can they? High above our heads a Degas girl in a feathered silver bird-suit bites on a noosed plumb line, makes geometry on string loops. Here's an elephant dancing with a tambourine, a fat Tarzan in spotted nylon G-string dangling from his mouth. Down tumbles a trapeze, and now three plump male fairies in skin-tight azure trunks swing from each other's fingertips. All five sibyls reappear carrying piles of encyclopedias, edge along the silvery high wire.

I'm wearing pink satin ballet shoes, their toes blocked. I go up on points, wobble. My shoes are filled with blood. I can't stop dancing.

I pirouette through an archway into what seems the vault of a museum, or the anteroom of a hospital. Broken capitals and columns are heaped pell-mell in a corner; fragments of memorial tablets cut with Latin inscriptions are set higgledy-piggledy into the wall, an incoherent poetry; cardboard boxes of pottery shards pile one on top of the other; oil paintings are stacked two foot deep against a table bearing a jumble of smashed sculptures, torn manuscripts, worm-eaten embroideries.

Here's Snow White, Keeper of Relics, holding a hacksaw.

– I'll cut your feet off, shall I? she offers: then you won't feel a thing.

She nods at the stack of corpses behind her. Like dolls they lie, rigid, eyes staring, shrouds pulled smooth, legs ending in bloody stumps.

– It's neater, Snow White giggles: I can't afford to buy shoes for all my little ones. The sweethearts. I collected this lot from the mortuary this morning. I like to get them while they're still fresh. The Third World War is breaking out, didn't you know?

There's been another bombing raid in the Middle East. I can't remember where, it's not my job to bother about details.

Under my feet the plaster dust of a fallen fresco. No, the ashes of six million Jews.

– Europe's dying, Snow White sighs: such a pity. All that lovely art and culture. No one will know what it was like. Gone up in flames. Irrelevant. We're washed out, all of us.

She waves her hacksaw and grins.

– But I like to keep busy, nonetheless. It's important to occupy oneself, you know, until one's Prince shall come. Hitler, Stalin, Mussolini, they all let me down. They weren't Mr Right. But I don't give up hope.

I limp off smartish, to the jerk of piano music.

Here's a fine tea table: snow of a white cloth, tiered cake-stand bearing plates of macaroons and gingersnaps, striped black and white humbugs, cucumber sandwiches. Around it are all the sibyls of the past, those whom I have not yet met, those whose names I do not know, those whose names I have not been allowed to know. All the women who have ever used the Ark are here. A reunion. A sort of Gaudy. Lazy librarian that I am: I have not browsed sufficiently in the bookstacks, the catalogue. I know so few of these women. I peer around for familiar faces.

Charlotte Brontë in a scarlet evening frock waves her cigar at Colette, whose ears are large and wing-shaped. Emily Dickinson, her hair in curl-papers, is arguing with Virginia Woolf, whose hands are full of pink betting-slips.

– I hate dinner parties, she yells above the hubbub of the Palm Court orchestra: but a quiet get-together with friends, that's different.

Katherine Mansfield catches my eye, waves her fork at me.

– Plenty of room for everyone, she cries, her mouth full of German sausage: pull up a chair.

I slide in, in between Dorothy Richardson, who is tap-dancing in tails and top hat amidst the teacups, and Aphra Behn, who is fighting a mock duel with Sappho, teasing her with brandysnaps.

– Ha, says the Nubian Sibyl through a mouthful of ripe peach: so you got here in the end, did you?

– How did *you* get here? I ask her: I thought you were out of town. You could have told me you were on board!

The Bombay Sibyl leans forward from her place beyond her friend.

– We were at a bookfair in Rome. Now we're on our way to a conference in some God-forsaken place called Gravesend. We thought we'd hitch a lift. And it seemed more fun down here.

– We took the opportunity, adds the Guatemalan Sibyl: to donate copies of our latest books to your library. Seems a little understocked in certain areas. You'll find them downstairs, in the Acquisitions Department. Better get down to some homework, girl.

– We aren't, murmurs the Kentish Town Sibyl, wiping mango juice off her fingers: merely the flavour of the month. You want to run a decent library, Mrs Noah, you'd better smarten up your act.

There are my five travelling companions munching bread pudding. There's the Gaffer pouring out tea. There's Hildegard of Bingen discussing gardening with Christine de Pisan and Marie de France. There's the Mills and Boon cohort alertly discussing structuralism with George Eliot. There's Madame de Sévigné offering the milk jug to Catherine of Siena. There's Anne Bradstreet scribbling poems on the tablecloth, Grazia Deledda playing cats-cradle with Simone de Beauvoir. There are all the other sibyls whose works I have yet to read. A feast of words. At least the table is big enough for us all: no hierarchies here; no one left out.

– It takes two to make a baby, murmurs Ahkmatova, bending forwards: why do people say literature has no sex? Meaning just one? Keep me in isolation from the male poets of my generation and you'll never understand my contribution to Russian poetry.

– Deny my friendship with Dickens, remarks Mrs Gaskell: and you'll never know what he learned from me.

– Forget the fact that Richardson read us, shout Jane Barker and Eliza Heywood in concert: and you'll never understand the origins of the English novel.

– Imagism had mothers as well as fathers, H.D. points out: and actually my name is Hilda. Ezra Pound, er, defrocked me.

The Gaffer leaps to his feet.

– History doesn't make sense without you, he cries: too many

272

so-called definitive anthologies, compiled by men of course, leave you out. The idea of the canon is a con. The great tradition is a fake. Select lists of great authors matter far less than *writing*. *Verbs* are what matter. *Doing* it.

He is radiant, ecstatic.

– It's time I told you all, he confesses: the truth about my book. I didn't write it all by myself. A group of us did. A team. I've taken all the credit all this time. My friends were so generous. They never betrayed me. I'm just a rip-off merchant.

He sits down again and hides his face behind a large meringue.

– But I like your book, Elizabeth Barrett Browning comforts him: I really do. You have real talent.

– Who is this guy? asks the Bangkok Sibyl: some sort of ageing hippy? Some sort of travelling salesman? Pass the fruitcake, will you? I'm still hungry.

– He must have been feeling a bit *lonely*, muses the Brixton Sibyl.

She leans across the table and touches the Gaffer's arm.

– I had a phone call half an hour ago, she says: from Donne and Wyatt, did I tell you? They're signing up for the next trip. That will cheer you up. You'll have some male company.

I'm confused. All the books in the Arkive bookstacks have come off their shelves and jostle as eager angry bodies in this room. Parents or writers? I can't sort them out. I can't tell one category from another. My library skills fail me. I need new words.

All this time I have been searching. All this time I have been wandering around the earth, going out, out, to look for a solution. Now at last I've found what I've been needing. Here.

Not Outsiders but Insiders.

This is the house of language. The house of words. Here, inside the Ark, the body of the mother, I find words.

The islands of faery. The blessed isles in the west. The earthly paradise. The country formed out of a single rock, surrounded by sea. With its walled garden, its precious minerals and spices, its singing streams, its beasts that talk. Here. Home.

I have darkness, I grope in darkness, I carve chunks out of it which are my words.

Home is the body. The bone-house. The room of my own is inside me. Each day I build it and each day it is torn down.

Creation starts here, in the Ark. Love actively shapes the work. My mother nourishes me with words, words of such power and richness that I grow, dance, leap. But the purpose of the Ark is that I leave it. The purpose of the womb is that I be born from it. So that when I'm forced to go from her, when I lose her, I can call out after her, cry out her name. I become myself, which means not-her; with blood and tears I become not-the-mother.

She points to the rainbow, umbilical cord connecting us. The curve of light in the rain joining belly to belly, the silver rope dangling earth, that mud baby. The symbol of the symbol, denoting the separation between worlds, the one I know and the one I have lost; also their connection.

Cutting the cord, she gives me speech. Words of longing for that world I've lost, words of desire to explore this absence-of-her. I must go further into absence, and find more words.

Ark. Imagination. Body. Home. Book.

The words juggle and swap, changing places, piling up on top of each other, jumping over semi-colons, free to move and play, to puncture syntax, tilt meanings, stand them on their heads. I'm inside the classification system of the Arkive, relating to everything under the sun and related to it. I'm inside the Ark and the Ark is inside me.

I have no name: I am Noah's wife. The Ark has drawn me onwards and has set me free. The Ark has made me want. The Ark has allowed me, in my turn, to become the virgin-whore who is both the mother and the wanderer; word that's been missing for so long; word that reliably keeps going away.

Delphi, Apollo's shrine, was the *omphalos*, the navel-centre of the universe. Here, inside. Daphne's place, where the hunt for meanings starts.

The sibyls and the Gaffer have plaited a rope of stories between them. I must add mine, while the sun shines in the rain, and finish the rainbow. Add the colour that's missing. A home at last: one that dissolves, is incomplete, and vanishes. As my child, in her time, will die. As my book, in its time, will rot.

274

Shaped against death, in the teeth of death, out of death, returning to death when the time comes. A pause between deaths, fought for by my hands.

Writer. Mother. Two words I have linked through this voyage on the Ark, this arc of stories, a distance of so many nights, such longing. This long twist of words spun out of loss.

The tea party's over, melted into shadows. The organ has stopped, the circus has packed up. I'm lying on a bed of cushions, in a tangle of clothes. Blearily I count. Fourteen arms. Fourteen legs. My right breast groans, and detaches itself, looms above me. Looking up, I stare at the Gaffer, then back down at the five sibyls entwined in sleep, each other, and us. What a muddle. I start to laugh, and cautiously to detach myself from my collapsed companions. The Gaffer pulls me to my feet, hands me bits of clothing. My mouth is dry, and my head aches.

– I need a glass of water, I croak; and I think I'll go up on deck and get some air.

The Gaffer wriggles into creased trousers. He coughs.

– I've never attended an orgy before. Though I must say it was very pleasant.

He blushes.

– What happened? I ask him, checking I've still got both earrings: I'm afraid I don't exactly remember.

A sea-monster, that we made between us, a creature with seven mouths sucking, seven pairs of hands caressing, innumerable openings to be explored and filled, expanse of skin to be licked and stroked, tasting of salt, fish, cheese, sugar. I shake my head, to clear it.

– You could say, admits the Gaffer: that the party got a little out of hand. We decided to celebrate the end of the voyage.

– What? I shout: where are we?

He stares at me.

– Don't you remember? We sighted land at dawn. We're docked. We're back in Venice.

41   The Ark looks like any other *vaporetto*. We come ashore together, turning our backs on it. We leave it behind.

Our farewells are brief. A hug, a kiss, a promise to keep on writing. Then I walk away, my eyes full of tears, leaving the others drinking coffee on one of the large café rafts bobbing alongside the Zattere. I stride along the edge of the Giudecca canal, concentrating on the wide pale green sky, the skip and race of the waters under the great boats gliding past the distant warehouses. I turn down the Rio S. Trovaso, towards the Accademia. I'm not ready to face Noah yet. I need to walk.

Now the city closes around me, streaked with green like onyx above and below. I stand on the Accademia bridge, listening to the clang of church bells. I become a needle, pushing my sharp inquisitive head through passages and alleys, whipping around the edges of *campi* and *piazze*, pulling my bright red thread behind me, stitching stone to stone, making a track, remembering, finding my way back.

The sun comes out slowly from behind pearly mist, at first just a faint warmth on my face, a delicate light on the red roofs of houses, then dry and sparkling. The *campo* I'm crossing becomes larger. Palaces tilt backwards. People stroll, don't hurry. Three dogs in black muzzles circle a dark smear on a paving-stone. Voices murmur in French, German, Italian. Heat laps my skin, dissolves me into the city. I find a bar, stand at the counter and order coffee, a brioche. I'm starving. I feel as though I haven't eaten for a long time. Needing sweetness, I sift sugar into my tiny cup with a long-handled silver spoon. The brioche is still warm, apricot jam at its heart. I eat a second one. A good breakfast. Now that I'm pregnant I must take proper care of myself.

I walk out again. I'm alone. No husband here. No Ark. Gone my anchor and maps, gone my compass, gone my passport into the world. I'm sailing alone now. Single, my eye driving forwards, into the wind. I should find Noah. But I can't return to that old world I shared with him. Will he be here in this new one?

Is it too much coffee, or morning sickness, or anxiety, that makes me feel suddenly dizzy and faint? The sun has gone in. I shudder. The *campo* is cold and black. After that I don't remember.

42 The Deftly Sibyl has taken over the garden shed. Lawn mower, hose, fork and spade, twig broom, all are cleared away into a corner. George's carpentry bench serves as desk. Pens and pencils bunch in a flowerpot, earthy, red. Discarded drafts rest on a sack of potting compost, there to rot like dry leaves and fertilize her brain. The typewriter purrs. Small square of dusty windowpane presses her nose against dripping green bushes, slime of cuckoo-spit on white flowers, slender black branches. Invisible: the sap running inside. Rain bounces on the corrugated-iron roof, clatters down its silver tilt. She has bolted the door, hung a notice outside. Danger: Woman at Work.

She has a house. She has hung red checked gingham curtains at the window, bought herself a bentwood chair from the local junkshop, provided herself with crockery from Woolworth's, a red and yellow tablecloth. Always carry a corkscrew in your handbag, her mother instructed her once, and she does. Meals of bread and cheese in her hermitage are feasts, savoured slowly in the silence broken only by the patter of rain above her head, the wet notes of blackbirds marking out their territory in the apple tree on the patch of grass between her and the other house where George sits writing an article. She doesn't know where the children are. She doesn't know what they are doing. Half term. George is in charge.

His face when she told him. Furious, grim. A day of argument brings no change. You are ruthlessly autonomous, he spits at her. Then pouts, sulks. The children save her: something new, this, a holiday from Mum. Dad will let them eat charred black sausages for breakfast every day, won't nag about changing shoes and making beds. They swear to be good, to leave him in peace. He caves in. She refuses their help in the

278

removal, carries over her belongings herself. She doesn't want them to come into her retreat. Campbed stacked against the wooden wall. Some nights she goes back to the house to sleep, but she departs early, cherishing her dawn cup of tea alone in the chilly shed. She creeps back to piss, too, using the outside lavatory in the yard. Then slinks off rapidly before she's seen.

She sits at her desk, an old quilt padding her knees; peace enters her, slides along her bones. On the shelf she has put up in the corner by the window stand her reassembled household gods: painted wooden doll from the USSR with a tiny replica in its belly; photograph of her sister; lump of blue glass worn smooth and round, a solid bit of sea; tiny folding shrine of gilded wood from Italy whose doors open to reveal a sad Madonna flanked by spiky angels.

Living in a dolls' house. Silly woman. How pathetic. How immature. Real writers (men) can write anywhere (in the middle of a battlefield or a riot), don't need to stake out this neurotic claim to personal territory (the world is theirs to start with).

She shakes her head, and the buzz of self-hate subsides. Her fingers touch the typewriter keys, re-order her world. Tap, tap, tap. Her small hammers reconstruct what she knows: a partial vision, limited, the joins showing. So be it. You do what you can, while the dispossessed line up on the path outside and beat at the door and she opens it. All the homeless pour into her heart and squat it, their anger and despair a further hammer fragmenting her even as she strives to build sentences that will last, to do her job capably. They dictate to her: a catalogue of wild cries.

A bang on the window. She starts up out of her pain-filled trance. Her daughter's face, staring and white. Come quickly Mum Johnny's cut himself with the carving knife blood quickly Mum come.

She hurries across the sopping lawn back towards the house.

The Forsaken Sibyl has taken a month-long job in Italy, house-sitting, while roof repairs are done on their flat in Florence, for a married couple who are cousins of her adoptive parents. She needs the money; and evacuated from her squat, her possessions stored in a friend's spare room, she also needs a temporary refuge until she sorts out what to do next. The Clellands introduce her to the builders, instruct her to call on their architect in case of problems, promise to despatch regular payments for building supplies and labour, then depart on their tour of Tuscany and Umbria.

She pushes open the green shutters, leans out of the study window. Below her, the impatient blaring queue of cars; the petrol fumes, rubbish heaps and dogshit of the narrow grey street; the busy shoppers; the children in pushchairs. Craning her neck one way, she can see the massive gate-arch marking the boundary of the city on its eastern side; looking the other way, she can just see the top of the Duomo, jewelled Easter egg.

But no time for sightseeing. She's here to work. She fingers her pocket dictionary, wondering whether her slender O-Level Italian will be sufficient.

The builders arrive next morning at eight, three sturdy dark brothers, wives and children left down south in Regio Calabria. They speak between themselves an impenetrable guttural code, translate for her into Italian when necessary. Eh, eh, no husband, all alone here? They laugh. It's better to be without women, wives belong in the house, a drag on a man.

She should have cleared out the big kitchen-living room last night. Frantically she packs china and glass into wicker baskets, carries the lighter furniture downstairs to the tiny storeroom, while they start knocking down the ceiling. Lumps of plaster clatter to the terracotta floor. More than dust: the kitchen is a gritty grey cloud. Next they tear down the woven cane-lining the plaster clung to, fragile basketry that has left its criss-cross print on the rubble below. Then the beams are exposed, thick logs, blackened and cracked. The large pieces of furniture huddle in the next room, widows draped in plastic veils heavy with grey powder. Fridge and cooker unplugged and hidden: she will live on fruit and water. Debris of broken bricks, ankle-deep, dust in her lungs and on her lips, her hair a stiff white wig.

Their job is to destroy, and hers to clear up after them. Noise of falling masonry as she crouches on the bed, her last oasis this one tiny room they will leave intact, trying to write. Her arms are about the house; trying to hold it up; while they huff and puff and blow her down. Beams dislodged, sawn up and vomited out of the study window into the waiting lorry, the roof can come off, heaved down in red handfuls. Women hold up half the sky? There is no sky. Just this gap. She is open-

280

mouthed to the rain. Pigeons shit in the bath. She is walled in air. The kitchen has vanished: she stands on a bombsite under dark winds, looking up at the stars, shuddering under hammer blows, iron wedges driven into her skull, fissuring it, she tumbles across the invisible floor, a litter of broken stones.

The days batter her with anxiety. Smashed light fittings dangle from the walls. The electricity fails. Neighbours complain about noise and mess. Invoices must be haggled over. Pall of thick dirt enters every pore of the house, dissolves it, dust to dust. At night she lies sleepless in her grimy bed, ears cocked for the scrabble of birds and rats across the gaping building site on the other side of her door. Open the door: step out into nothingness; the void; half the house swinging loose from a single hinge. She is lonely. By day she feeds on brief interchanges with the builders, with shopkeepers. By night, she thinks of Londoners in the last war, emerging from bomb-shelters in the morning to find their homes toppled and smashed, of the people across the world driven by war and poverty into refugee camps, squatting under cardboard shelters to await death, watching the children sicken, their bellies swell. Count their blessings? They are alive?

Self-pity breeds revolt. On the seventh day she decides to take time off. She hires a motorbike and roars off up into the hills to see the countryside.

The Correct Sibyl stands uncertainly on the edge of the pavement, peering about her. She has already lost Tom and Jessie. Still, they are old enough to be sensible. And they'll enjoy themselves more without her dogging them.

It is raining. The world is black and white and grey, shiny as celluloid. Texture and grain in monochrome. People bunch under umbrellas, waiting.

And then the first Carnival float leaps down Westbourne Grove towards her, a tongue poking out in showers of confetti colours, a dance of bright symbols unleashed, bobbing and circling, the street suddenly lit up as though by night in neon. The force of joy breaking out in her and unfurling along the tarmac is so great that she bursts into tears, fresh rain wetting her face.

Woman-spider, world-weaver, jogs along in her huge blue

281

and silver crinoline web. Bumblebees with furry knees jump up. Spacemen in silver-paper suits advance their hips. Drums beat, shrill whistles blow. A long narrow ceiling of plastic is held up against the rain by the file of dancers as they sway and step beneath it, and the watching people break free from the pavement and jig forwards under their umbrellas over the mud and refuse in the gutter, and the Correct Sibyl goes with them, released into this joy. All day long she sings and dances with these unknown neighbours in the dark streets which she helps illuminate. Repression lifts: the people lift their knees to the rhythm, splash in rain and music, twirl their hats, joggle their bones and shake their flesh free and get soaked. Lifting up their hands. No cars. No more division between pavement and road. Just this tide of bodies surging through the city and claiming it as theirs. The unconscious is out. Snaking serpent that coils and doubles back, that pours forward in primary colours and glitter shedding sparks and beer cans and streamers. A stranger darts in under her twirling umbrella and clasps her waist, putting his dark face next to hers, mixing sweat, tight black curls glistening, mouth amused, and they sway on together, swallowed up in the thrashing crowd, the wet.

The Babble-On Sibyl is building a new bed. She and Neil have designed it together, squabbling, grabbing the pencil from the other's fingers, furiously crossing out.

It must be *wide*, she insists. Wide enough for her to be able to lie on her stomach and scissor her legs out before she sleeps, wide enough that they can both loll surrounded by books. Wide enough that a child can tumble in with them of a weekend morning. No more of your rules of conduct, she tells Neil: I shall sleep late as often as I want, I shall lie in this bed on Sundays uncaring that I smudge the sheets with newsprint, I shall eat breakfast in bed, you will even bring me an early morning cup of tea.

They have sawn up the pine planks, which lie stacked on the carpet. They have agreed on the height of the headboard, the lack of curves and frills. Now they start to fit it all together.

He holds the wooden parts, she wields the screwdriver. Then they swap. Slowly, the bed assembles itself. Takes shape. She has not bought enough screws, and now the shops are shut.

Impatient, she runs to the kitchen door, prises from its top hinge the two long black flat-headed screws she needs. As supper time approaches, it is done. Sturdy, low, a frame of gleaming wood onto whose supporting struts they fit the new mattress.

The bed takes up most of the space in the tiny room. They edge around it, putting on the clean cotton sheets and pillowcases, tucking in the scarlet blanket. It is ready. Plump and soft, inviting.

– I'm not hungry yet, are you? she says: let's try it *now*.

Clothes off, sweat and grime rinsed away under the feeble lukewarm shower. Shivering, dry. Padding barefoot across the litter of wood-shavings, sliding naked between deliciously cold sheets. Bodies warmed by each other, by the blankets, air blowing in from the open window to curl around their necks. They design together how their bodies will fit; they manoeuvre arms and legs in intricate joins; carefully, according to no blueprint but this second by second of shared breathing and answering gestures, they begin to build. And all the time, even as she takes her pleasure and gives it, she is watching, considering, analysing; taking notes.

The Re-Vision Sibyl and Maria sit opposite each other at a small square table in the far corner of the restaurant. They've chosen the upstairs room, liking its old-fashioned decor, mournful and plain: brown walls lined with occasional mirrors, no plants or pictures. When they arrived, the restaurant was large, echoing. Now it is packed with people. Roar of noise buffets their ears, drowns their talk. They lean close, lipread in order to hear each other. Between them the thick white tablecloth, heavy white plates, silver knives and forks, glasses of mineral water alight with tiny bubbles, a dark red bottle of wine. Their hands, teasing crusts of bread, almost touch. They are underwater, swimming in this sea of shouts and babble, their faces looming up large, not quite bumping.

Maria's mouth is wide, full, red. Playing her role for tonight with scarlet lipstick, wide-shouldered forties suit, seamed silk stockings, little high-heeled shoes of black suede. She gestures with one hand, a crumpled white napkin. The lamp above her head is a bowl of dull yellow glass, opaque like milk. Her

283

shoulders are black, severely cut. The wall behind and beside her is painted brown. Her bright head bisects this angle coloured like mud. Her face breaks up, changes, frowns, smiles, as she shapes sentences and gesticulates.

Maria loves to talk, and to eat out in restaurants. She will pay the bill. She flings herself into her pleasure, talking rapidly and intensely, then letting herself float in pools of silence while she searches for words, and the Re-Vision Sibyl listens in joyful concentration, ears spread to catch the words issuing from Maria's mouth into this larger ocean of booming sound.

Love means a conversation. These words we carefully dredge up then cut and polish, offer each other, test between our teeth. Or given raw, smelling of salt. Pearl is grit. What else is love but this language we invent then share, these words we pass back and forth. Talking with Maria is coming, the same thing not different. This moment. Brown water lapping us.

These months of talking with Maria make love solid as a house of stone built into a hill. Foundations of trust. No game of enticing then slapping down, flirtatious dance promising all then giving nothing, need for control and holding back. She can say anything. She has a sense of being set completely free. She can reveal herself without fear. Peace. No more craving. Maria fills her with her words and she takes them in and is blessed.

Wine sinks in the dark red bottle, turning it dark green. Pizza slithers across their plates, puffed and blackened at the edges, shiny with melted cheese, blue puddle of Gorgonzola. She sticks her fork in, tears at it with her teeth.

Then it's over. Table cleared, cloth whisked off, chairs scrape back on the brown floor. Into the street, cold air on flushed face, arm in arm to the tube. Walking Maria home. Impossible to spend tonight together; baby-sitters; children; but it's all right.

Down her street under the huge dark blue clouds scudding under the wind tossing the tops of trees in the square. The iron railings are wet and black. She plunges into shadows, lets the wind fist her back, push her on. The joy of this, being out at night completely alone, hardly conscious of thought, the race of the indigo sky. Freedom and solitude. This too she cannot do without. For ten minutes only, tonight; coming home to her daughter.

43 I wake to a room full of darkness, darkness flowing between invisible walls, pressing outwards to make a shape I am boxed by. Cube of solid darkness one second, of dissolving darkness the next. Comfortable, comforting. I am part of the darkness, and I swim in it. Now I separate myself from it, make out the high rolled end of the bed, the black sheen of a mirror set above the soft cavern of blackness that must be a washbasin. I put out a hand, touch the marble top of the cabinet next to the bed, the cool swell of a lamp, the fringe of a linen towel.

A clock ticks somewhere. Inside me, my heart a pendulum pushing to and fro, pushing the darkness from side to side. The clock strikes eight, loud and resonant as the beat of a gong, hammer blows smoothing out the creases my fingertips find in my puzzled forehead. I know that clock. It's the one that stands outside our room in the Pensione Seguso, in the corridor.

So I'm back, then? So I must get up. Where's the light? Where are my clothes?

I fumble my way across the cold tiled floor to the window, throw back the shutters. There's the little canal flowing past the hotel, three floors below, and there's the walled garden opposite. I remember them now.

I stand in front of the washbasin and peer into the mirror. I haven't looked into one for so long that I've forgotten what I look like. Dark brown hair chopped off at chin length, thick brown eyebrows, green eyes, big nose, big mouth. I remember liking my face. This morning it's a collection of jigsaw pieces that don't make a whole. I feel too tall, too broad-shouldered. I take up too much space in this room, which has Noah's books, files and papers piled everywhere in it.

285

Then I spot a notebook, familiar, lying on the chair standing next to the basin, and pick it up, puzzled.

I remember now. I bought it late that first afternoon we arrived in Venice, on the way to the restaurant. It's a pretty object: A5 size, cover of thick paper marbled in blue and green, red silk headband, red silk marker. Here's the clutch of felt-tips I bought, and the two Chinese brushes, and the bottles of black and red inks. I was going to write, and I was going to enjoy myself. I was so lonely on that trip, which seems so long ago now: Noah out touring hospitals all day, I needed a friend. Then we got to Venice, for Noah's medical conference. And then?

I open the diary. I've hardly written in it at all. The two first pages are scribbled over in my untidy hand. The rest are blank. *Noah died last night . . . I should ask for forgiveness. But I can't. Not yet.* That's it. Must be a dream I had. I shake my head.

The door opens. I recognize the man who enters. It's Noah, wet black hair sleeked down, towelling dressing gown tied round his middle with his trouser belt, hands full of sponge bag and toothbrush. He looks at me, uncertain.

– How are you feeling?

I sit down on the bed. I'm wearing a white cotton nightdress. How?

– All right, I think, I tell him: but I can't remember much. What happened?

He treads towards me, rubber flip-flops slapping on the floor. Halts next to the bed and dumps his things on the cabinet. Doesn't touch me.

– We had a row last night. You were very angry with me. You were saying you'd had enough. You wanted a proper home as soon as we got back to London, no more living in my flat with no room for all your possessions. You wanted a baby too, and you were fed up with waiting. You said you'd been waiting for too long.

He pushes his hair back with one hand.

– Then you ran off and jumped into the canal. I fished you out. I think you banged your head going in. You were staggering about like a drunk. I had to get your clothes back on you and you were fighting me. I had a hell of a time getting you back here, both of us sopping wet. We were lucky no one saw us and fetched the police.

ARCHAEOLOGY AND BIBLE HISTORY

ARCHAEOLOGY AND BIBLE HISTORY

Joseph P. Free

REVISED AND EXPANDED BY

Howard F. Vos

ZondervanPublishingHouse

Grand Rapids, Michigan

A Division of HarperCollinsPublishers

Library of Congress Catalog Cataloging-in-Publication Data

Free, Joseph P.
    Archaeology and Bible history / Joseph R. Free; revised by Howard F. Vos.
        p.   cm.
    Includes bibliographical references and index.
    ISBN 0-310-47961-4
        1. Bible–Antiquities.   2. Bible–History of Biblical events.   I. Vos, Howard Frederic,
1925-   II. Title.
    BS621.F7   1992
    220.9'3–dc20   92-6108
                                                                                         CIP

Edited by Gerard Terpstra
Cover design by Church Art Works
Cover photos: left and center by Daniel Blatt; right by Shlomo Arad, SIPA

Printed in the United States of America

97 98 99 00 01 02 / DH / 11 10 9 8 7 6 5

CONTENTS

CHART, MAPS, AND ILLUSTRATIONS

TO THE READER

The Subject Matter and Development of This Book

This book deals with archaeology and Bible history, and not merely with archaeology and the Bible. Too often books on archaeology and the Bible contain a heterogeneous amount of material that lacks a unifying element. In this book I follow the sequence of Bible history as a unifying thread and show how archaeological discoveries illuminate and confirm the successive events of biblical history. Thus the following chapters serve as a summary of Bible history as well as a source of information on the bearing of archaeology on the Bible. This book is not exhaustive in any particular field but is rather introductory to many fields.

The Scope of This Book

Because the chief aim throughout the book is to be practical and helpful, I have not always limited myself to the most narrow interpretation of archaeology, which often restricts itself merely to data from the excavation of buried cities; nor have I necessarily broadened this study to its wide interpretation, which defines archaeology as "the study of ancient things." In general, the definition of archaeology followed here is that of the *Century Dictionary*, which describes archaeology as "that branch of knowledge which takes cognizance of past civilizations, and investigates their history in all fields, by means of remains of art, architecture, monuments, inscriptions, literature, language, implements, customs, and all other examples which have survived."[1] Occasionally I have departed from this definition when I felt that it would be helpful to deal with matters concerning chronology, supposed biblical contradictions and difficulties, and other topics chiefly relating to the validity and accuracy of the Scriptures.

The Author's Theological Position

My position is that of the Bible believer. Although in college days I came to the place where I wondered whether God existed, I now hold to the historic and traditional position of the Christian church, not merely because it is

[1]*Century Dictionary*, 1903 ed., 1:293; cited in G.A. Barton, *Archaeology and the Bible*, 7th ed. (Philadelphia: American Sunday School Union, 1937), xxxiii.

historic or traditional, but because I became convinced that it is true. The evidences from archaeology, fulfilled prophecy, Christian experience, and many other areas left me with no other choice than to acknowledge the Bible as the Word of God in the most complete sense.

Until recent years, the term "evangelical" or "conservative" could have adequately, or at least almost adequately, described my position. With the frequent appropriation of these terms by those who are neither evangelical nor conservative, their usefulness has been greatly diminished. Therefore, throughout this book the position that used to be designated "conservative" or "evangelical" will more often be designated by such phrases as "Bible believer's position," "orthodox position," "view of those who hold to the fundamentals of the faith," and, occasionally, "very conservative."

While I hold a very conservative position, I wish to emphasize that I always seek to be aware of what is going on in radical, liberal, and neo-orthodox circles, as well as developments in conservative and fundamentalist areas. We are counseled, "Test everything. Hold on to the good" (1 Thess. 5:21).

Bibliographical References and Footnotes

Each bibliographical reference is given in full the first time it appears, together with an abbreviation. For example, when the first reference is made to Chester C. McCown's book *The Ladder of Progress in Palestine* (New York: Harper, 1943), the author and title are given in full, followed by the letters, MLPP. Each successive reference is indicated only by the abbreviation followed by the page number. A list of abbreviations and the books they represent appear at the end of this book.

Bibliographical references include general works and secondary sources as well as primary sources. General works, such as Barton (BAB), Finegan (FLAP), and Price (PMOT), are included in the bibliographical material, inasmuch as source materials, such as Breasted's *Ancient Records of Egypt* (BARE), are not always available to many who will use this book.

It is helpful to remember that the documentation and additional information in the footnotes in a carefully prepared book often contain material that is as important as, and in some cases even more important than, the material in the text. Such material has been placed in footnotes in order to avoid breaking the line of thought but is available for those who wish "to know the reason why" or wish to pursue the matter further in other sources.

How to Use This Book

Those who are primarily interested in seeing how archaeology illuminates and confirms the Bible will find it profitable to read this book from beginning to end. Also, those who wish to get a sweep of biblical history will do well to read the book through, inasmuch as it summarizes the main sequence of events in the Scriptures, both Old and New Testaments, as well as the intertestamental period.

This book may also be used as a compendium on the subject "How Archaeology Confirms the Bible" by reading those sections whose headings contain the words "Archaeological Confirmation Concerning. . ." or some similar phrase. Likewise, this book may also be used as a compendium on the subject "How Archaeology Illuminates the Bible" by reading those sections that contain the phrase "Archaeological Light on. . ." or some similar expression. Many sections of this book give material that both illuminates *and* confirms the Bible.

Sunday school teachers who wish to use an example of archaeological illumination or confirmation to enliven a lesson will often find it profitable to check the section of this book that corresponds to the portion of the Scriptures from which the lesson is taken—they may find some archaeological material that will fit a point in the lesson or may be adapted to the lesson.

In my lifetime I have heard many messages or sermons that could have had some point driven home by the effective use of some archaeological item. While we are not called to "preach archaeology," we are responsible for getting our messages across, and the materials from archaeological discoveries constitute one of several useful areas from which progressive servants of God may draw material to bring home their message more effectively.

This book will be useful either as a text or as collateral reading in academic courses that deal with Bible survey, Bible history, or Bible archaeology.

It will also be useful for Sunday school and Bible class teachers who wish to have a series of lessons on the subject "Through the Bible." For the students in such classes this book will serve as a lesson help.

In the various uses made of this book, may it make more real the great events and the great truths of the Scriptures as they are illuminated and confirmed by archaeological discoveries.

Joseph P. Free

REVISER'S PREFACE

Joseph P. Free profoundly influenced a whole generation of students and laypersons alike. As professor of archaeology at Wheaton College in Wheaton, Illinois, he had an extensive outreach to the general public through articles in Sunday school quarterlies and other publications, and through public appearances and study tours to Bible lands. To us, his students, he did not merely impart information but challenged us to know what we believed and why. And he helped us to think perceptively about attacks on the Scriptures and to answer those attacks. Moreover, with the new insights that kept coming from research in Near Eastern studies, he helped to bring a new excitement to Bible study.

Not only was it my privilege to study with Dr. Free, but I also prepared the first edition of this book for the publisher. Now it has been my privilege to produce this new edition, which is based on the fourteenth printing of 1976. There have been some minor revisions along the way. I have followed Dr. Free's outline, his theological position, and his chronological framework. I have sought to bring the archaeological and historical material up to date and have modified the archaeological interpretation where necessary. The bibliography has required almost total replacement. It is my hope that this book will now continue to make the impact for which it was designed. May another generation of Bible students benefit from the profound insights of this dedicated scholar.

Howard F. Vos

Chapter 1

Bible Archaeology, Bible History, and Buried Cities

The Functions of Bible Archaeology

A friend once asked me, "What is the value of archaeology for biblical study, anyway?" I pointed out that numerous passages of the Bible that long puzzled the commentators have readily yielded up their meaning when new light from archaeological discoveries has been focused on them. In other words, archaeology illuminates the text of the Scriptures and so makes valuable contributions to the field of biblical interpretation and exegesis. In addition to illuminating the Bible, archaeology has confirmed countless passages that have been rejected by critics as unhistorical or contradictory to known facts. This aspect of archaeology forms a valuable part of the defense of the Scriptures—a discipline commonly known as apologetics. In summary it may be said that two of the main functions of Bible archaeology are the illumination and the confirmation of the Bible.

The Bible, a Historical Book

The Bible is a historical book, and the great truths of Christianity are founded on the historic facts revealed in it. If the fact of the Virgin Birth, the fact of the

Crucifixion, and the fact of the Resurrection are set aside, our faith is without foundation. Since the New Testament revelation stands upon the foundation of the Old Testament, the accuracy of the Old Testament is of great importance to us.

Although confirmation of one kind of truth (historical) does not demonstrate the validity of another kind of truth (theological), the veracity of the historical narrative of Scripture lends credence to the theological message. Those who do not accept the historical accuracy of the Bible find it easier to dismiss its theological claims. The accuracy and historicity of the Scriptures as God's Word and as his unique revelation has been denied by the destructive critic who has set aside the full validity of the Bible at point after point. For example, certain critics have said that the accounts of Abraham are legendary, that Mosaic legislation was formulated hundreds of years after the time of Moses, that such people as the Hittites were either legendary or insignificant, that the book of Judges was composed of "good stories" and not really historical accounts, and that various people ranging from Sargon to Sanballat were unhistorical. Yet archaeological discoveries have shown that these critical charges and countless others are wrong and that the Bible is trustworthy in the very statements that critics have set aside as untrustworthy.[1]

The Purpose and Nature of Bible History; Verbal Inspiration

Bible history is not primarily a record of humanity's seeking after God. It is rather a record of *God's revelation to humanity*. Pagan religions deal with humanity's seeking after God or gods, but the Scriptures are God's own revelation to us, telling how from the beginning in Eden God spoke to Adam and Eve and how he later directed Noah, called Abraham from Ur, spoke through the prophets, and finally gave the supreme revelation in his Son Jesus Christ.

Bible believers hold that this record of God's revelation is not only vital for all humankind but is accurate in all respects. We also hold that the Bible writers exercised their own personality, used their own vocabulary, and drew on their own memories, intuitions, and judgments and that at the same time they were prevented from making errors and were so guided by God that they expressed exactly what God wished to make known. This guidance was not so vague that it assured merely the general idea or concept that God wished to convey, but rather it extended even to the choice of words when it would be essential to convey his message. The foregoing description sets forth my view of "verbal inspiration,"

namely, that God guided even to the choice of words[2] when necessary. On the other hand, I reject the dictation theory of inspiration, which makes the process a mere mechanical operation, robs a writer of his personality, and makes him a mere machine. In summary, I agree with Gaussen's definition of inspiration, which holds that inspiration is "that inexplicable power which the divine Spirit put forth of old on the authors of Holy Scripture, in order to their guidance[3] even in the employment of the words they used, and to preserve them alike from all error and all omission."[4]

The Bible is not a textbook on science, yet when it speaks of matters relating to science, it is accurate. The Scriptures, for example, do not claim to be, nor are they, a treatise on astronomy, yet when Job speaks of the Bear (Job 38:32), he writes in accord with known astronomical facts. As has been said, "The Scriptures were written not primarily to tell us how the heavens go, but to tell us how to go to heaven." Yet the content of all Scripture is scientifically and historically accurate, and the scientific and historical allusions of the Bible are constantly illuminated and confirmed by modern discoveries.

Accuracy of the Text of the Bible

Bible believers do not hold that the translations of the Bible into English and other languages are inerrant. Nor do we maintain the inerrancy of existing manuscripts. But as believers in the fundamentals of the faith, we do hold that the *original* manuscripts were absolutely ac-

---

[1]For archaeological light on Abraham, see chapter 4; on Mosaic legislation, see chapter 9; on the Hittites, see chapter 10; on the book of Judges, see chapter 11; on Sargon, see chapter 17; on Sanballat, see chapter 22.

[2]The Latin word *verba* means "words"; hence the term "verbal inspiration" indicates that God guided even to the extent of the choice of the words when necessary. "Verbal inspiration" does not mean that God dictated the contents of the books of Scripture *verbatim*, or word for word.

[3]This expression "in order to their guidance" is probably a literal translation of the French original. In idiomatic English one would say "in order to guide them."

[4]L. Gáussen, *Theopneustia: The Plenary Inspiration of the Holy Scriptures* (Chicago: Bible Institute Colportage Association, n.d.), 34 [GT].

curate and without error. The question arises, "If we do not have the original manuscripts, how can we be sure of the accuracy of the manuscripts we do have?" In reply it should be said that hundreds of manuscripts have come down to us and that the variations in these manuscripts are so slight that none of them alter any vital Christian truth. Through the science of textual study, scholars are able to reconstruct a text so close to what the original text must have been that it is satisfactory to scholars of almost every degree of liberalism and conservatism. Hort, the great New Testament scholar of the nineteenth century, pointed out that "only about one word in every thousand has upon it substantial variation supported by such evidence as to call out the efforts of the critic in deciding between the readings."[5] The statement of Bentley, made many years ago, is still valid, that "the real text of the sacred writings is competently exact, nor is one article of faith or moral precept either perverted or lost, choose as awkwardly as you will, choose the worst by design, out of the whole lump of readings."[6]

Hort's statement that only about one word in one thousand in the New Testament would call out the efforts of scholars, is significant when we realize that the Westcott and Hort Greek New Testament is about five hundred pages long and that one one-thousandth of it would be only half a page. This does not mean that such an amount of the New Testament is necessarily inaccurate or wrong; it means merely that one one-thousandth of the material would require scholarly study to ascertain what were likely the original words.[7]

The surviving Hebrew Old Testament manuscripts show very little variation. A careful scholar of an earlier generation, William Henry Green said, "The Hebrew manuscripts cannot compare with those of the New Testament either in antiquity or number, but they have been written with greater care and exhibit fewer various readings."[8] In regard to the accuracy of the text of the Old Testament, Green concluded, "It may be safely said that no other work of antiquity has been so accurately transmitted."[9]

Light on Bible History From Buried Cities

A century and a half ago many familiar biblical cities such as Jericho, Samaria, Bethel, Shiloh, Bethshan, Gezer, Nineveh, Babylon, and Ur were shapeless mounds, the very identity of which, in some cases, had been forgotten.

Skepticism had been expressed concerning the details of the capture of Jericho; the ivory palace of Ahab at Samaria (1 Kings 22:39) was a puzzling reference in the Scriptures; the Wellhausen school of criticism doubted the actual existence of the tabernacle and minimized the importance of Shiloh, where the biblical record locates the setting up of the tabernacle in Palestine (Josh. 18:1); and the boasted glories of Nineveh and Babylon seemed more in keeping with the glowing reports of an overenthusiastic chamber of commerce than with sober historic fact.

Within the past hundred and fifty years, however, all of these cities have been uncovered, some receiving additional archaeological attention in recent

---

[5]B. F. Westcott and F. J. A. Hort, *The New Testament in the Original Greek* (New York: Harper, 1882), 2:2.

[6]Article on "Text," *International Standard Bible Encyclopedia* (Grand Rapids: Eerdmans, 1929), 2955 [ISBE].

[7]H. C. Thiessen, *Introduction to the New Testament* (Grand Rapids: Eerdmans, 1943), 77 [TINT].

[8]W. H. Green, *General Introduction: Text* (New York: Scribner, 1899), 179 [GIT].

[9]Ibid., 181.

years.[10] The importance of the discoveries is apparent when we realize that the excavation of these cities, and dozens more, has produced material that confirms the Scriptures at point after point. In addition to confirming the Bible, the excavations in the Near East have brought much illumination to the pages of Scripture. This phase of modern archaeological investigation is well summarized by Ira Maurice Price, late professor in the field of Old Testament at the University of Chicago: "The Old Testament is fast acquiring a fresh significance. Old Testament history has become incandescent with the wondrous archaeological discoveries in Bible lands. Almost every period of that old Book has been flooded with new light out of the ruins of the past."[11]

How Are Cities Buried?

Laypeople often ask, "How were these cities in the Bible lands buried?" They might suppose that the natural drifting of sands covered them over; and it did. But other processes were far more important in building up the mounds that represent the remains of Near Eastern cities. The repeated destruction and rebuilding of a city, a process that often went on during the course of many centuries, resulted in the formation of an artificial mound that may range from fifty to one hundred feet in elevation. Such a mound is known to archaeologists as a "tell," from the Arabic word for "hill."

The recurrent cycle is as follows: An invader captures a town, destroys many of the buildings, and possibly kills or carries off the inhabitants. In the course of time, some of the original inhabitants or perhaps another group level off the old ruins and build new buildings on the site of the old city. The layer of remains and debris from the first city forms a stratum that often measures from one to five feet in depth. During the course of many centuries, such a city is likely to go through many destructions and rebuildings, each one leaving what is called a "layer of occupation."

Some fourteen miles south of the Sea of Galilee, where the Jezreel and Jordan valleys meet, stands the mound that represents the biblical city of Beth Shan (called Tell el-Husn today, located near the modern town of Beisan, which retains the handed-down form of the name Beth Shan). Beth Shan is significant in biblical history as the place to which Saul's body was taken after he died in the battle against the Philistines at Mount Gilboa (1 Sam. 31:8–10). This site was excavated (1921–1933) by the University of Pennsylvania. The excavators went down over seventy feet through eighteen distinct strata.[12] Beneath them they found pits of unknown origin. The history of the city began perhaps as early as 3500 B.C. and continued down into the Christian era, with a possible gap that shows no evi-

---

[10]For archaeological light and confirmation concerning Jericho, see chapter 10; for Samaria, see chapter 15; for Shiloh, see chapter 12; for Babylon, see chapter 20.

[11]Ira Maurice Price, *The Dramatic Story of Old Testament History*, 2nd ed. (New York: Revell, 1935), 7 [POTH].

[12]Fitzgerald, reporting on the excavation, pointed out that by the end of 1931 they had gone through ten levels, measuring thirteen meters (43 feet). In resuming the work in 1933, they dug an area 24 x 16 meters through another eight definite levels (numbered XI to XVIII), measuring eight and one-half meters (about 28 feet), and then came to pit dwellings dug in the virgin soil by the earliest inhabitants of the site. Cf. Gerald M. Fitzgerald, "The Earliest Pottery of Bethshan," *Museum Journal* (University of Pennsylvania) 24, 1 (1935). See also, Michael Avi-Yonah, ed., *Encyclopedia of Archaeological Excavations in the Holy Land* (Englewood Cliffs, N.J.: Prentice Hall, 1975 for Vol. 1), 1:207–29 [EAEHL].

dence of occupation from 1000 to 300 B.C.[13] The stratification at Beth Shan of nearly twenty levels shows how cities of biblical times were built up through successive destructions and rebuildings. It is not uncommon to find remains of ten cities, one on top of the other.[14]

Invasion, however, was not the only cause of the destruction of a city in the Near East. Earthquake and fire struck from time to time, leaving a ruined site that may later have been rebuilt; pestilence sometimes decimated the inhabitants of a town to such an extent that it was abandoned and later reoccupied by others. Moreover, ordinary refuse and debris tended to accumulate in the streets of an oriental town and so added to the stratification. If a house (commonly made of mud brick) collapsed, much of the debris may have remained to form the base on which a new house was built. All of these causes of accumulation and stratification combined to make the city mounds of Bible lands grow upward, in many cases at the rate of about five feet per century.[15] City mounds or tells can usually be distinguished from natural hills because they tend to be more flat-topped. Such a configuration occurs because ancient city walls helped to hold debris in place and give definition to a mound.

Present-Day Archaeological Techniques

Modern archaeological method has been developed during the past one hundred years. In 1838 Edward Robinson, Professor of Biblical Literature at Union Theological Seminary, New York, went to Palestine and during a brief visit of only a few weeks, identified scores of biblical sites, many of which were excavated in the following years of the nineteenth and twentieth centuries. Not much actual excavating was done in Palestine until the Palestine Exploration Fund of England was formed in 1865 to foster research in Palestine. A few years earlier, in the 1840s, Nineveh was excavated in Mesopotamia. Much of the work done early in the nineteenth century consisted of "treasure hunts" rather than real scientific work. Even during the latter part of the nineteenth century, many excavations tended to be hunts for museum pieces.

Today the picture is entirely different. An archaeological excavation is a carefully planned scientific expedition. The governments of Near Eastern countries require prospective excavators to secure a government permit, which is granted only to competent individuals and recognized institutions. The staff of an archaeological expedition is ordinarily made up of a director and several assistants, including a photographer, a pottery expert, and, if possible, an architect.

The director of the "dig" lays out the surface of the buried city in squares, often ten meters on a side, with a narrow strip of soil known as a *balk* between. The balk serves as a walkway and a path on which wheelbarrows may be moved toward the dump. Each square has its own number, and all of the objects found in it are entered in the record book according to the number of the square and the depth at which they are found. This organization of a site is part of an excavation procedure developed by British archaeologists Sir Mortimer Wheeler and Kathleen

---

[13]Chester C. McCown, *The Ladder of Progress in Palestine* (New York: Harper, 1943), 152, 168, 169, 180 [MLPP].

[14]Melvin G. Kyle, *Excavating Kirjath-Sepher's Ten Cities* (Grand Rapids: Eerdmans, 1934), told of the excavation of ten levels at the mound of Tell Beit Mirsim, believed to represent the biblical town of Kiriath Sepher, mentioned in Joshua 15:15–16; Judges 1:11–12.

[15]For chart and information on levels of Beth Shan, cf. Alan Rowe, "The Discoveries at Beth Shan During the 1926 Season," *Museum Journal* 18,1 (March 1927): 12; Fitzgerald, "Earliest Pottery," 7–8, 15; J. McKee Adams, *Ancient Records and the Bible*, (Nashville: Broadman, 1946), 80 [AARB].

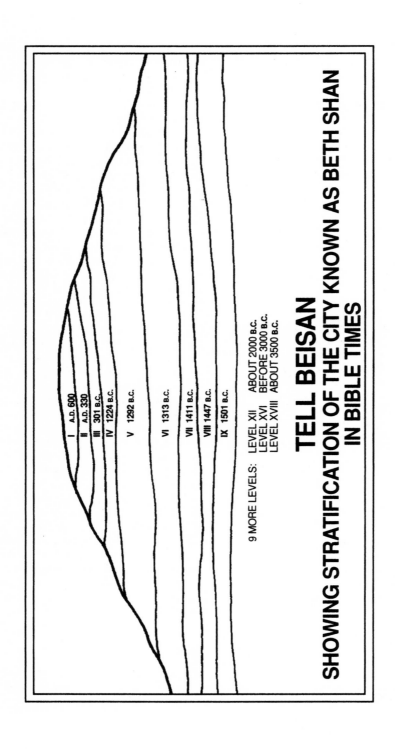

TELL BEISAN

SHOWING STRATIFICATION OF THE CITY KNOWN AS BETH SHAN
IN BIBLE TIMES

I   A.D. 600
II   A.D. 330
III 301 B.C.
IV   1224 B.C.
V   1292 B.C.
VI   1313 B.C.
VII 1411 B.C.
VIII 1447 B.C.
IX   1501 B.C.

9 MORE LEVELS: LEVEL XII   ABOUT 2000 B.C.
                  LEVEL XVI   BEFORE 3000 B.C.
                  LEVEL XVIII   ABOUT 3500 B.C.

Kenyon.[16] The actual digging is done by national workers or foreign students supervised by trained archaeologists of the staff. Surface soil is loosened with a pick. Then oversized hoes, about three or four times the size of a garden hoe, are used to scrape loosened soil into rubber buckets, made from old automobile tires, or baskets and then emptied into wheelbarrows. Wheelbarrow operators carry on a constant shuttle service to the dump. Workers use small hand picks, ice picks, trowels, and brushes to uncover and free objects as they surface.

As each layer of the mound is systematically cleared, every object is carefully recorded, and the more important objects are photographed in the actual position where they are found (*in situ*). No object is too insignificant to be recorded by the modern archaeologist, for all objects, large and small, combine to give a picture of the nature of ancient life. Archaeologists take note of everything, whether coins, seals, scarabs, pottery vessels, tools, statuettes, lifesize statues, or the foundations of houses and temples, and even the plan of the entire town.

The field archaeologist does not go out with a primary aim of illuminating some point in history or of confirming some biblical passage, but rather to find out what secrets the mound will yield. Needless to say, his discoveries often do illuminate some historical point or confirm some disputed reference in the Bible.

As archaeologists excavate, they are concerned about dating their finds. One of the most useful ways of doing so involves study of the pottery found in each level. Down through the centuries there were changes in the shape, decoration, type of clay, style, and other features of ancient bowls, jars, and dishes. The principle of dating levels by pottery found in them was first developed by pioneer

Egyptologist Sir Flinders Petrie at the end of the nineteenth century. And during more recent decades archaeologists have further refined the classification of the various types of pottery according to the periods in which they were used.[17]

Some of the generally accepted cultural periods (for Palestine) readily discernible by pottery chronology are as follows:

Neolithic Period, 6000–4300 B.C.
Chalcolithic Period, 4300–3300 B.C.
Early Bronze Period, 3300–2000 B.C.
Middle Bronze Period (age of Abraham, Isaac, etc.), 2000–1550 B.C.
Late Bronze Period (time of Moses, Joshua, Judges), 1550–1200 B.C.
Iron I Period (end of Judges, time of David, Solomon), 1200–1000 B.C.
Iron II Period (kings of Israel and Judah), 1000–586 B.C.
Iron III or Persian Period (end of Old Testament), 586–300 B.C.
Hellenistic Period (Intertestamental Period), 300–50 B.C.

After World War II another aid to the establishment of Near Eastern chronology appeared on the scene, this time as something of a by-product of atomic science. Willard F. Libby of the Institute for Nuclear Studies at the University of Chicago developed the Carbon 14 technique. Basic to this procedure are certain assumptions:

1. Carbon 14 (radioactive) ceases to be taken in by an organism when it dies.

2. After the organism dies, Carbon 14 disintegrates at a constant rate and has a half-life of 5,730 years. That is to say, an ounce of it would reduce to a half ounce in 5,730 years.

3. In the living organism, Carbon 14 and Carbon 12 have a constant proportion; after the death of the organism,

---

[16]See Mortimer Wheeler, *Archaeology from the Earth* (Baltimore: Penguin Books, 1954).

[17]An important book for the classification of Palestinian pottery is Ruth Amiran, *Ancient Pottery of the Holy Land* (Jerusalem: Massada Press, 1969).

Carbon 12 remains stable whereas Carbon 14 disintegrates.

In testing an object (which must be burned) the amount of Carbon 14 remaining can be measured against the Carbon 12 in the object in order to gain an indication as to how long the living organism has been dead. Charcoal, among other things, has proved to be very useful in Carbon 14 tests. Usually the Carbon 14 method yields dates valid within 5 to 10 percent of the time involved.[18] A discussion of the variables in the system and the doubts some scholars have expressed concerning it is beyond the scope of this book.

A third method of dating especially useful to archaeologists has come into its own during the last couple of decades, though the method was actually under development about the time of World War I. Known as Dendochronology, it seeks to establish a chronology by means of tree-ring dating.[19]

During the past three decades or so underwater archaeology has been scientifically developed. The basic principles are similar to those used on land. The excavation is divided into squares for record keeping (a grid of iron pipes commonly being used for the purpose), and excavation proceeds to go down stratum by stratum.[20]

[18]See Willard F. Libby, *Radiocarbon Dating*, 2nd ed. (Chicago: University of Chicago Press, 1955).

[19]A useful book on this subject is M. G. L. Baillie, *Tree-Ring Dating and Archaeology* (Chicago: University of Chicago Press, 1982).

[20]One of the authorities in this field is George F. Bass. See his *Archaeology Under Water* (Baltimore: Penguin, 1966).

Chapter 2

Creation

(Genesis 1–3: Creation, Fall, Promise of a Redeemer)

Two-Point Outline of the Book of Genesis

Genesis falls into two general parts: (1) chapters 1–11, which treat universal history and deal with Creation, the Fall, the Flood, and the tower of Babel, and (2) chapters 12–50, the patriarchal period, dealing with the lives of Abraham, Isaac, Jacob, and Joseph.

Treatment of the Material in the First Part of Genesis

Because of the nature of the material in the early chapters of Genesis, several subjects that lie at the fringe and sometimes beyond the limits of "Archaeology and Bible History" will be considered. One of my purposes in this book is to make departures from the immediate subject of archaeology and Bible history whenever I feel it will be helpful. Therefore I will briefly discuss such matters as the critical view of Genesis 1 and 2, the documentary theory, the time of the creation of man and the universe, gaps in genealogies, and, just now, the record of the creation of the universe and its implications.

Creation of the Universe, the World, and Its Inhabitants (Genesis 1)

One may speculate as to the origin of the world, but God has provided the eternal answer to the question in the opening verse of the Bible. "In the beginning God created the heaven and the earth" (Gen. 1:1). This verse answers unscriptural human theories and explanations concerning the creation or origin of the world. It answers *atheism*, which holds that there is no God, by setting forth the existence and work of God; it answers *agnosticism*, which asserts that we cannot know how things began, by stating that God did the creating; it answers *polytheism*, which holds that there were many gods, by setting forth God, not many gods, as the Creator.

The first chapter of Genesis records the creation of the universe, the world, and the inhabitants of the world. The second chapter develops certain points given in chapter 1, adding details concerning the manner of the creation of man, the nature of his surroundings (Eden), and the beginning of human activity.

Critical View of Genesis 1 and 2; Documentary Theory

According to the critical view of the Bible, Genesis 1 is ascribed to one writer and Genesis 2 to another. Genesis 2 supposedly represents a different and somewhat contradictory version of Creation. An examination of the details of this critical view shows that Genesis 1 is assigned to the so-called "priestly" writer, usually referred to as "P," who is supposed to have written about 500 B.C.[1] Genesis 2 is assigned to the writer (or school of writers) called "J," supposedly writing about 850 B.C.

This type of critical analysis of the Bible, usually known as the Documentary Hypothesis, is sometimes referred to popularly as the JEDP theory. This view holds that Moses (c. 1500–1400 B.C.) did not write the Pentateuch, but that it is made up of four main documents, written long after his time: J in the ninth century (c. 850 B.C.), E in the eighth century (c. 750 B.C.), D in the seventh century (621 B.C.), and P in the sixth to the fifth century (500–450 B.C.).

The J document was originally so designated because it supposedly used the name "Jehovah" for God, and the E document because of its use of "Elohim" for God. The document now called P was originally considered to be a part of the E document (until 1853), and one would expect it to use Elohim as the word for God. Subsequent studies have shown, however, that the use of Jehovah in the J document and of Elohim in the E and P documents did not always hold true.[2] In view of such difficulties in using the criterion of the divine names for dividing up the Pentateuch into documents, liberal scholars now lean more heavily on supposed differences in diction and style in assigning one part to J, another to P, and so forth. By way of answer to the critical view, it should be pointed out that when the writer of the Pentateuch moves from one subject to another, he would of necessity use different words. In short, one would expect differences in diction, vocabulary, and even style when the subject matter changes. Further demonstration of the many ways in which the critical criteria break down is given by Oswald Allis (AFBM, 40ff.), James Orr,[3] Robert Dick Wilson,[4] and other scholars.[5] In view of the many evidences for the unity of Genesis and of the Pentateuch, I can see no valid reason for denying the Mosaic authorship of the Pentateuch and for assigning it to various documents and writers in the late period (ninth to fifth centuries B.C.).

As a matter of fact, in recent decades scholars within the Wellhausen circle have questioned and repudiated almost every tenet of Wellhausen's system. The results of their study have not led them back to a Mosaic origin of the Pentateuch, however. They tend to make the whole Pentateuch postexilic (after 535 B.C.). Gleason Archer has provided an excellent survey of the development of recent pentateuchal scholarship and arguments for

---

[1]Robert H. Pfeiffer, *Introduction to the Old Testament* (New York: Harper, 1941), 139 [PIOT].

[2]Oswald T. Allis, *The Five Books of Moses* (Philadelphia: Presbyterian and Reformed, 1943), 25, 32, 38 [AFBM].

[3]James Orr, *The Problem of the Old Testament* (New York: Scribner, 1917) [OPOT].

[4]Robert Dick Wilson, *A Scientific Investigation of the Old Testament* (Philadelphia: Sunday School Times, 1926) [WSI]. Revised by Edward J. Young (Chicago: Moody, 1959).

[5]Cf. William Henry Green, *The Higher Criticism of the Pentateuch* (New York: Scribner, 1896) [GHCP]. The place of archaeology in answering the critical view is developed in M. G. Kyle, *The Deciding Voice of the Monuments in Biblical Criticism* (Oberlin: Bibliotheca Sacra, 1924) [KDVM], and in his *Moses and the Monuments: Light from Archaeology on Pentateuchal Times* (Oberlin: Bibliotheca Sacra, 1920) [KMM]. Edward J. Young, *An Introduction to the Old Testament* (Grand Rapids: Eerdmans, 1949) [YIOT], contains a concise history of the literary criticism of the Pentateuch from a conservative standpoint (109–53).

the Mosaic authorship of the first five books of the Old Testament.[6]

Answer to the Critical View of Genesis 1 and 2

An examination of Genesis 1 and 2 shows that they are not two divergent accounts of Creation. Genesis 1 is the record of the creation of the universe, the world, and the inhabitants of the world. Genesis 2, on the other hand, gives further details. It tells how man was created, describes the nature and location of his surroundings (Eden), records the test of obedience (not to eat of the Tree of Knowledge of Good and Evil), and relates the details of the creation of Eve (vv. 21–22). The two sections are not contradictory nor divergent, but the second supplements the first, and together they form an overall view of the broad sweep of Creation, along with the essential details.

In any modern book that gives a running narrative, one may find that a particular chapter will refer to a certain character in a passing remark, while a succeeding chapter will take up that character and give further details concerning him or her. The two chapters, written by the same author, are not contradictory but supplementary. In just such a way, Genesis 2 elaborates and supplements Genesis 1. Those who wish to see the unity of the first chapters of Genesis should read Genesis 1 and then skip to Genesis 3; they will notice that the preparation for Genesis 3 is lacking. Or if they begin with chapter 2, they will find that many essentials are missing, which are given only in Genesis 1. Genesis 1 is obviously an integral and essential part of the whole record of Creation. The unity of the book of Genesis was well demonstrated by a scholar of the last century, William Henry Green.[7] Oswald T. Allis, formerly professor at Princeton Theological Seminary, subsequently demonstrated the Mosaic authorship, the unity, and the validity of Genesis and the other books of the Pentateuch in his *Five Books of Moses* (AFBM).

Time of the Creation of Humankind

In the margin of many Bibles the date 4004 B.C. is given for Genesis 1. This date was computed about 350 years ago by an Irish clergyman, Archbishop Ussher (*Annals*, 1650), who used some of the indications of Scripture and research available to him at that time. Ussher's system is often referred to as the "short chronology" system. Essentially, his method was to add up all the genealogical figures in the Bible, assuming that they were complete. In the early nineteenth century Hales published a system (1809–1814), in which he took the Greek translation of the Hebrew Old Testament (known as the Septuagint, abbreviated LXX) as the basis for the patriarchal generations and computed the date of Creation as 5411 B.C.[8]

There are, however, many other systems of biblical chronology. Over 250 years ago (1738) Des Vignolles, a member of the Royal Society of Berlin, knew of some two hundred attempts to compute the earliest biblical date, ranging from 3483 B.C. to 6984 B.C.[9] Thus, if the computations of various scholars range from about 3500 to 7000 B.C., it is evident that the long-accepted date of 4004 B.C. is not in any sense final and absolute. We must remember that the Bible is not a textbook on chronology any more than it is a textbook on astronomy. The main pur-

---

[6]Gleason L. Archer, Jr., *A Survey of Old Testament Introduction*, rev. ed. (Chicago: Moody, 1974), 81–118 [ASOTI].

[7]William Henry Green, *The Unity of the Book of Genesis* (New York: Scribner, 1910) [GUG].

[8]William Smith, "Chronology," in *Dictionary of the Bible* (New York: Hurd and Houghton, 1871), 1:446–47 [SDB].

[9]*Cambridge Ancient History*, 2nd ed., "Chronology of Old Testament" (New York: Macmillan, 1924), 1:158 [CAH].

pose of the Bible is to give God's revelation to human beings and to show them their relation to God; nevertheless, when it speaks on matters relating to chronology or astronomy, or any other field, it is true and accurate.

However, the fact that the Bible was not written primarily to give chronological data does not mean that chronological indications are lacking in the Bible. The very fact that the suggested dates for the beginning, noted by Des Vignolles, range approximately from 3500 to 7000 B.C. shows that definite calculations are possible. But why are there such variations? The differences between the Hebrew and Greek texts of the Old Testament gave Ussher a date of 4004 B.C., based on the Hebrew, and Hales a date of 5411 B.C., based on the Greek. Some of the figures given in the Greek translation differ from those given in the Hebrew text. But variations in the interpretation of the Hebrew text make it possible to have other dates than either 4004 or 5411 B.C. In addition, we must entertain the possibility that there are gaps in the genealogies of Genesis.

Possibilities of Gaps in Biblical Genealogies

Genesis 5 and 11 give the genealogy of the descendants of Adam. The usual method of computing the date of Adam is to add the ages of all of his descendants, using the figures given for the age of each at the time of the birth of the son who carried on the line. Bishop Ussher's computation resulted in the date 4004 B.C., but others have arrived at different figures. This does not mean that there is any error in the Bible; it means rather that we do not know all the factors involved in computation. One pertinent question is whether these genealogies are complete

or whether they give only the main characters.

B.B. Warfield pointed out that there may be gaps in the biblical genealogies. This is not mere theory but is given possible support by the fact that certain genealogies omit some of the generations. The genealogy in Matthew 1:1–17 omits three kings (Ahaziah, Jehoash, and Amaziah) and indicates that Joram begat Uzziah, who was his great-great-grandson (Matt. 1:8)[10] One of the illustrations of a compressed genealogy in the Old Testament is found in Ezra 7:3, where six generations are omitted (which are given in a more complete genealogy in 1 Chronicles 7:7ff.). Such occurrences indicate that the Bible may not give a complete record in a genealogy but rather an indication of the line of descent.

The question arises: When the Bible states that one person begat another, must not the second person be the son or daughter of the first one, with no gaps in between? The possibility of a gap even in such cases is shown by Matthew 1:8, the text which states that Joram begat Uzziah. The term "son" is also used in the sense of "descendant," shown by the fact that some of those referred to in Genesis 46:18 as the "sons of Zilpah" were actually her grandchildren, and furthermore it is said that they were "born" by her. Thus we see that the expression "born by" may sometimes mean "had as a descendant."[11]

In addition to Warfield and Raven, more recent writers who hold to the fundamentals of the faith have pointed out this possibility of gaps in the genealogies. Oswald T. Allis deals with the problem involved in genealogical notations such as "After Terah had lived 70 years, he became the father of Abram. . ." (Gen. 11:26). Would we not have to allow just seventy years? An examination of the biblical text shows that the whole context

---

[10]B.B. Warfield, "On the Antiquity and Unity of the Human Race," in *Studies in Theology* (New York: Oxford University Press, 1932), 235–58 [WST].

[11]John Raven, *Old Testament Introduction* (New York: Revell, 1910), 134–35 [ROTI].

reads, "After Terah had lived 70 years he became the father of Abram, Nahor and Haran." As Allis points out, it seems improbable that all three of these sons were born the same year, and a comparison of scriptural references (Acts 7:4; Gen. 12:4) shows that actually Abraham was born sixty years later. The words of the verse apparently mean that at the age of seventy, Terah became a father. This does not accord with the theory that we are dealing with a rigid chronology (AFBM, 262). In view of such evidence of compression of genealogies, it seems safe to conclude that the creation of man took place probably sometime between 4000 and 8000 B.C.,[12] or perhaps somewhat earlier, although some conservatives have no hesitancy in allowing a very high age for man.[13]

Date of the Creation of the Universe

The date of the creation of the universe is an entirely different question from the date of the creation of man. The universe may have been created shortly before the creation of man or long before, depending on whether a long period of time is involved in the first two verses of Genesis and whether the days of Creation were twenty-four-hour days or long periods of time. I incline to the view that the days of Creation were literal twenty-four-hour days, but that a long period of time may have elapsed during the era described in Genesis 1:1-2. I recognize, however, the possibility of a second and third view that are sometimes set forth. The second holds that the days of Genesis were long periods of time, while the third states that no long period of time is involved in either the first two verses of Genesis or the creative days. All three views are discussed in the following paragraphs.

According to the first theory, the original creation of the universe and the earth is described in Genesis 1:1, "In the beginning God created the heavens and the earth." Then a period of time followed during which "the earth was formless and empty" (Hebrew, "the earth was desolation and waste," Genesis 1:2a). This period of time may have been of any length, from a few thousand to a few million years, and could include the geological ages observable in the earth's surface. During this period the fall of the angels (2 Peter 2:4; Jude 6), and the fall of Satan (Isa. 14:12-14) may have occurred. After this cataclysmic period, the putting of the world in order is described in Genesis 1:2b, 3ff., "And the Spirit of God was hovering over the waters, and God said, 'Let there be light,' and there was light." The succeeding creative acts took place in six days of twenty-four hours each and included the creation of plants, animals, and man. This view, in my opinion, is best supported by internal biblical evidence as well as by the external evidence from the world itself. Fur-

[12]For additional discussion of gaps in the biblical chronology see AFBM, 261-64; ASOTI, 185-89; Merrill F. Unger, *Introductory Guide to the Old Testament* (Grand Rapids: Zondervan, 1951), 192-94.

[13]Such a "limitless view" is set forth by Byron Nelson, who refers to the glacial age, which he says began to end "some twenty thousand years ago," and then asks, "Why should man not be very, very old, if that is the case? What is there in the Christian religion against it? What doctrine is in any way changed? Six thousand or sixty thousand or six hundred thousand years affect the fundamental situation set forth by the message of the gospel not a whit. Rather, the older man is the greater is the significance of the statement of the New Testament that Christ appeared in the 'last time,' and that we are now living in 'the last times.'" Byron Nelson, *Before Abraham: Prehistoric Man in Biblical Light* (Minneapolis: Augsburg, 1948), 95 [NBA]. Not all Christian scholars are convinced that there is conclusive evidence for placing man's beginning in remote antiquity. It is reassuring, however, to know that any future discoveries, pointing to an extremely early date for man's creation, can easily harmonize with the Scriptures, as shown by Byron Nelson's book.

ther reasons for assigning a long period of time to the first two verses of Genesis and taking the days as twenty-four-hour days will be discussed later when we consider the other two theories.

In the nineteenth century George H. Pember, in his book *Earth's Earliest Ages*, popularized this view that there may have been a long period or gap between Genesis 1:1 and 1:2, and it is sometimes charged that the whole idea is due merely to his book.[14] The possibility of such a gap has, however, been held by many competent theologians, including Hengstenberg (1802–1869), a German Lutheran scholar who became professor of theology at the University of Berlin in 1828; Franz Delitzsch (1813–1890), professor at Erlangen in Germany and an outstanding Old Testament scholar; and others such as Boehme, Oetinger, F. von Meyer, Stier, Keerl, and Kurtz.[15]

According to the second theory, the days of Genesis were long periods of time, perhaps corresponding to the various geological ages. This is sometimes referred to as the "day-age" theory. It is said that this view was held by Josephus, the Jewish historian of the first century A.D., by many rabbis, and by some early Christian fathers, including Irenaeus (2nd century), Origen (3rd century), and Augustine (4th century). Bible believers who hold this view today are not necessarily theistic evolutionists, inasmuch as the latter usually hold that God used evolution as a means of finally producing human beings, and they often attempt to fit the evolutionary process into the creative days of Genesis. On the contrary, most Bible believers who hold the view that the days of Genesis are long periods of time reject the theory of evolution.

I believe that a reasonable literal interpretation of the Bible does not give as much justification to an acceptance of the day-age theory of Creation as to the twenty-four-hour day theory (though I recognize that the day-age theory can be and often is held by a Bible believer who is true to the fundamentals of the faith). It is a principle of literal interpretation that we take a word in its usual sense unless there is definite evidence to show that it is used figuratively. Until rather conclusive evidence to the contrary is forthcoming, I prefer to take the days of Genesis as literal twenty-four-hour days because (1) this is the natural and usual use of the word; (2) the delimiting of the day by "evening and morning" (Gen. 1:5, 8, 13, etc.) would point to a literal day (holders of the day-age theory point out that "and there was evening and there was morning" may be figurative also, indicating the beginning and the end of an era, but this usage would seem a little strained in the light of the context); (3) the reference to the Sabbath day in the Ten Commandments refers to the six creative days and the seventh day of God's rest in such a way as to imply literal twenty-four-hour days (Exod. 20:11). An alternative to the day-age theory as usually stated is the idea that the creative days were literal days, but they were separated by extended periods of time.

According to the third view, the creation of the earth was followed immediately or at least very soon by the creation of plants, animals, and man during creative days of twenty-four hours. This view places the creation of the universe and the earth, as well as man and animal life, all within a brief period, perhaps since 10,000 B.C. Such a view is tenable, but there are factors that point to the possibility of a period of time between the creation of the earth and the creation of man: (1) In warning Israel of God's judg-

[14]George H. Pember, *Earth's Earliest Ages* (New York: Revell, c. 1876) [PEEA].

[15]A list of those holding the view that there was a gap is given by George Trumbull Ladd, *The Doctrine of Sacred Scripture* (1883), 1:265 [LDSS]. Ladd himself rejected the view but pointed out those who held it.

ment on backsliding, the prophet Jeremiah presented his vision of the earth as being "formless and empty" (Jer. 4:23), using the same Hebrew words as those applied to the earth in Genesis 1:2. Jeremiah was apparently led to think back to the desolation of the earth before the creation of man and compare it with the cataclysmic state that would result if God's judgment should fall on unrepentant Israel. This use of the very same words could point to a cataclysmic period in Genesis 1:2, which perhaps followed the sinning of the angels and Satan. (2) The geologic ages seem to give evidence of a period longer than a few thousand years. In some areas, several petrified forests have been found superimposed on one another. God could have created them this way, but it is possible that he permitted them to be formed over an extended period of time. Of course, natural scientists generally assign extended billions of years to the age of the earth, with no real degree of unanimity among them as to an approximate age.

Events of the Creation Days

The main events of the creative days may be easily summarized as follows:

First day: Light	Fourth day: Light bearers
Second day: Sky	Fifth day: Marine and aerial life
Third day: Dry land	Sixth day: Land animals and man

There is an orderly progression in the process of creation. The light of the first day corresponds to the light bearers of the fourth day; the sky ("expanse") is established on the second day, and the life that peoples the sea and the sky is brought forth on the fifth; the dry land is made to emerge on the third day, and the inhabitants of the dry land are created on the sixth.

On the first day, God spoke and there was light (Gen. 1:3). Skeptics like Voltaire have inquired, "How could there be light before there was any sun?" Modern science has shown the existence of light apart from the sun, as in the case of phosphorescence and the phenomenon of the Aurora Borealis (northern lights). Furthermore, the sun could have been created in the creative activity in Genesis 1:1–2, and could have already been in existence before the first day (or during the first day; cf. discussion of the fourth day). Sir James Jeans, a British physicist, referring to the words of Genesis that give the explanation of the origin of light, says, "The whole story of its creation can be told with perfect accuracy and completeness in the six words, 'God said, Let there be light.' "[16]

On the second, day, God made the expanse of the sky, dividing the earthly from the celestial waters (Gen. 1:6–8). The word *firmament* (KJV) may seem to imply that the Bible writer conceived of the sky as a solid vault ("something firm") in which the sun, moon, and stars are fixed like light bulbs. The liberal writer Skinner held that this was the unscientific view of the ancient Hebrew writers; he says, "The firmament is the dome of heaven, which to the ancients was no optical illusion, but a material structure. . . ."[17] A further analysis gives us the answer to the charge that the Bible is unscientific in this regard. The "firmament" is a mistranslation due to the false astronomy of the Greeks of the third century B.C., who believed that the sky was a solid crystalline sphere. Hence the Hebrew work *rakia'* was ren-

[16]*The Mysterious Universe*, cited in D.E. Hart-Davies, *The Genesis of Genesis* (London: James Clarke, 1932), 32 [HDGG].

[17]John Skinner, *Genesis*, International Critical Commentary (New York: Scribner, 1910), 21 [SG].

dered *stereoma* in the Greek translation of the Old Testament.[18] Then when Jerome translated the Old Testament into Latin,[19] he used the Latin word *firmamentum*, which in turn was rendered by the English word "firmament" in KJV. The original word in the Hebrew, *rakia'*, does not have the idea of something "firm" but comes from a root meaning that which is "stretched out," "attenuated," or "extended," and is best translated "expanse," as in the NIV. It perfectly describes the expanse of the atmosphere of our earth. In summary, the word "firmament" is faulty translation arising from the false science of the third century B.C. and incorrectly translates the original word. Hart-Davies well comments, "Thus, what has been frequently exhibited as a blunder in the Biblical narrative proves to be the product of a mistake in the realm of science; or, shall we say, a misguided attempt on the part of the modernists of two thousand years ago to 'restate' the ancient faith in terms of modern thought?" (HDGG, 39).

On the third day, God caused the waters of the earth to be gathered together, perhaps by the depressing of low places and the elevation of solid ground. The earth was now ready for vegetation, and God said, "Let the land produce vegetation: seed-bearing plants and trees. . . that bear fruit with seed in it" (Gen. 1:11).

On the fourth day, God said, "Let there be lights in the expanse of the sky. . . . God made two great lights. . . ." (Gen. 1:14, 16). There are two main views as to the instituting of the sun, moon, and stars. One view holds that the sun, moon, and stars were created in the original creation of Genesis 1:1ff., but that their light did not penetrate through the mists to the earth until the fourth day. This view is expressed by Jamieson, Fausset, and Brown: "The sun, moon, and stars were for the first time unveiled in all their glory in the cloudless sky."[20] It might be objected that God is said to have "*made* two great lights" (Gen. 1:16). The word rendered "made" (*'asah*), however, does not necessarily imply a creative act, being different from the word "create" (*bara'*) used in Genesis 1:1. Furthermore, in the next verse (v. 17) it says that God "set them [*nathan*] in the expanse of the sky," employing the Hebrew word usually translated "gave" (*nathan*), which is often used in the sense of "institute." Taking *nathan* in this sense of "institute," we could translate verse 17, "And God instituted [i.e., appointed] them in the expanse of the sky to give light on the earth." Hence this passage may refer to God's declaration of the function of the heavenly bodies rather than to their creation. The word "create" (*bara'*) is not used here. A second view holds that while light was created on the first day, it was concentrated in the sun on the fourth day; that is, at the word of God, the heavenly bodies came into operation as lights of the universe.[21]

On the fifth day, God caused the waters to bring forth marine life and the air to swarm with birds (Gen. 1:20). Why were birds and fish created on the same day? Older commentators (Calvin, Luther) explained it on the ground of their similarity, fins being like wings. It seems likely, however, that it is due to the fact that Creation proceeded from the lower to the higher; fish and birds occupy a lower place in the scale of life than land ani-

---

[18]The Greek translation of the Hebrew Old Testament is called the Septuagint, abbreviated LXX (probably made in the third or second century B.C.).

[19]The Vulgate translation, 4th century A.D.

[20]*A Commentary Critical and Explanatory on the Whole Bible*, single-vol. ed. (Grand Rapids: Eerdmans, 1935), 17 [JFB].

[21]C.F. Keil and F. Delitzsch, *Biblical Commentary on the Old Testament* (Edinburgh: T. & T. Clark, 1872), vol. 1, The Pentateuch, 56 [KD].

mals, especially the mammals (KD, 60–61).

On the sixth day, God made land animals and man (Gen. 1:24–27). Why does the creation of land animals and man fall on the same day? Lange points out that man has his being, as to his bodily appearance, from the earth in common with the animals; the land emerged on the third day of Creation, and now in the corresponding day in the second group of three, that is, the sixth day, the creatures that inhabit the earth were formed.[22] However, there is a great gulf between the animals and man, and one of the prime reasons is the fact that God created man in his own image, in his spiritual likeness (Gen. 1:26). This divine likeness was marred by the Fall, shattered by sin; but when a person puts his trust in Christ he becomes a new creation (2 Cor. 5:17) and "participate[s] in the divine nature" (2 Peter 1:4).

On the seventh day, God rested from his creative work and blessed the seventh day and sanctified it (Gen. 2:2–3). This shows that the sabbath principle of setting apart one day in seven existed from the beginning.

Critical View of Sabbath; Pan-Babylonian Theory

The Babylonian records tell of a certain special day that was observed on the seventh, fourteenth, twenty-first, and twenty-eighth of the month. Another special Babylonian day called *shabatum* was observed on the fifteenth of the month; *shabatum* is etymologically the same as the Hebrew *sabbath*.[23] The critical school has tended to hold that the Hebrew Sabbath was derived from these Babylonian special days. This whole critical tendency to trace the early records of

Genesis back to Babylonian religion and folklore, known as "Pan-Babylonianism," was forcefully presented to the world by Friedrich Delitzsch in his work *Babel und Bibel* (Babel and Bible), 1902, first given in the form of two lectures before the German emperor, Kaiser Willhelm II.[24] It made such a stir in Germany that even the cab drivers were discussing Delitzsch's ideas. It is said that a cartoon was published showing a dog baying at the moon, with the words coming out of his mouth, "Is Delitzsch right?" The emperor wrote a public letter proclaiming the need of orthodoxy. The evidence shows that the emperor was justified in his rebuke of Delitzsch, as we will see in the next section.

Answer to the Critical View of the Sabbath

An examination of some of the details of the Pan-Babylonian theory shows that it is not supported by the facts. The Babylonian special day differs from the biblical Sabbath in several ways: (1) The Babylonian special day was observed not only on the seventh, fourteenth, twenty-first, and twenty-eighth day, but also on the fifteenth and nineteenth days, and only the last was called *shabatum*. (2) The tablets call the seventh day "an evil day" or "an unlucky day," whereas Scripture describes it as "a holy day." (3) The restrictions on that day applied only to certain specified individuals, such as the king (shepherd of the great peoples), the seer, and the physician, whereas the Old Testament makes the Sabbath binding on everyone. (4) There was no cessation of business activity on Babylonian special days, in contrast to the Hebrew Sabbath. (5) Although Babylonians had special regard for days that were multiples of

---

[22]John Peter Lange, *Genesis* (New York: Scribner, 1870), 172 [LCG].

[23]George A. Barton, *Archaeology and the Bible*, 7th ed. (Philadelphia: American Sunday School Union, 1937), 310 [BAB].

[24]Article on Friedrich Delitzsch, in *Encyclopedia Britannica*, 14th ed., 7:168.

seven, those days rarely ever fell on the seventh day of the week in their lunar calendar and thus were not equivalent to the Hebrew Sabbath.[25] It does not seem, therefore, that there was any necessary connection between the Hebrew Sabbath and Babylonian special days.

Babylonian Creation Tablets

In the excavation of Nineveh by Layard and Rassam (1850–1854), the library of King Ashurbanipal (ruled 688–626 B.C.) was uncovered, with its multitudes of clay tablets.[26] Among these tablets was found the so-called Babylonian account of Creation, which tells of the conflict between the great god Marduk and the goddess of the deep, Tiamat. Marduk emerged from the conflict triumphant and was adored by both gods and men. During the course of the epic, reference is made to the creation of man.[27]

An examination shows some similarities between the Babylonian epic and the Genesis record of the creation of man: (1) The Babylonian account was written on seven tablets, perhaps corresponding to the seven days of creation. (2) The account of man's creation is found in the sixth tablet, parallel to the Bible's story of the Creation of man on the sixth day (BAB, 296).

The differences, however, are even more pronounced than the similarities: (1) The polytheistic Babylonian account with its many gods is in striking contrast to the majestic record of Creation by the one true and living God. (2) Mythology abounds in the Babylonian account, overlaid with fantastic ideas; Marduk, for example, cut Tiamat into two pieces and used one half as a covering for the heavens. (3) The order is different in many respects: in the Babylonian account the mention of the formation of the world does not occur until the fourth tablet, whereas in the biblical record the world appears early in the creation work of God. (4) A multitude of details is entirely different in the Babylonian account; e.g., Marduk and the lesser deities are all pagan inventions. (5) The whole nature of the Babylonian account is different, since it is basically a hymn to Marduk and has a political purpose. By portraying the preeminent place of her patron deity (Marduk) among the gods, Babylon could advance her cause in her bid for supremacy in Mesopotamia.

Connection Between Creation Tablets and the Bible

If there is any connection between the Babylonian tablets and the true account of Creation given in the Bible, it is likely that the facts regarding Creation were handed down and diffused among many peoples and finally appeared in this variant form in Babylonia with the addition of many legendary and polytheistic features. Our examination shows that the Pan-Babylonian theory of origins is not borne out.

Nature of Genesis 2; Location of Eden

Adam and Eve were placed in a "garden in the east, in Eden" (Gen. 2:8). The second chapter of Genesis, which tells of Eden, is not a variant account of the first, but gives additional details not recorded in Genesis 1. A careful examination shows that Genesis 1 and 2 harmonize. Some

[25]I.M. Price, O.R. Sellers, and E. Leslie Carlson, *The Monuments and the Old Testament* (Philadelphia: Judson, 1958), 109–11 [PMOT].

[26]H.V. Hilprecht, *Explorations in Bible Lands During the 19th Century*, (Philadelphia: Holman, 1903), 132, 133 [HEBL].

[27]Alexander Heidel has provided a translation and commentary in his book *The Babylonian Genesis*, 2nd ed. (Chicago: University of Chicago Press, 1951) [HBG]. See also James B. Pritchard, ed., *Ancient Near Eastern Texts Relating to the Old Testament*, 2nd ed. (Princeton: Princeton University Press, 1955), 60–70 [PANET].

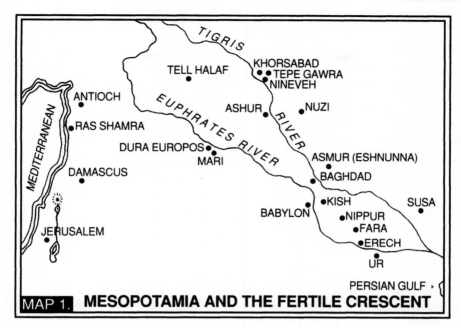

MAP 1. **MESOPOTAMIA AND THE FERTILE CRESCENT**

modern books are misleading when they suggest that there are "inconsistencies in details" between these two chapters.

One of the main purposes of Genesis 2 is to describe the nature of Adam and Eve's environment and the events leading up to the Fall. All of the essential facts are carefully recorded. Even the general location of the Garden of Eden may be ascertained from the facts given. The Bible records that two of the four rivers connected with the Garden of Eden are the Euphrates and the Hiddekel (Gen. 2:14). The Hiddekel River is the river we now call the Tigris. This is demonstrated by Babylonian clay tablets that apply the name Idiglat (of which Hiddekel is a variation) to the Tigris.

Thus we see that Eden was in the region of the Tigris and Euphrates, the area known geographically as Mesopotamia (Greek, meaning "between the rivers"), which today is the country known politically as Iraq.

Identification of the Pison and Gihon is a subject of conjecture. To say that they were ancient irrigation canals does not

seem to solve anything. The irrigation culture of ancient Mesopotamia did not develop until the fourth and especially the third millennia B.C., long after the Flood. Irrigation canals would not have existed as early as the Garden of Eden. The precise location of Eden within Mesopotamia is also a subject of pure conjecture. Probably we will never be sure exactly where it was located. The effects of the Noahic flood on the topography of the Near East may have been devastating, making it impossible to determine geographical locations in earliest times on the basis of present conditions. The courses of rivers could have been greatly altered, and some rivers could have disappeared entirely.

That there was such a place of perfection as the Garden of Eden seems to be reflected in the Sumerian account of the land of Dilmun, which was pure, clean, and bright, where "the lion kills not, the wolf snatches not the lamb," where there was no disease or pain, deceit, or guile [ANET, 38].

The land of Dilmun was both a paradise and a real land. In the minds of many, Bahrain Island in the Persian Gulf has been connected with the land of Dilmun even since Henry Rawlinson made the identification in 1861. A Danish expedition under the leadership of Geoffrey Bibby worked on the island for more than fifteen years (beginning in 1953) and believed it to have been the seat of power in a fairly extensive empire. Dilmun reached its zenith as a sea-trading power about 2000 B.C.[28]

Features of Mesopotamia
(Physical, Political)

Since the Garden of Eden was in the vicinity of Mesopotamia, it may be helpful to note some of the main features of this area, even though there has likely been some change since early time. The two main rivers of Mesopotamia are the Euphrates and Tigris. The Euphrates, meaning "that makes fruitful," is 1,780 miles long, and the Tigris, meaning "arrow," is 1,060 miles long. These rivers carry down mud or silt and deposit it along their banks and at the head of the Persian Gulf. Much of southern Mesopotamia consists of this fertile silt. In ancient times canals were maintained between the Euphrates and the Tigris in order to supplement the rainfall, which averages about ten inches per year. The main part of Mesopotamia measures about six hundred by three hundred miles. The terrain gently rises from sea level at the Persian Gulf to about a thousand feet above sea level at Haran in the north.

The earliest inhabitants of this area that can be described with certainty from the archaeological discoveries are the Sumerians, who came on the scene about 3000 B.C. or a little before. A high point of Sumerian culture is illustrated by the materials that Sir C. Leonard Woolley found in his excavation of the cemetery at Ur. These materials are now dated about 2500 B.C.[29] After the middle of the third millennium, Semites filtered into Mesopotamia, apparently coming from the Arabian Peninsula. They reached a prominent position under Sargon of Akkad about 2350. Sargon built the first Mesopotamian empire. From then on, there was a general decline in Sumerian civilization, except for some revival during the Ur III period (c. 2000). During the period 2000–1700, the city of Babylon became very important and gave the name of Babylonia to the area of Mesopotamia that it controlled; Hammurabi was the great king of this era. Following a period of Babylonian decline, the Assyrians emerged in Northern Mesopotamia. Although Old and Middle Assyrian empires may be identified and discussed, the Neo-Assyrian Empire (c. 900–612) is the Assyrian period most significant for biblical study.[30] The years 612–539 B.C. marked the period of Babylonian rule,[31] with Babylon and southern Mesopotamia coming into prominence; this is usually known as the Neo-Babylonian period. It was followed by the domination of the

[28]See Geoffrey Bibby, *Looking for Dilmun* (New York: New American Library, 1969).

[29]C. Leonard Woolley, *Ur of the Chaldees*, rev. by P.R.S. Moorey (London: Herbert Press, 1982) [WUC].

[30]The great kings of the Assyrian Empire included Shalmaneser III (858–824 B.C.), Tiglath-pileser III (745–427), Shalmaneser V (727–722), Sargon II (721–705), Sennacherib (704–681), Esarhaddon (680–669), and Ashurbanipal (668–627); see chapters 17–18. Most of these kings of Assyria came in contact with certain of the kings of Israel and Judah: Shalmaneser III received tribute from Jehu, the tenth king of Israel (for archaeological light, see "Archaeological Confirmation of Jehu," in chapter 16); Tiglath-pileser III received tribute from Menahem, the sixteenth king of Israel (see chapter 17); for other contacts between Assyria and Israel, see chapters 17–18.

[31]The great king of this period was Nebuchadnezzar II (605–562 B.C.). See chapter 20 for the section "Nebuchadnezzar's Control of Judah; Archaeological Evidence of His Building Activity in Babylon."

Persians,[32] 539–331. Alexander the Great brought the Persian Empire to an end in 331 B.C. But let us return to ancient Mesopotamia and Eden.

The Fall of Man (Genesis 3)

God placed Adam and Eve in an ideal environment, where they were tested in regard to obedience. Eve disobeyed, choosing her own self-interest in yielding to Satan's temptation to "be like God" (Gen. 3:5); Adam also sinned, likewise partaking of the Tree of the Knowledge of Good and Evil. When God questioned them, Adam sought to shift the responsibility to Eve (v. 12), and in turn, Eve said, "The serpent deceived me" (v. 13). The consequences of the Fall included the cursing of the ground, the requiring of exhausting labor to gain one's livelihood, and the imposition of temporal death; and in the spiritual realm, the Fall brought about the loss of innocence, the realization of guilt, and finally spiritual death (vv. 16–24).

Temptation Seals

At Tepe Gawra, a few miles north of Nineveh, where excavations were made in 1930–1932 by E.A. Speiser of the University of Pennsylvania, a seal was found that depicted a man, a woman, and a serpent. Since it was found in the level antedating 3000 B.C., Barton remarks, "It strongly suggests that the story of the temptation is very old" (BAB, 46; a picture is found in illustration 176½ in the back of Barton). In earlier excavations, made at Nineveh, another seal was found, now in the British Museum, showing a tree in the center, a man on the right, a woman on the left plucking fruit, and a serpent behind her standing erect (for a picture of this, see PMOT, 116). The significance of these seals lies in the fact that they may point back to the actual temptation in Eden.

Prophecy of Christ; God-Men of Pagan Religions

A prophecy of Christ is implied in the reference to the seed of the woman who would bruise the head of the serpent (Gen. 3:15). The fact that this coming One would be the seed of the woman rather than the seed of the man is an implied prophecy of the virgin birth of Christ, the One "born of a woman" (Gal. 4:4).

Critics have pointed out that pagan religions contain legends of supernatural men who were a combination of god and man. They often try to reduce the position of Christ to the level of the demi-gods of these pagan legends, citing as examples such heroes as the Babylonian Gilgamesh, who was two-thirds god and one-third man.[33] However, Christ was entirely different, because his being comprised no such proportion as two-thirds God and one-third man. Christ was completely God and completely man; all that God was, Christ was; all that man was, Christ was. This is an entirely different concept than the pagan fractional combinations.

---

[32]Cyrus was the first king of the Persian Empire, ruling 539–530 B.C., followed by Cambyses II (529–522). Cyrus gave the Jews permission to return from captivity, a policy illuminated by archaeological discovery (see "Archaeological Light on Cyrus' Policy" in chapter 21). For the other Persian kings, see chapter 22.

[33]James C. Muir, *His Truth Endureth* (Philadelphia: National, 1937), 15 [MHTE]. Muir does not hold this critical view; he merely describes the nature of Gilgamesh.

Chapter 3

Early Civilization

(Genesis 4–11: Cain and Abel, Flood, Babel)

Cain and Abel (Genesis 4:1–15)

After God cast Adam and Eve out of the Garden of Eden, Eve "gave birth to Cain. . . . Later she gave birth to his brother Abel" (Gen. 4:1–2). The Hebrew literally reads, "and she added to bring forth." On the basis of the Hebrew, many commentators believe that Cain and Abel were twins (JFB, 20; SG, 103).[1] Abel became a shepherd and Cain engaged in agriculture. It is evident that they had been instructed, probably by God, in the principle of sacrifice. Each brought an offering. Abel brought of the firstborn of his flock, and "the LORD looked with favor on Abel and his offering," but when Cain brought the products of the ground, the Lord was not pleased (Gen. 4:3–5).

Why was Abel's sacrifice acceptable? Some have thought that it was a matter of material, Abel's offering being animal, or that it was a matter of quality, Cain bringing something inferior, perhaps the first thing he laid his hands on. However, the divine commentary in Hebrews 11:4 shows that Abel's sacrifice was acceptable because his heart was right: "*By faith* Abel offered God a better sacrifice. . ." (MNG, 124). By implication, it is evident that Cain's offering was not acceptable because his heart was not right, for he had not truly trusted in God *by faith*. An external ritual, whether it be sacrifice, baptism, or church attendance, has little or no meaning unless one by faith has trusted in the Lord.[2]

When Cain became angry, God said, "If

---

[1]John Calvin, *Commentaries on the First Book of Moses, Called Genesis*, trans. from original Latin and compared with the French edition by John King (Edinburgh: Calvin Translation Society, 1847), 189 [CG].

[2]It is sometimes stressed that Abel's sacrifice was acceptable because, being a lamb, its blood was shed and this shedding of blood pointed forward to Christ. This is of course quite true, for "without the shedding of blood there is no forgiveness" (i.e., of sins, Heb. 9:22). The mere shedding of an animal's blood, however, could never make real atonement. In later times, when backslidden Israelites offered lambs but had not turned their heart to the Lord, God said through his prophets that he hated the people's sacrifices (Amos 5:21–22; cf. Isa. 1:11–16). God showed that an empty formality, though it included shedding of blood, was an abomination to him. By analogy, the sacrifice of Abel, though one of blood, could not have been acceptable if his heart had not been turned to the Lord.

you do not do what is right, sin is crouching at your door" (Gen. 4:7). The word sin (*hatta'th*) is often used in the sense of "sin-offering" in the Bible.[3] If it is taken in this sense, then God was actually saying, "If you do not do what is right, a sin-offering is lying at the door," which would seem to indicate that Cain's sin might be made right by a sin-offering that showed a change of heart. But Cain did not make things right with the Lord. When he and Abel were alone in "the field," i.e., the open country, he slew Abel. Even in the face of this sin, God did not forsake Cain, but, responding to Cain's words "whoever finds me will kill me" (Gen. 4:14), God put a mark on him that he might not be slain. Dodd, quoted in Clark's Commentary (p. 59), computed that the family of Adam and Eve and their sons could have increased to 32,000 by this time in Cain's life (cited in MNG, 125–26). Thus there could have been many whom Cain feared to meet.

Early Civilization (Genesis 4), Archaeological Light on Early Cities, Music, and Metal

Cain built a city (Gen. 4:17). When and where the earliest village life appeared is debated. Since the work of Kathleen Kenyon on the early levels of Jericho (1952–1958), many have classified Jericho as the oldest city in the world. Kenyon assigned a date of about 8000 B.C. to early village culture there.[4] But Mureybet (Mureybit), located in the bend of the Euphrates east of ancient Antioch (Modern Antakya), is probably fully as old.[5] And dates of 7500 to 6800 have been assigned to early village life at Çayönü, a town located between

the points where the Tigris and Euphrates originate at the north of Mesopotamia.[6] It is not possible, however, to be dogmatic about these dates, which are assigned largely on the basis of Carbon 14 tests, and scholars in the field have reservations about accepting them.[7] Presumably, too, these dates, if correct, have little to do with cities in the days of Cain, for he lived before the Flood. Such dates might do more to give some indication of the date of the Flood than when the earliest village life occurred, because probably the Flood totally wiped out the earliest villages. In any case, numerous early villages dating from 6000 B.C. on down have been excavated in Mesopotamia, where there was a civilization more advanced than anywhere else. Certainly the use of the wheel, writing, and other trappings of civilization appeared first in Mesopotamia, and there is no real debate over where civilization began.

One of Cain's family, a descendant named Jubal, is referred to as the "father of all who play the harp and flute" (Gen. 4:21). This reference implies an early knowledge of various types of instruments, the harp representing stringed instruments, and the flute, wind instruments. Archaeological discoveries have produced much evidence concerning the early development of musical instruments in the Bible lands. Most of the recent books on the history of music devote a large share of their beginning chapters to the evidence of early music found in the excavations, such as the harps and lyres discovered at Ur of the Chaldees and the string and wind instruments pictured on the Egyptian monuments.[8]

---

[3]CG, 202; W.H. Griffith-Thomas, *Genesis* (London: Religious Tract Society, n.d.), 64 [GTG].
[4]Kathleen Kenyon, *Archaeology in the Holy Land*, 3d ed. (New York: Praeger,, 1970), 331.
[5]James Mellaart, *The Neolithic of the Near East* (New York: Scribner, 1975), 45.
[6]Ibid., 52.
[7]See, for example, Hans J. Nissen, *The Early History of the Ancient Near East* (Chicago: University of Chicago Press, 1988), 4.
[8]See WUC; James B. Pritchard, *The Ancient Near East in Pictures*, 2nd ed. (Princeton: Princeton University Press, 1969), pictures 191–219, 794–97 [PANEP]. The article "Musical Instruments of Israel," by Ovid R. Sellers, appeared in the *Biblical Archaeologist* [BA] 4,3 (September 1941). It deals

A tower at Jericho that has been dated to about 8,000 B.C.

knowledge of iron long before 1200. At a site in Mesopotamia about fifty miles northeast of Baghdad, called Tell Asmar today, but known in ancient times as Eshnunna, Henri Frankfort of the Oriental Institute at the University of Chicago found evidence[9] of an iron blade from the level of 2700 B.C. A small steel ax from Ur and other very early objects of iron have also been found.[10] The fact that a greater abundance of iron has not been found seems to indicate that it was not widely used in early times, but another contributing factor may be that iron oxidizes more quickly and completely than copper, and, having disintegrated, would not be as readily detected in excavating. Numerous archaeological discoveries give evidence of the use of copper during the period 4300–3000. In summary, the excavations indicate some knowledge of metal in early times, as implied in the biblical record (Gen. 4).

Another man in the Cainitic civilization, Tubal-cain, is described as one who "forged all kinds of tools out of brass and iron" (Gen. 4:22). This reference reflects the early use of metal. It was formerly believed that the use of metal began very late, and it is certainly true that metal was probably not widely used in early times. Discoveries have shown, however, that metal was known and used much earlier than previously supposed. The usual date formerly given for the beginning of the Iron Age in the Near East was 1200 B.C., and this date is still used for convenience in listing the metal ages. Modern archaeology, however, shows that there was a

The Long-Lived Patriarchs of the Line of Seth (Genesis 5); Possible Reflection in the Clay Tablets

The descendants of Adam and Eve's son Seth were noteworthy for their longevity. Seth himself lived to be 912 years old, and in the seventh generation after Seth, Methuselah reached the greatest age of all—969 (Gen. 5:27). Most of those who came between Seth and Methuselah lived to be between 800 and 900 years of age.

It is reasonable to believe that people lived a long time when humankind was first on the earth. The effects of sin and disease and the debilitating aspects of civilization had not had time to work their full effect. Climate and diet may

primarily with musical instruments in the middle and later part of biblical history, c. 1000 B.C. and later.

[9]Rusted remains of a blade still clinging to a dagger handle were found by laboratory test to be iron. Oriental Institute Communication [OIC], no. 17, pp. 56ff., published by the University of Chicago; HSAB, article by Meek on Mesopotamia, 168.

[10]Millar Burrows, *What Mean These Stones?* (New Haven: American Schools of Oriental Research, 1941), 158 [BWMS].

have been different in antediluvian times. Considering all the factors, it would be rather surprising if the life span had not been considerably greater when the human family was in its infancy.

A possible reflection of the fact that humans did live to greater ages in early times is seen in some of the Babylonian clay tablets, which tell of early kings who ruled for fabulously long periods; one, named Dumuzi, held sway for eighteen thousand years, and another ruled for thirty-six thousand years.[11] These texts are certainly mythological, but they may well be a legendary account of the fact revealed in the Bible that people did live to greater ages in early times.

The Two Lines of Cain and Seth; Their Mingling (Genesis 4–6)

The ungodly line of Cain, described in Genesis 4:17–24, included Lamech, the first recorded polygamist (technically, polygynist; v. 19) and also the second recorded murderer (v. 23). The godly line of Seth, described in Genesis 5, included Enoch, the man who "walked with God; then he was no more, because God took him away" (Gen. 5:24). It is rather striking that the ages of those in the godly line of Seth are recorded, whereas the ages of those in the line of Cain are not.

Many scholars believe that the separation between the godly line of Seth and godless line of Cain broke down and that their intermarriage is described in Genesis 6:2, "The sons of God saw that the daughters of men were beautiful, and they married any of them they chose." It would appear that the "sons of God" were the god-fearing Sethites,[12] God's spiritual children, whereas the "daughters of men" were those of Cain's line who rose only to

the human level and were not God's children (MNG, 154).

There are several places in the world where clear and lucid rivers merge with muddy and murky rivers. As they join, there is at first no intermingling of the clear and muddy waters, but both flow along in the same river bed, the clear water on one side and the muddy water on the other, with almost a noticeable line of division between them. After some distance, however, the two streams begin to intermingle, and it is not long before the muddy water has made the clear water a turbid brown. From then on it is all muddy. So it was with the lines of Seth and Cain. As long as there was separation, the Sethite line brought forth those who walked with God. But after the beginning of intermarriage and the accompanying breakdown in separation, it was not long until "the LORD saw how great man's wickedness on the earth had become, and that every inclination of the thoughts of his heart was only evil all the time" (Gen. 6:5).

The Flood (Genesis 6–8); the Size of the Ark

Because of this culmination of the wickedness of the human race, God sent the Flood upon the earth. Noah and his family were saved from the waters by means of the ark. The ark is a good illustration of Christ, the One who saves us from the waters of judgment.

The size of the ark is given specifically as being three hundred cubits long, fifty cubits wide, and thirty cubits high (Gen. 6:15). We know, from a certain archaeological discovery, that the standard cubit in the days of the kings of Israel and Judah (900–600 B.C.) was about eighteen inches. In the later years of the nine-

---

[11]Stephen Langdon, *Oxford Editions of Cuneiform Texts* 2, 1 (1923) [LCT]; translation appears in BAB, 317, lines 15, 34.

[12]Some have held that the "sons of God" were fallen angels. This seems unlikely, inasmuch as the Bible indicates that there is no marriage among the angels (Matt. 22:30).

teenth century, archaeologists examined a tunnel in Jerusalem that was built in the days of Hezekiah (c. 700). An inscription at the entrance written in the old Hebrew alphabet tells that this tunnel is twelve hundred cubits long. Measurement of the tunnel revealed that it was about eighteen hundred feet long, thus demonstrating that the cubit was about eighteen inches. Cubits varied somewhat in the ancient world. The Egyptian cubit was about 20.5 inches, the Mesopotamian cubit about an inch shorter than the Egyptian. The "long" cubit of Ezekiel 40:5 may have been equal to the Egyptian cubit.

If the minimum length of the cubit (eighteen inches) is used as a basis for calculating the size of the ark, and if it is assumed that the ark was rather squarely built, then the three floors would give a displacement of 43,000 tons (MNG, 159). This would be just a little smaller than the largest of the pre-World War II Italian liners, the Rex, which had a displacement of about fifty thousand tons. By way of comparison, the *Queen Elizabeth*, built after the war had a displacement of 83,673 tons. There would certainly have been plenty of room in the three decks of the ark for Noah, his family, the animals, and their food.[13]

The Flood Tablets; Area Covered by the Flood

The excavation of Nineveh (1850–1854) produced clay tablets that later proved to be the Babylonian account of the Flood. In many ways this account is very similar

to the biblical record of the Flood, and it is a definite reflection of the fact that there must have been a flood.[14]

A tablet with a Babylonian flood account, from the library of Ashurbanipal of Assyria. Now located in the British Museum.

There are two main views among conservative Bible scholars as to the area covered by the Flood: (1) It covered the *inhabited* earth, that is, Mesopotamia and perhaps some of the surrounding lands, but not the whole earth, According to this view, there was no need for a worldwide deluge, because a flood over the inhabited earth would have been sufficient to bring life to an end. (2) The Flood covered the *entire* earth. I recognize the possibility of the first view, but I see no reason why the second view of a universal flood should not be adhered to. Scriptural evidence supports the universality of the

---

[13]Much has been written in recent decades about the search for Noah's ark. If a search is to be launched, it is necessary, first, to decide where to look. Genesis 8:4 says that the ark "came to rest on the mountains of Ararat," on the eastern border of Turkey. Although one peak is identified as the traditional site, there is no absolute certainty on the matter. Dozens of expeditions have ascended the traditional peak since World War II, but the ark has not yet certainly been found, though members of one or two expeditions have claimed a sighting or even brought back some pieces of wood. Carbon 14 tests on these samples have been inconclusive.

[14]For a discussion of the Mesopotamian Flood accounts, a translation of them, and their relation to the biblical account, see Alexander Heidel, *The Gilgamesh Epic and Old Testament Parallels*, 2nd ed. (Chicago: University of Chicago Press, 1949).

Flood: (1) The fact that every living creature was to be destroyed[15] would indicate that the whole earth was subject to the Flood (Gen. 7:4). Probably the animals had scattered over much of the earth; a universal flood would have been needed to destroy them. (2) All the high hills were to be covered (v. 9). (3) After the Flood was over, God referred to having "destroyed all living creatures" (Gen. 8:21); it would seem that a universal flood would be required to bring this result. There is also a physical reason for positing a universal flood: since water seeks its own level, it is difficult to imagine water being at a great height in Asia Minor and Mesopotamia, and not elsewhere over the earth (MNG, 193).

S.R. Driver objected that the covering of all the high hills by the waters of the Flood would imply a depth of five miles of water over all the earth and that it would be impossible to have this much water.[16] This is answered by two considerations: (1) We do not know how high the mountains were at the time of the Flood; the surface of the earth may have been quite different from what it is now. (2) The Flood was a miracle; whether it would be possible for it to occur today is entirely beside the point; it was God who caused it, and he could cause the earth to be covered to any depth that he chose.

The Noahic Covenant (Genesis 9)

After the Flood, God laid down the principles for the continuation of life on the earth: (1) Provision was made for the transmission of life, "Be fruitful and increase in number" (Gen. 9:1). (2) Provision was made for man's dominion over animal life: "The fear and dread of you will fall upon all the beasts of the earth" (v. 2).

(3) Provision was made for the means of sustaining life: "Every thing that lives and moves shall be food for you" (v. 3). (4) Provision for human government was implied in the statement, "Whoever sheds the blood of man, by man shall his blood be shed" (v. 6); if a man's life could be taken, anything less—his liberty, his property—could be taken. Thus the foundation for civil authority and civil government with penal regulation is given here (JFB, 1-vol. ed., 22; large ed., 104–5).

Noah's Drunkenness (Genesis 9:20–23)

After life began in the new period following the Flood, Noah planted a vineyard; and "when he drank some of its wine, he became drunk" (Gen. 9:20–21). Some commentators hold that Noah was ignorant of the effects of wine before he drank (KD, 155), while others hold that he formerly must have been an agriculturalist and would have known the characteristics of the grape. (In their commentary, Jamieson, Fausset, and Brown [JFB] suggest that because Noah was a pious man, his action may have been due to age or inadvertency.[17]

The Table of Nations (Genesis 10)

The descendants of Noah's three sons—Shem, Ham, and Japheth—are listed in Genesis 10, and the part of Shem's line that culminated in Abraham is given at the end of Genesis 11 (vv. 10–27). This list of the peoples living during the early history of humankind indicates the general direction of their migrations and the location of their settlement. *The descendants of Japheth* (Gen. 10:1–5) seem to have gone to the north and northwest in the direction of the Caspian Sea, the Black Sea, Asia Minor, and later

---

[15]The question has sometimes been raised as to whether all of the present varieties of animals could have developed since the time of the Flood. Certainly all of the main groups of animals were represented on the ark. The variations we observe today within the main groups of animals could have developed since the Flood.

[16]S.R. Driver, *Genesis*, 99ff. [DG], cited in MNG, 163.

[17]Unless otherwise noted, the references to JFB will be in the one-volume edition.

perhaps into Europe; Gomer, for example (v. 2), may have been the progenitor of the later Gimirrai, who came into Asia Minor from north of the Black Sea. *The descendants of Ham* (vv. 6–20) tended to go south and southwest, to Egypt, Africa, the east coast of the Mediterranean, and Arabia. One indication of the direction that Ham's descendants took is implied in the name Mizraim (v. 6), probably the progenitor of the Egyptians, since Mizraim is the Hebrew name for Egypt in the Bible. *The descendants of Shem* (vv. 21–31) settled in the Near East (Mesopotamia), with some groups going south (to Arabia) and southeast (to Persia, whose ancient name was Elam, v. 22). We do not know to which group some of the present-day peoples belong. Whether the Chinese, for example, form a subdivision of one of the Japhetic, Hamitic, or Semitic groups, or perhaps are a combination of two or more groups we do not know.

The table of nations in Genesis 10 is significant because it emphasizes the brotherhood of the human race in the sense that God is the *Creator* of all humankind. Humans are not united in a spiritual fellowship except by being born again of the Spirit of God. But there is a *natural fellowship* of humans implied in this table of nations and further emphasized by Paul in his message on Mars Hill at Athens when he said that "from one man [God] made every nation. . . that they should inhabit the whole earth" (Acts 17:26). The scriptural teaching concerning this natural brotherhood is a forceful answer to race prejudices that have resulted in race riots in various parts of the world. It is also the answer to the erroneous theories of racial superiority promulgated by totalitarian political groups in this century.

Failure of Man Under the Noahic Covenant; Tower of Babel (Genesis 11)

God laid down the principle of human government in the days of Noah. In the ensuing years, humankind increased and seemed to prosper, but all of this ended in a self-exaltation of humans and a forgetting of God. In a great united effort, people began to build a tower and a great city and to exalt *their* name. They urged each other on by saying, "Let *us* build *ourselves* a city, with a tower. . . that *we* may make a name for *ourselves* and not be scattered. . . ." (Gen. 11:4). God's name was conspicuously absent in their carefully laid plans. It was purely a human effort in which no cognizance was taken of God's sovereignty or directive power.

Archaeological Light on the Tower of Babel (Genesis 11)

At the sites of many ancient cities in Mesopotamia stand the remains of towers, built in several stages or stories. In the Babylonian clay tablets they are referred to as ziggurats and represent a part of the religious structures of the ancient dwellers of Mesopotamia. On top of these staged towers there was usually a shrine. Possibly these towers were modeled after the original tower of Babel.[18]

George Smith, the staff member of the British Museum who translated the Babylonian account of the Flood, published the translation of a fragment that tells of the destruction of one of these ziggurats: "The building of this temple offended the gods. In a night they threw down what had been built. They scattered them abroad, and made strange their speech. The progress they impeded."[19] This account may be a later reflection of what actually occurred when God came down

---

[18]Pictures of the ziggurat at Ur appear in WUC, 143, 148, 151–53. Other pictures of ziggurats may be seen in PANEP, pictures 746–48, 755, 759. A reproduction of the ziggurat at Babylon, sometimes referred to as "The Tower of Babel" but certainly not the original tower of Babel, may be seen at the Oriental Institute Museum of the University of Chicago. A picture of this ziggurat appears in this book on page 40.

[19]George Smith, *Chaldean Account of Genesis* (New York: Scribner, 1876) [SCAG], cited in CBS, 29.

A model of one of the ziggurats or staged towers of ancient Babylonia. On the top of this particular tower stood the temple of Marduk, the chief god of Babylon in the time of Nebuchadnezzar (c. 600 B.C.). These ziggurats were likely the later counterparts of the Tower of Babel (See "Archaeological Light on the Tower of Babel," pp. 39). Courtesy of the Oriental Institute of the University of Chicago.

at the time of the building of the tower of Babel and scattered the people abroad by confounding their language.

Original Unity of Language (Genesis 11)

Before the building of the tower of Babel, "the whole world had one language and a common speech" (Gen. 11:1), but after the rebellion, implied in the building of the tower of Babel, the Lord confounded the language of all the earth (v. 9). Max Mueller, a comparative philologist, declared concerning the common origin of speech, "We have examined all possible forms which language can assume, and we now ask, can we reconcile with these three distinct forms, the radical, the terminational, the inflectional, the admission of one common origin of human speech? I answer decidedly, Yes."[20] The linguistic scholar Swadesh stated, "The case for a single beginning seems

[20]Max Mueller, *Science of Language*, 329 [MSL], cited in MNG, 215. Mueller, 1823–1900, was born in Germany and later was made professor of comparative philology at Oxford; see *Encyclopedia Britannica* article on Mueller [EB].

fairly strong."[21] Roucek observed, "Scholars speculate that most languages originated in one universal parent language."[22] While some secular scholars still favor polygenesis in the origin of language, the trend is toward monogenesis.

Concerning the origin of language, the well-known philologist Otto Jespersen of the University of Copenhagen wrote, "Some scholars (among them quite recently W. Schmidt) see the insufficiency of the usual theories, and giving up all attempts at explaining it in a natural way fall back on the religious belief that the first language was directly given to the first men by God through a miracle."[23]

I see no reason for doubting the biblical indication concerning the original unity of language, or the implication that humankind had speech from the beginning.[24] No discovery, ancient or modern, has shown otherwise.

The Nature of Genesis 1–11

As we have seen, the first eleven chapters of Genesis deal with universal history, describing the creation of the universe and humankind, the fall of the human race, the Flood, and the tower of Babel. Humans were tested three times during this period, and each test ended in failure: first, in the disobedience in Eden; second, in the sin that brought the judgment of the Flood; and finally in humankind's self-exaltation and the forgetting of God, which culminated in the scattering of the people and the confusion of tongues at Babel.

Humankind as a whole had failed three times, and God now chose one man, Abraham, to be a witness to him and a blessing to the entire human race (Gen. 12:1–3). The call of Abraham and the events of his life are dealt with in the next chapter.

---

[21]Morris Swadesh, *The Origin and Diversification of Language* (Chicago: Aldine-Atherton, 1971), 215.

[22]Joseph S. Roucek, *The Study of Foreign Languages* (New York: Philosophical Library, 1968), 7.

[23]"Language," EB (1942), 13:702.

[24]Shown by several statements in Genesis 1–3: "The man said, 'This is now bone of my bones. . .'" (2:23); "The man gave names to all the livestock. . ." (2:20); cf. 3:2, 10, 12.

Chapter 4

Abraham's Early Life in Canaan

(Genesis 12–20)

The Time of Abraham

The era of Abraham is frequently thought to have begun about 2000 B.C., and that is a useful approximation. To arrive at a more precise date, it is necessary to work backward, with the use of fairly specific chronological reckonings. In this venture I prefer to stick with the Hebrew text of the Old Testament. Solomon probably began to reign in 970 B.C. According to 1 Kings 6:1, the Exodus took place 480 years before the fourth year of Solomon's reign, or about 1446. Exodus 12:40–41 puts the entrance of the patriarchs into Egypt 430 years earlier—about 1876. From a study of Genesis 12:4; 21:5; 25:26; and 47:9 we can infer that the patriarchs sojourned in Canaan 215 years, entering about 2091.[1] Since Abraham was seventy-five when he entered Canaan, his birth would be pegged at 2166 B.C.

Those who follow the Septuagint, the Greek translation of the Old Testament, arrive at a slightly later date for Abraham,

perhaps about 2085 B.C. for his birth and 2010 as the date for his entrance into Canaan. Many who cut themselves loose from the chronological specifics of the Old Testament text place the patriarchal period in a general way during the first half of the second millennium B.C. Among such there is no unanimity of opinion in regard to the chronology of the patriarchs.

The Genealogical Descent of Abraham
(Genesis 11–12)

Abraham's line of descent from Noah's son Shem appears in Genesis 11. This may be a complete geneaology, but on the other hand it may name only the important people in the line of descendants (See chapter 2, the section entitled "Possibilities of Gaps in Biblical Genealogies," 22–23). Abraham's line of descent from Shem is recorded as follows: Shem, Arphaxad, Salah, *Eber*, Peleg, Reu, Serug, Nahor, Terah, and Abraham (Gen. 11:10–

---

[1]In these references it is clear that Abraham entered Canaan at the age of 75. Isaac was born when Abraham was 100. Isaac was 60 at Jacob's birth, and Jacob was 130 when he stood before Pharaoh. A total of 215 years elapsed, then, between Abraham's entrance into Canaan and Jacob's entrance into Egypt.

26). Since the name *Eber* comes from the same Hebrew root as the word *Hebrew*, many Bible scholars believe that *Hebrew* is derived from *Eber*,[2] and that both the Hebrews of Abraham's line and several other related peoples were descendants of Eber. In the Old Testament, however, the term *Hebrew* is ordinarily applied to the Chosen People only, those descended from Abraham through Isaac and Jacob.[3]

Archaeological Light on the Place of Abraham's Birth

Abraham's father, Terah, lived in Ur of the Chaldees in southern Mesopotamia. Here Abraham grew up and spent his younger days. As a result of the archaeological excavations conducted at Ur (1922–1934) by C. Leonard Woolley, a great deal is now known about this city; in fact, the whole background and environment of Abraham can now be pictured. The type of house of the Abrahamic period was well illustrated at Ur. An average dwelling measured forty by fifty-two feet. The lower walls were built of burned brick, the upper of mud brick, and the whole wall was usually plastered and whitewashed. An entrance lobby led into the central court, onto which all the rooms opened. On the lower floor were located the servants' room, the kitchen, the lavatory, the guest chamber, and also a lavatory and wash place reserved for visitors. Thus all of the first floor was utilized for the servants and guests; the second floor housed the family. The entire house of the average middle-class person had from ten to twenty rooms (WUC, 191–204).

Other discoveries at Ur showed that education was extensive in the days of Abraham. Young scholars learned to write the cuneiform signs as they were demonstrated by the schoolmaster on a flattened lump of soft clay. They also had reading lessons. Other clay tablets showed that in mathematics they learned the multiplication and division tables, and as they progressed they were subjected to working at square and cube roots and simple exercises in geometry. When the results of this part of the excavation are reviewed, one finds that four thousand years ago, in the days of Abraham, the pupils had the same "reading, writing, and 'rithmetic" as their modern counterparts struggle with today.

The degree of literacy in Ur and the number of documents recovered from the site puts the biblical narrative in a new light. As a member of the upper class, Abraham could well have been able to read and write. If he could not, he had sufficient wealth to maintain a scribe to keep business accounts and to record historical events. Usually it is assumed that patriarchal history was passed down through oral tradition, and many doubt the veracity of numerous facets of it. But in the light of newer discoveries, it is entirely reasonable to expect that Abraham passed on written accounts, and Moses had some of those at hand when he wrote Genesis. Moreover, Moses himself was highly educated as a member of the court of Egypt and in later life presumably would have supervised whatever archives existed among the Hebrews at that time.[4]

Even evidence of the far-reaching extent of the commerce of that day was revealed when a bill of lading of about 2040 B.C. was unearthed. It showed that a ship had come up the Persian Gulf to southern Mesopotamia after a two-year cruise. The cargo included copper ore,

---

[2]The Hebrew word *eber* means "beyond." In this case it would designate the people who came from "beyond" the Euphrates, i.e., Abraham and his people.

[3]See Exodus 1:15–16, 19; 5:3; 10:3; 1 Samuel 4:6, 9; for other references consult a concordance.

[4]For a discussion of Sumerian education, see Samuel N. Kramer, *History Begins at Sumer* (Philadelphia: University of Pennsylvania Press, 1981), chapter 1. See also C.L. Woolley, *Abraham* (New York: Scribner, 1936), 103 [WA].

gold, ivory, hardwoods for the cabinet maker, and diorite and alabaster for making statuary. Several of these imported materials came from quite distant lands. But our knowledge of the business affairs of Ur during her golden age is not dependent on a single bill of lading. Other bills of lading, invoices, letters of credit, court cases, and tax records have also come to light (WA, 118–33).

The Call of Abraham

Terah took his family from Ur and moved to Haran in northern Mesopotamia, about six hundred miles northwest of Ur (ABB, 45). There he died (Gen. 11:32).

While Abraham was still in Mesopotamia, the Lord called him to leave his land and his people and go into the land that God would show him, which proved to be Canaan (Gen. 12:1).

Idolatry and Pagan Worship in the Days of Abraham; Light from Archaeology

Abraham was called to go out from the midst of idolatry and paganism. Several hundred years later when Joshua referred to the family of Abraham, he said that they had "served other gods" (Josh. 24:2). C. Leonard Woolley's excavation at Ur (1922–1934) shed much light on the pagan religion that flourished there in the days of Abraham. The chief deity of the city was the moon-god named Nanna (formerly spelled Nannar), whose temple and ziggurat were in a large area measuring 1,200 by 600 feet. The ziggurat was a tower consisting of a solid mass of brick 200 feet long, 150 feet wide, and about 70 feet high. Massive brick stairways led to the upper levels, and on the topmost (the third) rose a temple to the god. At the foot of the ziggurat stood a temple to Nanna, which he apparently shared with his wife,

the moon-goddess Ningal. Adjacent to the temple was a kitchen for the preparation of sacrifices that were shared by the god, the priests, and worshipers (WUC, 137–60). Nearby, excavators uncovered another temple, the Ekhursag, a worship center for the cult of the ruling king. Offerings were also made to the spirit of the king after he died (WUC, 161, 167).

The Abrahamic Covenant (Genesis 12:1–3)

God's covenant with Abraham included several promises:

1. *"I will make you into a great nation"* (Gen. 12:2). This has been fulfilled numerically.[5] Moreover, this promise has been fulfilled in the influence that both the nation Israel and individual Israelites have had, not only in spiritual spheres but also in the economic, cultural, and political affairs of the secular world.

2. *"I will bless you"* (v. 2). Abraham was blessed temporally (in cattle, silver, and gold—Gen. 13:2) and spiritually. These blessings have been shared by his descendants, particularly when they have kept their eyes on the Lord.

3. *"I will make your name great"* (v. 2). Abraham is revered even today by Jew, Arab, and Christian alike; particularly for the child of God, he is the "father of the faithful."

4. *"You will be a blessing"* (v. 2); this is better translated "Be a blessing," because the verb is in the imperative mood (the same form of the Hebrew verb is used in Genesis 17:1, "Be blameless"). God's command that Abraham be a blessing shows his missionary purpose for Israel. The nation was to give not only a passive testimony to the Lord, but also a positive witness—"Be a blessing."

5. *"I will bless those who bless you, and whoever curses you I will curse"* (v. 3). In

---

[5]In spite of Hitler's efforts to destroy the Jews during World War II, Jewish population worldwide stands at over 17,000,000 in 1991, *World Almanac and Book of Facts 1991* (New York: Pharos Books, 1990), 610.

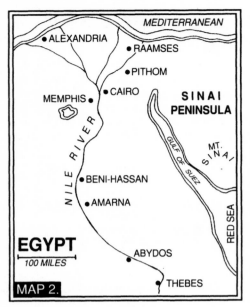

MAP 2.

ration for the Messiah and Savior (Isa. 53), and (4) a channel of blessing for the world (Rom. 15:8–12).

Abraham in Canaan; the Problem Concerning the Existence of Certain Towns in Abraham's Day (Genesis 12)

When Abraham came into Canaan, he lived for a time near Shechem (Gen. 12:6), about thirty miles north of Jerusalem, in a plain within the central mountain ridge of Palestine. Later he moved a few miles to the south and pitched his tent between Bethel and Ai (v. 8), some twelve miles north of Jerusalem. Here he built an altar to the Lord and worshiped.

The results of archaeological excavation seem to conflict with the biblical account at this point because all three of the places mentioned were uninhabited or virtually so when Abraham came through. In his work at Shechem, Wright found that there had been an extensive settlement there in the Chalcolithic period, in the fourth millennium B.C., and that the next major settlement began about 1850 (EAEHL, 4:1086). In his excavations at Et-Tell, identified with Ai, Callaway discovered that the early town there had been destroyed about 2400 B.C. and that the site had been abandoned until about 1200 (EAEHL, 1:49). At Bethel, Kelso found that the village dating to the period 2400–2200 was abandoned about 2200, and around 2000 a new period of occupation began (EAEHL, 1:192). What is one to do with this problem?

In the first place, Et-Tell probably is not to be identified with Ai.[6] Second, although Bethel has long been identified with Beitin, Bimson and Livingston question that conclusion also.[7] Obviously, if we have not yet found the location of either town with certainty, there is no conflict between the discoveries of archaeology and the intimations of Scripture. Third,

Abraham's own life this was observable, and in later years it has been apparent that those countries that have treated the Jews well have prospered.

6. *"All peoples on earth will be blessed through you"* (v. 3). This is messianic in its implications, as shown by the New Testament references to God's promises to Abraham (Gal. 3:8, 16). From Abraham came the line of descent that culminated in the human body of Christ. Through Christ true blessing has come to the earth, a fulfillment of the promise to Abraham that in him all families of the earth would be blessed.

With these promises to Abraham, God began to deal specifically with the Chosen People. His purposes for Abraham and the nation Israel were at least fourfold. Israel was to be (1) a witness to the rest of humankind regarding the reality and nature of God, (2) a depository of God's revelation (Rom. 3:1–2), (3) a prepa-

---

[6]See the discussion in chapter 10.
[7]See also the discussion in chapter 10.

A high place with altars for sacrifice at Et-Tell.

Abraham stopped only in the vicinity of the "site" of Shechem and at a point between Bethel and Ai. No contact with the inhabitants of these places is indicated, so it does not matter if they were largely deserted. The traditional locations would have been known in his day, and a few inhabitants may have lived in each place. As a matter of fact, in Palestine and much of Syria deurbanization had set in as early as the twenty-fourth century B.C. and certainly characterized the period 2200–2000. Then, gradually and later more rapidly, reurbanization of Palestine began during the twentieth century and was completed during the nineteenth.[8]

This deurbanization process permitted Abraham and Isaac considerable freedom to move about the country, but reurbanization would have restricted or threatened the activities of Jacob and his sons at a later time. Perhaps it is providential that the Hebrews were out of the country and living in Egypt while the Amorites and others were building the kind of power evident when the spies reconnoitered the land after the Exodus. Although there may be some problem connected with the existence of Shechem, Bethel, and Ai in Abraham's day, evidently archaeological discoveries do not show the Bible to be in error; and what we now know about the urbanization process in Palestine indicates that there was a considerable vacuum into which Abraham and Isaac could have moved if they were there in the twenty-second and twenty-first centuries B.C.

[8]See Suzanne Richard, "Toward a Consensus of Opinion of the End of the Early Bronze Age in Palestine-Transjordan," BASOR (Winter 1980), 5–34; Yohanan Aharoni, *The Archaeology of the Land of Israel*, trans. Anson F. Rainey (Philadelphia: Westminster, 1982), 81–97; John Bright, *A History of Israel*, 3rd ed. (Philadelphia: Westminster, 1982), 54–55.

Abraham in Egypt (Genesis 12:10–20); Archaeological Confirmation of "Strangers in Egypt"

The Genesis account declares that when a famine came to Canaan, Abraham went down to Egypt, where the Nile River almost always assured a harvest. The historian Diodorus indicated that Egypt was not open to strangers until about the seventh century B.C., thus seeming to contradict the biblical statement that Abraham went to Egypt.[9] Archaeological discoveries, however, show that people from the region of Palestine and Syria were coming to Egypt in the period of Abraham. This is clearly indicated by a tomb painting at Beni Hassan, dating a little after 2000 B.C. It shows Asiatic Semites who have come to Egypt.[10] Furthermore, the archaeological and historical indications of the coming of the Hyksos into Egypt c. 1900 B.C. provides another piece of evidence showing that strangers were allowed to come into that land (see beginning of chapter 7). Their entrance was almost contemporary with that of Abraham. The Bible is correct in this indication, and Diodorus was wrong.

Many other aspects of Abraham's sojourn in Egypt are illuminated or confirmed by archaeological discoveries. A possible reason for Abraham's saying that Sarah was his sister rather than his wife (Gen. 12:11–13) is furnished by the discovery of a papyrus document relating that Pharaoh had a beautiful woman brought to his court and caused her husband to be murdered. One can see why Abraham wished it to be understood that he was the brother of Sarah rather than her husband.

The Bible enumerates the various possessions that belonged to Abraham while he was in Egypt: "And Abram acquired sheep and cattle, male and female donkeys, menservants and maidservants, and camels" (Gen. 12:16). Archaeological monuments show the presence of sheep, oxen, and donkeys in Egypt. For example, such animals are portrayed on the walls of the beautiful temple of Hatshepsut at

[9]Popular books on archaeology in the past have frequently alluded to the critical view that strangers could not have come into Egypt in earlier times, and often traced the basis of such an idea back to the first-century historians Strabo or Diodorus, but ordinarily no further documentation was given. For example, Neatby said that the critic could quote Strabo, the Greek geographer and historian, who stated shortly before the time of Christ that "not till the time of Psammetichus [654 B.C.] did Egypt open its ports to strangers or grant security to foreign traders." T. Miller Neatby, *Confirming the Scriptures* (London: Marshall, Morgan and Scott, n.d.), 24 [NCS].

I have not felt that undocumented statements of this type were adequate. A detailed examination of the writings of Strabo and Diodorus has shown, however, that such an implication was given by Strabo, and a point-blank statement was made by Diodorus. They are provided below.

Strabo: "Now the earlier kings of the Aegyptians, being content with what they had and not wanting foreign imports at all, and being prejudiced against all who sailed the seas, and particularly against the Greeks (for owing to scarcity of land of their own the Greeks were ravagers and coveters of that of others), set a guard over this region and ordered it to keep away any who should approach" (*The Geography of Strabo*, E.T., Horace Leonard Jones, 8 vols. (London: Heinemann; New York: Putnam, 1932), 8:27, 29 (Book 17, 1, 6) [GS]).

Diodorus: "Psammetichus . . . regularly treated with kindness any foreigners who sojourned in Egypt of their own free will. . . and, speaking generally, he was the first Egyptian king to open to other nations the trading-places through the rest of Egypt and to offer a large measure of security to strangers from across the seas. For his predecessors in power had consistently closed Egypt to strangers, either killing or enslaving any who touched its shores" (*Diodorus of Sicily*, E.T., C.H. Oldfather, 10 vols. (London: Heinemann; New York: Putnam, 1933), 1:235 (Book 1, 67, 9, 10) [DS]).

[10]This painting, in the tomb of Khnumhotep at Beni Hassan, portrays the arrival of thirty-seven Semitic tribesmen who apparently came to trade with the local ruler, offering the fragrant cosmetics desired by the Egyptians. J.H. Breasted, *A History of Egypt* (New York: Scribner, 1912), 187 [BAHE].

A painting from the tomb of Khnumhotep at Beni Hassan, showing the arrival of Semitic tribesmen in Egypt shortly after 2,000 B.C.   Lehnert and Landrick, Cairo.

Dêr-el Bahri at Thebes (c. 1500 B.C.) and in the tomb of Ti at Saqqarah (c. 2200).

The casual reader usually takes no particular notice of the indication that Abraham had camels among his possessions in Egypt (Gen. 12:16). The critics, however, have set this aside as an error, asserting that camels were not known in Egypt until long after the time of Abraham. A study of archaeological material, however, reveals a knowledge of the camel in Egypt even before the time *MB of Abraham.[11] Archaeological evidence showing early knowledge of the camel in Egypt includes statuettes and figurines of camels, plaques bearing representations of camels, rock carvings and drawings, camel bones, a camel skull, and a camel hair rope. These objects, some twenty in number, range from the seventh century B.C. back to the period before 3000.[12] In recent years numerous indications of the domestication and use of the camel in Mesopotamia and Syria during the patriarchal period have come to light. K.A. Kitchen has collected some of this information.[13] Thus the evidence again shows the authenticity of the record concerning Abraham.

Abraham Again in Canaan; His Separation from Lot (Genesis 13); Archaeological Light

After Abraham returned to Canaan from Egypt, he found that frequently

[11]J.P. Free, "Abraham's Camels," *Journal of Near Eastern Studies* (July 1944), 187–93.

[12]Cf. chapter 14, the section entitled "The Visit of the Queen of Sheba. . . Camels and Sheba," pages 145–46.

[13]K.A. Kitchen, *Ancient Orient and Old Testament* (Chicago: InterVarsity, 1966), 79–80; idem, "Camel," *Illustrated Bible Dictionary* (Downers Grove, Ill.: InterVarsity, 1980), 1:228–30.

there was strife between his herdsmen and those of his nephew Lot. Abraham proposed that they separate and generously offered to have Lot choose any part of Canaan that he might wish (Gen. 13:9). Lot looked about and chose the Plain of Jordan (vv. 10–11), which includes the Jordan Valley and the area around the Dead Sea. Today this whole area is the hottest part of Palestine, with temperatures ranging from 104 to 118 degrees on some August days. The biblical record of Lot's choice of the Jordan Plain might seem to be an error. Why did he not choose the attractive maritime plain, or the hill country, or the central mountain ridge region of Palestine? Excavations at Khirbet Kerak, Beth Shan, Jericho, Teleilat el Ghassul, Bab ed-Dra, and other sites have demonstrated that many people were living in the Jordan Valley and region of the Dead Sea, the area of the "Plain of Jordan," in the third and second millennia B.C.

Some have thought that there may have been a drastic change in climate in the Jordan area during the earliest times, but Nelson Glueck reports that there is no evidence of such a change. Whatever the ultimate explanation, Glueck's explorations both before and after 1940 showed that the area had been "densely inhabited," for he discovered more than seventy ancient sites, many of them founded more than five thousand years ago.[14] Glueck concluded that there should be no more "prattle" of an "emptiness in the Jordan Valley!" Thus the archaeological discoveries have shown that no one who knows the facts can set aside as inaccurate the biblical record of Lot's choice of the Jordan area.

The Battle of the Four Kings Against the Five (Genesis 14); Archaeological Light and Confirmation

After Lot had moved down to the region of the Plain of Jordan and had established his home at Sodom, a military coalition of four kings from Mesopotamia came to this area and made war with five kings who lived near the Dead Sea, including the king of Sodom and the king of Gomorrah (Gen. 14:1–2). When the Mesopotamian kings started back to their native land, they took Lot along as part of their booty (vv. 11–12). Abraham pursued the army of these kings and recovered Lot (v. 16).

Genesis 14 has been regarded as unhistorical by such critics as Noldeke. These critics have said that (1) the names of the Mesopotamian kings are fictional or unhistorical; (2) in the days of Abraham there was no such extensive travel as indicated by this military expedition; and (3) there was no line of march east of Palestine, as indicated by Genesis 14:5ff.

Archaeological discoveries have helped to confirm the validity of Genesis 14. Inscriptions found in recent years have shown that the names of the Mesopotamian kings may in some cases be identified with names of persons already known from the discoveries, and that, in any case, they fit into the pattern of Babylonian names.[15]

---

[14]Nelson Glueck, *The River Jordan*, (Philadelphia: Westminster, 1946), 73 [GRJ].

[15]The old identification of Amraphel with Hammurabi is no longer held. Albright suggested equating Amraphel with Amud-pi-el ("enduring is the word of El"), a king named in the Mari tablets and powerful in Babylonia in the century before Hammurabi (D.J. Wiseman, "Hammurabi," *Zondervan Pictorial Encyclopedia of the Bible*, ed. Merrill C. Tenney, 5 vols. [Grand Rapids: Zondervan, 1975–1976], 3:26). Although reference to Chedorlaomer has not yet been found in the inscriptions, it is often pointed out that there are two Elamite elements in his name: *Chedor (Kudur)*, found in various Elamite names; and *laomer*, the softening of the name of an Elamite goddess, Lagamar. Tidal, king of Goiim, has been identified with Tudhalias (several Hittite kings were so named); and Arioch, king of Ellasar, has been identified with Arriwuk (a name appearing in the Mari texts). Whether or not these identifications are accepted, it can readily be seen that

Evidence concerning ancient travel in the days of Abraham has been discovered in a clay tablet found in Babylonia, and also in another group of tablets found at the edge of present-day Syria at the site of the ancient city of Mari. The Babylonian tablet contains a contract stipulating that a wagon was rented on condition that it *not* be driven over to the Mediterranean coastlands. It shows that in the days of Abraham travel from Mesopotamia to the Mediterranean was so common that when a person rented a wagon he ran the risk of having it worn out by being driven several hundred miles to the seacoast in the vicinity of Syria and Palestine. Certainly this gives an answer to any idea that extensive travel was improbable in the days of Abraham.[16] Moreover, as early as 2300 B.C. Sargon of Akkad (near Babylon) made raids on the Amorites of Syria and Palestine. Of particular significance for the present study is the fact that prior to Hammurabi's rule in Babylon, Kudur-Mabug, an Elamite king of Larsa (north of Ur), claimed to be "prince of the land of Amurru," which probably included Palestine and Syria.[17]

Evidence concerning the line of march to the east of Palestine was discovered by the American archaeologist W.F. Albright of Johns Hopkins University. He says he "formerly considered this extraordinary line of march as being the best proof of the essentially legendary character of the narrative."[18] Writers who follow the critical view in part or in whole are now inclined to give more credence to the validity of these events in the life of Abraham. Caiger, who made some con-

cessions to the critical view, came to acknowledge that "there seems to be no reason to question a factual basis of Genesis 14" (CBS, 34).

Abrahamic Covenant Confirmed (Genesis 15)

After Abraham recovered Lot, he might have feared some retaliation on the part of the Mesopotamian kings, but God reassured him with the comforting words, "Do not be afraid, Abram. I am your shield. . ." (Gen. 15:1). This was followed by the promise that Abraham's descendants should be as numerous as the stars of heaven. Abraham "believed the LORD, and he credited it to him as righteousness" (v. 6). This is a very significant verse, for here is the first appearance of the words *believe, credit,* and *righteousness.* Any study of the great Bible truths of belief or faith, of imputation, and of righteousness must take into account this important passage. We would call Abraham's belief in God "saving faith," for in all ages, human beings have been saved by faith in the Lord and have had God's righteousness imputed or put to their account. The Old Testament saints looked forward to the coming of the promised Seed (Christ), and they were saved by faith through his shed blood, just as believers today look back to the cross and are saved by faith "just as they are" (Acts 15:11). Old Testament saints, coming before the debt of sin was actually paid on the cross, were in the position of those who have an antedated check, a

---

Genesis 14 does not introduce fictional forms but good Near Eastern names. It may also be interesting to observe, in passing, that Babylonian clay tablets dating to the patriarchal period mention Abarama and Abamrama, very close in form to the Hebrew Abraham and often equated with Abraham, though of course they do not refer to the patriarch himself (FLAP, 73).

[16]A translation of this wagon contract may be found in G.A. Barton, *Archaeology and the Bible,* 7th ed., 346–47.

[17]A.T. Clay, *Light on the Old Testament from Babel,* 2nd ed. (Philadelphia: Sunday School Times, 1907), 137.

[18]W.F. Albright, *The Archaeology of Palestine and the Bible* (Cambridge, Mass.: American Schools of Oriental Research, reprint 1974), 142 [AAPB].

check for which the funds will surely be deposited.

Seeking a Posterity—Ishmael
(Genesis 16)

God's covenant and promise to Abraham that he would have a great posterity (Gen. 15:5), who would possess the Promised Land (vv. 18ff.), seemed to arouse in Sarah a desire to have an heir even though she had no children. Sarah gave her handmaid Hagar to Abraham as a secondary wife, and to Abraham and Hagar was born a son, Ishmael. In seeking posterity by this means, Abraham and Sarah were "running ahead of the Lord." God in his own time allowed them to have their own rightful child, Isaac.

Archaeological Light on Sarah's Giving Hagar to Abraham (Genesis 16)

Nowhere do we read that God instructed Sarah to give Hagar to Abraham as a secondary wife. It was quite evidently her own idea. Archaeological discoveries show us the probable source of the idea. The Code of Hammurabi[19] indicates that in Babylonia a wife might give a servant as a secondary wife to her husband in order to have children by the servant girl. Thus Abraham and Sarah were not following the directive will of God but rather the laws and customs of the old land out of which they had come.[20]

God's Covenant with Abraham; Circumcision and Archaeology (Genesis 17:1–14)

God next revealed himself to Abraham as El Shaddai, Almighty God (Gen. 17:1). He then changed Abram's name to Abraham (vv. 4–5) as a symbol of the covenant and the new relationship between Abraham and God and ordained circumcision (vv. 11–12) as an external sign of a covenant relation with God. Circumcision did not save Abraham or bring him and his posterity into vital relation with God, any more than baptism today saves a child or an adult; both are external tokens of a covenant with God and a trust in God.

Archaeological discoveries show that the practice of circumcision can be traced back to the days of Abraham. This surgical operation is pictured on the Egyptian reliefs that go back into Old

---

[19]The Code of Hammurabi codified many laws and practices that had been in use for generations. This is demonstrated by the subsequent publication of the Code of Lipit-Ishtar, which contains laws similar to those of the Code of Hammurabi and which antedates it by two centuries (Francis Steele, "The Lipit-Ishtar Law Code," *American Journal of Archaeology* [April–June 1947]:158–64).

Evidence of other early laws has been found in the excavation of Tell Hermel (1945ff.) in the region of modern Baghdad. A quantity of clay tablets was discovered that included many laws of the time of Bilalama (nineteenth century B.C., minimal chronology). One of these laws parallels a law in Exodus 21:35. (Cf. W.F. Albright, "A Decade of Middle Eastern Archaeology, 1939–1948," in *Palestine Affairs*, 4, 2 [February 1949]: 24). The code of Bilalama consists of a preamble and fifty-nine sections, covering business relations, specified prices and wages, penalties for non-fulfillment, trespass, marriage, deposit, sale, and torts and injuries caused by persons, animals, and things. See *Sumer*, 4, 2 (1948): 63–102; cited in AJA, 53, 4 (October–December 1949): 398.

For details of the discovery and nature of the Code of Hammurabi, see chapter 9. From what is said here, evidently the Code of Hammurabi was not the earliest law code, and it was not original. Some scholars now believe that its chief function was to bring up to date the common law of Mesopotamia. Of course it is the longest and most complete early law code of the region, and it antedates the Mosaic code by at least three or four centuries.

[20]This archaeological light is significant in refuting the idea that God sanctioned or even demanded polygyny (plurality of wives) in the Old Testament. The practice of polygamy in the Old Testament period was carried on under the permissive will of God, not under his directive will.

At the top of the Code of Hammurabi, Hammurabi portrays himself standing before the sun god Shamash, god of justice, to receive the laws of his code. This code, from the period 2000–1700 B.C., contains advanced laws similar to some of those in the Mosaic laws (1500–1400). In view of this archaeological evidence, the destructive critic can no longer insist that the laws of Moses are too advanced for his time. (See "Critical View of the Legislation of Deuteronomy . . . ," page 103.)   Located at Louvre Museum

Testament times.[21] Ancient burials in Egypt contain bodies that give evidence of circumcision, further showing the early establishment of this practice.[22]

Announcement of the True Heir— Isaac (Genesis 17:15–27)

Following the institution of circumcision, God announced to Abraham that he

and Sarah would have a son (Gen. 17:16, 19). Abraham laughed (v. 17), probably out of amazement because of his advanced age (one hundred) and that of Sarah (ninety). Later when the angelic visitors came to Abraham at Mamre, near Hebron (twenty miles south of Jerusalem), Sarah also laughed when she overheard their announcement that a son was to be born to her and Abraham (Gen. 18:12). Subsequently, when the child was born, he was named Isaac, meaning "laughter" (Gen. 21:6), because of the laughter of the two parents.

Announcement of Sodom and Gomorrah's Doom; the Angel of the Lord; Abraham's Intercession (Genesis 18)

In connection with the prediction made to Abraham of Isaac's coming birth, announcement was also made concerning the future judgment on the wicked cities of Sodom and Gomorrah (Gen. 18:20ff.). It seems that only one of the three angelic visitors made this announcement about Sodom and Gomorrah, and he is referred to as "the LORD" (v. 17). The other two angels went on to speak with Lot and met with him at the gate of Sodom, as recorded in the beginning of the next chapter (Gen. 19:1). The angel who remained with Abraham and who is referred to as "the LORD" is generally regarded as the "angel of the LORD," who appears throughout the Old Testament and is undoubtedly a preincarnation appearance of Christ.[23]

---

[21]For a picture of a circumcision operation from a tomb relief in Egypt, see PANEP, 206. This relief dates to about 2300 B.C. One of the Megiddo ivories, dating to the thirteenth century B.C., shows the prince of Megiddo, probably celebrating a victory. He drives naked, circumcised captives before his chariot. One is left to speculate whether these captives are Canaanite or Amorite or Hebrew. For a picture see PANEP, 111.

[22]James Henry Breasted, *The Oriental Institute* (Chicago: University of Chicago Press, 1933), 15 [BOI].

[23]An excellent study of the appearances of Christ in the Old Testament, often called "Christophanies" or "Theophanies," is found in E.W. Hengstenberg, *Christology of the Old*

At the Dan gate there is a platform (left) for a god or a king and benches for officials.

Abraham's intercession for the wicked cities is significant, not as an instance of bargaining, but rather as an example of the effect of repeated asking. The same truth is given in the parable of the unjust judge to whom the woman came again and again (Luke 18:1); it is a lesson in persistence in prayer. God has put the world together on the principle of prayer; he has "accorded to a created personality the right to assert itself in faith" (KD, 1:232).

Lot at Sodom; Significance of the Gate; Archaeological Light on Lot's House (Genesis 19)

Lot was sitting at the gate of Sodom when the angels came to the city (Gen. 19:1). Archaeological excavations show that the gates of Palestinian cities often had stone benches or seats as a built-in part of the structure, so that people might sit there and wait for their friends or engage in conversation with those whom they had agreed to meet at the gate. The

excavation by the Pacific School of Religion at Tell en-Nasbeh (1926–1935), believed by the excavators to be the site of the biblical Mizpah, revealed a gate lined with stone benches (MLPP, 211). People would sit at the gate in order to meet their associates, hear the news, and engage in trade. Here it was that legal transactions were carried on, as exemplified in the making of the marriage contract between Ruth and Boaz, which was arranged at the gate of the town (Ruth 4:1–2). The gate was the place of public proclamation; it was at the city gate that David waited to hear the news of Absalom, and then he went to the chamber over the gate to weep for him (2 Sam. 18:24, 33). Likely it was the place where the prophets made their proclamations. The significance of the gate becomes evident if one notes how often it is mentioned in the Old Testament. Archaeological discoveries have given us further light on the size and arrangement of the gates of biblical times and illuminate the importance of this structure in Near Eastern life. A particularly interesting gate, dating to the period of the divided monarchy (ninth–eighth century B.C.), has come to light at Dan as a result of the excavations there since 1966 under the leadership of Avraham Biran of the Israel Department of Antiquities. There a visitor to the site may see a stone bench about fifteen feet long that city fathers may have used for transacting business. Next to it was a canopied structure that may have protected the king's throne or a cult statue (See EAEHL, 1:320).

After meeting the visitors at the gate, Lot brought them to his house. The wicked men of Sodom crowded to the door of Lot's house and pressed heavily against it, but they could not get in (Gen. 19:9). Palestinian excavation has produced interesting information about Lot's mob-proof door. When Kyle and Albright

Testament, trans. Theodore Meyer (Edinburgh: T. & T. Clark, 1863) [HCOT]; pages 119–22 deal with this appearing of the angel of the Lord.

excavated the site of Tell Beit Mirsim (1926–1930ff.), identified with the biblical site of Kirjath-Sepher, they found evidence in the level of the Middle Bronze Age (2200–1600 B.C.) of strong walls and great doors. In one building, the very large door socket was still *in situ*, which shows the heavy construction of doors in the days of Lot. On the other hand, in the level of Early Iron II (900–600 B.C.), many houses and scores of doorways were unearthed, but scarcely a door socket; it was evident that in this late period the inhabitants used only archways or curtains. During this period, the kings of Israel and Judah were ruling; hence there was a strong central government. But in the early period of Abraham and Lot (c. 2000) there was no strong central government, and so sturdy doors and walls were necessary. The smaller the police force, the greater the doors. Lot's heavy door fits precisely in this period. The critics, however, date the writing of the accounts of Abraham in the ninth and eighth centuries B.C. How did the writer know the conditions a thousand years or more before his time? M.G. Kyle commented, "Was he an eminent archaeologist, who, while the Plain of Sodom was still uninhabited yet dug up that ancient civilization and so exactly described the condition that prevailed at that time that the description exactly conforms to the facts as found at Kirjath-Sepher?"[24]

Destruction of Sodom and Gomorrah; Archaeological Light (Genesis 19)

After Lot had been warned by the angels, he and his family left the city of Sodom. God then caused brimstone and fire to come down upon the cities of the plain to destroy them. There were five principal cities in this group, including Sodom and Gomorrah (shown by Genesis 14:2). An indication as to the location of these five cities may be seen in the fact that at the south end of the Dead Sea, there are five streams that may have been the respective sources of water for the five cities. Archaeological explorations at the south end of the Dead Sea, particularly at the site of Bab ed-Dra (possibly the place of pagan worship for the inhabitants of Sodom and Gomorrah), have shown evidence of a break in civilization about 2000 B.C.[25] Researches by Nelson Glueck also have shown a break in culture about 2000 in Transjordan, which he connects with the period of Abraham.[26]

It is possible that the cities of Sodom and Gomorrah are now covered by the shallow waters at the south end of the Dead Sea. There is evidence that the level of the Dead Sea has slowly risen over the centuries. In 1892 Dr. Kyle observed an island at the north end of the Dead Sea. Later, the rising waters caused it to disappear. When he rode over the same island in a motorboat in 1924, it was covered with several feet of water.[27] As a matter of fact, the level of the Dead Sea fluctuates considerably in relation to rainy and dry years and tectonic movements at the bottom of the sea. But it rose thirty-seven feet during the nineteenth century and then fell early in the twentieth century.[28] In recent years it has been visibly shrinking at the southern end because of water use for irrigation farther

[24]*The Evangelical Quarterly* (October 1930) [EQ]; cited in W.W. Prescott, *The Spade and the Bible* (New York: Revell, 1933), 94–95 [PSB]. Cf. Similar development in KEK, 197–98.

[25]See Howard F. Vos, *Archaeology in Bible Lands* (Chicago: Moody, 1977), 148.

[26]Nelson Glueck, *The Other Side of Jordan* (New Haven: American Schools of Oriental Research, 1940), 114 [GOSJ].

[27]W.F. Albright, *Annual of the American Schools of Oriental Research* 6:54–55 [AASOR]; two interesting articles on Sodom and Gomorrah by J. Penrose Harland appeared in BA, May 1942 and September 1943.

[28]Efraim Orni and Elisha Efrat, *Geography of Israel*, 3rd ed. (Jerusalem: Israel Universities Press, 1971), 98.

north in the Jordan Valley, and it may be possible to explore the bottom for location of the cities of the plain at an early date. In Josephus's day, at the end of the first century A.D., evidently the southern end of the Dead Sea did not cover the entire plain, because Josephus, the great Jewish historian, wrote, "Traces of the five cities are still to be seen" (*Wars of the Jews* IV.8.4). Presumably Josephus was an eyewitness to remains of Sodom and Gomorrah.

Chapter 5

Abraham, Isaac, and Jacob

(Genesis 21–37)

Birth of Isaac; Offering of Isaac (Genesis 21–22)

In due time a son was born to Abraham and Sarah (Gen. 21:1–2). He was named Isaac, meaning "laughter," because Abraham and Sarah had laughed in amazement at the Lord's announcment that they should have a son at their advanced ages (Gen. 17:17; 18:12; 21:6–7).

Several years later God tested Abraham, telling him to take Isaac to one of the mountains[1] of the land of Moriah and there offer him (Gen. 22:1–2). That God had no desire to have the child slain is shown by the outcome of the event — Isaac was not put to death. When Abraham went up to the mount and stretched forth his hand, he had already accomplished the sacrifice in his own heart and

had fully met the testing of God. God therefore immediately had the angel of the Lord intervene and show Abraham the ram that was the offering provided by God himself to be sacrificed in place of Isaac (KD, 250). The ram offered in Isaac's stead is a beautiful illustration[2] of Christ's substitutionary death. Christ died on the cross not only to pay for our sins, but actually in our stead, in our place, just as the ram died in the place of Isaac.

Problem of the Philistines (21:34)

At this time, Abraham was living at Beersheba in southern Palestine, in the region of "the land of the Philistines" (Gen. 21:32, 34). Abraham's having contacts with the Philistines in his day is a problem because the Philistines as they

---

[1]The writer of Chronicles applies the name "Moriah" to the mountain in Jerusalem on which Solomon's temple was built (2 Chron. 3:1). Some believe it is the same as the "land of Moriah" of Abraham's time.

[2]I prefer to call such events "illustrations" rather than "types," reserving the term "type" for Old Testament subjects and events that are specifically pointed out (usually in the New Testament) as types of biblical truth. For example, the veil of the tabernacle, described in the Old Testament, is set forth in the New Testament as a type of the body or flesh of Christ (Heb. 10:20). The rending of Christ's body on the cross opened up a more ready access to God, even as the rending of the veil of the temple (corresponding to the earlier tabernacle) opened in a literal sense the way of access to the inner sanctuary.

are known to archaeologists and historians seem to have entered Palestine in the twelfth century B.C. The common view is that they attacked Egypt by sea during the reign of Ramses III (1198–1167 B.C.),[3] that he repulsed them, and that they then settled in southern Palestine, in what is known as the Plain of Philistia. Subsequently they became a powerful people there and oppressed the Hebrews during the days of the judges and King Saul.[4]

Burrows of Yale says of this problem: "We have seen that the Philistines came into Palestine at the beginning of the Early Iron Age, not far from 1200 B.C. It is quite impossible to date Abraham and Isaac as late as this, yet the book of Genesis represents both as having dealings with the Philistines and their king, Abimelech (Gen. 21:22–32; 26:1–33)." Burrows says that this may be explained as "a convenient and harmless anachronism" and concludes, "At any rate, however the mistake may have come about, it is undoubtedly a mistake" (BWMS, 277). This type of supposed contradiction is often used by critics to support their statements that the Bible has "complicated problems and even direct contradictions in some cases" (BWMS, 278).

To deal with this problem, it is useful to note that the Old Testament says the Philistines came from the island of Caphtor (Jer. 47:4; Amos 9:7), commonly identified as Crete. Moreover, the term *Kherethites* (Cretans) is used to designate the Philistines in 1 Samuel 30:14; Ezekiel 25:16; and Zephaniah 2:5–6.

If the Philistines of about 1200 B.C. came from Crete, they would have been part of the warlike maritime culture known as Mycenean or else of the Sea Peoples who were pushed out of the Aegean by the Mycenean Greeks. And in Palestine they were warlike and a constant threat to the Israelites during the days of the judges and the early monarchy.

These were not the only ancient people to come from Crete, however. Minoan Cretans were establishing trading colonies around the Mediterranean by about 2000 B.C., and evidence of their contact with Palestine and Egypt during this early period is substantial. Moreover, the Philistines of Abraham's day appear to have been peace-loving agricultural people, as were the Minoans.

G. Ernest Wright has pointed out that the Hebrew word translated "Philistine" was used for all "Sea Peoples," of whom the Philistines were the most important for the inhabitants of Palestine.[5] Possibly the reference in Genesis should be translated by some other term. If it is, the problem evaporates completely.

Finally, it should be noted that the Gerar of Abimelech (Gen. 21, 26) has now been identified with Tell Abu Hureira, about eleven miles southeast of Gaza. In 1956 D. Alon excavated there and found that it had been inhabited continually through every period from Chalcolithic times to the Iron Age and was very prosperous during the Middle Bronze (the patriarchal) Age. He also found several smelting furnaces, giving evidence of Philistine iron working.[6] So some evidence of the culture of which Abimelech was a part has been found, but the name "Philistine" has not been connected with it. Clearly there are ways of resolving the problem of the Philistines even now, and it is not necessary to conclude that the Bible is in error. Further discoveries in the Mediterranean world may provide additional solutions.[7]

---

[3]For a picture of Ramses' great battle with the Philistines as portrayed on his temple at Medinet Habu at Luxor, Egypt, see PANEP, 114.

[4]For a discussion of the Philistines in the later period, see chapter 11.

[5]G. Ernest Wright, "Philistine Coffins and Mercenaries," *Biblical Archaeologist* (September 1959), 61.

[6]Edward E. Hindson, *The Philistines and the Old Testament* (Grand Rapids: Baker, 1971), 72.

[7]Actually, the whole issue of identifying or understanding the Philistines and the Sea Peoples is very unsettled at the present time. Any discussion of it is very technical and involved and far beyond the scope of this book. For two informed studies on this subject, see Alessandra Nibbi,

The mosque of Hebron covers the traditional Cave of Machpelah, burial place of Sarah and some of the patriarchs.

Death of Sarah; Purchase of the Cave of Machpelah (Genesis 23)

Sarah died at the age of 127 (Gen. 23:1). She is the only woman whose age is given in Scripture, perhaps because "as the mother of the promised seed she became the mother of all believers" in a spiritual sense (1 Peter 3:6; KD, 259).

After the death of Sarah, Abraham prepared to purchase the cave of Machpelah at Hebron, some twenty miles south of Jerusalem. The owner of the cave, Ephron, used bargaining tactics that were similar to the methods used even today in Near Eastern countries. By insisting on paying for the cave, Abraham obligated himself and had to consummate the bargain by giving a considerable sum. Actually Ephron was not a philanthropist, even though his words may sound so to the ears of Americans (Gen. 23:15).

When Abraham paid for the cave, he weighed out four hundred shekels of silver (Gen. 23:16). This shows that money was meausured by weight in those days and was not yet coined. Archaeological discoveries indicate that the minting of coins began somewhat before 700 B.C. in the kingdom of Lydia in Asia Minor, probably in response to intensive commerce between the Lydians and the Greeks.[8] Thus the implication that the shekel was a weight rather than a coin in the days of Abraham is another indication of the early date of the record concerning Abraham's purchase of Machpelah. A similar indication of the shekel as a weight rather than a coin is seen in the time of Joseph as well (Gen. 37:28, fn).

Abraham's ability to produce four hundred shekels of silver for the purchase of the cave of Machpelah indicates that he was not merely a nomadic sheikh engaging in commercial deals involving barter. He had, after all, come from a brilliant

The Sea Peoples and Egypt (Park Ridge, N.J.: Noyes Press, 1975), and N.K. Sandars, *The Sea Peoples* (London: Thames and Hudson, 1978).

[8]See, e.g., H.W. Perkin, "Money," *International Standard Bible Encyclopedia*, rev. ed., (Grand Rapids: Eerdmans, 1986 for vol. 3), 3:404. Excavations at Sardis, capital of Lydia and one of the seven cities of the Revelation, uncovered King Croesus' gold refinery there during the 1960s. See especially George M.A. Hanfmann, *Sardis from Prehistoric to Roman Times* (Cambridge, Mass.: Harvard University Press, 1983), especially chapter 3.

and highly developed commercial culture in southern Mesopotamia. The Genesis narrative presents him as wealthy and powerful, and numerous scholars not of a particularly evangelical bent have portrayed him in a new and significant light in recent decades. Cyrus Gordon developed the thesis that Abraham was a merchant prince and concluded that

> the patriarchal narratives, far from reflecting Bedouin life, are highly international in their milieu, in a setting where a world order enabled men to travel far and wide for business enterprise. . . . Abraham comes from beyond the Euphrates, plies his trade in Canaan, visits Egypt, deals with Hittites, makes treaties with Philistines, forms military alliances with Amorites, fights kinglets from as far off as Elam, marries the Egyptian Hagar, etc.[9]

Albright argued that Abraham was a "caravaneer," engaged in the rather extensive and lucrative caravan trade between Palestine and Egypt.[10] David Noel Freedman viewed him as a "warrior-chieftain" and a "merchant prince" who "belonged to urban culture and civilization."[11]

Today a Moslem mosque stands over the presumed site of the cave of Machpelah, and entrance into the cave is forbidden. During World War I, when General Allenby's troops were marching to Jerusalem, a British officer, Colonel Meinertzhagen, went into the mosque to seek the Turkish officials of Hebron, who were supposed to have fled there. Passing through a door in the limestone rock interior, the colonel slid down a steep incline and found himself in a cave about twenty feet square. In the cave stood a

block of stone about six feet long, three feet wide, and three feet high. The officer, not realizing the significance of the place, left without investigating. Later when Hebron had returned to a normal state, an effort was made to visit the cave, but the guardians of the mosque would not give permission.[12]

A new opportunity to explore the cave of Machpelah occurred in 1967, shortly after the Six-Day War when Moshe Dayan (Israel's Minister of Defense) took advantage of the Israeli victory and lowered a twelve-year-old girl named Michal through the small opening into the cave with a camera. By this means they discovered that the cave is twelve or thirteen feet deep and measures 9.65 by 9.26 feet. From the southeastern wall of this room a sunken step leads down to a doorway, and the doorway to a 57-foot-long corridor, which in turn leads to steps that ascend to another entrance in the floor of the mosque, now blocked. At the northwestern side of the room into which Michal was lowered stand three stone slabs, one of which may be a tombstone, and the others may block the entrance into other grottoes.[13]

Seeking a Bride for Isaac (Genesis 24)

When Abraham was well along in years, he sent his servant back to northern Mesopotamia to take a wife for Isaac from among Abraham's own kindred. The servant departed and went to the city of Nahor (Gen. 24:10). Confirmation of the existence of the city is found in the Mari

[9]Cyrus Gordon, "Abraham and the Merchants of Ura," *Journal of Near Eastern Studies* (January 1958), 30.

[10]William F. Albright, *Yahweh and the Gods of Canaan* (Garden City: Doubleday, 1968), 51, 62–73.

[11]David N. Freedman, "The Real Story of the Ebla Tablets," *Biblical Archaeologist* (December 1978), 158.

[12]Charles Marston, *New Bible Evidence* (New York: Revell, 1934–1935), 121–22 [MNBE]; Charles Marston, *The Bible Comes Alive* (London: Eyre and Spottiswoode, 1938), 54 [MBCA].

[13]Nancy Miller, "Patriarchal Burial Site Explored for First Time in 700 Years," *Biblical Archaeology Review* (May/June 1985), 26–43.

Tablets, which frequently mention it as Nakhur.[14]

At the well near Nahor the servant met Rebekah, who took him to the house of her father, Bethuel, a nephew of Abraham (cf. Gen. 11:29 with 24:24). At the home of Bethuel, the servant was well provided for, even being given water for washing his feet (Gen. 24:32). The archaeological discoveries at Ur of the Chaldees show that in the houses there was a drain in the corner of the lobby where a jar would be placed for washing feet (WUC, 198).

When it was proposed to Rebekah that she return with the servant to Canaan to become the bride of Isaac, she readily assented (Gen. 24:58). This beautiful chapter provides an excellent illustration of spiritual truth: Abraham as representing God the Father sent the unnamed servant, typifying the Holy Spirit who speaks not of himself, to seek Rebekah, illustrative of the church, the bride of Christ who is called out. Isaac represents the Bridegroom, Christ, whom the bride, having not seen, loves through the testimony of the servant.

Last Days of Abraham; Isaac's Sons, Jacob and Esau (Genesis 25); Archaeological Light on the Birthright

After the death of Sarah, Abraham married Keturah. Some commentators believe that Keturah was taken as a secondary wife or concubine before the death of Sarah, but I feel that this view is not substantiated by the biblical references. Years later, Abraham died at the advanced age of 175 (Gen. 25:7).

To Isaac and Rebekah were born two sons, Jacob and Esau (vv. 20–26). After the boys had reached maturity, Esau one day sold his birthright to Jacob for some lentil stew (vv. 27–34). Archaeological light on

this instance of selling one's birthright to obtain some desired object is furnished by the Nuzi tablets, found in Mesopotamia and dating from the patriarchal period. In one Nuzi tablet, there is a record of a man named Tupkitilla, who transferred his inheritance rights concerning a grove to his brother, Kurpazah, in exchange for three sheep. Esau used a similar technique in exchanging his inheritance rights to obtain the desired stew.[15]

Isaac and Abimelech (Genesis 26); Critical View and Answer

While Isaac was living at Gerar in the Philistine country, he told the local dwellers that Rebekah was his sister, rather than his wife (Gen. 26:6–7). Several years earlier Abraham had similarly told the people in this same area that Sarah was his sister (Gen. 20:2). The critics have held that this event happened just once, but that two different versions were circulated, one centering around Abraham and the other about Isaac. This theory of "doublets" is described by Knobel, a nineteenth-century German writer, who said, "It is held with good reason that one and the same event lies at the foundation of these. . . narratives" (LCG, 392). Even Sir Charles Marston, usually taking a definite stand against the critical view, said of Genesis 20: "It is probable that this chapter is a duplicate of Genesis 26, and the story really concerns Isaac, his son" (MBCA, 53).

These two chapters, however, deal with different events, one occurring in the life of Abraham and the other in the life of Isaac. The fact that similar incidents are recorded as occurring in the lives of both does not mean that these accounts are "doublets," having a single origin. An

---

[14]W.F. Albright, "Western Asia in the Twentieth Century B.C.: The Archives of Mari," *Bulletin of the American Schools of Oriental Research* 67 (October 1937): 27 [BASOR].

[15]Cyrus Gordon, "Biblical Customs and the Nuzu Tablets," *Biblical Archaeologist* (February 1940): 5. (Both terms are used, "Nuzu" and "Nuzi.")

One of the Nuzi tablets (1500-1400 B.C.) that describes a land sale in the form of an adoption. Other Nuzi tablets show that the background of the patriarchal records fits into the early period (2000-1500 B.C.), and not in the late period (900-600), as held in the liberal view of former years. For other significances of the Nuzi tablets, see "Last Days of Abraham . . . Archaeological Light on the Birthright," above.

examination of ancient or modern life shows many similar yet distinct events. A press release during World War II told of two Princeton University students who went through similar experiences, yet they were two different individuals:

> Amazing is the similarity of events that have happened to two brothers now in the Replacement Center at Fort Bragg, prior to and after the declaration of war. 1. William A. Wood Jr. and Thomas B. Wood were born twins. 2. Attended Princeton together in the class of 1938. 3. Both were active in college athletics. 4. Called to the Army on the same day, same order and sent to the same organization. 5. Held executive officer positions with respective batteries. 6. Both are first lieutenants. 7. Took command of batteries next door to each other. 8. Both are married and were presented with sons during the same month, recently.[16]

Certainly if all of these similar events could occur in the lives of these two boys, then Abraham and Isaac could each try to pass off his wife as his sister.

The Stolen Blessing (Genesis 27); Archaeological Light on Oral Blessing

When Isaac was getting along in years, he planned to bestow his blessing on Esau (Gen. 27:1, 7). Rebekah, however, arranged to have Jacob impersonate Esau and receive the blessing. When Isaac discovered the deception, he was filled with remorse, yet he did not revoke his oral blessing. We might wonder why. Archaeological light on oral blessings is found in the Nuzi tablets. One tablet shows that an oral blessing in patriarchal times had legal validity, even in a law court. This particular document recorded the lawsuit of a certain Tarmiya against his two brothers, who contested the right of the younger brother to take a woman by the name of Zululishtar as his wife. Tarmiya won the case and was awarded his bride because the court recognized the validity of his father's "blessing," which Tarmiya reported in this way: "My father, Huya, was sick and lying in bed and my father seized my hand and spoke thus to me: 'My older sons have taken

[16]Press release from Fort Bragg, N.C., printed in *The Princeton Alumni Weekly* 43,2 (September 25, 1942): 5, 9.

wives but thou hast not taken a wife and I give Zululishtar to thee as wife.' " This text parallels biblical blessings like those of the patriarchs in that it was an oral will, with legal validity, and was made to a son by his father. (In this case the father was dying, as was often the case in biblical blessings.)[17]

Jacob Away from Home (Genesis 28–31); Archaeological Light on the Teraphim

Jacob left home (Beersheba,[18] Gen. 28:10), after receiving the blessing through deception, and went to northern Mesopotamia to the home of his mother's brother, Laban. He served for Laban's daughters fourteen years and another six years for the flocks he was to receive. At the end of the twenty-year period, Jacob and his family prepared to leave Laban's home (Gen. 31:17–18).

Before they left, Jacob's wife Rachel stole the family images (Hebrew *teraphim*) of her father, Laban (Gen. 31:19). After Jacob, Rachel, and the rest of Jacob's family had departed, Laban learned of their unexpected departure and pursued them for seven days, a considerable journey. When Laban overtook them, he searched for the teraphim with great diligence but could not find them because Rachel had put them in a camel saddle and sat on them (v. 34). Why was Laban so anxious to find the teraphim? Certainly a man with his wealth would not need to make such a great commotion about some small idols. Commentators have struggled with this passage, suggesting that perhaps the teraphim were of gold, or had a superstitious value, but none of these explanations seemed to be completely satisfactory. The answer was found in the Nuzi tablets, which show that possession of the father's household gods played an important role in inheritance.[19] One of the Nuzi tablets indicated that in the region where Laban lived, a son-in-law who possessed the family images could appear in court and make claim to the estate of his father-in-law.[20] Since Jacob's possession of the images implied the right to inherit Laban's wealth, one can understand why Laban organized his hurried expedition to recover the images, It also explains why Rachel carefully concealed them in the saddle and sat on them.

Jacob's Return (Genesis 32–37); Archaeology and the Horites

After Laban departed from Jacob, Jacob and his family, continuing on their way, came down to the Jabbok River, which

---

[17]See BA (February 1940), 8.

[18]The biblical town of Beersheba has been located at Tel es-Saba (Tell Beersheba), about two miles northeast of the modern city. Yohanan Aharoni directed a Tel Aviv University excavation there from 1969 to 1976. He discovered that the town had a Hebrew foundation, built in the twelfth or eleventh century B.C. Apparently unwalled, the town probably was the place where the sons of Samuel judged the people (1 Sam. 8:2). Beersheba was fortified with a twelve-foot-thick wall in the tenth century. Aharoni found nothing at Tell Beersheba dating to the patriarchal period, and he concluded that patriarchal Beersheba was located near the valley and the wells, probably at Bir es-Saba, within the area of modern Beersheba (EAEHL, 1:160–68). Subsequent excavations at Tell Beersheba, seeking to find a patriarchal level, dug to bedrock and uncovered nothing earlier than 1250 B.C. See Ze'ev Herzog, "Beer-sheba of the Patriarchs," *Biblical Archaeology Review* (November/December 1980), 12–18.

[19]W.F. Albright, "Recent Discoveries in Bible Lands," supplement to *Young's Analytical Concordance to the Bible* (1936), 26 [ARDBL].

[20]Sidney Smith and C.J. Gadd, *Revue d'Assyriologie* 23 (1928): 126–27; E.A. Speiser, *Mesopotamian Origins* (Philadelphia, 1930), 162; cited by Allan A. MacRae, "The Relation of Archaeology to the Bible" [MRAB], in *Modern Science and Christian Faith* (Wheaton: VanKampen, 1948), 273 [MSCF].

flows through Transjordan[21] into the Jordan River. Here at the Jabbok, Jacob met a man, apparently the angel of the Lord, and they wrestled together. This experience was a spiritual turning point in the life of Jacob; from then on, he not only bore the name Israel ("he struggles with God"), but his self-seeking nature began to fade into the background.

Shortly after his experience at the Jabbok, Jacob met Esau, in reconciliation (Gen. 33), and then returned to a place in central Canaan near the city of Shechem (v. 18), about thirty miles north of Jerusalem. Following the difficulty with the Shechemites (Gen. 34), Jacob moved on south to Bethel (Gen. 35:1). Sometime later Jacob and his family left Bethel and journeyed farther south. Rachel died as they were traveling and was buried near Bethlehem (vv. 19–20). About a mile northwest of Bethlehem is a tomb still

pointed out as that of Rachel. Some time later, Jacob's father, Isaac, died at Hebron at the age of 180 (vv. 27–29).

At this point, the genealogy of Esau is given (Gen. 36). One of the groups of people mentioned in connection with Esau is the Horites. Because of the similarity of this word to a Hebrew word for "cave," the term "Horite" was formerly interpreted as "cave-dweller." For some decades it has been popular to identify the Horites with the Hurrians, an important group who entered northwestern Mesopotamia from the region of the Armenian mountains after 2400 B.C. But there are serious problems with that identification, and a recent theory holds that "Horite," Egyptian *Hurru*, is a general term the Egyptians applied to southern Transjordan and that the Hebrews adopted it from the Egyptians.[22]

---

[21]Area to the east of the Jordan.

[22]For the problem of identifying Horites with Hurrians and documentation on the current theory, see F.W. Bush, "Horites," ISBE, 2:756–57.

The mound of Dothan

The level of Elisha at Dothan

Chapter 6

Joseph in Egypt

(Genesis 37–50)

Joseph Taken to Egypt (Genesis 37); Dothan; the Pit

After the interlude of Esau's genealogy in Genesis 36, the account of the life of Jacob and his family is resumed in Genesis 37. When Joseph was a lad of seventeen, his father Jacob sent him to find his brothers, who were tending their flocks in the area to the north of Hebron (Jacob was living at this time at Hebron, which is about twenty miles south of Jerusalem). Joseph left the vicinity of Hebron and went to the region of Shechem, some thirty miles north of Jerusalem. Upon inquiry, Joseph learned that his brothers were about twenty miles still farther north, near a place called Dothan (Gen. 37:17). I began the excavation of the mound of ancient Dothan in 1953 and found specific evidence of the city dating from the time of Joseph, about 1900 B.C.[1]

When Joseph's brothers saw him coming, their jealousy prompted them to make plans to kill him and put him in a pit (Gen. 37:20). At Gezer (between Jerusalem and the Mediterranean coast) Macalister found a number of skeletons in an ancient cistern, illustrating the fact that the use of pits and cisterns was a means of disposing of people in Old Testament

[1]From 1953 to 1962 my wife, Ruby, and I, with our staff, carried on the excavation of the mound of ancient Dothan, some sixty miles by road north of Jerusalem. A deep sounding on the slope during the first season showed that Dothan began some 5000 years ago (3000 B.C.), and had a more or less continuous history until about 700 B.C. Two of the lower levels proved to come from the days of the patriarchs (2000–1600), thus confirming the biblical record of the existence of Dothan in the time of Joseph, 1900–1800 (Gen. 37:17). The upper levels on top of the mound yielded evidence of the city of Elisha's time (850–800), confirming the biblical record of the existence of Dothan in the days of that ancient prophet (2 Kings 6:13). The first eight seasons of excavation (1953–1962) disclosed the streets, the walls, the houses, the pottery and implements, and many other aspects of life at ancient biblical Dothan.

For accounts of the excavation, see Joseph P. Free, "The First Season of Excavation at Dothan," *Bulletin of the American Schools of Oriental Research* 131 (October 1953): 16–20; "The Second Season at Dothan," BASOR 135 (October 1954): 14–20; "The Third Season at Dothan," BASOR 139 (October 1955): 3–9; "Digging Down to Ancient Dothan," *Moody Monthly* (November 1954): 15–17ff.

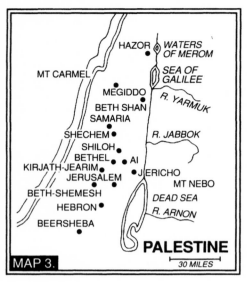

MAP 3.

PALESTINE

30 MILES

Map labels: HAZOR, WATERS OF MEROM, MT CARMEL, SEA OF GALILEE, MEGIDDO, R. YARMUK, BETH SHAN, SAMARIA, SHECHEM, R. JABBOK, SHILOH, BETHEL, AI, KIRJATH-JEARIM, JERUSALEM, JERICHO, MT NEBO, BETH-SHEMESH, DEAD SEA, HEBRON, R. ARNON, BEERSHEBA

times.[2] Such use of cisterns has also been noted in other places.

Reuben sought to save Joseph's life by suggesting that the lad be put into a pit alive. This they did, but before Reuben could deliver Joseph, the other brothers sold him to a passing caravan of Ishmaelites and Midianites, who took Joseph to Egypt and sold him to Potiphar, an officer of the pharaoh of Egypt (Gen. 37:36).

Joseph in Potiphar's House (Genesis 39); Joseph's Position; Archaeological Light on the Arrangement of Houses

Potiphar's purchase of Joseph is illuminated by the archaeological discoveries of papyrus documents in Egypt, which show that Syrian slaves were highly prized in Egypt. The word "Kan'amu" or

"Canaanites" even became a synonym for "slaves" in the Egyptian documents.[3] Joseph's position as overseer in the house of Potiphar also accords with what can be learned from the Egyptian monuments, which frequently mention the *merper*, or superintendent of the house in connection with the large dwellings of important Egyptians.[4]

The fact that Potiphar's wife was able to speak so easily with Joseph might be questioned (Gen. 39:10). Would not Joseph be in the steward's quarters, quite removed from the quarters of Potiphar and his wife? The excavations at Tell el Amarna in central Egypt, however, have revealed a number of house plans showing that the storerooms were at the back of the house and so were reached by going through the main part of the house. It is likely that Potiphar's house followed a similar plan. Thus Joseph, as steward of the house of Potiphar, would have had to pass through the inner apartments daily in order to inspect the storerooms and keep them replenished.[5]

Joseph in Prison (Genesis 39, 40); Egyptian Prisons; the Butler and the Baker

After Potiphar's wife falsely accused Joseph (Gen. 39:17ff.), he was put in prison. Abundant archaeological evidence demonstrates that there were important prisons in Egypt in Joseph's time. Several suggestions have been made as to which of these might be the one where Joseph was confined. The German Egyptologist Ebers identified Joseph's prison with a fortress at Memphis called "White

[2]R.A.S. Macalister, *A Century of Excavation in Palestine* (New York: Revell, 1925), 221 [MCEP]; also R.A.S. Macalister, *The Excavation of Gezer*, 2:429–30; [MEG]; also BAB, 223.

[3]A.H. Sayce, *Expository Times*, 10, 75 [ET], cited in G.A. Frank Knight, *Nile and Jordan* (London: Clarke, 1921), 108 [KN].

[4]A. Erman, *Life in Ancient Egypt*, 187 [ELAE].

[5]A diagram of one of these house plans is found in A. Erman, *Life in Ancient Egypt*, trans. H.M. Tirard (London: Macmillan, 1894), 179 [ELAE]. At the Oriental Institute of the University of Chicago there is a model of a rather elaborate Egyptian villa.

Wall."[6] The word used for the prison where Joseph was placed is the Hebrew term *sohar*, which literally means "house of roundness" and suggests a round tower, used as a state prison. The state prison at Thebes in the south of Egypt where Thothmes III (1501–1477 B.C.) confined his Syrian captives was called *suhan*; Knight suggests that *sohar* may be a Semitic equivalent of the Egyptian term (KNJ, 109). Yahuda notes an Egyptian word, similar to *sohar*, found in many inscriptions as a name of a fortress close to the Palestine frontier to which corrupt officials and notorious criminals were consigned. He believes this fortress is probably the prison where Joseph was held.[7]

Joseph, through God's help, ably interpreted the dreams of Pharaoh's butler and the baker who were confined in the same prison (Gen. 40:1ff.). The Egyptian monuments give abundant evidence of the presence of butlers and bakers in ancient Egyptian life. All of the phases of bread making are portrayed in the tomb paintings. These and other representations show bakers carrying baskets of bread and other baked goods on their heads, just as described to Joseph by the baker (vv. 16–17) (KNJ, 109).

Joseph as the Prime Minister (Genesis 41–42); Possibility of Joseph's Position

After the chief butler was released from prison, he forgot about Joseph until Pharaoh had his dream about the seven cows. Then the butler brought to Pharaoh's attention the fact that Joseph would be able to interpret the dream. Joseph's interpretation of Pharaoh's dream brought him the appointment to the office that we would call the prime minister of Egypt.

Doubt has been cast on the possibility of the promotion of a Canaanite slave such as Joseph to such a high position. Of course God was guiding the destiny of Joseph; but it can be demonstrated, even apart from this factor, that such a rise to power was possible. Egyptian archaeological discoveries tell of foreigners, including Canaanites, who achieved prominence in the course of Egyptian history. Erman points out that "amongst the court officials also we often meet with foreigners who may have been slaves" (ELAE, 106). One such Canaanite was the "first speaker of his Majesty," and at court he assumed the Egyptian name of "Ramses in the temple of Re" (ELAE, 106). This is a significant parallel to the giving of an Egyptian name to Joseph (Gen. 41:45). Also a Canaanite by the name of Dudu[8] rose to high favor in the Egyptian court. His high position is illustrated by a letter written to him by an Amorite, who wrote to Dudu, "Whatever is the wish of Dudu, let me know, and I will do it. . . . Thou sittest in the presence of the King my lord as a high dignitary."[9] Another

---

[6]G.J. Spurrell, *Notes on the Text of the Book of Genesis* (Oxford: Clarendon, 1896), 319 [SNG].

[7]A.S. Yahuda, *The Language of the Pentateuch in Its Relation to Egyptian* (Oxford University Press, 1933), 1:38–42 [YLP]. Albright issued this word of caution on Yahuda's works: "A.S. Yahuda's recent books on the subject of Egyptian materials in the Pentateuch, where the story of Joseph is treated in considerable detail, are unsound," ARDBL, 27. It is quite true that Yahuda does at times see connections between Egypt and the Bible that seem not to exist; however, some of his material is quite useful, when it is based solidly on a valid use of the archaeological materials. The above reference is cited merely as having a possible connection with the place of Joseph's imprisonment.

[8]W.F. Albright has pointed out (by oral communication) that the name Dudu is an Egyptian name but that Dudu's grandfather may have been a Canaanite; this would mean that Dudu was a Canaanite, though he bore an Egyptian name.

[9]CBS, 103–4; also in BAB, 368, lines 11–13, 28, from Winckler and Abel, *Thontafelnfund von El-Amarna*, no. 40. Cf. Knudtzon, *Die El-Amarna Tafeln*, no. 158. This is one of the Amarna Tablets that were found in Egypt by a peasant woman during the winter of 1887–1888. They proved to be

Canaanite by the name of Meri-Ra became armor-bearer to the pharaoh of Egypt (CBS, 61). But probably the position of Yankhamu, also a Canaanite, is even closer to that of Joseph. He acted as the deputy for the pharaoh of Egypt in the grain-growing district of Egypt (CBS, 104). Thus, Joseph's rise to power[10] is shown by the archaeological discoveries to have been entirely possible.

Egyptian Names Mentioned in Connection With Joseph; Critical View and Answer

Several Egyptian names are given in connection with Joseph, including that of his Egyptian wife, Asenath, and her father, Potipherah (Gen. 41:45). The critical view has held that these Egyptian names mentioned in connection with Joseph appear in a later period. Burrows says, "As a matter of fact the Egyptian names given in the Joseph story do not appear in Egypt before the time of the Hebrew monarchy" (BWMS, 53). In support of this idea he cites Albright, who says essentially the same thing (AAPB, 143). This assertion ties in with the critical idea that the Pentateuch was not written by Moses (c. 1500–1400 B.C.), but by late writers (850–450 B.C.), who would be familiar with the names common in the late period of Egyptian history. By way of answer to this contention that the Egyptian names of the Joseph account come in the late period, it is significant to note the acknowledgement of T. Eric Peet, Professor of Egyptology at the University of Liverpool, who was much more radical in his biblical criticism than either Burrows or Albright. Peet said, "Asenath is an Egyptian name meaning 'Belonging to the goddess Neit.' Names of this type are not absolutely wanting in the earlier periods, but they are extremely rare, and it is only in the XXIst Dynasty [c. 1100–950 B.C.] that they begin to be common."[11] Even though his admission is a grudging one, it is clear that he acknowledges the appearance of such names in the early period. Barton states the fact in more positive language: "The name of Joseph's wife, Asenath (in Egyptian *As-Neit*, 'favorite of the goddess Neith'), occurs from the eighteenth dynasty onward [1600 B.C. and after]" (BAB, 24). This provides another piece of evidence that harmonizes with the conservative view, holding to the early writing of the Pentateuch.

Joseph and His Brothers (Genesis 42–45)

The famine in Canaan caused Jacob to send his sons to Egypt to seek grain. They obtained grain from Joseph, who finally, after testing them, revealed himself to them on their second trip to Egypt. Joseph then instructed his brothers to return to Canaan and to bring their families and their father Jacob down to Egypt. Pharaoh added the provision that wheeled vehicles be sent along to aid in the moving venture.

Joseph's Titles (Genesis 45:8); Archaeological Light

In describing his position in Egypt to his brothers, Joseph referred to himself in a threefold way, as (1) father to Pharaoh, (2) lord of all his entire household, and (3) ruler of all Egypt (Gen. 45:8). The Egyptian monuments show that Joseph

---

letters written by rulers of various cities in Canaan and Syria to two Egyptian kings, Amenhotep III and Amenhotep IV, who ruled about 1400 B.C.

[10]Albright pointed out other evidence showing that Joseph was not the only Semitic prime minister in Egypt; the records tell of one who lived in the seventeenth century, B.C., bearing the good Hebrew name of Hur. Cf. W.F. Albright's article, "The Old Testament and Archaeology" [AOTA], in *Old Testament Commentary*, edited by Herbert C. Alleman and Elmer E. Flack (Philadelphia: Muhlenberg, 1948), 141 [AFOTC].

[11]T. Eric Peet, *Egypt and the Old Testament* (University Press of Liverpool, 1924), 101 [PEOT].

was applying the regular official Egyptian titles to himself.[12] Yahuda believes that "father to Pharaoh" refers to Joseph's position as vizier in its aspect of priestly dignitary, while "lord of his. . . household" describes his position as court chamberlain over the entire court, and "ruler of all Egypt" gives his position as supreme administrator of the entire land. Yahuda observes further that only someone who was familiar with Egypt would have known this.[13]

Jacob in Egypt (Genesis 46–50; Archaeological Light on Jacob's Few Years

When Joseph's message was brought by his brothers to their father, Jacob left for Egypt with all of his family (Gen. 46:1). According to God's provision, the nation Israel was to be blessed if it remained in the Promised Land of Canaan; God expressly stated this to Isaac when he said, "Do not go down to Egypt; live in the land where I tell you to live . . . and I will be with you and will bless you" (Gen. 26:2–3). Even though Jacob was going out of the Promised Land and thus departing from God's appointed place, yet God appeared to Jacob on the way (at Beersheba) and promised not only to go with him and his family, but also to bring them up again from the land of Egypt (Gen. 46:3–4). Scofield points this out as one of the many instances where a distinction between the directive and the permissive will of God must be made. God's directive will indicated Canaan as the place for his people, but God in his tenderness would not forbid the aged Jacob to go to Egypt to be with his family. God's permissive will allowed him to go and be with his

son Joseph (Scofield Reference Bible, note to Gen. 46:3).

When Jacob appeared before Pharaoh, Jacob referred to his own 130 years as "few and difficult" (Gen. 47:9). It strikes the modern occidental mind as somewhat strange to refer to such a goodly number of years as "few." The Egyptian archaeological sources help us understand that Jacob was observing a detail of etiquette in speaking thus to Pharaoh. Since the Egyptian king was regarded as an eternally living god, it was fitting for Jacob to refer to his own 130 years as "few."

The Pharaoh of Joseph's Day

Genesis does not name the Pharaoh before whom Jacob stood and of course whom Joseph served. To discover who he might have been, it is necessary first to establish a time frame for the events recorded. If we follow the chronology proposed at the beginning of chapter 4, the Exodus took place about 1446 B.C., and the children of Israel (Jacob and his sons) entered Egypt 430 years earlier (Exod. 12:40), about 1876. That would have been the era when the Hyksos were beginning to infiltrate from Canaan and when the Middle Kingdom of Egypt was in progress (c. 2000–1780). Politically the Middle Kingdom was very different from the Old Kingdom. In the earlier period (the pyramid age) kings were absolute and the land was apparently more prosperous. During the Middle Kingdom, kings had to contest with the nobles for political control, but by the end of the period they were successful in virtually restoring their absolutism.

Acceptance of 1876 B.C. for Hebrew

---

[12]KNJ, 115, citing Brugsch, *History of Egypt* (1891), 101, 357 [BHE], and Driver, in *Hastings Dictionary of the Bible*, 3:774 [HDB].

[13]A.S. Yahuda, *The Accuracy of the Bible* (London: Heinemann, 1934), 18 [YAB]. Albright's word of caution in regard to Yahuda's works has already been noted (footnotes). In connection with the relationship between Egypt and the Bible, Albright does acknowledge that in the Joseph story "there are many bits of Egyptian colouring in the narrative which have been beautifully illustrated by Egyptological discoveries," ARDBL, 27.

A lintel from a gate showing Sesostris III making an offering to the god Mentou. Sesostris may have been the pharaoh of Egypt in Joseph's day.   Lintel located in Louvre Museum.

entrance into Egypt would place the event during the reign of Sesostris III (or Senwosret or Sen-Usert). Although Egyptian chronologies vary, most Egyptologists conclude that Sesostris's regnal dates were 1878 to 1840. If these dates are right, the seven years of plenty and the beginning of Joseph's administration would have occurred during the reign of the previous pharaoh, Sesostris II (1897–1878). The Bible student will discover no evidence of a change of royal administration in the Genesis narrative, but that fact does not create a serious difficulty. As crown prince, Sesostris III presumably would have acquiesced to the policies inaugurated by his father. And he would have been king when the years of famine set in. An alternate chronology, held by some European scholars, puts the regnal years of Sesostris III at 1887–1850 and would envision him as in full control during the entire period of Joseph's leadership in Egypt. Interestingly, Sesostris III was a vigorous pharaoh who made great

progress in destroying the power of the nobles and in extending the boundaries of Egypt. He also pushed the southern frontier about two hundred miles south of Aswan, to the second cataract, and reconquered Nubia. Perhaps it is legitimate to speculate that he used the famine and the efforts of his prime minister, Joseph, to fasten royal control on all the populace of the land (see Gen. 47:13–26).

Death of Jacob and Joseph (Genesis 49–50); Mummification

After living seventeen years in Egypt, Jacob died at the age of 147 (Gen. 49:28). Before his death, the patriarch gathered his sons before him and bestowed his dying prophetic blessing on each of the individual sons and on the tribes they would beget (Gen. 49).

When Jacob died, his body was mummified, as was Joseph's when he died several years later at the age of 110 (Gen. 50:2, 26). Embalming was practiced generally at least by Egyptian royalty and nobility and is exactly what one would expect in the preparation of the bodies of Jacob and Joseph in Egypt. The elaborate preparation of the body required many days, as evidenced by the biblical statement that forty days were needed in the case of Jacob, with a mourning period of seventy days (Gen. 50:3). Light on the rather long period of time required in Egypt for embalming is furnished by the historian Herodotus, who, living at a later time when embalming had become a very elaborate process, gives seventy days as the period customarily observed; the historian Diodorus gives thirty.[14] The whole subject of embalming has been carefully studied and is not quite so shrouded in mystery as the layman ordinarily believes.[15] Archaeological records from Egypt indicate that the embalmers and undertakers used a liberal supply of fine linen, spice, oils, and rich perfumes.[16] The heart, liver, lungs, and viscera were removed and placed in four vessels known as canopic jars, and the body was soaked in natron before being wrapped in many yards of linen. The dry climate of Egypt was also a significant factor in the preservation of mummies, though this aspect of the matter is often overlooked by the layperson who considers the subject of mummification with some awe.

Time of Patriarchal Events; Accuracy of Patriarchal Accounts

Most current views of biblical chronology place the patriarchal period within the years 2000–1500 B.C., and the more conservative scholars restrict patriarchal activity to the first couple of centuries of that half millennium. Of course events of the period center around the life and times of Abraham, Isaac, Jacob, and Joseph. Although we have tried to refine the chronology of Abraham, 2000 is still a useful date to use for him when dealing in round numbers.

The critical view of past years held that the patriarchal accounts were legendary and included unreliable traditions that lacked historical basis. Julius Wellhausen well expressed this view when he said, "From the patriarchal narratives it is impossible to obtain any historical information with regard to the patriarchs."[17] The archaeological discoveries of recent decades, however, have led to a change of opinion on the part of many liberal scholars. W.F. Albright, trained in a liberal environment but having come to a view he described as neither liberal nor conservative in the usual sense of the word, acknowledged that the conclusion forced on us by recent archaeological discoveries is "that the saga of the patriarchs is essentially historical" (AAPB, 145). The archaeological discoveries that brought about this change of view in Albright include those concerning the cities of Abraham's day,[18] Lot and the Jordan Valley,[19] the line of march taken by the four kings,[20] light on Sodom and Gomorrah,[21] and many similar confirmations of the details and the background of patriarchal times (Albright deals with this line of thought specifically in AAPB, 129–51).

---

[14]KNJ, 117, citing Herodotus 2:86–89; Diodorus 1:91.

[15]For further discussion, see Howard F. Vos, *Genesis and Archaeology* (Grand Rapids: Zondervan, 1985), 106–9; A. Lucas, "Mummification," in his *Ancient Egyptian Materials and Industries*, 3rd ed. (London: Edward Arnold, 1948), 307–90.

[16]J.H. Breasted, *A History of Egypt* (New York: Scribner, 1912), 141 [BAHE].

[17]Julius Wellhausen, *Prolegomena to the History of Israel*, 3rd ed., 331; 1st ed., Edinburgh, 318 [WPHI].

[18]This book, chapter 4, section "Abraham in Canaan."

[19]Ibid., section "Abraham Again in Canaan."

[20]Ibid., section "The Battle of the Four Kings. . . ."

[21]Ibid., section "Destruction of Sodom and Gomorrah."

Chapter 7

Moses in Egypt

(Exodus 1–12)

The King Who "Did Not Know About Joseph" (Exodus 1:8ff.); Archaeological Light

The children of Israel increased in the land of Egypt until finally there arose a king "who did not know about Joseph" (Exod. 1:7–8). This pharaoh determined to prevent further increase of the Israelites by putting to death the male children at birth (vv. 15–16). Though the Bible does not tell which pharaoh this was, enough light has been shed on the general period in which these events occurred to ascertain which of the pharaohs is most likely to be identified with this one.

From historical and archaeological sources, we know that about 1570 B.C. the native Egyptians drove out the Hyksos rulers of Egypt, an Asiatic group that had governed the land for about 150 years, from c. 1730 to c. 1570. The Hyksos had probably begun filtering into Egypt about 1900 and finally gained control of the country by about 1730. It is generally believed that this pharaoh who did not know Joseph was one of the new line of native Egyptians, probably Ahmose I, who came to the throne when the Hyksos were driven out. Ahmose[1] reigned 1570–1545 B.C.[2]

If Ahmose, or one of the kings of his time, is the pharaoh who "did not know about Joseph" (i.e., who did not know Joseph's people), then the preceding period was that of the Hyksos domination of Egypt. Joseph and his people presumably would have been treated well up to this time, because the Hyksos, another Asiatic group, were in the land and likely would have been well disposed toward the Israelites, also a foreign group. Burrows indicates that this identification of Joseph's period with the Hyksos rule, a view that has long been held, is now generally accepted. He says, "Modern historians agree, on the whole, that the conditions of the Hyksos period afford a

[1]Ahmose's name is also spelled Ahmosis, Amosis, Aahmes, and Amasis. Egyptian names have a great variety of spellings, depending on whether they are in the form taken from Greek historians or are transliterated from the hieroglyphic inscriptions of Egypt. In the latter case, the vowels are inserted by conjecture because hieroglyphics are composed only of consonants.

[2]John A. Wilson, *The Burden of Egypt* (Chicago: University of Chicago Press, 1951), viii [WBE].

natural setting for Joseph's rise to power and for the settlement of Israel in Egypt" (BWMS, 71).

The Treasure Cities, Pithom and Raamses (Exodus 1:11); Archaeological Light

Beginning with the king who "did not know about Joseph," this new line of pharaohs put burdensome tasks on the Israelites. They required the people to build treasure cities (or store cities) and made their lives difficult with "hard labor in brick and mortar" (Exod. 1:11, 14). Light on the treasure cities specifically mentioned, Pithom and Raamses (or Ramses), apparently was found in 1883 by the Swiss archaeologist Naville when he excavated a site in the delta of Egypt called Tell el Maskhuta and found inscriptions containing the word *Pi-Tum*, meaning "House of the god Tum." This led Naville to identify Tell el Maskhuta with the Pithom built by the Israelites. He found that some of the bricks were actually made without straw.[3] In the light of more recent studies, however, Albright, among others, expressed the view that Pithom is to be identified with Tell er-Retabeh (ASAC, 194; AOTA, 142), which is eight and one-half miles west of Tell el-Maskhuta. He identified Tell el-Maskhuta with Succoth, which is mentioned in connection with Israel in Egypt (Exod. 13:20). Since these sites are near each other and both are referred to in the portions of Exodus dealing with Israel in Egypt, the brickwork found by Naville at Tell el-Maskhuta could still be connected with Israelite taskwork. Current scholarship is divided over whether Tell er-Retabeh or Tell el-Maskhuta is the site of Pithom, with preference possibly tilting toward the former.

The other treasure city specifically mentioned, Raamses (Exod. 1:11), has usually been identified with Tanis (AOTA, 142; FLAP, 114). The site of Tanis was excavated by Pierre Montet (1929–1932), who strongly maintained that it was the location of Raamses.[4] Tanis is some distance to the north of Tell el-Maskhuta and Tell er-Retabeh (see maps 2 and 4, pages 48 and 91).

Preparation of Moses, the Deliverer (Exodus 2ff.)

During the sojourn of Israel in Egypt, a child was born to an Israelite family, who concealed him at the edge of the Nile River in order to avoid having him put to death by the emissaries of Pharaoh. One day Pharaoh's daughter[5] went down to the river bank and, finding the child hidden in the reeds, took him to rear as her own son. She gave him the name Moses, "because I drew him out of the water" (Exod. 2:10). The name "Moses" could be derived from the Hebrew *masha*, "to draw out" (Gesenius-Robinson *Hebrew Lexicon*). Although it is hardly likely that Pharaoh's daughter, an Egyptian, would give a name based on a Hebrew word, the antecedent of "she" may be Moses' own mother instead of Pharaoh's daughter.[6]

---

[3]Naville, *The Store-City of Pithom and the Route of the Exodus*, 4th ed. (London: 1903), [NPRE], cited BAB, 26–27.

[4]*Revue Biblique* 39 (1930): 15–28; cited in FLAP, 114.

[5]Numerous writers consider Hatshepsut to have been this "Pharaoh's daughter" (e.g., CBS, 66; MNBE, 161; MBCA, 57). If Thutmose III or one of his line was the Pharaoh of the Oppression (see next section), Hatshepsut could have been the princess involved in the rescue of Moses. She was the daughter of Thutmose I, the wife of Thutmose II, and the stepmother of Thutmose III, according to George Steindorff and Keith C. Seele, *When Egypt Ruled the East* (Chicago: University of Chicago Press, 1942), 36–40 [SSWE].

[6]The question of whether Moses' name was derived from Hebrew or Egyptian is often debated and quickly becomes a very technical matter, quite beyond the scope of this book. See, e.g., ISBE, rev. ed., 3:417; *New Bible Dictionary*, 2d ed., 794.

Thutmose III, possibly the pharaoh who oppressed the Israelites   Lehnert and Landrock, Cairo

One day when Moses came upon an Egyptian striking a Hebrew, he intervened and killed the Egyptian. When Moses learned that the matter was known, he fled from Egypt, going out to the land of Midian (Exod. 2:15), which is to the east of Egypt, probably on the eastern side of the

Gulf of Akabah (the eastern arm of the Red Sea; see maps 2 and 4, pages 48 and 91). While in Midian, Moses married Zipporah, the daughter of Jethro (v. 21). Through tending the flocks of Jethro, Moses became very familiar with the whole region about Horeb (Exod. 3:1), which is the same as Sinai. In this time of preparation he had opportunity to learn all he needed to know about the Sinai area, so that he would be thoroughly ready to lead the children of Israel through Sinai years later when the Exodus from Egypt would take place.[7] Moses' forty years of preparation in the region of Sinai provides an illustration of the fact that God wants the believer to have adequate preparation for his tasks in life.

The Pharaoh of the Oppression (Exodus 2:23); Connection With the Fall of Jericho

While Moses was out in Sinai and Midian, "during that long period, the king of Egypt died" (Exod. 2:23). This particular king is usually known to Bible scholars as the "pharaoh of the oppression," because it was under his rule that the Israelites were particularly oppressed with their labors of making bricks and constructing buildings.

It has been a matter of interest (but not an article of faith) to Bible students to discover the identity of this pharaoh. The question of his identity depends on the date of Israel's Exodus from Egypt, as well as on the date of the fall of Jericho. The archaeological evidence from the pottery and scarabs at Jericho shows that this city fell about the year 1400 B.C. Among the factors supporting this date, John Garstang, the second excavator of Jericho, pointed out that not one piece of Mycenaean ware was found, suggesting that the walls of Jericho fell before the four-

---

[7]At the time of the wilderness journeys, God gave special help by leading Israel with the Cloud. That does not mean God could not also use a well-prepared man who knew the wilderness firsthand.

teenth century had begun.[8] Garstang's claim of an approximate 1400 date for the fall of Jericho seems supported by Kathleen Kenyon's work there (1952–1958), as recent publication of her excavation reports indicates.[9]

If Jericho fell about 1400, at the end of the forty years in the wilderness, then the Exodus occurred about 1440[10] or a little earlier. An examination of the history of Egypt shows that a great king of Egypt, Thutmose III, died in the year 1450 B.C.[11] (His name is also rendered Thutmosis Thothmes). This king could very well fit into the picture as the pharaoh of the oppression. He reigned for thirty-two years (1482–1450),[12] and thus his death came after a long period of rule, as implied in the biblical statement that "during that long period, the king of Egypt died" (Exod. 2:23; CBS, 68ff., has an interesting discussion of Thutmose III as the pharaoh of the Exodus).

It would be helpful, in trying to understand the situation of Israel in Egypt, to know something of this man who may have been the pharaoh of the oppression and who, in any event, was ruling during Israel's sojourn in that land. Thutmose III was one of the greatest, if not the greatest, of all the kings of Egypt. When he came to the throne, he reorganized the army of Egypt and began a campaign up into Palestine and Syria. When the Egyptian army approached the city of Megiddo in northern Palestine, they had a choice of three routes, one directly through a narrow mountain pass to Megiddo, and the other two less direct but through more open territory (SSWE, 53–54). Thutmose's military officers favored the two open roads, but Thutmose chose the direct route, and, personally leading his own army, he marched through the narrow defile and on into an open place, where early the next morning he formed his battle lines and attacked the Asiatic hosts. The latter fled to the city of Megiddo, but the inhabitants of the city had already closed the gates, making it necessary to haul the Asiatics up over the walls into the city by lowering clothing to them. The Egyptians could have had a striking victory by pursuing the enemy, but they were tempted by the plunder left outside the city by the Asiatic soldiers and stopped to get the horses, chariots of gold and silver, and the other valuables abandoned by the fleeing enemy (BAHE, 287–90). Shortly, however, Thutmose began the siege of the city, and finally those inside the walls surrendered. Still greater

[8]John Garstang, *Joshua Judges* (London: Constable, 1931), 146 [GJJ]. Mycenaean ware began to be imported about 1400 B.C.; see this book, chapter 10, section entitled "Date of the Fall of Jericho," page 112.

[9]See Bryant G. Wood, "Did the Israelites Conquer Jericho?" *Biblical Archaeology Review* (March/April 1990), 57.

[10]Biblical evidence also points to 1440–1450 as the time of the Exodus. 1 Kings 6:1 shows that the Exodus preceded the building of Solomon's temple by 480 years. Since the temple was begun in Solomon's fourth year, 966 B.C. or 967, this biblical reference points to an approximate date of 1446 for the Exodus.

[11]Albright favors a date of c. 1300 for the Exodus, ARDBL, 31; AOTA, 141; BWMS, 75; a large number of Bible scholars subscribe to this late date. For a discussion of this date, see chapter 8, section entitled "Date of the Exodus," pages 86–89.

[12]The dates followed here are those of Steindorff and Seele (George Steindorff and Keith C. Seele, *When Egypt Ruled the East*, rev. ed. [Chicago: University of Chicago Press, 1957], 274). If Thutmose's reign began in 1504, the year of his father's death, he reigned fifty-four years; but his stepmother Hatshepsut controlled the realm from 1504 to 1482. John A. Wilson (WBE, viii) and Alan Gardiner (*Egypt of the Pharaohs* [Oxford: Oxford University Press, 1961], 443) both put the dates of Thutmose III at 1490–1436. Such a chronology would have him ruling and aggressive at the time of the Exodus, if one subscribes to an approximate 1446 date. It seems unlikely that the Hebrews could have been moving around the Sinai when Thutmose III was making constant forays eastward and northward through the region and up into Canaan.

wealth came to Pharaoh from within the city, including 924 chariots, 2,238 horses, 200 suits of armor, 22,500 small cattle, and immense quantities of gold and silver (BAHE, 292; cf. SSWE, 55).

Year after year Thutmose III made expeditions into Palestine and Syria, subjugating the peoples and exacting tribute from them. He made seventeen campaigns in a period of nineteen years, until the people in Syria were quite beaten into submission (BAHE, 316–17). It is little wonder that this king has been called the Napoleon of ancient Egypt.

Moses' Return to Egypt (Exodus 4); His Excuses

At the proper time, God instructed Moses to return to Egypt (Exod. 4:19) to prepare to lead the children of Israel out of the land. Moses had objected when God appointed him to lead Israel from Egypt (3:10), saying that he could not undertake the task because the people would not listen to him (4:1) and because he was not eloquent (v. 10). God answered the first objection by showing Moses that he would be empowered to work miracles so the people would acknowledge him (vv. 2–9); and God answered the second objection by making Aaron, Moses' brother, his spokesman (vv. 11–17).

The Pharaoh of the Exodus (Exodus 5:1); Possible Identity

Moses and Aaron went in before Pharaoh to deliver God's message, "Let my people go" (Exod. 5:1). Bible scholars usually refer to this ruler as the "pharaoh of the Exodus" because it was during his rule that Israel made the Exodus from Egypt. If Thutmose III (1482–1450 B.C.) was the pharaoh of the oppression, then his successor, Amenhotep II (1452–1425, also spelled Amenophis) would have been the pharaoh of the Exodus, the one before whom Moses and Aaron went to deliver

the message that he should let Israel depart from Egypt.

Amenhotep II faced a rebellion of the tributary princes in Syria when they learned of the death of his father, Thutmose III. Marching into the Asiatic territory, he won victory after victory until he finally reached the great Euphrates River. He returned to Egypt with over five hundred north Syrian lords as captives, evidence of his triumphant campaigns to subdue these territorial lands (BAHE, 323–25). Not much is known about the person of Amenhotep II, although it seems that physically he was very strong, inasmuch as he boasts in the archaeological inscriptions that no man could draw his bow (BAHE, 326). The fact that his mummy is now preserved in the Cairo Museum is not an argument against his being the pharaoh of the Exodus, for Scripture does not say Pharaoh was drowned in the Red Sea at the parting of the waters; only part of his army was (Exod. 14:28).

Those who subscribe to a late date of the Exodus (c. 1290–1275 B.C.) will, of course, have a very different idea of who the pharaoh was at that time. An old view held that Ramses II (1299–1232) was the pharaoh of the oppression and Merneptah (1232–1222) the pharaoh of the Exodus. Inasmuch as the Merneptah Stele (now in the Cairo Museum), in which Merneptah records a victory over the Israelites in Palestine, views the Hebrews as settled in Palestine at the time (for inscription see PANET, 378; for picture see PANEP, 115), he could hardly have been the pharaoh of the Exodus. Those who hold to a thirteenth-century date now generally conclude that Ramses II was the pharaoh of the Exodus, and they do not usually concern themselves with identification of a separate pharaoh of the great oppression. Albright considered Seti I (1318–1299) to have been the pharaoh of the oppression (AOTA, 141).

Critical Objection to the Recorded Use of Straw in Brick Making (Exodus 5:13–18); Light From Archaeology and Chemistry

The forced labor of the Israelites was made more difficult when the Egyptian king withheld straw for making brick. The Israelites first had to gather straw for themselves (Exod. 5:7) and finally had to resort to collecting stubble (5:12). On the basis of the biblical record, it has usually been assumed that straw was necessary as binding material, that bricks could not be made satisfactorily without straw, and the Egyptian bricks generally contained a certain amount of straw.

On the contrary, T. Eric Peet, Egyptologist of the University of Liverpool, stated that the use of straw in making bricks was "somewhat rare" in ancient times and that the Nile mud coheres so well that any binding material would be quite unnecessary (PEOT, 99). He added that the reference to the use of straw in brick making is often used to demonstrate the biblical writer's acquaintance with Egyptian customs, but that it actually proves his ignorance of Egyptian practice (PEOT, 100). Peet's treatment of the matter leaves one with the impression that the Bible was wrong in implying that straw was necessary in making bricks.

Archaeological evidence does not bear out Peet's rather extreme assertion that the use of straw in bricks "is somewhat rare, more particularly in ancient times" (PEOT, 99). An ancient Egyptian document, the Papyrus Anastasi, contains the lament of an officer who had to erect buildings on the frontier of Egypt, probably in the region of the present-day Suez Canal. He could not work, he said, ex-plaining, "I am without equipment. There are no people to make bricks, and there is no straw in the district."[13] This document, then, definitely indicates that the overseer of building operations could not progress in his work because of a lack of straw for brick making.

I have examined many mud brick walls surrounding ancient temples in Egypt and have noted the presence of straw in many of the bricks. John Wilson, eminent Egyptologist of the University of Chicago, observed that straw was used as much as it was left out in Egyptian brick making.[14] In summary, it would be fair to state that Peet's extreme view must be definitely modified in view of the archaeological evidence.

There is, however, further evidence from another source. Edward G. Acheson, an American chemist, discovered by observation and experiment that clays were much easier to work when they contained certain organic matter.[15] In a further experiment, he boiled oat straw and added the water from the straw to clay. He found that this clay was much easier to work as a result of the admixture. This likely explains the Israelites' use of straw and, later, stubble, when the straw was not available for their brick making. Without straw or at least the organic material furnished by the stubble, the difficulty of brick making was greatly increased.

This discovery also shows that the presence of some bricks in Egypt containing no straw, as indicated by Peet in an overstatement, in no way detracts from the biblical indication of the desirability of straw in brick making. Lack of visible evidence of straw in bricks means either that straw or stubble was used in small enough quantities in some bricks to be

---

[13]ELAE, English ed., 1927, 204; cf. Alan Rowe, "The Palestine Expedition," *Museum Journal* 20 (1929): 58; also Yahuda, *The Accuracy of the Bible*, 75 [YAB].

[14]Oral communication, 1946.

[15]These findings were presented by Irving A. Cowperthwaite, a Boston industrial engineer, in a paper given at the meeting of the American Scientific Affiliation in 1946. It is concisely summarized by Allan A. MacRae in MRAB, 261, and earlier reported on in *Transactions of the American Ceramic Society*, 6:31.

invisible to the casual observer, or that bricks were made with water in which straw had been soaked, or that the bricks contain no such material and would have given the brick makers more difficulty in forming them. In any event, the basic biblical indication of the desirability of straw for making bricks is fully borne out.

The Hardening of Pharaoh's Heart
(Exodus 4–14)

The statement about the hardening of Pharaoh's heart has sometimes been used in attempting to illustrate the idea that God predestinates certain people to be lost. A study of the event does not support this extreme view of predestination, which seems to set aside man's free will. In analyzing the hardening of Pharaoh's heart, we find the following significant facts:

1. Pharaoh was a wicked man before the Lord dealt with him, for he first *hardened his own heart seven times* before God hardened it once. (Reference to Pharaoh's hardening his own heart may be found in Exodus 7:13, 14, 22; 8:15, 19, 32; 9:7.)

2. Furthermore, his heart was hardened, not with reference to salvation, but in reference to *public policy*. It was a question of whether he would let Israel go. "I will harden his heart so that he will not let the people go" (Exod. 4:21).

3. God predicted that he would harden Pharaoh's heart (4:21; 7:3), but God did not actually do it until after Pharaoh had hardened his own heart seven times. (The first time God hardened Pharaoh's heart is recorded in 9:12.)

4. Pharaoh hardened his own heart a *total of seven times* (7:13, 14, 22; 8:15, 19, 32; 9:7, 34, 35; 13:5), and ten times hardening is referred to God (4:21; 7:3 [predictive]; 9:12; 10:1, 20, 27; 11:10; 14:4, 8, 17).

5. *Three different Hebrew words* are used for "harden," perhaps implying dif-ferent degrees of resistance on the part of Pharaoh at different times. *Caved* is the weakest of the three words and means "to be dull, heavy"; it is used in 7:14; 8:15, 32; 9:7, 34. *Kashah*, meaning "to be hard," and in the causative stem (Hiph'il) "to make hard," is used in 7:3; 13:15. *Hazak*, the most intensive, implying fixed and stubborn resolution, is used in 4:21; 7:22; 8:19; 9:35.[16]

6. The hardening of Pharaoh's heart does not support the unscriptural and extreme view of predestination that seems to set aside free will. Predestination and free will are both firmly taught in the Scriptures, and both are equally true. If finite minds cannot completely understand the interrelationship between free will and predestination, there is still no justification for emphasizing free will at the expense of the sovereignty of God, or the sovereignty of God at the expense of free will. Free will is clearly taught in such Scripture passages as Matthew 23:37, where Christ said, "How often I have longed to gather my children together. . . but you were not willing," and in Revelation 22:17, "Whoever wishes, let him take the free gift of the water of life." Predestination, having a direct connection with God's foreknowledge, is clearly taught in such passages as Romans 8:29 and 1 Peter 1:2. Let us hold to both of these Scripture truths.

7. Keil and Delitzsch make the following helpful comments on the hardening of Pharaoh's heart: (1) The hardening of Pharaoh was due quite as much to his own act as to the decree of God. (2) After every one of these miracles, it is stated that Pharaoh's heart was *firm*, or *dull*, i.e., insensible to the voice of God and unaffected by the miracles performed before his eyes. (3) Not until after *the sixth plague* is it stated that the Lord made the heart of Pharaoh firm (9:12). (4) This hardening of his own heart was manifested first of all in the fact that he paid no

---

[16]*Pulpit Commentary*, 229 [PC], is helpful on this.

attention to the demand of Jehovah addressed to him through Moses and *would* not let Israel go (KD, 453–54).

The hardening of Pharaoh's heart is a good illustration of the principle laid down in Romans 1, that when people disregard the truth of God continually, God finally gives them up to their own wicked ways ("God gave them over"; cf. Rom. 1:24, 26–28).

The Plagues (Exodus 7–12); Their Significance in the Light of Archaeology

Each time Pharaoh refused to let Israel go, a plague was sent upon the land of Egypt. These plagues were a great nuisance and a great burden to the Egyptians, but more than that, they exposed the powerlessness of their gods. When the first plague struck, the Nile was turned to blood. The Egyptians worshiped the Nile as the source of life. So by the first plague, one of their very own gods was made a plague and a horror to them, and his powerlessness before the true and living God was demonstrated. Likewise other deities were shown to be powerless in the face of the succeeding plagues of frogs, lice, flies, death of cattle, boils, hail, locusts, darkness, and death of the firstborn.

Archaeological discoveries reveal the gross polytheism of the ancient Egyptians. For example, in addition to the Nile god (plague 1), they worshiped the frog god (Heqt, plague 2), the entire bovine family (cow, calf, bull, plague 5), various sun gods (plague 9), and the pharaoh himself as divine and a manifestation of

the sun god (plague 10, when the son of Pharaoh died).[17]

Miraculous Nature of the Plagues

Efforts have sometimes been made to explain away the plagues as natural phenomena in Egypt. It is quite true that unusual quantities of frogs and lice, unexpected darkness and the other serious heightening of natural phenomena have been known in Egypt. An examination of the plagues shows, however, that they were miraculous in at least five different ways: (1) *Intensification*—frogs, insects, plagues on cattle, hail, and darkness were all known in Egypt, but now they are intensified far beyond the ordinary occurrence. (2) *Prediction*—the time was set for the coming of the flies ("tomorrow," 8:23), the death of cattle (9:5), the hail (9:18), and the locusts (10:4). The removal time was also set: e.g., frogs (8:10) and thunder (9:29). Modern science cannot accurately predict the cessation of natural phenomena such as hail. (3) *Discrimination*—in Goshen there were no flies (8:22), no death of cattle (9:4), no hail (9:26), and so forth. (4) *Orderliness*—the severity of the plagues increased until they ended with the death of Pharaoh's firstborn. (5) *Moral purpose*—the plagues were not just freaks of nature, but carried a moral purpose in these ways: (a) The gods of Egypt were discredited, a purpose indicated in Exodus 12:12; the Nile-god, frog-god, and sun-god were all shown to be powerless before God. (b) Pharaoh was made to know that the Lord is God, and to acknowledge him (9:27; 10:16). (c) God was revealed as Savior, in rescuing Israel from the hands of the Egyptians (14:30).

[17]For an extended discussion of how the plagues attacked the gods and theology of Egypt, see John J. Davis, *Moses and the Gods of Egypt* (Grand Rapids: Baker, 1971).

Chapter 8

Out of Egypt

(Exodus 12–40)

The Passover (Exodus 12:1–11ff.)

At the time when Israel was preparing to leave Egypt, God gave instructions to offer the Passover sacrifice, a lamb for each house, unless the household was too small for one lamb (Exod. 12:3–4). The lamb was a type of Christ; it was to be without blemish (12:5), foreshadowing Christ's sinlessness; it was to be a lamb of the first year, in its prime, as Christ was in his prime at the time of his public ministry and death on the cross; its blood was to be shed by the whole congregation (12:6), symbolic of the fact that the whole world is responsible for the death of Christ; the blood was to be placed on the doorposts (12:7), illustrating the fact that Christ's blood must be appropriated for one to be saved.

Critical View of the Passover; Answer from Archaeology

The critical view has held that the Passover was merely an adaptation of an agricultural feast, presumably a Canaanite pagan feast. This view is widespread, as indicated by older as well as current standard Bible encyclopedias and well-known and accepted works on the Old Testament. Concessions to such a view have been made in the teaching at some seminaries in recent decades.

Archaeological discoveries, however, show the wide gulf between the Canaanite religious practices and the feasts revealed by God to the Israelites. A most striking discovery that throws light on the pagan religious practices of Canaan and Syria is that of the Ras Shamra tablets, found in 1929 after a farmer accidentally uncovered a subterranean passageway on the coast of Syria. These tablets show a sensual paganism, as illustrated in the description of the god El, who had several wives. One of the tablets describing El reads as follows, "Women, each a wife of El, even his servants,—he shall cleanse their lips, shall lift them up; their lips are sweet, sweet like the pomegranate. With them is kissing and conception. . ." (translation in BAB, 355, lines 48–51).

Albright well summarizes the significance of the Ras Shamra tablets in this respect when he says, "Every fresh publication of Canaanite mythological texts makes the gulf between the religions of Canaan and of Israel increasingly clear.[1] Thus the critical idea that the feasts of Israel are to be connected with the pagan Canaanite festivals does not find support, for every essential aspect of Canaanite religion is completely different from that of Israel, as shown by the Ras Shamra tablets. I reject the idea that the Passover was a Canaanite feast.

The Exodus (Exodus 12); the Sojourn and the Monuments; Archaeological Light

After the tenth plague, which resulted in the death of the firsborn, Pharaoh called for Moses and not only gave him permission but even urged him to leave Egypt and take the children of Israel with him (Exod. 12:30–32). They departed from Egypt after a sojourn of 430 years (Exod. 12:40–41). During that time they had increased from some seventy souls (Exod. 1:5) to a large multitude of six hundred thousand men (those over twenty, as indicated in Num. 1:45–46). With women and children, there would have been a total number of at least some two and a half million. (Most estimates of the total range from two to three million.)

Since the Israelites were in Egypt for a long period, one might expect some evidence concerning them on the Egyptian monuments. A study of the monuments, however, shows that the Egyptians did not record matters uncomplimentary to themselves. The plagues and the Exodus of Israel were a national calamity and surely would have been carefully avoided in the monumental records. Furthermore, when something was recorded that proved to be uncomplimentary or distasteful to a later regime, it was effaced at the first opportunity. For example, after the Hyksos were expelled (see chapter 7), their monuments were destroyed. Also, after the death of Hatshepsut (see chapter 7), Thutmose III chiseled away the name and representations of this queen (SSWE, 46; see also figure 5, p. 78). In view of this archaeological evidence of the Egyptian's ability at "chiseling," it is little wonder that nothing has been found on the monuments telling of Israel's sojourn in that land.

Of course there is more to consider than the monuments when explaining why there is no evidence of the Hebrew sojourn in Egypt. First, the Hebrews lived in the eastern delta, which is more moist than the rest of Egypt, and ancient remains decompose more rapidly and more thoroughly there. Second, they had been reduced to slavery, and the people who normally received recognition were royalty, nobility, and the priesthood of the official cults. Third, not many among the Hebrews were educated sufficiently to produce records, and papyrus materials would not have survived long in the delta. Fourth, if they did keep records on papyrus or animal skins, they would have taken them along at the time of the Exodus. Last, the area where they lived is now heavily populated, and early remains that may have survived are not likely to be excavated.

Date of the Exodus

Earlier discussions on biblical chronology have indicated that the Hebrew text of the Old Testament puts the date of the Exodus at about 1446 B.C. This is deduced primarily from 1 Kings 6:1, which says that the Exodus took place 480 years before the dedication of the temple,

---

[1]W.F. Albright, "Recent Progress in North-Canaanite Research," BASOR, 70 (April 1938): 24. Four useful books on Ras Shamra (ancient Ugarit) are Peter C. Craigie, *Ugarit and the Old Testament* (Grand Rapids: Eerdmans, 1983); Adrian Curtis, *Ugarit* (Grand Rapids: Eerdmans, 1985); Charles F. Pfeiffer, *Ras Shamra and the Bible* (Grand Rapids: Baker, 1962); Gordon D. Young, *Ugarit in Retrospect* (Winona Lake, Ind.: Eisenbrauns, 1981).

which occurred in the fourth year of Solomon's reign—967–966. If the Exodus is dated about 1440, the conquest should be placed about 1400, because the Israelites wandered in the wilderness for forty years before crossing the Jordan and beginning the conquest of Canaan.

As also already noted, John Garstang concluded from his excavation at Jericho (1930–1936) that the city fell about 1400 B.C. (GJJ, 147). Although many contested his conclusions, he reaffirmed them in a joint publication with his son after World War II, when he could once more gain access to his stored records.[2] When Kathleen Kenyon conducted the British School of Archaeology excavations at Jericho (1952–1958), she tended to put the fall of the town between 1350 and 1325.[3] But when the final report on her work came out after her death, information in it supported the fall of Jericho about 1400.[4]

Furthermore, an approximate date of 1400 for the beginning of the conquest fits admirably into the context of Egyptian history. At about that time the Amarna Age began and Egyptian control of Canaan rapidly disintegrated, explaining how it would have been possible for the Hebrews to invade a land where powerful Egyptian pharaohs had effectively campaigned. The situation was this. Amenhotep III (1412–1375) and especially Amenhotep IV (1387–1366) launched what is called the Amarna Revolution. This involved moving the capital from Thebes to Amarna (necessitating construction of the latter) and a religious shift to a quasi-monotheism. Instead of worship of the many gods of Egypt, the crown restricted worship to the sun god Aton, but this was

not a true monotheism, because the pharaoh was also considered divine. So during the period roughly from 1400 to 1365 the kings of Egypt were more interested in making religious reforms and expending the energies of the nation on gratifying their personal desires than they were on maintaining a powerful empire. The royal correspondence found at Amarna demonstrates that Egyptian puppet rulers of Palestine sent the pharaohs frequent calls for help during that half century. Local disturbances and the invasion of the Habiru (possibly related in some way to the Hebrews) were the occasions of such requests. But cushioned amid the luxuries of Egypt, the pharaohs chose the path of personal enjoyment rather than royal responsibility. The pleas went unheeded.

The early date of the Exodus is objected to by such scholars as Albright, who pointed out that Glueck's explorations in Edomite territory revealed that this area had no sedentary population until the thirteenth century B.C.[5] Therefore, the Israelites could not have been stopped by them on their way to Palestine at the beginning of the fourteenth century B.C. However, we may suggest with Unger[6] that as nomads the Edomites could have stopped the Israelites; certainly if the nomadic Israelites were able to carry on warfare, nomadic Edomites likewise could have done so. Or we could conjecture that Glueck's assignment of dates may need refinement. It should be pointed out that Glueck's conclusions are based on dates assigned to pottery fragments, and Albright himself stated that pottery evidence for dating some of the

[2]John and J.B.E. Garstang, *The Story of Jericho* (London: Marshall, Morgan & Scott, 1948), xiv [GSJ].

[3]Kathleen Kenyon, *Digging up Jericho* (New York: Praeger, 1957), 262.

[4]Bryant G. Wood, "Did the Israelites Conquer Jericho?" *Biblical Archaeology Review* (March/April 1990), 45–57.

[5]William F. Albright, *From the Stone Age to Christianity*, 2nd ed. (Baltimore: Johns Hopkins, 1957), 195.

[6]Merrill F. Unger, *Archaeology and the Old Testament* (Grand Rapids: Zondervan, 1954), 151.

copper mines west and south of Edom was not conclusive.[7]

Another major problem confronting one who accepts the early date of the Exodus is the fact that the Israelites built Pithom and Raamses (Exod. 1:11). Raamses I did not rule until about 1300. Unger suggested the difficulty here may be removed by concluding that Raamses is a modernization or renaming of the ancient place-name Zoan-Avaris. A similar situation occurs in Genesis 14:14, where *Dan* is substituted for the older city name of *Laish*.[8]

Nothing is solved by asserting, as many do, that the Exodus could not have taken place until after 1300 because the store city of Raamses was named after the ruling pharaoh. Moses was eighty at the time of the Exodus (Exod. 7:7). If the date of the Exodus is set at about 1275, Moses would have been born about 1355. The Hebrews built the store city of Raamses before the birth of Moses, long before the reign of the first Raamses (Exod. 1:11). So either Raamses may have been a modernization of Zoan-Avaris, or the town of Raamses may not have been named after the ruling king at all; possibly Raamses was a venerated royal or religious name of centuries' standing.

Third, Yigael Yadin, eminent excavator of Hazor, claimed that Hazor did not fall to the Israelites until the second third of the thirteenth century B.C. (EAEHL, 2:494). But Scripture indicates that Hazor fell to the Israelites twice: in the days of Joshua (Josh. 11:10–11), when Jabin I ruled, and in the days of Deborah and Barak (Judg. 4:2, 23–24), when another Jabin ruled. Yadin assumed that Joshua's conquest is to be related to a thirteenth-century destruction in the lower city of Hazor. There was, however, evidence of destruction at the site around 1400 B.C. or a little later in Areas H and K of the lower city (EAEHL, 2:481–82). What is more natural than to

conclude that the 1400 destruction dates to Joshua's day and the thirteenth-century destruction dates to the period of the Judges?

Fourth, it is argued that the palace's accessibility to Moses militates against the early date of the Exodus. The reasoning is that such accessibility indicates the palace was in the delta region, where the Israelites lived, and the periods when the palace was located in the delta were the days of Joseph and during the thirteenth century B.C. However, the pharaoh of the Exodus could have met Moses at a secondary palace or administrative center. The argument is not conclusive proof for the late date of the Exodus. Moreover, both Thutmose III and Amenhotep II, who together ruled from 1482 to 1425, were active in building projects in the delta.

Fifth, the destruction of Bethel, Lachish, and Debir, presumably by Israelites, is claimed to have occurred about 1230 and therefore to support a late date for the Exodus (see EAEHL; 1:192; 3:743; 1:177). Seemingly, this is strong evidence for the late date of the Exodus, but a second glance puts the matter in a different light. Those cities fell about the same time and near the beginning of the conquest, according to the Joshua narrative. But certainly the conquest did not occur as late as 1230, because the inscription on the Stele of Pharaoh Merneptah represents the Hebrews as settled in Canaan when Merneptah's armies attacked them about 1230. If adjustment in the dates assigned to the destruction of those sites needs to be made, how effective is the use of the evidence in establishing the date of the Exodus? Additionally, it is important to note that while Joshua captured Bethel, Lachish, and Debir, nothing is said about destroying them; he burned only Ai, Jericho, and Hazor (Josh. 6:24; 8:19; 11:13). Some of Joshua's conquests

[7]Albright, *Stone Age*, 195.
[8]Unger, *Archaeology*, 149.

were not permanent. We know that Debir had to be recaptured later (Josh. 15:13–17), and possibly the others did also. If dates of destruction at Bethel, Lachish, and Debir are correct, they may well refer to attacks during the days of the judges instead of to Joshua's conquests.

Finally, Beno Rothenberg, as a result of his excavations in the Timna Valley, south of the Dead Sea (1964–1970), concluded that the copper mining and smelting activity there did not date to Solomon's time but to the fourteenth to twelfth centuries (including the days of Raamses II) instead. This would mean that there was "large-scale Pharaonic industrial enterprise" in this region during the thirteenth century. With hordes of Egyptian troops and workers swarming all over the area during that century, it would seem unlikely that Hebrews in large numbers could have been there at the same time. He felt that his discoveries would require "reconsideration" of the thirteenth-century date of the Exodus, the prevailing view of Israeli scholars.[9]

In conclusion, it seems that archaeological discoveries increasingly support an approximate 1400 date for the conquest and a 1440 date for the Exodus.

Route of the Exodus: Critical View and Answer From Archaeological Evidence

In leaving Egypt, the Israelites went eastward through the delta, from Rameses to Succoth (Exod. 12:37), then to Etham (13:20), and finally to Baal-zephon by the shores of the Red Sea (14:2).

The route of the Exodus has been questioned by the critics. Peet says, "We are not in a position to discover what route the Israelites really followed, except in so far as we may conjecture it by the application of common sense to the problem. All we can hope to recover is the route which the compilers of the ninth century B.C. and onward thought that they followed, which is a very different thing" (PEOT, 126). Caiger reflects this same attitude when he says that "the dotted line showing the 'journey of the Israelites' in most of our Scripture atlases has no real authority" (CBS, 78). It is quite true that many of the sites given in the Bible as lying on the route of the Exodus and the wilderness journeys have not yet been identified.

Archaeological light, however, has been brought to bear periodically so that even Alan Gardiner, the Egyptologist, who long objected to the historicity of the route of the Exodus on topographical grounds, withdrew his objections in 1933. Albright pointed out Gardiner's change of view, and stated:

> With our present knowledge of the topography of the eastern Delta the account of the start of the Exodus given in Exodus 12:37 and 13:20ff. is perfectly sound topographically. . . . Many additional pieces of evidence for the substantial historicity of the account of the Exodus and the wandering in the regions of Sinai, Midian, and Kadesh can easily be given, thanks to our greatly increased knowledge of topography and archaeology. We must content ourselves here with the assurance that there is no longer any room for the still dominant attitude of hyper-criticism toward the early historical traditions of Israel. (ASAC, 194)

M.G. Kyle related that travelers who follow the coast of the Red Sea, along the line of the Exodus, need no other guidebook than the Bible. The whole topography corresponds to that mentioned in the biblical account.[10]

The Parting of the Red Sea (Exodus 14:21ff.)

After Israel had left Egypt, Pharaoh changed his mind and determined to

[9]Beno Rothenberg, *Were These King Solomon's Mines?* (New York: Stein & Day, 1972), 184.
[10]Floyd E. Hamilton, *The Basis of Christian Faith*, rev. ed. (New York: Harper, 1933), 172 [HBCF]. A third edition was issued in 1946.

pursue them (Exod. 14:9). When the Egyptians approached the stopping place of the Israelites, "Moses stretched out his hand over the sea, and all that night the LORD drove the sea back with a strong east wind" (Exod. 14:21). It is said that the driving back of water by a wind has been observed in modern times. General Tulloch reported a baring of the sands when a strong east wind drove back the waters of Lake Manzaleh seven miles.[11] Kyle says that such heaping up of waters by the wind is well known and sometimes amounts to seven or eight feet in Lake Erie.[12] The significant thing, however, in the parting of the waters for the Israelites was the time element. This was not just a freak parting of the waters by a chance wind, but rather the intervention of God in sending a wind at the time necessary to save Israel.[13] The time element is sometimes the major factor in a miracle.

Some have argued that *yam sûph* (translated "Red Sea" in KJV and other versions) should be correctly translated "Sea of Reeds" and have sought to relate it to a lake or lakes now part of the Suez Canal system. It is difficult to support such a position effectively, however. The Greek translation of the Old Testament (the Septuagint), Acts 7:36, and Hebrews 11:29 understand *yam sûph* to refer to the Red Sea (NIV mg. of Acts 7:36 and Heb. 11:29 reads, "That is, Sea of Reeds"). Moreover, Exodus 14:27 and 15:5, 8, 10 seem to require something more than one of the lakes of the Suez region. Furthermore, it has been observed that *yam sûph* in Exodus 10:19 would seemingly have to be more than marshy lakes of the Suez region; the Gulf of Suez is large enough to destroy hordes of locusts

and is properly placed for a northwest wind to blow the locusts into its waters. Certainly in Numbers 14:25 *yam sûph* is the Red Sea. Perhaps it is best, then, to conclude that the Hebrews journeyed southward to the west of the present canal system and crossed the Red Sea just south of the modern port of Suez.

The Journey to Sinai (Exodus 15–19)
(See Map 4.)

After the children of Israel had walked across the dry land on the bottom of the Red Sea and had safely reached the other shore (Exod. 14:22), they continued their journey into the Wilderness of Shur (15:22), on the east of the Gulf of Suez (the western arm of the Red Sea). The successive stages of the journey to Mount Sinai may be conveniently summarized as follows:

1. *Desert of Shur* (Exod. 15:22). No water was available there, and so Israel went on to Marah.

2. *Marah* (Exod. 15:23). Here they were unable to drink the bitter waters until the Lord showed Moses a tree that, when cast into the waters, made them sweet (15:25). Marah is sometimes identified with a site now called Huwara, about seven miles east of the Red Sea and about thirty miles south of the place where, according to tradition, the Israelites first stopped after crossing the Red Sea (BBHM, 80). At Huwara there is a basin about five feet in diameter still containing bitter water. The next stop was Elim.[14]

3. *Elim* (Exod. 15:27). Elim is described as having twelve wells of water and seventy palm trees. It is thought by some to be the present-day Wady Ghurundel,

---

[11]*Victoria Institute.*, 28:267, cited in POTH, 100–101.

[12]Article on "Moses," ISBE, 2086, citing Wright, *Scientific Confirmations of the Old Testament*, 106 [WSC].

[13]The Bible specifically states that "The LORD drove the sea back with a strong east wind" (Exod. 14:21).

[14]For an interesting discussion of the vast quantity of fossil water that lies under the Sinai Desert and comes to the surface in springs noted in Scripture, see Arie Issar, "Fossil Water under the Sinai-Negev Peninsula," *Scientific American* (July 1985), 104–10.

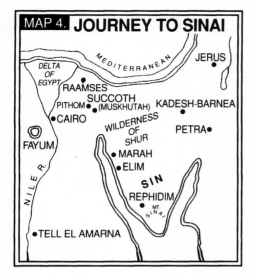

MAP 4. JOURNEY TO SINAI

five miles from Huwarah (possibly Marah), although it may be farther south. *Murray's Handbook* says of Wady Ghurundel:

> This may be safely identified with Elim. The whole desert is almost absolutely bare and barren, but Wady Ghurundel is fringed with trees and shrubs, forming a charming oasis. Here are the stunted palms, with their hairy trunks and dishevelled branches. Here, too, are the feathery tamarisks, with gnarled boughs, their leaves dripping with what the Arabs call manna. And here is the acacia, with its gray foliage and bright blossoms, tangled by its desert-growth into a thicket. Pleasant is the acacia to the sight, wearied by the desert-glare; but it has a higher and holier interest, as the tree of the 'burning bush,' and the 'shittim-wood' of the tabernacle.[15]

4. *Desert of Sin* (Exod. 16:1). The region of Sinai is a rugged area of rocks and ridges, varied in spots with shady nooks and ravines. For much of the way through Sinai, Israel traveled over rocky ascents and through narrow defiles. The Desert of Sin, however, is a contrast to much of Sinai, being an extensive sandy plain, stretching along the shores of the Red Sea (BBHM, 81).

While Israel was in the Desert of Sin, God sent the manna (Exod. 16;14–15ff.). Attempts to identify the manna of Scripture with the gum of the tamarisk tree and other substances are not successful (see above, the description of Wady Ghurundel, under "Elim"). There are many basic differences between the gum of the tamarisk tree and manna.

5. *Rephidim* (Exod. 17:1). From the Desert of Sin, the Israelites went toward the interior of the Sinai Peninsula, probably going through the valley that today is called the Wady Feiran (BBHM, 81). At the next important stop, Rephidim, Moses smote the rock to bring forth water (17:1, 6), and here also the Israelites were sustained by the Lord in their battle with the Amalekites (17:8).

6. *Mount Sinai* (Exod. 19:1–2), *the Sojourn at Sinai* (Exod. 19–Num. 10). Finally, in the third month after Israel's Exodus from Egypt, they journeyed the fifteen miles from Rephidim to Mount Sinai and camped before the mountain. Israel remained at Mount Sinai for about a year (Cf. Exod. 19:1 with Num. 10:11–12). All of the events in the remainder of Exodus, the material in Leviticus, and the happenings of the first part of Numbers through 10:10 took place at Sinai. In Numbers 10:11–12 we read of Israel's departure from Mount Sinai as they began their journey north to Kadesh.

Identification of Mount Sinai (Exodus 19)

Thirty-five times in the Old Testament Sinai is referred to as a desert or mountain, and seventeen times the same area or mountain is referred to by the name of Horeb. The terms are often used inter-

---

[15]*Murray's Handbook for Syria and Palestine*, [MHSP], 14, cited in BBHM, 80–81.

changeably, and thus it is evident that Sinai and Horeb refer to the same place.

Various locations for Sinai have been suggested, some authorities even placing this mountain far over in Midian, to the east of the Gulf of Akabah (the eastern arm of the Red Sea). The traditional view, however, has always held that Mount Sinai is to be identified with the mountain today called Jebel Musa. Edward Robinson, the pioneer American explorer in Palestine, thought that the peak next to Jebel Musa (called es-Sufsafeh) would fit the conditions better because from here one could see the large plain at the base of the mountain, and this plain was probably the place where the Israelites were encamped.[16]

There is, however, no compelling reason to abandon the traditional identification of Mount Sinai with Jebel Musa (meaning "Mount of Moses" in Arabic), and "it meets all the requirements indicated in the Old Testament" (ABB, 42). Jebel Musa, part of a great range of peaks, rises with imposing grandeur to a height of 7,370 feet. At the base of the mountain is a large plain, about a mile long, which is likely the place where the Israelites camped (RBR, 95).

The Ten Commandments (Exodus 20); the Purpose of the Law

While Israel was at Mount Sinai, Moses went up into the mountain and there received the Ten Commandments and the other laws that God revealed to him. The purpose of the law is at least threefold: (1) To reveal man's sinfulness. Man knows that he is a sinner by the testimony of conscience, but by the published law of God he has an intensified "knowledge of sin" (Rom. 3:19, speaking of what the law says, adds, "that every mouth may be silenced and the whole world held accountable to God"). (2) To reveal God's holiness. The nature of the commandments shows the holiness of God; but the ceremonial law and particularly the tabernacle with its Most Holy Place emphasizes the holiness of God. (3) To lead the sinner to Christ. This aspect of the law is set forth by Paul: "So the law was put in charge to lead us to Christ" (Gal. 3:24).[17] The law pointed to the cross of Christ (by its offerings, priesthood, and tabernacle) as the only way of salvation and access to God. (For development of the preceding material, see TSTS, 113.)

Our Relation to the Law

In the death of Christ the believer is delivered not only from the curse of the law (Gal. 3:13), but also from the law itself (Col. 2:14). May we then break the Ten Commandments? Paul shows that the answer is no, for he refers to being "not free from God's law but. . . under Christ's law" (1 Cor. 9:21). We "belong to another. . . that we might bear fruit to God" (Rom. 7:4). Every commandment of the Decalogue, except the fourth, is reaffirmed and sanctioned in the New Testament. The commandments are repeated in the New Testament for our instruction, that we may know what the will of the Lord is. The mere keeping of the commandments, however, will not save a person; it is only by trusting in Christ as Savior that one is saved. (For further discussion concerning our relationship to the law, see TLST, 170–71.)

Archaeological Light on the Prohibition of Image Worship; Critical View; No Images of Yahweh

The second commandment specifically says, "You shall not make for yourself an

---

[16]Edward Robinson, *Biblical Researches in Palestine*, 3rd ed. (Boston: Crocker and Brewster, 1868), 1:106–7 [RBR].

[17]"Schoolmaster" of the KJV obscures the intent of the Greek and the practices of the Roman world. *A paidagogos* (Greek) was a slave who had supervision of a child and took him to school, i.e., to the schoolmaster. A recent discussion of the term *paidagogos* is found in Norman H. Young, "The Figure of the *Paidagogos* in Art and Literature," BA (June 1990), 80–86.

idol. . ." (Exod. 20:4). The necessity for this commandment is indicated by archaeological discoveries, which show that the Canaanites of Palestine were given to image worship (BWMS, 189). Now that God was preparing Israel for entrance into Canaan, it was particularly fitting to emphasize the prohibition of idol worship, for Israel would be surrounded by idolatry in Canaan. The excavations in Palestine reveal figures of gods on stelae (stone monuments; singular, stele), such as the stele of the god Mekal, found in one of the Late Bronze Age temples of Bethshan (BWMS, 218). Small images in bronze are not uncommon and usually represent gods rather than goddesses. The most common representations of goddesses are the clay plaques or figurines. These figurines may have been household deities, like the teraphim of the Old Testament, or they may have been used in some part of sympathetic magic (BWMS, 219–20).

According to the critical view, the religion of Israel went through an evolutionary development, from animism (worship of spirits) through various stages to polytheism, and finally to monotheism. According to this theory, images were worshiped until the late period, when the prohibition against image worship was supposedly made. Thus the early date and the validity of the second commandment are denied, as seen in Wellhausen's statement that "the prohibition of images was during the older period quite unknown" (WPHI, 439).

If images were worshiped by Israel, as the critics have said, and if the prohibition against images was a late addition to the Scriptures, then we would expect to find images of Yahweh—i.e., the LORD. G. Ernest Wright, an American archaeologist, formerly of Harvard, points out that the excavations have not produced images of the LORD. A great amount of

material has been excavated, yet, says Wright, "we can nowhere place our hands on a figure of Yahweh."[18] Thus archaeology does not support the critical idea that images were worshiped by the true followers of the LORD. In fact, this prohibition seems to have been so rigidly ingrained that even backsliders did not make images of the LORD, but contented themselves with statues of Baal and of the fertility goddess.

Directions for Building the Tabernacle (Exodus 25–40)

The last sixteen chapters of Exodus are largely concerned with the directions for building the tabernacle, which was to serve as a meeting place between God and Israel. This purpose of the tabernacle was summarized in God's words to Moses regarding Israel: "Have them make a sanctuary for me, and I will dwell among them" (Exod. 25:8).

When Moses was preparing to direct the construction of the tabernacle, God told him to allow whoever was willing to bring an offering to provide the necessary materials (Exod. 35:4–5). Illumination and confirmation have come from the Near East concerning several of these materials. We will concern ourselves with two of them.

Material for the Tabernacle: The Skins of Sea Cows (Exodus 35:7, 23)

The material referred to as "badgers' skins" was used to make the last of the four coverings for the tabernacle (36:19). One notes, however, that the Hebrew word rendered "badgers' skins" in the KJV is translated "sealskins" in the text of the ASV, and "the hides of sea cows" in the NIV (Exod. 25:5). What reason is there for this variation, and what light is there on this word from a study of the languages and the animals of the Near East?

---

[18]G. Ernest Wright, "The Terminology of Old Testament Religion and Its Significance," *Journal of Near Eastern Studies* 1, 4 (October 1942): 413 [JNES].

The Hebrew word involved is *tahash*. The writers of the Talmud favored the idea that the word meant "badger." Superficially there is a resemblance between *tahash* and the Latin word *taxus* and the German word *Dachs*, both meaning "badger." This derivation was observed by the translators of the KJV. One difficulty with this translation is that badgers probably were not available to the Israelites when they were out in the Sinai wilderness, since this animal does not seem to be found in the region of Sinai nor in Egypt, although it is fairly abundant in Syria, in the Lebanon region to the north of Palestine.[19]

Another difficulty with the "badger" translation lies in the fact that Latin and German belong to families of languages other than Hebrew. Hebrew belongs to the group known as Semitic languages, which includes Arabic. In Arabic a word similar to the Hebrew *tahash* is the word *tuhas*, meaning "dolphin."[20] The Arabic *tuhas* was said by Tristram to be applied also to another marine animal called the dugong, or sea cow, which outwardly resembles dolphins and porpoises.

The dugong averages from five to nine feet in length. It is often found along the shore, where it feeds on seaweed. Since the dugong inhabits the seas in the region of Egypt and Sinai, it is quite likely that the Hebrew word refers to this marine animal. The Hebraist, Gesenius, as well as travelers in the Near East, have pointed out that the Arabs of Sinai wear sandals made of dugong skin.[21] This is significant, since shoes of "leather" (*tahash*) are referred to in Ezekiel 16:10.

While the seal and porpoise, as well as the dolphin and dugong, are all found in the waters near Sinai, and are possible candidates for the *tahash*, most recent writers favor the dugong.[22] The evidence given above would also favor this identification.

Materials for the Tabernacle: the Bronze Mirrors (Exodus 35:5, 24; 38:8); Critical View; Light from Archaeology

Copper was one of the important materials contributed for the construction of the tabernacle (Exod. 25:3; 35:5, 24). We are told that the laver was made of bronze, which was obtained from the contribution of the women's mirrors (Exod. 38:8).

The well-known nineteenth-century biblical critic Julius Wellhausen implied that this record of the laver made of bronze mirrors was a late addition to this part of the Bible when he said that it did not "belong to the original contents of the Priestly Code" (WPHI, 353). Critics usually date the parts of the Pentateuch called the "Priestly Code" (cf. the "P" document[23]) at about 500 B.C.[24] Wellhausen thus puts the record of the tabernacle entirely too late for the time of Moses (c. 1500–1400) and assigns the details concerning the making of the laver to a period even later than the so-called Priestly Code.

There is no valid reason for dating the record of the bronze mirrors in the late period, for it fits into the account as an integral part. Furthermore, the details that can be compared with external evidence are shown to fit into the early period. There is specific archaeological evidence showing the use of such bronze mirrors in the Empire Period of Egyptian

---

[19]A.E. Day, "Badger," ISBE, 1929 ed., 376.

[20]Brown, Driver, Briggs, *A Hebrew and English Lexicon of the Old Testament* (New York: Houghton Mifflin, 1906), 1065 [BDB].

[21]Day, "Badger," 377.

[22]Ibid.

[23]For a brief description of the "P" document, see the section "Critical View of Genesis 1 and 2," in chapter 2.

[24]R.H. Pfeiffer, *Introduction to the Old Testament* (New York: Harper, 1941), 256 [PIOT].

history (c. 1550–1100), the period contemporary with Moses and the Exodus. Excavations in Egypt have produced many bronze mirrors, showing their abundant use in that time. The reason why Israelite women happened to have such mirrors is that they had just come out of Egypt and had these mirrors as part of their possessions. They had even more mirrors than they ordinarily would have possessed, because the Egyptians gave[25] them many gifts at the time of the Exodus (Exod. 12:35–36), apparently because the Egyptians desired them to leave in order to avoid any more plagues. Such bronze mirrors from ancient Egypt may be seen in most of the large museums of the world (see PNEP index for pictures).

Critical View of the Tabernacle and the Lampstand; Archaeological Evidence to the Contrary

The critical view has tended to regard the tabernacle as a late "invention" of priestly writers and to deny, in effect, its existence in the days of Moses. Wellhausen set the critical pattern by denying the authenticity of the description of the tabernacle in Exodus (AAPB, 159), and more recent writers who hold the critical view reflect a similar attitude.

Even some of the details of the tabernacle are held to be late concepts. In recent decades some scholars have held that the seven-branched lampstand of the tabernacle reflects the Babylonian period (c. 600–500 B.C.) or the Persian period (c. 500–300) (AAPB, 161). This explanation fits in with the critical view that Exodus and Leviticus are late writings of about 500–450, assignable for the most part to the so-called "P" writer or school of writers.[26]

Archaeological excavations, however, do not support the critical idea that a sevenfold lamp is a late idea. In the excavations at Tell Beit Mirsim[27] it is precisely in the period of Early Iron I (1200–900 B.C.), never afterward, that we find pottery lamps with seven places for wicks, made by pinching the rim together seven times. Concerning the idea that the sevenfold lampstand reflects Babylonian or Persian times, Albright states, "Unhappily for this *a priori* conception. . . such lamps are found in Tell Beit Mirsim B, as well as in contemporary deposits elsewhere in Palestine" (i.e., c. 1200). Albright adds that he "wishes to protest most vigorously" against the idea that the priestly sources give "a fanciful account of the tabernacle," reflecting only "priestly ideals of the Exilic Age" (AAPB, 159).

During my sixth, seventh, and eighth seasons at Dothan (1959, 1960, and 1962) activities included the excavation of two tombs that dated to the Late Bronze II Period (1400–1200 B.C.) and the beginning of Iron I (1200–1100). Four different seven-spouted lamps were found in these early tombs, attesting further to the early date of the concept of the sevenfold lamp. For a photo of one of these lamps, see BASOR (December 1960), 14, figure 3.

One does not actually have to unearth the tabernacle and its appurtenances in order to produce evidence that the critical view asserting its lateness is incorrect. The critical argument is subjective. The moment we find one sevenfold lamp in the early period, we have objective evidence to show that the critical view is not sustained, at least at that point.

---

[25]The word really implies the idea of "gave," rather than "lent," in Exodus 12:36. Cf. BDB or any Hebrew lexicon.

[26]For the "P" document, see footnote 20.

[27]Identified as the site of the biblical Kiriath Sepher (cf. Judg. 1:12). This site was excavated by Kyle and Albright, 1926, 1928ff.

Chapter 9

Mount Sinai and the Wilderness

(Leviticus, Numbers, Deuteronomy)

The Book of Leviticus

While the children of Israel were encamped before Mount Sinai, God revealed to Moses the ceremonial laws found in the book of Leviticus. The purpose of Leviticus was to furnish a guidebook for the worship of the LORD and to give instructions to the priests as to the details of this worship. Chapters 1 to 7 give instructions concerning the presentation of five offerings: the burnt, meal, peace, sin, and trespass offerings, all typifying various aspects of the death and ministry of Christ. This section is followed by directions for the consecration of the priests (Lev. 8–10), and the laws of purity (chs. 11–15), which concern the food that might be eaten and the handling of leprosy. Chapter 16 gives the directions for the ceremony of the Great Day of Atonement, in which two goats were brought before the door of the tabernacle of the congregation, the one goat to be sacrificed and the other to be let go into the wilderness, bearing the iniquities of Israel. The two goats were symbolic of Christ's death, which removed transgressions from us. The remainder of Leviticus (chs. 17–27) concerns various laws of holiness, including directions for the

place of sacrifice, the significance of blood, the punishment of various sins, the feasts of the Lord (ch. 23), the sabbatical year (ch. 25), conditions of blessing in the Promised Land (ch. 26), and things dedicated to the Lord (ch. 27).

The Critical View of Levitical Laws; Light from Archaeology

The usual critical view holds that the code of Levitical laws was a late development, written down and codified about 500–450 B.C. This view was well expressed by R.H. Pfeiffer of Harvard University when he said concerning the Priestly Code: "It codifies in stereotyped and idealized form the current practices of the Second Temple, about 500 or perhaps in the next half century" (PIOT, 256). Thus, if the critical view were correct, it would mean that these laws are not Mosaic and do not date back to the period 1500–1400 B.C.

However, the fact that the Ras Shamra Tablets, dating back to about 1400 B.C., record several laws similar to those of Leviticus, shows that the critic has no right to deny the possibility of such a code of sacrificial laws as early as the time of Moses. Burrows, a liberal professor at Yale University, pointed out the presence of such offerings in the tablets: "Several of the terms employed in the Hebrew Old Testament for the various types of offering also have appeared in the Ras Shamra tablets, for example, the burnt offering, the whole burnt offering, the guilt offering, and the peace offering" (BWMS, 234).

As to why the Ras Shamra tablets contain references to sacrifices similar to those of the Mosaic laws in Leviticus, there are at least two possible answers. First, they may have been diffused from Israel at the time they were revealed to Moses (about 1450 B.C.) and have come into the practices of the Canaanites and people of Syria, being reflected in the Ras Shamra tablets (1400–1350). Second, the laws and statutes revealed by the LORD at a much earlier time (and later given in a codified form to Moses) were handed down among various peoples and appear in a modified and often corrupted form among such people as those of Ras Shamra. The fact that God gave early revelation of laws and statutes, long before the time of Moses, is shown by his saying to Isaac: "Abraham obeyed me and kept my requirements, my commands, my decrees and my laws" (Gen. 26:5).[1]

The Book of Numbers;
Contents; Outline

The fourth book of the Pentateuch is called Numbers because it tells of the two numberings or censuses of the people—one at Sinai, described at the beginning of the book (Num. 1), and the other when Israel was on the plains of Moab at the close of the wanderings (ch. 26). The contents of Numbers include directions for the arrangement of the tribes in the camp of Israel, directions for the service of the Levites in taking care of the taber-

nacle, the record of the sending out of the spies (ch. 13), and the events of the forty years in the wilderness, made necessary because of the unbelief of the people in not entering into the land (14:33–34).

The book of Numbers may be conveniently outlined as follows:

1. Israel at Mount Sinai, 1:1–10:10
2. Israel from Mount Sinai to Kadesh, 10:11–12:16
3. Israel at Kadesh, 13:1–19:22
4. Israel's wilderness wanderings, 20:1–33:49
5. Israel on the Plains of Moab, 33:50–36:13

Archaeological Light on the Numbering of the People

A detailed census of Israel, recorded at the beginning of Numbers, was taken while the people were still at Sinai (ch. 1) and another at the close of the wilderness wanderings when they were in the plains of Moab (ch. 26). Moses could easily have learned the methods of census taking during his life in Egypt, for the archaeological discoveries there show that it was a favorite custom of the pharaohs to compile exact statistics. Knight points out that papyri dating back to 3000 B.C. show that even at that early time strict census lists were made up, mention being made of the head of the house, resident female relatives, slaves, and young male children.[2]

Robert Dick Wilson demonstrates the way this material in Numbers fits into the early period of the time of Moses (c. 1500–1400 B.C.), and not into the late period (c. 900–400), to which the critics assign the Pentateuch. In this connection he says, "The form of the numeration of Numbers 1–4 bears many resemblances to those of the Annals of Tahutmes III"

---

[1]For a bibliography on Ras Shamra, see chapter 8, the section entitled "Critical View of the Passover," pages 85–86.

[2]KNJ, 181, citing Griffith, *Law Quarterly Review* (1898), 44–45.

(the same as Thutmose III or Thothmes III; see chapter 7, the section entitled "The Pharaoh of the Oppression," pages 79–81).[3]

From Sinai to Kadesh; Location of Kadesh

After Israel had encamped for nearly a year before Mount Sinai, the Lord directed the people to depart, then guided them with the cloud (Num. 10:11–36). Israel traveled north, finally coming to Kadesh, or Kadesh Barnea, the traditional site of which is about forty miles south of Beersheba.

The view was long held that Kadesh is to be identified with the present site called Ain-Kadis ('Ain Qedeis) in Arabic, forty-nine miles southwest of Beersheba. H. Clay Trumbull, former editor of the *Sunday School Times*, made a complete study of the question and wrote a book of nearly five hundred pages on the subject. He concluded that Kadesh was best identified with Ain-Kadis for several reasons: (1) It is in a region that is a strategic stronghold on the southern border of Canaan, near the principal roads into Canaan. (2) It is at the natural boundary line of southern Canaan. (3) It fits in with the other landmarks mentioned in the biblical text. (4) It integrates best with the journey of Israel after leaving Kadesh. (5) Ain-Kadis best corresponds with the biblical references to Kadesh.[4]

In later years other sites have been proposed as the location of Kadesh. The most important of these involved the work of C. Leonard Woolley and T.E. Lawrence, who in their exploration of the wilderness to the south of Palestine (1913–1914) concluded that 'Ain el-Qudeirat and its nearby Tell el-Qudeirat (five miles northwest of 'Ain Qedeis) was the site of Kadesh.[5] This identification is now generally accepted. 'Ain el-Qudeirat has the finest spring in the Sinai; it waters the largest oasis in northern Sinai. In 1956 M. Dothan for the Israel Department of Antiquities undertook an exploratory excavation on the tell. The excavation identified three periods of occupation: the first, dated by pottery to the tenth century B.C.; the second, consisting of a substantial fortress, perhaps of the time of Jehoshaphat around the middle of the ninth century; and the third, to the Persian period in the fifth and fourth centuries B.C.[6] Even if 'Ain el-Qudeirat is accepted as the site of Kadesh, it is likely that other springs in the general vicinity (Ain-Kadis, et al.) served the needs of the wandering Israelites.

Supposed Difficulties in Numbers; Formation for Travel; Number of Quail

Critics have often pointed out supposed difficulties and impossibilities in the book of Numbers. For instance, they have said it would have been impossible to get the large numbers of Israelites (two million or more) in formation to travel. According to this objection, the half million Israelites in each of the four main divisions could not have assembled into marching formation in any reasonable time, and after they formed, they would have stretched out a length of twenty-two miles, according to Colenso, or even six hundred miles according to Doughty. This means that it would have taken all day to get into marching formation and then there would not have been any day left in which to travel. An analysis of this situation, however, shows that such a difficulty would not necessarily exist. As

---

[3]Robert Dick Wilson, *A Scientific Investigation of the Old Testament*, with revisions by Edward J. Young (Chicago: Moody, 1959), 43 [WSI], referring to Petrie, *History of Egypt*, 2:103–4.

[4]H. Clay Trumbull, *Kadesh-Barnea* (New York: Scribner, 1884), 311–19 [TKB], summarized in PSB, 107–8.

[5]*The Wilderness of Zin*, Palestine Exploration Fund *Annual*, vol. 3, cited in BAB, 105–6.

[6]M. Dothan, "Kadesh-Barnea," EAEHL, 3:697–98.

Whitelaw points out, two divisions could start formation at six A.M., be ready to move at ten A.M., cover a distance of ten miles in four hours and then stop at two P.M. The other two divisions could fall in line at two P.M., arrive at six P.M. and be settled for the night by ten P.M. Moreover, there is no certain evidence that the Israelites formed a regularly constructed camp every night, and it is likely that this would be done only when they reached a spot where they were to halt for some time. Furthermore, the arranging of the four divisions for marching may have gone on simultaneously, since they were widely separated from each other, with Judah on the east side of the camp, Reuben on the south, Ephraim on the west, and Dan on the north.[7] In case such simultaneous formation occurred, a distance considerably greater than ten miles could have been covered in their daily march. In the absence of more details, the critic has no right to reconstruct a situation that is apparently impossible, particularly when the available records in the Bible can be understood so as to constitute no problem.

A second difficulty concerns the quail: when the Lord sent the quail to the Israelites in the wilderness, he let them fall "round about the camp, and as it were two cubits high *upon* the face of the earth" (Num. 11:31 KJV). Agnostics who have read this have hastily assumed that the quail were piled up two cubits (three feet) deep, giving each Israelite 2,888,463 bushels of quail for the month, or 69,620 bushels each meal! They have overlooked the fact that the Hebrew word translated "upon" in this verse is the word 'al, one of the regular meanings of which is "above," as in the NIV (BDB, 752, sec. 2). Inasmuch as this Hebrew word can mean either "upon" or "above," I take it as "above,"

since it fits the context better.[8] The quail, then, flew down *above* the earth about three feet, in other words, within easy reach of the Israelites so that they might take them for food. All of the ridiculous figures indicating that there were supposedly 69,620 bushels of quail for each Israelite for each meal are based on a false and deliberately misleading presupposition. A reasonable analysis of the other supposed difficulties and contradictions in Numbers shows no necessary improbability.

From Kadesh to the Plains of Moab (Numbers 13–36)

After the spies had been sent out from Kadesh to survey Canaan (Num. 13:1–2, 17ff.) and had returned with a report of the giants and the walled cities, the Israelites complained about going into the land (14:1–3). Only two of the twelve spies, Joshua and Caleb, wished to go on into the land, but the people refused their counsel (14:6–10). Because of the unbelief of the people and their lack of trust, the LORD said that they would remain in the wilderness for forty years (Num. 14:33). Some scholars believe that Israel was in the vicinity of Kadesh for most of this period, about thirty-eight years.[9]

When the Israelites finally left Kadesh, the Edomites refused them permission to go through the land of Edom (Num. 21:14, 21). So Israel went to the south, around the land of Edom (21:4), then north to the plains of Moab, where they encountered the prophet Balaam (ch. 22). After Balaam's dealings with Israel (chs. 22–24), God gave instructions through Moses to the people concerning the law of inheritance (ch. 27), the law of offerings (ch. 28), the preparation to enter the land of Canaan (ch. 34), and the provisions for

[7]T. Whitelaw, "Numbers," ISBE, 1929 ed., 2168.

[8]When a word has more than one meaning, what right has anyone to choose the reading that would constitute a problem?

[9]C.M. Cobern, *Recent Explorations in Palestine*, 98ff. [CREP].

cities of refuge (ch. 35). These closing events of the book of Numbers took place while Israel was at the plains of Moab,[10] near the north end of the Dead Sea. There they remained during the time that Moses spoke to them the words recorded in Deuteronomy (Deut. 1:5ff.).

The Book of Deuteronomy

Deuteronomy is made up principally of four main addresses of Moses to the people of Israel as they were encamped on the plains of Moab a few miles east of the Jordan River, somewhat north of the north end of the Dead Sea. These addresses begin successively at 1:5; 5:1; 27:1; and 29:1. The word "Deuteronomy" comes from two Greek words meaning "second law," and the term is used in the sense of a repetition of the law previously given in the Pentateuch. The purpose of Deuteronomy is to prevent a resumé of the law already given in Exodus and Leviticus for the benefit of the generation which had grown up in the wilderness, in order that they might be prepared for entering the land of Canaan. The subjects treated include:

1. Israel's journeys in the wilderness reviewed (chs. 1–3).
2. The Ten Commandments repeated (ch. 5).
3. Dietary laws (ch. 14), feasts such as Passover (ch. 16) reviewed.

4. Conditions of blessing in the Promised Land (ch. 28).
5. Moses' final instructions, his blessing of the tribes, and his death (chs. 31–34).

Critical View of the Date of Deuteronomy; Record of Moses' Death

The critical view holds that Deuteronomy was not written by Moses,[11] but was composed much later than his day. This position invaded many of the seminary faculties of mainline denominations in the United States during the first half of this century. For example, Otto Piper, professor at Princeton Theological Seminary, indicated his acceptance of the higher critical view when he stated that Deuteronomy was not written by Moses, but "by prophetic writers after his death."[12] S.A. Cartledge of Columbia Seminary (Decatur, Georgia), casually set aside the Mosaic authorship of many parts of the Pentateuch when he said, "Moses was considered the law giver par excellence, and so the priestly writers did not hesitate to ascribe new laws to Moses so long as they felt that they were in keeping with the spirit of Moses and the laws they did have from Moses."[13]

There are several reasons why liberals date the book of Deuteronomy late, usually in the seventh century B.C., and thereby deny the Mosaic authorship. Let us examine one of these reasons.[14] The last

---

[10]Numbers 36:13, last verse in the book.

[11]Cf. Pfeiffer (PIOT, 211), who concluded that the codes of the Pentateuch, which would include much of Deuteronomy, "could not have been promulgated by Moses."

[12]Otto Piper, *God in History*, 79 [PGH].

[13]Samuel A. Cartledge, *A Conservative Introduction to the Old Testament*, (Grand Rapids: Zondervan, 1943), 70 [CCIO]. This book was misnamed when it was titled *A Conservative Introduction*. It presented many liberal views with apparent approval. When Zondervan realized the implications of numerous statements in the book, they discontinued its publication. But the book was reissued by the University of Georgia Press.

[14]If this were a text in Old Testament Introduction (i.e., Old Testament Criticism), several other reasons and the answers would be developed. (For some material on the critical view of Deuteronomy in a book that is helpful, see ASOTI, 253–57). In summary, it could be said that another reason given by liberals for the late dating of Deuteronomy, often repeated in recent

chapter of Deuteronomy records the death of Moses (34:5ff.). Critics point out that since a man cannot write of his own death, Moses could not be the author of the book. This is not a new argument. Three hundred years ago, a Dutch philosopher named Spinoza (1632–1677) remarked about the record of the death of Moses, "Such testimony cannot have been given of Moses by himself . . . but it must have come from someone who lived centuries afterwards."[15] This argument has been repeated down to the present generation.

There are at least two possible explanations of this seeming discrepancy: (1) Moses was a prophet (Deut. 34:10) and consequently could have written of his death before it occurred, but that is highly unlikely. (2) Because Joshua was the assistant, the "minister" of Moses, what would be more natural than for him, as the successor to Moses, to add a few words telling of the death of his predecessor?

We may cite a modern illustration to show that the mention of an author's death within the confines of a book does not necessarily mean that the author could not have written the book in question. In 1938, the University of Chicago Press published a book called *They Wrote on Clay: The Babylonian Tablets Speak Today*, written by Edward Chiera, Professor of Assyriology at the University of Chicago. Professor Chiera was the author

of the book, yet on page vi we read of his "untimely death." Does this mean that Chiera could not and did not write the book, just as the reference to Moses' death in Deuteronomy 34:5 supposedly indicates that Moses could not and did not write Deuteronomy? A fuller knowledge of the facts gives the answer "No."

We find that Chiera did write the book, but he died before it was finished for publication, and a younger Assyriologist and associate of Chiera, George G. Cameron,[16] prepared the book for publication and wrote the preface, which tells of Chiera's death. The reference to Chiera's death was added at the beginning of his book, whereas in Deuteronomy the eight verses that tell of Moses' death were added at the end. If in the days of Moses books had been provided with full title pages, might we not read something like this: "*Deuteronomy*, by Moses, the servant of the Lord, with biographical note by Joshua, the minister of Moses"?

If the book of Deuteronomy only appears to have been written by Moses but actually was not, then we have a case of fraud; the critics of the past generation called it "pious fraud." Albright's examination of the ancient materials convinced him that the old critical theory of "pious fraud" is not sustained. He says, regarding the assumptions of the Wellhausen school, "A third assumption, that pious fraud and pseudepigraphy were common in Israel, is without parallel in the pre-

decades, is that its codes "reflect Palestinian conditions" (PIOT, 211). The liberal overlooks the obvious answer. In Deuteronomy Moses was giving instructions to Israel in advance concerning procedure in the agricultural economy in which they would find themselves after the conquest. The liberal erroneously assumes that the laws in Deuteronomy concerning an agricultural economy must indicate that they had already settled down in the land (e.g., laws prohibiting the removal of an ancient landmark or boundary stone, Deuteronomy 19:14). The Bible believer, on the other hand, acknowledges that God could and did give many of the provisions in Deuteronomy in order to prepare Israel for the conditions that would obtain in Canaan.

The objection to Deuteronomy on the ground that it contains laws too advanced for the time of Moses is dealt with in the next section entitled "Critical View of the Legislation of Deuteronomy."

[15]Benedict de Spinoza, *Tractatus Theologico-Politicus*, in *The Chief Works of Benedict de Spinoza*, 1670, trans. R.H.M. Elwes (London: George Bell, 1883), 124 [STTP].

[16]Subsequently head of the department of Near Eastern Studies at the University of Michigan.

Hellenistic Orient. . . there is hardly a single known case of *pia fraus*."[17]

Critical View of the Legislation of Deuteronomy; Bearing of Archaeology on the Problem

The critical theory has held that the social and moral level of the laws of Deuteronomy (as well as those of Exodus and Leviticus) were too advanced for the time of Moses and must be dated later in the history of Israel. This critical theory seemed to integrate with other reasons that were given for denying the Mosaic authorship of Deuteronomy and other books of the Pentateuch (see material in the preceding section).

Archaeological discoveries, however, have shown that the advanced laws of Deuteronomy and the rest of the Pentateuch do not have to be dated late in accordance with the supposition of the critical school. The Code of Hammurabi (written probably during the eighteenth century B.C.)[18] was found by a French archaeological expedition under the direction of M. Jacques de Morgan in 1901–1902 at the site of ancient Susa in what is now Iran, about 150 miles north of the head of the Persian Gulf. The code was written on a piece of black diorite, nearly eight feet high, and contained 282 sections or paragraphs. (See picture on page 55; also see PANET, 163–80.)

The Code of Hammurabi was written several hundred years before the time of Moses (c. 1500–1400 B.C.), and yet it contains some laws similar to those recorded by Moses. As noted in chapter 4, the Code of Hammurabi is actually late. It is similar in some respects to other ancient codes dating hundreds of years earlier. We now have traced the history of Mesopotamian

law codes back to the days of Abraham. In the light of this, the liberal has no right to say that the laws of Moses are too advanced for his time and could not have been written by him. This is acknowledged by Burrows, who says:

> Scholars have sometimes supposed that the social and moral level of the laws attributed to Moses was too high for such an early age. The standards represented by the ancient law codes of the Babylonians, Assyrians, and Hittites, as well as the high ideals found in the Egyptian Book of the Dead, and the early Wisdom Literature of the Egyptians, *have effectively refuted this assumption.*[19]

Some liberals have suggested in past years that perhaps Moses got his laws from the Code of Hammurabi. An examination of the Code during the earlier decades of this century has convinced most liberals, however, that there was no real connection between the Mosaic laws and the Code of Hammurabi. Such an acknowledgment was made by G.A. Barton, liberal professor at the University of Pennsylvania, who said, on the eve of World War II, "A comparison of the Code of Hammurabi as a whole with the Pentateuchal laws as a whole, while it reveals certain similarities, convinces the student that the laws of the Old Testament are in no essential way dependent upon the Babylonian laws" (BAB, 406). The Hammurabi Code contains many laws peculiar to itself, including those relating to soldiers, tax collectors, and wine merchants.

Why Were the Canaanites to Be Destroyed?

When Moses was giving his second address to Israel, he made it clear that the Israelites were not to compromise with

---

[17]W.F. Albright, "Archaeology Confronts Biblical Criticism," *American Scholar* 7, 2 (Spring 1938): 183 [AS].

[18]Note that the minimal chronology now dates Hammurabi 1728–1686 B.C. See W.F. Albright, "A Third Revision of the Early Chronology of Western Asia," BASOR 88 (December, 1942) and BASOR 106 (April, 1947), 19.

[19]BWMS, 56.

the natives of Canaan when the time of the conquest should come, but that they should drive out the Canaanites or destroy them (Deut. 7:1–5). The question has been raised as to how a good and loving God could order the driving out or destruction of great numbers of his creatures by their fellow creatures. The archaeological discoveries have given at least a partial answer, for they have shown that the Canaanites sacrificed their children, that their temples were places of vice, and that their morals were so low that they would inevitably corrupt the people of God if they remained in the land.

In fact, it may be argued that Canaanite morals and religious practices were so bad that they bred seeds of self-destruction. We should also observe that popular views of God today are far different from biblical views. To be sure, God is good and loving, but he is also just and holy and intolerant of sin, and he constantly reminds humankind of the ultimate judgment of sin. Also, there is a remarkable, blood-chilling verse tucked away in Genesis 15:16. In the context, God is talking with Abraham and is promising him and his descendants the land of Canaan as a permanent possession. But in the process God observes that the Hebrews will be out of the land for four hundred years and then will return once more, because "the sin of the Amorites has not yet reached its full measure," or quota. The intimation is that four hundred years later moral conditions among Amorites would be so bad that they would have reached divine limits, or their quota. Afterward, when the Israelites returned to the land, they were ordered to exterminate these foul people. Does God have quotas for all the peoples of the earth? If so, how near is contemporary society to the awful day of doom?

Copper out of the Hills
(Deuteronomy 8:9)

When Moses was giving the people the directions of the LORD concerning the conquest of Canaan, he said that Canaan was a land "where the rocks are iron and you can dig copper out of the hills" (Deut. 8:9). One day in Jerusalem, Nelson Glueck told me that many had thought the idea that copper might be found in Canaan was merely a "pious hope." It was Glueck who actually found the evidence of copper in the region to the south of the Dead Sea, showing the accuracy of this statement in Deuteronomy. In his explorations in southern Palestine, he found a large mining site at Khirbet en-Nahas, some twenty miles south of the Dead Sea. The surrounding hills were dotted with small ruined furnaces, and the whole area was black with heaps of copper slag. The rich copper veins that still protrude above the surface made mining a simple operation. Within a three-mile radius Glueck found three other large copper mining and smelting sites of which nothing had been recorded previously.[20] Referring to these copper and iron deposits, Glueck makes the interesting comment, "How accurate were the words of Scripture which spoke of 'a land whose stones are iron and out of whose hills you can dig copper' (Deut. 8:9)!" (GRJ, 146).

These ancient mines and mining camps are spread over an area of approximately four square miles in the western part of the Timna Valley, about thirteen to nineteen miles north of Eilat (Israel's port on the Red Sea). Earlier discoveries led to systematic Israeli exploration of the Timna Valley in 1959, to be followed by excavations in the area from 1964 to 1970 under the direction of Beno Rothenberg. Rothenberg showed that there were four periods of copper mining and smelting in this area. The first dated back to Chalcol-

[20]Nelson Glueck, "Explorations in Eastern Palestine and the Negeb," BASOR 55 (September 1934): 3–21, esp. 7–8. A photograph of a smelting furnace, made of stones, appears in GOSJ, 59.

ithic times in the fourth millennium b.c. The second occurred during the fourteenth through the twelfth centuries b.c., when the mining expeditions were royal projects of the Egyptian Nineteenth and Twentieth Dynasty pharaohs. This Egyptian activity came to an end by 1150 b.c. The mines were not operated again until the Roman period (1st–2nd centuries a.d.). During the Byzantine and Arab times a few minor sites were exploited.[21]

A Young Goat in Milk (Deuteronomy 14:21); Archaeological Light on This Rite

When Moses was giving certain restrictions and dietary laws, he repeated a command that appeared two times earlier in the Pentateuch, "Do not cook a young goat in its mother's milk" (Exod. 23:19; 34:26; Deut. 14:21). Though commentators have sought the explanation of this rather strange command, it was not until the discovery of the Ras Shamra tablets that a plausible explanation was forthcoming. A similar rite is recorded on the Ras Shamra tablets, which indicates that if one wishes to gain favor with a deity, he should slay a young goat in milk and present it to the deity. The discovery of this Ras Shamra text suggests why the

LORD prohibited this rite before the children of Israel entered Canaan. He was forewarning Israel of the pagan rites they would be tempted to practice in imitation of their pagan neighbors in Canaan.

Although a large number of scholars have followed this interpretation proposed by Harold L. Ginsberg in 1935, and it is commonly held today, Peter Craigie observes that more recent scholarship translates the Ugaritic text in question in a very different way and that it provides no background for Deuteronomy 14:21. He concludes, however, "It remains highly likely that the biblical text prohibits something central to the religion of Canaan and Ugarit."[22]

The Death of Moses (Deuteronomy 34)

After Moses had completed his fourth address and had pronounced his blessing on the tribes (Deut. 33), he died and the LORD buried him, "but to this day no one knows where his grave is" (Deut. 34:6). The fact that Moses' death is recorded at the end of Deuteronomy in no way proves that he could not or did not write the book itself (See the section entitled "Critical View of the Date of Deuteronomy," pages 101–2).

---

[21]See Beno Rothenberg, *Were These King Solomon's Mines?* (New York: Stein and Day, 1972).
[22]Peter Craigie, *Ugarit and the Old Testament* (Grand Rapids: Eerdmans, 1983), 76.

Chapter 10

The Conquest of Canaan

(Joshua)

**The New Leader—Joshua (Joshua 1);
Summary of Joshua's Earlier Life**

After the death of Moses, God commissioned Joshua to be the new leader of the people of Israel. Joshua first appeared in the history of Israel when the people were approaching the region of Mount Sinai and were attacked by the Amalekites at Rephidim (Exod. 17:8). Under Joshua's leadership the Israelites won a complete victory over the Amalekites (vv. 9–13). Later, Joshua is referred to as the aide of Moses, when he accompanied Moses to the foot of Mount Sinai, along with the other leaders. When Moses reached a certain point on the mountain, he told the other elders, "wait here for us until we come back to you" (Exod. 24:13–14). This seems to indicate that Joshua went on with Moses, being included in the "we." Blaikie believes that Joshua was with Moses during the six days when the glory of God remained on Mount Sinai and a cloud covered the mountain (vv. 15–16), but that when God called Moses to ascend still higher (vv. 16, 18), Joshua

remained behind, being in a place of rest halfway between the spot where the elders saw God's glory and the summit where God talked with Moses.[1]

Joshua was one of the twelve spies sent out from Kadesh to discover the condition of the land of Canaan and the people (Num. 13:1–3, 16–17); and of the twelve, Joshua and Caleb were the only ones who wanted to go right in and possess the land (Num. 13:30; 14:6, 8). Because of the unbelief of the people and because of their unwillingness to enter Canaan, God said that they should not see the land but would spend forty years in the wilderness, a year for each of the forty days that the spies had engaged in their surveillance mission (Num. 14:23, 33–34). In the account of the years of wandering, Joshua is not particularly referred to. It seems likely, however, that he continued to serve as Moses' aide, as he was doing at the time of the giving of the law on Sinai (Exod. 24:13). Now at the close of the forty years in the Sinai region and the wilderness, Joshua was appointed to succeed Moses as the new leader and received

[1]William Garden Blaikie, *The Book of Joshua*, The Expositor's Bible (New York: Funk & Wagnalls, 1900), 28 [BJ].

The Lion Gate at the entrance of the ancient Hittite capital at Boghaz-kale, east of Ankara

God's promise that "as I was with Moses, so I will be with you; I will never leave you or forsake you" (Josh. 1:5).

Archaeological Confirmation Concerning the Hittites (Joshua 1:4)

In describing the extent of the Promised Land to Joshua, God referred to "the Hittite Country" (Josh. 1:4). This is just one of almost fifty passages in the Bible that mention the Hittites. Even though they are referred to as often as this, some scholars in the nineteenth century expressed doubts as to the existence or at least the importance of such an ancient people. At the end of the nineteenth century, A.H. Sayce, a British Assyriologist, identified the Hittites of the Bible with the mysterious Hatti of the monuments (CBS, 98) and published his *Story of a Forgotten Empire* (1892), but E.A.W. Budge of the British Museum, writing in 1902, still expressed doubt concerning this iden-

tification, and said that it had been made "on insufficient grounds."[2]

Discoveries during the twentieth century, however, left no doubts concerning the Hittites. In 1906, Hugo Winckler of Berlin launched a German Oriental Society dig at Bogazköy (now officially Bogazkale, Hittite Hattusha), about 125 miles east of Ankara, Turkey, by modern road. The massive site of more than four hundred acres (compare the eight and one-half acres of biblical Jericho) proved to be the capital of the Hittite Empire. Within a year Winckler uncovered a large Hittite royal archive of over ten thousand clay tablets in the citadel area. This archive included a treaty between the Hittites and Ramses II (PANET, 201), dating to the thirteenth century B.C. The Germans continue almost annual excavations at Bogazkale, and excavations have proceeded at numerous other Hittite sites, including Sinjerli, Carchemish, Alishar, Malatya, Hama (Hamath), Tell Tainat, and Tell

[2]E.A. Wallis Budge, *Egypt and Her Asiatic Empire* (New York: 1902), 136.

Atchana. Of course efforts to translate Hittite have gone forward as well, and scholars at the University of Chicago are now preparing a Hittite dictionary. No longer is the existence of the Hittites questioned nor their importance doubted. One can earn a Ph.D. in Hittite studies at select universities in the United States and abroad.[3]

Sending the Spies to Jericho (Joshua 2); Location of Shittim

When Joshua prepared to send the spies to Jericho, Israel was encamped at Shittim (Josh. 2:1), the more complete name of which was Abel Shittim (Num. 33:49). The name apparently survived in Josephus' time (Josephus was a Jewish historian of the first century, A.D.) in the name Abila, a site that, according to Josephus, lay seven miles east of the Jordan River.[4] In this region potsherds have been found from the Late Bronze Age (1600–1200 B.C.), testifying to the occupation of this region in the period of Joshua (c. 1400). The area is bounded by two watercourses, giving evidence of availability of water even today. Garstang thinks this would have been a favored camping spot and that it seems to conform to the indications of the site of Shittim where the Israelites had their camp (GJJ, 127).

The spies, leaving Shittim, would have traveled six or seven miles west, crossed the Jordan, and then journeyed another six miles west to Jericho.

Archaeological Light on Rahab's House

At Jericho, the spies were given lodging in the house of Rahab (Josh. 2:1). She concealed them on the roof of her house when the king of Jericho ordered a search

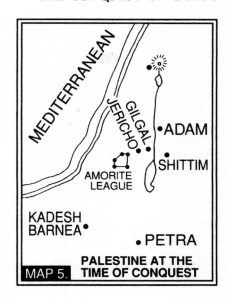

MAP 5. PALESTINE AT THE TIME OF CONQUEST

for these men, who were rumored to be in his city (vv. 2, 6). Rahab later let the men down from a window in her house, which was built on the town wall (v. 15). Excavations at Jericho now give an understanding of where Rahab's house may have stood. An outer stone revetment wall surrounded the mound on which the town was built. The revetment was in turn surmounted by a mud-brick wall. The revetment held in place a flat rampart, above which (higher up the slope) stood a second mud-brick wall that constituted Jericho's city wall proper. There were then two concentric walls with a flat area in between. When Ernst Sellin and Carl Watzinger excavated at Jericho before World War I, they found a number of houses just inside the revetment wall on the north side of the tell, and it is possible that one of these (the house of Rahab),

[3]For further information, see O.R. Gurney, *The Hittites*, rev. ed. (Baltimore: Penguin Books, 1961); J.G. Macqueen, *The Hittites*, rev. ed. (London: Thames & Hudson, 1986); C.W. Ceram, *The Secret of the Hittites* (New York: Knopf, 1956); Kurt Bittel, *Hattusha* (New York: Oxford University Press, 1970).

[4]Josephus, *Antiquities*, IV.8.1; V.1.1.

abutting the wall, had a window through the brick wall that stood on the revetment.[5] From such a window it would have been possible to lower the Israelite spies to the ground outside the city.

The Mountain to Which the Spies Went (Joshua 2:16)

When Rahab let the Israelite spies down from her house on the walls, she directed them to go to the hills to hide until their pursuers would return from their search (Josh. 2:16). A visit to Jericho makes it quite evident what Rahab was talking about when she mentioned the hills. Jericho lies in the plain of the Jordan, which at this point is about fourteen miles wide, with the Jordan flowing in the middle of the valley. Jericho is near the western edge of the valley. As one looks north, south, or east, no nearby hill meets the eye, only the flat plain of the Jordan. But just about a mile to the west lies the edge of a rugged plateau ridge, which is the beginning of the hills forming a part of the Judean Wilderness. Farther west these hills merge into the central mountain ridge of Palestine. The beginning of this mountain ridge, a mile west of Jericho, is so high that its shadow enfolds the city in the early afternoon. The cliff actually rises about fifteen hundred feet above the plain and presents numerous hiding places in the soft friable rock (GJJ, 133–34). It would have been to these hills that the spies hastened to conceal themselves for three days (v. 22), after which they would have traveled east across the plain, crossing the Jordan and continuing on to the camp at Shittim, where they reported to

Joshua the things they had seen (vv. 23–24).

Israel Crossing the Jordan; Room for Israel to Cross; Possibility of an Earthquake

Joshua led the children of Israel from the place where they encamped at Shittim across the plain some seven miles to the Jordan. At this point, the Jordan was ordinarily about one hundred feet wide, although at harvest time it was wider and measured about ten or twelve feet in depth.[6] God caused the Jordan to stop flowing so Israel could cross the river bed on dry ground. One might wonder how some two or three million Israelites would have room to cross the Jordan in a reasonable length of time. An examination of Scripture shows that the waters of the Jordan were stopped in the vicinity of the cities of Adam and Zaretan (Josh. 3:16). The location of Adam is marked by the present site of Damieh, some sixteen miles north of Jericho (GJJ, 136). Inasmuch as Jericho is a few miles north of the Dead Sea, this would give a stretch of at least twenty miles of dry river bed[7] over which Israel could cross. They would not have been restricted to a narrow passageway but could have crossed several hundred or even several thousand abreast. Even two or three million people could have crossed in a reasonable time.

I see no reason for accepting Garstang's idea that instead of six hundred thousand Israelite men there were only six hundred families, based on the idea that the Hebrew word *Alif* may mean "thousand" and also "family group" (GJJ, 120). By way of answer it may be said with

---

[5]Bryant G. Wood, "Did the Israelites Conquer Jericho?" *Biblical Archaeology Review* (March/April 1990), 46, 56 [WDICJ].

[6]It is difficult today to visualize what the Jordan was like in Joshua's day because Syrian, Jordanian, and Israeli use of water from the Jordan River system for irrigation and other purposes has reduced the river to an insignificant stream. This water use has also resulted in a continued shrinkage of the Dead Sea.

[7]This would include the sixteen miles north to Adam and the three or four miles from Jericho south to the Dead Sea.

Conder that the word Aleph (*Alif*) is used in the singular in Exodus 12:37, and so could not be rendered in the plural, "families." Furthermore, Keil and Delitzsch point out that the normal birthrate would produce six hundred thousand men after the four-hundred-year sojourn in Egypt (KD, 2:29).

It has been suggested that God may have used an earthquake to cause a landslide to stop the Jordan River. Scripture gives possible evidence of an earthquake at the time of Israel's entrance into Canaan. Referring to that time, Judges 5:4, says, "The earth trembled," and Psalm 114:3-4 says, "Jordan turned back; the mountains skipped like rams," which quite likely could be a poetic description of an earthquake.

At Damieh, the site of Adam, there are high banks that, when broken loose in a landslide, block the water. Such a blocking of the Jordan occurred in the year 1267 A.D., when a lofty mound overlooking the river on the west fell into it and dammed it up for sixteen hours (GJJ, 136-37). There was a similar occurrence in 1927, when a section of the cliff 150 feet high fell into the Jordan and blocked the water for twenty-one and a half hours (GJJ, 137). Whether God used an earthquake to effect a landslide to block the Jordan cannot be proved. It is certain, however, that at precisely the right time he caused the Jordan to cease flowing so that Israel could cross the river. The miracle would then be in the timing rather than in the means of accomplishing God's purposes.

Archaeological Light on the Walls of Jericho (Joshua 6)

God directed the Israelites to march around the walls of Jericho once each day for six days, and seven times on the seventh day (Josh. 6:3-4). They did so, and after the completion of the seventh circuit on the seventh day, the wall collapsed (v. 20).

When Garstang excavated Jericho (1930-1936) he found what he identified as the very walls of the ancient city. The discovery was so striking that a statement as to what was actually discovered was prepared and signed by Garstang; Père Vincent, a Catholic archaeologist; and by Clarence Fisher, a pottery and architectural expert. A part of this signed statement reads as follows:

> The outer wall suffered most, its remains falling down the slope. The inner wall is preserved only where it abuts upon the citadel, or tower, to a height of eighteen feet; elsewhere it is found largely to have fallen, together with the remains of buildings upon it, into the space between the walls which was filled with ruins and debris. Traces of intense fire are plain to see, including reddened masses of brick, cracked stones, charred timbers and ashes. Houses alongside the wall are found burned to the ground, their roofs fallen upon the domestic pottery within. (GJJ, 145-46)

Garstang summarized the evidence concerning the falling of the walls as follows: "As to the main fact, then, there remains no doubt: the walls fell outwards so completely that the attackers would be able to clamber up and over their ruins into the city" (GJJ, 146).

Excavations of Kathleen Kenyon at Jericho (1952-1958) demonstrated that the wall on top of the mound that Garstang dated to Joshua's day actually belonged to the period 3000-2000 B.C. and could have no connection with Joshua (WDICJ, 50). That fact does not alter Garstang's conclusions concerning the fall of the city, however. Kenyon herself discovered piles of bricks that had fallen down from the revetment wall surrounding the city (see "Archaeological Light on Rahab's House," page 109) and that would have enabled attackers to climb up into the city (WDICJ, 54). Moreover, in line with God's commands not to take from the city goods from which Israelites might benefit, abundant and valuable supplies of grain turned up in the excavation (WDICJ, 56).

Date of the Fall of Jericho

Garstang's findings in the excavations at Jericho (1930–1936) indicated that the city fell about 1400 B.C., shown in part by the fact that Mycenean ware did not appear in any quantity (GJJ, 146; cf. this book, chapter 7). This date also fits in with the biblical indication concerning the date of the Exodus,[8] which, on the basis of Garstang's interpretation of the Jericho material and on the basis of the biblical indications of chronology, would have been about 1446 B.C.

Some scholars, however, felt that the Jericho evidence pointed to a date later than 1400 for the fall of the city. Vincent dated the fall of Jericho between 1250 and 1200,[9] but G.E. Wright pointed out that the characteristic painted pottery of the period 1300–1200, with its scenes of animals, birds, and trees, is entirely absent at Jericho, and therefore the fall of Jericho must be earlier than 1300.[10] While Wright concluded that Jericho must have fallen before 1300, he saw no way to date it more closely than to put it within the period between 1475 and 1300.[11] Albright was reported (1942) to favor a date between 1375 and 1300,[12] and in a treatise published in 1948 (AOTA, 144), though undoubtedly written somewhat earlier, Albright concluded that Jericho fell "somewhere between 1400 and 1250."

Garstang, however, published a revision of his book *The Story of Jericho* in 1948 (GSJ). In this revision he sought to deal with opinions that conflicted with his conclusion that Jericho fell in 1400 B.C. (p. xiv). Garstang observed that few of these opinions were based on first-hand knowledge of the results of his excavation at Jericho and that many were lacking in logical reasoning or were based on preconceptions concerning the date of the Exodus. He stated that no commentator had as yet produced from the results of his excavation any evidence that City IV remained in being after the reign of the Egyptian king Amenhotep III (1413–1377 B.C.); the archaeological criteria of the age of the next Egyptian king, Akhenaton[13] (1377–1361), were "distinctive, plentiful, and well established," but the Jericho evidence did not include one fragment characteristic of the reign of this king. Garstang pointed out, furthermore, that Jericho was not mentioned in the Amarna Letters, which mentioned the other great cities of southern Canaan.[14] He saw no need to discuss the date of the fall of Jericho "as though it were a matter of debate," and said that if there had not been a controversy concerning the date of the Exodus, there probably never would have been any question of the date of Jericho's fall. He concluded that the date of 1400 B.C. was plainly indicated by the evidence, which the reader "may examine for himself" (p. xiv).

In regard to the absence of any quantity of Mycenean pottery, Garstang pointed out that it began to be imported from the Aegean area about 1400 B.C., and yet only one small fragment of this pottery was found inside the city, where the excavators examined more than 150,000 pieces of other types of pottery. Elsewhere, outside the city and in the tombs,

---

[8]See the sections entitled "The Pharaoh of the Exodus" (page 81) and "Date of the Exodus" (pages 86–89).

[9]Cf. H.H. Rowley, "The Exodus and the Settlement in Canaan," BASOR, 85 (February 1942): 31.

[10]G.E. Wright, "Two Misunderstood Items in the Exodus-Conquest Cycle," BASOR, 86 (April 1942): 33–34.

[11]Ibid., 34.

[12]Rowley, "Exodus," 31.

[13]Also spelled Ikhnaton.

[14]GSJ, 1948 ed., xiv, 126–27.

such specimens as were found were imitations of a later period and were not represented within the city's walls (p. 122).

Scholars generally were not prepared to accept Garstang's date for the fall of Jericho to the Hebrews. The debate about the matter contributed in part to Kathleen Kenyon's excavations at Jericho for the British School of Archaeology in Jerusalem (1952–1958). Although she concentrated on the neolithic levels at Jericho, she concluded that the city fell to Joshua somewhere between 1350 and 1325 B.C.[15] Kenyon's conclusion about various aspects of the Jericho dig led to a new round of debate that has continued to the present time. Kenyon herself died before the results of her fieldwork were published. These came in three separate volumes, which appeared in 1981, 1982, and 1983. Bryant Wood's independent assessment of this material concludes that Garstang was indeed right; Jericho fell about 1400 to the Israelites (WDICJ, 49–57).

The Capture of Ai (Joshua 7–8)

After the capture of Jericho, Joshua sent a detachment of men to capture the town of Ai, some fourteen miles to the northwest of Jericho. The three thousand Israelites were routed by the men of Ai (Josh. 4:4–5). The LORD permitted this defeat because one of the Israelites, Achan, had taken some plunder from Jericho at the time of its capture, contrary to God's command (Josh. 7:1, 20–21; cf. 6:18). After the sin of Achan had been judged, God told Joshua that Israel now would be able to take the city of Ai (Josh. 8:1). Joshua put an ambush of thirty thousand men between Bethel and Ai (vv. 3, 7), to which he added another ambush of five thousand (v. 12). The main body of the army under Joshua drew up on the north side of Ai, so that the people of Ai would see them and come out to attack (GJJ, 157). When the people of Ai attacked the main body of Israelites, the invaders fled, drawing their pursuers out toward the Jordan Valley, to the northeast (GJJ, 158). At this point, the ambush set fire to Ai (v. 19), and Joshua and his forces stopped their retreat and attacked the army of Ai (v. 21). The men of the ambush then came out of Ai, and the men of Ai found themselves in a pincers movement between the men of the ambush and the main army (v. 22). The pincers movement, used to so much advantage by Adolph Hitler during the early days of World War II, is not new; the Israelites used it against the men of Ai nearly 3,400 years ago. Following Israel's victory, Ai was burned (v. 28).

The site identified as Ai, now called Et-Tell, was excavated in 1934–1935 by Judith Marquet-Krause. She found that apparently the mound had not been inhabited between 2400 and 1200 B.C. (EAEHL, 1, 49). This constitutes a problem, since the Bible indicates that Ai was captured by Joshua and the Israelites, the probable date of which would be about 1400. It could not be as late as 1200 or as early as 2400. This does not mean that the Bible is wrong, but merely that we do not have the full light on the situation. Critics often use a case like this to demonstrate what they call the "inaccuracy of the Bible," when what is involved is incomplete knowledge. Years ago the biblical statements about Jericho, the ivory palace at Samaria, the tabernacle (see chapter 1), the Hittites, and many other items constituted problems and even supposed inaccuracies. One archaeological discovery after another has shown the accuracy of these biblical indications and a multitude of others. In the light of such discoveries even one who did not label himself as

---

[15]Kathleen Kenyon, *Digging Up Jericho* (New York: Praeger, 1957), 262; idem, *Archaeology in the Holy Land*, 3rd ed. (London: Ernest Benn, 1970), 211.

conservative[16] acknowledged, "Archaeological and inscriptional data have established the historicity of innumerable passages and statements of the Old Testament; the number of such cases is many times greater than those where the reverse has been proved or has been made probable" (W.F. Albright, AS, 181). I believe that further archaeological research will make it necessary to modify even the last part of this statement. I do not know of any cases where the Bible has been proved wrong. There are instances where we do not have full light, as in the case of the Philistines (see chapter 5) and the above-noted problem of Ai, but these do not prove error in the Scriptures.

A possible explanation of the problem concerning Ai was offered by the French Catholic archaeologist Père Vincent. He suggested that when the Israelites attacked Ai, the Canaanites of Bethel were merely using the site of the Early Bronze Age city as a fort or an outpost against the invaders.[17] This would mean that the outpost at Ai was of such modest proportions and temporary nature that it left no remains to betray its existence to the excavator. Other possible explanations have been offered, though none have been so widely received as that of Père Vincent (BWMS, 272–73).[18]

Perhaps the real solution lies in the suggestion of J. Simons[19] that Et-Tell is not to be identified with biblical Ai. He offered four objections to this identification: (1) Et-Tell is not particularly near Beitin (Bethel), whereas Joshua 12:9 indicates that Ai is "beside Bethel." (2) Et-Tell is a large site, whereas Joshua 7:3 describes the people as "few." (3) Et-Tell was not a ruin in the postconquest period, whereas Joshua indicates that Ai was destroyed (8:28). (4) There is no broad valley to the north of Et-Tell, whereas Joshua 8:11 indicates the existence of a valley near Ai.

When Professor Joseph A. Callaway of Southern Baptist Theological Seminary led a new expedition to Et-Tell in 1964, he concluded, "Nothing in the present evidence warrants an identification of the

---

[16]W.F. Albright well described his theological position in his "Memoriam" article on Melvin Grove Kyle. There he said, speaking of their association prior to 1919, "In those days, the fact that we were apparently at antipodes with regard to most crucial Biblical and oriental problems seemed to preclude all real friendship." Then he told of his association with Kyle in archaeological work in Palestine over a period of years (1921ff.) and added, "We seldom or never debated Biblical questions, but there can be no doubt that our constant association with the ever-recurring opportunity for comparing Biblical and archaeological data has led to increasing convergence between our views, once so far apart. To the last, however, Dr. Kyle remained staunchly conservative on most of his basic positions, while the writer has gradually changed from the extreme radicalism of 1919 to a standpoint which can neither be called conservative nor radical in the usual sense of the terms" (BASOR, 51 [September 1933], 5–6). By 1933, then, his position had come to be "neither conservative nor radical."

Writing in 1938, Albright described his position in similar terms. After pointing out the triumph of criticism in certain areas and institutions, he stated, "By now the reader doubtless considers the writer an extreme liberal, full of enthusiasm for the triumph of scholarship, as represented by Wellhausenism, over obscurantist orthodoxy. Actually, this is not true, and the writer's position is as far removed from the former as it is from the latter, as will become clear in the coming pages" ("Archaeology Confronts Biblical Criticism," American Scholar 7, 2 (Spring 1938), 179 [AS]).

In an oral communication to me in 1946, Albright indicated that he held essentially the same views as those expressed in the article in the American Scholar (1938).

[17]Revue Biblique (1937), 231–66 [RB], cited in BWMS, 76, 273.

[18]The explanation that it was Bethel that was captured and that the story was later transferred to Ai is hardly acceptable. This view is presented in G.E. Wright and F.V. Filson, The Westminster Historical Atlas to the Bible, rev. ed. (Philadelphia: Westminster, 1956), 116.

[19]Summarized in "Archaeological Digest" of the American Journal of Archaeology (July–September 1947), 311.

village with the city of 'Ai captured by Joshua as described in Joshua 8:1–29."[20] Apparently Callaway never quite gave up on the idea that Et-Tell was Ai, however. In a 1975 publication (after seven seasons of excavation at Et-Tell, 1964–1972) he seemed to accept the identification (EAEHL, 1:36). Presumably his chief problem was that no other more likely candidate for the site of Ai had yet turned up. More recently, John Bimson and David Livingston have proposed Khirbet Nisya, eleven miles north of Jerusalem, as the site of Ai, and they have excavated there for six seasons (1979–1986).[21] The jury is still out on this proposal, however.

If Et-Tell is not to be identified with Ai, then the indication that Et-Tell was not in existence in 1400 or 1250 B.C. has no bearing on the biblical indication concerning Ai. Or if Père Vincent's suggestion that Ai was a fortress, which would leave little or nothing in remains, is correct, again the biblical narrative offers no difficulty. Of course, if Khirbet Nisya or some other site should be identified as Ai, the problem would also be eliminated. In view of such possible solutions, it is inadvisable to *insist* that the Bible must be wrong.

The Southern Campaign (Joshua 9–10)

After the defeat of the people of Ai, a group of the native dwellers of Canaan, called the Hivites, came to Joshua and asked to make a league with him and the Israelites (Josh. 9:6). The Hivites pretended to have come from a great distance, and to carry out the deception, they wore old shoes and old garments and carried dry and moldy bread with them (vv. 12–13). Joshua made a league with them (v. 15) and thus obligated himself to come to the aid of the Hivites, who came from the four cities of Gibeon, Chephirah,

Beeroth, and Kirjath-jearim, all of them just a few miles to the northwest of Jerusalem. (For excavation at Gibeon, see chapter 13, "Establishment of David as King," page 133.)

When another group of native dwellers of Canaan, called the Amorite league, heard that the Hivites, headed by the town of Gibeon, had made a league with Joshua, they determined to make war with the Hivite league (Josh. 10:1–5). The men of Gibeon sent word to Joshua at Gilgal, where the Israelites were encamped, and Joshua made a night march from Gilgal to Gibeon, a distance of about twenty-four miles. Joshua and the Israelites fought against the Amorite league and defeated it (v. 10). It was during this battle that the miracle of the sun's standing still took place (vv. 12–14). The Amorite league was made up of five cities— Jerusalem, Hebron, Eglon, Lachish, and Jarmuth (vv. 5, 23), all in the south of Palestine (see map on page 109). With the conquest of these southern cities, the southern campaign was finished and the Israelites were ready for the northern campaign.

The Northern Campaign; Division of the Land

The northern Canaanites were gathered in a confederacy under the leadership of Jabin, king of the city of Hazor (Josh. 11:1). The Israelites defeated this coalition and burned the city of Hazor (vv. 11, 13). The site of Hazor, examined by Garstang, gave evidence of being burned about 1400 B.C. (GJJ, 197, 383).

Yigael Yadin, in his subsequent Hebrew University excavation at Hazor (1955–1958, 1968), claimed that Hazor did not fall to the Israelites until the second third of the thirteenth century B.C. (EAEHL, 2:494). But Scripture indicates that Hazor

---

[20]Joseph A. Callaway, "The 1964 'Ai (et Tell) Excavations," BASOR (April 1965), 27–28.

[21]John J. Bimson and David Livingston, "Redating the Exodus," *Biblical Archaeology Review* (September/October 1987), 48.

fell to the Israelites twice: in the days of Joshua (Josh. 11:10–11), when Jabin I ruled, and in the days of Deborah and Barak (Judg. 4:2, 23–24), when another Jabin ruled. Yadin assumed that Joshua's conquest was to be related to the destruction in the thirteenth century of the lower city of Hazor. There was, however, evidence of destruction at the site around 1400 B.C. or a little later in Yadin's Areas H and K of the lower city (EAEHL, 2:481–82). What is more natural than to conclude that the 1400 B.C. destruction dates to Joshua's day and the thirteenth-century destruction dates to the period of the judges?

Most of the remainder of the book of Joshua concerns the division of the land of Canaan among the twelve tribes of Israel.

Archaeological Light on the Period of the Conquest from the Amarna Tablets

The Amarna Tablets comprise a group of letters written by the kings of various Palestinian and Syrian cities to the two kings of Egypt who lived about 1400 B.C.[22] The tablets illuminate and confirm the picture the Bible gives of Palestine at that time. Canaan in the period of the conquest was subject to many local kings who ruled over individual cities with perhaps their surrounding territory. The book of Joshua (12:9–24) lists some thirty-one such kings with whom Joshua and Israel came in contact during the military campaigns in Canaan. At times some of these little city-states banded together for mutual aid against Joshua, as in the case of the king of Gezer who came to help the city of Lachish (Josh. 10:33). Sometimes they sought an alliance with Joshua, notably in the instance of the Hivites (Gibeonites), who forsook the group of Amorite cities banded together against Joshua, and asked that Joshua make a league with them (Josh. 9:11). As noted above, for their betrayal of the Canaanite-Amorite cause, the Hivite group was attacked by a coalition of five Amorite kings (Josh. 10:5). The Amarna Tablets confirm this picture of Canaan, for they were actually written by such kinglets who ruled over various cities. Seven of the letters were written by the king of Jerusalem, and others were from the kings of such places as Tyre and Sidon (BAHE, 383). They reflect the same general lack of unity among the city-states of Canaan as indicated in the biblical record.

Several of the Amarna Tablets tell of the invasion by a group called the Habiru. Some scholars believe that the Habiru are to be identified with the Hebrews under Joshua (BWMS, 271); it is at least possible that the Amarna Tablets reflect the conquest from the standpoint of the native dwellers of Canaan.

---

[22]See PANET, 483–90; Charles F. Pfeiffer, *Tell El Amarna and the Bible* (Grand Rapids: Baker, 1963); F.F. Bruce, "Tell el-Amarna," in *Archaeology and Old Testament Study*, ed. D. Winton Thomas (Oxford: Clarendon, 1967), 3–20.

Chapter 11

The Period of the Judges

(Judges)

The Book of Judges; Causes of Failure; Outline of the Book

The book of Judges recounts the history of Israel during the three and one-half centuries following the conquest of Canaan and the settlement of the land. According to Garstang's computation, the main part of the period of the judges falls between the oppression of Cushan[1] in 1367 B.C. and the beginning of the reign of Saul about 1025, giving a span of 342 years (GJJ, 62–65). The last part of this era, concerning Eli and Samuel, is described in the early chapters of 1 Samuel.

The book of Judges records the failure of Israel and their turning aside from the LORD. Their moral and spiritual decline was due to at least three factors: (1) failure to drive out the pagans (Judg. 1:21, 27, 29, 33), (2) idolatry (2:12–13), and (3) intermarriage with the pagans (3:5–6). The LORD had given specific instructions that the people of the land should be driven out or destroyed, but this command had not been carried out completely, and the people remained to corrupt the Israelites. In the era of the judges, Israel reaped the result of their disobedience in not driving out the degraded pagan peoples.

The book of Judges is often called "The Book of Failure," and as such, it may be conveniently outlined as follows: I. Cause of the Failure: presence of the pagans, idolatry, intermarriage with the pagans (1:1–3:6); II. Course of the Failure: apostasies, servitudes, and deliverances (3:7–16:31); III. Conditions Growing out of the Failure: apostasy, idolatry, civil war (chs. 17–21).

Authorship of the Book of Judges

Rabbinic tradition makes Samuel the author of the book of Judges, and the internal evidence confines it to Samuel's period. The expression "In those days Israel had no king" (Judg. 17:6 et al.) shows that the writer was familiar, as Samuel was, with the era when kings were ruling in Israel; and the indication that Jerusalem had not yet been taken by Israel shows that it was written before the time of David, for it was David who took the city (Judg. 1:21; cf. 2 Sam. 5:6–8).

[1]Rendered Cushan-rishathaim in Judges 3:8.

OPPRESSING NATION	TIME	DELIVERING JUDGE
1. Mesopotamia, under Cushan-Rishathaim	8 years	Othniel
2. Moab, under King Eglon	18 years (3:14)	Ehud
3. Canaanites, under Jabin of Hazor (4:2)		Deborah, Barak
4. Midian	7 years	Gideon
5. Abimelech (8:33–35 shows this fifth apostasy)		
6. Ammonites (10:9)	18 years (10:8)	Jephthah
7. Philistines (13:1)	40 years (13:1)	Samson

The Nature of the Office of the Judges; the Number of Judges

The office of the judge in Israel was unlike that of a judge today. The judges were primarily military leaders, raised up for particular national crises, but they also exercised an executive function.

By most commentators, the number of judges is computed as either twelve or thirteen. Some omit Barak, considering him the helper of Deborah; some omit Abimelech, considering him a petty king rather than a judge; Eli and Samuel are ordinarily omitted from the list of those strictly considered judges. In the following list, those who are usually considered judges are numbered. The most significant judges are italicized:

1. *Othniel*, of the tribe of Judah (3:9)
2. *Ehud*, a Benjamite (3:15)
   Shamgar (omitted in BBHM, 141)
3. Deborah, a prophetess (4:2) Barak (included with Deborah, BBHM, 141)
4. *Gideon*, of Manasseh (6–8)
5. Abimelech, son of Gideon (9:1; cf. 7:1. Raven makes him a king, ROTI, 161; BBHM, 141, includes him as a judge)
6. Tola, of Issachar (10:1, 2)
7. Jair, of Gilead (10:3)
8. *Jephthah*, of Gilead (11:1)
9. Ibzan, of Bethlehem (12:8)
10. Elon, of Zebulun (12:11)
11. Abdon, a Pirathonite (12:13; Pirathon, possibly six miles southwest of Nablus)
12. *Samson*, of Dan (13:2)

The Seven Cycles of Apostasy, Servitude, and Deliverance in the Book of Judges

Each time Israel went into apostasy and spiritual decline, God used one of the surrounding nations to punish the people and bring them to repentance. When the people cried for help, God sent a deliverer in the person of a judge, who, as military leader, delivered Israel from the oppressor nation.

This sequence of apostasy, servitude, and deliverance occurred seven times, and may be outlined in the chart (above).

Critical View of Judges: "Good Stories"; Garstang's Statement; Archaeological Confirmation

The critical view holds that Judges is made up of stories about Israel that were handed down and finally committed to writing in a late period, about 550 B.C. according to Pfeiffer (PIOT, 315). The beginning and end of the book (1:1–2:5 and chs. 17–21) were supposedly added even later, probably in the third century B.C. (PIOT, 337).

I took a course a few years ago in the Hebrew text of the book of Judges. Quite often the professor would remark, "These are *good stories* and I like them; they're just like the stories the Arabs tell around the campfire today over in the Near East." The Bible believer, however, wants to know whether these are just "good stories," containing a mixture of myth, legend, and fact, or are really the Word of God, recording actual events in this period of Israel's history.

Garstang's statement in regard to the historicity of Judges is significant, particularly so because he held to the documentary theory.[2] Garstang wrote:

> We find no reason to doubt that the historical narrative contained in the Books of Joshua and Judges, so far as it was derived from the old sources J and E, was founded upon fact. Further, in view of the remarkable accuracy and fullness of topographical detail. . . it is difficult to believe that these records were not written down in any form until the ninth or eighth century B.C. (GJJ, 341)

Archaeological discoveries have confirmed one item after another in the book of Judges, showing its accuracy and validity. We will now consider some of these confirmations.

Canaanite Leaders (Judges 1:10); Archaeological Evidence of These Names

The first chapter of Judges states that two Canaanites, apparently leaders of Hebron, were named Ahiman and Talmai. These names also appear as Canaanite names in the Ras Shamra Tablets (AOTA, 145), showing that they fit in the same general period as the time of the judges.

Jerusalem Not Captured (Judges 1:21); Archaeological Indications Concerning Other Cities

We find the indication in Judges 1:21 that at the time of the Israelite conquest of Canaan, they did not drive out the inhabitants of Jerusalem. The fact that Israel did not take Jerusalem is confirmed by the Amarna Tablets, which show that the king of Jerusalem remained loyal to the pharaoh of Egypt.[3]

According to the Bible, Bethel was destroyed during the early period of the judges (1:23–25), and excavations there in 1924 showed that the town was completely destroyed during that period (AOTA, 145). The Bible indicates, on the other hand, that during this same period Bethshan, Megiddo, and Gezer were thriving towns (1:27, 29), but not subject to the Israelites. The excavations at these latter sites show the correctness of this indication that they were not held by Israel at the time of the judges (AOTA, 145).

Archaeological Evidence of the Early Existence of Hazor (Judges 4:2)

The third group that oppressed the Israelites during the period of the judges were the Canaanites, under King Jabin of Hazor (Judg. 4:2). If these stories in Judges are a late creation, reflecting both myth and legend, how would the writers of the stories know that such places as they mention really existed in the days of the judges (1350–1050)? As an example, consider the city of Hazor. The archaeological work there showed that it was in existence in the days of the judges and, in fact, was destroyed during the second half of the thirteenth century. The excavator, Yigael Yadin, attributed this destruction to the forces of Joshua, though I have

---

[2]The JEDP analysis. See chapter 2, the section entitled " Critical View of Genesis 1 and 2," pages 22–23. See also chapter 2, footnotes 2–7.

[3]For details, see GJJ, 218. The Amarna Tablets apply to this situation in the conquest and the time of the judges if one accepts the early date of the Exodus (1446 B.C.). See chapter 8, section entitled "Date of the Exodus," pages 86–89.

The temple of the house of Berith, Shechem

argued earlier that it occurred during the days of the judges.[4] Likewise, destruction at Debir (Judg. 1:11) and Bethel (v. 22) took place during the thirteenth century, as shown in the excavations.[5] Thus the book of Judges again commends itself as trustworthy, as excavations at sites referred to in the book have shown these places to have been in existence and to have suffered destruction during the thirteenth century B.C.

Writing in the Days of Gideon (Judges 8:14); Archaeological Evidence

The fourth oppression of the Israelites was imposed on them by the Midianites for a period of seven years (Judg. 6:1). In this instance the Lord raised up Gideon to deliver Israel. Gideon did so with his hand-picked commando group of three hundred men (7:7–25). Following the expulsion of the Midianites, Gideon, wishing to learn the names of the chief men of Succoth, caught a young man

from this place and had him write down the names of the principal men of the town (8:14). According to the older critical view, that writing was not well developed until about 800 B.C., Gideon's young man would likely have been unable to write the list of names. Archaeological discoveries have abundantly answered this older view concerning writing, by revealing well-developed writing before the days of Gideon, not only in the other Bible lands but in Palestine as well. Albright pointed out that archaeological evidence from the Palestinian sites of Lachish, Bethshemesh, and Megiddo indicates the use of the Hebrew alphabet written in ink in the fourteenth and thirteenth centuries B.C. (ASAC, 193). Moreover, Albright reported that the earliest known alphabetic inscriptions, dating between 1800 and 1500 B.C., were found at Gezer, Shechem, and Lachish in Palestine.[6] Burrows acknowledges that "the fact that Gideon could find a young man who was able to write

[4]EAEHL, 2:494. See discussion under "The Northern Campaign," in the preceding chapter, pages 115–16. Yadin led an excavation at Hazor for five seasons from 1955 to 1958 and in 1968.
[5]See discussion under "Date of the Exodus," in chapter 8, pages 86–89.
[6]Noted in correspondence with the reviser, Howard F. Vos.

indicates a high degree of literacy in the Early Iron Age population of Transjordan (Judg. 8:14)" (BWMS, 183).

The House of Berith (Judges 9); Archaeological Evidence of Burning

The son of Gideon, Abimelech, sought to gain power in Israel but soon found himself opposed by the men of Shechem. When Abimelech and his followers attacked the town of Shechem, the Shechemites shut themselves in an inner fortress called the "stronghold of the temple of El-Berith" (Judg. 9:45–46). In order to gain this stronghold, Abimelech and his men gathered wood, piled it about the structure, and set fire to the wood pile (v. 49). Archaeological confirmation of such a burning was found in 1926 in the excavations of the German archaeologist Sellin. He found a building from this period that he identified with the "House of Berith." The pottery evidence showed that it had been built about 1300 B.C. and was finally destroyed by burning about 1150 (BAB, 113–14). The event therefore falls within the period of the judges in which Abimelech lived. This correlation between the destruction recorded in Judges 9 and archaeological investigation was confirmed by the Drew-McCormick excavation at Shechem (1956–1966) under the direction of G.E. Wright (See EAEHL, 4:1092).

Archaeological Light on the Philistines in the Days of Samson (Judges 13–16)

God raised up Samson to deal with the Philistines. The Bible clearly shows that the Philistines not only existed but also exercised extensive power at this time. Much of the biblical indication concerning the Philistines, however, used to be doubted by the critics. Pfeiffer, speaking of the time of Samson, referred to the "legendary and fabulous beginnings of

the conflict with the Philistines" (PIOT, 342). Archaeology, on the contrary, has given factual evidence concerning the power of the Philistines. It is probably this evidence that caused Pfeiffer himself to admit that in the days of Eli and Samuel (1 Sam. 4) "the author continues the story of the same conflict on solid historical ground" (PIOT, 342).

Philistine archaeology is just beginning to come into its own. An introduction to Philistine study (now somewhat dated) is Edward E. Hindson, *The Philistines and the Old Testament* (Grand Rapids: Baker, 1971). The most definitive treatment of the Philistines and the various Philistine sites is Trude Dothan, *The Philistines and Their Material Culture* (New Haven: Yale University Press, 1982). This book describes Philistine remains at twenty-eight sites in Palestine. Dothan continues to excavate at Ekron (Tel Mikne), one of the five major centers of the Philistines (Gaza, Ashdod, Ashkelon, Gath, and Ekron). The only Philistine cultic center excavated to date has appeared at Tel Qasile (on the northern outskirts of Tel Aviv), as a result of the work of Amihai Mazar.[7] With every passing year we experience an increase in our knowledge of the Philistines during the days of the judges. There is no longer any doubt about the significance of this ancient people.

The Dark Days at the Close of the Period of the Judges (17–21); the Crime at Gibeah; Civil War; Archaeological Confirmation of the Burning of Gibeah

The last chapters of the book of Judges (17–21) give us the picture of apostate priests (17:1ff.), idolatry (v. 3), sexual crimes (19:25), civil war (20:14), and almost every other type of sin. The mistreatment of the Levite's concubine by the wicked men of Gibeah (19:25) caused her death.

---

[7]See Amihai Mazar, *Archaeology of the Land of the Bible* (New York: Doubleday, 1990 [MALB]), 300–328, for a discussion of the Philistines in general and Qasile in particular.

The holy of holies of the Philistine temple at Tel Qasile

The Levite then cut her body in pieces and sent a piece to each of the districts of Israel as a horrible reminder of the event (vv. 23–30). Since the crime had occurred at the town of Gibeah, in the territory of Benjamin, the rest of Israel determined to fight against the Benjamites and particularly against the town of Gibeah (20:8–9). The men of Benjamin mustered their troops, twenty-six thousand strong (20:13), including their slinger division of seven hundred left-handed slingers (v. 16). The civil war culminated in the defeat of the Benjamites (v. 35) and the burning of Gibeah (vv. 37, 40). The historicity of these events that culminated in the burning of Gibeah has often been doubted. Confirmation of the burning of the town, however, was found in Albright's excavation of that site.[8] The first stratum of remains in the fortress, dating from the time of the judges, had been burned as described in the Bible (v. 40). The sin and confusion in the period of the judges is well summed up in the last verse of the book: "Everyone did as he saw fit" (Judg. 21:25).

As we have examined the events of the book of Judges, we have found that archaeological discovery has helped to confirm the validity of the records. The book cannot be set aside as a collection of "good stories such as are told about the campfire in the Near East."

[8]AAPB, 47; AOTA, 147; BWMS, 281.

Chapter 12

The Beginning of the Monarchy

(1 Samuel: Eli, Samuel, Saul, David)

The Book of First Samuel; Contents

The two books of Samuel were originally a single volume in the Hebrew Bible, as shown by the Talmud. When the Greek translation of the Old Testament (Septuagint) was made, it required more space because the vowels were not written in the ancient Hebrew language; hence the book of Samuel was divided into two books when it was translated into Greek (probably in the second or third century B.C.). The Hebrew text was divided into two books for the first time in 1516 A.D. in the edition of Daniel Bomberg, and thereafter this division became current. In the Greek and Latin Bibles, the books of 1 and 2 Samuel and 1 and 2 Kings are called I, II, III, and IV Kingdoms (PIOT, 338; ASOTI, 282).

The contents of 1 Samuel deal with two main subjects—the judgeship of Samuel (1–7) and the reign of Saul (8–31). The book may be analyzed by chapters as follows:

1. Birth of Samuel
2. Childhood of Samuel
3. Vision of Samuel
4. Eli's death
5. Ark a curse to the Philistines
6. Ark returned
7. Revival and victory over Philistines
8. Israel's demand for a king
9. Saul chosen
10. Saul anointed (privately, v. 1; publicly, vv. 17, 25)
11. Saul's conquest of the Ammonites
12. Samuel's proclamation of the kingdom (v. 13)
13–15. Wars of Saul and his rejection
16. David chosen
17. Goliath killed
18. David's marriage to Michal
19–23. Enmity of Saul toward David
24–26. David's sparing of Saul's life
27–30. David in Philistia
31. Saul's death

The Character and Work of Samuel

Samuel is called a judge[1] and also a prophet (1 Sam. 3:20), and as such he is sometimes characterized as the last of the judges and the first of the prophets. Samuel established the schools of the

[1]Samuel's work as judge is recorded in 1 Samuel 7:6, 15, 17.

prophets at Rama (about five miles north of Jerusalem); he also served as the leader who anointed Saul (10:1, 24) and David (16:1, 13) as kings of Israel.

Childhood of Samuel; Last Days of Eli; Power of the Philistines (1 Samuel 1–4)

During the time that Samuel was growing up under the guardianship of Eli at the tabernacle (1 Sam. 2:18ff.), Israel was having difficulties with the Philistines. Finally the elders of Israel thought that if they took the ark of the covenant with them to battle, they might overcome the powerful Philistines (1 Sam. 4:3–4). The presence of the Philistines in Canaan at this time is specifically illuminated by archaeological discoveries (see the preceding chapter).

At the bidding of the elders, the people of Israel brought the ark of the covenant from Shiloh in order to take it with them as they went out to meet the enemy Philistines (1 Sam. 4:4–5). During the battle that ensued, the Philistines took the ark, and the sons of Eli were slain (4:11). When Eli received the report of these events, the shock was so great that he fell over backward and broke his neck (4:17–18).

The Ark in the Temple of Dagon (1 Samuel 5); Archaeological Light on Dagon

After the Philistines had captured the ark of the covenant, they brought it to Ashdod to the temple of their god, Dagon (1 Sam. 5:1–2). The next morning they found Dagon fallen on his face before the ark. They set him in his place, but the following morning they found the god not only fallen again, but with his hands broken off (vv. 3–4). When other calamities came upon the Philistines, they finally sent the ark back to the Israelites (1 Sam. 6–7).

Archaeological light and confirmation concerning the god Dagon have been brought out by excavations. A temple of Dagon, identified by the inscriptions, has been found at Ugarit (the ancient name of Ras Shamra), as well as two steles erected to the same god.[2] The Ras Shamra tablets also mention Dagon, the grain-god, whose son was Baal (AARI, 74). Albright points out that actually Dagan[3] was one of the oldest Accadian deities and was worshiped all through the Euphrates region as early as the twenty-fifth century B.C.; he believed that Dagan was undoubtedly a vegetation deity, though the original meaning of the name is as yet unknown (AARI, 74). Interestingly, there is a town called Bet or Beit Dagan in Israel today, located about halfway between the airport at Lod and the city limits of Tel Aviv. The name, meaning "house of Dagon," preserves the name of the ancient deity Dagon, the god of the Philistines.

Why Was the Ark Brought to Kiriath Jearim? (1 Samuel 6–7): Archaeological Confirmation Concerning Shiloh

In order to send the ark back to the Israelites, the Philistines put it on a cart drawn by two cows, which took it to the town of Beth Shemesh, a few miles to the southwest of Jerusalem (1 Sam. 6:7–8, 10, 12). Word was sent ahead to the men of the town of Kiriath Jearim, a few miles nearer to Jerusalem, who brought the ark to their town, where it remained (1 Sam. 7:1).

The question arises, "Why was the ark brought to Kiriath Jearim, to remain there, rather than to Shiloh (nineteen miles north of Jerusalem), where it had been taken earlier by the Israelites?" It is likely that Shiloh had been destroyed by

---

[2]W.F. Albright, *Archaeology and the Religion of Israel* (Baltimore: Johns Hopkins Press, 1942), 42, 106 [AARI].

[3]An early Semitic form DAGAN, could easily give, as a later form, DAGON.

the Philistines either after the battle of Ebenezer (1 Sam. 7:11–12), or a little later (AARI, 104). Jeremiah definitely indicates that the Shiloh sanctuary was desolate in his day (Jer. 7:12, 14; 26:6, 9), about 600 B.C., and it is quite likely that this desolation dated from its probable destruction by the Philistines about 1050 (PIOT, 343; AARI, 104).

Confirmation of the biblical indication of the desolation of Shiloh was found in the excavation by the Danes, under Aage Schmidt, 1922–1931 (BAB, 127–128). This excavation showed that Shiloh was occupied from the thirteenth to the eleventh centuries B.C., but not for some centuries after about 1050. This is exactly what one would expect, for the Israelites established the ark at Shiloh in the fourteenth or thirteenth century (Josh. 18:1), and later the site became desolate, probably about 1050, and at least the area of the sanctuary was still desolate in the days of Jeremiah, as this prophet tells us. Robinson comments, "Indeed, all that has been found by the Danes at Shiloh agrees exactly with what is implied in the Old Testament" (RBA, 172). Although Pfeiffer is very weak in his inclusion of material on archaeology in his book on Old Testament introduction,[4] he does acknowledge this archaeological discovery at Shiloh in a two-line footnote (PIOT, 343).

Since 1981, I. Finkelstein of Bar-Ilan University in Tel Aviv has been excavating at Shiloh. The expedition confirmed that the town was destroyed by an intense fire in the mid-eleventh century B.C. and that it remained desolate until a small settlement was established there during the Iron II period (900–600).[5]

The archaeological discoveries at Shiloh are all the more significant because scholars holding the critical view frequently asserted in the past that the story of the tabernacle at Shiloh was a late fiction (AOTA, 147). This view was based, in large part, on the theory that the part of Exodus telling of the tabernacle was a late document (see chapter 2, section entitled "Documentary Theory," pages 22–23), dating from the sixth century B.C. However, when the Danish excavation showed that Shiloh was at the height of its prosperity in the period of the judges, as indicated in the Bible, and that it was destroyed by a fire in the days of Eli and Samuel (c. 1050), it was evident that the skeptical attitude toward the historicity of these events was "sheer nonsense" (AOTA, 147).

The Beginning of the Monarchy; Saul as King (1 Samuel 8–15)

The chronology of the events and characters involved in the establishing of the monarchy is outlined by Garstang (GJJ, 65) as follows:

(1) Eli	1065–1045 B.C.	20 years as leader	
(2) Samuel	1045–1025 B.C.	20 years as leader	
(3) Saul	1025–1010 B.C.	15 years as king	
(4) David	1010–971 B.C.	40 years as king	

During the later days of Samuel, Israel asked for a king. Samuel was displeased at this request, but the LORD pointed out that Israel had not rejected Samuel but in reality had rejected the LORD as their ruler (1 Sam. 8:7). Saul was then chosen to be king, and Samuel anointed him (1 Sam. 10:1) in a private ceremony, and later in a public ceremony before all of Israel (vv. 17, 25). Saul engaged in war against the Ammonites (1 Sam. 11:11ff.), against the Philistines (13:1ff.), and against the other enemies of Israel (14:47).

During the time of strife with the Philistines, Saul intruded into the office of

---

[4]Albright criticized him for this in his review of Pfeiffer's book (JBL [June 1942], 112).

[5]*Excavations and Surveys in Israel* (Jerusalem: Israel Department of Antiquities and Museums, 1984), 2, 100.

The sanctuary area at Shiloh

the priesthood, offering a sacrifice himself (1 Sam. 13:9–10). Samuel told Saul that he had disobeyed the commandment of the LORD, and he announced that Saul's kingship would not continue indefinitely (v. 14). Saul's line did not continue on the throne of Israel after his death, but was supplanted by David and his descendants. Even during this period of Saul's life, the LORD indicated that David would be the next king (1 Sam. 16:1ff.).

Davidic Music (1 Samuel 16ff.); Critical View; Archaeological Light

David's musical ability was evident from the time he was a young man, for when Saul requested a man who could play well, David was brought to play for him (1 Sam. 16:17, 21, 23). David's interest in music is also shown by the fact that the author of Chronicles attributes to David the organization of the guilds of temple musicians (1 Chron. 23:5–6).

As Albright points out, the critical theory holds that the formal establishment of classes of temple musicians and musical guilds is strictly postexilic (after c. 538 B.C.), and that the attribution of their

founding to David is aetiological in origin (AARI, 125). An aetiological story is one that is invented to explain a known fact, like the story, for example, that the robin got its red breast by getting too close to the fire. According to the critical view, some late writer tried to explain the existence of the temple choirs and classes of musicians in Israel, supposedly a late development, by attributing their founding to David. Albright pointed out in 1942 that "until the past year or two this position was difficult to refute, since external evidence was totally lacking" (AARI, 125).

Archaeological discoveries show, however, that the critic has no right to say that David could not have developed the temple music, for the excavations show a definite development of music and musical instruments not only in David's time (c. 1000 B.C.), but also very much earlier (see chapter 3). The tombs at Beni-Hassan in Egypt, about 170 miles south of Cairo, dated about 1900 B.C., show Asiatic Semites coming into Egypt with musical instruments; one of them carries a lyre, which antedates David's time by nearly a thousand years.[6] Tomb No. 38 at Thebes in Egypt (c. 1420) portrays a girl with a lyre and another girl with a double oboe.[7] A vase from Megiddo (c. 1025) pictures a lyre that came from the time of David.[8] Pictorial representations and material remains from Egypt, Mesopotamia,[9] and Palestine show a high development of musical instruments from an early period (before 2000) down to the time of David and later.

For example, from the Royal Cemetery at Ur, dating to about 2500 B.C. have come the remains of nine richly ornamented lyres, a harp, and a set of pipes (see, e.g., PANEP, 61 and index). The so-called Standard of Ur, picturing a banquet scene with entertainment provided by a male lyre player and a singer dates from the same period. And from the Ur III period (twenty-first century B.C., the time of Abraham) come numerous hymns replete with musical terminology.[10] Unfortunately, most of the critical views concerning the Bible were spun out in the days before Near Eastern studies began to come into their own. Many of these positions no longer seem to have much validity as archaeological discoveries throw increasing light on the civilizations that provided the cultural context for the ancient Israelites.

Albright believes that evidence for the antiquity of the musical guilds is to be seen in the Canaanite character of some of the names of these guild musicians. The name Chalcol (Calcol) appears in 1 Chronicles 2:6, and the same name appears on the Megiddo ivories, dating from the thirteenth century B.C. Two other of these musicians, Ethan and Heman (1 Chron. 2:6) are closely paralleled by scores of abbreviated names found at Ras

Shamra (Ugarit) and elsewhere in the late second millennium B.C. (AARI, 127). Albright says that these names, thanks to archaeological discoveries (AARI, 127), prove the correctness of the biblical indication concerning early musical guilds. Although I do not agree with every implication of Albright's development of this idea, it is certainly true that the evidence supports the conservative view of the Bible in a very definite way.

The Later Life of Saul and His Death (1 Samuel 17–31); Archaeological Light on Ashtaroth and Beth Shan

After David killed Goliath (1 Sam. 17), Saul's hostility toward David increased. On more than one occasion Saul tried to kill David, but David was spared. Twice when David came upon Saul, he had opportunity to harm him, but with generosity of spirit he did not take advantage of the king (1 Sam. 24, 26). For some time it was necessary for David to take refuge with the Philistine people (1 Sam. 27–30). Happily he was spared the bitterness of having to fight with the Philistines against his own people, since some of the Philistines, fearing treachery on David's part (1 Sam. 29:4, 9), did not wish to have him with them. Finally Saul engaged in battle with the Philistines at Mount Gilboa in northern Palestine (1 Sam. 31:1ff.). Saul was wounded and, in order to avoid being taken by the Philistines, fell on his own sword (1 Sam. 31:3–4). When the Philistines found the body of Saul, they took it to the city of Beth Shan, fastened it to the wall of the city and put Saul's armor in the temple of Ashtaroth, referred to in the Bible as "the house of Ashtaroth" (v. 10). Our archaeological and historical

---

[6]For picture of this tomb painting, see PANEP; also see article by O.R. Sellers, *Biblical Archaeologist* (September 1941), 37. Also, BAB, figure 1; POTH, 80; PMOT, 170.

[7]Sellers, *Biblical Archaeologist*, 39.

[8]Ibid., 33.

[9]Evidence of early musical instruments in Mesopotamia is noted in chapter 3 under "Early Civilization," 36–37.

[10]See D.A. Foxvog and A.D. Kilmer, "Music," ISBE, 1986 ed., 3:436–49.

The mound of Beth Shan

sources show that Ashtaroth was one of the best known fertility goddesses. She was known in certain areas in the Near East under the names Ashtart and Astarte, and to the Babylonians as Ishtar. She is pictured on a seal found at Bethel (BWMS, 230).

The excavations at Beth Shan, where Saul's body was placed, showed that the city was destroyed between 1050 and 1000 B.C., the approximate period of David and Saul. It is likely that the destruction of the town was due to military action on the part of David after the death of Saul (AAPB, 40; BWMS, 251).

Archaeological Light on the Temples of Ashtaroth and Dagon at Beth Shan (1 Samuel 31:10; 1 Chronicles 10:10)

The University of Pennsylvania expedition at Beth Shan (1921–1933) unearthed a temple the excavators identified with the temple of Ashtaroth, in which Saul's armor had been placed (1 Sam. 31:10). This temple was found on the extreme south side of the tall summit and had been built, as shown by the excavation, before the time of Saul, and therefore would have dated back to his time. It was about twenty-four meters long (c. 80 feet) and nineteen meters broad (c. 62 feet), with its axis running west to east, and contained a long central hall with three circular stone bases on either side. It was assumed that wooden columns must have been set on these bases. At the center column base on the south side of the wall was discovered a foundation deposit, consisting of a container filled with ingots, rings, and earrings of gold and silver.[11]

Within the temple, a monument of basalt was found. It bore a figure of the goddess Ashtaroth, depicted as wearing a long dress and the conical crown customary for all Syrian goddesses, with two feathers attached. She held a sceptre in her left hand and the sign of life in her right hand. She is referred to as "Anaitas" (Antit), which Rowe, the excavator, says is

[11]Alan Rowe, "Discovery of the Temple of Ashtaroth: Report of the Expedition to Palestine," *Museum Journal* 16, 4 (December 1925): 311.

a variant form of the name Ashtaroth.[12] Rowe concludes that all the available evidence shows that the temple was constructed by the Egyptian dwellers in Beth Shan in honor of the goddess Ashtaroth.

As indicated in 1 Chronicles 10:10, there was a second temple at Beth Shan, namely, the house of Dagon, where Saul's head was placed. The excavations revealed a temple to the south of the house of Ashtaroth, which Rowe identified with this second temple mentioned in the Bible. He asserted, in conclusion, that the Chronicles reference indicates two temples at Beth Shan during the Philistine regime, and the excavations have certainly "proved that such was the case."[13]

[12]Ibid., 310.

[13]Alan Rowe, "The Temples of Dagon and Ashtoreth at Beth-shan," *Museum Journal* 17, 3 (September 1926): 298.

Chapter 13

David's Reign

(2 Samuel; 1 Chronicles 11–29)

The Report of the Amalekite Concerning Saul's Death; Explanation (2 Samuel 1)

The report of Saul's death was brought to David by an Amalekite who escaped from the camp of the Israelites after the Philistines defeated Israel (2 Sam. 1:2–3). According to the Amalekite, he came upon Saul and slew him at his request (2 Sam. 1:9–10). On the other hand, the record at the end of 1 Samuel indicates that Saul fell on his own sword and died (31:4–5). These accounts are not necessarily contradictory, for there are at least two possible explanations of the facts as we have them: (1) The Amalekite was lying. Many commentators hold this view, explaining that possibly the Amalekite saw Saul's act of suicide and then thought of turning it to his own advantage by fabricating the story that he had acceded to Saul's request to kill him (JFB, 195; Lange [LC], 363). (2) Saul's armorbearer merely thought that Saul was dead (1 Sam. 31:5), but Saul was not actually dead, only wounded; he later raised himself on his spear and begged the Amalek-

ite to kill him. In this case the Amalekite was telling the truth![1]

Pfeiffer says critics have generally concluded that the same author could not have written both accounts of the death of Saul. But Pfeiffer, in this case, does not follow the critical view, for he says, "After giving the true version of Saul's death in I Samuel 31, the author has a right to assume that the reader will recognize the falsehood of the Amalekite's report in II Samuel 1" (PIOT, 350–51). As noted above, the facts may harmonize very easily in at least two different ways.

David's Elegy Over the Death of Saul (2 Samuel 1:17–27)

In the Hebrew text of the Bible David's elegy over the death of Saul is entitled "the bow" (2 Sam. 1:18), and the KJV supplies the words "The use of," thus giving us the reconstructed full title, "The use of the bow." The ASV suggests a better phrase, perhaps, to fill out the sense, "The song of the bow." The NIV calls it the "lament of the bow."

In regard to authorship, even one as liberal as Pfeiffer acknowledges the rela-

[1]Note on 1 Samuel 31:3 in Scofield Reference Bible.

131

tionship of this passage to David: "His authorship of the poem is unquestionable. The deep pervading emotion shows that it was composed immediately after the battle of Gilboa, under the first shocking impression of the calamity. . . . The poet's grief is intense and sincere but nevertheless virile" (PIOT, 351).

Blaikie fittingly says of the song, "The song embalms very tenderly the love of Jonathan for David," and he likewise points out the implied patriotism: "The thought of personal gain from the death of Saul and Jonathan is entirely swallowed up by grief for the public loss" (BBS, 9). David shows a true love for his enemies, mourning the death of Saul as that of a friend. Some of the thoughts of the poem have become a part of our everyday language, particularly the phrase "How are the mighty fallen" (vv. 25, 27 KJV).

Possible Archaeological Light on the Text of David's Elegy (2 Samuel 1:21)

The remarkable agreement among the various manuscripts of the Bible has long been recognized by scholars. Regarding the New Testament, Hort pointed out that only one word in a thousand appears with sufficient variation in different manuscripts to make necessary the services of a scholar in deciding between the readings. The Hebrew manuscripts of the Old Testament that have survived also show very little variation, as pointed out by William Henry Green (see this book, chapter 1, section entitled "Accuracy of the Text of the Bible," pages 14–15).

Sometimes, however, scribes have made "slips of the pen" in copying the ancient manuscripts of the Bible, and occasionally ancient documents recovered by excavation have enabled us to correct such readings. An interesting possibility of a case of this type has been suggested by H.L. Ginsberg (JBL, 1938,

209–13) and is summarized by Burrows (BWMS, 39). It concerns the verse in David's lament over Saul and Jonathan which reads, "Ye mountains of Gilboa, let there be no dew, neither let there be rain, upon you, nor fields of offerings" (2 Sam. 1:21 KJV). The expression "fields of offerings" seems somewhat strange, for in this context one would expect, as parallel to dew and rain, some reference to water, rather than to "fields of offerings." Commentators have never found a completely satisfying explanation of this awkward expression.

In one of the Ras Shamra tablets that records the poem of "Dan'el," Ginsberg pointed out a passage that curses the land in words similar to those of David: "Seven years may Baal fail, even eight the Rider of the Clouds; *nor dew, nor rain, nor upsurging of the deep*, nor sweetness of the voice of Baal!" The word in the Ras Shamra tablets rendered "deep" is related to the Hebrew word translated "deep" in Genesis 1:2 (*tehom*), which is similar in appearance to the word for "offerings" in 2 Samuel 1:21. The Hebrew word for "fields" also looks like the Ras Shamra word rendered "upsurging" if both are written in Hebrew characters.[2] On this evidence, Ginsberg has suggested that the original text of David's poem read, instead of "fields of offerings," the similar looking words "upsurging of the deep," referring to the mountain springs that were fed by the fountains of the deep. According to this explanation, the present text would be due to the error of a copyist who was misled by the resemblance of the words, and the original text would have read, "Ye mountains of Gilboa, let there be no dew, neither let there be rain upon you, nor upsurging of the deep." Burrows acknowledges that one cannot say this explanation is certain but feels that it does offer an interesting and possible explanation of a difficult passage (BWMS, 39).

---

[2]Also cf. H.L. Ginsberg, "Ugaritic Studies and the Bible," BA (May 1945), 56.

In regard to the discoveries that concern the actual text of the Bible, Burrows acknowledges that

> on the whole such evidence as archaeology has afforded thus far, especially by providing additional and older manuscripts of the books of the Bible, strengthens our confidence in the accuracy with which the text has been transmitted through the centuries. . . they have also shown that not only the main substance of what has been written but even the words, aside from minor variations, have been transmitted with remarkable fidelity, so that there need be no doubt whatever regarding the teaching conveyed by them. Regarding what Amos, Isaiah, Jesus, or Paul thought and taught, our knowledge is neither increased nor altered by any of the manuscripts discovered" (BWMS, 42).

The Establishment of David as King; Fall of Ishbosheth (2 Samuel 2–5)

Following the death of Saul, there were actually two kings reigning in Israel. David was anointed to be king by the men of Judah at the town of Hebron (2 Sam. 2:3–4), some twenty miles south of Jerusalem, and Ishbosheth, the fourth son of Saul, was established as king by Saul's military commander at the town of Mahanaim (v. 8), in the territory of Transjordania, east of the Jordan River.

At one point in the struggle between the two kings, a meeting of the followers of Ishbosheth and the followers of David took place by the pool of Gibeon (2 Sam. 2:12–13). When negotiations apparently broke down, the two groups fell upon each other with the sword. The site of Gibeon, identified with present-day El Jib, a few miles north of Jerusalem, was excavated from 1956 to 1962 by Professor James Pritchard of the Church Divinity School of the Pacific. He discovered a large rock-cut pool nearly thirty-eight feet in diameter which he identified with the pool where the followers of Saul's son and of David fought. (EAEHL, 2, 447).

A series of events led to the downfall of Ishbosheth. Abner, the military commander of Saul and Ishbosheth, took a concubine of Saul as his wife, and Ishbosheth rebuked him for doing so (2 Sam. 3:7). Abner, angered by the rebuke, proposed to turn the kingdom over to David (v. 12), but during the negotiations, Joab, the military commander of David, slew Abner at the gate in Hebron (2 Sam. 3:27). A short time later, two of Ishbosheth's captains murdered Ishbosheth (2 Sam. 4:2, 5–6), and the northern tribes of Israel then acknowledged David as their king (5:3).

The Capture of Jerusalem; Method of Conquest (2 Samuel 5:6–9; 1 Chronicles 11:4–8)

The conquest of Jerusalem is described briefly in 2 Samuel 5:6–9 and 1 Chronicles 11:4–8. From these verses the general situation is clear. The Jebusites felt secure behind virtually impregnable fortifications—so much so that they said the blind and lame could ward off the attacks of David. David was determined, however, and offered the captaincy of the armed forces to the one who would lead a successful attack against the Jebusite defenders. Joab earned the reward promised by David.

A problem arises, however, in interpreting the method Joab used to accomplish this military feat. Second Samuel 5:8 speaks of ascending the "gutter" in the KJV, the "watercourse" in the ASV, and the "water shaft" in the RSV and NIV. In recent decades, the common opinion has been that the city water supply was in view here and that the "watercourse" was to be identified with a discovery of Sir Charles Warren at Jerusalem. He found that since there was no natural water supply within the walls of the ancient city, a water channel had been cut leading from a point inside the walls to the Spring Gihon, or the Virgin's Fountain, on the outside. More specifically, a horizontal tunnel leading from the spring had been dug into the hill on which the city was located; this ended in a cave that served as a cistern. Above the cave rose a 52-foot vertical shaft, which connected with a sloping passageway 127 feet long. The entrance to this passageway was inside the city wall. Women could then descend the sloping passage to the vertical shaft and lower their waterskins into the cave to procure a water supply, in spite of military forces that might be encamped outside the walls. Joab supposedly discovered this water system, ascended the passageway, and entered the city at night, delivering it into the hands of David.

J. Garrow Duncan took issue with this suggestion, asserting that it is almost humanly impossible to scale the shaft, which is very steep. Furthermore, the sides of it have been worn almost smooth by the constant rubbing of waterskins, to say nothing of the fact that it is so narrow at one point that a large man could not even get through.[3] A. Rendle Short claimed, however, that some British army officers were able to accomplish this feat in 1910.[4] The water system was finally cleared in 1980, and two young Americans subsequently did manage to ascend the shaft.

Duncan also argued that Warren's Shaft led into the lower part of the Jebusite city only, and thus still would not have given David access to the fortress area. In reporting his excavations at Jerusalem, he claimed that part of the eastern wall of the lower city was battered in during Davidic times and that David therefore forced his way into the lower city.[5]

Duncan, puzzled with the meaning of tsinnor, translated "watercourse" in the

ASV, pointed out that in Aramaic and Arabic its connotation is "hook."[6] Albright believed that was the real solution to the matter and identified it as a hook used in scaling ramparts.[7] The resultant translation, then, would be "whoever gets up by means of the hook and smites the Jebusites." The NEB follows Duncan and Albright by translating tsinnor with the word "grappling-iron."

Kathleen Kenyon, in her 1961–1967 excavations at Jebusite Jerusalem, discovered that the city wall was not located as far up the slope of the hill as Duncan, Macalister, and others would have put it. Therefore if Joab and his men had ascended the channel of the city water supply in their conquest of Jerusalem, they would have been able to enter the strategically important parts of the town. And she concluded that David's men did indeed capture the city in this way when they made it the capital of Israel about 1000 B.C.[8]

In his new 1990 study, Amihai Mazar of the Hebrew University in Jerusalem concludes that Warren's Shaft should probably be dated to the period of the divided monarchy (after the division at Solomon's death in 931 B.C.) and before the days of Hezekiah (716–687) (MALB, 480–81) and that it definitely was not the "Sinnor" of the Jebusites (MALB, 31).

To complicate the discussion further, the Revised English Bible, published in 1989, reversed itself on the translation of 2 Samuel 5:8 and now phrases the passage as follows: "Everyone who is eager to attack the Jebusites, let him get up the water-shaft to reach the lame and the blind." At least two issues currently face the biblical interpreter: (1) What is the meaning of the Hebrew word tsinnor?

[3]J. Garrow Duncan, The Accuracy of the Old Testament (London: SPCK, 1930), 136–38.

[4]A. Rendle Short, Modern Discovery and the Bible, 3rd ed. (London: InterVarsity, 1952), 182.

[5]Duncan, Accuracy of the Old Testament, 138–41.

[6]Ibid., 141.

[7]William F. Albright, "The Old Testament and Archaeology," in Old Testament Commentary, ed. Herbert C. Alleman and Elmer E. Flack (Philadelphia: Muhlenberg, 1948), 149.

[8]Kathleen Kenyon, Royal Cities of the Old Testament (New York: Shocken, 1971), 24–27.

(2) When should Warren's Shaft be dated? At the present time a final answer to either question does not seem to be forthcoming.

The Capture of Jerusalem; Archaeological Light on Millo (2 Samuel 5:6–9; 1 Chronicles 11:4–9)

The city of Jerusalem had not been taken over by the Israelites in the days of Joshua and the judges.[9] But now David, after a rule of seven and a half years in Hebron (2 Sam. 5:5), went against Jerusalem and captured it through the strategy of his military commander, Joab (vv. 7–8; 1 Chron. 11:5–6).

In connection with David's building activities after taking Jerusalem, the Bible says that he "built the city round about, even from Millo" (2 Sam. 5:9; 1 Chron. 11:8 KJV). Commentators have not been sure just what the word "Millo" referred to; some have suggested that it was "perhaps a corner tower" (JFB). The Hebrew word means "filling," being a form of the word used in Genesis 1:28, where the Lord told Adam and Eve to "fill the earth" (the KJV reads "replenish"; it is really the word "fill"). Possible archaeological light on the identity of this Millo or "filling" was found by Macalister in his excavation at the northern end of the ancient Jebusite city of Jersalem. He found a breach or opening in the north wall and the remains of a fortress that had apparently been constructed to fill the gap in the wall. Macalister identified this fortress as the Millo, or filling (MCEP, 106). Duncan, who was associated with Macalister in this excavation, also believed that Millo was at the north end of the early city of Jerusalem.[10] Thus archaeology illuminates the "Millo," which oth-erwise would be merely a word to us. The NIV has "supporting terraces."

Jerusalem the Political and Religious Capital of Israel (2 Samuel 5–6)

In making Jerusalem the political and religious capital of Israel David took three important steps: (1) he captured the city (2 Sam. 5:8) and thus made it the possession of Israel; (2) he had a palace built for himself there (2 Sam. 5:11); and (3) he brought the ark from the house of Abinadab (Obed-Edom), where it had remained after it was returned by the Philistines (1 Sam. 7:1–2), and placed it in the tent he had erected for it in Jerusalem (2 Sam. 6:12, 17). Thus with the establishment of the palace and the worship at Jerusalem, this city effectively became the political and religious center for Israel. The significance of Jerusalem for Israel (and eventually for the church and the world) down through the centuries may be traced back to the days of David (c. 1000 B.C.).

King Hiram of Tyre (2 Samuel 5:11); Archaeological Light

David was aided in the construction of his palace at Jerusalem by Hiram, the king of Tyre (2 Sam. 5:11; 1 Chron. 14:1). Possible archaeological light on King Hiram was found when a French excavation of Jebeil or Byblos[11] in 1923–1924 uncovered a sarcophagus[12] on which was inscribed in Phoenician writing the name Ahiram, equivalent to the biblical Hiram (BAB, 128). This may possibly be a reference to the biblical King Hiram, or one of his line, inasmuch as the inscription dates no earlier than the eleventh or twelfth

---

[9]Judges 1:21. Also see this book, chapter 11, section entitled "Jerusalem Not Captured."
[10]J. Garrow Duncan, *Digging up Biblical History* (New York: Macmillan, 1931), 115 [DDBH].
[11]Called Gebal in Bible times. See Ezekiel 27:9.
[12]Montet, *Syria*, vols. 3 and following, cited BAB, 128.

century B.C. (ARDBL, 18; AARI, 40), and may be dated as late as 975 B.C.[13]

One should be cautious here, however, for the sarcophagus was found at Byblos, and the biblical Hiram was king of Tyre. Of course the inscription does show that someone by the name of Hiram was important in Phoenicia about 1000 B.C., about the time of David, and it gives a greater ring of authenticity to the biblical narrative.

The Davidic Covenant (2 Samuel 7)

The realization that the ark of the covenant resided in a tent caused David to propose that he build a house or temple for the LORD (2 Sam. 7:2). The Lord showed David that one of his family or "seed" would build the house for the Lord instead (7:12–13), and at the same time God made several other promises to David, which are usually known as the Davidic covenant. According to 7:16, this covenant provided that David should have (1) a "house," that is, a posterity; (2) a "throne," that is, royal authority; (3) a "kingdom," that is, a successor on the throne; and (4) perpetuity of the kingdom, that is, a throne that should last "forever." This last provision is to be fulfilled in the reign of Christ, for as the angel announced to Mary, "the Lord God will give him the throne of his father David." Christ "will reign over the house of Jacob forever," as the rightful heir of David (Luke 1:32–33).

David's Victories (2 Samuel 8–10)

David smote the Philistines (2 Sam. 8:1), Moabites (8:2), and the Syrians of Damascus (8:5) and extended his control to the south, over the area of Edom (8:14). When the emissaries of David went over into the Ammonite region to the east of the Jordan, the Ammonites shaved off the beards and cut off half the clothes of David's men and then sent them back. When David heard how the Ammonites had insulted his emissaries, he went out against the Ammonites, who were joined by the Syrians in battle against David (2 Sam. 10:7–8).

Archaeological Light on the Extent of the Davidic Empire (2 Samuel 8:1ff.)

Albright pointed out a tendency, inaugurated by scholars such as Hugo Winckler and developed by men like Hermann Guthe, to reduce the extent of the Davidic empire. The Bible indicates that David's empire included Damascus and the area of Zobah (2 Sam. 8:3, 6; 1 Chron. 18:3, 6). But liberal scholars have excluded Damascus from the empire of David and have located Zobah, the land of King Hadad-ezer (whom David conquered), in the Hauran, the area to the east of the Sea of Galilee. Archaeological discoveries, however, have given us much light on the Assyrian provincial organization and have demonstrated conclusively that Zobah, which the Assyrians called Subatu, lay north of Damascus and not south of it.[14] Thus the biblical indication that David's empire extended up to the north of Damascus in the area of the city of Homs (Hums) is confirmed by these archaeological discoveries. Albright concluded, "It follows that the biblical narrative is perfectly reasonable geographically. . . . David's empire then extended from the Gulf of Aqabah in the south to the region of Hums in the north, and it remained,' at least nominally, in Solomon's hands until his death or shortly before" (AARI, 131).

---

[13]As indicated by the sherds found by Dunand in the tomb of Ahiram. This has been pointed out by Albright in his *Archaeology of Palestine* (Harmondsworth-Middlesex, Penguin Books, 1949), 191 [AAP].

[14]E. Forrer, *Die Provinzeinteilung des assyrischen Reiches* (1921), 62, 69, cited in AARI, 131; AOTA, 149.

David's Sin; God's Punishment
(2 Samuel 11-12)

During the war between Israel and the Ammonite-Syrian coalition, Israel was able to overcome the Syrians (2 Sam. 10:18-19), but it was necessary to continue the battle against the Ammonites and to besiege their city of Rabbah (2 Sam. 11:1ff.). At this time David made the acquaintance of Bathsheba and committed adultery with her (11:3-4) while her husband, Uriah, was fighting in the armies of Israel against Rabbah. David tried to cover up his sin, but when this failed (vv. 5-9), he had Uriah assigned to a front-line battle position so that he would be killed (vv. 14-17). After the death of Uriah, David took Bathsheba as his wife (v. 27).

God's punishment of David for his sin was threefold. The Lord told David that (1) the sword would never depart from his house (12:10); that is, he would have wars and rebellions; (2) others would commit sin with his wives (v. 11); and (3) the child that would be born to him by Bathsheba would die (v. 14).

Several lessons are connected with the sin of David: (1) David was a great man, yet he sinned; how foolish are those who trust their own hearts rather than in the Lord to direct their ways. (2) David's sin is not excused, but condemned. It was a wicked act, and God so labels it. (3) David repented deeply (Ps. 51) and confessed his sin; but because he had given the enemies of the Lord occasion to blaspheme, the threefold punishment was not removed (2 Sam. 12:13-14).

David's Later Days (2 Samuel 13-24)

David's later days were beclouded by the rebellion of his son Absalom (2 Sam. 13-19), by the rebellion fostered by Sheba (2 Sam. 20:1ff.), by the three-years' famine (2 Sam. 21), and by David's sin of numbering the people (2 Sam. 24).

Chapter 14

Solomon's Reign

(1 Kings 1–11; 2 Chronicles 1–9)

The Book of 1 Kings; Contents; Outline

In the Hebrew Bible, 1 and 2 Kings were originally one book, and, as in the case of 1 and 2 Samuel, when the Hebrew text was translated into Greek, it was divided into two books. In modern Hebrew Bibles, the material has been divided into two books ever since the publication of the Rabbinic Bible of Daniel Bomberg at Venice in 1516 (ASOTI, 282).

The contents of 1 Kings deal with three main subjects: (1) The last events of the life of David (1:1–2:11); (2) the reign of Solomon (2:12–11:43); and (3) the events of the first seventy-five years of the divided kingdom (12–22), running from about 931 B.C. (the death of Solomon) through the reign of Ahab (874–853), and into part of the reign of Ahab's son Ahaziah (853–852).

The contents of 1 Kings may be outlined by chapters as follows:

1. Anointing of Solomon
2. Death of David
3. Wisdom chosen by Solomon
4–5. Alliance with Hiram
6–8. Temple built and dedicated

9–11. Greatness of Solomon and his reign
12–22. Divided kingdom

David's Last Years; Adonijah's Rebellion (1 Kings 1)

David was approaching the age of seventy as he came to the end of his forty-year reign (2 Sam. 5:4). At this time, David's fourth son, Adonijah, the oldest one living, laid plans to seize the throne (1 Kings 1:5). It is evident that Adonijah was a good example of a spoiled child, for we are told that "his father had not displeased him at any time" (v. 6). As Lange well comments, "A perverted parent love is self-punished" (LC, 27), for if the father does not "trouble" the son, the son will "trouble" the father.

Adonijah secured the help of the military leader, Joab, and the aid of the priest, Abiathar (1 Kings 1:7). Abiathar's willingness to help in the rebellion may have been due to fear that Zadok, another priest, might replace him. Adonijah now felt that he had the "church and the army" behind him; but his plans were upset when Nathan the prophet and Bathsheba, the mother of Solomon, advised David of the situation (vv. 11, 15, 24).

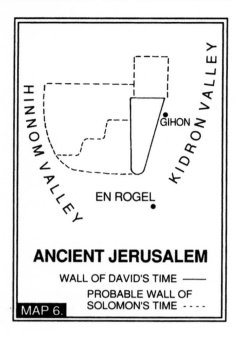

ANCIENT JERUSALEM

WALL OF DAVID'S TIME ——
PROBABLE WALL OF
SOLOMON'S TIME - - - -

MAP 6.

mon was here at Gihon, while Adonijah and his friends were at the spring En Rogel, some seven hundred yards farther south in the Kidron Valley. A knowledge of the relative positions of Gihon and En Rogel permits a vivid reconstruction of this event. Solomon and Adonijah were out of sight of each other due to the terrain of the Kidron Valley, yet they were close enough that the shout of the multitude at Gihon could have been heard by the followers of Adonijah at En Rogel (v. 9 shows that Adonijah was at En Rogel). See map 6.

When Adonijah's friends heard that Solomon had been anointed king (1 Kings 1:43), the meeting broke up very quickly and they dispersed (v. 49). Then Adonijah became afraid of Solomon (v. 50), his ostentation and boasting ending in cowardice and cringing.

David settled the matter of succession by ordering that his son Solomon be anointed by Zadok the priest at the spring Gihon (vv. 33–34). Solomon was duly anointed, and when the assembled people shouted, "God save the king," the shout reached the ears of Adonijah and his guests, who were gathered near En Rogel (vv. 39–41; cf. v. 9), some distance away.

Topographical Light on Solomon's Anointing Ceremony as Heard by Adonijah

How could Adonijah have heard so readily the shout of the people at the anointing ceremony of Solomon (1 Kings 1:41)? The older commentaries are wrong in locating the spring Gihon on the west side of Jerusalem (LC, 24). Gihon is to be identified with the source of water that today is called the Virgin's Fountain, located just under the brow of the southeastern hill, some four hundred yards north of the south end of the hill. Solo-

David's Charge to Solomon; Death of David (1 Kings 2)

As David came to his closing days, he charged his son Solomon to walk in the ways of the Lord. The play on words in David's injunction "Observe what the Lᴏʀᴅ your God requires" (2:3) is best appreciated in the original language, which may be rendered, "Observe the observances," since the two words are from the same verbal root.

David's charge concerning Joab indicated that he was not to be allowed to live (1 Kings 2:5–6), and an examination of the situation shows the reason. Joab was guilty of the following offenses: (1) the murder of Abner (2 Sam. 2:27ff.), (2) the murder of Amasa (2 Sam. 20:8ff.), and (3) active conspiracy against Solomon on behalf of Adonijah (1 Kings 1:7).

David died at the age of seventy, having begun his reign at the age of thirty. He ruled for seven years at Hebron and thirty-three years at Jerusalem, following the capture of that city. The dates of his reign are probably 1010–971 B.C.

Solomon the King; Alliance with Pharaoh; Choice of Wisdom
(1 Kings 3)

After the death of David, Solomon began his reign of forty years (971–931 B.C.).[1] Solomon soon made himself a relative of the pharaoh of Egypt by marrying his daughter (1 Kings 3:1). The identity of this pharaoh has always been a matter of interest to Bible students. Barton believes that it was either Siamon (976–958) or Pesibkhenno II (958–945) (BAB, 20). Knight also indicates Pesibkhenno II as the pharaoh with whom Solomon made an alliance.[2] The tomb of this king was found in excavations in the delta of Egypt and was opened in March, 1939. The royal sarcophagus was opened about February, 1940.[3] Breasted, however, feels that the pharaoh with whom Solomon had to deal was the next king of Egypt, Sheshonk I (945–924),[4] because the biblical description fits an energetic king such as Sheshonk I, and not the degenerate kings at the end of the twenty-first dynasty, such as Siamon or Pesibkhenno II (BAHE, 529). Future discoveries may enable us to determine with certainty which of these pharaohs was the father-in-law of Solomon.

The Lord appeared to Solomon in a dream and said, "Ask for whatever you want me to give you" (1 Kings 3:5). Solomon asked for an understanding heart, and in response God said that he would give him (1) a wise and understanding heart (v. 12), (2) riches and honor (v. 13), and (3) length of days if he would walk in God's ways and keep his statutes (v. 14). The first two were unconditional, and the last one was conditional. Solomon asked only for an understanding heart, but the Lord gave him much more, showing that if one asks for the right thing, God will also give many other things. "Seek first his kingdom and his righteousness, and all these things will be given to you as well" (Matt. 6:33).

The Greatness of Solomon's Empire
(1 Kings 4:21; 2 Chronicles 9:26)

The greatness of Solomon's empire is definitely indicated in Scripture (1 Kings 4:21; 2 Chron. 9:26), yet because of the great empires of Assyria on the Euphrates and Egypt on the Nile, it might seem unlikely that such a kingdom as Solomon's could have existed. Archaeological discoveries show us, however, that precisely during the period 1100–900, when the kingdom of Israel was being built up, the "weak and inglorious twenty-first dynasty" was ruling in Egypt, Assyria had gone into a period of decline, and the Hittite Empire in Asia Minor had come to an end, and the glory of the Myceneans had disappeared in Greece. There was a power vacuum in the Mediterranean world and the Near East. Thus God in his providence overruled so that "Solomon ruled over all kingdoms from the River to the land of the Philistines, as far as the border of Egypt" (1 Kings 4:21).

Solomon's Phoenician Friends (1 Kings 5:1; 2 Chronicles 2:3); Archaeological Light on Phoenician Activity

When Solomon prepared to build the temple, he received aid from King Hiram of Tyre. We have already seen that the name Hiram, in the form Ahiram, was found on a sarcophagus excavated at Jebeil in Syria (see chapter 13). The biblical references to the Phoenician king Hiram and to his subjects indicate that the Phoenicians were a people of some

---

[1]The factors involved in the chronology of the period of the kings are dealt with at the beginning of chapter 15.

[2]KNJ, 270. He spells the name Pasebkhanut; it is rendered Psou Sen Nef by others.

[3]See *Illustrated London News* (March 9, 1940) [ILN].

[4]Spelled Shishak in the Bible (1 Kings 14:25).

importance (1 Kings 5:8–9, 18; 9:27), yet earlier in the twentieth century, writers such as Salomon Reinach and Julius Beloch denied the validity of such references to important Phoenician activity as early as this period.[5] Archaeological inscriptions, however, in the Cyprus Museum and on the Island of Sardinia, dating back to the ninth century B.C., reveal early Phoenician activity in the Mediterranean, as implied in the biblical references to Solomon's relations with the Phoenicians. Albright comments on the significance of these inscriptions in this way: "Once more we find that the radical criticism of the past half century must be corrected drastically. . . . Incidentally the Biblical account of Solomon's reign is again proved to be historically reasonable."[6]

Solomon's Temple; Its Size and Appearance (1 Kings 6ff.; 2 Chronicles 3:1)

The temple proper was sixty cubits long and twenty cubits wide (1 Kings 6:2), just twice the size of the tabernacle (Exod. 26:16, 18). If the cubit is taken as a foot and a half, as shown by the Siloam tunnel and inscription,[7] then the floor plan of the temple would have been ninety by thirty feet. It was divided into two rooms. The inner one, the Most Holy Place or the oracle, was a cube, twenty by twenty cubits (1 Kings 6:16, 20); the outer chamber, or Holy Place, was forty by twenty cubits.

The floor and walls were of stone, covered with cedar, and in turn overlaid

with gold (1 Kings 6:16, 21–22). Around the temple on the two sides and back, chambers were constructed (vv. 5–6), and across the front there was a porch twenty cubits long and ten cubits wide (v. 3), decorated with two large pillars (1 Kings 7:15, 21).

Archaeological Light on the Temple

Wright[8] points out that with the information given in the Bible and

with the aid of a wealth of archaeological data it is possible to reconstruct it in a general way, even though no remains of it have ever been found in Jerusalem. . . . It was a comparatively small building standing on a platform in a walled-in courtyard. . . . The over-all interior length, including the width of the dividing walls, would thus have been c. 135 feet, and the interior width c. 35 feet. . . . The structure was probably built entirely of the type of hewn and carefully bonded stone which we have previously noted in Solomonic construction at Megiddo, but the interior was lined with cedar and was highly decorated with Phoenician motifs. . . . In the rear room (Holy of Holies) were two olivewood cherubim, standing c. 17 feet high and overlaid with gold leaf, under whose outstretched wings the Ark was placed. . . . In the exterior court were the large altar of burnt offering, the lavers, and the bronze "sea." The latter was a tremendous bowl, c. 17 feet in diameter, c. 8 feet high, and holding c. 10,000 gallons of water. It was cast in the clay beds of the Jordan Valley at Adamah. The "sea" and the bronze pillars placed in front of the Temple (1 Kings 7:15ff.) were so large that we marvel

---

[5]W.F. Albright, "New Light on the Early History of Phoenician Colonization," BASOR, no. 83 (October 1941): 14–15.

[6]Ibid., 22. In a lecture at the Archaeology Conference at Wheaton College, October 16, 1961, Albright reported on Phoenician materials dating to the tenth–ninth centuries B.C. that were discovered in Spain during the late 1950s.

[7]See chapter 3, the article entitled "The Flood; the Size of the Ark," pages 38–39.

[8]G. Ernest Wright of McCormick Theological Seminary, Chicago, and Harvard. His field was archaeology and Old Testament studies.

at the genius of the artisan Hiram who cast them.[9]

Archaeological Light on Solomon's Use of "Dressed Stone and Trimmed Cedar Beams" (1 Kings 7:12)

The record in 1 Kings tells us that the courts of Solomon's palaces were constructed of "three courses of dressed stone and one couse of trimmed cedar beams" (1 Kings 7:12). Archaeological light on this type of construction was found in the University of Chicago excavation at Megiddo. There the remains of a large building consisted of well-cut stone foundations, the upper surfaces of which were burned black. Fragments of mud brick and ashes from the superstructure lay scattered about. From these ashes was taken a piece of charred wood, which was shown by chemical analysis to be cedar, indicating that the superstructure was built with a "half timber" type of construction similar to the courts of Solomon, which were made with rows of hewn stone and cedar beams. Guy, the excavator, was inclined to see Hittite influence in this type of construction, though it may be indirect influence.[10]

Solomon's Stables (1 Kings 9:19; 2 Chronicles 8:6); Archaeological Confirmation

The Bible indicates that Solomon had whole cities given over to the stabling of his horses (1 Kings 9:19), yet such features of the glorious reign of Solomon were once thought to be late legendary additions to Scripture, and it was easy to suggest that "Solomon was really a very insignificant ruler" (AAPB, 46). The University of Chicago excavation at Megiddo

(1925–1939) identified the fourth stratum as Solomonic and discovered there two stable compounds capable of housing about 450 horses (EAEHL, 3: 830–55; for a picture of a stable and reconstruction, see PANEP, 232). J.W. Crowfoot subsequently sought to date these stables a little later than Solomon's time and to assign them to the days of Omri and Ahab,[11] and when Yigael Yadin excavated at Megiddo (1960–1970), he came to the same conclusion.[12] Yohanan Aharoni of Tel Aviv University defended the University of Chicago dating of the stables as Solomonic, and W.F. Albright concluded that they were built in Solomon's time and used down through the period of Omri and Ahab (AAP, 124, and oral communication to me). Albright's position seems to take into account all the facts in the case. Such discoveries confirm the biblical indication concerning this phase of Solomon's building activity and show that the splendor of his reign can no longer be doubted.

Solomon's Seaport (1 Kings 9:26; 2 Chronicles 8:17–18); Archaeological Light

The Bible records that Solomon had a seaport named Ezion Geber, located on the eastern arm of the Red Sea. The site has been identified with Tell el-Kheleifeh, midway between Jordanian Aqabah and Israeli Eilat in no-man's-land about five hundred yards from the shore of the Gulf of Aqaba. Nelson Glueck led a Smithsonian-American Schools of Oriental Research dig there during the spring seasons of 1938 to 1940. He found a wall two and a half to three yards thick, originally easily twenty-five feet high, surrounding a site of an acre and a half. Near the

---

[9]G.E. Wright and F.V. Filson, *The Westminster Historical Atlas to the Bible*, rev. ed. (Philadelphia: Westminster, 1956), 49 [WFWA].

[10]*Oriental Institute Communications*, 9:35 cited in BWMS, 127.

[11]See J.P. Free, "Oriental Institute Archaeological Report on the Near East, 1941," *American Journal of Semitic Languages* 58, 4 (October 1941): 410 [AJSL].

[12]Yigael Yadin, "New Light on Solomon's Megiddo," BA (1960), 62–68; see also Yadin, EAEHL, 3:853–56.

The foundations of Solomon's stables at Megiddo.   Courtesy of Oriental Institute of the University of Chicago

A model of Solomon's stables, reconstructed on the basis of the excavations.   Courtesy of Oriental Institute of the University of Chicago

southwest corner of the town and facing the sea stood a triple gate. In the northwest corner of the site he found an installation that he identified as a smelting and refining plant used for finishing ore that had been partially smelted in the Arabah to the north. Glueck found five periods of occupation from Solomon's day to the fourth century B.C.

In recent years there have been numerous modifications to the dramatic story spun around Solomon's having built a fleet and established a mining industry. In the first place, doubt arose as to the nature of the "smeltery" Glueck found, and he himself decided it was a citadel also used as a storehouse or granary.[13] Then he concluded that Tell el-Kheleifeh may have been only a satellite of Ezion Geber instead of the port itself. There is no evidence of port facilities at the tell, and it is not on the seacoast.

Moreover, Rothenberg and others have suggested the possibility that the island of Jezira Fara'un, about three hundred yards from the shore at Eilat, may have been the site of Ezion Geber. Rothenberg has observed further that no great fortress and port installation would have been necessary for the occasional use that Egyptian miners, Solomon, and Jehoshaphat of Judah required in the area.[14] So, evidently archaeologists have not yet found Solomon's seaport, but that fact has not thrown any doubt on its existence at the head of the Gulf of Aqaba.

Rothenberg has also shown that what used to be called Solomon's copper mining industry in the area south of the Dead Sea was incorrectly dated. Instead, the Egyptians operated the mines there during the fourteenth to the twelfth centuries B.C., and Egyptian mining activity there came to an end by 1150. The mines were not operated again until the Roman period.[15]

The Visit of the Queen of Sheba (1 Kings 10:1ff.); Archaeological Light on Camels and Sheba

When the Queen of Sheba heard of Solomon's fame, she came to visit him at Jerusalem, bringing with her a great caravan that included camels bearing gold, spices, and precious stones (1 Kings 10:1-2). This casual mention of a camel caravan is significant in view of the doubt that has been expressed in past years concerning the early use of the camel.[16] Archaeological discoveries show, however, that the effective domestication of the camel came at least as early as the period 1200-1000 B.C. It is during this period that the camel appears in cuneiform inscriptions, on the monument known as the Black Obelisk of Shalmaneser (FSAC, 120; for a picture see PANEP, 120), and on a sculptured stone relief from Halaf showing a one-humped dromedary with a rider sitting on the saddle.[17] Thus the archaeological evidence shows the effective domestication of the camel even before the time of the Queen of Sheba (c. 950 B.C.). Actually some knowledge of the camel, even in Egypt, goes back to at least 3000, as I have shown.[18] To set aside the reference to Abraham's having camels in Egypt (Gen. 12:16) is presumptuous in the light of such evidence as camel statuettes, bones, and other evidences that appear in archaeo-

[13]Nelson Glueck, "Ezion-geber," BA, 28 (September 1965), 75.

[14]Beno Rothenberg, *Were These King Solomon's Mines?* (New York: Stein & Day, 1972), 206-7.

[15]Ibid.

[16]As done by T.E. Peet (PEOT, 60), R.H. Pfeiffer (PIOT, 154), and others.

[17]Max Freiherr von Oppenheim, *Der Tell Halaf* (1931), Pl. XXIa (facing p. 136) and p. 140; cf. FLAP, 55 and figure 25.

[18]J.P. Free, "Abraham's Camels," *Journal of Near Eastern Studies*, University of Chicago (July 1944), 187-93.

logical materials beginning before 3000.[19] Albright came to acknowledge that "partial sporadic domestication may go back" several centuries before 1100 B.C. (FSAC, 120), and that "it is by no means impossible that successful efforts to domesticate this animal" were made in the Patriarchal Age (AOTA, 146).

The Queen of Sheba lived in southern Arabia and probably controlled the southern caravan routes and possibly the sea commerce that passed through the straits called Bab-el-Mandeb, the southern entrance into the Red Sea. It is possible that she discussed commercial interests when she visited Solomon, inasmuch as Solomon's merchant ships sailed down the Red Sea and probably came within the "sphere of interest" of the Queen of Sheba's enterprises.

James A. Montgomery[20] has pointed out that some scholars have dismissed the record of the visit of the Queen of Sheba to Solomon as "a romantic tale." It was objected that no such cultured Sheba existed at that early time, since any culture that appeared to exist in that area apparently belonged rather to the Minaeans (another people of Arabia). The archaeological discoveries, however, have produced historical inscriptions of several Assyrian kings[21] showing that the Sabaeans (people of the country of Sheba), though appearing to some extent in northwest Arabia, were purveyors of the South-Arabian trade. Professor Montgomery points out that this is a parallel to the Queen of Sheba's activity involved in bringing the precious gifts of the South to

Solomon, and in this connection he observes that the biblical setting is "quite correct."[22]

Further evidence of relations between Palestine and South Arabia (Sheba area) came in the discovery of an inscribed South Arabian clay stamp in the third season of excavation at Bethel (1957). Partly broken, it was originally about three by four inches and evidently used to seal bags of cargo such as frankincense and myrrh.[23]

The stamp is significant because it is the earliest and possibly the first South Arabian object found in Palestine, and it proves that contact had already been set up between Israel and South Arabia early in the first millennium B.C., near the time of the visit of the Queen of Sheba to Solomon. Van Beek concludes, "While the substantial historicity of this event has been increasingly accepted in recent years, this object carries us closer to that period than most scholars had dared hope."[24]

Archaeological Light on Tarshish
(1 Kings 10:22)

A part of Solomon's commercial activity included the operation of a "fleet of trading ships" at Tarshish, which brought gold, silver, ivory, and apes from far away places (1 Kings 10:22). The word *tarshish* is explained by Albright as a loan word from Akkadian (Babylonian) meaning "smelting plant" or "refinery."[25] The location of the site referred to in the Bible as Tarshish has usually been assumed to be

---

[19]Cf. chapter 4, the section entitled "Abraham in Egypt," pages 50–51.

[20]Professor of Hebrew and Aramaic at the University of Pennsylvania; deceased 1949. For "Memoriam" article on Professor Montgomery, see BASOR, no. 115 (October 1949): 4–8.

[21]Tiglath-Pileser, Sennacherib, and others.

[22]James A. Montgomery, *Arabia and the Bible* (Philadelphia: University of Pennsylvania Press, 1934), 180.

[23]G.W. Van Beek, BASOR (October 1958).

[24]A similar stamp, found earlier, was reported in BASOR (October 1961).

[25]W.F. Albright, "New Light on the Early History of Phoenician Colonization" BASOR, no. 83 (October 1941): 21.

Tartessus in Spain,[26] but one of the Phoenician inscriptions found at Nora on the Island of Sardinia gives the name Tarshish immediately before the name Sardinia, which indicates that Tarshish was likely the Phoenician name for Nora.[27] The name Tarshish has also been found in an inscription of Esarhaddon,[28] referring to a Phoenician land at the opposite end of the Mediterranean from the Island of Cyprus (AOTA, 151). In light of the archaeological evidence available up to the present, Tarshish was in the western Mediterranean, and likely was the Phoenician name for Nora on the Island of Sardina.

But perhaps the foregoing discussion does not tell the whole story. First Kings 10:22 mentions "apes" and "ivory"; these would not have come from the western Mediterranean. "Ships of Tarshish" were not necessarily ships connected with a specific locale, but were ships constructed for transporting ore and other heavy cargoes, as Unger has pointed out.[29] As such, they would compare with large ships the Egyptians built in the third millennium B.C. for long-range shipping. These were called "Byblos travelers" and were used especially but not exclusively in trade with Byblos in Lebanon.[30]

Solomon's Spiritual Decline (1 Kings 11)

Solomon married many foreign women (1 Kings 11:1), even though the Lord had warned against such a practice (v. 2; Deut. 7:3). These foreign wives turned Solomon's heart away after other gods, and he turned his attention to such pagan deities as Ashtoreth (vv. 4–5). From the archaeological discoveries we actually have a seal impression, found at Bethel, which pictures this goddess.[31] She was one of the best known of the fertility goddesses; she was known in Greek as Astarte and was worshiped in Babylonia under a slightly different form of the name—Ishtar (BWMS, 230–31).

Solomon finally came to build a high place of worship for the pagan god Chemosh on the "hill that is before Jerusalem" (1 Kings 11:7), probably the Mount of Olives.

Because of these sins of Solomon, God said that he would rend the kingdom from him, but because of David, his father, he would not do this until the time of Solomon's son. One tribe would remain to the descendants of Solomon (1 Kings 11:11–13).

During the reign of Solomon there came to prominence a young man named Jeroboam, who later was to be the king of the northern tribes after the division of the kingdom. The prophet Ahijah had predicted this as he tore Jeroboam's garment into twelve pieces, symbolic of the rending of Solomon's kingdom at the time of Solomon's death (1 Kings 11:30–31). Solomon seems to have become suspicious of Jeroboam, and Jeroboam found it advisable to flee to Egypt and to remain there until Solomon finished his reign of forty years and rested with his father (vv. 42–43).

---

[26]Brown, Driver, Briggs, *A Hebrew and English Lexicon of the Old Testament* (New York: Houghton Mifflin, 1906), 1076. For a discussion see Paul MacKendrick, *The Iberian Stones Speak* (New York: Funk & Wagnalls, 1969), chapter 2.

[27]Albright, "New Light," 21, AOTA, 151.

[28]King of Assyria from 681–668 B.C.

[29]Merrill F. Unger, *Archaeology and the Old Testament* (Grand Rapids: Zondervan, 1954), 226.

[30]See Charles F. Pfeiffer and Howard F. Vos, *The Wycliffe Historical Geography of Bible Lands* (Chicago: Moody Press, 1967), 190.

[31]BWMS, 230. See chapter 12, section entitled "The Later Life of Saul and His Death," pages 127–28.

Chapter 15

The Divided Kingdom

(1 Kings 12–22; 2 Chronicles 10–20; Jeroboam Through Ahab, 931–853 B.C.)

Division of the Kingdom; Rehoboam's Policy (1 Kings 12; 2 Chronicles 10)

After the death of Solomon (931 B.C.), Rehoboam, his son, prepared to ascend the throne (1 Kings 12:1ff.). The people of the northern tribes, Israel, asked Rehoboam to make their lot easier (vv. 3–4). Rehoboam consulted with the older men, who counseled him to accede to the request of the people; but later he counseled with the young men who were his associates, and they advised him to add to the yoke of the people. Rehoboam foolishly followed the advice of the young men (vv. 13–14), telling the people of Israel that he would add to their yoke, whereupon the northern tribes rallied around Jeroboam, making him the new king of the ten northern tribes (v. 21). Rehoboam prepared to fight against the secessionist tribes, but the Lord sent a message through his prophet Shemaiah telling him not to subdue the rebellious tribes, explaining, "This is my doing" (v. 24). It evidently was not God's original

plan[1] to have a division, but the situation that had come to exist made the division necessary. If the north and south had remained together, it is possible that the idolatry of the north would have penetrated deeply into the southern kingdom of Judah and brought corruption there all the sooner.

Data for Determining the Dates of the Kings of Israel and Judah; Chronology

The reader will notice that the date of 931 B.C. has been indicated for the death of Solomon and the division of the kingdom. However, in older books a date forty or fifty years earlier was usually given for the death of Solomon; Raven, for example, gave this date as 979 B.C. (ROTI, 175). All books written in the light of recent discoveries date Solomon's death in the 930s B.C.

How is it possible to fix a date of 931 B.C. or thereabouts for the death of Solomon and the division of the kingdom? A partial answer will prove helpful. Fortunately the

---

[1]This does not mean that God changes his mind in human fashion and that therefore his character is changeable. It means, rather, that when humans change or fail, God alters his dealing with them in accordance with the situation. His character never changes.

Assyrians kept lists of years, noting their principal events and ruling officials. These we call Eponym Lists; an eponym was a year named for a person who held office during that year. Archaeological excavations have produced tablets that give specific lists from 893 to 666 B.C. (BAB, 57). One of these lists mentions an eclipse that occurred at Nineveh in May–June, 763 B.C. Astronomers have checked this eclipse, and thus we have a fixed date in the eponym lists, from which we can calculate other dates in the period 900–600.

From these Assyrian records, we know that the great battle of Qarqar was fought in the year 853 B.C. The archaeological records of King Shalmaneser III (858–824) tell us that he was opposed in the battle of Qarqar by a coalition of twelve allies, one of whom was King Ahab of Israel.[2]

Since Ahab fought in the battle of Qarqar in 853, the dates of Ahab must include this year. Apparently the battle came near the end of Ahab's reign (ORHI, 291), and so Ahab's rule is to be dated 874–853. Since the Bible gives us the length of reign for each of the kings of Israel and Judah, we can figure back from Ahab to the death of Solomon and arrive at the date of approximately 931. The preceding development provides an example of some of the processes employed in working out the chronology of the period of the Hebrew kings.

Problems in Connection With the Chronology of the Period of the Kings; Pfeiffer's Acknowledgment

Why is it that the date given by an assortment of scholars for the death of Solomon and the division of the kingdom varies by several years? The answer is that there are problems in connection with the chronology of the kings of the Bible concerning which we did not have full

light in the past. For example, we find that the length of time from Jeroboam I to Jehoram in Israel should be the same as the time from Rehoboam to Ahaziah in the southern kingdom of Judah. This is true because Jehoram and Ahaziah met their death simultaneously at the hands of Jehu. However, when we add up the reigns of the kings in each line, we arrive at the following result:

ISRAEL

Jeroboam I	22 years
Nadab	2 years
Baasha	24 years
Elah	2 years
Zimri	7 days
Omri	12 years
Ahab	22 years
Ahaziah	2 years
Jehoram	12 years
Total	98 years, 7 days

JUDAH

Rehoboam	17 years
Abijam	3 years
Asa	41 years
Jehoshaphat	25 years
Jehoram	8 years
Ahaziah	1 year
Total	95 years

Thus we see that the same period of time adds up to ninety-eight years and seven days for Israel, and only ninety-five years for Judah. Such problems have caused some scholars to feel that the chronological data from the Old Testament is of such a nature that a valid chronology cannot be constructed.

Archaeological discoveries, however, have led writers as liberal as Pfeiffer to acknowledge the value of the Old Testament chronological indications. He says,

[2]D.D. Luckenbill, *Ancient Records of Assyria and Babylonia* (Chicago: University of Chicago Press, 1926), 223 [LARA]; PANET, 278–79.

"The chronology of the histories of the kings of Judah and Israel—the synchronisms—are genuine, though not errorless" (PIOT, 394). He adds on the next page, "In spite of these discrepancies, inaccuracies, and errors, the chronology of Kings is not fantastic. . ." (PIOT, 395). But what about the apparent discrepancies such as appear in the above chart?

Thiele's Work on Chronology; Significance of the Work

E.R. Thiele[3] wrote his doctoral dissertation at the Oriental Institute of the University of Chicago on the chronology of the period 900–600 B.C. It was published in substance in the *Journal of Near Eastern Studies* under the title "The Chronology of the Kings of Judah and Israel" [JNES],[4] and in book form by the University of Chicago Press under the title, *Mysterious Numbers of the Hebrew Kings* (1951). In a revised edition, it has now been published by Zondervan (1983). A spokesman at Paternoster Press in Britain has called Professor Thiele's work "the basis of all subsequent investigation in this field, and the standard authority on the subject."

Thiele discovered that the chronological data in the period of kings in the Old Testament harmonize in a most wonderful way. He utilized several factors that many scholars have only partially taken into consideration and in this way was able to solve many apparent problems and contradictions in the length of reigns. Of these, the principle factors are as follows:

1. In Israel the regnal year began with the month Nisan, while in Judah it began with the month Tishri.
2. At the time of the division of the kingdom, Judah reckoned the years of its kings according to the accession-year system. In this system, the fraction of the year the king ruled when he first came to the throne was regarded as his accession year, and not as his first year. His first year was reckoned as beginning with the month Tishri following his accession to the throne. Judah continued to follow this system until the fall of the kingdom, except for the period from Jehoram to Joash, when they employed the nonaccession-year system. Israel, on the contrary, during her early history employed the nonaccession-year system, whereby the part of the year during which the king first reigned was counted as his first year, and his second year began with the first of Nisan following his accession. Israel followed this system until the reign of Jehoash in 798, when they shifted to the accession-year system. Thus, during the later history of the two kingdoms, they were using the same system.
3. Both Judah and Israel, when computing the years of each other's kings, did so according to the method of reckoning in force in their own countries and not according to the system used by their neighbors.
4. Both Israel and Judah made use of co-regencies, but in neither nation did interregna occur.
5. When there were co-regencies, the years of the king were usually counted from the beginning of the co-regency.

The Dates of the Kings of Israel and Judah

A serviceable list of the kings of Israel and Judah, with dates of their reigns, is given by Pfeiffer (PIOT, 375–76), by Robinson (ORHI, 463–64), and in recent encyclopedias. Generally these place the division of the kingdom between 936 and 931 B.C. and are quite usable. However, because of Thiele's use of factors that harmonize the data, we are presenting an adaptation of his results below. (Many of

---

[3]Then professor in the field of Biblical Studies at Andrews University, Berrien Springs, Michigan.
[4]3,3 (July 1944): 137–86.

ISRAEL	Reign	Co-regency	JUDAH	Reign	Co-regency
1. Jeroboam	931–910		1. Rehoboam	931–913	
2. Nadab	910–909		2. Abijam	913–911	
3. Baasha	909–886		3. Asa	911–870	
4. Elah	886–885		4. Jehoshaphat	870–848	873–870
5. Zimri	885		5. Jehoram	848–841	853–848
Tibni	885–880	885–880			
6. Omri	880–874	885–880	6. Ahaziah	841	
			Athaliah	841–835	
7. Ahab	874–853		7. Joash	835–796	
8. Ahaziah	853–852		8. Amaziah	796–767	
9. Jehoram	852–841		9. Azariah	767–740	791–767
10. Jehu	841–814		10. Jotham	740–736	750–740
11. Jehoahaz	814–798		11. Ahaz	736–716	
12. Jehoash	798–782		12. Hezekiah	716–687	
13. Jeroboam II	782–753	793–782	13. Manasseh	687–642	696–687
14. Zechariah	753–752		14. Amon	642–640	
15. Shallum	752		15. Josiah	640–609	
16. Menahem	752–742		16. Jehoahaz	609	
17. Pekahiah	742–740		17. Jehoiakim	609–597	
18. Pekah	740–732	752–740	18. Jehoiachin	597	
19. Hoshea	732–723, 722		19. Zedekiah	597–586	

these dates will approximate and others will equate with the chronologies mentioned above.)

Jeroboam, the First King of Israel (1 Kings 12); Archaeological Light on His Name

Jeroboam was chosen to be the first king of the northern tribes after their secession from Rehoboam (1 Kings 12:20). Archaeological confirmation of the name Jeroboam was found in the excavation by the German expedition at Megiddo (1903–1905) directed by Gottlieb Schumacher. In the fifth stratum from the bottom, in a palace of the Hebrew period, they found a seal bearing an inscription that read, "Belonging to Shema, servant of Jeroboam."[5] We do not know whether this Shema was the servant of Jeroboam I (931–910 B.C.) or Jeroboam II (782–753),

but in any event the seal does reveal the presence of this personal name in the time of the monarchy of Israel.

Jeroboam's Calf Worship; Critical View; Light From Archaeology

Shortly after Jeroboam became king of Israel, he established calf worship by setting up a calf at Dan far in the north and another one at Bethel in the southernmost part of the northern kingdom. His purpose in doing this was to prevent the people of his kingdom from going to the temple at Jerusalem, where they might be influenced to return to the allegiance of Rehoboam (1 Kings 12:27). A. Biran in his excavations at Tel Dan has uncovered the high place of the town (an almost square platform about fifty-nine by sixty feet), which he thought was erected

[5]BAB, 110, 456.

Ruins of the high place at Dan, built by Jeroboam I

by Jeroboam I and enlarged during the reigns of Ahab and Jeroboam II.[6]

Critics have often held that Jeroboam was merely continuing an older form of worship in which the Lord was represented as a bull. The archaeological discoveries in Egypt, however, show the presence of bovine worship there. The sacred bull was an object of worship in Egypt, its tomb being found at Memphis during the last century. The sacred cow was the symbol of the goddess Hathor. In the light of this evidence, it is more likely that Jeroboam became acquainted with bovine worship when he fled to Egypt while Solomon was yet alive (1 Kings 11:40; 12:2) and upon his return to Palestine introduced the worship he had observed in Egypt. The German Egyptologist Steindorff and the American Old Testament scholar George L. Robinson both reflect this view (RBA, 66). The question is sometimes raised as to how Jeroboam could get the Israelites to switch from worship of an invisible God to calf worship. A possible explanation is seen in the artistic illustrations of several ancient Near Eastern peoples that pictured their gods as standing or sitting on the back of an animal, such as a bull or lion, with the animal sometimes thought of as being there invisibly.[7]

---

[6]These excavations, under the auspices of the Israel Department of Antiquities and Museums, have been in progress since 1966. See EAEHL, 1:320.

[7]For example, for the Hittites see O.R. Gurney, *The Hittites*, rev. ed. (Baltimore: Penguin Books, 1961), 143; for the Assyrians, see PANEP, 180–81.

Rehoboam, the First King of Judah (1 Kings 12, 14); Archaeological Confirmation of Shishak's Invasion

During the reign of Rehoboam, Sheshonk I (spelled "Shishak" in the Bible) came from Egypt to Palestine and took the treasures of the temple at Jerusalem (1 Kings 14:24ff.). Archaeological confirmation of this campaign of Shishak is found in his inscription on the wall of the great temple of Karnak in Egypt. The inscription shows his god Amon leading by cords rows of Asiatic captives, undoubtedly Israelites. On the relief 156 captives are represented and on the bodies of these people are inscribed names of many Palestinian towns, such as Taanach, Gibeon, Ajalon, and Beth Shan (see PANEP, 118, and ANET, 242–43). The archaeological material adds further light to what is revealed in the Bible, showing that Shishak went to other towns in addition to Jerusalem and even invaded the northern kingdom.

Omri, the Sixth King of Israel; Archaeological Light on Samaria, His Capital

For six years (885–880 B.C.) Omri ruled in opposition to the usurper Tibni. But finally the followers of Omri prevailed over the people who followed Tibni, and Omri gained sole rule over Israel (880–874; 1 Kings 16:21–22). He established the capital at Samaria (v. 24), confirmation of this being found when Harvard University excavated the site (1908–1910) under the direction of G.A. Reisner. On the native rock a large palace was found, identified as that of Omri (BAB, 120; EAEHL, 4:1041–42). Thus the biblical indication that Samaria was founded by Omri is confirmed. Burrows acknowledges this in his statement that "Samaria was built at a time corresponding to the statement that Omri established it as the capital of the northern kingdom. The examples of such confirmation which might be given are almost innumerable" (BWMS, 281).

The Progress of Idolatry in the Northern Kingdom

The progress of idolatry in the northern kingdom is well outlined by William G. Blaikie in his *Manual of Bible History*. This outline is retained in the revision (though the revision, having been done by a liberal, has suffered in many other respects—cf. BBHM). Blaikie's outline is as follows:

1. Idolatry taking root (under Jeroboam: calf worship, etc.)
2. Idolatry rampant (under Omri, Ahab, Jezebel; Elijah and Elisha raised up to combat the progress of idolatry and Baal worship)
3. Idolatry slightly checked (Jehu, Jeroboam II; Elisha)
4. Idolatry terminating in destruction (the northern kingdom finally ended in a series of murders in the palace.) (BBHM, 207, 211, 227, 229).

Ahab's Reign; His Marriage; Elijah and Elisha (1 Kings 16:30ff.)

Ahab (874–853 B.C.), the seventh king of Israel, married Jezebel, the daughter of the king of the Sidonians (1 Kings 16:31). Jezebel brought in the worship of Baal from her home in Phoenicia. When this new curse was about to engulf the kingdom, God raised up Elijah, and later Elisha, to sustain the true believers in Israel. We might wonder why Elijah and Elisha did not cry out against the calf worship (see earlier section in this chapter entitled "Jeroboam's Calf Worship," pages 152–53), but as Albright points out, the Baal worship was so much worse that Elijah and Elisha spent their energies on the most serious problem in this hour of crisis (AARI, 156).

Archaeological Light on Baal Worship in the Northern Kingdom

Archaeological discoveries show that the name "Baal" appears in the personal names of people who lived in the northern kingdom, being evidenced in the seals and inscriptions that have been found. On the other hand, it is very significant that the seals and inscriptions from Judah, which become more common in the eighth century and are very numerous in the seventh and early sixth, never seem to contain any names of Baal (AARI, 160).

In the Harvard excavation at Samaria, a number of inscribed potsherds (called ostraca) were found,[8] sixty-three of which contained writing in ancient Hebrew, which was fairly legible.[9] These inscribed ostraca served as notations concerning payments of oil and wine that had been sent in by individuals as revenue or taxes to the storerooms of the royal palace.[10] Ostracon No. Two tells that in the tenth year of the king, there was sent to Gaddiyau, the royal steward (or tax collector), from the town of Azah, two jars to be credited to Abibaal, two to be credited to Ahaz, one to Sheba, and one to Meribaal. It reads literally, "In the tenth year, to Gaddiyau, from Azah, Abibaal 2, Ahaz 2, Sheba 1, Meribaal 1."[11] It is significant that these ostraca, dating from about 775 B.C.,[12] contain many names formed with Baal,[13]

showing what a great impact the Baal worship introduced by Jezebel had on the land of Israel. (See also EAEHL, 4: 1044.)

Archaeological Light on Ahab's Ivory House (1 Kings 22:39)

The biblical summary of Ahab's life refers to "the palace he built and inlaid with ivory" (1 Kings 22:39). The excavations at Samaria revealed a palace platform 315 feet from north to south.[14] The remains of the palace structure found on this site dating from Ahab's period gave evidence of walls faced with high-quality white limestone, which would, in itself, give the appearance of an "ivory" palace as it stood there gleaming in the Palestinian sun. But, more than that, numerous ivory decorations were found, in the form of plaques and panels for decorating furniture and wall paneling (FLAP, 187–88).[15] As Clarence Fisher, one of the excavators of Samaria, remarked to me, there was a double reason for calling Ahab's palace an "ivory house"—the gleaming white walls and also the ivory decorations.

---

[8]BAB, 120–21.

[9]J.W. Jack, *Samaria in Ahab's Time; Harvard Excavations and Their Results* (Edinburgh: T. & T. Clark, 1929), 37 [JSAT].

[10]Ibid., 97–98.

[11]Hand copies of these ostraca are published in George Andrew Reisner, *Israelite Ostraca from Samaria*, Harvard University. Three are reproduced in Albright's *Archaeology of Palestine* (AAP, 135, figure 40).

[12]The Samaria Ostraca were formerly dated in the reign of Ahab (874–853 B.C.), but on the basis of the forms of the letters and the contents, Albright later dated them in the reign of Jeroboam II (782–753, according to Thiele's chronology. Albright's dates for Jeroboam are 774–766 in AARI, 41; and 782–742 in AOTA, 152).

[13]Note the two names Abibaal and Meribaal in the inscription given above; cf. AARI, 160; BWMS, 252.

[14]A.T. Olmstead, *History of Palestine and Syria* (New York: Scribner, 1931), 372 [OHPS].

[15]For another significance of the ivory decoration, see chapter 17, the section entitled "Archaeological Light on Amos' Condemnation of the Idle Luxury of Samaria," 166–67. On the Samaria ivories, cf. also AAP, 137, and AOTA, 152.

A public building at Hazor from the time of King Ahab

Steps leading to the temple to Augustus at Samaria, constructed by Herod the Great in New Testament times

The Greco-Roman theater at Samaria, also constructed by Herod the Great

Chapter 16

The Northern and Southern Kingdoms, Israel and Judah, c. 850–750 B.C.

(2 Kings 1–14; 2 Chronicles 21–25. Israel: Ahaziah Through Jeroboam II, 853–753 B.C. Judah: Jehoram to Azariah (Uzziah), 848–767 B.C.)

Ahaziah's Illness and Elijah's Message (2 Kings 1)

In dealing with the kings of Israel and Judah, it will be helpful for the reader to refer constantly to the chart of kings on page 152, in order to keep in mind the relative relationship of the various kings and their approximate dates of rule.

After the death of Ahab (874–853 B.C.), the seventh king of Israel, his son Ahaziah (853–852) came to the throne and continued the wicked practices of his father by worshiping Baal (1 Kings 22:51–53). When Ahaziah became sick, he sent messengers to inquire of the god of Ekron, in the Philistine territory, whether he would recover from his disease (2 Kings 1:2). The messengers were met on their way by Elijah, who first asked why they should go to Ekron when there was a God in Israel and then told them that the king would not recover from his illness but would surely die (2 Kings 1:3–4). In accordance with Elijah's prophecy, Ahaziah died; he was succeeded by his brother Jehoram (852–841), another son of Ahab.

Elijah's Translation; Elisha's Ministry, c. 850 B.C. (2 Kings 2–8)

Elijah had been raised up to cry out against the introduction and spread of

Baal worship, which was fostered and spread by the Phoenician wife of Ahab, Jezebel, in the period c. 875–850 B.C. (see chapter 15). Elijah's ministry came to an end about 850, when the great prophet was taken to heaven by the Lord without suffering death (2 Kings 2:11).

Elijah's successor, Elisha, had asked that he might inherit a double portion of Elijah's spirit (2 Kings 2:9b). It is often assumed that Elisha was asking to excel his master in spiritual power and that the granting of his request is seen in Elisha's performing fourteen recorded miracles in comparison to Elijah's seven. But on the face of it, that is not a very "spiritual" or kind request, and it does not fit Hebrew thought patterns or customs. Apparently what Elisha was asking for was not to excel his master but to receive the double portion of the eldest son as inheritance rights under Hebrew law (Deut. 21:17). That is, he was asking to be the true heir and successor of Elijah. It is true, however, that Elisha did perform fourteen miracles, and they are summarized as follows: (1) He made the bad water of a spring wholesome (2:19–22). (2) He cursed children who mocked him (2:23, 24; the Hebrew word does not indicate

159

little children, but rather "young men"; they may have been participants in the idolatrous Baal practices). (3) He provided water for the armies (3:11–20); the armies of Israel and Judah were fighting against the Moabites, and were about to succumb because of lack of water; God showed Elisha that water would be provided; at Elisha's direction, ditches were dug and were found to be filled with water the next day. (4) He multiplied a widow's oil (4:1–7). (5) He raised the Shunamite woman's son (vv. 8–37). (6) He healed the deadly pot of stew (v. 38–41). (7) He miraculously fed one hundred men (vv. 42–44). (8) He cleansed the leper Naaman by having him bathe in the Jordan River (5:1–19). (9) He smote Gehazi with leprosy when Gehazi accepted gifts from Naaman without Elisha's permission (vv. 20–27). (10) He caused the iron ax head to swim (6:1–7). (11) He revealed the movements of the Syrian army (vv. 8–13). (12) He struck the Syrians with blindness (vv. 14–19). (13) He healed the blindness of the Syrians (vv. 20–23). (14) He raised a dead man (13:20–21).

Intimate Relations Between Israel and Judah, c. 850 B.C.

King Jehoshaphat (870–848 B.C.), the fourth king of Judah, had introduced a period of intimate interrelationships between Israel and Judah, with the royal families intermarrying (2 Kings 8:18, 26), adopting the same names for their children (2 Kings 3:1; 8:16), and visiting each other (2 Kings 8:29; 2 Chron. 18:1–2). They made joint ventures in foreign trade, establishing a merchant marine at Ezion Geber (2 Chron. 20:35–36), where Solomon had established his seaport about a century earlier (see chapter 14); and at various times Israel and Judah made a joint disposition of their military forces, as in the case of the battle at Ramoth Gilead (1 Kings 22:29ff.), and the alliance

between Jehoram of Israel and Jehoshaphat of Judah to put down the rebellion of the Moabites (2 Kings 3:6–7). These entangling alliances brought no real gain to Judah but merely served to yoke her unequally with the kings of idolatrous Israel and to undermine her own spiritual progress. Elisha specifically spoke a word of rebuke concerning this last mentioned alliance of Israel and Judah against the Moabites (2 Kings 3:13–14).

Archaeological Light on the Moabite Rebellion (2 Kings 3:4–27; c. 850–840 B.C.); the Moabite Stone

During the days of Ahab, seventh king of Israel (874–853 B.C.), the king of Moab, Mesha, had been subject to Israel. After the death of Ahab, Mesha rebelled, and the ninth king of Israel, Jehoram (852–841), proceeded to ally himself with Jehoshaphat (870–848), the fourth king of Judah, for the purpose of subjugating Mesha again (2 Kings 3:5–7).

Interesting light and confirmation on Mesha is found on the Moabite Stone, a monument that was seen in Dibon in Transjordan in 1868 by a German clergyman, F.A. Klein. The Germans and the French both tried to obtain the stone, and during the negotiations some Arabs heated it and poured cold water on it, causing it to break in many pieces. According to one theory, this was done in the hope of making more profit out of the fragments. Fortunately, much of the stone was recovered, and with the aid of a "squeeze"[1] made previously, it could be read. (For a picture of the reconstructed Moabite Stone, now in the Louvre in Paris, see PANEP, 85.)

The inscription on the Moabite Stone confirms the fact of Mesha's rebellion and also the fact that he had been subject to Israel. On the stone, Mesha says, concerning his subjection to Israel, "Omri, king of Israel—he oppressed Moab many days

[1] A type of impression or cast.

... and his son succeeded him, and he also said I will oppress Moab" (PANET, 320–21).

Some scholars have thought that there is not complete harmony between the statements of the Moabite Stone and the Scriptures. Barton, for example, says, "There are some differences of statement which are perplexing" (BAB, 462). Significant work, however, was done on this problem by John D. Davis, formerly of Princeton Seminary, who showed how the two accounts may be harmonized.[2] Davis correctly observes, "Mesha is in no wise contradicting, but only unintentionally supplementing the Hebrew account" (RBA, 167). For a summary of Davis' analysis, see Robinson (RBA, 167–69); Caiger also briefly shows the harmonization of the Moabite Stone and the scriptural records (CBS, 135–38).

Excavations at Dibon, forty miles south of Amman, were carried out by the American School of Oriental Research in Jerusalem, 1950–1955. A fragment bearing the same script as that of the Moabite Stone was discovered.[3] The walls of the old Moabite city, destroyed by Nebuchadnezzar in 582 B.C., were explored, Unfortunately, a Nabatean temple was built on the apparent site of Mesha's palace, thus destroying much of the evidence of the earlier period (see EAEHL, 1: 330–33).

Ben-Hadad's Advance Against Israel in the Days of Jehoram (852–841 B.C.) (2 Kings 6–7)

During the days of Jehoram, the ninth king of Israel, the Syrian king Ben-Hadad came up against Israel and besieged the city of Samaria, capital city of Israel (2 Kings 6:24ff.). Elisha promised that the Syrian siege would be lifted (2 Kings 7:1ff.), and this occurred when the Syrians wrongly assumed that the Hittites and Egyptians were coming to the aid of the

Israelites (2 Kings 7:6–7). This false assumption caused the Syrians to flee, and Elisha's promise was fulfilled.

The Bible indicates that Elisha sojourned at Dothan in the period 850–800 B.C. (2 Kings 6:12–13). Certain critics have been skeptical of the scriptural record of Elisha, and some have even doubted his existence. In view of these doubts, it is significant that my excavations at Dothan (1953–1962) have uncovered areas of the city of Elisha's day in the upper stratification of the ancient mound. Dothan was a thriving city in the days of that prophet, as implied in the biblical record and confirmed by our excavations (see BASOR, Nos. 131, 135, 139).

Archaeological Light on Hadad; Connection with Ben-Hadad (2 Kings 6:24ff.)

The significance of a name is often illuminated by archaeological discoveries. The name Ben-Hadad, meaning "son of Hadad," is intelligible when we know that Hadad was one of the most prominent of Near Eastern deities, being the Aramean storm god. An archaeological reference to this god was found on a stone statue of about 800 B.C. at Zinjirli in northern Syria; it bears an Aramaic inscription stating that King Panammu had dedicated the statue to Hadad. The Amarna Tablets also show that Hadad was already a prominent figure in the religion of Palestine in the Bronze Age, i.e., before 1200 B.C. (BWMS, 228).

Archaeological Confirmation of Hazael the Usurper (2 Kings 8:7–15)

Ben-Hadad, the Syrian king, came to a sudden end when Hazael suffocated him with a cloth and usurped the throne (2 Kings 8:15). Archaeological confirmation of the fact that Hazael succeeded Ben-Hadad and gained the throne but

---

[2] "The Moabite Stone and the Hebrew Records," *Hebraica* 7 (1891): 178–82, cited in RBA, 167.
[3] BASOR 125 (February 1952): 20–23.

was not of royal blood or in the royal line of succession was found in an inscription of Shalmaneser III of Assyria (860–825 B.C.), which reads, "Hazael, son of nobody, seized the throne" (PANET, 280–81).

Further confirmation of Hazael was found on some ivory decorations discovered at Khadatu in northwestern Mesopotamia. One of these ivory objects bears the name of Hazael, king of Damascus (ARDBL, 34).

Climax of Elisha's Fight Against Baalism—the Anointing of Jehu as King (2 Kings 9:1–13)

Ahab and his wife, Jezebel, had fostered the introduction and growth of Baal worship in Israel. The successor of Ahab, his son Ahaziah (853–852 B.C.), had continued the worship of Baal (1 Kings 22:53), and the next king, another son of Ahab, Jehoram (852–841), still continued in the sins of Jeroboam, although he did "put away the image of Baal that his father had made" (2 Kings 3:2–3). The house of Ahab was still on the throne, and Baalism could again flourish in all its power at any moment. God used Elisha to initiate the train of events that would preclude the fostering of any further Baal worship by the family of Ahab. Elisha had Jehu anointed to become the next king of Israel and to bring to an end the house of Ahab (2 Kings 9:7–8), thus avenging the crimes perpetrated by the followers of the Baal cult.

The Activity of Jehu, the Tenth King of Israel, 841–814 B.C. (2 Kings 9–10)

After Elisha directed one of the prophets to anoint Jehu as king over Israel (2 Kings 9:1–3), the prophet carried out the instructions, and in addition told Jehu that he would smite the house of Ahab (v. 7), and the house of Ahab would perish (v. 8). The army subsequently acknowledged Jehu as king of Israel (v. 13).

Jehu set out for the town of Jezreel in north central Palestine, where Jehoram,[4] the ninth king of Israel (852–841 B.C.) had returned after being wounded in battle with the Syrians (2 Kings 8:28–29). Ahaziah, the sixth king of Judah (841), had already come to see Jehoram at Jezreel, because he was sick (8:29; 9:16). The watchman on the tower in Jezreel saw Jehu's military company approaching and surmised that it was Jehu, for, as the watchman said, "the driving is like that of Jehu the son of Nimshi—he drives like a madman" (2 Kings 9:20).

Upon hearing the news that the approaching company was that of Jehu, Jehoram of Israel and Ahaziah of Judah went out to meet him (2 Kings 9:21). Both kings were slain (vv. 24, 27), and at the direction of Jehu, Jezebel was thrown down from an upper window and killed (v. 33). Jehu also had the sons of Ahab put to death (10:1ff.) and the prophets of Baal slain (vv. 19–25); he finally concluded his purge of Baal worship by burning the images of the house of Baal and breaking down the house of Baal (vv. 16–28).

Jehu's reforms brought in the third period in the progress of idolatry in Israel, a period in which idolatry was slightly checked (see Blaikie's outline, page 154). Jehu stopped short of a complete spiritual house-cleaning in Israel, for he allowed the worship of the golden calves at Bethel and Dan to continue (2 Kings 10:29), thus perpetuating the sins of Jeroboam I, the first king of divided Israel, who had had these calves erected (v. 31). Jehu's incomplete obedience shows that he went far enough in the reform to seat himself securely on the throne by killing Ahab and his family but did not completely serve the Lord by thoroughly destroying idolatry.

Hazael of Damascus attacked the borders of Israel on the north and east during the latter part of the reign of Jehu

---

[4] Often rendered in the shorter form, Joram.

(2 Kings 10:32–33). Jehu died after a reign of twenty-eight years (v. 36).

Archaeological Confirmation of Jehu: the Black Obelisk of Shalmaneser

A monument called the Black Obelisk of Shalmaneser was found by Layard at Nimrud (Calah), south of Nineveh, about the middle of the nineteenth century. The second register from the top pictures the tribute brought to Shalmaneser III of Assyria (860–825 B.C.) by the Hebrew caravan. One of the panels shows Jehu or his envoy bowing down before King Shalmaneser III. (For a picture of this, see PANEP, 120–22, 290–91.) The inscription of this panel reads, "Tribute of Jehu, son of Omri" (PANET, 281). In the Assyrian cuneiform the name Jehu was rendered by the syllables Ya-u-a; it was Hincks, an Irish clergyman and cuneiform scholar, who, in 1851, first recognized in these syllables the equivalent of the biblical name Jehu (CBS, 141). The Black Obelisk of Shalmaneser is in the British Museum in London. It is a specific confirmation of the reign of Jehu and supplements the Scriptures by telling us of the tribute he paid to Shalmaneser III.

Athaliah of Judah (2 Kings 11)

After Jehu had slain Ahaziah, king of Judah (841 B.C.), Ahaziah's mother, Athaliah, took the throne of Judah, slaying all those who might be heirs to the throne except Joash, who was concealed from the fury of Athaliah (2 Kings 11:1–2). After Athaliah had ruled for six years (841–835), a movement was instituted by Jehoiada the priest resulting in the overthrow of Athaliah and the elevation of Joash to the throne (vv. 4–18). Jehoiada the priest was able to break down the house of Baal (vv. 17–18) and to make repairs on the temple (vv. 9–16).

The Seventh and Eighth Southern Kings: Joash (835–796 B.C.) and Amaziah (796–767) (2 Kings 12–14)

After the six-year rule of Athaliah (2 Kings 11:3), Joash came to the throne of Judah at the age of seven (12:1). Jehoiada the priest probably guided the fortunes of Judah until Joash was old enough to reign. When Hazael of Damascus headed for Jerusalem, Joash sent him the sacred treasures of the temple (vv. 17–18). Joash died in a palace conspiracy (v. 19) and was succeeded by his son, Amaziah, who suffered an invasion from Jehoash, king of Israel (vv. 13–14).

The Eleventh, Twelfth, and Thirteenth Northern Kings: Jehoahaz (814–798 B.C.), Jehoash (798–782), and Jeroboam II (782–753) (2 Kings 13–14)

In Israel, Jehu was followed by his son, Jehoahaz (2 Kings 13:1), who made concessions to idolatry (v. 2), yet had some regard for the things of God (v. 4). Jehoahaz was followed by his son Jehoash (v. 9), who took the temple treasures from Jerusalem (14:13–14), and Jehoash was followed by his son Jeroboam II (v. 23), who was able to restore the eastern borders of Israel (v. 25), which had earlier been smitten by Hazael of Damascus in the days of Jehu (10:32–33).

A reconstruction of the palace of Sargon II of Assyria at Khorsabad   Courtesy of the Oriental Institute of the University of Chicago

A great stone winged bull from the palace of Sargon II, carved from a single block of stone and weighing forty tons   Courtesy of the Oriental Institute of the University of Chicago

Chapter 17

The End of the Northern Kingdom, c. 750–722 B.C.

(2 Kings 15–17; 2 Chronicles 26–28. Israel: Zechariah Through Hoshea, 753–722 B.C. Judah: Azariah [Uzziah] Through Ahaz, 767–716 B.C.)

ISRAEL		JUDAH	
13. Jeroboam II	782–753	9. Azariah	767–740
14. Zechariah	753–752		
15. Shallum	752		
16. Menahem	752–742	10. Jotham	740–736
17. Pekahiah	742–740		
18. Pekah	740–732	11. Ahaz	736–716
19. Hoshea	732–722		
End of Northern Kingdom	722	12. Hezekiah	716–687

The Last Kings of Israel; Their Contemporaries in Judah (2 Kings 15–17)

For convenience in dealing with this period, the last kings of Israel and their contemporaries in Judah are listed above.

The Prophets of the Mid-Eighth Century: Amos and Hosea (c. 750 B.C.)

Amos prophesied during the reign of Jeroboam II of Israel and Azariah (Uzziah) of Judah. Scholars generally agree in dating him about 750 B.C., though some have placed him as early as 760. Amos did not belong to the regular schools of the prophets (1 Sam. 19:20) but was a herdsman and a gatherer of sycamore figs (Amos 1:1; 7:14), whom the Lord called to prophesy (7:15). Although Amos lived in the kingdom of Judah, at Tekoa, some ten miles south of Jerusalem (Amos 1:1), he took to task not only his own southern kingdom for her sins (Amos 2:4–5), but also the northern kingdom of Israel in particular (vv. 6ff.), singling out for rebuke the capital city of Samaria in the north (4:1) and the idolatry of Bethel, where Jeroboam's calf was erected (v. 4). Amos scored the decadent and luxury-loving people of Israel for their extortion from the poor (5:11), their crookedness and use of bribes (v. 12), and their use of sacrifice and offering to cover up their sins—a form of hypocrisy, which God hates (vv. 21–22). After portraying this sordid picture, Amos pointed forward to the time of the restoration of the Davidic kingdom (9:11), and the time of prosperity (vv. 13–

15) that will be brought in with the millennial reign of Christ.

The prophet Hosea, a contemporary of Amos, prophesied in the time of Jeroboam II (782–753 B.C.) against the sins of the northern kingdom of Israel. Hosea used his own family experience as a symbol of the situation in Israel. This prophet had taken an unchaste woman, who bore him children whose names were symbolic (Lo-ruhamah, "no mercy," Lo-ammi, "not my people"; Hosea 1:6, 9). Hosea's wife, it seems, forsook him for an adulterous life (2:1–2) but was restored to him after a time (3:1–3). Hosea used the fact of her adultery as a symbol of the apostasy (spiritual adultery) of Israel, and her restoration as an illustration of the fact that one day Israel will be restored in the future Davidic kingdom (v. 5). Hosea pointed out the many sins of Israel, their forgetting of the things of God (4:6), their idolatry (v. 13), their adultery (7:4), and all manner of other sins. It was a stern rebuke, but it was greatly needed in the days of low spirituality and low morality in the era of Jeroboam II.

Archaeological Light on Amos's Condemnation of the Idle Luxury of Samaria (Amos 6:4, 6)

Amos pointed out the dishonesty, extortion, and crookedness of the decadent luxury-loving people of Samaria, who took their ease "on beds inlaid with ivory," drank "wine by the bowlful," and anointed themselves with the "finest lotions [oils]" (Amos 6:4, 6). The excavation of Samaria begun in 1931 under the direction of J.W. Crowfoot uncovered from the citadel area of the city numerous fragments of ivory inlay, which illuminate Amos' reference to the "beds inlaid with ivory." Most of these ivory pieces are in the form of plaques or panels bearing reliefs, and apparently formed part of the inlay decoration of the furniture. The subjects portrayed in the reliefs include lotus, lilies, papyrus, lions, bulls, deer, winged figures in human form, sphinxes, and figures of Egyptian gods, such as Isis and Horus (FLAP, 185–88).

Several of the Samaria ostraca,[1] which record the payment of taxes to the royal treasury at the capital or income from the royal estates, list such payments in wine and oil. A typical ostracon (No. 1) tells that in the tenth year contributions of wine were sent to Shemaryo, the royal steward from the town of Beeryam, by Raga son of Elisha, Uzza, Eliba, Baala son of Elisha, and Yedayo. The words on the potsherd read literally, "In the tenth year, to Shemaryo from Beeryam, jars of old (wine), Raga son of Elisha, Uzza," etc.[2] Another ostracon (No. 17) reads, "In the tenth year, from Azzah to Gaddiyo, a jar of fine oil,"[3] These ostraca show that the payment of taxes in wine and oil provided a source for the wine that the ease-loving people of Samaria were drinking, and also a source for the fine oil they used to anoint themselves (Amos 6:6). There is some debate over the date of the Samaria ostraca. When they were initially found, the excavators dated them to the reign of Ahab. Albright and others have since placed them during the general time of Amos' ministry, c. 785–750 B.C. (EAEHL, 4:1044).

Earlier in his message of rebuke, Amos referred to the statement that the Lord would "tear down the winter house along with the summer house" (3:15). Archaeological discoveries show that the winter and summer houses were characteristic of that period, being included among the

---

[1]See chapter 15, section entitled "Archaeological Light on Baal Worship. . . ," pages 154–55.

[2]Hand copies of these ostraca appear in George Andrew Reisner, Clarence Stanley Fisher, David Gordon Lyon, *Harvard Excavations at Samaria*, 1908–1910, vol. 1, Text (Cambridge: Harvard University Press, 1924), 239 [RHES]; cf. JSAT, 85–86; PANET, 321.

[3]RHES, 239; JSAT, 87; FLAP, 187.

buildings of Syrian royalty in the eighth century. In an inscription found at Shamal in Syria, dated about 740 B.C., the king, Bir-Rakeb, said that his royal predecessors had three palaces, including a winter house and a summer house (AOTA, 167).

Murder in the Palace of Israel: Zechariah, Shallum, Menahem (2 Kings 15)

The materially prosperous yet sinful era of Jeroboam II (782–753 B.C.), the thirteenth king of Israel, was followed by bad times in the northern kingdom. The wickedness of the nation caught up with it, and the last years were characterized by greater sin, with murder even in the royal palace.

Jeroboam II was succeeded by his son Zechariah, the fourteenth king of Israel. Zechariah ruled only six months (2 Kings 15:8), and was then slain by Shallum (v. 10). This brought to an end the dynasty of Jehu, with the death of his fourth descendant, who occupied the throne of Israel. God had promised Jehu that four generations of descendants would sit on the throne (2 Kings 10:13).

Shallum, the fifteenth king of Israel, usurping the throne after he had murdered Zechariah, ruled for only one month, during the year 752 B.C. and then was slain by Menahem (2 Kings 15:14), who became the sixteenth king of Israel (752–742).

The Kings of Assyria; Their Relationship with Israel

After 750 B.C., the kings of Assyria pushed down into Syria and Canaan from time to time and came in direct contact with the kings of Israel and Judah. In order to integrate these kings of Assyria with the biblical record, it will be helpful to list them:

Tiglath-Pileser III	745–727
Shalmaneser V	726–722
Sargon II	721–705

Tiglath-Pileser III was a usurper, apparently a general who put himself on the throne, took the name of the famous Tiglath-Pileser I (c. 1100 B.C.), and then boasted about the kings of his fathers (OHA, 175). Tiglath-Pileser III reorganized the army of Assyria and then made a drive for an empire. He annexed the area southeast of his own country, that is, Babylonia, and thereafter proceeded to extend control over Syria and Palestine. Menahem, the sixteenth king of Israel (752–742 B.C.), paid tribute to Tiglath-Pileser III, as recorded in 2 Kings 15:20, where Tiglath-Pileser is called Pul (for an explanation, see the next section).

Archaeological Light on the Problem of Tiglath-Pileser III and Pul

As noted above, it is recorded that Menahem, the sixteenth king of Israel (752–742 B.C.), paid tribute to Pul, the king of Assyria, when the Assyrian king came against the land of Israel (2 Kings 15:19–20). Another biblical reference refers to both Pul and Tiglath-Pileser as involved in the affairs of Israel at this time: "And the God of Israel stirred up the spirit of Pul king of Assyria, *and* the spirit of Tilgath-pilneser [Tiglath-Pileser] king of Assyria, and *he carried* them away. . ." (1 Chron. 5:26 KJV). In trying to harmonize the facts, some scholars argued in the past that Pul and Tiglath-Pileser III were two different individuals, and the above-mentioned reference in 1 Chronicles referring to "Pul *and* Tiglath-pileser" was cited to support this view. Horner pointed out, however, that the Hebrew word for "carried" is in the singular (therefore correctly rendered "he carried"), and that the word "and" in the middle of the section would in this context more properly be translated "even," as may be done in accordance with Hebrew usage. In view of these considerations, the verse should read, as in the NIV: "So the God of Israel stirred up the spirit of Pul king of Assyria (that is, Tiglath-Pileser king of Assyria). . . ." Thus this verse does not indicate that Pul and Tiglath-Pileser were different individuals, but is rather a definite piece of evidence that they were the same.[4] The newer Bible versions follow this approach to Hebrew usage. The NASB uses the word "even" to equate Pul with Tiglath-Pileser; the NKJV also equates the two kings.

In addition to the biblical indication that Tiglath-Pileser and Pul are the same, archaeological evidence of the identification has long since been established by Schrader (TCK, 155; TMN, 141). Specific evidence is found in two clay tablets that give similar material about this period of Assyrian history, with the name of Tiglath-Pileser in one tablet and Pul as the corresponding name in the other (translations of these records appear in TCK, 156; TMN, 140).

Furthermore, archaeological light as to why Tiglath-Pileser had these two names has surfaced in other inscriptional material. When Tiglath-Pileser III annexed Babylonia to the Assyrian Empire, he went through the ceremony used for assuming the kingship of Babylonia. And it seems that in order to spare the tender susceptibilities of the Babylonians, he even permitted them to use a separate name for him, Pul (Pulu), so that they would feel they had a king of their own. This explains why he is called Pul in the book of Kings (OHA, 181) and enables us also to understand why he is called Pulu from time to time in the cuneiform records (BWMS, 102).

Tiglath-Pileser and Menahem

When Tiglath-Pileser came with his army against Israel, Menahem paid him a thousand talents of silver, a considerable sum, to induce him to allow Menahem to remain securely on his throne (2 Kings 15:19). The usual date assigned for this campaign of Tiglath-Pileser has been 738 B.C., but Thiele produced evidence to show that it could have been in the year 743 B.C. (TCK, 156–63, esp. 156, 161; TMN, 108, 121, 139–62). Thus it would have occurred during the dates of Menahem's reign, as now correctly understood (752–742).

Archaeological Light on Tiglath-Pileser and Azariah of Judah (767–740 B.C.)

The archaeologicl records of Tiglath-Pileser III (745–727 B.C.) reveal that he came in contact with Azariah of Judah in his campaign to the region of Syria and Canaan (the same one in which he received tribute from Menahem as noted above). The Bible does not tell us anything about the contact of Azariah with Tiglath-Pileser, and so this is a case of further illumination from the archaeological discoveries. As Thiele points out, there is no reason to doubt the identification of "Azriau of Yaudi" in the Assyrian inscription with Azariah of Judah (TCK, 156).

Archaeological Light on Tiglath-Pileser and Pekah of Israel (740–732 B.C.)

Menahem (752–742 B.C.), the sixteenth king of Israel, was followed by his son, Pekahiah (2 Kings 15:22–23), who reigned for two years (742–740). Pekahiah was murdered by one of his military officers, Pekah (v. 25), and Pekah became the eighteenth king of Israel (740–732).

The Bible records that in the time of Pekah, Tiglath-Pileser III came into the northern part of Israel, the region around Galilee and the land of Naphtali. From there he carried off some of the inhabitants and apparently subjugated the area (2 Kings 15:29). Archaeological evidence of the extension of Tiglath-Pileser III's sway over northern Palestine is indicated in his inscription, which reads in part,

---

[4]Joseph Horner, "Biblical Chronology," *Proceedings of the Society of Biblical Archaeology* (1898), 237 [PSBA], cited in TCK, 155; Edwin R. Thiele, *The Mysterious Numbers of the Hebrew Kings*, new rev. ed. (Grand Rapids: Zondervan, 1983), 189 [TMN].

"...the border of Bit-Humria [House of Omri, i.e., Israel] ... the wide land of Naphtali, in its entirety, I brought within the border of Assyria" (LARA, 1: 292, paragraph 815; CBS, 146).

Jotham, the Tenth King of Judah
(2 Kings 15:32–38; 740–736 B.C.)

When Azariah, the ninth king of Judah, was smitten with leprosy, his son Jotham ruled with him as co-regent (2 Kings 15:5), and after the death of Azariah, Jotham ruled for several years as king of Judah (740–736 B.C.). Jotham had some interest in the things of God, for we are told that "he walked steadfastly before the LORD his God" (2 Chron. 27:6), but all was not well in Judah, because the high places of pagan worship were not removed (2 Kings 15:35).

Ahaz, the Eleventh King of Judah
(2 Kings 16:1–20; 736–716 B.C.)

After the death of Jotham, Ahaz his son became the eleventh king of Judah (2 Kings 15:38). He proved to be a wicked king, aping the idolatrous "ways of the kings of Israel and [he] even sacrificed his son in the fire" (16:3). When Ahaz went up to Damascus to see Tiglath-Pileser III, he noticed a pagan altar there and sent the pattern back to Jerusalem to have a copy of this altar produced. Upon his return from Damascus, he used the new pagan altar (16:10, 12).

Ahaz and Tiglath-Pileser III
(2 Kings 16:7ff.)

The king of Syria (Rezin) and the king of Israel (Pekah) fought against Ahaz, apparently with plans to punish him for not coming into an alliance with them against Tiglath-Pileser. Ahaz sought help from Tiglath-Pileser, seeking to gain favor by the payment of the wealth of the temple and the palace to him (16:8).

Tiglath-Pileser went up against Damascus and gave the Syrians a thorough beating, killing the king, Rezin, and carrying the people into captivity (16:9). The archaeological records of Tiglath-Pileser tell of the attack on Damascus (LARA, 1:279, paragraph 777).

Hoshea, the Last King of Israel; the
End of the Northern Kingdom
(2 Kings 17)

Pekah, the eighteenth king of Israel, came to a sudden end when he was slain by Hoshea in a conspiracy (2 Kings 15:30). Hoshea became the nineteenth king of Israel (732–723, 722 B.C.) and was the reigning king when the northern kingdom was brought to an end with the siege of Samaria by the Assyrians.

The Siege of Samaria (2 Kings 17:3–6)

When Tiglath-Pileser died in 727 B.C., Hoshea apparently became tired of paying his huge annual tribute in gold and silver to Assyria, and looked to Egypt for help in resisting Assyria (POTH, 302). The new king of Assyria, Shalmaneser V (726–722), swept into Canaan and besieged the city of Samaria. After a three-year's assault, the city fell (2 Kings 17:5–6). The principal inhabitants of the northern kingdom were carried off into captivity by the Assyrians, bringing to an end the northern kingdom and beginning the captivity of Israel, in about 722.

The King Who Captured Samaria

Sargon, in his inscriptions claimed that he captured Samaria (PANET, 284–85). Most writers have accepted this assertion and have held that, although Shalmaneser initiated and carried on the siege of Samaria, it was Sargon who completed the capture of the city. According to this view, Sargon is to be identified with the "king of Assyria" in 2 Kings 17:6, who took the inhabitants of Samaria to Assyria. Olmstead pointed out, however, that Sargon was silent concerning the capture of Samaria in his own accounts inscribed at the beginning of his reign, and that a Babylonian chronicle seems to justify ascribing the capture to Shalmaneser V just at the end of his reign, in 723–722 B.C., rather than to Sargon during his first year of rule, 722–721. Thus it is likely that Shalmaneser V, and not Sargon II captured Samaria[5] and that, with the passing of the years, Sargon's "press corps" ascribed the siege to this latter king. It is only in the royal chronicles recorded in the later part of his reign that Sargon is credited with taking Samaria. Apparently what happened is that Samaria fell during the fighting season (spring or summer) of 722 B.C. Shalmaneser died late in December, and Sargon then took the reins of government. He finished mopping up in 721 and collected the prisoners and established a government for the defeated province. His claim to have carried off 27,290 inhabitants (PANET, 284–85) may well be accurate; the government probably tried to establish accurate records of booty and prisoners that could be sold into slavery or used for construction projects. Such a number was too large to have come from the town of Samaria alone and must represent captives from the whole province of Samaria. Presumably, at least some of these captives were used on the construction gangs when Sargon started to build his new capital and palace at Khorsabad, about twelve miles northeast of Nineveh. For pictures of the great stone winged bull at the entrance of Sargon's palace and an artist's reconstruction of the palace, see page 164.

Archaeological Confirmation Concerning Sargon's Existence

Though certain verses in the Bible that speak of "the king of Assyria" may refer to King Sargon, the name "Sargon" actually occurs only once in the Bible: "In the year that the supreme commander, sent by Sargon king of Assyria, came to Ashdod and captured it" (Isa. 20:1). Up to a century ago, no evidence of the existence of such a king had been found in other available historical records.[6] A.T. Olmstead[7] pointed out that scholars once argued that Sargon was the same as Shalmaneser.[8] Such an absence of Sargon's name from historical records made it easy for some critics and historians to doubt "his very existence."[9]

In 1843 the French consular agent at Mosul began digging at Khorsabad (FLAP, 174), some twelve miles north of the site of ancient Nineveh, and there found the great palace of Sargon. The palace area occupied some twenty-five acres, and the walls of the palace proper varied from nine and one half to sixteen feet in thickness (HEBL, 86). No longer was there doubt about the existence of Sargon. (A restoration of his palace based on the excavations appears in PANEP, 236; and a picture of Sargon in PANEP, 154.)

One of the large stonewinged bulls that stood at the entrance of Sargon's palace was found in later excavations made by Chiera (1929ff.) and was brought to the University of Chicago, where it may now be seen in the Oriental Institute Museum. This winged bull is sixteen feet long, sixteen feet high, and weighs forty tons. Fortunately for purposes of transporta-

---

[5]A.T. Olmstead, "The Fall of Samaria," *American Journal of Semitic Languages* [AJSL] 21 (1904–1905): 179–82; idem, *Western Asia in the Days of Sargon*, 45ff., n. 9; cited in TCK, 173. See also FLAP, 208–10.

[6]Finegan points out that "for a long time" the reference in Isaiah was the sole place in extant literature where Sargon's name appeared (FLAP, 209).

[7]Professor of Oriental History at the Oriental Institute of the University of Chicago until his death in 1945.

[8]A.T. Olmstead, *History of Assyria* (New York: Scribner, 1923), 282 [OHA].

[9]Noted by George L. Robinson, RBA, 96.

tion, this large monument was found broken in several pieces, the largest one weighing nineteen tons. Even this partial "fragment" constituted somewhat of a transportation difficulty when it began its land and sea journey. The various pieces, assembled into a unit, form "without doubt the most valuable ancient work in the Institute collection."[10] A marvelous collection of reliefs and stonewinged bulls from the palace of Sargon is on display at the Louvre Museum in Paris.

[10]James Henry Breasted, *The Oriental Institute* (Chicago: University of Chicago Press, 1933), 368 [BOI].

Chapter 18

Judah, 722–640 B.C.

(2 Kings 18–21; 2 Chronicles 29–33.
Hezekiah, Manasseh, Amon)

The Date of Hezekiah, the Twelfth King of Judah (2 Kings 18)

Most recent writers believe that Hezekiah began to reign sometime between 730 and 720 B.C. Their dates are based for the most part on the synchronism of 2 Kings 18:1, which indicates that in the third year of Hoshea, the last king of Israel, Hezekiah began to reign in Judah. Since most recent chronologies give about 730 or a little later for the beginning of Hoshea's reign, Hezekiah's reign is ordinarily indicated as beginning shortly after that.

Thiele, however, feels that the synchronisms of 2 Kings 18:1, 9–10 are "open to question" (TCK, 165; TMN, 134–38), and that therefore other criteria must be taken into consideration. The passage in 2 Kings 18:13 tells of Sennacherib's invasion of Judah when he came up against the cities of Hezekiah's land. This invasion is recorded as being in the fourteenth year of Hezekiah, and in turn the Assyrian records give reasonable indication that this was in the year 701 B.C.[1]

Fourteen years prior to 701 would give the year 716–715 as the inaugural year of the reign of Hezekiah (TCK, 174; TMN, 134–35). This would mean that the northern kingdom had come to an end with the capture of Samaria several years earlier, about 722.

Several details noted by Thiele seem to show that the northern kingdom was at an end in the days of Hezekiah. When Hezekiah sent out invitations to the Passover, held early in his reign, he included the northern tribes of Ephraim and Manasseh (2 Chron. 30:1) and even Zebulun (v. 10). These tribes inhabited areas that would more likely be open to the envoys of the southern kingdom after the northern kingdom had fallen (TCK, 174). Furthermore, after the Passover, when the people went out to break down the pagan images and groves, they extended their activity to Ephraim and Manasseh (2 Chron. 31:1)—another indication that the northern kingdom was at an end and that her territory was open to contact with Judah (TCK, 175). These are some of the considerations that led Thiele, in his

[1]D.D. Luckenbill, *The Annals of Sennacherib* (Chicago: University of Chicago Press, 1924), 10–14 [LAS].

chronology, to date the beginning of Hezekiah's reign in 716 B.C.

Future study may throw more light on the synchronisms of 2 Kings 18:1, 9–10, which Thiele holds are "open to question" (TCK, 165). Thiele correctly points out the competence of the Old Testament writers in keeping the biblical chronology and comments that in this complex procedure they were able to "keep their bearings" and pass on records to us which are so straight that we can unravel the seemingly tangled skein (TCK, 177).

Hezekiah's Reforms (2 Kings 18:3–7; 2 Chronicles 29–31)

Reacting sharply against the wickedness of his father, Ahaz, who had participated in the detestable ways of the nations (2 Kings 16:3–4), Hezekiah opened the doors of the house of the Lord and repaired them (2 Chron. 29:3) and then fostered the resumption of the normal worship with the keeping of the Passover (2 Chron. 30:15ff.). The resultant spiritual awakening caused the people to break down the images and the groves and destroy the high places of pagan worship, even in parts of the northern area (2 Chron. 31:1). Hezekiah's attitude in spiritual matters is well summarized by the writer of Kings: "He held fast to the LORD and did not cease to follow him; he kept the commands the LORD had given Moses" (2 Kings 18:6).

Isaiah and Hezekiah

The prophet Isaiah states that he carried on his ministry in the days of Uzziah (Azariah), Jotham, Ahaz, and Hezekiah (Isa. 1:1). His great transforming vision came in the year that King Uzziah died (Isa. 6:1), probably about 740 B.C. This means that Isaiah lived through the rule of Jotham (740–736) and the wicked reign of Ahaz (736–716), who sacrificed his own son in the fire (2 Kings 16:3) and who also copied the pagan altar at Damascus for the temple of God in Jerusalem. It ap-

pears that Isaiah's words of admonition concerning these ravages made upon the worship and the temple of the Lord were disdained, ignored, and scorned by Ahaz (POTH, 309). The period of Ahaz figures to some degree in much of the material in Isaiah 1–35. This part of the book of Isaiah falls into several sections and in most cases the events of a given section begin in the reign of Ahaz.

Isaiah's great opportunity for influence at the court came after the death of Ahaz, when Hezekiah came to the throne. It seems likely that Isaiah had had close contact with Hezekiah during his boyhood, and this influence now bore fruit, undoubtedly being largely responsible for the reforms that Hezekiah instituted in the breaking down of the pagan images, the destruction of the high places, and the fostering of the resumption of the normal worship in Jerusalem. Isaiah 36–39 describes events during the reign of Hezekiah, when Sennacherib came into Judah, besieged Jerusalem, and suffered defeat because the Lord delivered the city (Isa. 36:36). The last chapters of Isaiah (40–66) were probably written during the reign of Manasseh (687–642), the wicked king who succeeded Hezekiah; in these chapters the prophet turns from the sad condition in Judah and looks forward to the glorious redemption that the Lord promised would come after the Exile.

Archaeological Light on Isaiah's Words to the Vain Women of His Time (Isaiah 3:16–24)

When Isaiah pointed out the greed of the rich and their oppression of the poor (3:14–15), he went on to ridicule some of the women of his day for their "outstretched necks," their "flirting" eyes, their "mincing" walk, their elaborate hairdressing, their "sweet-smell," and their overindulgence in the use of cosmetics and other fineries (Isa. 3:16–23). M.G. Kyle, describing the excavations at Kiriath

Sepher,[2] remarked that while the women of that day had different names for their cosmetics than women have today, nevertheless their fashions in make-up most remarkably resembled the extremes of fashionable "make-up" that we are accustomed to see in modern times. Scarcely a day went by during their excavating, he said, that they did not find, in the city of the days of the late monarchy, a vanity pallette of one of these pampered ladies. As Kyle wrote in his report concerning the excavation at Kiriath Sepher, "It seems as if every Jewess in the town had one" (KEK, 199–200).

Discovery of an Ancient Isaiah Manuscript

One day in the spring of 1948, John C. Trever,[3] one of the Fellows at the American School of Oriental Research in Jerusalem, taking a phone call for the school, learned that Father Sowmy of the Syrian Orthodox Convent wished some information on five ancient Hebrew scrolls recently acquired by the convent from some Arabs.[4] After the scrolls were brought to the school, Trever examined and photographed one manuscript, which later proved to be a complete copy of the book of Isaiah. A photograph was

---

[2]Carried on from 1926 to 1932; KEK, 189ff.

[3]John Trever gave his account of the Jerusalem scrolls in *The Biblical Archaeologist* (September 1948). A preliminary report was presented in the same publication in May 1948 by G. Ernest Wright.

[4]In addition to Albright, also Burrows of Yale, Sukenik of the Hebrew University in Jerusalem, and Trever, who photographed the manuscript, were all convinced that it was ancient. Further studies showed that little value was to be attached to the suggestion that it dated from the Middle Ages (made by Solomon Zeitlin, Professor of Rabbinical Literature at Dropsie College in Philadelphia) (Report on Zeitlin's suggestion published in *New York Times*, summarized in *Presbyterian Guardian* [March 1949], 57; also see article by Zeitlin in *Jewish Quarterly Review* [January–March 1949]).

An Associated Press dispatch from Jerusalem dated March 18, 1949, reported that the cave where the Arabs found these scrolls had been examined by Lankester Harding, Director of Antiquities in Transjordan, and by Father De Vaux of the Dominican Bible School in Jerusalem. Regarding their finding, O.R. Sellers, director of the American School of Oriental Research in Jerusalem, reported that they found late Hellenic pottery in the cave, which would point to the first or second century B.C. (Article in *Philadelphia Inquirer* [March 1949]; substantially the same report was given in the *Biblical Archaeologist* 12, 2 [May 1949]: 32.) The pottery, then, also supports the date of 100 B.C. for the manuscript.

Writing in the February 1949 issue of the *Bulletin of the American Schools of Oriental Research*, John Trever reported that he had examined the individual letters used in the Isaiah manuscript, had made comparisons with other early manuscripts, and had concluded that the Isaiah manuscript should be dated about 125–100 B.C. In the same issue, Solomon Birnbaum, one of our ablest palaeographers, reported that he had made comparisons between the Isaiah manuscript and documents of Jewish colonists settled in Egypt in the third century, and also with the boundary stones of about 100 B.C. and several other inscriptions, and that on the basis of those studies, he had concluded that the first half of the second century B.C. suggested itself as the date of the writing of the Isaiah manuscript (Solomon A.Birnbaum, "The Date of the Isaiah Scroll," BASOR 113 [February 1949], 33).

In view of the pottery evidence from the cave and the studies of Albright, Burrows, Sukenik, Trever, and Birnbaum, there appears to be no reason to doubt the date of c. 100 B.C. that has been assigned to this Isaiah manuscript.

Reporting further in the October 1949 issue of BASOR, Albright pointed out that further study, including examination of a new infrared photograph of the Nash Papyrus (containing the Ten Commandments and the Shema passage and dated in the first or second century B.C. by Albright, Birnbaum, et al.) only adds additional evidence for the early date of the Isaiah manuscript (first or second century B.C.). Albright also observes that the rapid progress of discovery and publication of material concerning the Isaiah manuscript will soon render discussions like Zeitlin's "antiquated" (W.F. Albright, "On the Date of the Scrolls from Ain Feshkha and the Nash Papyrus," BASOR 115 [October 1949]: 10–19).

sent to W.F. Albright of Johns Hopkins University, who concluded that the form of the script would indicate a date of about 100 B.C. Such an early manuscript of Isaiah is of great significance, inasmuch as the oldest manuscript up to that time dated from about 900 A.D. Even more important was the close agreement between this newly found Jerusalem manuscript and the traditional Hebrew text, which was copied much later. Millar Burrows of Yale indicates that there is nothing in this manuscript that can be called "a major addition or omission" and that there is "no important dislocation or disarrangement of the text."[5] The substantial agreement between this ancient manuscript and those of a thousand years later shows the care with which biblical manuscripts were copied and adds to our assurance concerning the substantial accuracy of the later manuscripts from which our English translations were made.

This manuscript became available to the scholarly world at the time when the RSV translation committee was preparing the new version. They finally decided to adopt only thirteen readings for their translation based on the new manuscript. Millar Burrows, a member of the translation committee, later concluded that even some of these were unwarranted and that in five of the thirteen instances the Masoretic reading should have been retained.[6]

Burrows observed further, "It is a matter for wonder that through something like a thousand years the text underwent so little alteration. As I said in my first article on the scroll, 'Herein lies its chief importance, supporting the fidelity of the Masoretic tradition' " (BDSS, 304). In fact, he concluded that at many points the Isaiah manuscript had readings inferior to those in some of the medieval manuscripts already possessed (BDSS, 303).

In time a second Isaiah manuscript, from the same cave at Qumran and not complete, became available to biblical scholars. In commenting on this discovery, Gleason Archer noted that it "proved to be word for word identical with our standard Hebrew Bible in more than 95 percent of the text. The five percent of variation consisted chiefly of obvious slips of the pen and variations in spelling" (ASOTI, 25).

More Manuscript Discoveries

As the world generally knows now, the discovery of the Isaiah manuscripts in a cave at Qumran, adjacent to the Dead Sea, was only the tip of the iceberg. Eventually the State of Israel came into possession of a whole collection of scrolls from what is now called Cave 1 at Qumran. These include a complete scroll of Isaiah, a partial Isaiah, the Habakkuk Commentary (including two chapters of Habakkuk), the Manual of Discipline (rules for members of the religious community who lived nearby), Thanksgiving Hymns, a Genesis Apocryphon (apocryphal accounts of some of the patriarchs), and Wars of the Sons of Light Against the Sons of Darkness (an account of a real or spiritual war between some of the Hebrew tribes and the tribes east of the Jordan—Ammonites, Moabites, etc.).

The magnificent collection from Cave 1 raised the possibility of finding treasures in other caves of the Qumran area. A massive search of the region between 1949 and 1956 resulted in the discovery of biblical manuscripts in a total of eleven caves. Excavation of Cave 2 turned up about one hundred fragments of Exodus, Leviticus, Numbers, Deuteronomy, Jeremiah, Job, Psalms, and Ruth. In Cave 3, in addition to inscribed fragments of hide and papyrus, there was the curious cop-

---

[5]Article on "The Contents and Significance of the Manuscripts," *The Biblical Archaeologist* (September 1948), 60–61.
[6]Millar Burrows, *The Dead Sea Scrolls* (New York: Viking, 1955), 305 [BDSS].

Cave 4 at Qumran

A jar in which Dead Sea Scrolls were stored at Qumran   Courtesy of Palestine Archaeological Museum in Jerusalem

Aerial view of the excavations at Qumran   Courtesy of Palestine Archaeological Museum in Jerusalem

per scroll (about twelve inches high) with directions to over sixty sites containing hidden treasure. To date no treasure has been found, and there is a variety of speculations concerning this scroll. Cave 4 was in many ways the most exciting of all. It provided some forty thousand fragments of an unknown number of manuscripts, about four hundred of which have been identified. About one hundred were biblical scrolls and represent all Old Testament books except Esther. There were fragments from thirteen scrolls of Deuteronomy, twelve of Isaiah, ten of Psalms, six of Exodus, and five of Genesis. A fragment of Samuel, dating to the third century B.C., is thought to be the oldest known piece of biblical Hebrew. Caves 5 through 10 had a variety of scroll fragments too diverse to list here. Prize pieces from Cave 11 included very fine portions of Psalms and Leviticus. The former included forty-eight psalms—forty-one biblical and seven nonbiblical.

After Cave 1 was excavated, attention centered on Khirbet Qumran, a ruin on a plateau between Cave 4 and the Dead Sea. Excavated between 1951 and 1956, it turned out to be the center of a religious community. Presumably Caves 1–11 constituted the library of the community, and some of the manuscripts found there were no doubt produced in the writing room or scriptorium of the community.

It is not possible in a survey book of this sort to tell the story of the Dead Sea Scrolls and their significance.[7] Nevertheless, some of the significance of the scrolls can be briefly told. First, as noted,

the discovery of the scrolls pushed back the history of our Hebrew manuscript collection by a thousand years. Second, again as noted, during the long period of copying the Old Testament text by hand, there was a remarkable—can we say miraculous—degree of preservation of the text. What could be said for the Isaiah manuscripts was approximately true of the rest of the scrolls as well. Third, evidently the standardization of the Hebrew text as we now know it was taking place during the first Christian century. Fourth, the early date of some of the Dead Sea Scrolls has helped to answer critical views on the nature and date of composition of some Old Testament books—e.g., the unity of Isaiah and the second-century B.C. date of Daniel. Last, the discovery of this large body of literature, biblical and nonbiblical, has provided a means for a better understanding of the meaning of Old Testament words.

The Assyrian Kings of Hezekiah's Time and After

We have already noted the Assyrian kings of the middle of the eighth century (see chapter 17). The Assyrian kings contemporary with Hezekiah and following his time are as follows:

Sargon II	721–705 B.C.
Sennacherib	704–681 B.C.
Esarhaddon	680–669 B.C.
Ashurbanipal	668–627 B.C.

Either Sargon or probably his predecessor captured the city of Samaria and

---

[7] For a fuller study of the subject read one or more of the following books: F.F. Bruce, *Second Thoughts on the Dead Sea Scrolls*, 2nd ed. (Grand Rapids: Eerdmans, 1961); Millar Burrows, *Burrows on the Dead Sea Scrolls* (a combination of *The Dead Sea Scrolls* and *More Light on the Dead Sea Scrolls*) (Grand Rapids: Baker, 1978); Frank M. Cross, *The Ancient Library of Qumran and Modern Biblical Studies* (Grand Rapids: Baker, 1958); Philip R. Davies, *Qumran* (Grand Rapids: Eerdmans, 1982); William S. LaSor, *The Dead Sea Scrolls and the Christian Faith* (Chicago: Moody Press, 1962); idem, *The Dead Sea Scrolls and the New Testament* (Grand Rapids: Eerdmans, 1972); Charles F. Pfeiffer, *The Dead Sea Scrolls and the Bible* (Grand Rapids: Baker, 1969); R. de Vaux, *Archaeology and the Dead Sea Scrolls* (London: Oxford University Press, 1973); Geza Vermes, *The Dead Sea Scrolls in English*, 2nd ed. (Harmondsworth, Middlesex, England: Penguin Books, 1975); Howard F. Vos, *Archaeology in Bible Lands* (Chicago: Moody Press, 1977), chapter 6; Yigael Yadin, *The Message of the Scrolls* (New York: Simon & Schuster, 1957).

brought the northern kingdom to an end (see chapter 17). Sargon's successor, Sennacherib, pushed into southern Palestine, into the territory of Judah and not only besieged and took Lachish[8] (2 Kings 18:14; 19:8), but also came up against Jerusalem. The Lord delivered the city of Jerusalem from the hosts of Sennacherib (2 Kings 19:35; Isa. 37:36). A few years later, Esarhaddon subjugated Manasseh (2 Chron. 33:11). Let us now look more closely into the reign of these monarchs.

Sargon Against Ashdod; Archaeological Light (Isaiah 20:1)

Isaiah indicates that Sargon's army came against the city of Ashdod (Isa. 20:1), which is in the plain of Philistia in southwestern Palestine. Confirmation of this is found in the records of Sargon, in which he says, "Azuru, king of Ashdod, plotted in his heart to withhold tribute and sent (messages) of hostility to the kings round about him. . . . Against Ashdod, his royal city, I advanced in haste. Ashdod, Gimtu (Gath), and Asdudimmu, I besieged, I captured" (LARA, 2:13–14, paragraph 30; PANET, 286). For a discussion of the archaeological confirmation of the existence of Sargon, see chapter 17.

Sennacherib's Invasion of Judah (2 Kings 18:13ff.); Archaeological Confirmation of Hezekiah's Payment of Tribute

When Sennacherib made his invasion into Judah (701 B.C.), he took many of the cities (2 Kings 18:13) and finally threatened Jerusalem. Hezekiah then paid trib-

ute to Sennacherib, including thirty talents of gold and three hundred talents of silver (2 Kings 18:14). The inscriptions of Sennacherib tell us of this tribute in the following words, "In addition to 30 talents of gold and 800 talents of silver, (there were) gems, antimony, jewels, large sandu-stones . . . ivory, maple, boxwood, all kinds of valuable treasures . . . which he had them bring after me to Nineveh, my royal city. To pay tribute and to accept servitude he dispatched his messengers" (LARA, 2:121, paragraph 240; also see BAB, 472; PANET, 288). The biblical and the Assyrian records agree exactly in the reference to thirty talents of gold, but the biblical figure of three hundred talents of silver at first appears to be contradicted by the eight hundred talents of silver recorded in the Assyrian inscription. It is quite possible, however, that Sennacherib counted some other payment or valuables in his figure of eight hundred talents of silver, which is more than the three hundred talents given in the Bible. It has also been suggested that the numbers were really equivalent to one another, the divergence being due to textual corruption (BAB, 473). Schrader explains it as due to the difference between the Babylonian and the Palestinian talent (RBA, 100).

Archaeological Confirmation of Sennacherib's Failure to Capture Jerusalem (2 Kings 19:35–36)

When Sennacherib's army came up against Jerusalem, God spoke through Isaiah the prophet (2 Kings 19:20ff.) and

---

[8]Sennacherib devoted considerable space to his conquest of Lachish on bas reliefs produced to decorate the walls of his palace at Nineveh. These are on display in one of the Assyrian rooms at the British Museum in London, and a cast of them may be seen in the Oriental Institute Museum of the University of Chicago. David Ussishkin, current excavator of Lachish, has produced a stunning book portraying Sennacherib's conquest of the city, *The Conquest of Lachish by Sennacherib* (Tel Aviv: Tel Aviv University Publications, 1982). A review of the book with detailed discussion of the Assyrian destruction of the city appears in BAR (March/April 1984), 48–65. This is followed in the same issue of the magazine by Ussishkin's article entitled "Defensive Judean Counter-Ramp Found at Lachish in 1983 Season," 66–73. Excavations indicate that the Israelites put up a fierce resistance against the Assyrians. As the Assyrians built a siege ramp on the outside of the walls, the Israelites built a counterramp inside the walls.

promised to defend the city (2 Kings 19:34; Isa. 37:35). The angel of the Lord went forth and smote the Assyrian army, leaving 185,000 "dead bodies" (2 Kings 19:35; Isa. 37:36).[9] Sennacherib returned to Nineveh without capturing the city of Jerusalem (2 Kings 19:36).

To the rationalist, this story of the angel's smiting an army and causing a great king to return to his native land without capturing a city seems beyond the realm of historical possibility. However, confirmation of the fact that Sennacherib did not take Jerusalem was found in an inscription on a prism called the Taylor Cylinder, discovered at Kouyunjik, the site of ancient Nineveh, in 1830 by J.E. Taylor, the British Vice-Consul at Basra. The Taylor Cylinder is now in the British Museum in London. An almost indentical inscription is found on the Oriental Institute Cylinder, purchased by the Oriental Institute of the University of Chicago in 1920 (PMOT, 316, figure 136). In the inscription Sennacherib says that he made other Palestinian cities yield, but when he comes to describe his campaign against Jerusalem, he fails to mention the capture of that city and its king, Hezekiah. Rather the text of the inscription tells of King Hezekiah in these words, "As for himself, like a bird in a cage is his royal city Jerusalem, I shut (him) up" (PANET, 288). Since Sennacherib did not capture Jerusalem (as indicated in the Bible), he made as good a story out of the siege as possible. Actually, Hezekiah was reposing quite safely in his "cage."

There is no evidence in the archaeolog-ical records that Sennacherib ever re-turned to the region of Palestine. The Bible gives us an adequate reason—the loss of his army before the walls of Jerusalem.

Archaeological Confirmation Concerning Sennacherib's Death (2 Kings 19:36–37)

The Bible states that Sennacherib final-ly met his death at the hands of his own sons (2 Kings 19:37; Isa. 37:38). Esarhad-don (680–669 B.C.), Sennacherib's son and successor, tells of this very event in the following inscription:

> In the month Nisanu, on a favorable day, complying with their exalted command, I made my joyful entrance into the royal palace, the awesome place, wherein abides the fate of kings. A firm determination fell upon my brothers. They forsook the gods and turned to their deeds of violence, plotting evil. . . . To gain the kingship they slew Sennacherib, their father.[10]

Archaeological Light on the Military Officers of Sennacherib: Tartan, Rabsaris, and Rab-Shakeh (2 Kings 18:17 KJV)

Archaeological discoveries in Babylonia show that the names of the military officers of Sennacherib (2 Kings 18:17) are not proper names but rather Assyrian

---

[9]The number seems excessive (one of the greatest problems in the Old Testament is the transcription of numbers). The Assyrians could and did amass large armies. For example, Shalmaneser III moved across the Euphrates westward with an army of 120,000 men in 845 (H.W.F. Saggs, The Might That Was Assyria [London: Sidgwick & Jackson], 253). But after the 183,000 died on this occasion, there was apparently a substantial army left to return to Assyria. If one assumes that the figure is accurate, it might be arrived at by including Assyrian fighting men, camp servants, Judean defectors or impressments into the Assyrian force, and even some captives (many of whom may have become collaborators). The parallel passage in 2 Chronicles 32:21 leaves unspecified the number of men killed. Another explanation is that the Hebrew of 2 Kings 19:35 could possibly be translated "one hundred and eighty and five thousand"—i.e., 100 + 80 + 5,000 = 5180.

[10]LARA, 2:200–201, paragraphs 501–2.

The Oriental Institute Cylinder, which gives an account of Sennacherib's campaign against Judah and against Jerusalem in particular
Courtesy of the Oriental Institute of the University of Chicago

military titles (BWMS, 43). Tartan is the Assyrian *tartanu*, indicating the second in command, the field marshall.[11] Rabshakeh is rendered *rab-shaqu* in Assyrian meaning "chief officer." Rabsaris is rendered *rabu-sha-reshi* in Assyrian and originally had the meaning of "chief eunuch" (BWMS, 43–44).

[11]BWMS, 43; cf. AOTA, 161.

Archaeological Light on Merodach-Baladan's Embassy to Hezekiah (2 Kings 20:12)

After Hezekiah's illness (2 Kings 20:1ff.), the king of Babylon, Merodach-Baladan, sent letters and a present to Hezekiah, seemingly to congratulate him on his recovery. The archaeological discoveries, however, indicate that there was a further purpose behind Merodach-Baladan's friendly gesture, a diplomatic reason. Merodach-Baladan had been able to hold out for a number of years against Sennacherib, the king of Assyria. Sennacherib himself gives us evidence of this, for he tells of going down to Babylon to subjugate Merodach-Baladan:

> In my first campaign I accomplished the defeat of Merodach-Baladan, king of Babylonia, together with the army of Elam, his ally, in the plain of Kish. In the midst of that battle he forsook his camp and made his escape alone; so he saved his life. The chariots, horses, wagons, mules, which he left behind at the onset of battle, my hands seized. Into his palace which is in Babylon, joyfully I entered. I opened his treasure house:—gold and silver, precious stones of every kind, goods and property without limit. . . . I counted as spoil. (LARA, 2:116, paragraph 234)

In another record, Sennacherib tells about many of the rebellious tactics of Merodach-Baladan:

> At the beginning of my reign, when I solemnly took my seat on the throne, and ruled the inhabitants of Assyria with mercy and grace, Merodach-Baladan, king of Babylonia, (whose heart is wicked), an instigator of revolt, plotter of rebellion, doer of evil, whose guilt is heavy, brought over to his side Shutur-Nahundu, the Elamite, and gave him gold, silver and precious stones, and (so) secured him as an ally. (LARA, 2:128–29, paragraph 257)

Thus it seems clear from these Assyrian accounts that Merodach-Baladan's real motive in sending the present to Hezekiah was to seek an alliance with him against Assyria (BAB, 475; cf. CBS, 153), even as he had similarly persuaded Shutur-Nahundu to become his ally against Assyria.

Hezekiah's Conduit (2 Kings 20:20; 2 Chronicles 32:30); Archaeological Light from the Siloam Inscription

The Bible tells us of the pool and the conduit that Hezekiah made to bring water into the city (2 Kings 20:20) from the spring Gihon (2 Chron. 32:30). This tunnel may be seen today at Jerusalem still connecting the spring of Gihon with the pool that Hezekiah made at the south end of the city, within the wall. It seems likely that Hezekiah constructed it so water would be available in a convenient place within the walls when the Assyrians would finally besiege the city of Jerusalem. The tunnel is nearly eighteen hundred feet long and about six feet in height throughout its length (MALB, 483–85).

At the south end of the conduit, where it enters the pool of Siloam, an inscription was found in 1880. The discovery is said to have been made when a small boy, wading in the water, slipped and fell. As he scrambled out, he noticed some letters carved on the wall of the tunnel (CBS, 154–55; PMOT, 326). It was brought to the attention of archaeologists, and later Sayce visited the spot and deciphered the inscription, sitting in mud and water to accomplish his task (CBS, 155). The inscription of six lines tells how the stone-diggers, who began at each end of the tunnel, could finally hear each other as they approached the place where they ultimately met; it also tells that the tunnel was twelve hundred cubits long. (For a translation of this Hebrew inscription see MALB, 484; PANET, 321.) Since the tunnel is nearly eighteen hundred feet long, it gives us an indication that the cubit was about one and one-half feet at that time. The place where the two parties of diggers met can clearly be seen today, being marked by a difference in the level of the tunnel and a change in the direction of the pickmarks (BWMS, 262). The inscription is now in the Museum of the Ancient Orient in Istanbul.

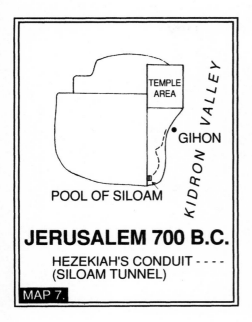

TEMPLE
AREA

GIHON

KIDRON VALLEY

POOL OF SILOAM

JERUSALEM 700 B.C.

HEZEKIAH'S CONDUIT - - - -
(SILOAM TUNNEL)

MAP 7.

Manasseh, King of Judah (2 Kings 21);
Archaeological Light

Manasseh (687–642 B.C.) was a contrast to Hezekiah,[12] his father. He built up the high places of pagan worship that his father had destroyed and erected altars to Baal (2 Kings 21:3). Archaeological light on Manasseh comes from the inscriptions of Esarhaddon, king of Assyria (680–668) who tells of the subservience of Manasseh to his domination.[13] Esarhaddon's domination extended to Egypt as well, the conquest of which is celebrated in a rock-hewn inscription—north of Beirut, Lebanon (see picture in PMOT, 332). Manasseh's son, Amon (642–640), walked in the idolatrous ways of his father and after two years was slain, being succeeded by his eight-year-old son, Josiah.

[12]The casual student of 1 and 2 Kings may wonder why a good king like Hezekiah could have such an idolatrous son as Manasseh or how other good kings could have such bad offspring—or how bad kings could have devout sons. Of course we recognize that this sort of thing often happens in modern society, but there is another dimension to the subject that comes clear from a study of history and archaeology. Often a Hebrew king was able to suppress idolatry when foreign intervention (especially Assyrian) was weak and he could pursue an independent policy. Conversely, when Assyrian influence was strong, royal opposition to idolatry could not be so effective and might even be neutralized. Note that Manasseh was firmly under the Assyrian control, while Hezekiah had successfully opposed the Assyrians.

[13]LARA, 2:265, paragraph 690; CBS, 163–64; BAB, 476; PMOT, 333.

Chapter 19

The End of Judah, 640–586 B.C.

(2 Kings 22–25; 2 Chronicles 34–36; Jeremiah)

Josiah (640–609 B.C.), the Fifteenth King of Judah; His Reform

Josiah came to the throne as a small boy of eight (2 Kings 22:1) and ruled for thirty-one years. His reign stood in striking contrast to that of his father, Amon, and his grandfather, Manasseh, with their shedding of innocent blood and fostering of degrading idolatry (2 Kings 21:16, 21). Josiah "did what was right in the eyes of the LORD" (22:2). He directed the repairing of the temple, in the course of which the "Book of the Law" was found (v. 8) and later read by Shaphan the scribe to King Josiah (v. 10). Josiah had the law read to the people of Judah and Jerusalem (23:1–2) and then made a covenant, in which the people concurred, to keep the commandments of the Lord and to walk in the way of the Lord (v. 3).

Quickened to action by the reading of the Word of God, Josiah proceeded to put away the idols and idolatry that had been promoted by his father and grandfather. He had all the vessels that had been made for Baal worship brought out to the region of the Kidron (east of Jerusalem) and burned (23:4). He put down the surviving idolatrous priests (v. 5), broke

down the houses of the Sodomites (v. 7), and defiled both the high places of pagan worship (v. 8) and the place of child sacrifice where Josiah's predecessors had sacrificed their sons and daughters "in the fire to Molech" (v. 10).

Josiah's reforms were characterized not merely by the purging out of idolatry and paganism but also by a positive and aggressive movement to foster spiritual growth and worship of a true nature. He commanded the people to keep the Passover, and this proved to be a high point in their spiritual awakening, for there had been no Passover such as this one in all the days of the judges and the kings (2 Kings 23:20–21). Josiah had turned to the Lord "with all his heart and with all his soul and with all his strength" (v. 25).

The Finding of the Book of the Law (2 Kings 22:8); Archaeological Light

The Book of the Law found during the repair of the temple was probably the Pentateuch and certainly was at least the book of Deuteronomy. Critics hold that the book of Deuteronomy was written

185

largely in the seventh century B.C.[1] and, except for some traditions that may have been handed down, it has no vital connection with the time of Moses. According to this view, after the book of Deuteronomy was found in the temple in 621 B.C. during the repairs, it underwent a series of editorial expansions between 621 and about 400 (PIOT, 181, 187).

The Bible definitely indicates that Deuteronomy is a record of the words of God to Moses (1500–1400 B.C.) and of the words of Moses to the people. This is shown by many statements telling of God's speaking to the great lawgiver and by Moses' direct messages to Israel (Deut. 1:1; 5:1; 10:1; 27:1; 29:1; 31:1). Thus the internal biblical evidence does not support the idea that the book of Deuteronomy first came into definite form as a forgery in the seventh century shortly before it was found during the temple repairs of 621.

Archaeological discoveries throw interesting light on the possible reason for the repairmen's finding the Book of the Law during their labors on the temple. It is possible that this was the copy of the Pentateuch that had been placed in the cornerstone of the temple several hundred years earlier in the days of Solomon when he directed the building of the temple (c. 967). From archaeological discoveries we now know that it was customary to place documents in the foundations of ancient buildings, just as papers and documents are placed in the cornerstones of buildings at the present time. Nabonidus, king of Babylon in the middle of the sixth century B.C. (555–539), was quite an antiquarian—in fact, almost an archaeologist. He delighted in digging into foundations of buildings ancient in his time and finding the records placed there centuries earlier. He tells of his work on the temple of Shamash at Sippar,

in Mesopotamia, which had been restored by King Nebuchadnezzar but had fallen into decay in his day. He describes his activities in detail:

> When I had brought out Shamash from within it, and made him dwell in another house, that house I tore down, and I made a search for its old foundation record; and I dug to a depth of eighteen cubits, and the *foundation record* of Naram-Sin the son of Sargon (I), which for 3200 years no king that preceded me had discovered, Shamash the great Lord of Ebabbara, the temple of the dwelling of his heart's delight, permitted me, even me, to behold. (translation in PMOT, 306)

If a copy of the law had been placed in the foundation of Solomon's temple (tenth century B.C.), as is likely from the archaeological evidence already cited, then this document would necessarily date back nearly three hundred years before the time of the supposed forgery. It would obviously invalidate the critical theory that the book of Deuteronomy was forged in the seventh century, "found" in the temple later in the seventh century, and passed off by priests as the work of Moses. The implications of the archaeological evidence do not support this critical view of Deuteronomy.

Josiah's Reform Concerning Molech (2 Kings 23:10): Archaeological Light on Molech

As noted previously, Josiah's reform included the defiling of the place of child sacrifice, where his predecessors had sacrificed their sons and daughters "in the fire to Molech" (2 Kings 23:10). The usual view of Old Testament scholars has been that *Molech* was a variant of the Hebrew word *melek*, meaning "king," and was applied to one of the pagan gods as a proper name (Baal, for example, actually

---

[1]For several aspects of the critical view of Deuteronomy, see chapter 9, the sections entitled "Critical View of the Date of Deuteronomy" and "Critical View of the Legislation of Deuteronomy," pages 101–3.

is the word for "Lord"). On the basis of archaeological discoveries, the Old Testament scholar Eissfeldt proposed another explanation of Molech. In North Africa a number of Latin inscriptions have been found that contain the name *molchomor*, a term applied to a type of sacrifice. In view of the fact that parts of North Africa were settled by the Phoenicians, who spoke a Semitic language, and in view of the fact that *molchomor* must be a Semitic rather than a Latin word, Eissfeldt believes that it is made up of two Phoenician words, the first of which is probably *molk*, a variant form of which would be *molech* (molek). Since the compound word referred to a type of sacrifice, Eissfeldt concluded that Molech of the Old Testament was not a god but rather a sacrifice. Burrows states as his opinion that, while some of Eissfeldt's theory is questionable, he has definitely established that there was a Semitic sacrifice called *molk* (BWMS, 227). R.K. Harrison argues, however, that whenever it mentions Molech, "the OT clearly referred to a specific deity."[2]

The Decline and Fall of Assyria, 626–612 B.C.; Archaeological Light from Records of Ashurbanipal

During Josiah's reign (640–609 B.C.), Assyria went into political decline, and finally its capital of Nineveh was captured in 612 by the Babylonians under Nabopolassar in alliance with the Medes (POTH, 341). The last great king of Assyria was Ashurbanipal (668–627 B.C.), who was a ruthless warrior but also a scholar. As a young boy Ashurbanipal had studied the languages that were ancient to him, in particular Sumerian. He tells of his labors in these words:

> I have read the artistic script of Sumer and the dark (obscure) Akkadian, which is hard to master, (now) taking pleasure in the reading of the stones (i.e., steles) (coming) from before the flood, (now) being angered (because I was) stupid and addled by the beautiful script. . . . At the same time I was learning royal decorum, walking in the kingly ways, I stood before the king, my begetter, giving commands to the nobles. (LARA, 2:379, paragraph 986)

(Those whose brains have been "addled" by Greek and other ancient languages may take comfort from Ashurbanipal in his struggle with Sumerian.)

Ashurbanipal did a great service in collecting the clay tablets of his time and putting them in his extensive library at Nineveh. Many of these documents are copies of tablets that were ancient in his day, and thus the learning of Mesopotamia of early times has been brought down to us. In the middle of the nineteenth century, Ashurbanipal's library was found by Layard and Rassam. The tablets included such important documents as the Babylonian record of the Flood.[3]

The discouraging description of Ashurbanipal's last days gives us a picture of the beginning of decline in Assyria. In a clay tablet, he says, "Enmity in the land, strife in the house, do not depart from my side. Disturbances, evil words, are continually arrayed against me. Distress of soul, distress of body have bowed my form. I spend my days sighing and lamenting. . . . Death is making an end of me, is weighing (me) down" (LARA, 2:378, paragraph 984).

After the death of Ashurbanipal (627 B.C.), Assyria's decline culminated in the fall of the capital city of Nineveh in 612 to a coalition of Babylonians, Medes, and Scythians (FLAP, 219). Part of the Assyrian army fled to the west toward Harran and made it a temporary capital. The king of Egypt, Pharaoh Neco, came to the aid of the Assyrian remnant and their king,

---

[2]"Molech," ISBE (1986), 3:401.
[3]For further details on Ashurbanipal's library, see chapter 3.

Ashur-uballit, who stood at bay for several years at Carchemish, once the great city of the Neo-Hittite empire (FLAP, 129).

Death of Josiah at the Hands of Neco (2 Kings 23:29); Archaeological Light on the Problem Concerning Josiah's Action

The Bible recounts that Pharaoh Neco, king of Egypt, went *against* the king of Assyria in the region of the Euphrates (2 Kings 23:29 KJV). Thereupon Josiah went out against Neco, and Neco killed him. Historians of past generations were puzzled as to why Josiah, king of Judah, went against Neco when Neco was on his way to take action against Assyria, the ancient enemy of Israel and Judah. The discovery of a clay tablet published by Gadd of the British Museum explains the reason. It shows that Nineveh had already fallen, and that Neco was not going against the remnant of the Assyrian army but was actually going to its aid (as indicated above). Josiah, not wishing to have any aid reach the Assyrians, went out to Megiddo to stop Neco but was killed by the Egyptian. The word translated *against* in 2 Kings 23:29 (KJV) is a Hebrew word that also has the meaning "on behalf of," and so in this context it is clear that Pharaoh Neco was actually going up to the Euphrates region *on behalf of* the king of Assyria, to help him against the Babylonians under Nabopolassar and Nebuchadnezzar.

Neco actually suffered overwhelming defeat at the hands of Nebuchadnezzar, and the city of Carchemish, crushed, lay under its own debris until it was excavated a hundred years ago.[4] The excavations revealed what violent treatment the city received at the hands of Nebuchadnezzar's army (BWMS, 252).

Jehoahaz, the Sixteenth King of Judah (609 B.C.) (2 Kings 23:30–33)

Jehoahaz, son of Josiah, made king after the death of his father at the hands of Neco (2 Kings 23:29–30), reigned only three months. He was deposed by Neco (v. 33), evidently on Neco's return from the north (TCK, 181; TMN, 182), and taken to Egypt, where he died (v. 34). In order to visualize the succession of kings in Judah, refer to the list in chapter 15, page 152, from time to time.

Jehoiakim, the Seventeenth King of Judah (609–597 B.C.) (2 Kings 23:34–24:6)

After Jehoahaz had been deposed by Neco (2 Kings 23:33), another son of Josiah was put on the throne of Judah by Neco. His name was changed from Eliakim ("God establishes") to Jehoiakim ("the LORD establishes"). This king paid tribute of silver and gold to his master Neco, king of Egypt (v. 35), but soon, when Nebuchadnezzar, the new king of Babylonia (605–562 B.C.) controlled Palestine, Jehoiakim shifted his allegiance to him (2 Kings 24:1).

Jeremiah and Jehoiakim (Jeremiah 36)

Jeremiah had received the word of the Lord from the thirteenth year of Josiah, i.e., 627 B.C. (Josiah 640–609), and had also ministered during the time of Jehoiakim and Zedekiah, the latter being the last king of Judah (Jer. 1:1–2). In the days of Jehoiakim, the Lord gave Jeremiah a message that pointed out the sins of the people of Judah and their need to turn

---

[4]A British Museum team excavated there in 1878–1881, again in 1911–1914, and thereafter sporadically until 1920. They traced the history of the city back to the fifth millennium B.C. Carchemish suffered repeatedly at the hands of invaders. Particularly severe was its suffering in 717 when Sargon II destroyed it, deported its Hittite inhabitants, and resettled it with Assyrians, and in 605 when Babylonians destroyed it. At that time it was the chief anchor of Pharaoh Neco's Syrian empire. See R. Youngblood, "Carchemish," ISBE (1979), 1:616–17.

from their wicked ways (Jer. 36:3). Jeremiah had the message written down on a roll by his amanuensis, Baruch (v. 4). The roll was later brought before Jehoiakim and read to him. The king took it, cut it with his pen-knife, and cast it into the fire on the hearth (v. 23). But the word of God was not so easily destroyed. Jeremiah dictated a second time to Baruch, causing the words that had been on the first roll to be recorded again (vv. 27–28, 32).

Jehoiakim's treatment of the roll of Jeremiah was in accordance with his other wicked acts described in Kings, where he was said not only to have shed blood but also to have "filled Jerusalem with innocent blood" (2 Kings 24:4).

Jehoiachin, the Eighteenth King of Judah (597 B.C.) (2 Kings 24:6–16); Archaeological Evidence of Jehoiachin's Name

When Jehoiakim died in 597 B.C., his son Jehoiachin came to the throne (2 Kings 24:6), probably beginning his reign on April 22, 597.[5] He was king for only three months. When Nebuchadnezzar came against Jerusalem in 597, Jehoiachin surrendered and was taken to Babylon (vv. 11, 15). This constituted what is usually called the second deportation, the first one apparently being in 605. Some writers inclining to the liberal view have given up the idea of a first deportation in the period 606–604, even though there is evidence for it. I see no valid reason for assuming it to be fictitious. The evidence for this first deportation is discussed in chapter 20 in the section entitled "The Three Deportations That Began the Exile," pages 193–94.

Archaeological evidence of the name of Jehoiachin was found in the excavation of Tell Beit Mirsim, thirteen miles southwest of Hebron, believed to represent the site of the biblical town of Kiriath Sepher (Josh. 15:15–16; Judg. 1:11–12). The work was directed by W.F. Albright and M.G. Kyle in 1926, 1928, 1930, and 1932. In the upper stratum (dated a little after 600 B.C.) the excavators found two stamped jar handles with the same seal impression, reading, "Belonging to Eliakim steward of Yokin" (AAPB, 125). Yokin is a shortened form of the name rendered "Jehoiachin" in the Bible, so the seal impression says in effect, "Belonging to Eliakim steward of Jehoiachin." An identically inscribed jar handle was found in the excavation of Beth Shemesh by Elihu Grant in 1930. Careful examination showed that all three jar handles had been impressed with the same seal (AAPB, 125; KEK, 200; cf. BAB, 116). Evidently Eliakim was charged with the administration of Jehoiachin's property while the king was in exile in Babylon.

Archaeological Confirmation of Jehoiachin's Exile in Babylon (2 Kings 25:27–30); His Ration Receipts

The Bible states that Jehoiachin was a political prisoner in Babylon for thirty-seven years. At the end of that period, Evil-Merodach, king of Babylon, brought him out of prison, changed his prison garments, and gave him a daily allowance of food for the rest of his life (2 Kings 25:27–30). Confirmation of this aspect of Jehoiachin's life was found on a clay tablet from Babylon that lists the payment of rations of oil, barley, and other food, to captives and skilled workmen around Babylon; it lists Youkin (Yokin), king in Judah, equivalent to Jehoiachin, and his five sons as recipients of these issues of food.[6] It is thrilling to be able to find even

---

[5]TCK, 182; TMN, 187, based on R.A. Parker and W.H. Dubberstein, *Babylonian Chronology 626 B.C.–A.D. 45* (Chicago: University of Chicago Press, 1942), 26.
[6]W.F. Albright, "King Joiachin in Exile," BA 5 (1942): 49ff.; citing Ernest F. Weidner, "Joiachin, Koenig von Juda, in babylonischen Keilschrifttexen," *Mélanges Syriens offerts a Monsieur René*

the "ration receipts" of King Jehoiachin from over 2,500 years ago.

Zedekiah, the Nineteenth King of Judah (597–586 B.C.); the End of Judah and the Destruction of Jerusalem (2 Kings 24–25)

After taking Jehoiachin off the throne of Judah, Nebuchadnezzar made the uncle of Jehoiachin the nineteenth king of Judah; his name, Mattaniah, was changed to Zedekiah (2 Kings 24:17). Zedekiah later rebelled against Nebuchadnezzar, and the latter again invaded Judah, in 588 (the ninth year of Zedekiah, who began to reign in 597 B.C.; cf. 2 Kings 25:1). The siege of Jerusalem began on January 15, 588 B.C. (TMN, 190) and was temporarily lifted by Pharaoh Hophra of Egypt, who invaded Palestine and sent his fleet against Phoenicia (cf. Jer. 37:5–11; Ezek. 17:15–17). Finally in the eleventh year of Zedekiah, on July 18, 586 B.C., Jerusalem fell to the Babylonians (2 Kings 25:1–4), and on August 14 the Babylonians began the final destruction of the city (TMN, 190). A great number of the people were taken to Babylon in this third and final deportation; only the poor of the land were left as farmers for the country of Judah (2 Kings 25:11).

Archaeological Light from the Lachish Letters on the Detractors of Jeremiah (Jeremiah 38:4)

As the fall of Jerusalem approached in the days of King Zedekiah, Jeremiah faithfully proclaimed the message, given him by the Lord, that the Babylonians (Chaldeans) would come and take the city of Jerusalem and destroy it (Jer. 37:8). The royal officials[7] of Zedekiah's court denounced Jeremiah to the king and asked

that he be put to death for "discouraging [lit., weakening the hands of] the soldiers" (38:4), presumably because his prophecy of the fall of Jerusalem would give the soldiers fighting against the Babylonian army a defeatist attitude.

In the excavation of the site called Tell ed-Duweir, now identified with the biblical town of Lachish, J.L. Starkey found (in 1935) a group of eighteen potsherds bearing on their surface several military messages written by an army officer to his superior officer stationed at Lachish.[8] W.F. Albright pointed out[9] that in one of these letters (No. 6) the army officer complained that the royal officials (sarim) had sent out circular letters that were said to "weaken the hands" of the people. The army officer who wrote this Lachish letter used the expression "weaken the hands" to describe the effect of the overoptimism of the royal officials, whereas the officials referred to in the book of Jeremiah (38:4) had used the same expression in describing the effect of Jeremiah's realistic prophecy concerning the approaching fall of Jerusalem. The royal officials were deemed guilty of the very action they sought to ascribe to Jeremiah.

Archaeological Confirmation Concerning Lachish and Azekah from the Lachish Letters (Jeremiah 34:7)

In the days of Jeremiah when the Babylonian army was taking one town after another in Judah (589–586 B.C.), the Bible states that the two cities of Lachish and Azekah had not yet fallen (Jer. 34:7). Striking confirmation of the fact that these two cities were among those still holding out is furnished by the Lachish letters. Letter No. 4, written by the army officer at a military outpost to his supe-

Dussaud, Paris, 1939, I, 923–35. "Joiachin" is a shorter form of "Jehoiachin." See also FLAP, 225–27.

[7]Hebrew, sarim.

[8]R.S. Haupert, "Lachish—Frontier Fortress of Judah," BA 1, 4 (December 1938): 30; MLPP, 137.

[9]W.F. Albright, "A Brief History of Judah from the Days of Josiah to Alexander the Great," BA 9, 1 (February 1946): 4.

The mound of Lachish

rior officer at Lachish, says, "We are watching for the signals of Lachish according to all indications which my Lord hath given, for we cannot see Azekah."[10] This letter not only shows how Nebuchadnezzar's army was tightening its net around the land of Judah, but also evidences the close relationship between Lachish and Azekah, which are similarly linked in the book of Jeremiah.

Biblical Names in the Lachish Letters (Jeremiah 36:10)

The Lachish letters, written in the time of Jeremiah, contain a number of names that occur in the Bible. It is not certain whether the names in the Lachish letters refer to the same individuals as given in the Bible, but it is significant that at least three of the names in the letters appear in the Old Testament only in the days of Jeremiah: Gemariah (Jer. 36:10; 29:3), Jaazaniah (35:3), and Neriah (36:4). Other names include Mattaniah and Jeremiah, which occur in other periods as well as that of Jeremiah; the name "Jeremiah" in the letters does not necessarily refer to the prophet. Thus we have military dispatches written at the time Jeremiah was living in Judah and even giving names mentioned by the prophet. It is no wonder Haupert remarks that we have had no archaeological discovery up to recent years that has had a more direct connection with the Bible than the Lachish letters. They provide us with a virtual "supplement to Jeremiah."[11]

[10]W.F. Albright, "The Oldest Hebrew Letters: the Lachish Ostraca," BASOR no. 70 (April 1938): 14; AOTA, 163; FLAP, 192–95; MLPP, 138 Cf. W.F. Albright, "The Lachish Letters After Five Years," BASOR 82 (April 1941): 21.

[11]Haupert, *Lachish*, 32.

Excavations at Lachish; Reinterpretation of the Lachish Letters

Lachish, now identified with Tell ed-Duweir, thirty miles southwest of Jerusalem, was the second most important city in the kingdom of Judah. That fact had led to the ferocious attack of Sennacherib of Assyria on that city in the days of Isaiah, in 701 B.C., as described above. The first excavation at the site took place in 1932–1938, under the leadership of J.L. Starkey. C.H. Inge and G.L. Harding continued to dig there from 1938 to 1940, and Yohanan Aharoni of Tel Aviv University led an Israeli dig there in 1966 and 1968. In 1973 David Ussishkin of Tel Aviv University began the latest excavations at Lachish.

For our present purposes, the most interesting results of the excavations concern the attacks by Sennacherib in 701 and Nebuchadnezzar in 589. Ussishkin has been able to demonstrate that Level III was the city Sennacherib attacked.[12] At that time Lachish was a large garrison city surrounded by massive battlements. The inner gatehouse was the largest of its kind ever found in Israel (BAR, 52). The Assyrians built a siege ramp on the southwest of the city, and the Judeans built a counterramp against them.[13] After conquering the site, apparently the Assyrians forced all the inhabitants to leave and then burned Lachish to the ground (BAR, 53). Probably King Josiah rebuilt Lachish, for it was again a strong bastion to meet the Babylonian onslaught.

One of the most interesting discoveries dating to the period of the Babylonian attack was that of the Lachish letters, discussed partially above. In 1935 Starkey found eighteen ostraca in a guardroom between the outer and inner gates of the city, in a layer of ash deposited by the fire Nebuchadnezzar had kindled when he destroyed the city. Probably the Chaldeans breached the walls late in 589 B.C. after the olive harvest, because numerous burned olive pits appeared in the nearby ruins. Nebuchadnezzar then laid siege to Jerusalem in January of 588. In 1938 three other letters were found at Lachish. All of these texts were written in black carbon ink on pieces of broken pottery (See EAEHL, 3: 645–46). The standard interpretation subscribed to over the years is that these letters were written by a subordinate officer at an outpost to the commander at Lachish, and that is the position taken above. But Yigael Yadin has presented a new interpretation that they were rough drafts of correspondence that the commander at Lachish was about to send to Jerusalem. Such an interpretation would explain why, e.g., the sender or addressee is so frequently omitted and why some of the texts are so fragmentary. Yadin marshaled an impressive list of arguments for his position, which certainly is appealing.[14]

[12]David Ussishkin, "Destruction of Judean Fortress Portrayed in Dramatic Eighth-Century B.C. Pictures," BAR (March/April 1984), 51.

[13]See David Ussishkin, "Defensive Judean Counter-Ramp Found at Lachish in 1983 Season," BAR (March/April 1984), 66–73.

[14]See Oded Borowski, "Yadin Presents New Interpretation of the Famous Lachish Letters," BAR (March/April 1984), 76–77.

Chapter 20

The Exile, c. 605–536 B.C.

(2 Kings 25; Jeremiah; Daniel; Ezekiel)

The Three Deportations That Began the Exile (Daniel, Ezekiel, 2 Kings), 606–586 B.C.

Bible scholars in the past have usually held that there were three deportations of the people of Judah, who were taken from Palestine to Babylonia by Nebuchadnezzar in 605, 597, and 586 B.C. Some critics have doubted the fact of a deportation in 605; Price, for example, says that the writer of Daniel 1:1 implies that there was a deportation in the third year of Jehoiakim (c. 606–605), but that "to such a captivity at that time no other reference is found" (POTH, 358). There is, however, very good evidence for the deportation of 605, in that the book of Daniel specifically indicates such a siege of Jerusalem, with a deportation of some of the people, including Daniel and certain of the princes of the house of Judah (Dan. 1:1, 3). Moreover, as Wiseman points out, Josephus preserved an important witness of the historian Berosus (a Babylonian priest, c. 300 B.C.) concerning such a campaign. The statement indicates that while Nabopolassar was still king of Babylonia, hearing that the territory to the west had revolted, he sent his son Nebuchadnezzar (the crown prince) to put down the revolt among the Jews and others.[1]

The *Babylonian Chronicle*, coming from the court records of ancient Babylon, specifically states, "At that time Nebuchadrezzar [alternate spelling] captured the whole area of the Hatti-country" (WCCK, 69). This includes all Syria and Palestine south to the border of Egypt. In the midst of the campaign, on the eighth of Av (August 16), King Nabopolassar died (WCCK, 69), and Nebuchadnezzar hurried back to Babylon to take the throne left by his father. Twenty-three days later he "sat on the royal throne in Babylon" (WCCK, 69). In his rush Nebuchadnezzar committed the captives, including "Jews, Phoenicians, and Syrians" to some of his friends.[2] When we examine the archaeological evidence further, we find that the last two texts of Nabopolassar are dated

---

[1]Donald J. Wiseman, *Chronicle of the Chaldean Kings* (London: British Museum, 1956), 26 [WCCK].

[2]Josephus, *Against Apion*, I.19.

in the months that would correspond to May and August, 605 B.C. and that the first two records of Nebuchadnezzar are dated in September and October, 605.[3] All this integrates with the biblical indication of the first siege of Jerusalem and first deportation in 605 B.C. It does not really matter that there may not have been much of a siege of Jerusalem at that time and that Jehoiakim apparently submitted to Nebuchadnezzar voluntarily with the surrender of numerous captives or hostages (WCCK, 26). The spring or summer of 605 B.C. would be the probable time of year for the campaign of Nebuchadnezzar, and there should be no further doubt of the historicity of the event.

The first deportation, then, was in 605 B.C. and included Daniel among those who were deported (Dan. 1:1–3, 6). The second deportation occurred in 597 and included Ezekiel among the captives. The third deportation took place in 586, when Nebuchadnezzar captured Jerusalem and burned the city and the temple (2 Kings 25:9–10).

Ezekiel, the Prophet to the Exiles in Babylonia (Ezekiel 1:1ff.)

Ezekiel was carried away to Babylonia with the deportation that included King Jehoiachin in the year 597 B.C. This second deportation in the days of Nebuchadnezzar (2 Kings 24:10–16) is also specifically confirmed in the *Chronicles of the Chaldean Kings*:

> In the seventh year, the month of Kislev [December, 598], the king . . . marched to the Hatti-land, and encamped against [i.e., besieged] the city of Judah and on the second day of the month of Adar [March 15, 597 B.C.] he seized the city and captured the king. He appointed there a king of his own

choice . . . , received its heavy tribute and sent [them] to Babylon. (WCCK, 73)

Ezekiel relates that he was among the captives in Babylonia by the Kebar River (Ezek. 1:1, 3). The Kebar (Kabaru or Kabari) was one of the navigable canals that ran between Babylon and the city of Nippur to the south. Nippur was excavated by an American expedition under Peters, Haynes, and Hilprecht during the years 1888–1900 (BAB, 37).[4] Tens of thousands of clay tablets were found at this site, including a Sumerian version of the Flood. Just how close to Nippur (sixty miles southeast of Babylon) the colonies of deported Jews were located we do not know. But into this rich valley they were brought, and there they worked for the seventy years of captivity. Ezekiel, though warned of the stiff-hearted nature of his people by the Lord (Ezek. 2:4), yet was commissioned to bring to them a message of comfort and encouragement, with a prediction of the future regathering of the people and a new spiritual awakening in the Promised Land (Ezek. 11:1ff.). Ezekiel looked forward to the time of Christ's earthly kingdom, yet future, when the dry bones of Israel will come to life and the nation of Israel will be restored to the Promised Land (Ezek. 37:1–14).

Archaeological Confirmation of the Validity of Ezekiel's Method of Dating (Ezekiel 1:1; 8:1ff.)

When I first took a course in biblical criticism, I was told that the critics had not touched the book of Ezekiel and that the validity of the book was accepted by liberal and conservative alike. However, subsequently the book was attacked from several angles, but, as W.F. Albright pointed out, this critical attitude is not

---

[3]Richard A. Parker and W.H. Dubberstein, *Babylonian Chronology 626 B.C.–A.D. 45*, 2d ed. (Chicago: University of Chicago Press, 1956), 9 [PDBC].

[4]The University of Chicago and the University of Pennsylvania resumed excavations at Nippur in 1948 on a plan to work there every second year. Only the University of Chicago has sponsored the excavations there since 1965. The great temple of Inanna and the religious center of the city, as well as the residential and administrative parts of this great site, have been largely uncovered.

justified in the least, and to his way of thinking there seems to be every reason for going back to a more conservative attitude toward Ezekiel (AOTA, 164).

One of C.C. Torrey's[5] principle arguments against the authenticity of the book concerned the unusual dating of events by the years "of king Jehoiachin's captivity" (AOTA, 164). This method of dating, however, now turns out to be an "inexpugnable argument" (AOTA, 164) in favor of the genuineness of Ezekiel, as shown by archaeological discoveries. From the seal impression on three jar handles[6] bearing the reference to "Eliakim steward of Jehoiachin," it was deduced that Eliakim was the administrator of the crown property that still belonged to Jehoiachin while he was in exile. Evidently Jehoiachin was still considered king by the people of Judah, and Zedekiah was regarded as king only in the sense of being regent for his captive nephew, Jehoiachin. Thus it was quite in harmony with the attitude of the Jewish people for Ezekiel to date events according to the reign of Jehoiachin, even though he was in exile.

Any doubt that Jehoiachin was still considered king was removed by the discovery of clay tablets in Babylon that refer to "Jehoiachin the king of the land of Judah." This shows that even the Babylonians still referred to Jehoiachin, their prisoner, as the king of Judah (AOTA, 165).

Therefore, when Ezekiel tells of his vision when the elders of Judah sat before him in the "sixth year" (Ezek. 8:1), he is dating the event according to Jehoiachin's captivity (FLAP, 225–27), or as most Jews probably regarded it, his "reign" in absentia. (By way of further interest, it may be pointed out that this vision of the sixth year would have been in the year 592 B.C., which is the very date of the tablet that mentions Jehoiachin.)

The ususual system of dating in the book of Ezekiel, then, is not an evidence of its lack of authenticity, but, in the light of the archaeological evidence, "proves its authenticity in a most striking way" (AOTA, 165).

The Colony That Remained in Palestine (2 Kings 25; Jeremiah 39–41); Gedaliah

When Nebuchadnezzar captured Jerusalem, he carried away about twenty-five thousand persons, mostly inhabitants of Jerusalem, into captivity in Babylonia (POTH, 352). This constituted the third deportation. The poor of the land, however, were left to be the vinedressers and husbandmen of Palestine (2 Kings 25:12). There was little likelihood that these folk would organize a rebellion against the Babylonian control of the land, after the political leaders had been either killed or deported (vv. 11, 19–21).

Nebuchadnezzar appointed a Jew named Gedaliah to rule over the Jews who remained in Palestine (2 Kings 25:22). This man set up his capital at Mizpah (v. 23), about seven miles north of Jerusalem. Here Jeremiah came to be with him after the chief military officer of Nebuchadnezzar had released the prophet and counseled him to return to Gedaliah (Jer. 40:1, 5).

Archaeological Evidence of the Desolation of Palestine at the Time of the Exile

The invasions of Nebuchadnezzar in 605, 597, and 589–586 B.C. caused much damage and destruction in Judah. Archaeological evidence shows that many of the cities of Judah were destroyed and not rebuilt, a fact particularly evidenced in the excavations at Azekah, Beth Shemesh, and Kiriath Sepher, and also by

[5]Torrey was formerly a professor at Yale University.
[6]For a description of these jar handles, see chapter 19, the section entitled "Archaeological Confirmation of Jehoiachin's Exile in Babylon," page 189–90.

surface examination elsewhere (BWMS, 107). The excavation of Lachish also gave evidence of Babylonian destruction there (see chapter 19). The last invasion, in 589, culminated in the siege and destruction of Jerusalem followed by the final deportation in 586.

Nebuchadnezzar's Control of Judah; Archaeological Evidence of His Building Activity in Babylon (Daniel 4:29–30)

For twenty years, Judah had suffered from the invasions of Nebuchadnezzar II, beginning with the campaign of 605 B.C. and ending with the capture of Jerusalem and the last deportation in 586. For another twenty-five years, Judah was subject to the rule of Nebuchadnezzar; his reign lasted from 605 to 562 (PDBC, 10).

Daniel, one of the captives deported by Nebuchadnezzar in the invasion of 605 B.C. (Dan. 1:1–3, 6), lived in Babylon for nearly three quarters of a century. He gives us a good thumbnail sketch of Nebuchadnezzar's building activities. Daniel relates that one day Nebuchadnezzar considered the great city and then remarked, "Is not this the great Babylon I have built as the royal residence, by my mighty power and for the glory of my majesty?" (Dan. 4:30). The archaeological excavations in Babylon have produced inscriptions that tell of Nebuchadnezzar's great building activities. The East India House inscription, now in the British Museum, has six columns of Babylonian writing telling of the stupendous building operations the king carried on in enlarging and beautifying Babylon. He rebuilt more than twenty temples in Babylon and Borsippa and directed construction work on the docks and defenses of the city.[7] Many of the bricks taken out of Babylon in the archaeological excavations bear the name and inscription of Nebu-

chadnezzar stamped on them. One of the records of Nebuchadnezzar sounds almost like the boast that Daniel recorded, as noted above (Dan. 4:30); it reads, "The fortifications of Esagila and Babylon I strengthened and established the name of my reign forever" (BAB, 479; PMOT, 302).

Significance of Daniel's Reference to Nebuchadnezzar's Building Activity; Failure of Archaeology to Support the Critical View in This Matter

Daniel's indication (4:30) that Nebuchadnezzar was responsible for the extensive building operations of Babylon was abundantly confirmed, as noted in the preceding section, by the excavation of Koldewey beginning in 1899 and continuing until the First World War. The German excavators found a vast system of fortifications, buildings, canals, palaces, and temples (FLAP, 224). Nebuchadnezzar was responsible not only for rebuilding Babylon but also for adding a whole new section on the west bank of the Euphrates and for linking the two parts of the city with a bridge across the Euphrates. The latter was an especially great achievement for his day.[8]

Many critical scholars hold that the book of Daniel was not written in the time of Daniel (sixth century B.C.) but that it was composed some four hundred years later, about 168–165 (PIOT, 765). However, on the basis of the critical view, it is difficult to explain how the supposed late writer of the book of Daniel knew that the glories of Babylon were due to Nebuchadnezzar's building activities. Pfeiffer, though setting forth the critical view, acknowledges that "we shall presumably never know" how the writer of Daniel knew that Babylon was the result of Nebuchadnezzar's building projects, as

---

[7]For a picture of this inscription, see PMOT, 213.

[8]For a discussion of Babylon, see especially James G. Macqueen, *Babylon* (London: Robert Hale, 1964), chap. 6; and James Wellard, *Babylon* (New York: Saturday Review, 1972), chap. 13.

The city of Babylon, reconstructed on the basis of the excavations, with the Ishtar gate in the foreground   Courtesy of the Oriental Institute of the University of Chicago

the excavations have proved (PIOT, 759). For one who accepts the time of Daniel's life as the period of the writing of the book, there is no problem.

Discovery of Ancient Fragments of the Book of Daniel

Among the Dead Sea Scrolls there are eight fragments of Daniel.[9] The forms of the letters are similar to those of the Isaiah manuscript, pointing to the first or second century B.C. as the date for these fragments of the Daniel text. It is significant that the text is substantially the same as that in the Hebrew Bibles that we have had all along, the chief differences having to do with the spelling of words. This provides another piece of evidence

[9]See James A. Sanders, "The Dead Sea Scrolls—A Quarter Century of Study," BA (December 1973), 136; and G. Ernest Wright, BA (May 1949), 33.

for the care with which the text of the biblical books has been brought down to us.

Moreover, a manuscript of Daniel dating about 120 B.C. brings into question the alleged Maccabean date (mid-second century B.C.) of its composition.[10] Gleason Archer has discussed at length the critical questions concerning the date of Daniel's composition (ASOTI, 379–93), including new evidence from the Dead Sea Scrolls; he concludes, "In the light of this newly discovered linguistic evidence, therefore, it would seem impossible to maintain any longer a second-century date for the book of Daniel" (ASOTI, 393).

The End of Gedaliah; Archaeological Light from Mizpah

The rule of Gedaliah as the governor of Judah by Nebuchadnezzar's appointment (2 Kings 25:22), did not last long. A Jew by the name of Ishmael, who probably considered himself a "patriot," and Gedaliah a "quisling," leading a group of ten men in a conspiracy, killed Gedaliah at his headquarters in Mizpah (v. 25) and also the other officials who were with him (Jer. 41:2–3); they cast their bodies into a pit at Mizpah (v. 9).

The site called Tell en-Nasbe, about seven miles north of Jerusalem, was excavated by the Pacific School of Religion of Berkeley, California, under the direction of F.W. Badé. The excavators found several jar handles stamped with what was apparently the word *Mizpah*, which led them to identify the site with the Mizpah of Scripture (BAB, 132). At Tell en-Nasbe, Badé found a pit filled with rubbish and potsherds, the latest material dating from a little after 600 B.C., indicating that the cistern was closed at approximately the time of the Exile. This led him to surmise that this might even be the pit into which

Gedaliah was cast after he had been murdered by Ishmael (BAB, 133). Muir says that in one cistern there was a large number of human skeletons, and he asks, "Were these the victims of Ishmael's treachery?" (MHTE, 207). The fact that cisterns were sometimes used as a convenient means of disposing of bodies was indicated at Gezer, where Macalister found fifteen skeletons in a cistern (BAB, 223).[11]

The Flight to Egypt (2 Kings 25:26; Jeremiah 41–43)

After Ishmael had slain Gedaliah at Mizpeh (Jer. 41:2), he took the important people who remained in Mizpeh and fled with them to the east, toward the country of the Ammonites, on the east of the Jordan (v. 10). However, Johanan and the other military leaders heard of Ishmael's doing and went to find him (vv. 11–12); they located him and recovered the people whom Ishmael had abducted, but Ishmael escaped (vv. 13–15). Because of fear of retaliation from the forces of Nebuchadnezzar, Johanan with his cohorts made plans to go to Egypt (vv. 17–18). He first consulted Jeremiah, who told the group that the Lord would not have them to go down into Egypt (42:19). Johanan and his companions, feeling that Jeremiah had not spoken aright (43:2), proceeded to take the whole group who had formerly been at Mizpeh, including Jeremiah, down to Egypt (vv. 5–7).

Jeremiah in Egypt; Archaeological Light from Tahpanhes (Jeremiah 43:8–10)

Johanan brought the group to the town of Tahpanhes, in the eastern delta of Egypt. Here the Lord directed Jeremiah to act out a prophecy: he was to take stones and hide them in the brick pavement at

---

[10]Edwin M. Yamauchi, "The Dead Sea Scrolls," *Wycliffe Bible Encyclopedia* (Chicago: Moody Press, 1975), 159.

[11]A summary of the Tell en-Nasbe excavations may be found in EAEHL, 3:912–18.

A nilometer on the island of Elephantine in the Nile River, used to measure the flood level of the Nile in ancient times

the entrance of the palace in Tahpanhes. This was to be an indication that Nebuchadnezzar would come into Egypt and set up his pavilion there (Jer. 43:8–10).

The site of Tahpanhes survives today as Tell Defenneh, about twenty-seven miles south-southwest of Port Said. Sir Flinders Petrie excavated there in 1883–1884 and laid bare a large brick building in front of which was a pavement identified with the one mentioned in Jeremiah.[12] Fulfillment of the prophecy that Nebuchadnezzar would invade Egypt finally occurred in Nebuchadnezzar's thirty-seventh year, as one of his inscriptions indicates (PANET, 308). Presumably Nebuchadnezzar did not intend to add Egypt to his empire but to launch a punitive expedition to humble Egypt and keep the Egyptians out of Asia.

Archaeological Evidence of a Colony of Jews in Egypt a Century and a Half After the Time of Jeremiah

At the beginning of the twentieth century, a fascinating discovery was made on the island of Elephantine, located at the first cataract in the Nile, some 583 miles south of Cairo (BAB, 3). As early as 1895, evidence of papyrus documents had been found on the island by native diggers, and in 1904, the Service of Antiquities in Egypt made excavations that uncovered many papyri, including documents written in the Aramaic language by a colony of Jews in the period 500–400 B.C. (PMOT, 320–32). One of the documents was a letter written to the Persian governor of Jerusalem in the year 407 or 408, asking for permission to rebuild the temple on the island of Elephantine. Whether these were actually some of the descendants of the Jews who came down with Johanan and Jeremiah we cannot say, but at least they may well have been some of the same. Albright believed that the Elephantine documents were written by Jews probably connected with the migration to Egypt described in Jeremiah 41–44, not long after 586 B.C. (ARBDL, 36).

Events in Babylon, c. 562–560 B.C.; Archaeological Light on Jehoiachin and Evil-Merodach (2 Kings 25:27–30)

Nebuchadnezzar died in 562 B.C. He was succeeded by his son, Evil-Merodach (POTH, 366), who released Jehoiachin from prison and gave him an allowance of provisions (2 Kings 25:27–30). We have already noted the discovery of clay tablets at Babylon listing the payment of rations of oil, barley, and other food to workmen and political prisoners. Among those listed as recipients of these provisions was Jehoiachin of Judah (see chapter 19, the section entitled "Archaeological Confirmation of Jehoiachin's Exile in Babylon," pages 189–90).

[12]See Carl E. DeVries, "Tahpanhes," ISBE (1988), 4:715–16.

Archaeological evidence of King Evil-Merodach (Amel-Marduk in Babylonian) was found on a vase at Susa in Persia, reported by the French archaeological expedition there.[13] This vase bore an inscription that read, "Palace of Amel-Marduk, King of Babylon, son of Nebuchadnezzar, King of Babylon." The people of Persia (called Elam in ancient times) had apparently carried this vase from Babylonia to Persia at the time of one of their military invasions of the Mesopotamian area (BAB, 479).

Last Events in the Neo-Babylonian Empire, c. 560–539 B.C.; Nabonidus and Belshazzar (Daniel 5)

Evil-Merodach ruled for only two or three years (562–560 B.C.) and was then assassinated by his brother-in-law, Neriglissar (Nergalsharezer), who was the Nergalsharezer of Jeremiah 39:3. After a rather successful administration of four years (560–556), Neriglissar died, leaving the throne to his infant son, Labashi-Marduk, who was deposed by the priestly party in nine months and replaced by Nabonidus (Nabu-na'id), a Babylonian of the priestly group.

Nabonidus (556–539 B.C.) tells us in his inscriptions that he had been a trusted general in the army of his predecessors. As king, Nabonidus maintained the stability of the empire and spent much time in directing the building and strengthening of the fortifications on the Euphrates River. One of this great joys came in the rebuilding of ruined temples. His record telling of the rebuilding of the temple of Shamash at Sippar (PMOT, 306) and the finding of the foundation record of Naram-Sin has already been cited (see chapter 19, the section entitled "The Finding of the Book of the Law," pages 185–86).

Whereas the secular sources indicated Nabonidus as the last king of the Neo-Babylonian Empire, the Bible indicates that Belshazzar was the last ruler (Dan. 5). This apparent contradiction and difficulty has been resolved by the archaeological discoveries of recent years. It is dealt with in the following section.

Archaeological Confirmation Concerning Nabonidus and Belshazzar (Daniel 5)

A college student once wrote me the following letter:

> I am a history major at the university. This semester I am taking a course in Ancient History.
>
> As my religious beliefs are orthodox and some of Dr. ——'s are not, there are naturally quite a few points where we do not agree. The particular point which she and I are discussing at the present time concerns the book of Daniel. Dr. —— believes that Daniel errs in his book when he speaks of Belshazzar as king of the Chaldeans in Daniel 5:1. She says that Nabonidus was king of Babylon at the time of its fall and not Belshazzar. She takes the position that Belshazzar was never king, and, from the way she has spoken, I believe she even doubts his actual existence. She also has taught that Daniel errs when he says that Babylon was taken by siege. According to other accounts there was not a siege of Babylon. It was just handed over to Cyrus.
>
> I feel as though I should have proof for my beliefs whenever it is possible to obtain it. I am writing to you to ask you if you would be willing to give me your point of view on the matter or refer me to some source which, in your opinion, states the facts correctly.

I replied to the above letter basically as follows: The biblical statements concerning Belshazzar have been used for a long time by critics to demonstrate that the Bible is not accurate. It is quite true that up to one hundred years ago our historical sources (outside of the Bible) showed that Nabonidus was the last king of Babylon and was not killed when the city

---

[13]De Morgan, *Délégation en Perse*, 14:60, cited in BAB, 479.

was taken by the Persians but was given a pension by his conquerors. Ancient historians such as Berossus (c. 250 B.C.) and Alexander Polyhistor give us this information that Nabonidus was the last king of Babylon. On the other hand, the Bible indicates that Belshazzar was the last ruler of Babylon and that he was killed when the city was taken (Dan. 5:30). Modern liberal commentators, such as Hitzig, have taken the view that the name Belshazzar was a pure invention on the part of the writer of Daniel 5.[14]

Archaeological discoveries, however, show that the Bible is accurate in regard to its indications concerning Belshazzar. About the middle of the nineteenth century a great number of clay tablets were excavated in the region that was ancient Babylonia and were sent to the British Museum. During the last half of the nineteenth century many of these tablets were examined by Theophilus G. Pinches, a prominent Assyriologist of London. One of them contained the name Belshazzar, showing that such a man actually existed. Another tablet was found to bear the names of Belshazzar and Nabonidus (PANET, 310), indicating that there was some connection between these two people, and still another tablet referred to Belshazzar as the king's son (PMOT, 307). Furthermore, another tablet proved to be a contract containing an oath taken in the name of Nabonidus and Belshazzar.[15] In ancient Babylonia oaths were taken in the name of the reigning king. This tablet, then, gave indication that Belshazzar was actually a co-ruler with his father, Nabonidus.

In subsequent years, the work of Raymond P. Dougherty, then professor of Assyriology at Yale University, furnished further illumination on the situation concerning Belshazzar.[16] Dougherty showed that during the latter part of his reign Nabonidus spent a great deal of his time in Arabia (cf. PANET, 306), probably for the purpose of consolidating that part of his empire, though some scholars have suggested that he was doing what we would call archaeological work, and others have suggested that he stayed in Arabia because he liked the climate. In any event the clay tablets show us the reason for the raising of Belshazzar to the position of ruling monarch—namely, the absence of his father from Babylon. The English scholar Sidney Smith published an inscription that evidently refers to Nabonidus; it reads, "He entrusted the kingship to him," indicating the bestowal of royal authority on Belshazzar.[17]

I know of no first-rate critic today who urges this old objection concerning Belshazzar. An example of the way in which liberals recognize the facts in the case may be taken from the book *What Mean These Stones?* by Millar Burrows (BWMS, 276–77). The author points out that "the solution of this apparent discrepancy was apparent when evidence was found that during the last part of his reign Nabunaid (Nabonidus) lived in Arabia and left the administration of the government to his son Belshazzar."

The detailed facts are that Nabonidus, in one sense the last king of Babylon, was not killed by the invading Persians but was given a pension by his conquerors. On the other hand, Belshazzar, elevated to the position of ruler of Babylon by his father, was killed when the city of Baby-

[14]Hitzig, *Commentary on Daniel*, 75.
[15]This tablet was published by Pinches in the *Expository Times* (April 1915).
[16]R.P. Dougherty, *Nabonidus and Belshazzar* (New Haven: Yale University Press, 1929) [DNB].
[17]Ibid., 108.

lon was taken, as indicated in Daniel 5:30. The matter concerning Belshazzar, far from being an error in the Scriptures, is one of the many striking confirmations of the Word of God that have been demonstrated by archaeology.

Chapter 21

The Return from Exile, 536–458 B.C.

(Ezra, Haggai, Zechariah)

The End of the Neo-Babylonian Empire (612–539 B.C.); the Fall of Babylon (539)

Nabonidus (556–539 B.C.), the last king of the Neo-Babylonian Empire (612–539), was ruling with his son, Belshazzar, when Cyrus of Persia swept across western Asia and captured Babylon in the year 539. One of Cyrus' own clay cylinders tells that the priests of Babylon opened the gates of the impregnable city and let him come in. Cyrus felt that he was the man of destiny for his day (For Cyrus' account of his capture of the city of Babylon, see PANET, 315–16).

When Cyrus captured Babylon, he had effectively launched the Persian Empire. Coming to the throne of the principality of Anshan (north and east of the head of the Persian Gulf) in about 559 B.C., he had rebelled against his Median overlord and had conquered the Medes during the 550s, had overrun Lydia in 546, and now had subdued the Neo-Babylonian Empire in 539. The empire he established lasted for some two hundred years, until Alexander the Great conquered it in 331 B.C. One of Cyrus' early acts after taking Babylon was to permit the Jews to return to Palestine after their seventy-year captivity.

Archaeological Light on Cyrus' Policy (2 Chronicles 36:22–23; Ezra 1:1–4)

The Bible indicates that after Cyrus gained control of Babylon (on October 29, 539 B.C.) he made a proclamation permitting those people of Judah who had been deported by Nebuchadnezzar to go back to Palestine and rebuild the temple (2 Chron. 36:22–23; Ezra 1:1–4). Thus Cyrus reversed the policy of deportation that had been used by Tiglath-Pileser III (745–727 B.C.), Sargon II (721–705), and other Assyrian conquerors, as well as by the Babylonian king, Nebuchadnezzar (see chapters 17 and 20).

Archaeological evidence that Cyrus pursued a liberal and tolerant policy toward deported peoples, such as the Jews whom he found in Babylonia, was discovered during the nineteenth century by Rassam, who found the Cyrus Cylinder. This cylinder states concerning such groups, "I [also] gathered all their [former] inhabitants and returned [to them] their habitations. Furthermore, I resettled upon the command of Marduk, . . . all the gods . . . in their [former] chapels"

(PANET, 316). The cylinder tells of Cyrus' taking the city of Babylon without violence and, later, of returning people to their former dwellings. Not only was Cyrus a humane man, he was also a wise administrator. Certainly he realized that disaffection of subject peoples and their ill will toward the central administration would be eliminated if they were free to return to their ancestral homes. Presumably almost none of them did return; we do not have their records. We know about the Jewish action because of their religious devotion and the preservation of the account of resettlement in the Bible. Cyrus' humaneness and administrative wisdom were also buttressed by his polytheistic superstition or faith. He wanted the subject peoples and their gods to be well disposed toward him, and he wanted their prayers. "May all the gods whom I have resettled in their sacred cities ask daily Bel and Nebo for a long life for me and may they recommend me [to him]; to Marduk," he wrote on the Cyrus Cylinder (PANET, 316).

Preparations of the Jews to Return from Captivity (Ezra 1:5–11)

The decree of Cyrus allowing the Jews to return to Palestine was made in his first year, 539–538 B.C. (Ezra 1:1); the actual return must have gotten under way at least by 537 or 536. Those who prepared to return were given vessels of silver and gold, as well as animals and precious things (v. 6), and Cyrus even had the vessels that Nebuchadnezzar had taken from the temple in Jerusalem restored to Sheshbazzar, one of the leaders of the Jews (vv. 7–8).

The Return Under Sheshbazzar and Zerubbabel (Ezra 2); Archaeological Light on the Names of the Leaders

Prominent among those who led the people back to Palestine were Sheshbazzar (Ezra 1:11) and Zerubbabel (Ezra 2:2). A detailed listing of the various people whom they led back appears in Ezra 2, with a summary of the total at the end of the chapter, amounting to nearly 50,000 (congregation of 42,360, servants numbering 7,337, and singers numbering 200— giving a total of 49,897; see Ezra 2:64).

Archaeological light has been found on the names of these two leaders of the Jews who spent their early years in Babylonia; for it is now known from discoveries in this area that the names of Zerubbabel and his uncle, Sheshbazzar, were good Babylonian names (Zer-Babel and Shin-ab-usur) (ARDBL, 36).

Gifts for Rebuilding the Temple; the Altar Set Up (Ezra 2:3)

When the Jews returned to Jerusalem and saw the condition of the temple, which had been burned by Nebuchadnezzar's troops more than a generation before (2 Kings 25:9), some of the fathers gave freely for its restoration (Ezra 2:68). Their gifts amounted to more than a thousand "drachmas" of gold and five thousand pounds of silver (v. 69). (For an explanation of "drachmas," see "Archaeological Confirmation of the Reference to the Drachma in Nehemiah," pages 213–14.)

At the time of the return many of those whose ancestral home had been elsewhere than Jerusalem had apparently gone to their home town (Ezra 2:70), but now in the seventh month, October (according to Jewish system, see article on "Calendar," ISBE), the people gathered themselves together "as one man" in Jerusalem (Ezra 3:1), and the altar was erected so that they could offer burnt offerings according to the law of Moses (v. 3).

Materials for Rebuilding the Temple; Archaeological Light on the Use of Cedar Wood (Ezra 3)

In preparation for rebuilding the temple, payment was sent to the people of Sidon and Tyre in Phoenicia for bringing cedar trees for the construction work (Ezra 3:7). Archaeological discoveries illuminate the use of cedar wood from the Lebanon mountains in Phoenicia for the building of important structures. Long before the restoration of the temple in Jerusalem, a ruler in the city of Lagash[1] in Babylonia by the name of Gudea (c. 2100 B.C.) rebuilt a temple of Ningirsu, and for this purpose he sent to the Amanus mountains for cedar wood. The Amanus mountains were a part of the same general range as the Lebanons, lying along the Mediterranean to the north of the Orontes River. Gudea said, "From Amanus, the mountain of cedar, cedar wood, the length of which was 60 cubits, cedar wood, the length of which was 50 cubits, ukarinnu-wood, the length of which was 25 cubits, for the dwelling he made; (from) their mountain they were brought.[2]

Archaeological light on the use of cedar wood for construction also comes from Egypt. About 1100 B.C. a man named Wenamon was sent from Egypt to the Lebanon region to secure "timber for the great and august barge of Amon-Re," as Wenamon tells us in the record he left.[3]

The archaeological discoveries also show that Nebuchadnezzar (605–562 B.C.) had been to the Lebanon mountains. In speaking of the beautiful trees there, he said, "Mighty cedars they were, tall and strong, of wonderful beauty, whose dark appearance was remarkable—the mighty products of mount Lebanon. . . ."[4] A little later Darius I of Persia brought cedar of Lebanon to Susa (the biblical Shushan) for use in his royal palace (FLAP, 243). And, of course, Solomon had bought cedar of

Lebanon from Hiram of Tyre for use in the first Hebrew temple (2 Kings 5:6 et al.).

The Foundation of the Restoration Temple Laid (Ezra 3)

After sending for the Lebanon cedar wood, the builders of the temple proceeded to lay the foundation (Ezra 3:10). When the foundation had been laid, the people sang praises and gave thanks to the Lord (v. 11), but many of the old people wept aloud (v. 12). These were the people who had seen Solomon's temple before it was destroyed in 586 B.C. by the troops of Nebuchadnezzar (2 Kings 25:9). Barton believes that these old people did not weep because the restoration temple was any smaller than that of Solomon, but rather because it was less ornate. He feels that the second temple was built on the lines of the first, which were probably still traceable in the debris, and that the builders used much of the stone from Solomon's temple, which still lay on the temple hill (BAB, 243).

The Adversaries from Among Those Brought in by "The Great and Noble Asnapper" (Ezra 4:1–10 KJV); Archaeology and Asnapper

Adversaries arose among some of those living in the land of Palestine who were descendants of foreign peoples deported from other countries to Palestine in the days of Esarhaddon and Asnapper (Ezra 4:2, 10). These people came to Zerubbabel and asked to be allowed to help build the temple, saying that they had sought the

---

[1]Lagash, the city of Gudea, is represented today by the site of Telloh, which was excavated by de Sarzec at intervals from 1877 to 1901 and later by Genouillac beginning in 1928; large quantities of clay tablets were found, one room alone containing an archive estimated at thirty thousand tablets (BAB, 36).

[2]Sarzec, Découvertes en Chaldée, p. ix, col. v. 28ff.; Thureau-Dangin, Les Inscriptions de Sumer et d'Akkad (Paris, 1905), 109; idem, Sumerischen und akkadischen Konigsinschriften (Leipzig, 1907), 68ff., all cited in BAB, 455.

[3]J.H. Breasted, Ancient Records of Egypt 4:278ff. [BARE].

[4]BAB, 478, translated from Pognon, Les inscriptions babyloniennes du Wadi Brissa, Pl. xiii f, and Recueil de traveaux relatifs à la philologie et à l'archeologie égyptiennes et assyriennes 28:57; see also Langdon, Neubabylonishcen Königsinschriften, 174ff.

God of the Jews. Zerubbabel and the fathers of Israel declined their offer of help (v. 3); they may have remembered that idolatry had been one of the chief causes of the downfall of Judah and feared that to associate with these people, whose religion was a mixture of paganism and perhaps some truth, would be another subversive factor in the new start that was being made in the reestablishment of the worship in Jerusalem (POTH, 381).[5]

Asnapper (Osnappar in NIV, Osnapper in KJV, et al.) is referred to in Ezra 4:10 as "the great and honorable Ashurbanipal" who brought into Palestine these peoples who sought to help the Jews build the temple. He is evidently the famous Ashurbanipal (668–626 B.C.) who collected the great library at Nineveh and who studied the ancient languages such as Sumerian, discovering that he was "addled" by the beautiful script (see chapter 19). To him we owe a debt of gratitude for the extensive library that was found by Layard and Rassam in the nineteenth century and from which came such important records as the Babylonian creation account and the flood record.

Archaeology and the Validity of the Letters of the Adversaries (Ezra 4:11–16); Significance of Elephantine Papyri in This Demonstration

The adversaries of the Jews wrote a letter to the Persian king, telling him that these Jews who had come to build Jerusalem would not pay their taxes to him after the city was built (Ezra 4:13). This section of Ezra is written in Aramaic. Most critical scholars have denied the essential authenticity of these Aramaic letters recorded in Ezra (AAPB, 170), but

archaeology has given a definite answer to the critical view. Specific evidence comes from the Elephantine papyri, which are letters written in Aramaic by a colony of Jews on the island of Elephantine in Egypt during the period 500–400 B.C. (see chapter 20, the section entitled "Archaeological Evidence of a Colony of Jews in Egypt. . . ," page 199). The similarity of the Aramaic in the Elephantine papyri and in Ezra shows that the Aramaic of Ezra may easily date back into the fourth century, if not even to the end of the fifth century (AAPB, 170). Albright points out that these edicts and letters of Ezra 4:7ff. are almost certainly the original text, as has been demonstrated from ancient parallels by Eduard Meyer and H.H. Schaeder (1930) (ARDBL, 36). Thus the critical view that holds that Ezra, Nehemiah, and Chronicles were all written about 250 B.C. (PIOT, 812) is not sustained. The Elephantine papyri show that Ezra need not be dated late on the ground that a late type of Aramaic is used (ASOTI, 413–16).

Cessation of the Work on the Temple Until 520 B.C. (Ezra 4)

Ezra 4 is an account of efforts of the people living in the land to prevent the Jews from rebuilding the temple. They kept on trying to discourage them or to "frustrate their plans" and kept on troubling them. They even "hired counselors" (or "bribed officials") to discredit them or to order a stop to the work altogether. The result was cessation of the work through the remainder of the reign of Cyrus and down into the reign of Darius, a period of some fifteen years (Ezra 4:5).[6]

[5]See also Howard F. Vos, Ezra, Nehemiah and Esther (Grand Rapids: Zondervan, 1987), 42ff. [VENE].

[6]For discussion of the opposition to the Jews detailed in Ezra 4 and the historical references included there, see VENE, 42–47.

The Encouragement of Haggai and Zechariah to Resume Work on the Temple (Ezra 5); the Temple Completed (Ezra 6)

In the second year of the reign of Darius (520 B.C.) the prophets Haggai and Zechariah encouraged the people to resume the building of the temple, which had been started some sixteen years earlier, about 536. Haggai pointed out that the people had become unduly interested in their own paneled houses, but now it was time to think of going to the mountain, getting wood, and building the house of the Lord (Hag. 1:4, 8). When the people began to rebuild the temple under the leadership of Zerubbabel and Jeshua (Ezra 5:2), Tattenai, the Persian ruler of the district, raised a question about who had authorized the Jews to build the temple. When the Jews stated their case, Tattenai wrote to Darius (v. 7), explaining that Cyrus had given them permission to rebuild their "house of God" (v. 13). Darius caused a search to be made in the palace and found the decree of Cyrus (6:1–3ff.). Then Darius ordered that the Jews be left alone so that they might continue the work (v. 7), and he even authorized that supplies be given from the royal treasury to help in the work (v. 8).

The work on the temple proceeded, and it was finally completed in the sixth year of Darius, which was the year 515 B.C., some twenty years after it was begun, in about 536. A great dedication service was held (6:16–17), and the observance of the Passover was restored (6:19–20).

The Sixty-Year Silence in the Book of Ezra

The sixth chapter of Ezra ends with the completion of the restoration temple in 515 B.C., and the seventh chapter begins with events in the life of Ezra in the year 438 B.C. Thus there is approximately a sixty-year gap in the historical account. This is probably due to the fact the Ezra's purpose seems to have been to deal with the reestablishment of the temple, the religious institutions, and the religious life of Judah. Apparently the next important step in this progression came in the life of Ezra in 458, and for that reason he does not deal with the intervening period.

The Period of Esther

Darius reigned 521–486 B.C. He was succeeded by Xerxes (485–465), who invaded Greece, in 480 and was initially successful, but his forces were nearly annihilated at Plataea in 479. The Ahasuerus of the book of Esther is identified with this Xerxes. The book of Esther opens in the third year of the reign of Ahasuerus (Xerxes), 483, at which time he gave a great feast in connection with preparation for the Greek invasion. King Ahasuerus commanded that Vashti, the queen, be brought before the people at the feast, but Vashti refused. The king then had Vashti deposed as queen, at the advice of his counselors (Esther 1:10–22).

The deposing of Vashti as queen occurred in the year 483 B.C. During the next four years Ahasuerus (Xerxes) was engaged in his battles against the Greeks. After his defeat at Plataea in 479, he returned to his capital at Shushan. It seems likely that the remaining events in the book of Esther (Est. 2–10) come in this period of the life of Ahasuerus, after 479. During this time Esther became the queen of Persia and was able to save her people, the Jews, from the machinations of Haman, who earlier had persuaded Ahasuerus to have the Jews killed (Est. 3:8–9, 13).

Archaeological Light on Susa, the Capital of Persia in the Days of Esther

The winter capital of Persia in the days of Darius and Xerxes (Ahasuerus)[7] was at Susa, known as Shushan in the Bible (Est. 1:2; Neh. 1:1). It is located about 150 miles northeast of the head of the Persian Gulf. In the summer the court moved to Ecbatana or Pasargadae in the mountains.

Susa has been excavated longer than any other site in Iran. Marcel and Jeanne Dieulafoy conducted the first systematic excavation there from 1884 to 1886. In 1897 the French delegation in Persia went out to start work at Susa under the leadership of Jacques de Morgan and continued until World War I. De Morgan found the Code of Hammurabi there in 1901. R. de Macquenen assumed directorship at the dig for the delegation after the war, to be followed by Roman Ghirshman. After Ghirshman's retirement in 1967, M. Jean Perrot took over leadership of the Susa excavation.

Susa is a very large site. Four gigantic mounds, covering an area of three hundred acres, stand up out of the plain on the east bank of the Shaur River, and a smaller mound rises west of the river.[8] Of special interest is the great Apadana mound, the southern part of which is covered with the magnificent palace of Darius (820 x 490 feet). This is normally described as a collection of rooms surrounding three open courts, a characteristic arrangement of Mesopotamian residences. But Frankfort casts doubt on this interpretation of the finds and questions whether a Mesopotamian element was introduced into otherwise typical Persian architecture.[9] The northern part of the Apadana mound was occupied by the great Apadana or audience hall or throne room. Originally built by Darius I, it burned and was later reconstructed by Artaxerxes II (404–359). The central hall had thirty-six majestic columns with bell-shaped bases and bull capitals, and the porticoes on two sides brought the total number of columns to seventy-two. The palace was decorated on the interior with glazed-brick panels that served as murals. Subject matter included Persian archers and spearmen, human-headed lions wearing Babylonian crowns, winged bulls, sphinxes, and griffons (FLAP, 243). Many of the remains from the site are now housed in the Susa rooms at the Louvre Museum in Paris.

[7]The Hebrew name Ahasuerus is fairly close to the Persian Khshayarsha; Xerxes was a name that the Greeks assigned to him.

[8]For a description of this site, see Sylvia Matheson, *Persia: An Archaeological Guide* (Park Ridge, N.J.: Noyes, 1973), 147–52.

[9]Henri Frankfort, *The Art and Architecture of the Ancient Orient*, rev. ed. (Harmondsworth, England: Penguin Books, 1970), 354.

Chapter 22

Rebuilding the Walls of Jerusalem

(Ezra, Nehemiah, Malachi, c. 458–435 B.C.)

The Persian Kings of the Fifth and Fourth Centuries B.C.

Since Palestine was subject to Persia, it will be helpful to list the Persian kings of the fifth and fourth centuries B.C. for reference in dealing with the backgrounds of this period of Bible history (that is, the period of Ezra and Nehemiah, as well as the last of the Old Testament prophets, Malachi):

Darius I	521–486
Xerxes (Ahasuerus)	485–465
Artaxerxes I known as Longimanus ("Longhand")	464–424
Darius II know also as Darius Nothus	423–405
Artaxerxes II	404–359
Artaxerxes III	358–338
Arses	338–336
Darius III	335–330

Darius I was the Persian king who gave permission to resume the building of the temple at Jerusalem (Ezra 6:1–3, 7) and Xerxes was the Ahasuerus of the book of Esther (see the preceding chapter).

The Return of Ezra c. 458–457 B.C. in the Reign of Artaxerxes I, 464–424 (Ezra 7)

The first six chapters of Ezra deal with events that took place more than a generation before the time of Ezra. In these chapters, Ezra tells of the return under Sheshbazzar and Zerubbabel (Ezra 1:11; 2:2) about 536 B.C., of the laying of the foundation of the temple (3:10), the efforts of the adversaries to stop the work (4:1ff.), the encouragement of Haggai and Zechariah to complete the rebuilding of the temple (5:1ff.), and the completion of temple in the year 515 (Ezra 6:15).

As has been noted, there is about a sixty-year silence in the book of Ezra between chapters six and seven, including the years 515–458 B.C. (see page 207); during this time the events of the book of Esther took place.

In chapter 7, Ezra begins with the events of his own life in the year 458 B.C. He tells that in the seventh year (458) of the reign of Artaxerxes, king of Persia, he went from Babylon to Jerusalem (Ezra 7:6–8), taking with him quite a company of people (8:1–20).

Ezra received the support of King Artaxerxes I, who made a decree that any of the people of Israel who were still in the region of Babylon would be permitted to return to Jerusalem with Ezra (7:12–13). Artaxerxes even made contributions of silver and gold to Ezra and his companions for the temple at Jerusalem (7:15, 20).

Arrival of Ezra in Jerusalem; Significance of the Twelve Bullocks; Revival and Reform (Ezra 8–10)

When Ezra and his companions arrived in Jerusalem (Ezra 8:32), they brought the treasures they had carried from Babylonia into the temple (v. 33), and also offered sacrifices, including twelve bullocks for all Israel (v. 35). The offering of the twelve bullocks for "all Israel" is an indication that the twelve tribes were in existence. This does not support the theory that ten of the tribes became lost and some of these lost tribes migrated across Europe to England and are the ancestors of the English people of today. The ten tribes were never lost, as shown by the offering of these twelve sacrifices representing all of the twelve tribes. Furthermore, the archaeological discoveries show that a large percentage of the people were not taken into captivity. Sargon, for example, tells us that he deported 27,290 of the inhabitants of Samaria.[1] This represented only a small fraction of the people in the northern kingdom; thus many people of the various tribes were never carried away, so no tribes could become "lost."

Ezra learned that the people of Israel who were living in the land had not kept themselves separated from the pagan people and their abominations (Ezra 9:1) and had also intermarried with the daughters of these people (v. 2). He prayed to the Lord and confessed the iniquities of the people (vv. 5–6), who then, taking cognizance of their sins, acknowledged that they had trespassed in taking strange wives (10:1–2) and set the matter aright.

The Return of Nehemiah in 444 B.C. (Nehemiah 1–2)

Nehemiah, a Jew, was a cupbearer in the court of Artaxerxes I (Neh. 1:11), at Shushan, where the capital of the Persian Empire was located. (Archaeological discoveries at Susa have already been noted in the preceding chapter.) In the twentieth year of Artaxerxes, 445–444,[2] Nehemiah heard from his brother Hanani that the walls of the city of Jerusalem were in a broken-down condition (vv. 1–3). Nehemiah was grieved with this news, and his sadness was noticed by King Artaxerxes, who asked what the reason might be (2:1–2). Nehemiah told the king of the condition of the walls of Jerusalem and of his desire to return and build them. Artaxerxes gave Nehemiah permission and also letters of commendation to the Persian officials whom Nehemiah would meet when he got beyond the Euphrates River in his thousand-mile journey to Palestine (vv. 7–9). Nehemiah was also accorded an escort of horsemen from the army of the king, apparently arranged at the suggestion of Artaxerxes, for we have no mention of Nehemiah's requesting such a guard (v. 9).

Archaeological Confirmation of the Time of Nehemiah's Return

Nehemiah tells us that it was in the reign of Artaxerxes that he returned to Jerusalem to direct the rebuilding of the walls (Neh. 2:1). The question might arise as to whether this was Artaxerxes I or one of the other Artaxerxes who succeeded him (see the list of Persian Kings on page 209). Some scholars have tried to place the return of Ezra in the reign of Artaxerxes II (404–359). Confirmation con-

---

[1]LARA, 1:26, paragraph 55; PANET, 285.

[2]According to Nehemiah 1:1, the message from Palestine arrived in Chislev (Kislev), equivalent to December of 445 B.C. Thus Nehemiah's return to Jerusalem occurred in 444 B.C.

cerning the time of Nehemiah's return is found in the Elephantine papyri (see the section concerning the colony of Jews in Egypt, page 199), which show that it was in the reign of Artaxerxes I. These papyri were written in the generation after Nehemiah (about 408–407) and refer to some of the very persons mentioned as the contemporaries of Nehemiah in his book (BWMS, 83; FLAP, 238). Thus the return of Nehemiah occurred before 408 and of necessity in the reign of Artaxerxes I, since Artaxerxes II did not begin to rule until 404.

Archaeological Confirmation of Sanballat and Tobiah, Nehemiah's Adversaries (Nehemiah 2:10, 19; 4:1–3, 7–8; 6:1ff.)

Even before Nehemiah told of his arrival in Jerusalem (Neh 2:11), he said that Sanballat and Tobiah were grieved when they heard of his coming to seek the welfare of the children of Israel (v. 10). Sanballat and Tobiah proved to be the adversaries of Nehemiah and his people in their work to rebuild the wall of the city (v. 19; 4:1–3ff.). Archaeological confirmation of Sanballat is also found in the Elephantine papyri, which refer to Sanballat, governor of Samaria, and his two sons (AAPB, 170; BWMS, 108). In writing to the governor of Judea, the Jews of Elephantine tell of their desire to rebuild their temple; they conclude by saying, "Also the whole matter we have set forth in a letter in our name to Delaiah and Shelemiah the sons of Sanballat, governor of Samaria."[3]

Archaeological light on Sanballat's henchman, Tobiah, is also forthcoming from Egypt. The Zeno papyri were discovered at Gerza in the oasis of Egypt called the Fayum (AAPB, 170). They were written in the third century B.C., in the reign of Ptolemy II Philadelphus (285–246 B.C.),

and frequently deal with Palestine; one of these documents was actually written by a Tobias, a governor of Ammon in the region of Palestine to the east of the Jordan; this Tobias was undoubtedly a descendant of Nehemiah's adversary, "Tobiah the Ammonite" (Neh. 2:10; BWMS, 111).

Archaeological light on the family of Tobiah was also found in Transjordan itself. At Araq el-Emir, almost directly east of present-day Amman, are the ruins of a building that was the castle of the family of Tobias (BWMS, 133). The tombs of the Tobiad family are nearby, and the name Tobiah can be seen, deeply cut into their external wall in an archaic Aramaic script (AAPB, 171). Albright believed that the type of script could date back to 400 B.C., the time of Tobiah I (AAPB, 222, n. 111).

Nehemiah's Inspection Tour of the Walls of Jerusalem (Nehemiah 2:12–16)

After Nehemiah had been in Jerusalem only three days (Neh. 2:11), he made an inspection tour of the walls of the city by night (v. 12). Apparently he did not want to have any of the emissaries of Sanballat and Tobiah observing his actions so that they might lay plans to hinder the work of rebuilding the walls.

Nehemiah went out of Jerusalem by the Valley Gate, near the southwestern corner of the city and rode eastward along the wall in the Hinnon Valley, coming to the Dung Gate (Neh. 2:13) in the southern wall, and then to the Fountain Gate, which was probably near the Pool of Siloam, where the Siloam Conduit emptied out (see chapter 18, the section entitled "Hezekiah's Conduit," page 182).

When Nehemiah reached the Fountain Gate and the King's Pool, he says, "There was not enough room for my mount to get through; so I went up the valley by night, examining the wall" (Neh. 2:14–15).

---

[3] A. Cowley, *Aramaic Papyri of the Fifth Century B.C.* (Oxford: Clarendon, 1923), 114, Aramaic Papyrus No. 30 [CAP].

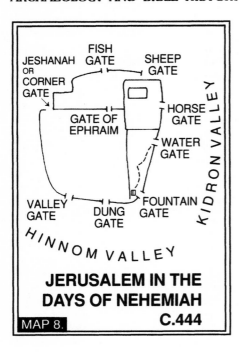

**JERUSALEM IN THE
DAYS OF NEHEMIAH**

MAP 8.   **C.444**

interpretation he turned back, retracing his steps to the Valley Gate and entering the city again at this point from where he had gone out some time earlier (Neh. 2:15). We are not told why Nehemiah did not complete the circuit of the walls. Burrows suggests that he may have been able to see the condition of the rest of the wall without continuing his excursion, or that perhaps the breaches in the wall were the most serious on this side, or that he wished to gain only a general impression of the condition of the wall and, in order to avoid attracting attention, chose a relatively unfrequented part of the wall.[5] According to another interpretation of Nehemiah 2:15, Nehemiah just continued his survey, moving around the north of the city and thus returning to the point from which he had started. This is the intimation of the NASB, the REB, and the Jewish Publication Society translation.

Rebuilding the Walls and Gates of Jerusalem (Nehemiah 2:17–20; 3:1–32)

After surveying the wall of Jerusalem on his night tour of inspection, Nehemiah made a proposal to the people, saying, "Come, let us rebuild the wall of Jerusalem" (Neh. 2:17). Sanballat and Tobiah mocked and ridiculed them, but, undaunted, they went ahead with the construction work. Different sections of the wall and different gates were assigned to particular groups. The repair and rebuilding of the various gates with adjoining sections of wall is described in detail in Nehemiah 3. The names of the gates are given as follows:

1. Sheep Gate (v. 1)
2. Fish Gate (v. 3)
3. Jeshanah Gate (v. 6), elsewhere called the Old Gate or Corner Gate

The question as to what the valley was and why Nehemiah could not continue to ride his donkey has intrigued Bible scholars. Burrows points out that the term valley (Hebrew *nahal*, ravine) is often applied to the Kidron Valley (2 Sam. 5:23; 1 Kings 2:37; 15:13; 18:40; 23:6, 12, et al.). He believes that Nehemiah had, up to this point, been following the base of the wall along the southern side of the city but now came to the eastern wall, which was on the crest of a steep slope that was almost like a cliff and did not leave room at the foot of the wall for even a donkey to find his way. For this reason, Nehemiah proceeded along the stream bed at the bottom of the Kidron Valley.[4]

After Nehemiah had gone north along the Kidron Valley for a way and had inspected the wall, according to one

---

[4]Millar Burrows, "Nehemiah's Tour of Inspection," BASOR 64 (December 1936); 18–20; VENE, 92–94.

[5]Ibid., 21.

4. Broad Wall[6] (v. 8), running from the Jeshanah Gate to the Tower of the Ovens
5. Tower of the Ovens (v. 11)
6. Valley Gate (v. 13)
7. Dung Gate (v. 14)
8. Fountain Gate (v. 15)
9. Water Gate (v. 26)
10. Horse Gate (v. 28)
11. East Gate (v. 29)
12. Inspection Gate (v. 31)

Sanballat and his henchman, Tobiah, mocked the Jews again, Tobiah remarking that if a fox went up on the wall, he would break it down (Neh. 4:3). Nehemiah looked to the LORD and continued the work, finding it necessary when the opposition grew fierce to have the builders wear their swords while they labored on the wall with their hands (v. 18). In spite of all the opposition, the walls were completed in fifty-two days (6:15). Then the people assembled and Ezra read the word of God to them (8:1–8).

Archaeological Confirmation of the Reference to the Drachma in Nehemiah (7:70)

In connection with some of the gifts that were given for the work of rebuilding at Jerusalem, one gift of one thousand drachmas is recorded (Neh. 7:70). The Hebrew word translated "dram" in the KJV and "daric" in the ASV is actually the Hebrew word for drachma and is so translated in the NASB, the NIV, and other newer versions. Some scholars have doubted the validity of this reference to

the drachma, a Greek coin, in the book of Nehemiah on the basis of a preconceived idea that the system of Greek coinage would not have been spread abroad until after the conquests of Alexander the Great (c. 330 B.C.). This would be over a century too late for the time of Nehemiah (c. 450). Some scholars, including C.C. Torrey, have used this reference to the drachma as an argument for dating the composition of Nehemiah much later than the time when Nehemiah actually lived (ARDBL, 37; AOTA, 154). This line of argument supported the critical view of Nehemiah, which holds that Ezra, Nehemiah, and Chronicles were all written by the same man, who is usually referred to as "the Chronicler" and is dated about 250 B.C. (PIOT, 812–13, 830).

Information on the drachma came to hand when the site of Beth Zur, several miles south of Jerusalem, was excavated in 1931.[7] The excavators found in the Persian level (c. 530–330 B.C.) six drachma coins (AAPB, 227), proving that the drachma was known in Palestine in the Persian period and that Nehemiah could have mentioned it about 450 B.C. without being "ahead of himself." This confirmation was effectively pointed out by W.F. Albright, who stated that the critical arguments for the late date of the "chronicler" have been disproved by such discoveries as the Elephantine papyri[8] and the evidence for the use of the drachma standard in Palestine during the period 450–330.[9] Albright commented that Pfeiffer was "far behind the van of Old Testament scholarship" when he assigned the "Chronicler" to the period of 250 B.C. and described the

---

[6]Nahman Avigad, in his recent excavations in the Jewish Quarter, on the Southwestern Hill in Jerusalem, uncovered a two-hundred-foot section of this wall, which was about twenty-three feet thick. He ascribed the wall to the building activities of Hezekiah. See Nahman Avigad, "The Upper City," in *Biblical Archaeology Today* (Jerusalem: Israel Exploration Society, 1985), 471.

[7]O.R. Sellers, *The Citadel of Beth-zur* (Philadelphia: Westminster, 1933), 69–71ff. [SCB].

[8]See this book, chapter 21, for the significance of the Elephantine papyri.

[9]See W.F. Albright's review of Pfeiffer, PIOT, in JBL (June 1942), 126. Cf. AJA (April–June 1944), 185, which points out that an Attic drachma imitation was found near Hebron and that Athenian silver money had become almost international currency in the fifth century B.C.

memoirs of Ezra as "confused and legendary"[10] (see also ASOTI, 410–16).

Later Years of Nehemiah

During the years following 444 B.C., Nehemiah was not in Jerusalem all of the time. His brother Hananiah was put in charge of the city (Neh. 7:2), but in the year 433–432 (the thirty-second year of Artaxerxes, Neh. 13:6–7), Nehemiah found it necessary to return to Jerusalem and set some things aright. The Levites had not been given their portion (v. 10), the Sabbath was not observed by some (v. 15), and intermarriage with pagan people had been practiced by others (vv. 23ff.).

Malachi; the End of the Old Testament; the Four Hundred Silent Years

The prophet Malachi fits into the time of Nehemiah. The references to offerings (Mal. 1:7, 10) and to the temple (3:1) show that the temple had already been rebuilt (515 B.C.) and the worship established. The sins that Malachi rebuked are similar to those denounced by Nehemiah, among them intermarriage with pagans (Mal. 2:11). Pfeiffer dated Malachi too early (460 B.C., PIOT, 614). Raven suggested that Malachi may have written in 432, when Nehemiah was at the court at Susa (ROTI, 249), possibly indicated by the fact that when Malachi refers to the governor of the Jews, he does not mention Nehemiah but merely refers to "the governor" (Mal. 1:8). On various bases, Archer concludes that the date of Malachi was about 435 (ASOTI, 431–32), and he is probably right.

With the writing of Nehemiah and Malachi, the Old Testament books come to an end, shortly before 400 B.C. The intervening period of silence that came to an end with the writing of the New Testament books is often called the "Four Hundred Silent Years," for there was no recorded prophetic utterance until the days of John the Baptist. Persia (539–331 B.C.) and Greece (331 and after) were the great powers during this time. References to these powers during this period of four hundred years are not entirely lacking in the Bible, inasmuch as the Persians facilitated Jewish return to Palestine and Daniel gave specific prophecies concerning them. We will study this era in the next chapter.

---

[10]Albright, review of Pfeiffer, 126.

Chapter 23

Palestine Under Persia, Greece, and Egypt in the Intertestamental Period, c. 435–200 B.C.

The Close of the Old Testament, c. 435 B.C.

The Old Testament books had all been written by the time of the later years of Ezra, about 425–420 B.C., the last books being Nehemiah and Malachi, whose internal evidence points to the period 435–430. Critics hold that some of the books of the Old Testament were written later than 400, placing Ezra, Nehemiah, and Chronicles about 250 (PIOT, 812, 830), Daniel about 168–165 (PIOT, 765), and Esther about 125 (PIOT, 742). Many archaeological and linguistic discoveries present a formidable argument against the dating of these books in the late period. Events once supposed by critics to have been late are now known to have been early, for example, the return of Nehemiah has been shown to have been before 400, rather than after, through the evidence of the Elephantine papyri.[1]

Conservatives have held in the past that the Old Testament was completed by about 425–420 B.C., and true conservatives still maintain that. Liberals have presented no conclusive evidence to alter this view. Furthermore, there are specific reasons for adhering to this early date. We may cite, in addition to archaeological evidence, the following reasons for holding to the date of 425–420, in the days of Ezra, as the time when the Old Testament was completed:

1. *The testimony of Josephus*. The Jewish historian Josephus (first century A.D.) indicated that the canon of the Old Testament was completed in the reign of Artaxerxes Longimanus (464–424 B.C.; he is Artaxerxes I; see list on page 209), which would be in the time of Ezra.[2] As Green remarks,

> Strenuous efforts have been made to discredit this statement of Josephus, but without good reason. It has been said that it is not based on reliable historical information, nor the general belief of his time, but is

---

[1]See the preceding chapter; cf. also the significance of the discovery of the drachma in showing that Nehemiah need not be dated late on the ground of the mention of this Greek coin; see chapter 22, pages 213–14.

[2]W.H. Green, *General Introduction to the Old Testament: The Canon* (New York: Scribners, 1898), pp. 37, 38 [GIC]. For a new study of the canonicity of both the Old and New Testaments, see F.F. Bruce, *The Canon of Scripture* (Downers Grove, Ill.: InterVarsity, 1988).

merely a private opinion of his own. It is obvious, however, that this cannot be the case. Josephus was a man of considerable learning, and had every facility for acquainting himself with the history of his own nation, upon which he had written largely in his "Antiquities." His priestly origin afforded him special opportunities for becoming familiar with the religious opinions of his countrymen . . . he gives no intimation that what he here says is simply his own opinion. It is stated as a certain and acknowledged fact.[3]

2. *The character of Ezra.* Ezra was especially concerned with the sacred books; he is called "the scribe" (Neh. 8:1, 4, 9, 13), and also "a teacher well versed in the Law of Moses" (Ezra 7:6). His concern with the books of Scripture would make him a likely and appropriate person to have collected the books of the Old Testament.

3. *The nature of Ezra's time.* Ezra's time was such that the collection of the sacred books may have appropriately been made then. After the Exile, the people were founding anew the religious institutions of the nation. What would be more natural than to gather the volumes of the sacred library? (ROTI, 33).

The Jews in Palestine During the Intertestamental Period (After 420 B.C.)

There is a paucity of material on this period of history in Palestine after 420 B.C. Our two main sources are the Jewish historian, Josephus, and the apocryphal books of the Old Testament.[4] From the

indications in the last books of the Old Testament (Nehemiah, Ezra, and Malachi) and from Josephus, we know that there was no longer a king ruling in Jerusalem, as there had been before the Exile. The House of David had disappeared from sight,[5] and now the leader was the high priest, and his family was the royal family. The life of the people of Palestine from this time on was ecclesiastical rather than political. The priests ruled by the law, which was impressed upon the people by public reading, evidenced already in the days of Ezra, when he read the Book of the Law to the assembled multitude in Jerusalem (Neh. 8:1ff.). Gregg says that the priests held the people to the law and the people held the priests to the law; this was a step toward democracy because it elevated the law to the place of king and made both the priests and the people guardians of the rights defined by the law. The people as well as the priests then had a voice, making for democracy, in the opinion of Gregg (GBT, 49–50). The political situation in Palestine during this period after 420 B.C. is dealt with in the next section.

Palestine Subject to Persia Until 331 B.C.

The main period of Persian history began with Cyrus' capture of Babylon in 539 B.C. (see chapter 20; for a list of the main Persian kings see chapter 22, page 209). During the rule of Cyrus (539–530), the Jews were allowed to return from captivity to the land of Judah (southern

---

[3]Green, *General Introduction*, 38.

[4]David Gregg, *Between the Testaments, or Interbiblical History* (New York: Funk and Wagnalls, 1907), 49 [GBT]. For a new translation of the apocryphal books, see *The Revised English Bible with the Apocrypha*, 1989. For some useful books on the Intertestamental period, see William Fairweather, *The Background of the Gospels*, 4th ed. (Edinburgh: T. & T. Clark, 1926); Michael Grant, *From Alexander to Cleopatra* (New York: Scribner, 1982); Peter Green, *Alexander to Actium* (Berkeley, Calif.: University of California Press, 1990); Erich S. Gruen, *The Hellenistic World and the Coming of Rome*, 2 vols. (Berkeley, Calif.: University of California Press, 1984); Charles F. Pfeiffer, *Between the Testaments* (Grand Rapids: Baker, 1959).

[5]This does not mean, however, that God had broken the Davidic covenant. The Davidic line continued, though not on the throne, and reappeared with the birth of Christ. The Davidic line, culminating in Christ, is summarized in the genealogy of Christ (Matt. 1:1–17).

Palestine). With the permission of Darius (521–486) they were allowed to resume the rebuilding of the temple at Jerusalem, which was finished in 515 (see chapter 21). The events of the book of Esther took place during the reign of Xerxes (Ahasuerus of the book of Esther, 485–465; see this book, chapter 21). The next Persian king, Artaxerxes I (Longimanus, 464–424), allowed Ezra to return to Palestine in 458–457 and gave permission for Nehemiah to return in 444 to supervise the rebuilding of the walls of Jerusalem (see chapter 22). If the Jewish historian Josephus is correct when he states that the Old Testament was completed in the reign of this same Artaxerxes, this would indicate a date of about 425–420 at the latest, since the usual date given for the end of the reign of Artaxerxes I is either 424 or 423.[6]

With the successors of Artaxerxes I (464–424 B.C.), we enter the intertestamental period. When Artaxerxes I died, there was a struggle for the throne among three of his sons. The one who gained the day, by means of forming an army to back him, came to the throne as Darius II, also known as Darius Nothus (423–405). At this time Egypt was a part of the Persian Empire. When the Persian ruler of Egypt, Arsames, left the land temporarily to make a report to Darius II in the year 411, native Egyptians attacked the Jewish colony on the island of Elephantine, located at the first cataract (RHAP, 197). The Jewish temple on the island was destroyed; three years later, in 408, these Jews wrote to Bigvai, the Persian governor in Jerusalem, to enlist his aid in persuading the chief Persian authorities to give them permission to rebuild their temple. These very letters were found about 1900 A.D. on the island of Elephantine and are known as the Elephantine papyri; they even mention such biblical characters as Sanballat, the opponent of Nehemiah (see chapter 22, the section entitled "Archaeological Confirmation of Sanballat. . . ," page 211; see also chapter 20, the section entitled "Archaeological Evidence of a Colony of Jews in Egypt. . . ," page 199).[7]

When Darius II died in 405 B.C., two of his sons, Arsikas and Cyrus the Younger sought the throne. Arsikas gained the throne, taking the name of Artaxerxes II (404–359). Cyrus, however, did not give up hope of taking the throne of Persia. Earlier, in 408, he had been appointed Persian ruler (satrap) over the territory of Lydia in Asia Minor and had established a power base there. Cyrus was able to build up an army consisting of a great number of Greek mercenaries, and finally in the year 401 he was ready to attack his brother, Artaxerxes II, who was on the throne of Persia. Cyrus marched across Asia Minor and finally joined battle at Cunaxa, probably the modern site of Kunisch, about fifty-one miles north of Babylon.

During the battle, the forces of King Artaxerxes II gave way in a rout. Cyrus saw the king and rushed upon him, ready to give the death blow in another moment, but Cyrus himself fell, the victim of a javelin thrust. "So died Cyrus; a man the kingliest and most worthy to rule of all the Persians who have lived since the elder Cyrus: according to the concurrent testimony of all who are reputed to have known him intimately" (Xenophon, *Anabasis*, I, 9, cited in RHAP, 212). Some 10,000 of the Greek mercenaries who had been in the army of Cyrus the Younger began their trek back to the west, a journey described in the famous *Anabasis* of Xenophon. Of the original 10,000, some 8,600

---

[6]The Parker-Dubberstein date is 423 B.C. The evidence from the clay tablets shows that Artaxerxes I was recognized as king until the end of December 424, and possibly as late as the following February. Darius II was king, and tablets were dated as in his reign, by the middle of February 423 (PDBC, 16).

[7]Rogers, RHAP, 198, gives a good brief bibliography of the publication of the Elephantine papyri.

came through to the Black Sea (RHAP, 216).

Artaxerxes II was succeeded by a son, Ochos, who took the name Artaxerxes III (358–338 B.C.). He died in 338, poisoned by a physician at the behest of the court eunuch, Bagoas (RHAP, 255). Bagoas then put a son of Artaxerxes III on the throne, one named Arses, but Arses had too much a mind of his own, and Bagoas had him put out of the way also. Bagoas then put another man of the royal line on the throne, who, adopting the name Darius, set about to make sure that he had a firm grip on the throne. Seeing what Bagoas had done to others, he anticipated his schemes; Bagoas was poisoned, as he had poisoned others, and thus Darius III was able to occupy the throne with more assurance. He became king in 335, a few months after Alexander the Great became king of Macedonia. These two monarchs were to confront each other in the ensuing years.

During all of this time Palestine was also a part of the Persian Empire. The empire was divided into provinces, called satrapies, each one being governed by an officer called a satrap. Palestine fell within the boundaries of the Fifth Persian Satrapy, with its capital either at Damascus or Samaria.

The Conquests of Alexander the Great, 334–323 B.C.

In 336 B.C. Alexander the Great became king of Macedonia, the region to the north of Greece. Before his accession to the throne, his father Philip had defeated the city states of Greece at the battle of Chaeronea in 338 and had formed the League of Corinth, which he dominated. When Alexander took the reins of government, many of the Greek states were still very restless. Thebes revolted, and Alex-

ander resubjugated and utterly destroyed it, sparing only the house of the great poet, Pindar.[8] This act of ferocity cowed the rest of Greece, and Alexander was free to pursue his father's goal of launching a Panhellenic War against the Persians.

In the year 334 B.C. Alexander crossed the Hellespont and invaded Asia Minor. He had a formidable army of about 48,000 and some 16,000 support personnel, for a total of about 65,000. The cavalry units consisted of over 6,000 horses.[9]

At the River Granicus, which flows into the Hellespont, Alexander met the Persian forces of the western satraps (334 B.C.). He crossed the river unopposed and engaged the Persian forces in battle, putting them into hopeless flight. The victory was significant, for it showed the superiority of the Greek cavalry to that of the Persians. The psychological effect was important also, for the Persian Empire began to crack, with the cities of western Asia surrendering to Alexander without battle (RHAP, 272–73). After the victory at the Granicus, Alexander pushed boldly eastward, following the route of the 10,000 of Cyrus the Younger (see preceding section), traversing the difficult pass at the Cilician Gates near the northeastern corner of the Mediterranean (BCC, 433), and descending into the Plains of Issus.

There Alexander met the main army of Persia under the personal command of Darius III (335–330 B.C.) in the year 333. As the two armies joined battle, Alexander himself was in charge of one cavalry unit, 12,000 strong, which drove into the Persian left wing with great force, causing the opposing unit to yield ground at once. The rest of the Persian army made a sturdy resistance, and their superior numbers gave them great advantage, but Alexander drove into the flank of the mercenaries of Darius, and it broke in confusion. This turned the tide, though

---

[8]J.H. Breasted, *The Conquest of Civilization* (New York: Harper, 1926), 431 [BCC].

[9]Donald W. Engels, *Alexander the Great and the Logistics of the Macedonian Army* (Berkeley, Calif.: University of California Press, 1978), 18.

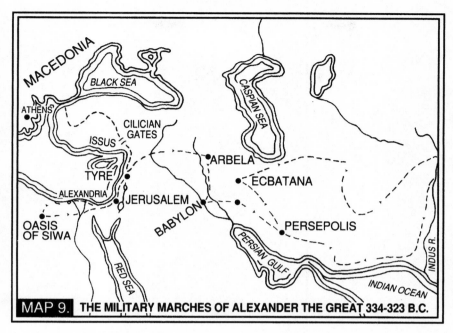

MAP 9. THE MILITARY MARCHES OF ALEXANDER THE GREAT 334-323 B.C.

much hard fighting remained to be done. At the first opportunity Alexander headed for Darius in person, knowing that he would be sitting in royal splendor in a chariot behind the center of the army. As Alexander and his unit fought in this direction, Darius was soon surrounded with the wounded and dead who fell before the Macedonians, and it was only with great difficulty that Darius was extricated by his brother and placed on a lighter chariot so that they were able to flee to the rear. He escaped none too soon, for if they had stayed a little longer, Darius would surely have been captured or killed (RHAP, 289–90). A representation of Alexander's attack on the bodyguard of Darius III at the Battle of Issus was found in the excavations at Pompeii in 1831; it is over 2000 years old, since Pompeii was destroyed by volcanic action in 79 A.D. The scene is a mosaic, made to form a floor pavement; it shows Alexander's spear piercing the body of one of the noblemen who is protecting Darius as the Persians are hastily removing Darius from the field of battle. (For a reproduction of this mosaic, see BCC, figure 169, p. 432.)

Darius's flight from the Battle of Issus continued until he finally crossed the Euphrates River (RHAP, 291). He sent a letter to Alexander, asking for terms of peace and offering to accept the Euphrates as the boundary between their domains (BCC, 434). Alexander replied with a stiff letter, which began,

> Your forefathers came into Macedonia and into the rest of Greece and did us harm, without any previous injury from us. Now I, having been appointed leader of the Greeks and wishing to punish the Persians, have crossed into Asia. . . . My father was killed by conspirators whom you instigated, as you have boasted to everybody in your letters.

Alexander closed by saying that if Darius wished to receive his mother, his wife,

A street in the city of Tyre during the Roman period

and his children,[10] he should come before him, and whatsoever was just should be his; furthermore Darius was to address him as Lord of Asia, not as an equal, and to speak of him as lord of all his possessions; if Darius disputed his right to the kingdom, he would have to fight for it (RHAP, 296–97).

Alexander then decided to march south from Issus, going through Syria, Phoenicia, Palestine, and down into Egypt (RHAP, 294). His fame preceded his army, and as he moved south, one city after another surrendered, including Aradus, Byblus, and Sidon (RHAP, 297). When Alexander came to the city of Tyre, it was a different story.

Alexander's Siege of Tyre a Fulfillment of Ezekiel's Prophecy (Ezekiel 26)

More than 250 years before the time of Alexander, the prophet Ezekiel predicted that the city of Tyre would be destroyed (Ezek. 26:3). Specifically, he foretold that Nebuchadnezzar would besiege Tyre, breach the walls, and destroy the city (Ezek. 26:7–12). (Parenthetically, it should be noted that Tyre was a two-part city: a formidable bastion on land and a well-fortified island city about a half mile from the coast.) This part of the prophecy was fulfilled a few years after it was made, for the army of Nebuchadnezzar came up against Tyre and besieged the city for thirteen years (585–573 B.C., RHAP, 298). Before the fall of the land city of Tyre, however, the inhabitants moved most of their possessions to their island city. The ruins of the land city were left there, but the island city continued on and was a thriving metropolis when Alexander came down this part of the Mediterranean coast in 333–332.

Through Ezekiel God had also prophe-

---

[10]When Darius fled at Issus, he abandoned his mother, his wife, his two daughters, and his infant son (OHPE, 504).

sied, "They will throw your stones, timber, and rubble into the sea. . . . I will make you a bare rock, and you will become a place to spread fishnets" (Ezek. 26:12, 14). How amazing to take the worthless remains of a city and dump them in the water! Surely manpower could be put to a more useful task than that. The fulfillment, however, came in the campaign of Alexander against Tyre.

When Alexander first approached the island city of Tyre, there was a willingness to surrender. But when he demanded permission to enter the city and offer worship at the temple of the god Melkart, he was refused (RHAP, 297). The citizens of Tyre declined to accept his request on the ground that they wished to maintain neutrality in the conflict between Macedonia and Persia. Alexander began the siege of the city and found it necessary to labor for seven months before capturing it (RHAP, 298). He decided to build a causeway, using cedars from the Lebanon Mountains as piles and the debris from the old land city as material for constructing it. As the water became deeper farther out, the difficulties of the workmen increased; they were also hindered in every possible way by the people of Tyre, who had a good navy. In order to meet this challenge, Alexander left the construction of the causeway to his "army engineers" and went north to collect ships. The kings of Aradus and Byblus on the coast of Syria placed their ships at his disposal; from the island of Cyprus he was able to secure 120 ships, from Sidon about 80. With a fleet of some 220 warships, Alexander was more than a match for the sizeable, but smaller fleet of the Tyrians (RHAP, 299). After seven months, the causeway was brought up to the walls of the island city of Tyre in August 332 B.C.[11] The wall was breached from the cause-

way, and part of the fleet of Tyre was sunk. With the capture of the city, thousands of the inhabitants were sold in the slave market, 13,000 according to Arrian, and 30,000, according to Diodorus (RHAP, 300).

Ezekiel's prophecy concerning the throwing of the stones, timber, and rubble into the sea (Ezek. 26:12) was specifically fulfilled when Alexander's engineers built the causeway and used the remains of the ancient land city of Tyre, throwing them into the water.

Alexander's Siege of Gaza, 332 B.C.

After the siege of Tyre, Alexander proceeded down the coast of Phoenicia and Palestine, receiving the submission of the towns he encountered until he came to Gaza in southern Palestine, some 150 miles south of Tyre (RHAP, 301). Gaza had once been on the seacoast, but its harbor had silted up, and the city now lay about two miles inland on a mound over sixty feet high. Its elevation made it impossible for an army to attack it with siege machines in the usual manner. Alexander decided to build a mound beside the city, from which to attack with his siege machines. From this elevation he was able to break through the massive fortifications. After fierce combat with the gallant garrison of Gaza, Alexander took the city, and 10,000 men were slain, according to the ancient historians (RHAP, 302). The rest of the population was sold into slavery. The siege had required two months but was well worth the effort, for it raised the prestige of the Macedonian army another notch; and furthermore, valuable stores from the rich commercial city of Gaza had been added to the quartermaster department of Alexander's military machine.

---

[11]There is an excellent account in Dodge, *Alexander*, 327ff., cited in RHAP, 298. These dramatic events are summarized in A.T. Olmstead, *History of the Persian Empire* (University of Chicago Press, 1948), 506–7 [OHPE].

Josephus's Record of Alexander's Visit to Jerusalem

Josephus, the Jewish historian of the first century A.D., relates that after Alexander had taken Gaza, he made haste to go to the city of Jerusalem.[12] According to Josephus's story, the high priest Jaddua was at first frightened, but God had warned him in a dream that he should meet Alexander without fear of any evil consequences. Jaddua was to appear in his priestly garments, and the people were to be dressed in white garments. When Alexander approached Jerusalem, he saw the procession of priests and people and saluted the high priest. When one of Alexander's men asked why he treated the high priest so respectfully, Alexander replied that he had seen this very person in these very clothes in a dream while he was still in Macedonia.[13] In the dream, the high priest told Alexander to come over with his army, and he would have dominion over the Persians.

After the meeting with the high priest and the other priests, Alexander is said by Josephus to have gone to the temple in Jerusalem and to have offered sacrifice to God. When the book of Daniel was shown to Alexander, and he saw where Daniel indicated that one of the Greeks should destroy the empire of the Persians, Alexander supposed he was that person.

Whether or not this event actually occurred cannot be proved. It is likely that some of the details are in error, even if the story as a whole is substantially correct. Albright has pointed out that it is unlikely that Jaddua would have been the high priest as late as 332 B.C., since the Elephantine papyri showed that his father, Johanan, was high priest as early as 411, some eighty years earlier (ARDBL, 36–37). In any case, it is an interesting story and probably at least reflects the Jewish attitude toward Alexander.

Alexander in Egypt, 331 B.C.

From southern Palestine, Alexander made a hard march of seven days and arrived in the delta of Egypt (RHAP, 303), going from there to the city of Memphis at the south end of the delta. Here Alexander paid every honor to the cult of the Apis bull, enlisting the support of the Egyptian people. From Memphis, he went north to the Mediterranean and determined to build a city on the northwestern corner of the delta, to bear the name Alexandria. Even Alexander could not have envisaged at that time what this city would become, for by 60 B.C. it had a total population of half a million and was considered the greatest city in the world (RHAP, 306). While Alexander's architect was sketching plans for the new city, the king went two hundred miles westward along the Mediterranean coast and then due south another two hundred miles to the oasis now known as the Oasis of Siwa, where in ancient times was located the famous temple dedicated to the Egyptian god Amon.[14] One day as Alexander left the shrine of the god, the high priest of the temple addressed him as the son of Zeus-Amon (BCC, 440). This idea that he was a deity became a part of Alexander's plan for establishing his control over his empire.

Alexander at Arbela (331 B.C.); the End of His Life

Early in the spring of 331 B.C., Alexander left Egypt, marching up the coast of Palestine and Phoenicia to the city of Tyre. After completing governmental arrangements at Tyre, he left in June or July 331, going up the Lebanon Valley, and then by way of the Orontes Valley to

---

[12]Josephus, *Antiquities of the Jews*, XI.8.4 [JAJ].
[13]Ibid.
[14]For a drawing of this oasis, see BCC, Fig. 171, p. 441.

Antioch and on to the Euphrates, which he crossed with two bridges of boats, prepared by the engineers (RHAP, 317–18). He moved north and crossed the Tigris River on September 20, 331. On October 1, 331, Alexander and Darius were ready to begin the conflict (RHAP, 321) at Gaugamela, eighteen miles northeast of Nineveh. Darius had not kept up on the progress of military developments, and his army was as out of date as that of France in 1940. The Persians had devised one new weapon, a body of chariots with scythes attached to the sides for the purpose of mowing down the enemy (BCC, 436). But this was no more effective in gaining the day than was the Maginot Line in saving France in World War II. The army of Alexander crushed the Persians, and Darius III departed in ignominious flight, only to be stabbed a little later by his own treacherous attendants (BCC, 437). When Alexander arrived at the spot, he threw over the lifeless body of Darius III his own red robe in token of royal respect. Later he sent the body to Persepolis and gave it a royal burial (RHAP, 342).

After stopping at Babylon, Alexander went on to Susa and then to Persepolis, where he set fire to the Persian palace with his own hand (BCC, 437). After touching at Ecbatana in the north, Alexander proceeded across the Iranian plateau, across the Idus River, and into the frontiers of India, stopped only by the murmuring of his troops, who were not inclined to go farther eastward. He descended the Indus, touched the waters of the Indian Ocean, and finally undertook the arduous journey back to Mesopotamia, arriving at Babylon in 323 B.C., more than seven years after he had left it (BCC, 438). There he contracted a fever (perhaps malaria) and died after only a few days of illness, at the age of thirty-three.

The Division of Alexander's Kingdom; Palestine Subject to Ptolemy of Egypt, 301–198 B.C.

After the death of Alexander, a struggle followed among his generals. Macedonia finally came under the control of Antigonus, the grandson of Alexander's great general of the same name. Most of the territory in Asia that had formerly been included in the Persian Empire came under the rule of Alexander's general, Seleucus, whose line of successors is known as the Seleucid rulers, with their center at Antioch. Africa came into the possession of Ptolemy, one of the cleverest of Alexander's Macedonian leaders. His successors formed the Ptolemaic line in Egypt, with headquarters in Alexandria. Palestine ultimately fell to Ptolemy as part of his domain and remained under the Ptolemies from 301 to 198 B.C. The introduction of Greco-Macedonian culture (Hellenism) into Palestine was actively pursued by Ptolemy Philadelphus (285–246), who rebuilt such places as Ashod and Askelon, and restored the city of Rabbath-Ammon in Transjordan under the name of Philadelphia.

The Ptolemies seem to have been quite moderate in their treatment of the Jews. They encouraged a large colony of Jews to settle in Alexandria, Egypt, where they soon forgot their native tongue and required a translation of the Hebrew Bible into Greek. Produced during the period of about 250–150 B.C., this translation is called the Septuagint. Other aspects of Hellenism also made their inroads into Judaism, and some Jews came to follow a Hellenistic mindset and way of life, including a denial of the supernatural. Many Palestinian Jews also became Hellenized, and some of them became ancestors of the later Sadducees.

Chapter 24

Palestine Under Syria, the Maccabees, and the Hasmoneans in the Intertestamental Period, c. 200–63 B.C.

Seleucid Kings of Syria in the Second Century B.C.

The background of the history of Palestine in the second century B.C. is connected with the Seleucid kings of Syria, who are listed below:

Antiochus III, the Great	223–187
Seleucus IV, Philopator	187–175
Antiochus IV, Epiphanes	175–163
Antiochus V, Eupator	163–162
Demetrius I, Soter	162–150
Alexander Balas	150–145
Demetrius II, Nicator	145–139, 129–125

Palestine Passes to Syria in the Reign of Antiochus III, the Great (223–187 B.C.), in the Year 198 B.C.

For about one hundred years, Palestine had been subject to the Ptolemies of Egypt. In the year 202 B.C., Antiochus the Great of Syria pushed into the south of Palestine as far as Gaza but was driven north again by the Egyptian army under a man named Scopas. Finally at the battle of Panion (or Banias), at the sources of the Jordan in northern Palestine, Antiochus gained an overwhelming victory over Scopas in the year 201–200. Scopas fled with the remnant of his army to Sidon, where Antiochus besieged him; the garrison was finally starved out by 199, and Scopas surrendered. By 198 all of Syria, including Palestine, was subject to Antiochus. His policy toward the Jews was friendly, following the pattern of the Ptolemies of Egypt in their treatment of the Jews in Palestine.

The Pro-Egyptian Party and the Pro-Syrian Party in the Days of Antiochus IV (175–163 B.C.)

For many years, the high priesthood of the Jews was vested in the house of Onias, but in the days of Antiochus IV the house of Tobias rose in opposition. Josephus tells how Onias got the upper hand and cast the sons of Tobias out of Jerusalem, and they fled to Antiochus IV.[1] Thus it appears that the house of Onias was pro-Egyptian and favored the orthodox Jews who clung to the faith and the practice of their religion as it had been handed down, while the house of Tobias represented the pro-Syrian party.

[1]Josephus, *Wars of the Jews*, I.1.1.

Antiochus IV Takes Advantage of the Rivalry in the Priestly Group

At this point something of a bidding war for the high priesthood seems to have taken place. Joshua, Onias's brother, evidently in the pro-Syrian party, paid a huge bribe for appointment as high priest and the right to build a gymnasium in Jerusalem (2 Macc. 4:8–10). Taking the Greek name Jason, Joshua proceeded to build a gymnasium to introduce athletic competition in the nude and to encourage other actions totally repugnant to the orthodox Jews. The orthodox organized under the name *Hasidim* (pious), a movement from which the Pharisees eventually came.

After three years in office (175–172), Jason was deposed by a close associate, Menelaus, who outbid him in the bribery game (2 Macc. 4:23–26), and Jason fled to Transjordan. Menelaus proved to be an even more thoroughgoing Hellenist than Jason and more unscrupulous as well. Jason waited impatiently in Transjordan for a chance to regain his lost position. Finally, in 168, when Antiochus was busy with a military campaign in Egypt, Jason raised a force and attacked Jerusalem. The disorders that followed evidently were clashes primarily between those loyal to Jason and Menelaus on the one hand and the pro-Egyptian and pro-Syrian factions on the other, but Antiochus chose to regard them as open rebellion against his rule. He sent a force to Jerusalem that broke down the walls, destroyed many houses, slaughtered countless inhabitants, and built a fortified citadel for a Syrian garrison.

Light from the Books of the Maccabees on the Situation in Palestine in the Reign of Antiochus IV of Syria (175–164 B.C.)

Much of our knowledge of the activities of Antiochus IV (175–163 B.C.) in relation to the Jews in Palestine comes from two apocryphal books called First and Second

Maccabees which appear in modern English in *The Revised English Bible with the Apocrypha* (1989). Although we do not regard the apocryphal books as inspired, they are often helpful in supplying historical background and details not otherwise available. In dealing with this period of intertestamental history in the second century B.C. (c. 175–135), the books of the Maccabees provide material that otherwise would be lacking.

The Abominations of Antiochus IV (175–164 B.C.) Against the Jews

The quarrel between Onias and Jason concerning the high priesthood, and the subsequent machinations of Menelaus gave Antiochus IV the opportunity he apparently desired to wreak his hatred on the Jews in the spoliation of Jerusalem, the defilement of the temple, and a horrible persecution.

First Maccabees relates that Antiochus entered the sanctuary of the temple and took away the golden altar, the lampstand, and the other sacred vessels (1 Macc. 1:23) and then slaughtered many of the men (v. 25). Antiochus decreed that the people should forsake their own law, and as a result many of the Jews sacrificed to idols and profaned the Sabbath (vv. 43, 45). He order that idols be erected, pagan altars set up, and sacrifices of unclean animals offered (v. 50). Those who refused to act according to the word of Antiochus were to be put to death, and many of the people of Israel chose to die rather than to be defiled by unclean things (v. 65).

In 168 B.C. Antiochus IV reached a peak in his abominable crimes against the Jews. On the holy altar at Jerusalem he erected a pagan altar on which he sacrificed the flesh of swine, an animal unclean to the Jews. Both the first book of the Maccabees (1:50, 57ff.) and Josephus (JAJ, XII.5.4) tell of this sacrifice of pigs in the holy place and of the further command that the Jews were not to circumcise their children. Women who were found to have circumcised their sons were hanged on crosses and their children hanged about their necks. If any copy of the Bible was found, it was destroyed, and those with whom it was found perished miserably (ibid.).

Antiochus IV had the surname of Epiphanes, meaning "God made manifest." He was soon nicknamed Antiochus Epimanes, which means "Antiochus the madman."

The Maccabean Revolt Against Antiochus (168 B.C.)

The bitter persecutions of Antiochus IV led inevitably to a reaction among the Jews. The first effective resistance was initiated by a man named Mattathias, a priest, living at the town of Modin in Judah to the west of Jerusalem. One of the ancestors of Mattathias was named Hasmon, and from this name was derived the title Hasmonean, which was applied to the later descendants of Mattathias (cf. "The Hasmoneans," pages 228–29).

When the emissaries of Antiochus IV came to the town of Modin to compel the inhabitants to carry on pagan sacrifices and to depart from the law of God (1 Macc. 2:15), Mattathias and his five sons stood firm, refusing to bow to the coercion of the king of Syria; the father as spokesman declared categorically that he and his sons would obey the laws of their fathers and would not listen to the words of Antiochus (vv. 20, 22). When Mattathias had finished speaking, a renegade Jew came to the pagan altar that had been erected in Modin and prepared to sacrifice to the idols (v. 23). Mattathias was grieved, and his anger rose; running up to the man, he slew him, together with the emissary of Antiochus who was compelling the Jews to offer this sacrifice, which was unlawful for them (vv. 24–25). Mattathias proclaimed that everyone who had

a zeal for the law should follow him, and thereupon he and his sons fled to the hills, where they maintained themselves (vv. 27–28).

Judas Maccabaeus (166–160 B.C.)

Mattathias apparently was well along in years when he began the resistance to the decrees of Antiochus IV in 168 B.C. He died in 166 and left the work of carrying on the resistance to his five sons, appointing Simon as counselor and Judas as the military leader of the movement (JAJ, XII.6.1).

Judas proved to be a real leader. The name Maccabaeus was first applied to him. Two possible derivations of this word have been suggested: (1) It is derived from the Hebrew word *makkabah*, meaning "hammer" and (2) it is made up from the initial letters of a phrase meaning "Who is like unto thee among the mighty, O Yahweh?" (*Mi Camoca Ba'elim Yahweh*). The first explanation seems more likely.

The military genius of Judas reminds one somewhat of Joshua. In fighting against the Syrian generals, Judas used the technique of night attack and was able to scatter the armies of his Syrian opponents. Finally in 165 B.C. Judas captured Jerusalem and purified and rededicated the temple, which had been defiled by the abomination of Antiochus IV. The Jewish "Festival of Lights," or Hanukkah, or Rededication came into existence in connection with this deliverance of the Holy City.[2]

But Judas was not home free. Lysias, commander of the Syrian forces now descended on Judah, defeated Judas, and besieged Jerusalem. At that juncture, however, hearing news of an enemy force marching on the Syrian capital of Antioch, Lysias offered peace, the repeal of the laws proscribing Judaism, the removal of Menelaus from the high priest-

---

[2] 1 Maccabees 4:52–59; John 10:22; Josephus, *Antiquities*, XII.7.7.

hood, and amnesty for Judas and his followers. The Hasidim accepted the terms because their goal of religious liberty had been achieved. Judas, however, was not satisfied with anything less than full political liberty and left Jerusalem with a small force. When the new high priest, Alcimus, seized and executed a number of Hasidim, Judas renewed the war. With greatly reduced forces, he was defeated and killed on the battlefield in 161.

Jonathan (160–143 B.C.)

The place of Judas was taken by his younger brother Jonathan. Living as a virtual freebooter in the wilderness of Tekoa and adjacent regions, as David had done, he gradually augmented his forces and was finally ready to go on the attack. At that point, dynastic quarrels in Syria made it possible for him to manipulate the situation to his own advantage, and he gained considerable power. His brother Simon became military governor of coastal Palestine from Tyre to the Egyptian border. Although a Syrian general finally killed Jonathan in 143, the Maccabean cause was too well established to be snuffed out. Simon rushed to Jerusalem and took over leadership of the nationalist movement and gained the independence of the Jews from Syria the following year.

The Hasmoneans (143–63 B.C.)

At the time of the death of Jonathan, the only one of the five sons of Mattathias who remained was Simon. He was declared by the Jews to be "their prince and high priest for ever" (1 Macc. 14:41), that is, until there should arise a prophet worthy of credence. With the naming of Simon as both prince and priest, the Maccabean leaders assumed a temporal leadership that was really a kingship, going beyond the priestly and military leadership held by the previous Maccabees. Beginning with Simon in 143 B.C., we

usually think of these leaders as forming the Hasmonean line of kings (the name of this dynasty is also called "Asmonean.") The Roman Senate recognized Simon as a friendly, independent ruler (1 Macc. 14:16–19, 24; 15:15–24). In international affairs, for the next eighty years the Romans valued the Hasmonean dynasty as a counterbalance to the Seleucid state. Domestically, the Hasmoneans depended on the aristocratic Sadducean party with its power base in the temple.

Simon was the first of the Maccabees to strike his own coinage. Archaeological excavations in Palestine have often produced such coins, giving evidence of the activities of Simon as an actual monarch (for a picture of a half-shekel of Simon see BAB, figure 192).

Simon soon fell victim to the treachery of the governor of Jericho in 135 B.C. and was succeeded by his son, John Hyrcanus (135–105), who ruled both as prince and as high priest as his father had done. Since the book of 1 Maccabees ends with the death of Simon, our sources for the next events are rather sparse, and most of our information comes from Josephus.

John Hyrcanus (135–104 B.C.) began his reign fighting for his life and his kingdom but ended it with the Jewish state at the height of its power. Avowedly expansionistic, he first reestablished control of the coastal cities of Palestine. Then he conquered the enemy east of the Jordan and followed that with the capture of Shechem and the destruction of the Samaritan temple on Mount Gerizim. Next he subjugated the Idumeans (Edomites) in the south and forced them to accept Judaism and be circumcised.

Aristobulus (104–103 B.C.), the eldest son of Hyrcanus, emerged as victor in the dynastic struggle that erupted after the death of Hyrcanus. Then he proceeded to imprison his brothers and his mother to guarantee his position as chief of state. He continued the expansionist policies of his father and extended Jewish rule into Galilee. He also continued the Hasmonean tendency to transform the religious community into a secular state, adopting the title "Philhellene" (love of things Greek) and taking the title of king.

When Aristobulus died, his widow, Salome Alexandra, released his brothers from prison and married the eldest, Alexander Jannaeus (103–76 B.C.). Jannaeus continued the expansionistic policies of his predecessors, and by the time he died he had extended the border of the Jewish state to include nearly all the territory that Solomon had ruled. He was almost constantly at war, however, and more than once came close to total disaster.

When Jannaeus died, his widow, Salome Alexandra (76–67 B.C.), succeeded him on the throne, as she had when Aristobulus, her first husband, died. Because she was a woman, she could not exercise the high priesthood. Her eldest son, Hyrcanus II, filled that position. Her more able second, son, Aristobulus II, received command of the army. The Pharisees, who had enjoyed little influence under earlier Hasmonean rulers, now played an important role in the government. In general, Alexandra's reign was peaceful and prosperous. When she died at the age of seventy-three, the days of Jewish independence were nearing an end and Roman power loomed on the horizon. As a matter of fact, it was sparring between Alexandra's two sons that gave the Romans a chance to add Palestine to their empire.

Three months after the death of Alexandra, Aristobulus managed to defeat the forces of Hyrcanus at Jericho, and the latter gave up all rights to the high priesthood and the crown and retired to private life. All might have gone well for Aristobulus, had it not been for the ambition of Antipater, military governor of Idumea and father of Herod the Great. Antipater saw that he could manipulate the weak Hyrcanus but had no future under a strong leader like Aristobulus. So with the help of Aretas, king of the Nabateans, he managed to put Hyrcanus on the throne in the Jewish state.

Chapter 25

Palestine Under Roman Rule, 63 B.C. and After

(End of the Intertestamental Period and Beginning of the New Testament Period)

Pompey's March into Palestine, 63 B.C.

The Roman general Pompey finally put an end to the struggle between John Hyrcanus II and Aristobulus and made Palestine a Roman province. What happened was this. Pompey had become involved in conquests in the East, in Pontus and Armenia. In 66 B.C. one of his lieutenants visited Judea, where he heard appeals from representatives of both brothers and made some tentative decisions, pending later action of Pompey. Three years later Pompey came to Damascus and there heard appeals from the two brothers, promising a decision after a campaign against the Nabataeans (JAJ, XIV.3.2–3).

When Pompey's general, Gabinius, returned, he found that Aristobulus had locked the gates of Jerusalem against him. Gabinius then issued an arrest warrant for Aristobulus. Soon the followers of Hyrcanus opened the city gates, and Pompey launched a siege of Aristobulus's forces holding out in the citadel. When the battle was over, Palestine came under Roman rule. All non-Jewish areas (the Mediterranean coastlands, Transjordan, and Samaria) were detached from the Jewish state, and what was left was

placed under the rule of Hyrcanus II as high priest. Thus Hyrcanus (with Antipater at his elbow) controlled the Jewish state, at the pleasure of the Romans. Aristobulus was taken to Rome, where he marched in Pompey's triumphal parade, along with many Jews who were sold into slavery in the capital. In later years, as many won their freedom, they became the nucleus of the Jewish community there.

The Rise of Herod the Great

The Herods were not of Jewish stock but were descendants of Esau, the brother of Jacob. The descendants of Esau, called the Edomites, settled to the south of the Dead Sea in the region of Mount Seir and the great city that was later called Petra. About 300 B.C., the Edomites were driven out by a group of people called the Nabataeans, and they migrated to the west into the southern part of Palestine, which came to be known as Idumaea, and the people were known as Idumaeans, a Greek form of the word Edomite. The chief city of the Idumaeans, Hebron, was taken by Judas Maccabeus in 165 B.C. (1 Macc. 4:29, 61; 5:65). John Hyrcanus later subdued their territory and made the people become Jews and submit to circumcision.

The first ancestor of Herod the Great who was of any importance was a man named Antipas (died 78 B.C.). He had been appointed governor of Idumaea (the part of Palestine south of Judea) by the Hasmonean king Alexander Jannaeus (103–76, see preceding chapter). Antipas was succeeded as governor of Idumaea by his son, Antipater (the father of Herod the Great). Antipater had all of the overweening ambition of his son, Herod the Great, and saw his opportunity to gain a powerful position in the declining Hasmonean house. When John Hycranus II and Aristobulus II were both seeking to gain the throne of the Hasmoneans, Antipater took the side of John Hyrcanus II and induced him to seek the aid of the Romans. When Pompey came against Jerusalem in 63, Hyrcanus aided the Romans in their siege of the inner fortifications.

John Hyrcanus II, as ruler of Judea, and Antipater, as governor of Idumaea, continued to support the Roman general Pompey until Pompey was defeated at the Battle of Pharsalus in 48 B.C. Thereafter Hyrcanus and Antipater submitted to Julius Caesar, now the leader at Rome. Julius Caesar confirmed their political position in Judah.

Herod the Great Becomes King of Judea, 37 B.C.

Julius Caesar as head of the Roman State brought in a new order of things in Judea. He, however, was assassinated on March 15, 44 B.C., and a train of unfortunate days followed for the little territory of Judea. Antipater died in 43, poisoned by a rival. He left four sons—Phasael, Herod the Great, Joseph, and Pheroras—and a daughter, Mariamne. The second of

these sons, Herod the Great, is famous in biblical history as the ruler of Judea in the days when Christ was born (Matt. 2:1).

Herod had begun his political career as a young man, ruling as governor over the territory of Galilee in northern Palestine, a post to which he was appointed by his father, Antipater (JAJ, XIV.9.1–2). Josephus says that Herod was only fifteen years of age when he came to this post, but it is quite evident that he must have been twenty-five.[1] As governor of Galilee, Herod was successful in ridding his territory of freebooters, and even more successful in raising the tribute money that was due the Roman authorities. Politically he advanced rapidly, and Mark Antony, who ruled in the East after the death of Julius Caesar, appointed Herod and his brother Phasael tetrarchs of Judea in 41 B.C. The following year Antony made Herod king of the Jews.

At that point the Parthians on Rome's eastern frontier took advantage of Rome's political and military weakness created by the period of civil war (involving first Pompey and Julius Caesar and later Augustus Caesar and Mark Antony) and invaded Syria and Palestine. They made Antigonus, son of Aristobulus II, king and high priest of the Jews (40–37 B.C.). The Jews hailed the Parthians as deliverers from the Romans, and all classes supported the rule of Aristobulus. Of course the Romans counterattacked, and Herod, with Roman help, managed to take much of Palestine. After the fall of Jerusalem (37), Antony ordered the execution of Antigonus. Now Herod became king in fact and ruled until his death in 4 B.C.[2] He remained loyal to Antony until Octavian (Augustus) defeated him (31 B.C.). Then Herod offered his total loyalty to Augustus as he had given it to Antony, and the Roman emperor accepted it.[3] Augustus

---

[1] Note in Whiston edition of Josephus, 346.

[2] It is known that the calendar is somewhat in error. Christ was born up to a couple of years before Herod died, perhaps in 6 B.C.

[3] A biography of Herod appears in Josephus, *Antiquities*, Books XV–XVII and *War* 1:18–33. See also A.H.M. Jones, *The Herods of Judaea* (Oxford: Clarendon, 1930); Stewart Perowne, *The Life and Times of Herod the Great* (New York: Abingdon, 1956).

gave Herod additional territories along the Mediterranean coast and Jericho, all of which had belonged to Cleopatra, and later the wild regions east of the Jordan. Herod held the position of an allied king with local autonomy but subject to Rome in foreign affairs. Rome used him as they did other allied kings to pacify a recalcitrant frontier province and prepare it for a stage when Rome could directly appoint governors. Those direct appointees ruled Judea in the days of Jesus and Paul.

Herod the Great, King of Judea, 37–4 B.C.: His Atrocities

Herod's rule began with crimes of violence, involving the execution of many of his enemies at the time of his conquest of Jerusalem (JAJ, XV.1.1–2). Soon thereafter he had his wife's brother, Aristobulus, the high priest, drowned in a "swimming accident" (JAJ, XV.3.3). His vengeful, jealous, and suspicious nature later led him to execute his wife, Mariamne, and her mother, Alexandra (JAJ, XV.7.4–8).

The death of Mariamne in 28 B.C. caused Herod to suffer great remorse, and he would often call for her as though she were still alive. He tried to divert his mind by ordering all kinds of feasts and assemblies, but it was to no avail (JAJ, XV.7.7). He had lost the one person whom he ever really seems to have loved. Even this remorse did not cure Herod's inclination to violence, for in 7 B.C., shortly before his own death, he had his own sons by Mariamne strangled to death (JAJ, XVI.11.7). And of course we are familiar with his massacre of the infants in Bethlehem in an effort to destroy Jesus (Matt. 2:16–18).

Herod's Lack of Understanding of the Jews

In spite of an apparent desire to understand his subject people, Herod the Great found it difficult to understand them adequately and impossible to get along with them. Two significant factors hindering Jewish acceptance of Herod were that he was not a Jew but an Idumaean and that he aligned himself with the Romans for support. A further source of estrangement lay in the fact that Herod had displaced the Hasmonean dynasty. Herod sought to win the confidence of his people by royal charity in the time of famine and by other means, but in vain. They saw in him only a usurper on the throne of David. There were innumerable plots against his life, but with almost superhuman cunning, Herod was able to defeat them and continue his rule (JAJ, XV.8).

Archaeological Light on Herod the Great's Building Activities

Herod's outstanding city constructions in Palestine were at Samaria and Caesarea. Samaria he renamed Sebaste in honor of Augustus (which in Greek is *Sebastos*) and built there a temple to Augustus, a theater, an agora with a Roman basilica, a Greek-style colonnaded main street lined with shops, and more. Harvard University excavated at the site under the leadership of G.A. Reisner in 1908–1910, and in 1931–1935 in conjunction with four other institutions. Then J.W. Crowfoot was the director (see EAEHL, 4:1032–1050, and this book, chapter 15).

About twenty-five miles south of the modern city of Haifa, Herod rebuilt the great city of Caesarea (22–9 B.C.), about half the size of Manhattan Island, again named in honor of Augustus Caesar. This was a thoroughly Greco-Roman city, flung down on the coast of Palestine. Its temple to Augustus, hippodrome, theater, magnificent man-made harbor and port facilities, and other accouterments qualified it to be a first-class Roman capital of Palestine. Robert J. Bull of Drew University is the director of the joint expedition to

Ruins of the temple of Augustus that Herod the Great built at Caesarea in the emperor's honor

The Greco-Roman theater that Herod the Great built at Caesarea

Caesarea Maritima, which has been working at the site since 1971.[4]

In Jerusalem Herod built a theater and an amphitheater. Other examples of Herod's building activities include his reconstruction of Antipatris, northeast of modern Tel Aviv; the construction of the fortresses of Machaerus in Transjordan, of Masada along the Dead Sea, and of the Herodion, south of Bethlehem; and the palace complex at Jericho and his great palace in the western part of Jerusalem. His zeal for Hellenism and his desire to enhance his own reputation also led him to get involved in numerous building projects all over the eastern Mediterranean — in Rhodes, Greece, Lebanon, and Syria. The glory of Antioch when Paul launched his three missionary journeys from there was due in part to the beneficence of Herod.

Herod's palace in Jerusalem occupied the citadel area on the west side of the city. According to Josephus, it consisted of two main complexes surrounded by parks and gardens (Josephus, *War* V) and had three towers on the city wall, which guarded the palace's northern side. Of the three towers (Phasael, Hippicus, and Mariamne), nothing has survived except the base of the main tower, Phasael, now called the Tower of David. It is 66 feet square and approximately 66 feet high. This palace was the headquarters of Herod's government and of the Roman procurators who followed him. Here it was that Christ appeared before Pilate for his trial. Benjamin Mazar reported that excavations there revealed that the palace and gardens covered more than 4.5 acres and that the palace itself was built on a podium measuring 1,000 by 430 feet. Nothing was found of the superstructure.[5]

Herod's Rebuilding of the Temple at Jerusalem

The temple of the Jews in Jerusalem at the beginning of Herod the Great's reign was the same building that had been reconstructed some five hundred years earlier when the Jews returned from the Babylonian Captivity (see chapter 21). Herod's penchant for building new edifices prompted him to make plans to rebuild the temple at Jerusalem. In order not to offend the sensitive feelings of the Jews, Herod chose a thousand priests, many of whom were trained to be stonecutters and carpenters, so that no profane hand would have to touch the shrine of the temple (JAJ, XV.11.2).

The main part of the temple, begun in 20 B.C., was completed within eighteen months, but the final touches were still being added in the days of the ministry of Christ. It was for this reason that the Jews, speaking to Christ, could say that it had taken forty-six years to build the temple (John 2:20). It was not completely finished until A.D. 64, only six years before it was destroyed by the legions of Titus when Jerusalem was taken in 70. The temple occupied the same ground plan as that of its predecessor, but Herod did increase its elevation to one hundred cubits (BAB, 250). The temple complex was arranged in terraces, with the temple itself at the highest point. The outer court was the court of the Gentiles, then came the court of the women and the court of the Israelites, and finally the temple precincts.

After the Six Day War in 1967, Israeli archaeologists were free to explore the Temple Mount. In February, 1968, Benjamin Mazar began excavations south and southwest of the Temple Mount on behalf of the Hebrew University and the Israel

---

[4]See especially, Kenneth G. Holum et al., *King Herod's Dream: Caesarea on the Sea* (New York: Norton, 1988); EAEHL, 1:270–85. The latter also describes other explorations and excavations at the site.

[5]Benjamin Mazar, *The Mountain of the Lord* (Garden City, N.Y.: Doubleday, 1975), 78–79 [MML].

THE HERODIAN LINE

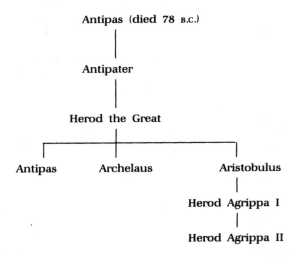

Antipas (died 78 B.C.)

|

Antipater

|

Herod the Great

|

Antipas   Archelaus   Aristobulus

|

Herod Agrippa I

|

Herod Agrippa II

Exploration Society. This work has continued until the present time.[6] Some of the more significant finds are the following: First, the Herodian Western Wall, often called the Wailing Wall, extends 69 feet (19 courses of masonry) below the present surface to bedrock. Second, the enormous arch near the southwestern corner of the western wall has been reinterpreted. This is called Robinson's Arch because Edward Robinson first identified it as part of a bridge from the Temple Mount across the Tyropoeon Valley to the Upper City. Excavations showed that this was the end of a monumental staircase that led up from the Tyropoeon Valley rather than the end of a bridge. Third, archaeologists uncovered along the western wall part of what was Jerusalem's main street during the Herodian period. Fourth, along the southern wall the Hulda Gates were discovered; the western gate was a double gate (43 feet wide) and the eastern gate a triple gate (50 feet wide). Fifth, these were approached by massive stone stairways. The one facing the western Hulda Gate is 215

feet wide and consists of thirty steps. The stairway leading to the eastern Hulda Gate has been torn away. Sixth, numerous ritual immersion baths, *mikvehs*, were uncovered in the area between the two stairways. It is interesting to note that these would have provided facilities for the multitude of believers to be baptized on the Day of Pentecost (Acts 2:41).

Herod Antipas (4 B.C.–A.D. 39)

When Herod the Great died in 4 B.C., his son Herod Antipas was assigned rulership over the northern province of Galilee and the transjordan area called Perea. Antipas had married a daughter of the king of Arabia, King Aretas of the Nabataeans, but he sent her back to her father and lived with Herodias, his brother's wife. It was this illicit union that John the Baptist rebuked, and for this rebuke John ultimately lost his life (Mark 6:16–18). It was to Herod Antipas that Christ was sent by Pilate during the trial, because Christ came from Galilee, the place of Herod Antipas's jurisdiction (Luke 23:6–12).

[6]The outstanding early account of Mazar's excavations may be read in his own words in MML. See especially pages 131–52 for a summary of some of the most significant finds.

A stone stairway that led to the Hulda Gate of the temple in Jerusalem

The Herodion, a fortress built by Herod the Great and the place where he was buried

The peristyle garden in the Herodion

Antipas launched numerous construction projects, including Tiberias on the sea of Galilee, named for Tiberius Caesar.

Herod Archelaus (4 B.C.–A.D. 6)

Herod Archelaus was the oldest son of Herod the Great. Upon the death of his father, he came to rule over Judea and Samaria and ruled with such an iron hand and incurred such dislike that he finally had his possessions taken from him by the Roman government and was banished to Vienna in Gaul.[7] At this time Judea was placed under the rule of a Roman procurator (see the last section in this chapter, pages 238–39).

Herod Philip (4 B.C.–A.D. 34)

A third son of Herod the Great, Herod Philip, became the tetrarch of Trachonitis, Batanea, and Gaulanitis (the area northeast of the Sea of Galilee). He apparently ruled justly and well. He built as his capital Caesarea Philippi (Matt. 16:13; Mark 8:27). Excavations at Caesarea Philippi (Banias) began in May, 1988, under the auspices of the Israel Department of Antiquities and the Nature Reserves Authority, with the participation of three American universities. Attention centered on a series of well-preserved vaults, nine of which were excavated, dating to the first century A.D. The use of these vaults, which apparently stood in the center of the New Testament city, has not yet been determined. Apparently superstructures stood on these vaults. Later in the summer, excavation was conducted at the temple of Pan at the site.[8] V. Tzaferis directed this first season of excavation.

Herod Agrippa I (A.D. 40–44)

Herod Agrippa I was the grandson of Herod the Great and Mariamne (and the son of their son, Aristobulus, whom Herod the Great had put to death in 7 B.C.). Herod Agrippa I hated his uncle, Antipas, and in 39, when Antipas was banished, he received his uncle's territory of Galilee and Perea. The next year, by currying the favor of the emperor of Rome, Herod Agrippa I received Judea and Samaria as well. He endeavored to be tactful with the Jews, taking sides against the Christians and even killing James the apostle with the sword (Acts 12:1–3).

Herod Agrippa II (A.D. 44–70 as King; Died c. A.D. 100)

When Herod Agrippa died in 44, his son, Herod Agrippa II, was only seventeen years old and was considered too young to rule. The country was placed under the care of a Roman procurator, but later Herod Agrippa II was given certain territories, including the area to the east of the Sea of Galilee. Herod Agrippa II is mentioned in the New Testament in connection with the apostle Paul, who appeared before him (Acts 25:13, 26:1ff.). When the Jews planned to rebel against the Romans, Herod Agrippa II warned against the rebellion. In spite of this warning, the Jews revolted, and when Jerusalem fell in A.D. 70, the Romans remembered Agrippa's loyalty to them, allowing him to come to Rome and live. Here he became a praetor (Roman official) and finally died in the year 100 at the age of seventy.

The Relationship of Pontius Pilate to the Government of Palestine in the New Testament Period

As noted above, the province of Judea was under the jurisdiction of Herod Archelaus from 4 B.C. until A.D. 6, when he was deposed from office. Judea was then put under a Roman provincial ruler who

---

[7]JAJ, XVII.13.1–2.

[8]See *Excavations and Surveys in Israel 1988/89* (Jerusalem: Israel Antiquities Authority, 1990), 10–11.

held the title of "procurator," and was directly responsible to the emperor. Pontius Pilate was the fifth of these procurators to rule over Judea after the deposing of Herod Archelaus and was the one who sentenced Christ to the cross (Matt. 27:2, 11ff.). Josephus tells us that Pilate held this office for ten years (JAJ, XVIII.4.2), a tenure that probably lasted from 26 to 36.

Tiberius was the emperor who appointed Pilate to his post in the province of Judea, and Pilate reciprocated in part by dedicating a small temple to the worship of the emperor in Caesarea. An inscription mentioning this dedication and naming both Pilate and Tiberius came to light in the theater of Caesarea during an Italian excavation there in 1961.[9] This is the first time that archaeological evidence of an inscriptional nature attesting to the existence of Pontius Pilate has been found.

---

[9]Kenneth G. Holum, *Caesarea on the Sea* (New York: Norton, 1988), 109–10.

Chapter 26

The Life and Ministry of Christ

(Matthew; Mark; Luke; John)

Prophecies of Christ in the Old Testament

The Old Testament abounds with prophecies that give details of the birth, life, and ministry of Christ. For example, Isaiah 7:14 predicted that he would be born of a virgin; Micah 5:2 indicated that he would be born in Bethlehem; and Isaiah 53:3 showed that he would be "a man of sorrows." His triumphal entry into Jerusalem was predicted in Zechariah 9:9, his betrayal for thirty pieces of silver in Zechariah 11:12, the use of the betrayal money for a potter's field in Zechariah 11:13, and the nailing of his hands in Zechariah 13:6 and Psalm 22:16. The fact that not a bone in his body was to be broken is indicated in Psalm 34:20, his death in the presence of criminals in Isaiah 53:8–9, his provision of atonement in Isaiah 53:4–5, and the fact of his resurrection in Psalm 16:10 ("You will not let your Holy One see decay"). The rejec-

tion of Christ is indicated in Micah's statement "They will strike Israel's ruler on the cheek with a rod" (5:1).

The Amazing Significance of the 332 Prophecies Concerning Christ

Many other prophecies, in addition to those given above, are found in the pages of the Old Testament. The great significance of the number of these prophecies was pointed out by Canon Liddon of England.[1]

Canon Liddon is the authority for the statement that there are 332 distinct prophecies in the Old Testament that have been literally fulfilled in Christ (HBCF, 156). Someone with a flair for mathematics has figured out that the mathematical probability of all these prophecies being fulfilled in one man is represented by an amazing fraction, the numerator of which would be one and the denominator represented by a figure

---

[1]Henry Parry Liddon, 1829–1890, educated at Oxford, vice-principal of St. Edmund's Hall at Oxford, delivered lectures in the Bampton Lectures series on the subject "The Divinity of Our Lord." In 1870 he was made canon of St. Paul's Cathedral in London and also professor of exegesis at Oxford. In 1882 he resigned his professorship and traveled in Palestine and Egypt, and in 1886 he was made chancellor of St. Paul's.

written with the number eighty-four followed by ninety-seven zeros (HBCF, 157). The chances of all these prophecies being fulfilled in one man are so overwhelmingly remote that there is no way they could be the shrewd guesses of mere men; rather, they were given by God to holy men who "spoke from God as they were carried along by the Holy Spirit" (2 Peter 1:21).

The Birth of Christ at Bethlehem (Matthew 2:1); Significance of the Prophecy

Some seven hundred years before the birth of Christ, the prophet Micah predicted that he would be born in Bethlehem Ephrathah (Mic. 5:2). Such foreknowledge is an evidence of the supernatural nature of the Bible, and the prophecy is all the more striking when we remember that there were two Bethlehems—one in northern Palestine, Bethlehem of Zebulun, and one in southern Palestine, Bethlehem Ephrath, or Bethlehem of Judah. Guided by the Holy Spirit, Micah not only stated that the birthplace of the "ruler in Israel" would be Bethlehem but he also indicated which Bethlehem it would be—Bethlehem Ephrathah. Seven hundred years later the prophecy was fulfilled in the birth of our Lord.

The Date of the Birth of Christ, Probably Between 6 and 4 B.C.

Because of an error in the ancient calendar, Christ was not born in the year one, as we now compute dates, but was actually born a few years B.C. His birth took place while Herod the Great was still alive (Matt. 2:1), and Herod died sometime between March 12 and April 11 in the year of 4 B.C.[2] Moreover, the visit of the wisemen had also occurred before the death of Herod. By the time they arrived, the holy family was no longer in the

stable but in a "house" (Matt. 2:11), and the baby was now called a "child." Herod, determined to eliminate this possible competitor for his throne, decided to kill all the boys in Bethlehem "two years old and under, in accordance with the time he had learned from the Magi" (Matt. 2:16). On this basis we could push the date of Christ's birth back to 5 or possibly the end of 6 B.C.

A second means of determining the date of Christ's birth concerns establishment of the date of the census (Luke 2:2). At the end of a lengthy discussion of this subject, Finegan concluded that it may have been in 6 or 5 B.C. He noted that while this census is only "concretely affirmed" by Luke 2:2, Justin Martyr and Tertullian (second century A.D.) stated that the record of this census was in the archives in Rome (FHBC, 234–38).

A third criterion used to peg the date of Christ's birth involves the construction of the temple. John 2:20 says that Herod's temple had been under construction forty-six years by the time Christ was thirty years of age (Luke 3:23). The temple was begun in 733 A.U.C. (*ab urbe condita*, from the founding of the city, i.e., Rome). If we add 46 to 733, we get 779. Subtract Christ's age at the time, 30, and we get 749 A.U.C. or 5 B.C. for the date of his birth. Since he was a little over 30 and the temple may have been in the process of being built slightly over 46 years, the date of Christ's birth could easily be pushed back to 6 B.C.

Archaeological Confirmation of the Validity of Luke's Reference to the Census at the Time of the Birth of Christ (Luke 2:1–3)

Luke tells us that at the time of the birth of Christ, Caesar Augustus sent out a decree that "a census should be taken of the entire Roman world." Luke also

---

[2]Jack Finegan, *Handbook of Biblical Chronology* (Princeton: Princeton University Press, 1964), 231 [FHBC].

indicates that this was done when Cyrenius was governor of Syria, and that everyone had to go to his "own town" for the enrollment (Luke 2:1–3).

Earlier it was believed that Luke had made almost as many mistakes as could possibly be made in these few lines, for it was thought that he was in error with regard to (1) the existence of such an imperial census, (2) Cyrenius's being governor at the time (Luke 2:2), and (3) everyone's having to go to his ancestral home. Archaeological discoveries remarkably confirmed and illuminated all of these statements of Luke, attesting his reliability in the very items noted above: (1) the discovery of the number of papyrus documents relating to census taking shows that a census was made every fourteen years, and these documents point back to a census taken 9–6 B.C.;[3] (2) though earlier references seemed to show that Cyrenius was governor of Syria in A.D. 6, which would be too late for the time of Christ's birth, an inscription was found at Rome in 1828 indicating that Cyrenius had been governor twice; and shortly before World War I, Ramsay found a monument in Asia Minor likewise implying two governorships for Cyrenius. Thus he could have been governor at the time of Christ's birth, as well as at a later period, in A.D. 6 (CNAD, 538); and (3) an edict made in A.D. 104 by the governor of Egypt (which was under Roman rule, just as Palestine was) showed that at the time of the census people were to return to their ancestral homes.[4] In summary, it is evident that archaeological discoveries testify to the validity of Luke's statements.

Evidence Outside of the Bible for the Existence of Jesus Christ

Especially since the rise of modern rationalism in the eighteenth century, some have doubted the very existence of Christ on earth. And in spite of accumulating evidence to the contrary, there are still voices who argue against Christ's historicity. Therefore we pause to restate some of the evidence.

First, there were the Roman writers. Tacitus, the "dean" of Roman historians (c. A.D. 60–120), among other works wrote the *Annals*, a history of the Julio-Claudian emperors from Tiberius to Nero (A.D. 14–68). In the section on Nero, Tacitus briefly described the persecution of Christians and in the process named their leader: "Christus, from whom their name is derived, was executed at the hands of the procurator Pontius Pilate in the reign of Tiberius."[5]

Second, Pliny the Younger (c. 62–113), while governor of Bithynia and Pontus in Asia Minor (modern Turkey), was faced with the issue of how to treat Christians, who were by then an illegal sect. In about 111 or 112 he wrote to the emperor Trajan for advice on the suject. In the process he bore witness to the innocent lives of Christians and their allegiance to Christ, their founder.[6]

A third witness to the person of Christ is Lucian of Samosata (c. 125–190), regarded by many as the most brilliant writer of revived Greek literature under the Roman Empire. During his later years he held a government post in Egypt. Of particular interest is his satire on Christians, published under the title *The Passing of Peregrinus*, in about 170. He described Christ as the originator of the cult of Christianity and mentioned that he was "crucified in Palestine" for having originated this cult.[7]

An especially important first-century Jewish historian was Josephus, who in his *Antiquities* (A.D. 93) made a rather

---

[3]Camden M. Cobern, *New Archaeological Discoveries*, 9th ed. (New York: Funk & Wagnalls, 1929), 46–47 [CNAD]; FLAP, 260.
[4]Adolf Deissmann, *Light from the Ancient Past* (New York: Harper & Brothers, 1922), 271 [DLAE].
[5]Tacitus, *Annals*, 15.44.
[6]Pliny the Younger, *Correspondence of Trajan*, Epistle, 10.96.
[7]Lucian, *Passing of Peregrinus*, 1.11.13.

evangelical-sounding reference to Jesus. He spoke about how Pilate condemned him to death and how he appeared alive again to his followers on the third day (JAJ, XVIII.3.3). Some critical scholars used to regard this passage as an insert by later Christian writers to gain respectability for their movement, but the general attitude today is that the reference is an embellished account of Josephus's more restrained reference to Jesus. They observe that Josephus, as an outstanding historian, quite likely made some reference to Christ. Moreover, later on he did speak of James as "the brother of Jesus, who was called Christ" (JAJ, XX.9.1). Writers who argue about the earlier longer passage tend to ignore this unembellished statement that has a ring of authenticity and may be accepted as a bona fide witness to Jesus' life on earth.

Of course there are numerous works of the church fathers of the first and second centuries that speak in great detail of the reality of the Christ. And the New Testament, now recognized to be a first-century document, must be accepted as a reliable witness to Jesus' historicity.

Christ's Birth at Bethlehem; the Manger; the Inn (Luke 2:7)

When Christ was born at Bethlehem, he was laid in a manger (Luke 2:7). The probable location of the birth of Christ is a matter of interest to the Christian world, and, fortunately, we do have some light on this subject. One of the church fathers, Justin Martyr (c. 110–165), indicated that in his time a cave in Bethlehem was pointed out as the birthplace of Christ.[8]

There are a number of old houses in Bethlehem today that are built over caves in the limestone rock, and these caves are used for stabling cattle even at the present time (CANT, 81).[9] Caves were certainly used for the same purpose in the time of Christ, and it is quite likely that his birth took place in such a grotto. Today the Church of the Nativity stands over a cave that has been pointed out for hundreds of years as the scene of the birth of our Lord. We can trace this tradition back to 325. In that year, the Bishop of Jerusalem, Macarius, informed the Emperor Constantine that in Bethlehem there was a cave that the people of the town venerated as the birthplace of Christ. The emperor gave orders for the construction of a church to enshrine the scene of the Nativity, and the work began in 326. This church has suffered various changes and destructions and rebuildings, but the cave still remains beneath it and can be seen today. High authorities generally believe that the cave of the Nativity is the birthplace of Christ, and there is no reason to doubt the tradition. The cave is about forty feet long and twelve feet wide (CANT, 79; FLAP, 532–35)

The Church of the Nativity as it now stands is a product of the extensive building activity of Justinian (emperor A.D. 537–565, but reportedly he was angry that the church did not turn out to be more grand, so he punished the builder (FLAP, 534). Minimal excavations under the present church were conducted in 1934 by William Harvey, and he found remains of the Constantinian church (FLAP, 535). The visitor to the church today can see under the floor of the nave

---

[8]S.L. Caiger, *Archaeology and the New Testament* (London: Cassell, 1939, 77) [CANT]. We do not have Justin Martyr's own statement on this, but another church father, Origen, c. 250, refers to Justin's writings that tell of this cave; Origen's reference is in his work, *Against Celsus*, I, 51.

[9]Morton picturesquely describes some of the caves of Bethlehem over which present-day houses are located. The caves are level with the road, and the one-room house is reached by a flight of stone steps numbering fifteen or twenty. The caves are still used as stables for animals, which enter from the road level. In most of the caves one can see a stone trough, or manger, cut from the rock, with iron rings to which the animals are tied at night. See H.V. Morton, *In the Steps of the Master* (New York: Dodd, Mead, 1937), 144 [MSM].

some of the floor mosaics of Constantine's church.

Jesus was born "in a manger, because there was no room for them in the inn" (Luke 2:7). Ordinarily there would be inns or stopping places (caravansaries) for caravans every twenty or twenty-five miles, the length of a day's journey. Bethlehem, however, is only five miles south of Jerusalem, and we might wonder why there would be an inn there. The answer lies in the fact that there was a branch route that came to Bethlehem from the Dead Sea region, and Bethlehem would have been the natural stopping place for those coming along this branch route, which made a junction with the main route at Bethlehem.

The Infancy of Christ; the Years of Silence

The name "Bethlehem" means "House of Bread," and in itself seems almost prophetic of Christ, who was the "Bread of Life." After Christ was born, an angel of the Lord told the shepherds near Bethlehem of the great event (Luke 2:9–11). The shepherds' fields where the shepherds were watching their flocks are still pointed out on the northeast of Bethlehem. After the visit of the shepherds, the Magi came from the East (Chaldea or Persia) for the express purpose of worshiping the newborn king (Matt. 2:11). During this period, Jesus was circumcised according to the Mosaic Law (Lev. 12:3), and Mary offered the pigeons for her purifying, according to Leviticus 12:8.

The suspicion of Herod the Great and the fear of losing his kingdom prompted him to order the slaughter of the innocent children in Bethlehem. This act was entirely in accord with his character as we have it delineated in our ancient sources, particularly in Josephus. A man who had his own wife and her mother put to death, his brother-in-law forcibly drowned in a swimming pool, and his own sons strangled (see chapter 25, page 233) was certainly capable of giving the order that the children under two years of age in Bethlehem should be slain (Matt. 2:16).

The Lord directed Joseph to take Mary and the Christ child to Egypt to escape the wrath of Herod (Matt. 2:13–15). After Herod the Great died, they could safely return to Palestine, but this time the Lord directed Joseph to take his family to Galilee, for Archelaus, the worst of the sons of Herod the Great, now ruled in his father's place in Judah (4 B.C.–A.D. 6; see chapter 25, page 238).

The Gospels are silent concerning the life of Christ from the time of the return from Egypt to Galilee until his baptism by John the Baptist (c. A.D. 27), except for the record of his visit to the temple in Jerusalem when he was twelve years old. After talking with the learned men in the temple, Jesus said to his concerned parents, "Didn't you know I had to be in my Father's house?" (Luke 2:49)—an indication of his own self-consciousness of his mission.

The Baptism of Christ and the Early Judean Ministry

Up to the time that Christ appeared before John the Baptist, John apparently did not know him (John 1:31). But when John saw him, he intuitively recognized Christ as the One whose coming he was to herald. After his baptism, Christ devoted himself to his public ministry and his messianic mission. Immediately following the baptism, Christ was tempted by Satan in the Judean desert in respect to body, mind, and spirit. Satan first tempted Christ to satisfy his physical hunger by turning stones into bread (Matt. 4:3), an appeal to the need of the body. The second temptation was intended to influence Christ to presume upon God by toying with his supernatural powers in casting himself down from the pinnacle of the temple (Matt. 4:5–6), an appeal to the pride of mind. The third temptation was designed to cause Christ to seek a shortcut to world sovereignty by merely yielding to one act of homage to Satan (Matt. 4:8–9), but Christ had come to do the will of God. He would adhere to the way of the Cross. At each temptation, Christ answered Satan by quoting Scripture. It is significant to note that in answering Satan, our Lord quoted from the book of Deuteronomy, a work denied to Moses by the critics and explained by them as a forgery (see chapter 9, pages 101–2).

The Gospel of John provides information about the early Judean ministry of Christ. This period includes the witness of John the Baptist, in which he pointed out the Lord as "the Lamb of God, who takes away the sin of the world" (John 1:29). This testimony was a commendation of Christ to two of John the Baptist's disciples, Andrew and John; they followed Christ and became the first two disciples (v. 37). They immediately told others, Andrew bringing Simon his brother (vv. 40–41). Our Lord called Phillip, who in turn sought out Nathanael (vv. 43–45), probably the same person known as Bartholomew the apostle.

During an interval in the Judean ministry, Christ went to Galilee, where he performed his first miracle of turning water into wine at the wedding feast at Cana (John 2:1–11). Afterward he returned to Jerusalem to keep the Passover, at which time he cleansed the temple, driving out the wrangling money changers and the sellers of animals from the court of the temple (vv. 14–16). When the Jews asked Jesus by what sign he did this, he replied with the enigmatic answer, "Destroy this temple, and I will raise it again in three days" (v. 19), referring to his body. Even here Christ had reference to the conflict that would end in his rejection and death, though the disciples did not really comprehend this until after his resurrection (v. 22). A short time later, Nicodemus came to Jesus by night and learned the truths of the new birth (John 3).

The Galilean Ministry (27–29)

On the way from Judea to Galilee, Jesus passed through Samaria, and there talked to the woman at the well (John 4), explaining to her that he would give living water, a picture of salvation. From there, Christ journeyed on to Galilee, probably ministering there for about two years. During this time, Jesus healed the nobleman's son (John 4:43–54) and visited Nazareth, where he read the Scriptures in the synagogue, declaring that they spoke of him. But he was not received by his own people; the Nazarenes drew him to the brow of the hill on which their city was built and would have thrown him down, but "he walked right through the crowd and went on his way" (Luke 4:29–30).

Christ went from Nazareth to Capernaum, on the shores of Galilee, and there made his headquarters (Matt. 4:13), for it is later referred to as "his own town" (Matt. 9:1). At this time, the Lord enabled Simon to make the miraculous catch of fish (Luke 5:1–9), and Christ said then that he would make them to be "fishers of men" (Matt. 4:19). Much of Christ's activity was carried on in Capernaum and the vicinity. Here he healed Peter's wife's mother (Matt. 8:14ff.), healed the paralytic (Mark 2:1ff.), and called Matthew from his task of tax collector to the position of disciple (Matt. 9:9ff.)

Edward Robinson first identified the site of Capernaum (Tell Hum) on the northwest shore of the Sea of Galilee in 1838. Small excavations there in 1856 and 1881 prompted looting of stones, and the Franciscan Order purchased the site in 1894 to protect it. H. Kohl and C. Watzinger excavated the synagogue beginning in 1905, and since 1968 V. Corbo and S. Loffreda have been excavating there. Attention has especially focused on the synagogue, which probably dates to the

Excavated fishermen's quarters at Capernaum

Octagonal church at Capernaum that covered an early Roman house, believed to be that of Peter

third century A.D. and therefore could not be the one in which Jesus ministered. The structure of two stories was built of white limestone and measured about sixty-six feet long and sixty feet wide, with a side room that could serve as a school and social hall. In 1981 excavations below the floor of the synagogue uncovered

247

what were believed to be remains of the synagogue in which Jesus preached. In front of the synagogue stood a residential area (now cleared), and in front of that stood an octagonal church, which the excavators have dated to the mid-fifth century. Below the church was a house dating to the first century; the excavators believe this house to have been the house of Peter. Progress is now being made on uncovering some of the residential section behind the synagogue.[10]

It was in Galilee, on a hill overlooking the northwestern shore of the Sea of Galilee, that Christ gave the great Sermon on the Mount (Matt. 5–7), which presents principles of character and conduct for those who are members of the kingdom. By Galilee Christ fed the five thousand (Matt. 14:13–21) and then gave the great discourse on the bread of life (John 6:22–71). From time to time there were disputes with the Pharisees, in which Christ rebuked their inward sin, which was veneered with an outward and pretended purity (Matt. 15:1–20; Mark 7:1–23).

At Caesarea Philippi, near the sources of the Jordan, some fifty miles north of Galilee, Peter gave his great confession: "You are the Christ, the Son of the living God" (Matt. 16:16). Christ at this time said that he would build his church upon the rock, the rock being symbolic of the truth that Peter had confessed.[11] It is significant that one of the early sermons in the church, recovered through archaeological discovery, is entitled "Peter the Rock." It goes to great lengths to explain that Peter was not the rock (CNAD, 279). A few days after Peter's confession of Christ, the Transfiguration took place, probably on a slope of Mount Hermon, during which there was a foreview of the coming glory of Christ (Matt. 17).

Christ's Last Journey to Jerusalem

While Christ was still in the vicinity of Galilee, he sent out the seventy disciples to prepare the way in the towns to which he would come (Luke 10:1ff.). The messengers were to announce to the people whom they met that the kingdom of God was near (Luke 10:9), referring to the impending visit of Christ who was to come after these disciples. During the course of his journey from Galilee, Jesus came into Perea, the region to the east of the Jordan. Here he answered the lawyer's question "Who is my neighbor?" by giving the parable of the Good Samaritan (Luke 10:25ff.)

A little later, Jesus went to Jerusalem on the visit described in John 10:22–29, for the Feast of Dedication, which was held in December in commemoration of the cleansing of the temple and restoration of worship by Judas Maccabeus in c. 165 B.C. after it had been defiled by Antiochus Epiphanes (in 168 B.C.; see chapter 24, pages 227–28). At this time Jesus set forth again the clear claim to his deity in the statement, "I and the Father are one" (John 10:30), and the Jews picked up stones to stone him.

Leaving Jerusalem, Jesus went to the place where John had first baptized (John 10:40) but was called back to Bethany on the occasion of the death of Lazarus (John 11), after which he withdrew again from the vicinity of Jerusalem to Ephraim, a place near the wilderness (John 11:54). During this time Christ healed the lepers in the vicinity of Samaria (Luke 17:11–19), and in his discourses dealt with the subject of divorce (Matt. 19:3–12), the coming of the kingdom (Luke 17:20–37), the parable of the unjust judge (Luke 18:1–8), and the fact of his coming cru-

---

[10]See especially EAEHL, 1:286–90; James F. Strange and Hershel Shanks, "Has the House Where Jesus Stayed in Capernaum Been Found?" BAR (December 1982), 26–37; V. Corbo, *The House of Saint Peter at Capharnaum* (Jerusalem: Franciscan Printing Press, 1972); and Stanislao Loffreda, *A Visit to Capharnaum* (Jerusalem: Franciscan Printing Press, 1973).

[11]For a discussion of the meaning of the rock, see Howard F. Vos, *Matthew* (Grand Rapids: Zondervan, 1979), 118–20.

cifixion and resurrection (Matt. 20:17–19), which the disciples found so hard to believe.

Subsequently, Jesus came to Jericho, where he healed blind Bartimaeus (Matt. 20:29–34) and called Zacchaeus to come down from a sycamore tree to hear the words of life (Luke 19:1–10). Soon afterward, Jesus arrived in Bethany, just east of Jerusalem, six days before the Passover (John 12:1), and then began the events that quickly led to the betrayal, trial, and crucifixion of our Lord.

Archaeological Discoveries in Egypt Relating to the Greek Language of the New Testament

During the nineteenth century, scholars assumed that many words in the New Testament were peculiar to the Bible and were not found in the ordinary language of the first century A.D. Kennedy found about 550 such words in the New Testament, which he considered to be "biblical" words (CNAD, 119). Some even suggested that New Testament writers invented words in order to convey certain ideas. Such a practice would, however, really hinder the message of the New Testament from reaching the people, for they would readily understand only those words that were familiar to them and would have difficulty in understanding the meaning of "invented" words.

Archaeological discoveries in Egypt during the later years of the nineteenth century brought a startling discovery. Thousands of papyrus documents—including letters, wills, receipts, tax records and the like—were found in the excavations in Egypt, where the hot dry sands had preserved them for some two thousand years. The significance of these papyrus documents was brought to the attention of the scholarly world by a young German scholar named Adolph Deissmann in 1895, when he pointed out that these records of everyday life were written in the same type of Greek as that used in the New Testament (CNAD, 30). This demonstrated that the New Testament was not written in some artificial language containing many "invented" words, but was actually written in the language in common use and therefore would be intelligible to everyone. God's purpose in making the gospel known to everyone is seen even in the type of Greek used—*koine* (common) Greek.

The significance of this great discovery is seen in the fact that dozens of words once thought peculiar to the New Testament are now known to have been good everyday words in the first century A.D., known to and used by all people of the Greek-speaking world, which in those days included the entire Roman Empire and the Near East all the way to the Indus River in India. We have seen that years ago Kennedy listed 550 such "biblical" words, whereas Deissmann, as a result of his study of the papyri, reduced this to a list of only about fifty words not yet found in other writings (CNAD, 119).

The papyri have not only demonstrated that some words thought to be invented were in standard use, but they have also clarified the meanings of many words inadequately understood before and have breathed new life into the meanings of others. A few examples will demonstrate the contribution of the papyri in this connection.

In the Sermon on the Mount Jesus condemned externalism and told those who made a public show of piety that they had their reward in the recognition accorded them (Matt. 6:2, 5, 16). In the papyri the construction used here was a technical term for granting a receipt and indicated payment in full, with no expectation, in this case, for any further reward in heaven. Thus the NIV translates the clauses in these three verses, "they have received their reward in full."[12]

Second, Peter urged in 1 Peter 2:2 that believers crave "sincere" milk (KJV), or "pure spiritual" milk (NIV), of the word. Of course no one has seen or tasted "sincere" or "spiritual" milk. In the papyri the word signifies "unadulterated" and refers to wheat unadulterated or unmixed with barley, or oil unmixed with impurities (DBS, 256). Now the meaning of the 1 Peter reference is clear.

Third, the word translated "forgiveness" in the New Testament is used in the papyri in the economic sense of remission of debt, but it is also used in a very beautiful and refreshing connotation that might not occur to us. In Egypt it was used in the irrigation of land and was the technical expression for releasing of water by opening the sluice gates. So forgiveness may be viewed as the divine opening of the sluice gates of mercy and the pouring of life-giving water over the dry and thirsty soul (DBS, 89–101).

Fourth, Hebrews 11:1 takes on a whole new significance as a result of the contribution of the papyri. We are not quite sure what to think when we read that "faith is the substance of things hoped for" (KJV). In the papyri the word translated "substance" is a legal term used to denote the collection of papers bearing on the possession of a piece of property; we would use the word "deed."[13] Now we come up with the glorious translation, "Faith is the title-deed of things hoped for," and faith loses some of its abstract or nebulous character.

In addition to what the papyri do for word meanings, they also contribute to our understanding of Greek grammar. In the past, scholars sometimes observed that passages in the New Testament seemed to have been written in bad grammar, compared to what appeared in classical literature. Critics occasionally commented that grammatical errors could be expected from unlettered fishermen who had become apostles. But we all recognize that grammatical usage changes. For example, in the past few years it has become acceptable in English usage to split infinitives. When we engage in a careful study of the papyri, we find that numerous shifts in grammatical usage took place between the classical and New Testament periods and that what appears in the New Testament is good grammar judged by the standards of its own time.

Zacchaeus the Tax Collector (Luke 19:1–10); Archaeological Light on Tax-Collectors and Taxes in Ancient Times

When Jesus was at Jericho, he called Zacchaeus down from a sycamore tree into which Zacchaeus had climbed in order to better see the Lord as he passed by (Luke 19:1–5). Zacchaeus was a tax collector; by his own confession (that he would make restoration if he had taken too much) he showed the traits of the tax collector of ancient times, who extorted all of the money he could from the people. Several papyri have been found concerning the extortions of tax collectors, and they bring vividly to mind the popular feeling that there must have been against Zacchaeus, as well as against Matthew, who was also a tax collector (Matt. 9:9) (CNAD, 29).

A study of taxation under the Romans reveals that opposition to tax collectors did not necessarily arise from overcharging on allowable rates. The real problem sometimes came with payment; in extending credit, agents might engage in what amounted to loan sharking. Moreover, in Palestine Jewish tax collectors employed by the Roman government were looked on as agents for an oppressive, occupying power, in some sense

---

[12]G. Adolph Deissmann, *Bible Studies* (Edinburgh: T. & T. Clark, 1903), 229 [DBS].

[13]George Milligan, *Here and There Among the Papyri* (London: Hodder & Stoughton, 1922), 72.

disloyal to their own people. Thus they might be hated even if they were scrupulously honest.

The need for tax collectors in the ancient world is revealed by the documents excavated in Egypt. The custom house receipts of a town named Socnopaei Nesus show that there was a heavy tariff rate on both exports and imports and that the individual merchants and tradesmen of every kind had to pay heavy taxes. There were taxes on land and farm stock, on goats and pigs of the temple, and on every item, in fact, that was taxable. In Bible times a very heavy force of collectors must have been necessary (CNAD, 85), and for this reason we should not be surprised to encounter tax collectors such as Zacchaeus and Matthew in the New Testament.

Archaeological Light on the Apparent Contradiction Concerning the Healing of Blind Bartimaeus (Matthew 20:29; Mark 10:46; Luke 18:35)

Just before the Lord met Zacchaeus at Jericho (Luke 19:1ff.), he healed the blind in the same vicinity (Luke 18:35ff.). Matthew (20:29) says that this healing took place as Christ *left* Jericho, whereas in Luke (18:35) the indication is that it took place *on the way into* Jericho. Some have suggested that these were two different events, and that is a possibility.

Archaeology, however, has thrown additional light on this apparent discrepancy. Early in the twentieth century Ernest Sellin of the German Oriental Society conducted excavations at Jericho (1907–1909). He showed that the Jericho of Jesus' time was a double city (CNAD, 361). The old Jewish city was about a mile away from the Roman city. In addition to what Sellin found, Josephus spoke of a theater (JAJ, XVII.vi.3), and amphitheater (viii.2), and a hippodrome (vi.5) there. So far, excavators at Herodian Jericho have uncovered part of the Hasmonean palace and the adjacent swimming pools (where

Herod drowned Aristobulus) and a good part of the palace of Herod the Great and his son Archelaus (EAEHL, 2:565–70). The great structures to which Josephus referred and the residential area await the work of the archaeologists.

It is possible that Matthew wrote about the Jewish city that Christ had left, whereas Luke wrote about the Roman one, at which Christ had not yet arrived. Thus, on his way from the old to the new city, Christ met and healed the blind Bartimaeus. Therefore, if these three passages in Matthew, Mark, and Luke refer to the same event, there is not any contradiction; and if they refer to different healings, there would of course be no contradiction either.

The Trial and Crucifixion of Christ

As noted previously, Christ arrived in Bethany near Jerusalem "six days before the Passover" (John 12:1), probably on a Friday evening. On Saturday evening, a supper was given in honor of Jesus; at this time Mary anointed his feet with costly pure nard (John 12:3), showing her love for him. On the next day, Palm Sunday, Jesus made his triumphal entry into Jerusalem, where the multitude hailed him as "King of Israel" (John 12:12–13), and that evening he returned to Bethany (Mark 11:12).

On Monday, Jesus and his disciples were again on the way into the city. A fig tree, having nothing but leaves, was cursed by the Lord and withered away (Matt. 21:18–22); as to whether the record of the cleansing of the temple at this point (vv. 12–13) is a second cleansing or is the same act as described by John at the beginning of the ministry of Christ is difficult to determine.

Tuesday of the Passion Week was a most eventful day. When Christ appeared at the temple, the scribes, priests, and elders, representing the Sanhedrin, asked him by what authority he acted (Matt. 21:23). Jesus met this effort to ensnare him with a counterquestion, "John's baptism—where did it come from? Was it from heaven, or from men?" His questioners were stymied, for they realized that if they said that the baptism of John was from heaven, Christ would ask why they did not believe him concerning his testimony about Christ; but if they said that John's baptism was of men, they would have to fear what the people might do and say, for John was esteemed by the people. Other ensnaring questions, such as the question of tribute to Caesar (Matt. 22:17), were also effectively answered by the One who is the source of all wisdom. Our Lord then turned the sword of verbal condemnation on his prosecutors and denounced them as hypocrites making only a pretense (Matt. 23:13–14), as fools and blind (23:17), and as a brood of vipers (23:33).

On this same day as the apostolic company was leaving the temple, the disciples pointed to the magnificence of the temple, which brought forth Christ's prophecy that not one stone should be left upon another (Matt. 24:2), a prophecy that was fulfilled within forty years. The remainder of Matthew 24 contains Christ's predictions of events yet to be fulfilled, including his second coming (v. 30). To this discourse on the future (Olivet Discourse, Matt. 24), Christ added the great parables of Matthew 25 on the wise and foolish virgins, the talents, and the sheep and goats—the last one dealing with the judgment of the nations. On Tuesday evening Christ forewarned the disciples of his approaching crucifixion (Matt. 26:2).

Jesus may have spent Wednesday in retirement in Bethany, in preparation of his spirit for the last great conflict (although some scholars arrange the events of this day a little differently).

On Thursday, the fourteenth of Nisan, Jesus gave instructions to the disciples to make preparations for the observance of the Passover (Matt. 26:17–19); they followed the man bearing the pitcher of water and were shown the upper room prepared for their use (Mark 14:13–16). At evening Jesus and the Twelve gathered, and he washed their feet (John 13:2–20); this was followed by the observance of the Passover, now instituted as the Lord's Supper (Matt. 26:26). Here in the Upper Room, Christ foretold his betrayal (John 13:21ff.) and Peter's denial (v. 38), followed by his wonderful words of comfort in John 14, "Do not let your hearts be troubled," and the promise of giving the Counselor or Comforter, the Holy Spirit (John 14:16ff.). He then gave the lesson on the vine and the branches (John 15), and closed with the wonderful intercessory prayer of John 17.

It was still Thursday evening when Jesus and his disciples came to the Garden of Gethsemane, on the east side of Jerusalem (Matt. 26:36). Following the agony in the garden, Jesus was arrested by Roman soldiers, sent by the chief priests (Matt. 26:39–47) and led there by the traitor Judas. Our Lord's surrender was voluntary, demonstrated by the fact that the Father would have sent more than twelve legions of angels if he had but asked (v. 53; in the Empire Period of Rome a legion numbered between 5,000 and 6,000 men; this would mean between 60,000 and 72,000 angels). But this was not a battle against flesh and blood but against sin.

It would have been about midnight Thursday when Jesus was hurried to the house of Caiaphas, the high priest (Matt. 26:57). The whole trial of Christ abounds with illegalities. To mention only a few, it was held at night, there was lack of a definite charge, an interrogation of the accused was made, and there was haste in condemning Christ. He was then brought before Pilate (Matt. 27:11), who against his own convictions and through fear of a charge of disloyalty to Caesar yielded up the One whom he had declared guiltless. Pilate sent Jesus to Herod Antipas, who had jurisdiction over Galilee but happened to be in the city at that time (Luke 23:6–11). Jesus did not answer the questions of Herod or the false accusations heaped upon him by the priests and scribes as he stood before them (v. 9); Herod and his men mocked Christ, putting a robe on him, and then sent him back to Pilate.

During the morning hours of Friday, Pilate finally yielded to the mob, who shouted that if he released Jesus he would not be the friend of Caesar (John 19:20). Christ, bearing the crown of thorns made by the soldiers (Matt. 27:29), was led out to Calvary, and there, between two thieves, was crucified (Matt. 27:35, 44). From the sixth to the ninth hour (12:00 to 3:00 P.M.) there was darkness (Matt. 27:45); it was as though nature herself were veiling her face from the greatest crime ever perpetrated. The Holy One of Israel was being made sin for us.

It was three o'clock by the time Christ had given up his spirit. The Sabbath began at evening, and in order that his body might not remain on the cross on the Sabbath, Joseph of Arimathea sought and obtained permission from Pilate to bury Jesus (Matt. 27:57–60). The body of Christ was placed in Joseph's own new tomb, and the door was closed with the rolling stone. Some of the priests and Pharisees asked that it be sealed and were given permission to seal the stone (Matt. 27:66).

Location of Calvary

Ever since the British hero General Charles George Gordon identified a certain hill just north of the Damascus Gate in Jerusalem as Calvary in 1883, the popular acceptance of this site has grown. In recent years over a hundred thousand tourists and pilgrims have visited there annually. The proposed hill of Calvary stands just north of the present city wall, and by some effort one can imagine that it looks like a skull. On its western side, just 820 feet north of the Damascus Gate is a cave that many have come to believe was the actual burial place of Christ. In 1894 the Garden Tomb Association of Great Britain bought the cave and the surrounding garden, and the tomb is now called the Garden Tomb. Protestants, who have no special rights in the use of the Church of the Holy Sepulcher, have been especially enamored with this site as the location of Calvary and the tomb of Christ. By no means have all Protestants been convinced of its validity, however. The best that some can say is that a visit to the Garden Tomb is satisfying because it permits one to visualize an early empty tomb without the kind of decorative impediments of the Church of the Holy Sepulcher.

Among arguments in favor of Gordon's Calvary are that it resembles a human skull, is close to the city, and is not far from the Damascus Gate and that a cemetery containing a tomb identified as that of Christ is located nearby. Answers to these points include the following: The spot has not looked like a skull for more than a couple of centuries; the continued use of sand and stone from the mound has brought it to its present appearance. Moreover, the city walls and the great North Road are not in the same locations as in New Testament times. In Jesus' day the city wall ran far south of where it does now.

This is where the subject stood until the last few years. Now it must be viewed in a different light. After the Israeli occupation of East Jerusalem and the West Bank in 1967, it has been possible for Israeli archaeologists to work in East Jerusalem. Amihai Mazar made a study of the burial caves north of the Damascus Gate and concluded that the whole area had been an Iron Age cemetery (during the general period of the eighth to the seven centuries B.C.).[14] Gabriel Barkay, who teaches at Tel Aviv University and the American Institute of Holy Land Studies, has made a new study of the case for the Garden Tomb and has concluded that it was first hewn in the Iron Age II period, during the eighth to the sixth centuries B.C., and was not used again for burial purposes until the Byzantine period. So it is not the tomb in which Jesus was buried.[15]

The traditional site of Calvary and the tomb of Jesus is in the Church of the Holy Sepulcher, now located deep inside the old city of Jerusalem. But was it outside the city in New Testament times? As a result of various discoveries in recent decades, the line of the wall has now been established; the wall was about 500 feet to the south and 350 feet to the east of the church.[16] If the church was outside the wall, the next issue is the legitimacy of the claim that Jesus was buried there.

The church as it now stands is essentially a Crusader structure, begun after the Crusaders captured Jerusalem in 1099. The prior history of the site requires a considerable amount of space to describe it in full (for details, see FLAP, 527–32), but the main outline can be briefly put. By and large the Crusader church replaced a church erected by Constantine and dedicated in 335, though parts of the edifice had been destroyed and rebuilt. Apparently what Constantine constructed was a rotunda covering the tomb of Jesus, before which (on the east) lay a garden open to the sky and surrounded by a portico of columns. In the southeastern corner of the garden stood the rock of Calvary. Then on an axis with the tomb and to the east of the garden Constantine put up a basilica church (Bahat, 36; FLAP,

527–28). Reportedly all Constantine had to do when he built his church was to remove a small temple built by Hadrian to Venus/Aphrodite on that site when he rebuilt Jerusalem early in the second century A.D. Local Christians had identified this as the place of Christ's death and burial to Queen Helena, Constantine's mother, when she visited Jerusalem in A.D. 326 (Bahat, 35). Eusebius, the noted church historian, who preached in the church soon after its construction, reported how after the removal of the temple of Venus the tomb of Christ reappeared.[17] The Crusader church covered the site of the tomb, the garden, Calvary, and Constantine's basilica.

In recent times the Crusader Church of the Holy Sepulcher became quite decrepit. A restoration plan was finally agreed on in 1959 by the religious bodies having access to the church, and the following year Virgilio Corbo of the Franciscan School in Jerusalem was appointed archaeologist for the project. The Franciscan Printing Press published the three-volume report, the *Holy Sepulcher of Jerusalem*, in 1981–1982. The restoration involved a considerable amount of excavation under the church. Beneath the north wall of the rotunda lies a tomb traditionally attributed to Joseph of Arimathea (Bahat, 31). After completing his study on the Church of the Holy Sepulcher, Finegan concluded, "We may with confidence seek beneath the roof of this structure the true place of Golgotha and the sepulcher of Christ" (FLAP, 532).

The Resurrection and Ascension of Christ

On the morning of the first day of the week (Sunday), the two Marys came to the

[14]Amihai Mazar, "Iron Age Burial Caves North of Damascus Gate Jerusalem," *Israel Exploration Journal* 26 (1976): 1–8.

[15]Gabriel Barkay, "The Garden Tomb—Was Jesus Buried Here?" BAR (March/April 1986), 57.

[16]Dan Bahat, "Does the Holy Sepulcher Church Mark the Burial of Jesus?" BAR (May/June 1986), 38.

[17]Charles Coüasnon, *The Church of the Holy Sepulcher Jerusalem* (London: The British Academy, 1974), 13–14.

tomb and found that Christ had risen (Matt. 28:1ff.). Ten appearances of Jesus after his resurrection are recorded in the Gospels, five of them occurring on the resurrection day. Among the significant ones are his meeting with the disciples on the Emmaus road (Luke 24:12–35) and with the Eleven on the day of his resurrection (vv. 35ff.), his appearance at the Sea of Galilee when the disciples were fishing (John 21:1ff.), and his meeting them at the mountain in Galilee where he gave the great commission to go into all the world and preach the gospel (Matt. 28:16–20). The last appearance of Christ on earth was on the slopes of the Mount of Olives, near Bethany, where he ascended to heaven (Luke 24:50–51). As he went up, two angels appeared and assured the disciples that he would return (Acts 1:11), an event for which we wait and pray.

Archaeological Evidence Against New Testament "Form Criticism"

A new type of biblical criticism has developed since 1919 under the leadership of Martin Dibelius and Rudolph Bultmann, both of Germany (AAP, 242). It is called "form criticism"[18] because it holds that the oral traditions of the church developed into definite literary "forms," such as the miracle stories, parables, and sayings of Jesus (ASAC, 294). Form critics usually hold that much of the content of the Gospels was adapted or in other cases invented to correspond to situations that developed in the church after the days of the apostles (AAP, 242). This means, according to form criticism, that much of the material in the Gospels really reflects a later period in the church and merely appears to describe

the early apostolic era. The gospel of John, to cite an example, is held by this school (e.g., Bultmann) to contain practically no original historical material, but to reflect a period in the second century A.D.

In 1942 historian A.T. Olmstead[19] reacted against this critical view of John. He insisted that the narratives of John were written down in Aramaic before A.D. 40 and were later rendered in Greek (AAP, 243). (Truly conservative scholars hold to 85–90 as the date of John's gospel, on the basis of internal as well as external evidence; TINT, 173.) While Olmstead probably went too far in the reverse direction from those who hold to a second-century date for John, it is refreshing to see an objective historian object to these subjective extremes of form criticism. More recently Bishop John A.T. Robinson (Anglican), lecturer in theology at Cambridge University, rejected many of his earlier radical views and concluded in 1977 that the New Testament books were written between A.D. 47 and 70.[20]

Archaeological discoveries have given definite evidence that the background of the gospel of John reflects a knowledge of the situation in Palestine prior to A.D. 70. This evidence is well summarized by W.F. Albright (AAP, 244–48). Only two items from this body of evidence will be given here: First, very often in the gospel of John the Aramaic term *rabbi*, rendered in Greek as *didaskalos*, "master, teacher" (John 1:38; 20:16), is applied to Christ. Rabbinic scholars have held that the use of this term was a borrowing from current usage in the second century, when it appeared in the Mishnah[21] and other sources. This would mean that the employment of "master" was an evidence of the late date of the gospel of John.

---

[18]Known in German as *Formgeschichte*. For brief descriptions, see AAP, 242ff.; ASAC, 298; TINT, 118ff.; Donald Guthrie, *New Testament Introduction*, 3rd ed. (Downers Grove: InterVarsity, 1970), chap. 6.

[19]At the Oriental Institute of the University of Chicago until his death in 1945.

[20]John A.T. Robinson, *Can We Trust the New Testament?* (Grand Rapids: Eerdmans, 1977), 63.

[21]The Mishnah (or text) is one of the two main parts of the Talmud, the other being the Gemara, or commentary.

Excavations by E.L. Sukenik, however, produced an early ossuary[22] in 1930 from Mount Scopus (across the Kidron Valley from Jerusalem) on which the Greek word *didaskalos* ("master") was applied as the title of a man named Theodotion, whose personal name was written in Aramaic characters (AAP, 244). This discovery shows that one may not charge the gospel of John with an anachronism in the use of the term "master" (*didaskalos*).

Second, some scholars formerly held that personal names used in the gospels, particularly in John, were fictitious and had been selected because of their meaning and not because they referred to historical persons. Such speculations are not supported by the ossuary inscriptions, which preserve many of the biblical names. Those occurring include Miriam (Mary), Martha, Elizabeth, Salome, Johanna, and Sapphira (Acts 5:1), as well as Jesus (equivalent to the Old Testament Joshua), Joseph, and an abbreviated form of the name Lazarus (AAP, 244). While no one would insist that the biblical characters bearing these names are necessarily the same as those recorded on the ossuaries, nonetheless the ossuary inscriptions show that these names fit in the

early New Testament period and that the form critic is left without archaeological support for using this criterion of personal names for his late dating of New Testament material, particularly the gospel of John.

As noted before, conservative scholars hold that the gospel of John was written about 85–90.[23] In addition to the ossuary evidence, discoveries of papyrus manuscripts also support this date, as against a later date in the second century, held by adherents of form criticism. In 1935 C.H. Roberts identified a fragment of the Gospel of John that had been excavated several years earlier by Grenfell and sent to the John Rylands Library in England (often referred to as "Rylands John"). This fragment contains only five verses (18:31–33, 37–38), but it is most significant because papyrus experts agree in assigning it to the first half of the second century. Kenyon points out that the copy of the gospel from which this fragment came would have circulated in Egypt in the period 130–150. This means that the original Gospel of John must have been composed sometime earlier than 130, which would bring us so near to the traditional date that "there is no longer

---

[22]An ossuary is a bone chest in which bones of those long dead were placed so that the tomb could be reused for another burial. An inscription bearing the name of the person to whom the bones belonged was usually inscribed on the ossuary.

[23]This is based on a number of factors. The church fathers gave indications that John was written after the other gospels: Irenaeus (c. 140–203) placed it after Matthew, Mark, and Luke, and Clement of Alexandria (c. 155–215) said that John wrote "last of all." Jerome (c. 340–420) gives a similar indication. The way in which the gospel of John refers to "the Jews" implies that it was written after that nation had become confirmed enemies of the church and many years after the author had been absent from Palestine. The lack of reference to the destruction of Jerusalem in 70 seems to require that the gospel be dated sometime before that event, or sufficiently afterward to allow for it to have become somewhat incidental. Since the evidence would point to a date sometime after 70 rather than before, it would likely be sometime between 85 and 90. (Other factors noted below would preclude its being much later.) Irenaeus declares that John wrote this gospel at Ephesus and that he lived until the time of the Roman emperor Trajan, who began to rule in 98. Since John did not get to Ephesus until about 69 or 70 (following Paul's last visit there in 65 or 66; cf. TINT, 170), it must have been written sometime after 70, inasmuch as no reference is made to the Jewish troubles of 66–70 or the destruction of the temple in 70. Since John lived until the time of Trajan (98), it appears logical on the basis of all these indications to date the Gospel 85–90. Westcott, the well-known New Testament scholar of the nineteenth century, substantially agreed to this date, placing it late in the first century. For development and documentation of this material, see TINT, 172–73.

any reason to question the validity of the tradition."[24]

Other evidence for the early date of John and the other Gospels appeared in the discovery of some papyri fragments that were published by H.I. Bell and T.C. Skeat of the British Museum. The document from which these fragments came must have been written in the first half of the second century A.D. and contains material that Kenyon assigns to the first century. It records the stories of the healing of the leper (Mark 1:40–42) and the question of paying tribute to Caesar (Matt. 22:17–18; Mark 12:14–15; Luke 20:21–25), and reflects the language of not only the first three Gospels but also of John (KBMS, 22–23). Here also, Kenyon says, is "confirmatory evidence of the existence of the Fourth Gospel by about the end of the first century" (KBMS, 23).

Kenyon points out that if the fourth Gospel was written by A.D. 90, and if it was preceded by Matthew and Luke, and earlier by Mark, about 65, then there was not time enough for the elaborate process required by Dibelius's form criticism. This theory presupposes, first, the diffusion of stories about Jesus, then their collection and classification into groups according to their literary form, and finally the formation of continuous narratives in which they were utilized. Kenyon aptly remarks that there simply is "not time for elaborate processes of literary workmanship and development" (KBMS, 52). The discoveries thus show that the speculations of the school of form criticism are not supported[25] and that the Gospels must have been written in the first century A.D.

The General Critical View of the Date of the Gospels; the Bearing of Archaeology

As we have seen in the preceding section, an integral part of the theory of form criticism is the late dating of the Gospels. This was first developed by F.C. Baur (1792–1860) and others in the Tübingen school of German criticism. They set forth the view that the Gospel of John could not have been written until 160 (BAB, 588).

The same evidence that refutes form criticism's late dating of the Gospels is applicable to a more general theory holding to their late date. This would include the archaeological evidence showing an early background for John, such as the indications on ossuaries of the early use of the term "master" and of New Testament names, as well as Rylands John and the Gospel fragments published by Bell and Skeat (see preceding section). All of this evidence points to the existence of the Gospel of John by the end of the first century, which is the date held by true conservatives.

In regard to the Synoptic Gospels (Matthew, Mark, and Luke), it is refreshing to see that one of the greatest French liberal scholars of the last generation, Maurice Goguel, puts them in the first century in his work *The Early Church*.[26] Most significant of all, of course, is not the opinion of the scholars, but rather the internal evidence from the Gospels, the evidence from the archaeological discoveries and papyrus documents, which point to the early date and validity of the Gospels.

Something has been said about the contribution of the early papyrus fragment of the Gospel of John to the dating

---

[24]Frederic G. Kenyon, *The Bible and Modern Scholarship* (London: Murray, 1948), 21 [KBMS]. Sir Frederic Kenyon was formerly Director of the British Museum; his field of specialization is in New Testament manuscripts.

[25]There is other evidence against form criticism that for the sake of conciseness cannot be treated here. For summary, see TINT, 118–21.

[26]*L'Église primitive (Jésus et les origines du Christianisme)* (Paris: Payot, 1947); cf. review written by C.C. McCown in JBL 68, 3 (September 1949): 270.

of the books of the New Testament. There are two other contributions the papyri make in this regard. This first concerns the argument based on historical grammar. We are familiar with the fact that language keeps changing, and even the less technically educated person can, for instance, spot the difference between the English of Shakespeare's or Thomas Jefferson's day and contemporary American prose. Just so, the person who has studied the papyri knows what the Greek style and vocabulary was like in the first century and knows that the New Testament uses the language of the first century, not the second or third. The conclusion of Millar Burrows in this regard is significant: "Unless we resort to the wholly improbable hypothesis of a deliberate and remarkable successful use of archaic language, it is evident therefore that the books of the New Testament were written in the first century" (WMTS, 54).

Second, the biblical papyri, dating from the second or third centuries help to destroy the old critical view that the oral traditions, and especially the miraculous nature of Christ's ministry, evolved over time and finally came to their present form in the third or fourth century.

The Dead Sea Scrolls and the Ministry of Christ

Soon after the Dead Sea Scrolls began to make their impact, a literature developed that sought to rob Christ and Christianity of all their uniqueness. Some found Christ to be merely the "reincarnation of the Teacher of Righteousness" of the Qumran community, and the church to be merely an extension of the community there. A detailed and definitive answer to these assertions is not possible in a few words here, nor is it necessary. William S. LaSor in his definitive work *The Dead Sea Scrolls and the New Testament* has carefully handled all aspects of these issues. He showed that John the Baptist either was not a Qumranian or, if he ever had been, he had broken completely with the community's viewpoint. He demonstrated the tremendous difference between the church and the Qumran community. And answering some of the earlier assertions, LaSor concluded that the "Teacher of Righteousness" was really totally unlike Jesus Christ. Contrary to claims of likeness, there is no record of his crucifixion, burial, resurrection, or promise of return.[27]

---

[27]William S. LaSor, *The Dead Sea Scrolls and the New Testament* (Grand Rapids: Eerdmans, 1972), 152, 247–54. See also R.K. Harrison, *Archaeology of the New Testament* (London: English Universities Press, 1964), chapter 6, "Qumran and the New Testament." Charles F. Pfeiffer in his *Dead Sea Scrolls and the Bible* (Grand Rapids: Baker, 1969) has a helpful chapter entitled "Qumran Messianism."

Chapter 27

The Beginning of the Church

(Acts 1–12)

The Day of Pentecost; the Beginning of the Church (Acts 1–2)

After the ascension of Christ (Acts 1:9), Matthias was chosen to replace Judas among the apostles (vv. 15–26). The next important event occurred on the Day of Pentecost. Pentecost was one of the Old Testament festivals, referred to in the Pentateuch as the "Feast of Weeks" (Exod. 34:22), because it was celebrated seven weeks, or fifty days, after the Passover (Lev. 23:16). On that day, two loaves were presented, along with the offering of lambs and other animals (v. 18). It was to be a day of rejoicing, as well as a day in which Israel remembered that they had been bondservants in the land of Egypt, a reminder to observe the statutes of the Lord (Deut. 16:11–12).

When the disciples gathered on this Day of Pentecost, it was fifty days after the resurrection of Christ, or just ten days after his ascension (since his postresurrection ministry was forty days). The Holy Spirit came upon the disciples, and they spoke with other tongues, so that the strangers who were in Jerusalem could understand what they were saying (Acts 2:6). Thus we see that there was a specific purpose for the speaking in tongues—it was to enable the visitors in Jerusalem to understand the message.

The coming of the Holy Spirit on Pentecost is generally recognized as marking the beginning of the church.[1] The apostles were now changed, and the outpouring of the Holy Spirit on them enabled them to become effective wit-

---

[1]Those who hold that the church began in Old Testament times would say, rather, that Pentecost was a turning point in the church. Both views present a definite aspect of truth: to say that the church began in Old Testament times is to emphasize the fact that people in all ages are saved by the shed blood of Christ. It is evident that a change took place in the operation of the Holy Spirit beginning with Pentecost. From then on the Holy Spirit indwells the believer, whereas in Old Testament times he came upon individuals for special tasks. As to salvation, it is clear that whether the church began at Pentecost or in Old Testament times, in all ages people have been saved only by the substitutionary death of Christ. Old Testament saints looked forward to the promised Seed, whereas those in the Christian era look back to him and his finished work on Calvary. Peter states the truth of the unity of the plan of salvation when, referring to Old Testament believers, he says, "It is through the grace of our Lord Jesus that we are saved, just as they are" (Acts 15:11).

nesses of the resurrection of Christ as the fundamental fact in Christianity and to extend the church by preaching the gospel according to the Great Commission.

Archaeological Evidence of Jews in Many Countries in the New Testament Period

Among the people who heard the disciples speak in tongues on the Day of Pentecost were those from Phrygia, Egypt, Rome, and many other places (Acts 2:10). Many of them, perhaps most of them, were descendants of Palestinian Jews who years earlier had gone to other countries and there lived and learned the language of their adopted land. Archaeological evidence of Jews in these other lands has been forthcoming in the excavations. Ramsay's work in Asia Minor in the region of ancient Phrygia showed that there were many Jews in that area in the New Testament period. Some two thousand families of Jews had been brought from Babylon to Phrygia about 200 B.C. and had populated the district; with succeeding generations they increased in numbers and influence, and many of them grew rich. With the passage of time, they even forgot their own language (CNAD, 417). It was undoubtedly for Jews of this type who may have been visiting Jerusalem that the miracle of the tongues at Pentecost occurred; it was necessary in order that these Jews could understand the message.

Egypt is also mentioned among the countries represented by the hearers of the disciples on the Day of Pentecost (Acts 2:10). The presence of Jews in Egypt in the New Testament period has been shown by several excavations, including evidence from a large oasis called the Fayum, about forty miles south and a little west of Cairo (CNAD, 65). Here was a Jewish colony, named Samaria, where the Jews were, among other things, bankers, tax gatherers, and police officers (CNAD, 79). The entire fourth quarter of the great

city of Alexandria, named for Alexander the Great, was a Jewish district.

The Bible refers to Rome as one of the places represented on the Day of Pentecost (Acts 2:10). Evidence for Jews living at Rome in that era appeared in the excavation of several early cemeteries in that city that proved to be Jewish. One cemetery on the Via Portuensis yielded 119 inscriptions, some of them showing the seven-branched lampstand, and others giving such Jewish names as Jacob, Judas, Anna, and Rebecca (CNAD, 517–18).

Peter's Message on the Day of Pentecost (Acts 2:14–39)

After the apostles had spoken in different tongues on the Day of Pentecost, those who had heard were amazed, and some mocked, saying they had had too much wine (Acts 2:12–13). Peter stood up and addressed the group. He pointed out that Jesus of Nazareth, whom God had raised, was the One foretold by David (v. 25), the One who would not see corruption (Ps. 16:10, a prophecy of the resurrection of Christ). Peter then called on Israel to repent, to be baptized in the name of Jesus Christ for the remission of sins, and to receive the Holy Spirit (Acts 2:38). Many gladly received the message, and about three thousand were baptized and added to those who already believed. This constituted the beginning of the church.

Peter's Second Sermon; the Opposition That Followed (Acts 3–4)

After Peter and John healed the lame man at the Beautiful Gate (Acts 3:1–11), a group of people gathered at Solomon's porch, and Peter took the opportunity to address them (3:11–12). He called on Israel to repent that their sins might be blotted out, pointing to Christ as the One whom God had raised up, the One sent to turn them from their iniquities (vv. 19, 26).

The priests and Sadducees were greatly disturbed at this preaching of Jesus and the resurrection (Acts 4:1–2), and they seized the disciples and confined them. But the seed had already been sown, and in spite of the detention of the disciples, about five thousand men had believed (v. 4). Peter was given opportunity the next day to address the Jewish council known as the Sanhedrin; he preached to them the truth of the crucifixion and resurrection of Christ, in whom alone there is salvation (vv. 10–12). The Jewish leaders ordered them to preach no more in the name of Christ (v. 17), but Peter and John candidly answered, "We cannot help speaking about what we have seen and heard" (v. 20).

Mutual Aid in the Early Church; the Sin of Ananias and Sapphira (Acts 4:32–37; 5:1–11)

It seems that, in order to meet an emergency in the early church, there was a temporary practice of pooling the resources of the believers. Those who had property sold it and brought the proceeds to the apostles, who distributed according to every person's need.[2]

A man and his wife, Ananias and Sapphira, sold some property and brought only a part of the money to the apostles, keeping back a part, yet pretending to have brought all of it. There was no compulsion for them to have brought anything. Their sin lay in the fact that they lied, pretending that they had brought it all (Acts 5:2). Upon hearing the charge against him, Ananias fell down and died. When his wife, Sapphira, came in, she likewise lied about the matter, and died when confronted with the fact of her sin.

Archaeological Light on the Name Sapphira (Acts 5:1)

Until earlier in this century, no evidence of the name Sapphira had been found outside of the Bible. In 1933, a report was published of the discovery of several ossuaries and other objects contemporary with New Testament times on which was written the name Sapphira (HSAB, 84), showing that it was a perfectly good name and fits into this period.

The Second Persecution of the Church (Acts 5:17ff.)

The works and words of the apostles caused more and more people to turn to

---

[2]Some have thought that this temporary pooling of resources by members of the early church at Jerusalem gives justification to communism as a legitimate form of government. An examination of the situation shows just the opposite. First, it was a *temporary* measure designed to meet an immediate need. Doubtless many Jews who became Christians were unable to continue their former means of employment because of prejudice on the part of employers (and for other reasons as well), and there was need for helping them over this transition stage while the church was in the process of being established and until there could be set up a regular "fund" to take care of such contingencies. Not only did the local converts have financial needs, but also many pilgrims who had come to Jerusalem for the Feast of Pentecost were in great distress. Some of them wished to stay longer for spiritual enrichment and had no resources to do so, and others feared to return home and face the economic and social discrimination they would encounter there. Second, as shown by the case of Ananias and Sapphira, there was no compulsion on them or anyone else to put anything in the common pool. Those who did so gave *voluntarily*, an entirely different situation from the communistic idea, which sets aside the rights of voluntary giving and virtually, by decree, makes the property of the thrifty the property of the indolent. Third, this was a *local* practice carried on, as far as we know, only at Jerusalem to meet an immediate need—the poverty of some of the new believers. There is no evidence that such communism was practiced at Philippi, Corinth, Ephesus, or other more affluent places. This temporary measure was merely an outworking of true Christian charity and bears no resemblance to the political communism prevalent in many countries of the world in much of the twentieth century. The idea of one man's enterprise being penalized by another man's laziness is foreign to the Scriptures. It is clearly stated that "if a man will not work, he shall not eat" (2 Thess. 3:10).

the Lord (Acts 5:12–14). This in turn aroused the ire of the high priest and his company, and they put the apostles in prison (vv. 17–18). When they were brought before the council, the apostles were asked why they had not ceased to teach in the name of Christ. Peter and the other apostles gave their unanswerable reply: "We must obey God rather than men" and then continued to exalt Christ as the One who could forgive sins (vv. 28–31). The council considered putting the apostles to death, but one of the Pharisees, Gamaliel, warned that if this movement were of men, it would fail, but if it were of God, they could not overthrow it (vv. 38–39). Gamaliel's wise council influenced them to abandon their thought to kill the apostles, and they were content to beat them and let them go with the admonition that they should not speak in the name of Jesus. The apostles went out, rejoicing that they were considered worthy to suffer for his name, and they did not stop teaching and preaching the good news of Jesus Christ (v. 42).

The Appointment of Deacons (Acts 6:1–7)

A complaint arose within the church because certain of the widows were being neglected in the provision that should have been made for them. The apostles realized that if they busied themselves too much with the necessary everyday routine, they would neglect the preaching of the Word of God. They therefore decided to appoint deacons, who would take care of serving the needy. This first deacons' board consisted of seven members, one of whom was Stephen (Acts 6:5).

The Third Persecution, Initiated by the Synagogue of the Freedmen and Others (Acts 6:8–15)

Stephen set a good example, not restricting himself to serving the needy but also doing great spiritual wonders among the people. This aroused the wrath of those in the synagogue of the Freedmen and other groups of Jews, who stirred up the people so that they again brought one of the believers, this time Stephen, before the Jewish council (Act 6:12).

Archaeological Evidence of the Synagogue of the Freedmen (Acts 6:9)

In 1913, Captain Weill excavated at Jerusalem and found an inscription stating that a certain "Theodotus" (Greek translation of the name Nathanael) had "constructed the synagogue. . ." (for translation, see BAB, 564). The father of Theodotus had a Latin name, Vettenos (shown by the inscription), which probably means that the father was one of the Jews captured by Pompey (63 B.C.; see chapter 25), taken to Rome, and later liberated, becoming a "libertine" or freedman and returning to Jerusalem. Thus it seems likely that this inscription, bearing a name appropriate for a freedman, may come from this very synagogue of the freedmen who initiated the persecution against Stephen (BAB, 564). It is interesting to note that, according to the inscription, the synagogue Theodotus constructed had a hospice connected with it "for the needy from abroad." These needy might have included freed Jews returning from Rome with plans to resettle in Palestine. This name Vettenos is the type of name that would be given by a man named Vettius to his slave; Clermont-Ganneau has suggested that this Vettius might be the very man of the same name who acted for Cicero, the Roman orator, as his agent in money matters (MCEP, 197).

Stephen's Message (Acts 7)

When Stephen was brought before the council, the council set up false witnesses against him, who charged that he spoke blasphemous words against the holy place and the law (Acts 6:13–14). Stephen was then asked by the high priest if these things were so; his answer forms the

seventh chapter of Acts. He began with
the call of Abraham, telling how God had
brought him into the Promised Land and
had watched over him and all of his
descendants, showing his favor to Joseph,
Jacob, Moses, and a host of others. But
Israel had been stiffnecked and had persecuted the prophets and slain those
who proclaimed the Righteous One to
come, the very One whom they had
murdered.

The First Appearance of Saul, Later Called Paul (Acts 7:58)

The words of Stephen cut his accusers
to the quick, and they threw him out of
the city and stoned him (Acts 7:57–58).
One of the witnesses of the stoning of
Stephen was a young man named Saul, at
whose feet the murderers of Stephen laid
their clothes. Stephen's calm committal of
himself to his Lord must have made an
impression on Saul—but what type of
impression we do not know. Outwardly, it
seemed merely to spur Saul on to a
greater persecution of the Christians, for
he continued to try to destroy the church,
committing believers to prison whenever
he could.

The Ministry of Philip; Archaeological Light on Candace (Acts 8)

In the meantime, the ministry of the
church went forward. Philip went to
Samaria and preached Christ (Acts 8:5).
He was carrying out the commission of
Christ, to take the Gospel beyond Jerusalem and Judea to Samaria and more
distant regions (v. 8). Sometime later Philip was traveling in the south, toward
Gaza, and there he met an Ethiopian
eunuch, a man of authority in the government of Queen Candace of Ethiopia.
Archaeological light on the group of
queens called Candace was found by
McIver in his excavations in Nubia, 1908–
1909. In the Christian period these Nu-
bians still called their queen Candace;
they gave her milk to drink, regarding

obesity an attribute of royalty (BAB, 30). In
the British Museum there is a large relief
showing one of these queens named
Candace.

Philip found the Ethiopian eunuch
reading the fifty-third chapter of Isaiah
and tactfully asked him if he understood
what he read. Then, receiving an implied
invitation, he proceeded to explain the
Scripture passage and to lead the man to
a knowledge of Christ (Acts 8:35–36).

The Conversion of Paul (Saul) (Acts 9)

Saul set out for Damascus, planning to
look for Christians whom he might bring
bound to Jerusalem (Acts 9:1–2). As he
journeyed along the road to Damascus, a
light engulfed him; he fell to the ground
and heard a voice calling to him, "Saul,
Saul, why do you persecute me?" Saul
asked, "Who are you, Lord?" and received
the answer, "I am Jesus whom you are
persecuting" (vv. 4–5). Saul asked what he
should do, and the Lord told him to go on
into Damascus. When Saul arose and
opened his eyes, he could see no one. He
was brought to Damascus to the house of
Judas on Straight Street. There he stayed
three days and was then met by a man
named Ananias, who put his hands on
him, and immediately the scales of
blindness fell from his eyes. (Later Saul's
name was changed to Paul.)

Peter's Ministry to the Gentiles (Acts 10)

The Lord revealed to a Roman army
officer, a centurion named Cornelius, that
he should send to Joppa for Peter (Acts
10:5). When the messengers arrived at
Joppa, Peter went with them to the home
of Cornelius at Caesarea, some distance
to the north of Joppa (v. 24). To the
household of Cornelius Peter preached
Christ as the One who could give remission of sins (v. 43), and they believed.
With the preaching of the Gospel to this
household, the ministry to the Gentiles
was definitely begun.

The Church at Antioch; First Use of the Name "Christian" (Acts 11:19–30)

The persecution of Stephen had resulted in the scattering of many believers, some of whom came to Antioch and preached the Word to the Jews (Acts 11:19–20). The Jerusalem church heard the good news of the church at Antioch and sent Barnabas to visit the believers there (v. 22). From Antioch, Barnabas went on to Tarsus and brought Paul back to Antioch, where they both taught the people for a whole year (v. 26). It was here at Antioch that the believers were first called Christians.[3] During the famine that occurred in the reign of the Roman emperor Claudius (41–54), the Christians at Antioch took up an offering and sent it for the relief of the believers in Judea (vv. 28–30).

The Imprisonment of Peter; Death of Herod Agrippa I (A.D. 40–44) (Acts 12)

At this time (c. 40–44) Herod Agrippa I put James the brother of John to death, and imprisoned Peter (Acts 12:1–3). The believers prayed for Peter, and the Lord sent an angel who brought Peter out of prison (v. 7). Herod reigned for only a short time, dying in 44. The Antioch church now prepared to send Paul and Barnabas on the first missionary journey (Acts 13:1–3).

Antioch, the Great Apostolic Center

Antioch was not only the place where believers were first called Christians; it was also the city that became the early headquarters of Christianity and from which the church sent the apostle Paul on all three of his missionary journeys. It was the third most important city of the Roman Empire—after Rome and Alexandria. Metzger estimated the population of Antioch to have been about a half million during the first Christian century and believed that about one-seventh of them were Jews.[4] The city was located on the Orontes River in Syria, about sixteen miles from the Mediterranean. Its seaport was Seleucia.

In 1931 the Syrian government gave permission to Princeton University and the National Museum of France to excavate at Antioch for a period of six years. By means of these excavations and historical references, it has been possible to reconstruct some of the main features of the city as it appeared during the New Testament period.

As one entered the gate in the northeast wall, he would have found himself on an open roadway thirty feet wide paved with Egyptian granite. All along both sides of this four-and-a-half-mile-long thoroughfare (running from northeast to southwest) stood covered colonnades, each thirty feet wide. As a result of this construction, a pedestrian could walk the entire length of the city protected from sun and rain. Houses and public buildings could be entered between the columns of the walkway. Augustus and Tiberius, with the assistance of Herod the Great of Judea, built this street with its walks in the period from 23 B.C. to A.D. 37.

Side streets intersected the main street, and the more important were colonnad-

---

[3]Modern believers must often wonder how the term *Christian* originated and what it implied. In the Greek the term is *Christianos*. The adjective ending (*ianos*) originally applied to a slave belonging to a great household and subsequently was regularly used to denote adherents of an individual or party. So a Christian might be regarded as a slave of Christ or simply an adherent of Christ (J. Dickie, "Christian," ISBE, 1:657). Head, working from the papyri, observes that a *Kaisarianos* was an imperial slave or soldier belonging to the divine Caesar; the parallel form, *Christianos*, would signify a slave or soldier belonging to the divine Christ (Eldred D. Head, *New Testament Life and Literature as Reflected in the Papyri* [Nashville: Broadman, 1952], 50). As bondslaves we have been bought with a price (1 Cor. 6:19–20); as Christian soldiers we are to "fight the good fight of faith" (1 Tim. 6:12; cf. Eph. 6:11–17).

[4]Bruce M. Metzger, "Antioch-on-the-Orontes," BA 11 (December 1948): 81.

ed. Public fountains stood at the corners of the streets, where women and children could get the family water supply. There were numerous squares where children played, shopkeepers sold their wares, philosophers taught, and entertainers performed. In the middle of the city the main thoroughfare opened into a plaza where a striking bronze statue of Tiberius stood, erected by the grateful city for all the emperor's benefactions.

In the river to the north of the city lay an island some two miles long by two miles wide. There had stood the palaces of the Seleucids, and Roman royal residences had succeeded them. On the island was also a hippodrome with an arena over sixteen hundred feet long, built in the first century.

Along the southeast bank of the river and south of the island was located the city's original quarter as established by Seleucus Nicator in 300 b.c. Here barges discharged cargoes at stone quays. Near-by stood an agora (covering four city blocks) and a temple of Zeus.[5]

An especially interesting find, presumably unearthed at Antioch, is the famous Chalice of Antioch, now in the Metropolitan Museum of Art in New York, reportedly found in 1910 by workmen who were digging a well. The chalice is of two parts: a plain inner cup of silver, about seven and a half inches high and six inches in diameter, and an outer gilded holder with twelve figures displayed on the outside. Much has been written about the date and interpretation of this piece. The outer cup has been said to represent Christ and his disciples, and the inner cup has even been identified as the Holy Grail, used by Christ at the Last Supper. Dates as early as the first century have been assigned.[6] Perhaps the best that can be said about this chalice is that it is an early piece of Christian art of some century later than the first and that Christ or some of the disciples may be intended by the artistic representations.

[5]See Glanville Downey's *Ancient Antioch* (Princeton: Princeton University Press, 1963) and his *History of Antioch in Syria* (Princeton: Princeton University Press, 1961).

[6]For a discussion see H. Harvard Arnason, "The History of the Chalice of Antioch," BA (December 1941), 49–64, (February 1942), 10–16; Floyd V. Filson, "Who Are the Figures on the Chalice of Antioch?" BA (February 1942), 1–10.

Chapter 28

Paul's Journeys

(Acts 13–28)

Paul's First Missionary Journey
(Acts 13–14)

The church at Antioch in Syria was led by the Lord to commission Paul and Barnabas to go on the first missionary journey (Acts 13:1–3). They left Antioch and went some sixteen miles to the seaport of Seleucia (v. 4) on the Mediterranean. There they took a ship to travel across a seventy-nine-mile stretch of the Mediterranean to the island of Cyprus, where they landed at the port of Salamis (v. 5). At Salamis they preached in the synagogues (see map 10).

The harbor at Seleucia, from which Paul's first and third missionary journeys were launched

Archaeological Work at Salamis

Salamis was the great port on the eastern side of Cyprus, and it was the chief city of the island during the Roman period. Unfortunately, because of destructive earthquakes in the region, it may be impossible ever to visualize the city as it was when Paul and Barnabas preached there about A.D. 45. For instance, an earthquake destroyed the city in 76/77. Rebuilt under the emperors Trajan and Hadrian, it was again hit by a severe earthquake in 332 and another ten years later—this time accompanied by a tidal wave. Again, during the seventh century, Arab raids destroyed the city, and it was finally abandoned in favor of Famagusta, about five miles to the south.

Although digs did take place at Salamis in the nineteenth century, serious work did not begin there until the Cyprus Department of Antiquities launched annual campaigns at the site beginning in 1952. Much of what they uncovered dated either to the city's early history (eleventh to seventh centuries B.C.) or to the Byzantine period (fourth century A.D. or later). Two finds are of interest to the New Testament student, however. Not far from the harbor stood the theater of Salamis.

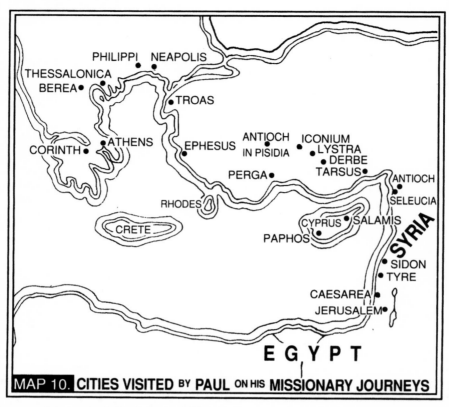

MAP 10. CITIES VISITED BY PAUL ON HIS MISSIONARY JOURNEYS

Discovered in 1959, it had an orchestra area about 87 feet in diameter and a cavea of 50 rows of seats. The structure is estimated to have seated over 15,000 people. It was built early in the first century A.D. and was therefore in use when Paul and Barnabas came through.

In the late 1960s the department worked extensively at the stone forum, located several hundred yards south of the theater. Considered to be the greatest in the Roman Empire, this town center was 750 feet long and 180 feet wide. Along the sides were 27-foot-high columns spaced 15 feet apart and topped with Corinthian capitals. Behind the colonnades stood the usual shops of a Greek agora. At the south end of the forum or agora stood the temple of Zeus, of which only the high podium remains. The cella measured about 50 feet square. Unfortunately, Turkish occupation of the site since 1974 has made it impossible for the Department of Antiquities to continue to work there.[1]

Archaeological Light and Confirmation Concerning Sergius Paulus
(Acts 13:6–12)

Paul and Barnabas, with their companion John Mark (the author of the gospel of Mark), left Salamis and traversed the island of Cyprus to the western end, coming to the city of Paphos (Acts 13:5–6). There they met the ruler of the area, the proconsul named Sergius Paulus. In

---

[1]See Vassos Karageorghis, *Salamis in Cyprus* (London: Thames & Hudson, 1969); idem, *Salamis* (Nicosia: Department of Antiquities, 1970).

1912 Ramsay found a block of stone at Antioch with this inscription on it: "To Lucius Sergius Paullus, the younger, one of the four commissioners in charge of the Roman streets. . ." (CNAD, 539). Another inscription told of a woman named Sergia Paulla. According to Ramsay, these two people probably were the son and daughter of the Sergius Paulus who was proconsul of Cyprus in the days of Paul. Ramsay even believes that the inscription about the daughter hints that she may have been a Christian, training her children in the Christian faith. (He infers this from the indication that her husband dropped out of public life, perhaps because he had become a Christian, CNAD, 540.) Concerning the spelling of Paulus, Ramsay said, "The spelling of the Latin name is always 'Paullus' but the Greeks always spelled it with one 'l,' Paolos. This rule is almost universal. Thus even in orthography Luke's accuracy is confirmed" (CNAD, 539, footnote 91).

Confirmation of Sergius Paulus's Title (Acts 13:7)

Luke indicates that the title of Sergius Paulus was that of proconsul (English, "deputy," Acts 13:7). The discoveries show that this was the correct designation of the title of the ruler of Cyprus in the time that Paul and Barnabas were there. Cyprus was originally an imperial province in the Roman State, but in 22 B.C. Augustus transferred it to the Roman Senate, and it was therefore placed under the administration of proconsuls. The archaeological confirmation of this is indicated in the Cyprian coins that have been found.[2] Before Paul and Barnabas left Paphos, Sergius Paulus believed, being astonished at the doctrine of the Lord (v. 12).

Paul and Barnabas Journey to the Mainland of Asia Minor; Ministry at Antioch (Acts 13:13–50)

When their ministry was finished on the island of Cyprus, the apostle Paul and his companions crossed the Mediterranean to the mainland of Asia Minor, coming to Perga, which was twelve miles inland from the coast. It was at this point that John Mark left Paul and Barnabas and returned to Jerusalem (Acts 13:13).

Paul and Barnabas journeyed on north to the city of Antioch in Pisidia and there ministered to the Jews in the synagogue. Paul preached, telling how Jesus Christ had come from the seed of David, had been crucified, had risen again, and was the One who justified those who believe in him (Acts 13:14–44). Opposition to Paul grew on the part of the Jews (vv. 45, 50), and so he and Barnabas turned to the Gentiles, and preached the Word to them (vv. 46–49).

Archaeological Light on the Region Between Perga and Antioch; Possible Reason for John Mark's Return to Jerusalem (Acts 13:13)

When Paul wrote to the Corinthians later and pointed out his earnestness in preaching the Gospel, he indicated that in his journeys he had been "in danger from rivers, in danger from bandits. . ." (2 Cor. 11:26). Conybeare and Howson, well-known New Testament scholars, suggest that Paul was referring to the journey between Perga and Antioch when he told of these perils, particularly from bandits. This is supported by the archaeological discoveries that have been made in the region of Pisidia, the territory in which Antioch is located. Ramsay pointed out a number of archaeological inscriptions in the Pisidian area that refer to the armed policemen and soldiers who kept the peace in this region, while other

---

[2]C.M. Kerr, "Paulus, Sergius," ISBE (1929 ed.). See also the revision of this article in the 1986 edition of ISBE by J.J. Hughes.

inscriptions "refer to a conflict with robbers, or to an escape from a drowning in a river."[3] It may have been for this reason that John Mark decided to go home when Paul and Barnabas reached Perga (Acts 13:13), for the next region they had to traverse in order to come to Antioch in Pisidia was this very region that was shown by the archaeological inscriptions to require armed soldiers to keep the peace. Perhaps the prospect of an encounter with brigands helped John Mark to decide to return home at this juncture. It may, of course, have been for other reasons as well.

Excavations at Antioch of Pisidia

As the 1924 University of Michigan excavations have shown,[4] life at Antioch in Paul's day centered around two paved squares, the Square of Tiberius and the Square of Augustus. The former lay at a lower level, and scattered around on its three thousand square feet of paving stones were many incised circles and rectangles on which residents in their idle hours could play all kinds of games. From the lower square, twelve steps about seventy feet long led into the Square of Augustus through a magnificent triple-arched gateway. The façade of this propylaea was faced with two pairs of Corinthian columns that flanked two enormous reliefs of Pisidian captives (representing Augustus's victories on land) and had a frieze with tritons, Neptune, dolphins, and other marine symbols (commemorating Augustus's victories on the sea, especially at Actium).

At the east end of the Square of Augustus a semicircle was cut out of the native rock, before which rose a two-story colonnade with Doric columns below and Ionic above. In front of the center of the semicircle stood a Roman temple, the base of which was cut out of native rock and the superstructure built of white marble. It had a portico of four Corinthian columns across the front. The frieze of this temple, apparently dedicated to the god Men and to Augustus, consisted of beautifully executed bulls' heads (the symbol of Men) bound together with garlands of all sorts of leaves and fruits. What the rest of the city was like the excavators were not able to determine.

Paul's Ministry in Iconium; the Flight to Lystra and Derbe (Acts 14)

After Paul and Barnabas turned from the Jews to preach to the Gentiles at Antioch, the Jews stirred up many of the chief people of the city of Antioch, and Paul and Barnabas were expelled from the region (Acts 13:46, 50). They went on to the town of Iconium, which was east of Antioch. There they spoke in the synagogue, and again the Jews stirred up opposition to the point that Paul and Barnabas were about to be stoned. They fled to the towns of Lystra and Derbe, farther to the southeast (Acts 14:1–6; see map 10).

Archaeological Confirmation Concerning Luke's Indication of the Relationship of Iconium, Lystra, and Derbe (Acts 14:6)

When Luke, the author of the book of Acts, describes Paul's departure from Iconium, he says, "They . . . fled unto Lystra and Derbe, cities of Lycaonia" (Acts 14:6). This implies that Lystra and Derbe were in the territory of Lycaonia and Iconium was not (see maps 10 and 11). Roman writers such as Cicero, however, indicated that Iconium was in Lycaonia, and on the basis of such evidence, many

---

[3]W.M. Calder, "Pisidia," ISBE (1929 ed.), 4: 2401.

[4]David M. Robinson, "A Preliminary Report on the Excavations at Pisidian Antioch and at Sizma," AJA 28 (October 1924): 435–44; William M. Ramsay, *The Bearing of Recent Discovery on the Trustworthiness of the New Testament* (Grand Rapids: Baker, reprint 1979), chapter 4 [RBRD].

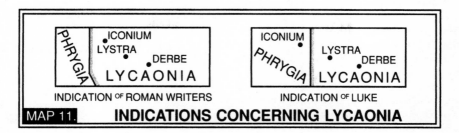

MAP 11.   INDICATIONS CONCERNING LYCAONIA

critical scholars have held that the book of Acts was not written by Luke but was an untrustworthy work written much later.

A monument found in 1910 in Asia Minor by Sir William Ramsay showed, however, that Iconium was considered to be not a Lycaonian, but rather a Phrygian city. Further discoveries demonstrated that the Iconians had distinguished themselves as being citizens of a Phrygian city. Luke's accuracy was definitely confirmed.

The Conclusion of Paul's First Missionary Journey (Acts 14); Archaeological Light on Zeus and Hermes

Paul and Barnabas preached the gospel at Lystra and healed a lame man (Acts 14:7–10). This miracle caused the people of Lystra to consider the apostles to be gods, and they called Barnabas, Jupiter, and Paul, Mercury (vv. 11–12). Jupiter and Mercury were the Roman equivalent for the Greek gods Zeus and Hermes.

Archaeological light on the worship of Zeus and Hermes in the region of Lystra was found on two inscriptions discovered in the neighborhood of Lystra in 1909. One of these monuments was erected to "priests of Zeus," and another one tells of two men who, "having made in accordance with a vow at their own expense [a statue of] Hermes Most Great along with a

sun-dial dedicated it to Zeus the sun-god" (RBR, 48–49).

When the people of Lystra, thinking that Paul and Barnabas were gods, prepared to make sacrifices to them, Paul talked to them, urging them to turn from these vanities to the living God (Acts 14:13, 15). Their ministry in Lystra was interrupted by Jews from Iconium and Antioch who caused Paul to be stoned and left for dead; Paul got up, however, and they retraced their steps through Lystra, Iconium, and Antioch in Pisidia, encouraging the believers in these regions (vv. 22–23). Continuing their return journey, they came back to the home base at Antioch in Syria, where they gave their "missionary report," relating the things that God had done with them, and "how he had opened the door of faith to the Gentiles" (v. 27).

The Jerusalem Council (Acts 15)

While Paul and Barnabas were in Antioch in Syria, after returning from their first missionary journey, certain men from Judea came to Antioch, teaching that believers must be circumcised according to the law of Moses before they could be saved (Acts 15:1). This was nothing but legalism; it put the believer under law rather than grace. Paul and Barnabas disputed with these legalists; they determined to go to Jerusalem and ask the elders there about the question. In the council held at Jerusalem, Peter pointed out that we are saved through the grace of the Lord Jesus Christ (v. 11). Then James declared as the official position of the council that the Gentiles should not be put under any obligation to the law as a means of salvation, but that it would be well for the Gentiles to abstain from meat sacrificed to idols so that this would not be a stumbling block to the Jewish Christians (vv. 19–29).

Paul's Second Missionary Journey (Acts 15:36–18:22); the Call to Macedonia

Some time after the Jerusalem Council, Paul proposed to Barnabas that they make a journey to visit the believers in the cities where they had preached on the first missionary journey (Acts 15:36). Barnabas wanted to take John Mark with them, but Paul remembered how John Mark had left them in the middle of the first journey and decided not to take him. When Paul and Barnabas separated over the issue, Barnabas took John Mark with him, and they went to Cyprus (v. 39); but Paul chose Silas, and they went overland to the north and west again, visiting Derbe and Lystra, the home of Timothy (Acts 16:1ff.).

Paul and Silas, continuing across Asia Minor, traveled to the northwest and finally reached Troas. There Paul had a vision, in which a man appeared to him and said, "Come over to Macedonia and help us" (Acts 16:9). In response to the vision, Paul and Silas sailed from Troas and came to Neapolis in Macedonia and then went on to the city of Philippi. At this point in the book of Acts, the first person plural pronoun "we," is used, indicating that Luke[5] had joined the party on the journey from Troas to Neapolis and Philippi (vv. 10–12).

Archaeological Confirmation Concerning Luke's Reference to a "District" of Macedonia (Acts 16:12)

When Paul and his companions came to Philippi, Luke refers to it as being in "that district" of Macedonia. He uses the Greek word *meris* for the word translated "district." F.J.A. Hort, a well-known New Testament scholar, believed that Luke was wrong in this usage, and asserted, "*Meris* never denotes simply a region, province, or any geographical division: when used of land, as of anything else, it means a portion or share." Since a writer would not be expected to use the expression "that share of Macedonia" when he meant "that district of Macedonia," Hort suggested that there had been a primitive error in the text and a conjectural emendation.[6]

Archaeological excavations in the Fayum in Egypt, however, have shown that the colonists there, many of whom came from Macedonia where Philippi was located, used this very word *meris* to describe the divisions of the district. Thus these documents show that Luke knew more about the geographical terminology of Macedonia than one of the greatest experts on the Greek language in recent times. All scholars now agree that this word *meris* was used by Luke in a legitimate sense that is particularly associated with Macedonia (CNAD, 546). Thus archaeology corrected Hort and again showed the accuracy of Luke.

Archaeological Confirmation of Luke's Reference to the Rulers of Philippi as "Magistrates" (Praetors) (Acts 16:20)

While Paul was in Philippi, he and his companions led Lydia, a seller of purple, to a knowledge of the Lord Jesus (Acts

---

[5]That Luke was the author of Acts is indicated by, among other evidences, the similar beginning of the gospel of Luke and the book of Acts and the similar Greek style of the two books.

[6]In other words, according to Hort, a scribe found an obvious error in the text, conjectured what he thought it said originally, and changed (emended) the text to read *meris*, which, according to Hort, was incorrect also. See Westcott and Hort, *Greek Testament*, vol. 2, Appendix, 96.

The Agora at Philippi, where the mob scene of Acts 16 took place

16:14–15). Some time later, Paul cast a demon out of a girl who was possessed (vv. 16–18). This angered the masters of the girl, who had used her for soothsaying, and they had Paul and Silas brought before the magistrates, who had them beaten and committed to prison (vv. 20–24).

Luke, the author of Acts, refers to the rulers of Philippi as "magistrates" (*praetors*). This term was not technically correct for the officials of Philippi, inasmuch as the town normally would have been governed by two *duumvirs*.[7] The archaeological inscriptions have shown, however, that the title of *praetor* was used as a "courtesy title" for the supreme magistrates of a Roman colony. As usual, Luke moved on a plane of educated conversation rather than on the plane of technicality.[8]

While Paul and Silas were in prison at Philippi, an earthquake shook the foundations of the building, and the doors were opened. This gave Paul and Silas an opportunity to lead the jailor to a knowledge of Christ (Acts 16:25–34). The next day, the magistrates sent an order to have the two men freed, and when they learned that they were Roman citizens, they were all the more eager to have them leave (vv. 38–39).

Archaeological Work at Philippi

The French School at Athens worked at Philippi from 1914 to 1938, and the Greek Archaeological Service has been active there since World War II. As usual, attention has focused on a limited number of major structures in the middle of town. The agora, center of Greek life, where the mob scene and judgment of Acts 16 took place, is a large rectangular area 300 feet long and 150 feet wide. On its northern side stood a rectangular podium with steps leading up to it on either side. This apparently was the place where magistrates dispensed justice. Although the agora was largely rebuilt during the reign of Marcus Aurelius in the second century

[7]Roman officials in towns of the empire who paralleled the two consuls in Rome.

[8]Hogarth, *Authority and Archaeology*, 351–52; also Ramsay, *St. Paul the Traveller* (Grand Rapids: Baker, reprinted 1979), 218; CNAD, 546–47.

A.D., the general plan presumably is essentially the same as it was in Paul's day. Along its north side ran the Egnatian Way, the Roman highway across northern Greece. The acropolis of Philippi, over one thousand feet high, towers above the town. On its eastern slope are the well-preserved remains of a Greek theater, which in its original form dates back to the fourth century B.C. when Philip of Macedon founded the town; but it was radically altered in the Roman period.

The early success of the Gospel at Philippi is evident from the fact that imposing ruins of great churches may be seen. At the south side of the agora stand the remains of a sixth-century church known as Basilica B. Just north of the agora, across the modern highway, lie the ruins of a large fifth-century church known as Basilica A. East of the agora in an area of recent excavation may be seen the remains of another fifth-century church flanked by a third-century bath (FLAP, 350–51).

In the past few years excavations have gone forward at the east end of the agora and at the city's east wall and gate. Archaeological work is slow, and as is true with most other sites in Bible lands, excavation at Philippi has uncovered only a fraction of the ancient town.

Archaeological Light and Confirmation Concerning Thessalonica

After they left Philippi, Paul and Silas went on to the city of Thessalonica (Acts 17:1). Archaeological light and confirmation have been discovered concerning several items connected with Thessalonica. Two examples follow. First, Luke's use of the word "politarch" for the rulers of Thessalonica was once thought to be an inaccuracy, but the discovery of seventeen inscriptions at Salonika (modern name of Thessalonica) containing this term shows the accuracy of this usage.

Second, the use of the word meaning "turn upside down" (*anastatoō*) in connection with the accusation made by the adversaries at Thessalonica is illuminated by an ancient letter found in Egypt, written by a spoiled child to his father, who had gone up to Alexandria.[9] In this letter, this child described how his mother had been terribly disturbed; he writes, "And she said, 'He quite upsets me. Off with him!' " The same word appears here for "upset" (*anastatoō*) as is used in the accusation against Jason and the others who were said to have "turned the world upside down." A study of this picturesque word shows that just as a spoiled child upset his mother and drove her to distraction, so Jason, Paul, and the others were upsetting the complacency of the unsaved in Thessalonica, and are described as "turning the world upside down."

Archaeological Research at Athens

From Thessalonica, Paul journeyed to Athens (Acts 17:15). A knowledge of the archaeological remains of Athens enables us to fill in the colorful background of his visit to this city.

When Paul arrived in Athens, he probably headed straight for the agora. There, at the hub of public life, he could learn best where he might lodge and how to arrange his affairs. In fact, he reasoned there "daily" about the Christian faith with individuals he was able to engage in conversation (Acts 17:17). The agora was excavated by the American School of Classical Studies from 1931 to 1940 under the leadership of T. Leslie Shear and from 1946 to 1960 by Homer A. Thompson. In 1969 new excavations began at the north end of the agora, and they continue to the present time.

Now one can visualize the Athenian agora as Paul knew it. Along the east side stood the great stoa of Attalos, built by

---

[9]J.H. Moulton, *From Egyptian Rubbish Heaps* (London: Charles H. Kelly, 1916), 37–39.

Attalos II, king of Pergamum, in the second century B.C., and rebuilt by the excavators as the agora museum. Some 385 feet long and 64 feet wide, it was faced with a two-story colonnade of forty-five columns on each level—Doric on the first story and Ionic on the second. Behind the colonnade were twenty-one shops on each level. Directly opposite the stoa in the middle of the agora stood the odeion, or music hall, of Agrippa, built about 15 B.C. and seating one thousand people. Extending across the agora from the south end of the stoa of Attalos sprawled the middle stoa (450 feet long), which was connected to the south stoa by a small east stoa. At the west end of the south stoa was the *heliaia,* or law court, adjacent to which was the southwest fountain.

The west side of the agora was the political side. At the south was the round *tholos,* the office of the *prytany,* a committee of the city council. The official set of standard weights and measures was kept there. North of that was the public record office, behind which rose the home of the Council of Five Hundred. North of this complex was the temple of Apollo and the stoa of Zeus, a favorite haunt of Socrates. On the hill behind the temple of Apollo stood the temple of Hephaestus (god of the forge), one of the best preserved of all Greek temples (104 feet long by 45 feet wide). Across the north of the agora extended the "Painted Stoa," a kind of historical picture gallery with scenes of Athenian struggle with the Persians at Marathon, among others. Here philosophers held forth, one of the better known of which was Zeno, founder of the Stoic school.

A few hundred feet east of the Greek agora lay the Roman market. Made necessary by the expansion of Athenian commercial affairs, it particularly housed wine and oil shops. This center was built by Julius Caesar and Augustus Caesar. The structure consists of an interior courtyard 269 by 187 feet and paved with marble, surrounded by an Ionic colonnade, through which entrance was gained to the shops. At the east end of the market stands the Tower of the Winds, a hydraulic clock arranged with sundials. This is an octagonal tower in white marble measuring 26 feet in diameter and about forty feet in height. Excavation of this market was undertaken by the Greek Archaeological Society in 1890 and carried on intermittently until 1931; much is yet to be done there.

At the south end of the Greek agora stands the Areopagus or Mars Hill, where Paul probably spoke to many of the intelligentsia of Athens. This 377-foot hill stood just west of the Acropolis. And as he delivered his Mars Hill speech, Paul must have gestured toward the Acropolis when he spoke of "temples built by hands" (Acts 17:24).

Undoubtedly Paul visited the Acropolis. A visitor to Athens could hardly have avoided it. Besides, Acts 17:23a may be translated, "For as I went about and examined objects of your religious devotion, . . ." indicating that the apostle went sight-seeing in the city. The magnificent *propylaea* with its adjacent Nike temple and statue of Athena, the Erechtheum, and the Parthenon must have inspired Paul's admiration. The Parthenon was, of course, still in perfect condition. Built of white Pentelic marble, it measured 238 feet in length and 111 feet in width. Its encircling row of forty-six fluted Doric columns stood at a height of 34 feet. Encircling the structure above the colonnade was the Doric frieze with 92 panels depicting legendary and mythological scenes dear to the hearts of Greeks. Inside the colonnade the Ionic frieze encircled the temple below the roof. This continuous frieze, 524 feet in length, consisted of six hundred figures and portrayed the annual Panathenaic procession up to the Parthenon to honor Athena. The pediment on the east end of the temple depicted the birth of Athena, and the one on the west portrayed the struggle between Athena and Poseidon for control of Attica. Inside was the great gold-and-ivory statue of Athena. To the north of the Parthenon stood the Erechtheum, temple of Athena and Poseidon-Erechtheus with its beautiful porch of the maidens (caryatids).

On the southeast slope of the Acropolis lay the great theater of Dionysus, where the leading dramatists of ancient Greece aired their productions. The theater seated about 17,000 people. Just east of it stood the Odeion of Pericles, probably used for musical events.

From 1884 to 1891, Greek archaeologists examined the whole Acropolis area down to bedrock. The Greek Archaeological Society also excavated the remains of Pericles' odeion in the 1920s. Several German scholars studied the theater of Dionysus. The American School of Classical Studies excavated the north slope of the Acropolis from 1931 to 1939 under the direction of Oscar Broneer.

Some distance to the southeast of the Acropolis stood the great temple of Zeus. It was excavated by the Greek Archaeological Society from 1886 to 1901 and by the German School from 1922 to 1923. Begun in the latter part of the sixth century B.C., it was still open to the sky in Paul's day and was not completed until the second century A.D. The structure had 104 Corinthian columns of Pentelic marble 56 feet high. These were arranged in two rows on the sides and three rows at the ends and rested on a foundation 354 feet long and 135 feet broad. The height was over 90 feet to the top of the pediments.[10]

Paul at Corinth; Archaeological Light

From Athens Paul journeyed to Corinth, the great commercial center of Greece in New Testament times. The city gained significance from its location on the Isthmus of Corinth, across which goods flowed in quantity, not having to follow the longer and more dangerous route around the southern tip of Greece. The economic opportunities there and the biennial Isthmian Games held nearby brought throngs of businessmen, athletes, and sports enthusiasts to whom Paul could minister; and he stayed at Corinth for eighteen months (Acts 18:11), being second only to Ephesus in length of evangelistic effort. As a result of the work of the American School of Classical Studies, conducted at Corinth since 1896, except for war years, we now know something of what the city was like when Paul ministered there.

At the center of the city stood the agora—the agora being the hub of activity in any Greek city. It measured about 600 feet in length (east-west) and 300 feet in width (north-south). Following the natural configuration of the land, the southern section stood about six feet higher than the northern part of the agora. At the dividing line of the two levels stood the bema or podium where public officials could address crowds and render judgment. No doubt Paul stood before Gallio here (Acts 18:12–13). The bema was flanked by a row of central shops. A south stoa extended some 500 feet along that side of the agora. Among other things, it housed the city council and office of the supervisors of the Isthmian Games.

The road from the port of Lechaion entered the agora on the north. On the west side of the road at the entrance to the agora stood a basilica, which along with basilicas on the south and east of the agora provided court facilities where the litigious Corinthian Christians could have been involved in court cases (1 Cor.

---

[10]For a detailed discussion of the agora, see John M. Camp, *The Athenian Agora* (London: Thames & Hudson, 1986). For further information on the agora and other excavations in Athens, see Paul MacKendrick, *The Greek Stones Speak*, 2nd ed. (New York: Norton, 1981), 429–40; FLAP, 352–58.

Reconstructed Stoa of Attalos in the Athenia agora

The bema or judgment seat at Corinth, where Paul stood before Gallio

The inscription of Erastus in the theater at Corinth, thought to be the Erastus Paul knew (Rom. 16:23)

6). On the east side of the road near the agora entrance a stone was found bearing the inscription "Synagogue of the Hebrews," thought by some to be the lintel of the synagogue in which Paul may have preached (Acts 18:4). A little farther away along the Lechaion Road stood shops of the meat and wine merchants, in one of which was found an inscription indicating it was a *makellon*, the word used in 1 Corinthians 10:25. This must be the very meat market where, Paul said, believers could shop with a clear conscience, not worrying whether the meat sold there had at one point been offered to idols.

On a rocky terrace adjacent to the northwest corner of the agora stood the temple of Apollo, dating to the sixth century B.C. It measured 176 feet long by 69 feet wide, and the 38 columns of the peristyle rose almost 24 feet in height. These fluted Doric columns were more impressive than many in Greece because they were made of single blocks instead of being built up with drums of stone. In the side of the hill northwest of the temple was the 14,000-seat theater of Corinth. In the pavement near the stage area one can still see an inscription saying that the *aedile* Erastus laid the pavement at his own expense. Scholars commonly believe that this is the same Erastus, one of Paul's converts, to whom the apostle referred in Romans 16:23, when he wrote the epistle to the Romans from Corinth.

Some five miles east of ancient Corinth on the Saronic Gulf the American School of Classical Studies has been excavating the site of the Isthmian Games. There, near the end of the modern Corinth Canal, one can see remains of the temple of Poseidon, a theater, and part of the stadium. The stadium of Paul's day lay some 800 feet away in a natural depression. The Isthmian Games were held every two years and probably drew larger crowds than the Olympic Games. The Isthmian Games provided the backdrop for Paul's comments about the race in 1 Corinthians 9:24–27.[11]

Archaeological Light on the Date of Paul's Sojourn at Corinth—A.D. 50 (Acts 18:12)

While Paul was at Corinth, the Jews had him brought before the ruler of the city, Gallio the proconsul (Acts 18:12). Archaeological discovery has given us a definitely fixed point for Paul's sojourn in Corinth, for an inscription found at Delphi shows that Gallio was proconsul of Achaia in 52. (BWMS, 86). The account of Paul's trial before Gallio suggests that Gallio had recently come to office.[12] Since Paul had already been there eighteen months (v. 11), it is likely that he came to Corinth about A.D. 50.[13]

1 and 2 Thessalonians Written from Corinth, A.D. 50–51 (Acts 18:12)

Paul wrote 1 and 2 Thessalonians from Corinth, as internal evidence in these epistles shows (TINT, 193, 198). It is likely that these letters were written within a few months of each other, probably during the years 50–51.

The Conclusion of the Second Missionary Journey (Acts 18:18–22)

After Paul left Corinth in 51–52, he stopped at Ephesus and then continued on to Palestine, landing at Caesarea (Acts

---

[11]For documentation, see Jerome Murphy-O'Connor, "The Corinth That Saint Paul Saw," BA (September 1984), 147–59; idem, *Corinth* (Wilmington, Del.: Michael Glazier, 1983); FLAP, 358–63; Jack Finegan, *The Archaeology of the New Testament* (Boulder: Westview, 1981), 142–52 [FANT].

[12]The biblical context seems to indicate that the coming of Gallio induced the Jews to bring Paul to trial. If this is so, it means that Paul's trial before Gallio occurred early in the latter's proconsulship (TINT, 194).

[13]BAB, 560–61; BWMS, 86; CNAD, 502; TINT, 194; Deissmann, *St. Paul*, 246–47, 280–81.

18:22). He concluded the second missionary journey at the home base of Antioch in Syria.

Paul's Third Missionary Journey (Acts 18:23–21:16); Archaeological Light on His Stay at Ephesus

Paul's third missionary journey began at Antioch in Syria (Acts 18:22–23). From there he went north and then west, through the territory of Galatia and Phrygia (v. 23), where Iconium and Antioch of Pisidia were located, and then on to the city of Ephesus (Acts 19:1ff.) in the western part of Asia Minor (see map 10, page 268).

Ephesus was a great city when Paul arrived. With a population in the hundreds of thousands, it probably ranked fourth in size in the Empire behind Rome, Alexandria, and Antioch of Syria. The importance of the city at that time was threefold: political, economic, and religious. It had become the de facto capital of the province of Asia, and the Roman governor resided there. Its economic prowess lay in the fact that it stood astride the great route to the interior of Asia Minor and the north-south road through western Asia Minor. Religiously, Ephesus was a leading center for the worship of Diana, or Artemis. Ephesus was therefore a very strategic center for evangelization. From this one spot not only the whole province of Asia but also many other parts of the Roman Empire could be reached with the Gospel.

The archaeological history of Ephesus began on May 2, 1863, when the British architect John T. Wood started his search for the temple of Diana, one of the seven wonders of the ancient world. He did not discover the ruins of the temple until December 31, 1869, and then worked five more years at the temple site. The temple platform was 239 feet wide and 418 feet long. On that stood the temple itself, which measured 180 feet wide and 377 feet long, its roof supported by 117 sixty-

foot columns. These columns were six feet in diameter, and 36 of them were sculptured at the base with life-sized figures.

The Austrian Archaeological Institute began to excavate in the ancient city of Ephesus in November 1897 and excavated there continuously for sixteen years. Members of the institute resumed work there between the world wars (1926–35) and have continued annually since 1954. To date they have uncovered only about 25 percent of the ancient city. In recent years they also have done some work on the temple of Diana.

The excavation of Ephesus is one of the most impressive of all archaeological projects in Mediterranean lands. If one walks through the Magnesian Gate into the city of Ephesus in a westerly direction, on his right are the east baths (from the second century A.D.). A short distance farther on the right stands an odeion, or covered concert hall (A.D. 150), which increasingly is being interpreted as the meeting place of the town council (capacity about 1400). Next to it is the town hall, built about the time of Christ's birth. Facing these two civic structures on the left is a long basilica (built about the beginning of the first century A.D.), which served as a court building. This was the northernmost structure of the Roman state agora.

When one reaches the end of the basilica, he enters the open roadway of Curetes Street (which runs northwest). This is lined on both sides with inscribed statue bases and excavated structures. Immediately on the left is a plaza, at the back of which stands a temple of Domitian, built during his reign near the end of the first century, when John was living there. On the right is the Memmius monument (erected at the end of the first century B.C.) in honor of a grandson of the dictator Sulla.

Here at the beginning of Curetes Street is a gateway formed by two pillars adorned with reliefs of Hermes or Mer-

The great theater at Ephesus, where the mob scene of Acts 19 took place

cury. As one descends the street, he will soon see on the right a fountain of Trajan and then the temple of Hadrian (both of the early second century). Behind the temple of Hadrian stand the baths of Scholastica (built c. A.D. 100 or earlier). Across the street from the temple of Hadrian on a hillside rise villas of the first century A.D., now partially restored.

Passing other minor structures, one comes to the junction of Curetes and Marble streets. On the left in a little plaza is the early second-century A.D. library of Celsus (now restored). On the right of this plaza is a monumental gate that leads into the Hellenistic commercial agora. The gate, too, has been completely restored. An inscription above the gate dates to the reign of Augustus Caesar; thus the gate was there while Paul lived in the city.

We now walk down Marble Street. Behind the wall on the left of Marble Street (which goes north) spreads the great Hellenistic commercial agora 360 feet square and surrounded with shops,

including some where silversmiths marketed their wares. On the right of the street rises Mount Pion and the great Hellenistic theater where the mob scene of Acts 19 took place. Measuring some 495 feet in diameter, the theater held about 25,000 people. The cavea of the theater was divided into three bands of twenty-two rows of seats each, and twelve stairways divided the cavea into huge wedge-shaped sections. Much restoration work has been done on the theater and its stage area.

From the theater, the Arcadian Way, 1,735 feet long, led westward to the harbor. This marble-paved street, 36 feet in width, was lined on both sides by a colonnade behind which were shops. At both ends of the street were monumental gateways. While this street, in the form the excavators found it, dates from about A.D. 400, there was a magnificent street on the site during the first century. As one walks from the theater to the harbor, one passes a late-first-century gymnasium and bath. If one returns to the theater and walks on an extension of Marble Street, he will pass, on the right, the city stadium built during the reign of Nero while Paul was there.

Ephesus is sacred to the memory of the apostle John, as well as to Paul. On the hill of Ayasoluk, overlooking the temple of Diana, the apostle John lived and was buried according to Christian tradition of the second century. At first marked by a memorial, the grave was enclosed by a church in the fourth century. The emperor Justinian (527–565) took down the old church and erected a domed basilica over the tomb. Restorations at the site of the church have been going on in recent years (for documentation on Ephesus see FLAP, 345–49; FANT, 155–71).

Paul remained in Ephesus for over two years (Acts 19:10) and during that time wrote the first epistle to the Corinthians, probably in the spring of 54 or 55 (TINT, 205). When Paul left Ephesus, he went into Macedonia (Acts 20:1), and there evidently wrote the second epistle to the Corinthians, probably some seven or eight months after writing 1 Corinthians. The second epistle would have been written late in 54 or 55 (TINT, 209).

From Macedonia, Paul went on to Greece, where he spent three months (Acts 20:2–3). While he was there, he wrote Galatians (TINT, 217), seeking to set right the Galatian people who had come under the influence of Judaizers. During that same sojourn in Greece, Paul was in Corinth for a time, where he wrote the epistle to the Romans, probably in 56 (TINT, 226).

Paul left Greece, returning through Macedonia to Philippi (Acts 20:6), and went on to Troas. From there Paul and his company sailed down the coast of Asia Minor, passing near Ephesus (v. 17), where Paul gave an account of his ministry to the Ephesian elders, pointing out that he had never hesitated to declare "all

the counsel of God" (v. 27). Paul's return journey took him on across the Mediterranean, past the island of Rhodes and the island of Cyprus, to Tyre (Acts 21:7), and then to Caesarea, from where Paul and his companions went to Jerusalem (vv. 8, 15).

Paul Imprisoned at Caesarea; His Voyage to Rome (Acts 21–28)

While Paul was in Jerusalem, after his return from the third missionary journey, some of the Jews in Jerusalem thought they saw him bring Gentiles into the court of the temple (Acts 21:20–29). They stirred up a riot in order to kill Paul, but order was restored by the Roman guard (vv. 31ff.). Paul gave his defense before the assembled mob (22:1–21) and later before the Jewish council of the Sanhedrin (23:1–6). Some of the Jews conspired to kill Paul (vv. 12ff.), but when the Roman authorities at Jerusalem learned of the plot, they sent him to Caesarea (for a discussion of excavations at Caesarea, see chapter 25), where he was imprisoned for more than two years (24:27). Paul appealed his case to Caesar (i.e., the Roman emperor, who was Nero at that time, 25:11) and was sent by ship from Palestine to Italy (Acts 27:1–28:16).

Paul was in Rome for two years (Acts 28:30). He probably arrived in 59 and was released in 61 (TINT, 185). The book of Acts must have been written in about 61, for it closes with the record of Paul's detention at Rome for these two years.

During the two-year stay at Rome, Paul wrote the Prison Epistles: Ephesians, Philippians, Colossians, and Philemon. They were probably written in the following order: Colossians, Philemon, Ephesians, and Philippians (TINT, 228), during the years 60–61 (TINT, 233, 251). Paul's second imprisonment is treated in chapter 29.

Chapter 29

The Development
of the Early Church

(Paul's Later Life: Pastoral Epistles; General Epistles;
Book of Revelation; Development of the Church)

Paul's Release from Prison (A.D. 61) and Further Travels

Paul's first imprisonment lasted two years, probably from 59 to 61, during which time he wrote the Prison Epistles. The book of Acts ends with a description of this imprisonment and the statement that Paul was detained in Rome for two years (28:30). However, we can trace Paul's travels after his release from this first imprisonment in 61 from early church sources and certain of his expressed purposes, including his plan to see the Philippians (Phil. 2:23–24) at Philippi in Macedonia and to visit Philemon at the town of Colosse in Asia Minor (Philemon 22).

Leaving Rome in 61, Paul probably took the main highway across Italy to Brundisium (modern Brindisi) on the Adriatic Sea, then crossed the Adriatic to Apollonia or to Dyrrhachium, where he took the main highway across Greece (the Egnatian Way) to Philippi in Macedonia. Prob-

ably he did not stay long in Philippi, but hurried on to Ephesus and visited Colosse and other cities of Asia Minor in this vicinity (TINT, 261). These travels probably took most of the year (61–62), after which Paul may have made a voyage to Spain. The probability of a voyage to Spain is indicated by Paul's purpose to visit that country, expressed when he wrote to the Romans in about 56 (Rom. 15:24). Also, the early church writer Clement of Rome seems to imply that Paul went to Spain (Clement *ad Cor.* 5), and the fact of such a journey is stated in the Canon of Muratori.[1] It is thought that Paul may have remained in Spain for two years, probably 62–64 (TINT, 261–63). Robertson thought that Paul may have been in Spain when Rome was burned on July 19, 64.[2]

Paul's First Epistle to Timothy and His Epistle to Titus (64–65)

Some time after Paul left Spain, he wrote the first epistle to Timothy, about

---

[1]The Canon of Muratori is a fragment of a document, so named because it was discovered by an Italian named Muratori in the Ambrosian Library at Milan in 1740. It dates from A.D. 170 or a little later (TINT, 22).

[2]A.T. Robertson, "Paul the Apostle," ISBE (1929 ed.), 4:2286.

64 or 65 (TINT, 263). Timothy was carrying on ministerial duties in the church at Ephesus, acting as Paul's temporary representative in his apostolic capacity (TINT, 262). Paul wrote to encourage Timothy to oppose false teachers and not give heed to myths (1 Tim. 1:4). He also wrote to instruct him in the qualifications of church officers (1 Tim. 3) and to exhort him to faithfully discharge his pastoral duties (1 Tim. 4:6ff.).

A short time later, probably during the year 65 (TINT, 266), Paul wrote the epistle to Titus. Titus was Paul's representative on the island of Crete, not actually being the "bishop of Crete," as Eusebius calls him (TINT, 265). The subject matter of Paul's words to Titus ranges in content from urging him to complete the organization of the work at Crete (Titus 1:5) to warning him against false teachings and teachers (3:9–10).

Defense of the Pauline Authorship of the Pastoral Epistles (1 and 2 Timothy and Titus)

Critics have said that the Pastoral Epistles (1 and 2 Timothy and Titus) could not have been written by Paul because they differed in style and language from the other Pauline epistles. Cobern suggests that the difference may be due to the fact that ancient writers used scribes, and a different scribe would produce a different style (CNAD, 102). It is not necessary, however, to posit the idea of various scribes producing varying style and vocabulary in the Pastoral Epistles, because a comparison shows that these epistles did not have a vocabulary that differed greatly from the other epistles Paul wrote. An actual count shows that 1 Timothy has 82 new words not found elsewhere in the New Testament; 2 Timothy has 53 such words; and Titus 33—a total of 168. On the other hand, the epistles from Romans through Philemon contain 687 such words.[3]

Why is there some difference in vocabulary between the Pastoral Epistles and the other letters of Paul? The answer lies in the fact that different subjects require different words. When Paul wrote the Pastoral Epistles, he would obviously use different words in dealing with ministerial duties and responsibilities from those he would use when he wrote concerning justification by faith or when he dealt with the errors of Gnosticism.[4]

1 and 2 Peter (A.D. 65–67)

In about 65 Peter wrote his first epistle to the believers in Pontus, Galatia, Cappadocia, Asia, and Bithynia—all provinces of Asia Minor. It is possible that Peter had visited these regions of Asia Minor, or converts of Paul may have evangelized the area (TINT, 283–84). Peter wrote to comfort these Gentile believers in their trials (1 Peter 1:7) and to remind them that they had been redeemed, not with silver and gold, but with the "precious blood of Christ" (1 Peter 1:19).

The second epistle of Peter was written in about 66 or 67 (TINT, 291). He urges believers to go on in the faith, adding to their faith the godly virtues that should characterize believers, including brother-

---

[3]John Rutherford, "The Pastoral Epistles," ISBE (1929 ed.), 4:2261.

[4]A detailed discussion of the supposed problems of authorship of the Pastoral Epistles appears in Everett F. Harrison, *Introduction to the New Testament*, rev. ed. (Grand Rapids: Eerdmans, 1971), 351–63, with the conclusion that they came from Paul's pen. Harrison also mentions the testimony to Paul's authorship in the early church. Donald Guthrie in his *New Testament Introduction*, 3rd ed. (Downers Grove: InterVarsity, 1970), 584–622, provides an even more exhaustive discussion of the authorship of the Pastorals and likewise tends to support the traditional view of Pauline authorship. Certainly the idea that the Pastorals were composed in the second century is totally unacceptable, because, as noted earlier (chapter 26), the argument from historical grammar, developed from the contribution of the papyri, requires that all the New Testament books were written during the first century (BWMS, 53–54).

ly kindness (2 Peter 1:7). Peter also warns against false teachers who bring in heresies, even denying the atonement of Christ (2:1) and his return in glory (3:4).

Answer to the Critical Opinion Concerning 2 Peter

Critics have held that Peter did not write 2 Peter because of differences in style and vocabulary between the two epistles. A possible answer to this supposed difficulty is supplied by the internal evidence of 1 Peter, which shows that Peter used Silvanus as a scribe or amanuensis to write the epistle (1 Peter 5:12). This means that Silvanus could have suggested and made stylistic improvements in Peter's dictation (TINT, 285–86). If Peter used another amanuensis or wrote with his own hand when he composed the second epistle, this would explain the differences between the two letters. We should not be surprised that the Greek of 2 Peter "jars on us" (CNAD, 115), since Peter and John are referred to in the New Testament as "unschooled" (Acts 4:13). There are some differences between the vocabularies of 1 and 2 Peter, but the work of Dods and Zahn show that there are also some very remarkable similarities.[5] The likelihood of 2 Peter's being a forgery is well answered by H.C. Thiessen's question, "Would a forger risk detection by neglecting closer attention to the style and language of I Peter?" (TINT, 288).

Hebrews (A.D. 67–69)

Whether Paul wrote the epistle to the Hebrews cannot be proved or disproved conclusively (TINT, 300–301), but there is some indication of the time of its composition. The internal evidence of the book makes it clear that the temple had not yet been destroyed (this occurred in A.D. 70), being shown by the references to priests offering gifts (8:4), to the offering of sacrifices from year to year (10:1), and to other activities of the temple referred to in the present tense. The people addressed had evidently been Christians for a long time. Putting all these factors together, it seems likely that the book of Hebrews was written about 67–69 (TINT, 304). The writer of Hebrews sets forth Christ as superior to the angels, to Moses and Joshua (Heb. 3–4), and to the earthly priests of the Old Testament.

Paul's Last Epistle—2 Timothy; the End of His Life (A.D. 67–68)

When Paul wrote to Titus in about 65, it is evident that he planned to spend the winter in Nicopolis (Titus 3:12). Since there were eight places named Nicopolis, it is not possible to ascertain which one was the location of Paul's sojourn, but the prevailing opinion holds to the Nicopolis in Epirus (now divided between Greece and Albania). Paul probably left Nicopolis when the Neronian persecution became severe and fled across Macedonia to Troas in Asia Minor, where he was shown hospitality by Carpus. He seems to have departed from Troas suddenly, for he left his cloak, some books, and the parchment manuscripts of the Old Testament there (2 Tim. 4:13). We are not certain of Paul's travels from this point on, but we know that he was arrested and taken to Rome for trial (TINT, 268).

During this second imprisonment at Rome, Paul wrote 2 Timothy, in about 67–68 (TINT, 269), exhorting Timothy to be strong in the grace that is in Christ (2 Tim. 2:1) and warning him to watch out for apostasy—for people who would not endure sound doctrine (4:3).

---

[5]Dods, *An Introduction to the New Testament*, 210–11; Theodor Zahn, *Introduction to the New Testament*, 2:289–90, cited in TINT, 288. For a more extended discussion of the authorship of 2 Peter, see Harrison, *Introduction to the New Testament*, 411–26. Harrison defends Petrine authorship.

Paul apparently was put to death by the Roman government shortly before the death of Nero, who died June 8, 68. Thus the end of Paul's life may be placed in the spring of 68. According to tradition, he was led out along the Ostian Way and was beheaded there. A grove is still pointed out in the countryside beyond Rome as the traditional scene of the execution of the great apostle.

Jude (A.D. 75), 1, 2, and 3 John (A.D. 85–90)

The epistle of Jude was probably written in about 75 (TINT, 296), to warn concerning false teachers and their teaching, urging believers to "contend for the faith" against those who deny our only Master and Lord Jesus Christ (Jude 3–4). Many of the church fathers held that Jude quoted from the apocryphal books known as the Assumption of Moses (v. 9) and the book of Enoch (v. 14), and it was rejected as canonical on this ground. Philippi, however, denied that Jude quoted from these apocryphal books, asserting that Jude wrote from oral tradition, and this is quite possible. Moorehead points out that even if Jude did cite two passages from noncanonical books, it does not mean that he accepted those books as true; Paul quoted from three Greek poets—Aratus, Menander, and Epimenides[6]—but that does not mean he endorsed all that those poets wrote. When Jude cited the prophecy from Enoch that the Lord would come (v. 14), this does not mean that he accepted the whole book as true, but rather that he received this particular prediction as from the Lord (TINT, 294–95).

The three epistles of John were all written in the period from 85 to 90. John was probably living in Ephesus at this time, as indicated by Irenaeus (TINT, 308), and he seems to have written his first epistle to the churches in the surrounding area, such as Smyrna, Pergamos, Thyatira, Sardis, Philadelphia, and Laodicea. John wrote to these believers, pointing out the provision for daily cleansing from sin by confession to the Lord (1 John 1:9), showing that the walk of the believer should not be in sin (3:9), warning against apostasy (2:18), and assuring the believers that they may be certain of their salvation (5:1, 13).

The second epistle of John is a letter addressed to "the chosen lady" (v. 1), probably a believer and her family who lived in one of the towns in Western Asia Minor near Ephesus. John commended these people for walking in the truth (v. 4), warned them against spiritual deceivers (v. 7), and expressed a hope to visit them soon (v. 12).

The third epistle of John was written to a friend of Paul named Gaius (v. 1). Paul knew men by that name residing at various places, including Macedonia (Acts 19:29), Derbe (Acts 20:4), and Corinth (Rom. 16:23; 1 Cor. 1:14). We do not know whether he was one of these individuals or perhaps another not mentioned in any other part of the New Testament. John wrote to this Gaius to express his joy in hearing of Gaius's walk in the truth (v. 3); to commend him for his hospitality to visiting ministers (vv. 5–6); to tell of his plans to rebuke the trouble-maker, Diotrephes (vv. 9–10); and to express his hope of seeing him personally in the near future (vv. 13–14).

The Book of Revelation (A.D. 95)

The true title of this book is given in the opening verse, "The Revelation of Jesus Christ," and it is often referred to as "the book of the Revelation," or "the book of Revelation," or just "Revelation." In any event it is not the revelation of John, for it is not John but rather Christ who is revealed in this book written by John.

The book of Revelation may be dated

---

[6]Acts 17:28; 1 Corinthians 15:33; Titus 1:12.

The temple of Artemis at Sardis in Asia Minor, with a little chapel built into it at the left, showing the triumph of the Gospel there

about 95, on the basis of indications in the church fathers Irenaeus, Clement of Alexandria, and Eusebius to the effect that John's banishment to the island of Patmos was in the latter part of the reign of the Roman emperor Domitian (81–96). Under Domitian, Christians were persecuted for not worshiping the emperor, a situation seemingly implied in John's statement that he was on the island of Patmos "because of the word of God and the testimony of Jesus Christ" (Rev. 1:9) (TINT, 323).

The book of Revelation falls into three great divisions that are unequal in length: (1) Chapter 1 concerns John's vision of Christ in the midst of the seven lampstands, commanding John to write about the seven lampstands, which are the seven churches (Rev. 1:13, 19–20). (2) The second section (chapters 2–3) records the messages from the Lord to each of the seven churches: Ephesus, Smyrna, Pergamum, Thyatira, Sardis, Philadelphia, and Laodicea. (3) The third division com-

prises the bulk of the book of Revelation (chapters 4–22). This last section deals with events yet future to our time, including details on the rule of the Antichrist, the dark days of the Tribulation, the coming of Christ in glory to establish justice and righteousness on earth (19:11–16), his thousand-year rule in the Millennium (20:1–6), the white throne judgment at the end of the Millennium (20:11–15), and the ushering in of the eternal ages with the new heaven, the new earth, and the new Jerusalem (21:1–2). The book closes with the prayer that is anticipatory of the coming again of Christ, "Amen. Come, Lord Jesus" (Rev. 22:20).

Answer to the Objections Concerning the Linguistic Nature of the Book of Revelation; Archaeological Light

The book of Revelation is inferior to the gospel of John in its linguistic qualities (CNAD, 115; TINT, 322). Some have tried to explain this fact by positing that Revelation was written by John in the 60s, before he had learned much Greek, and then, after a lapse of some thirty years during which his Greek improved, he wrote the gospel of John in the 90s.[7] This explanation does not fit the facts very well, for it seems that the gospel of John was probably written in about 85–90 (TINT, 173) and the book of Revelation a few years later, about 95 (TINT, 323).

What, then, is the explanation of the difference in the vocabulary and style of the gospel of John and Revelation? Several factors supply the answer:

1. Many constructions in Revelation that were once thought to be bad Greek are now known from the archaeological discoveries to have been forms in common every-day usage. For example, in Revelation 14:19, the expression "the great winepress" is so construed that the word "winepress" is in the masculine and the word "great" is in the feminine gender. This would constitute a violation of the grammatical principle that a modifying adjective should agree with its noun in gender (such a violation of a grammatical idiom is called a "solecism"; an example in English would be the construction, "between you and I," instead of "between you and me"). The New Testament archaeological discoveries made in Egypt have shown, however, that the construction with two different genders between a noun and its modifier (as in Revelation 14:19) is also found with this same word in the papyri.[8] A number of other textual discoveries show that many of the supposed blunders and solecisms of New Testament writers are merely grammatical forms common among the middle classes of the first century A.D.

2. A second objection to the language of Revelation was that it contained expressions characteristic of the Hebrew language; however, the papyri show that in this case as well, many forms of speech once supposed to be Hebraic or Semitic were not such at all but were expressions used by the non-Jewish population of the apostolic period (CNAD, 115).

3. It is quite true that there are some expressions in Revelation that are Hebraistic in style, but as H.C. Thiessen points out, this is only what we might expect in a book that makes a copious use of Old Testament imagery (TINT, 320).

4. A careful study shows that there are significant similarities between the book of Revelation and the other writings of John, such as "the Word," "he who overcomes," "water of life," "show," "little lamb," and others (TINT, 320).

Other differences between Revelation and the gospel of John may be explained by such factors as change of subject matter and circumstances and difference of amanuensis (TINT, 320).

Archaeological Light on Date of the Book of Revelation

Nikolaus Morosow set forth the eccentric theory that the book of Revelation was written as an astrological exercise by John Chrysostom on or about September 30, 395.[9] Chrysostom was one of the church fathers who lived in the fourth century; he died shortly after 400. The answer to this fantastic idea of Morosow is furnished by archaeological discoveries in Egypt. At a site called Oxyrhynchus,[10] Grenfell and Hunt found a beautiful edition of the book of Revelation written on vellum, dating from the main part of the fourth century. This shows that the book of Revelation had been in circulation for some time previously, long before the

---

[7]S.A. Cartledge, *A Conservative Introduction to the New Testament* (Grand Rapids: Zondervan, 1943), 198 [CCIN].

[8]CNAD, 111; citing Moulton, *Prolegomena*, 60, who speaks of this loss of gender distinction.

[9]Nikolaus Morosow, *Die Offenbarung Johannes*, 1912, 100–110; cited in CNAD, 104–5.

[10]About 120 miles south of Cairo, CNAD, 6.

impossible date suggested by Morosow (CNAD, 104–5).

Moreover, as has already been noted, the argument from historical grammar indicates that all New Testament books were written during the first century A.D. By way of review, this argument, based on discoveries in the papyri from Egypt, observes that the New Testament books as we have them are now known to have been written in the grammar and vocabulary of the popular Greek of the first century, not in the language of some subsequent period.

Archaeological Light on Places of Worship in the New Testament Period: Synagogues, Catacombs, Churches

Synagogues. The synagogue of the Jews was not abandoned at first by Christians in the early part of the New Testament period. Christ himself, as was his custom, went into the synagogue at Nazareth and read the Scriptures on the Sabbath (Luke 4:16ff.). When Paul went from town to town on his missionary journeys, he customarily went to the synagogue first and told the Good News to the assembled Jews (as at Salamis, Acts 13:5; Antioch in Pisidia, 13:14; Iconium, 14:1). Evidence of first-century synagogues is now coming to light. First, as noted in the discussion of Capernaum (chapter 26, pages 246–48), some remains of what appears to have been the Capernaum synagogue of Jesus' day have been found under the floor of the extensively preserved third-century synagogue there. Second, Yigael Yadin found a fairly well-preserved synagogue at Masada that was certainly in use at the time of the destruction of the temple in A.D. 70. Yadin thought that its earliest use may date back to the days of Herod the Great.[11] Third, V. Corbo found a synagogue at the Herodium (Herod's great fortress seven miles due south of Jerusalem), which was introduced during either

the first revolt (A.D. 66–70) or the second revolt 132–135) (EAEHL, 2:502–10). There are, of course, many more synagogues excavated at biblical sites and dating from the second, third, or fourth centuries (e.g., Capernaum, Chorazin, or Sardis), but it is not the purpose of this book to attempt a history of the synagogue in the ancient Near East.

Catacombs. The catacombs at Rome were constructed for underground burial, but at times when the persecutions were severe, they were used as places of refuge and worship (BWMS, 207). Several of the catacomb passages connect with small chapels, which were likely used in connection with the burial services during ordinary times but may well have served as regular meeting places when it was not safe to meet above ground. These chapels are probably the oldest preserved places of Christian worship.

Catacombs were used by Christians as burial places during the first to the fourth centuries, the end of their use coming at the time of the invasion of Rome by Alaric the Visigoth (CNAD, 385). During the tenth to the sixteenth centuries, the catacombs were almost completely forgotten. In the sixteenth century one of the catacombs was accidentally discovered, but the true discoverer of the catacombs was de Rossi (1822–1894), who thoroughly explored them and published his results in three splendid volumes (CNAD, 386).

A study of the area has shown that the passageways of the various catacombs near the city of Rome would total 550 miles if they were extended in a straight line, according to de Rossi (CNAD, 384), and it is estimated that there are nearly two million graves in them. They covered a surface area of about 615 acres (FLAP, 455). The oldest inscription that can be dated in the catacombs was made in 72 (CNAD, 394), and the use of the catacombs continued unabated through the second and third centuries, with a de-

[11]Yigael Yadin, *Masada* (New York: Random House, 1966), 181–87.

cline in the fourth century when Christianity became the state religion and catacomb burials were no longer necessary. At least thirty-five Christian catacombs are known at Rome (FLAP, 455).

The painting on the walls of the passageways and rooms of the catacombs show us what the early Christians thought and believed. The most common scenes pictured are the raising of Lazarus, the escape of Noah from the deluge, the escape of Daniel from the lions, and the escape of Jonah from the great fish. All of these scenes have the one underlying motif of escape or deliverance and are an evidence of the fact that the early Christians were looking to Christ for deliverance. These scenes often appear in the oldest catacombs, such as the Catacomb of Domitilla, the Catacomb of Priscilla, and the Catacomb of Lucina, all of which are accepted by scholars as dating back to the first century (CNAD, 384) or, at the latest, to the middle of the second century A.D.[12] Just before the outbreak of World War II, my wife and I spent a month in Rome, devoting most of our time to an examination of the catacombs. Our study strikingly demonstrated that the early Christians who used them left a wholehearted testimony to a trust in Christ and his saving power.

Churches. Both because of the persecution of Christians and the fact that they often came from the lower classes of society in the early days of the church, we would not expect to find remains of very early church buildings. Moreover, it was common for groups of believers to meet in homes (see, e.g., Rom. 16:5, 14–15), and

wealthy believers sometimes either made their property available for church services or gave it to the church for its use. Private homes provided greater secrecy than public structures in the event of persecution (see, e.g., FLAP, 495).

The earliest church yet to be excavated and dated with certainty was uncovered at Dura, a ruin on the Euphrates River, about halfway between Aleppo and Baghdad. Although there was some excavation at the site earlier, the definitive work took place from 1928 to 1937 under the sponsorship of Yale University and the French Academy of Inscriptions. During the 1931–32 season, excavators found in a house a chapel that had been made by joining two rooms and installing a platform. An adjacent room served as a baptistry. The numerous scenes on the walls included those of Jesus walking on the water to meet Peter, the Marys before the tomb of Jesus, the temptation of Adam and Eve, David and Goliath, the healing of the paralytic, and more—all in an extraordinary state of preservation. A dated inscription on the wall fixed construction or renovation to A.D. 232.[13]

When we move into later centuries, there is an abundance of ruins of churches in Bible lands. There are some remains of Constantine's fourth-century Church of the Nativity at Bethlehem (under the present church) and his basilica at the site of Mamre near Hebron. There are the Capernaum church over the presumed house of Peter (mid-fifth century), basilicas at Philippi dating to the fifth and sixth centuries, baths at Hierapolis converted into a Christian church during the

---

[12]Paul Styger's researches into the origins of the catacombs seem to indicate that the oldest Christian catacombs go back to about A.D. 150, a date that is still very early in the history of the church. In the case of the Catacomb of Domitilla, it appears from the inscriptions that this property was made available to a group of pagans who used it as a burial place in the first century and that their descendants accepted Christianity about the middle of the second century and established three underground burial places on the property as Christian burial chambers. Cf. FLAP, 462, and Paul Styger, *Die römischen Katakomben, archäoligische Forschungen üier den Ursprung und die Bedeutung der altchristlichen Grabstätten*, 1933.

[13]See Clark Hopkins, *The Discovery of Dura-Europos* (New Haven: Yale University Press, 1979), 90–96; Marie-Henriette Gates, "Dura-Europos: A Fortress of Syro-Mesopotamian Art," BA (September 1984), 166–81.

The magnificent temple of Bacchus at Baalbek

fifth century, unexcavated churches at Sardis dating to the fifth and sixth centuries, and many, many more.

Christianity Confronts Paganism; the Great Temple Complex at Baalbek

Although the advance of the Gospel during the first Christian centuries was phenomenal, paganism did not just roll over and play dead. Numerous older pagan worship centers were maintained, and new ones sprang up all over the Roman Empire; a few grandiose projects were launched. Perhaps the greatest of these was at Baalbek, located on a superb site fifty-three miles east of Beirut.

Probably as early as the reign of Augustus, the massive temple complex at Baalbek was begun. Inscriptions show that work on the temple of Jupiter was well under way during Nero's reign. And the temple of Bacchus apparently was begun about the middle of the first century A.D. For over two centuries construction went on at the site to produce a magnificent complex exuding a sense of power, size, and glorious magnificence.

A huge substructure—from 24 to 42 feet above the ground—was built for the temples to fulfill a psychological function—to render them more imposing by lifting them high above the neighboring landscape. Worshipers would enter the temple complex through a tower-flanked propylaea 165 feet wide and 38 feet deep, with columns brought from faraway Aswan in Egypt. They would then pass through a hexagonal court into a great altar court 350 feet square. On either side of the altar were large stone basins (actually tanks) 68 feet long by 23 feet broad and 2 feet 7 inches high for ritual washing.

From this court a magnificent stairway led to the temple of Jupiter. Surrounded by a colonnade of fifty-four columns, the cella, or holy of holies, was 290 by 160 feet, over five times as large as that of the Parthenon. Six of the great one-hundred-ton Corinthian columns of the peristyle remain standing. Sixty-five feet high, they are the tallest in the Greco-Roman world. Atop the columns is a 16-foot entablature ornately decorated with lions' and bulls' heads.

Adjacent to the temple of Jupiter on the south and at a lower level is the temple of Bacchus with a cella 87 by 75 feet, originally surrounded by a peristyle of forty-six columns 56 feet high. Beautifully preserved, no better example of a Roman temple interior survives. East of the Acropolis was a round temple, rare in Syria, that was probably a temple of Venus, constructed about A.D. 250.

Huge stones appear in the temple complex substructure, the three largest being about 64 feet long, 14 feet high, and 11 feet thick and each weighing over a thousand tons. The largest stone of all never made it out of the quarry and may be seen about a mile south of the modern town. It measures 70 by 14 by 13 feet.

A German archaeological mission under the leadership of Otto Puchstein and Bruno Schulz dug at Baalbek from 1900 to 1904, thoroughly studying the acropolis area. From 1943 to 1975 the Lebanese Antiquities Service under the direction of Maurice Chehab and architect H. Kalayan conducted restoration work at the site.[14]

Palestine from New Testament Times to the Present

In A.D. 66 the Jews revolted against the Romans, and after four years of fierce warfare (described by Josephus), the Romans captured Jerusalem and destroyed the temple in A.D. 70. The tenth Roman legion was left at Jerusalem to maintain order (BAB, 162). Evidence of their occupation of Jerusalem appears even today when, from time to time, tiles are found bearing the inscription of this legion. In 132 a revolt of the Jews was led by a man named Simeon, who was called Bar Cochba, or Kokhba (Aramaic, meaning "son of the star"). This insurrection was not put down until 135 by the forces of the Roman emperor Hadrian. Hadrian determined to erase the Jewish city of Jerusalem from the map, and to accomplish this he rebuilt the city, making it a Roman colony and naming it Aelia Capitolina. He built a pagan temple to Jupiter on the site of the Jewish temple (BAB, 162). Jerusalem in this form continued on until the time of Constantine (c. 325).

The emperor Constantine made Christianity a legal religion of the Roman Empire. As at least a nominal Christian, he took an interest in the Holy Land. His mother, Queen Helena, made a trip to Palestine and sought to identify many scenes of gospel events. On the site selected by her as the location of the tomb of Christ a church was built in about 325. After many destructions and vicissitudes, it stands today and is still know as the Church of the Holy Sepulchre. Pilgrimages were frequent during the 300 years (300–600) after its construction, and many monasteries and churches were built in Palestine during this time. Queen Helena was also instrumental in the construction of churches at Bethlehem and Mamre near Hebron.

In 615 Chosroes II of Persia overran Palestine. The Persians controlled Palestine until 628, when it was regained by the Byzantine kings of the Roman Empire. It remained under Byzantine control for only a few years, 628–638, when the Muslims conquered it.[15]

After 638 Palestine was ruled by Muslims from various areas and dynasties in the Near East, including the Caliphs of Medina, Damascus, and Baghdad; the Fatimid Caliphs of Egypt, and the Seljuk Turks. Seljuk mistreatment of Christian

---

[14]While there are numerous works on Baalbek, most of them are not now readily available. Probably the best current work is Friedrich Ragette, *Baalbek* (Park Ridge, N.J.: Noyes Press, 1980).

[15]Palestine continued under the Muslims from 638 to 1917, except for a period of 89 years (1099–1188) when the Crusaders from Europe governed the area.

pilgrims to the Holy Land and pressure on the borders of the Byzantine Empire led to the organization of Crusades in Western Europe. The first Crusade resulted in the establishment of the Latin Kingdom of Jerusalem, which lasted from 1099 to 1188. Archaeological materials from the Crusader period are often found on the top or at least near the surface of many tells and ruins in Palestine.

Crusader involvement in the construction of the Church of the Holy Sepulchre has already been noted. A second major Crusader bastion on which archaeologists have concentrated is at Caesarea (see EAEHL, 1:282–85). Probably pride of place goes to the magnificent Crusader construction at Acre, however. There between 1955 and 1965 the great Refectory of the Order of St. John was cleared. The large two-aisled hall is under the present government hospital. It had three chimneys to facilitate its use as a refectory. The hall is built in the transitional style, from Romanesque to Gothic. Three huge columns, each about nine feet in diameter, support the heavy cross-rib vaults of the ceiling. Presumably the structure was erected about 1148, when Louis VII, leader of the Second Crusade, lived in Acre (EAEHL, 1:20).

After the fall of the Latin Kingdom in 1188, Palestine again came under Muslim control. The Sultans of Egypt controlled Palestine until 1517, when the Ottoman Turks captured it and survived as the rulers of Palestine during a long period of misrule.

The Allied Forces took Palestine during World War I, and in 1917 Palestine was freed from the domination of Muslim rulers. General Allenby was able to deliver Jerusalem without firing a shot in the Holy City. The League of Nations gave Great Britain a mandate to administer Palestine, and the Holy Land was opened up for the return of the Jews to their ancestral home by the provisions of the Balfour Declaration.[16] Seemingly the impossible occurred when the State of Israel was proclaimed on May 14, 1948, under United Nations auspices. Certainly the return of the Jews to Palestine is a foreshadowing of the time when the Lord "will reach out his hand a second time to reclaim the remnant that is left of his people . . . and gather the scattered people of Judah from the four quarters of the earth" (Isa. 11:11–12).

Prospects for the Future in Archaeology

Edward Chiera,[17] in his fascinating book on the clay tablets,[18] estimated that 99 percent of the Babylonian clay tablets remain undug, and A.T. Olmstead[19] pointed out, shortly before his death in 1945, that something like half a million clay tablets that have already been excavated are yet to be read and appraised.[20] It has been estimated that there are some five thousand ruin heaps in Palestine (including tells), only a few hundred of which have been excavated at all, and of these only about thirty have been the scenes of major digs. The Iraq Department of Antiquities has records of over 6,500 tells (mounds of buried cities) in the

---

[16]The Jewish population of Palestine was largely exterminated during the first (A.D. 66ff.) and second (132–135) Jewish revolts, and Arabs occupied the land during medieval and modern times. Extensive Jewish repatriation began with Theodor Herzl and the Zionist movement in the 1890s.

[17]Late Assyriologist at the Oriental Institute of the University of Chicago.

[18]George Cameron, ed., *They Wrote on Clay* (Chicago: University of Chicago Press, 1938), 233.

[19]Near Eastern specialist and historian at the Oriental Institute of the University of Chicago.

[20]A.T. Olmstead, "History, Ancient World, and the Bible," JNES 2, 1 (January 1943): 32. Although Olmstead wrote long ago, the situation has not improved since his day because more tablets have been found than have been translated since the time he compiled his estimate.

country; well over 6,000 of them have not yet been excavated at all. Nor has the day of "diminishing returns" been reached in Near Eastern archaeology—that is, in excavating one does not find a mere duplication of materials and information that is already known from previous excavations. Considering all of this, one is thrilled at the propects for the future in the field of archaeological research.

The Usefulness of Archaeology Today

In the meantime, there is already available abundant material that should be appropriated and put into use by Bible students in their study and teaching of the Scriptures. I once thumbed through the book of Genesis and mentally noted that each of the fifty chapters was either illuminated or confirmed by some archaeological discovery—the same would be true for most of the remaining chapters of the Bible, both the Old and New Testaments. With such an amount of material at hand to help us understand the Scriptures better and to show their validity, we need only to use it in order to enable others not only to appreciate the historical sequence of events in the Bible but also to realize afresh the significance of the great spiritual truths revealed in it. This book has been an effort in that direction.

BIBLIOGRAPHIES

BIBLIOGRAPHY

Some General Works on Archaeology and the Bible
(usually reliable but holding a variety of theological positions)

Albright, W.F. *The Archaeology of Palestine*. Harmondsworth, Middlesex, England: Penguin Books, 1949.

_____. *The Archaeology of Palestine and the Bible*. Cambridge, Mass.: ASOR, 1974.

_____. *Archaeology and the Religion of Israel*. Baltimore: Johns Hopkins Press, 1942.

_____. *From the Stone Age to Christianity*. Baltimore: Johns Hopkins Press, 1940.

_____. *Yahweh and the Gods of Canaan*. Garden City, N.Y.: Doubleday, 1968.

Barton, George A. *Archaeology and the Bible*. 7th ed. Philadelphia: American Sunday School Union, 1937.

Burrows, Millar. *What Mean These Stones?* New Haven: American Schools of Oriental Research, 1941.

Finegan, Jack. *Light from the Ancient Past*. 2nd ed. Princeton: Princeton University Press, 1959.

_____. *Archaeological History of the Ancient Near East*. Boulder, Colo: Westview, 1979.

Kenyon, Frederic. *The Bible and Archaeology*. New York: Harper, 1940.

Kitchen, Kenneth A. *Ancient Orient and Old Testament*. Chicago: InterVarsity, 1966.

Mazar, Amihai. *Archaeology of the Land of the Bible*. New York: Doubleday, 1990.

Price, Ira M., O.R. Sellers, and E. Leslie Carlson. *The Monuments and the Old Testament*. Philadelphia: Judson, 1958.

Robinson, George L. *The Bearing of Archaeology on the Old Testament*. New York: American Tract Society, 1941.

Schoville, Keith N. *Biblical Archaeology in Focus*. Grand Rapids: Baker, 1978.

Thomas, D. Winton, ed. *Archaeology and Old Testament Study*. Oxford: Oxford University Press, 1967.

Thompson, J.A. *The Bible and Archaeology*. 3rd ed. Grand Rapids: Eerdmans, 1982.

Unger, Merrill F. *Archaeology and the Old Testament*. Grand Rapids: Zondervan, 1954.

Vos, Howard F. *Archaeology in Bible Lands*. Chicago: Moody Press, 1977.

Wright, G. Ernest. *Biblical Archaeology*. Philadelphia: Westminster, 1961.

Works Opposing the Critical View of Scripture
(based on archaeology, linguistics, etc.)

Allis, Oswald T. *The Five Books of Moses*. Philadelphia: Presbyterian and Reformed, 1943.

Archer, Gleason L., Jr. *A Survey of Old Testament Introduction*. Rev. ed. Chicago: Moody Press, 1974.

Green, W.H. *The Unity of the Book of Genesis*. New York: Scribner, 1910.

_____. *The Higher Criticism of the Pentateuch*. New York: Scribner, 1896.

Guthrie, Donald. *New Testament Introduction*. 3rd ed. Downers Grove: InterVarsity, 1970.

Hamilton, Floyd E. *The Basis of Christian Faith*. 3rd ed. New York: Harper, 1946.

Harrison, Everett F. *Introduction to the New Testament*. Rev. ed. Grand Rapids: Eerdmans, 1971.

Harrison, Roland K. *Introduction to the Old Testament*. Grand Rapids: Eerdmans, 1969.

Kyle, M.G. *The Deciding Voice of the Monuments in Biblical Criticism*. Oberlin: Bibliotheca Sacra, 1924.

————. *Moses and the Monuments*. Oberlin: Bibliotheca Sacra, 1920.

————. *The Problem of the Pentateuch: A New Solution by Archaeological Methods*. Oberlin: Bibliotheca Sacra, 1920.

Orr, James. *The Problem of the Old Testament*. New York: Scribner, 1917.

Raven, John H. *Old Testament Introduction*. New York: Revell, 1910.

Thiessen, Henry C. *Introduction to the New Testament*. Grand Rapids: Eerdmans, 1943.

Unger, Merrill F. *Introductory Guide to the Old Testament*. Grand Rapids: Zondervan, 1951.

Wilson, Robert D. *A Scientific Investigation of the Old Testament*. Revised by Edward J. Young. Chicago: Moody Press, 1959.

————. *Is the Higher Criticism Scholarly?* 9th ed. Philadelphia: The Sunday School Times, 1948.

Young, E.J. *An Introduction to the Old Testament*. Grand Rapids: Eerdmans, 1949.

Works on the Dead Sea Scrolls

Bruce, F.F. *Second Thoughts on the Dead Sea Scrolls*. 2nd ed. Grand Rapids: Eerdmans, 1961.

Burrows, Millar. *Burrows on the Dead Sea Scrolls* (a combination of his *Dead Sea Scrolls* and *More Light on the Dead Sea Scrolls*). Grand Rapids: Baker, 1978.

Charlesworth, James H., ed. *John and the Dead Sea Scrolls*. New York: Crossroad, 1990.

Cross, Frank M. *The Ancient Library of Qumran and Modern Biblical Studies*. Grand Rapids: Baker, 1958.

Davies, Philip R. *Qumran*. Grand Rapids: Eerdmans, 1982.

LaSor, William S. *The Dead Sea Scolls and the Christian Faith*. Chicago: Moody Press, 1962.

————. *The Dead Sea Scrolls and the New Testament*. Grand Rapids: Eerdmans, 1972.

Murphy-O'Connor, Jerome, and James H. Charlesworth, eds. *Paul and the Dead Sea Scrolls*. New York: Crossroad, 1990.

Pfeiffer, Charles F. *The Dead Sea Scrolls and the Bible*. Grand Rapids: Baker, 1969.

Sanders, James A. "The Dead Sea Scrolls—A Quarter Century of Study." BA (December 1973).

deVaux, R. *Archaeology and the Dead Sea Scrolls*. London: Oxford University Press, 1973.

Vermes, Geza. *The Dead Sea Scrolls in English*. 2nd ed. Harmondsworth, Middlesex, England: Penguin Books, 1975.

Vos, Howard F. *Archaeology in Bible Lands*. Chicago: Moody Press, 1977. Chapter 6.

Yadin, Yigael. *The Message of the Scrolls*. New York: Simon & Schuster, 1957.

Yamauchi, Edwin M. "The Dead Sea Scrolls." In *Wycliffe Bible Encyclopedia*. 2 vols. Chicago: Moody Press, 1975. 1:434–42.

Works on the Monuments and the Bible

Breasted, James H. *Ancient Records of Egypt*. 5 vols. Chicago: University of Chicago Press, 1906.

Luckenbill, D.D. *Ancient Records of Assyria and Babylonia*. 2 vols. Chicago: University of Chicago Press, 1926.

Pritchard, James B., ed. *Ancient Near Eastern Texts Relating to the Old Testament*. 2nd ed. Princeton: Princeton University Press, 1955.

Works on Bible Geography

Adams, J. McKee. *Biblical Backgrounds*. Revised by Joseph A. Callaway. Nashville: Broadman, 1965.

Aharoni, Yohanan. *The Land of the Bible*. London: Burns & Oates, 1967.

————, and Michael Avi-Yonah. *The Macmillan Bible Atlas*. New York: Macmillan, 1968.

Baines, John, and Jaromir Malek. *Atlas of Ancient Egypt*. New York: Facts on File, 1980.

Beitzel, Barry J. *The Moody Atlas of Bible Lands*. Chicago: Moody Press, 1985.

Cornell, Tim, and John Matthews. *Atlas of the Roman World*. New York: Facts on File, 1982.

Levi, Peter. *Atlas of the Greek World*. New York: Facts on File, 1980.

May, Herbert, ed. *Oxford Bible Atlas*. 2nd ed. New York: Oxford University Press, 1974.

Orni, Efraim, and Elisha Efrat. *Geography of Israel*. 3rd ed. Jerusalem: Israel Universities Press, 1971.

Pfeiffer, Charles, and Howard F. Vos. *The Wycliffe Historical Geography of Bible Lands*. Chicago: Moody Press, 1967.

Pritchard, James B., ed. *The Harper Atlas of the Bible*. New York: Harper & Row, 1987.

Ramsay, William M. *The Historical Geography of Asia Minor*. New York: Cooper Square, reprint 1972.

Rasmussen, Carl G. *Zondervan NIV Atlas of the Bible*. Grand Rapids: Zondervan, 1989.

Roaf, Michael. *Cultural Atlas of Mesopotamia*. New York: Facts on File, 1990.

Smith, George A. *The Historical Geography of the Holy Land*. London: Hodder and Stoughton, 1897.

Wright, G.E., and F.V. Filson. *The Westminster Historical Atlas to the Bible*. Rev. ed. Philadelphia: Westminster, 1956.

A Few of the More Useful Encyclopedias

Blaiklock, Edward M., and R.K. Harrison, eds. *The New International Dictionary of Biblical Archaeology*. Grand Rapids: Zondervan, 1983.

Bromiley, Geoffrey W., ed. *International Standard Bible Encyclopedia*. Rev. ed. 4 vols. Grand Rapids: Eerdmans, 1979–88. This replaces the 1929, 5-vol. set. Both editions are used in this book.

Buttrick, George A., ed. *Interpreter's Dictionary of the Bible*. 4 vols. Nashville: Abingdon, 1962.

Douglas, J.D., ed. *Illustrated Bible Dictionary*. 3 vols. Leicester, England: Inter-Varsity, 1980.

Tenney, Merrill C., ed. *Zondervan Pictorial Encyclopedia of the Bible*. 5 vols. Grand Rapids: Zondervan, 1975.

Archaeology and the New Testament

Blaiklock, E.M. *The Archaeology of the New Testament*. Grand Rapids: Zondervan, 1970.

Cobern, C.M. *The New Archaeological Discoveries and Their Bearing upon the New Testament*. 9th ed. New York: Funk and Wagnalls, 1929.

Deissmann, Adolf. *Light from the Ancient East*. New York: Doran, 1927.

Harrison, R.K. *Archaeology of the New Testament*. London: English Universities Press, 1964.

Finegan, Jack. *The Archaeology of the New Testament: The Life of Jesus and the Beginning of the Early Church*. Princeton: Princeton University Press, 1969.

————. *The Archaeology of the New Testament: The Mediterranean World of the Early Christian Apostles*. Boulder, Colo.: Westview, 1981.

McRay, John. *Archaeology and the New Testament*. Grand Rapids: Baker, 1991.

Unger, Merrill F. *Archaeology and the New Testament*. Grand Rapids: Zondervan, 1962.

BIBLIOGRAPHY

Arranged Alphabetically by the Abbreviations Used in This Book

AAP   Albright, W.F. *The Archaeology of Palestine*. Harmondsworth,
           Middlesex: Penguin Books, 1949.

AAPB   ——————. *The Archaeology of Palestine and the Bible*. Cambridge,
           Mass.: ASOR, 1974.

AARB   Adams, J. McKee. *Ancient Records and the Bible*. Nashville:
           Broadman, 1946.

AARI   Albright, W.F. *Archaeology and the Religion of Israel*. Baltimore:
           Johns Hopkins Press, 1942.

AASOR   *Annual of the American Schools of Oriental Research*.

AFBM   Allis, Oswald T. *The Five Books of Moses*. Philadelphia: Presbyterian
           and Reformed, 1943.

AFOTC   Alleman, H.C., and E.E. Flack, *Old Testament Commentary*.
           Philadelphia: Muhlenberg, 1948.

AJA   *American Journal of Archaeology*.

AJSL   *American Journal of Semitic Languages*.

AOTA   Albright, W.F. "The Old Testament and Archaeology." In AFOTC.

ARDBL   ——————. "Recent Discoveries in Bible Lands." In Young's *Analytical
           Concordance to the Bible*. 20th ed. New York: Funk and Wagnalls,
           c. 1936.

AS   *American Scholar*.

ASAC   Albright, W.F. *From the Stone Age to Christianity*. Baltimore: Johns
           Hopkins Press, 1940.

ASOTI   Archer, Gleason L., Jr. *A Survey of Old Testament Introduction*. Rev.
           ed. Chicago: Moody Press, 1974.

BA   *Biblical Archaeologist*.

BAB   Barton, G.A. *Archaeology and the Bible*. 7th ed. Philadelphia:
           American Sunday School Union, 1937.

BAHE   Breasted, J.H. *A History of Egypt*. New York: Scribner, 1912.

BAR   *Biblical Archaeology Review*.

BARE   Breasted, J.H. *Ancient Records of Egypt*. 5 vols. Chicago: University of
           Chicago Press, 1906.

BASOR   *Bulletin of the American Schools of Oriental Research*.

BBH   Blaikie, William G. *A Manual of Bible History*. Rev. ed. London, New
           York: Nelson, 1923.

BBHM   ——————. *A Manual of Bible History*. Revised by Charles D.
           Matthews. London: Nelson, 1940; reissued by Ronald Press, New
           York: 1942.

BCC   Breasted, J.H. *The Conquest of Civilization*. New York: Harper, 1926.

BDB   Brown, Driver, Briggs. *A Hebrew and English Lexicon of the Old
           Testament*. New York: Houghton Mifflin, 1906.

BHE   Brugsch. *History of Egypt*. 1891.

BJ   Blaikie, William G. "The Book of Joshua." In *The Expositor's Bible*. New York: Funk and Wagnalls, 1900.

BOI   Breasted, J.H. *The Oriental Institute*. Chicago: University of Chicago Press, 1933.

BS   Blaikie, William G. "The First Book of Samuel." In *The Expositor's Bible*. New York: Armstrong, 1901.

BSS   _____. "The Second Book of Samuel." In *The Expositor's Bible*. New York: Armstrong, 1893.

BWMS   Burrows, Millar. *What Mean These Stones?* New Haven: American Schools of Oriental Research, 1941.

CAH   *Cambridge Ancient History*. 2nd ed. New York: Macmillan, 1924.

CANT   Caiger, S.L. *Archaeology and the New Testament*. London: Cassell, 1939.

CAP   Cowley, A. *Aramaic Papyri of the Fifth Century*. Oxford: Clarendon, 1923.

CBE   Chadwick, G.A. "The Book of Exodus." In *The Expositor's Bible*. London: Hodder and Stoughton, 1896.

CBS   Caiger, S.L. *Bible and Spade*. London: Oxford University Press, 1936.

CCIN   Cartledge, S.A. *A Conservative Introduction to the New Testament*. Grand Rapids: Zondervan, 1943.

CCIO   _____. *A Conservative Introduction to the Old Testament*. Grand Rapids: Zondervan, 1943; reissued by University of Georgia Press, Athens, Ga., 1944.

CG   Calvin, John. *Commentaries on the First Book of Moses, Called Genesis*. Revised by John King. Edinburgh: Calvin Translation Society, 1847.

CHJ   Case, Shirley Jackson. *The Historicity of Jesus*. Chicago: University of Chicago Press, 1912.

CNAD   Cobern, C.M. *The New Archaeological Discoveries and Their Bearing upon the New Testament*. 9th ed. New York: Funk and Wagnalls, 1929.

CREP   Cobern, C.M. *Recent Explorations in Palestine*. Meadville, Pa.: Tribune, c. 1915.

DBS   Deissmann, G. Adolf. *Bible Studies*. Edinburgh: T. & T. Clark, 1903.

DDBH   Duncan, J. Garrow. *Digging up Biblical History*. New York: Macmillan, 1931.

DG   Driver, S.R. *The Book of Genesis*, Westminster Commentaries. 4th ed. London: Methuen, 1905.

DNB   Dougherty, R.P. *Nabonidus and Belshazzar*. New Haven: Yale University Press, 1929.

DS   Diodorus of Sicily. E.T. by C.H. Oldfather. 10 vols. New York: Putnam, 1933.

DTH   Driver, S.R. *A Treatise on the Use of the Tenses in Hebrew*. Oxford: Clarendon, 1892.

EAEHL   Avi-Yonah, Michael, ed. *Encyclopedia of Archaeological Excavations in the Holy Land*. 4 vols. Englewood Cliffs, N.J.: Prentice Hall, 1975–78.

EBLT   Ellis, William T. *Bible Lands Today*. 1926.

EDC   Engberg, R.M. *The Dawn of Civilization*. Chicago: University of Knowledge, 1938.

EHR _____. *The Hyksos Reconsidered.* Studies in Ancient Oriental Civilization (SAOC). Chicago: University of Chicago Press, 1939.

ELAE Erman, A. *Life in Ancient Egypt.* Translated by H.M. Tirard. London: Macmillan, 1894.

EQ *Evangelical Quarterly* (Edinburgh).

FANT Finegan, Jack. *The Archaeology of the New Testament.* Boulder, Colo.: Westview, 1981.

FHBC _____. *Handbook of Biblical Chronology.* Princeton: Princeton University Press, 1964.

FLAP _____. *Light from the Ancient Past.* 2nd ed. Princeton: Princeton University Press, 1959.

GBT Gregg, David. *Between the Testaments.* New York: Funk and Wagnalls, 1907.

GHCP Green, W.H. *The Higher Criticism of the Pentateuch.* New York: Scribner, 1895.

GIC _____. *General Introduction to the Old Testament: The Canon.* New York: Scribner, 1898.

GIT _____. *General Introduction to the Old Testament: The Text.* New York: Scribner, 1899.

GHH Garstang, John. *Joshua, Judges.* London: Constable, 1931.

GOSJ Glueck, Nelson. *The Other Side of Jordan.* New Haven: American Schools of Oriental Research, 1940.

GRJ _____. *The River Jordan.* Philadelphia: Westminster, 1946.

GS *The Geography of Strabo.* E.T. by Horace Leonard Jones. 8 vols. London: Heinemann; New York: Putnam, 1932.

GSJ Garstang, John, and J.B.E. Garstang. *The Story of Jericho.* Rev. ed. London: Marshall, Morgan and Scott, 1948.

GT Gaussen, L. *Theopneustia: The Plenary Inspiration of the Holy Scriptures.* Cincinnati, 1859; reissued by Moody Press, Chicago.

GTG Griffith-Thomas, W.H. *Genesis.* London: Religious Tract Society, n.d.

GUG Green, W.H. *The Unity of the Book of Genesis.* New York: Scribner, 1910.

HBCF Hamilton, F.E. *The Basis of Christian Faith.* 3rd ed. New York: Harper, 1946.

HBG Heidel, Alexander. *The Babylonian Genesis.* 2nd ed. Chicago: University of Chicago Press, 1951.

HCH Harper, R.F. *The Code of Hammurabi, King of Babylon about 2250 B.C.* Chicago: University of Chicago Press, 1904.

CHOT Hengstenberg, E.W. *Christology of the Old Testament.* Translated by Theodore Meyer. Edinburgh: T. & T. Clark, 1863.

HDB Hastings, James. *Dictionary of the Bible.* Rev. ed. New York: Scribner, 1927.

HDGG Hart-Davies, D.E. *The Genesis of Genesis.* London: Clarke, 1932.

HEBL Hilprecht, H.V. *Explorations in Bible Lands During the 19th Century.* Philadelphia: Holman, 1903.

HHMM Harper, W.R. *Introductory Hebrew Method and Manual.* Revised by J.M.F. Smith. New York: Scribner, 1921.

HSAB *The Haverford Symposium on Archaeology and the Bible.* Edited by Elihu Grant. New Haven: American Schools of Oriental Research, 1938.

BIBLIOGRAPHIES

ILN	*Illustrated London News.*
ISBE	*International Standard Bible Encyclopedia.* Edited by James Orr. 5 vols. Severance, 1929. Reprinted by Eerdmans, 1939. (Revised ed., edited by Geoffrey W. Bromiley. 4 vols. Grand Rapids: Eerdmans, 1979–88. This edition is also referred to in this book.)
JAJ	Josephus. *Antiquities of the Jews.* Translated by William Whiston.
JBL	*Journal of Biblical Literature.*
JFB	Jamieson, Robert, A.R. Fausset, and David Brown. *A Commentary Critical and Explanatory on the Whole Bible.* Rev. ed. 1 vol. Grand Rapids: Eerdmans, 1935.
JNES	*Journal of Near Eastern Studies.*
JSAT	Jack. J.W. *Samaria in Ahab's Time: Harvard Excavations and Their Results.* Edinburgh: T. &. T. Clark, 1929.
JSKL	Jacobsen, Thorkild. *The Sumerian King List.* Chicago: University of Chicago Press, 1939.
KA	Kroeber, A.L. *Anthropology.* New York: Harcourt, Brace, 1948.
KBA	Kenyon, Frederic. *The Bible and Archaeology.* New York: Harper, 1940.
KD	Keil, C.F. and F. Delitzsch. *Biblical Commentary on the Old Testament.* Edinburgh: T. &. T. Clark, 1872.
KDVM	Kyle, M.G. *The Deciding Voice of the Monuments in Biblical Criticism.* Oberlin: Bibliotheca Sacra, 1924.
KEK	_____. *Excavating Kirjath-Sepher's Ten Cities.* Grand Rapids: Eerdmans, 1934.
KMM	_____. *Moses and the Monuments.* Oberlin: Bibliotheca Sacra, 1920.
KNJ	Knight, G.A. Frank. *Nile and Jordan.* London: Clarke, 1921.
LARA	Luckenbill, D.D. *Ancient Records of Assyria and Babylonia.* Chicago: University of Chicago Press, 1926.
LAS	_____. *The Annals of Sennacherib.* Chicago: University of Chicago Press, 1924.
LC	Lange, John Peter. *A Commentary on the Holy Scriptures: Critical, Doctrinal, and Homiletical.* New York: Scribner, 1870.
LCG	_____. *Commentary on Genesis.* New York: Scriber, 1870.
LDSS	Ladd, George Trumbull. *The Doctrine of Sacred Scripture.* 1883.
MACR	Möller, Wilhelm. *Are the Critics Right?* New York: Revell, n.d. [c. 1899].
MALB	Mazar, Amihai. *Archaeology of the Land of the Bible.* New York: Doubleday, 1990.
MBCA	Marston, Charles. *The Bible Comes Alive.* London: Eyre and Spottiswoode, 1938.
MCEP	Macalister, R.A.S. *A Century of Excavation in Palestine.* New York: Revell, 1925.
MCG	Murphy, J.G. *Critical and Exegetical Commentary on the Book of Genesis.* Boston: Estes, 1873.
MEG	Macalister, R.A.S. *The Excavation of Gezer.* New York: Revell, 1912.
MHTE	Muir, James C. *His Truth Endureth.* Philadelphia: National, 1937.
MLPP	McCown, C.C. *The Ladder of Progress in Palestine.* New York: Harper, 1943.
MNBE	Marston, Charles. *New Bible Evidence.* New York: Revell, 1934–35.

MRAB MacRae, Allan A. "The Relation of Archaeology to the Bible." In MSCF.

MSCF *Modern Science and Christian Faith*. Wheaton: Van Kampen, 1948.

MSM Morton, H.V. *In the Steps of the Master*. New York: Dodd, Mead, 1937.

NCA Neatby, T. Miller. *Confirming the Scriptures*. London: Marshall, Morgan and Scott, n.d.

NOTP Noordtzy, A. *The Old Testament Problem*, printed in issues 388, 389, 390 of *Bibliotheca Sacra*, and reprinted as booklet, 1940–41, by Dallas Theological Seminary.

NPRE Naville, E. *The Store-City of Pithom and the Route of the Exodus*. London, 1903.

OHA Olmstead, A.T. *History of Assyria*. New York: Scribner, 1923.

OHPE ————. *History of the Persian Empire*. Chicago: University of Chicago Press, 1948.

OHPS ————. *History of Palestine and Syria*. New York: Scribner, 1931.

OIA Oesterley, W.O.E. *An Introduction to the Books of the Apocrypha*. New York: Macmillan, 1935.

OIC *Oriental Institute Communications*. Chicago: The Oriental Institute of the University of Chicago, n.d.

OJJ Oesterley, W.O.E. *The Jews and Judaism During the Greek Period*. London: SPCK; New York: Macmillan, 1941.

OPOT Orr, James. *The Problem of the Old Testament*. New York: Scribner, 1917.

ORHI Oesterley, W.O.E., and Theodore H. Robinson. *A History of Israel*. Oxford: Clarendon, 1932.

PAK Poebel, A. "The Assyrian King List from Khorsabad," JNES, 2, 1 (January 1943).

PANEP Pritchard, James B., ed. *The Ancient Near East in Pictures*. 2nd ed. Princeton: Princeton University Press, 1969.

PANET ————. ed. *Ancient Near Eastern Texts Relating to the Old Testament*. 2nd ed. Princeton: Princeton University Press, 1955.

PC *Pulpit Commentary*.

PDBC Parker, R.A., and W.H. Dubberstein. *Babylonian Chronology*, 626 B.C.–A.D. 45. Chicago: University of Chicago Press, 1942.

PEEA Pember, G.H. *Earth's Earliest Ages*. New York: Revell, c. 1876.

PEOT Peet, T. Eric. *Egypt and the Old Testament*. Liverpool: University Press of Liverpool, 1924.

PGH Piper, Otto. *God in History*. New York: Macmillan, 1939.

PIOT Pfeiffer, R.H. *Introduction to the Old Testament*. Rev. ed. New York: Harper, 1948.

PMOT Price, Ira Maurice, et al. *The Monuments and the Old Testament*. Philadelphia: Judson, 1958.

POTH Petrie, Flinders. *Palestine and Israel*. London: SPCK, 1934.

PSB Prescott, W.W. *The Spade and the Bible*. New York: Revell, 1933.

PSBA *Proceedings of the Society of Biblical Archaeology*.

RBA Robinson, George L. *The Bearing of Archaeology on the Old Testament*. New York: American Tract Society, 1941.

RBR Robinson, Edward. *Biblical Researches in Palestine*. 3rd ed. Boston: Crocker and Brewster, 1868.

BIBLIOGRAPHIES

RCP	Rogers, R.W. *Cuneiform Parallels to the Old Testament*. 2nd ed. New York: Abingdon, 1926.
RENG	Ryle, H.E. *Early Narratives of Genesis*. London: Macmillan, 1904.
RGGT	Robertson, A.T. *New Short Grammar of the Greek Testament*. London: SPCK, 1931.
RHAP	Rogers, R.W. *A History of Ancient Persia*. New York: Scribner, 1929.
RHES	Reisner, G.A.; C.S. Fisher; D.G. Lyon. *Harvard Excavations at Samaria, 1908–1910*. Cambridge: Harvard University Press, 1924.
ROTI	Raven, John. *Old Testament Introduction*. New York: Revell, 1910.
RRB	Rogers, R.W. *The Religion of Babylonia and Assyria*. New York: Eaton and Mains, 1908.
SBT	Harold R. Willowby, ed. *The Study of the Bible Today and Tomorrow*. Chicago: University of Chicago Press, 1947.
SDB	*Smith's Dictionary of the Bible*. New York: Hurd and Houghton, 1871.
SG	Skinner, John. *Genesis*. International Critical Commentary. New York: Scriber, 1910.
SHL	Smith, J.M.P. *The Origin and History of Hebrew Law*. Chicago: University of Chicago Press, 1931.
SNG	Spurrell, G.J. *Notes on the Text of the Book of Genesis*. Oxford: Clarendon, 1896.
SSWE	Steindorff, George, and Keith C. Seele. *When Egypt Ruled the East*. Rev. ed. Chicago: University of Chicago Press, 1957.
STTP	Spinoza, Benedict de. *Tractatus Theologico-Politicus*. In *The Chief Works of Benedict de Spinoza, 1670*. Translated by R.H.M. Elwes. London: George Bell, 1883.
TCK	Thiele, E.R. "The Chronology of the Kings of Judah and Israel." JNES 2, 3 (July 1944): 137–38.
TINT	Thiessen, H.C. *Introduction to the New Testament*. Grand Rapids: Eerdmans, 1943.
TKB	Trumbull, H. Clay. *Kadesh-barnea*. New York: Scribner, c. 1884.
TMN	Thiele, Edwin R. *The Mysterious Numbers of the Hebrew Kings*. New rev. ed. Grand Rapids: Zondervan, 1983.
TSTS	Theissen, H.C. *Lectures in Systematic Theology*. Rev. ed. Grand Rapids: Eerdmans, 1979.
UNBG	Urquhart, John. *The New Biblical Guide*. Chicago: Blessing, n.d.
VENE	Vos, Howard F. *Ezra, Nehemiah, Esther*. Grand Rapids: Zondervan, 1987.
WA	Woolley, C.L. *Abraham*. New York: Scribner, 1936.
WBE	Wilson, John A. *Burden of Egypt*. Chicago: University of Chicago Press, 1951.
WCCK	Wiseman, Donald J. *Chronicle of the Chaldean Kings*. London: British Museum, 1956.
WCI	Wright, G.E. *The Challenge of Israel's Faith*. Chicago: University of Chicago Press, 1944.
WDICJ	Wood, Bryant G., "Did the Israelites Conquer Jericho?" BAR (March/April 1990), 44–59.
WDP	Woolley, C.L. *Digging Up the Past*. New York: Scribner, 1931.
WFWA	Wright, G.E., and F.V. Filson. *The Westminster Historical Atlas to the Bible*. Rev. ed. Philadelphia: Westminster, 1956.

WPHI   Wellhausen, Julius. *Prolegomena to the History of Israel*. Edinburgh: Black, 1885.

WSC   Wright, G. Frederick. *Scientific Confirmations of Old Testament History*. Oberlin: Bibliotheca Sacra, 1913.

WSEB   *The Westminster Study Edition of the Holy Bible*. Philadelphia: Westminster, 1948.

WSI   Wilson, Robert Dick. *A Scientific Investigation of the Old Testament*. Revised by Edward J. Young. Chicago: Moody Press, 1959.

WST   Warfield, B.B. *Studies in Theology*. New York: Oxford University Press, 1932.

WUC   Woolley, C.L. *Ur of the Chaldees*. Revised by P.R.S. Moorey. London: Herbert, 1982.

YAB   Yahuda, A.S. *The Accuracy of the Bible*. London: Heinemann, 1934.

YLP   ————. *The Language of the Pentateuch in Its Relation to Egyptian*. New York: Oxford University Press, 1933.

INDEX

INDEX

Abimelech, 63
Abraham
  ancestry, 45
  birthplace, 46
  call, 47
  covenant, 47-48, 53-54
  in Egypt, 50
  time of, 45
Adonijah's rebellion, 139-40
Ahab, 154-59
Ahasuerus, 207
Ahaz, 169
Ahaziah, 159, 162
Ai, 48-49, 113-15
Albright
  accuracy of Ezekiel, 194-95
  alphabet, 120
  Ai, 114
  excavation of Kiriath Sepher, 189
  Exodus, 81, 87
  Lachish Letters, 190
  line of march, 53
  Patriarchs, 75
  Phoenicians, 142
Alexander the Great, 218-23
Amarna, 87, 116, 161
Amenhotep II, 81
Amos, 165-66
Ananias, 261
Antioch of Pisidia, 269-70
Antioch of Syria, 264-65, 267
Antiochus IV of Syria, 225-26
Antipater, 229
Archaeology
  biblical, function of, 13
  excavation technique, 17-18
Aristobulus, 228
Artaxerxes I, 209-10, 217
Ashdod, 179
Ashurbanipal, 30, 187, 206
Asnapper, Osnappar, 205-6
Ashtaroth, 128-29
Athaliah, 163
Athens, 274-77
Azariah, 168

Baalbek, 291-92
Babel, tower of, 41
Babylon, 196-97, 203
Babylonian creation tablets, 30
Bartimaeus, 251
Beersheba, 65
Belshazzar, 200-202
Ben-Hadad, 161
Beni Hassan, 50-51, 126

Bethel, 48-9, 88, 114, 119
Bethlehem, 242
Beth Shan, 128
Bible
  accuracy, 14
  inspiration, 14
  birthright, 63
  blessing, stolen, oral, 64
  bricks made with straw, 82

Caesarea, 233-34, 281
Cain, 34-37
Calf worship, 152-53
Calvary, 253-54
Camels in Egypt, 51; cf. 145-46
Cannanites, destruction of 103-4
Candace, 263
Capernaum, 246-48
Caphtor, 60
Catacombs, 289-90
Churches, early, 290-91
Church of Holy Sepulcher, 254
Church of the Nativity, 244-45
Circumcision and archaeology, 54
Cities, how buried, 16
Civilization, beginnings, 36ff
Commandments, Ten, 92
Communism in early church, 261
Copper in Palestine, 145
Corinth, 276-78
Creation
  answer to critical view, 23
  Babylonian creation tablets, 30
  biblical statement, 21
  creative days, 27-28
  critical view, 22
  time of 23-27
Cubit, 182
Cyrus, 203, 216

Dabon, 128
Dan, 56, 153
Daniel, 193, 196-97
Darius I, 206-9, 217
Dating, Carbon 14, 19, 20
  dendochronology, 20
  pottery chronology 19
David, 126-27, 131-40
Dead Sea Scrolls, 175-78, 197, 258
Debir, 88
Deir-el Bahri, *see* Der-el Bahri
Der-el Bahri, 50
Dibon, 161

Eden, 30-32
Edom, Edomites, 100